WE, THE DROWNED

Carsten Jensen was born in 1952. He first made his name as a columnist and literary critic. As a journalist he has reported from many regions of conflict, including the Balkans and most recently, Afghanistan. His essays, novels and travel books have won numerous literary awards, including the coveted Golden Laurels and the Danish Bank Literary Prize. In 2010 he received the prestigious Olof Palme Prize, awarded for his contribution to the defence of human rights. *We, The Drowned* has sold more than 300,000 copies in Scandinavia alone and was voted best Danish novel of the past twenty-five years.

ALSO BY CARSTEN JENSEN

I Have Seen the World Begin
Earth in the Mouth

CARSTEN JENSEN

We, The Drowned

TRANSLATED FROM THE DANISH BY
Charlotte Barslund
with Emma Ryder

VINTAGE BOOKS
London

Published by Vintage 2011

10

First published with the title, *Vi, De Druknede* in 2006 by Gyldendal, Copenhagen

First published in Great Britain in 2010 by Harvill Secker

Vintage
Random House, 20 Vauxhall Bridge Road,
London SW1V 2SA

www.vintage-books.co.uk

Addresses for companies within The Random House Group Limited
can be found at: www.randomhouse.co.uk/offices.htm

The Random House Group Limited Reg. No. 954009

A CIP catalogue record for this book is available from the British Library

ISBN 9780099512967

This translation has been published with the support of the Danish Arts Council.

The author is grateful for financial assistance from the following: Statens
Kuntsfond, Litteraturrådet, Autorkontoen, Statens Kunstråds Litteraturudvalg,
Politikens Fond, J. C. Hempels Fond, Konsul Georg Jorck og hustru Emma
Jorcks Fond, Fonden Erik Hoffmeyers Rejselegat

Penguin Random House is committed to a sustainable future for
our business, our readers and our planet. This book is made from
Forest Stewardship Council® certified paper.

Printed and bound in Great Britain by Clays Ltd, St Ives plc

For Lizzie
the love of my life

CONTENTS

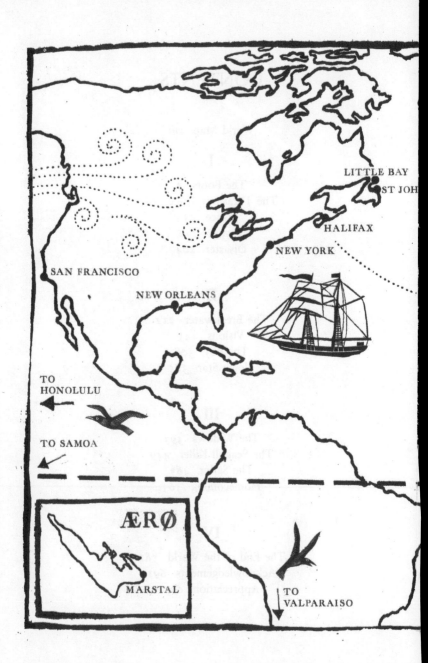

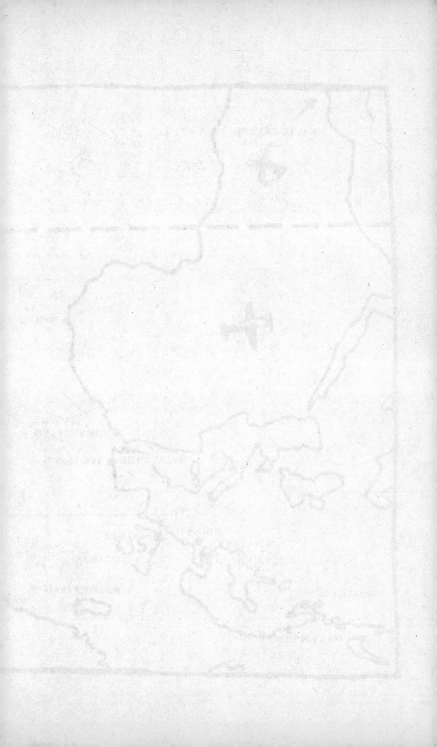

I

The Boots

MANY YEARS AGO THERE LIVED A MAN CALLED LAURIDS MADSEN, who went up to heaven and came down again thanks to his boots.

He didn't soar as high as the tip of the mast on a full-rigged ship; in fact he got no further than the main. Once up there, he stood outside the Pearly Gates and saw St Peter – though the guardian of the gateway to the hereafter merely flashed his bare arse at him.

Laurids Madsen should have been dead. But death didn't want him, and he came back down a changed man.

Until the fame he achieved from this heavenly visit, Laurids Madsen was best known for having single-handedly started a war. His father, Rasmus, had been lost at sea when Laurids was six years old. When he turned fourteen he shipped aboard the *Anna* of Marstal, his native town on the island of Ærø, but the ship was lost in the Baltic only three months later. The crew was rescued by an American brig and from then on Laurids Madsen dreamed of America.

He'd passed his navigation exam in Flensburg when he was eighteen and the same year he was shipwrecked again, this time off the coast of Norway near Mandal, where he stood on a rock with the waves slapping on a cold October night, scanning the horizon for salvation. For the next five years he sailed the seven seas. He went south around Cape Horn and heard penguins scream in the pitch-black night. He saw Valparaiso, the west coast of America, and Sydney, where the kangaroos hop around and the trees shed bark, not leaves, in winter. He met a girl with eyes like grapes by the name of Sally Brown, and could tell stories about Foretop Street, La Boca, Barbary Coast and Tiger Bay. He boasted about his first equator crossing, when he'd saluted Neptune and felt the bump as the ship passed the Line; his fellow sailors had marked the occasion by forcing him to drink salt water, fish oil and vinegar; they'd baptised him in tar, lamp soot and glue; shaved him with a rusty razor with dents in its blade; and tended to his

3

cuts with stinging salt and lime. They'd made him kiss the ochre-coloured cheek of the pockmarked Amphitrite and forced his nose down her bottle of smelling salts, which they'd filled with nail clippings.

Laurids Madsen had seen the world.

So had many others. But he was the only one to return to Marstal with the peculiar notion that everything there was too small, and to prove his point, he frequently spoke in a foreign tongue he called American, which he'd learned when he sailed with the naval frigate *Neversink* for a year.

'*Givin nem belong mi* Laurids Madsen,' he said.

He had three sons and a daughter with Karoline Grube from Nygade: Rasmus, named after his grandfather, and Esben and Albert. The girl's name was Else and she was the oldest. Rasmus, Esben and Else took after their mother, who was short and taciturn, while Albert resembled his father: at the age of four he was already as tall as Esben, who was three years his senior. His favourite pastime was rolling around an English cast-iron cannonball, which was far too heavy for him to lift – not that it stopped him trying. Stubborn-faced, he'd brace his knees and strain.

'*Heave away, my jolly boys! Heave away, my bullies!*' Laurids shouted in encouragement as he watched his youngest son struggling with it.

The cannonball had come crashing through the roof of their house in Korsgade during the English siege of Marstal in 1808, and it had put Laurids' mother in such a fright that she promptly gave birth to him right in the middle of the kitchen floor. When little Albert wasn't busy with the cannonball it lived in the kitchen, where Karoline used it as a mortar for crushing mustard seeds.

'It could have been you announcing your arrival, my boy,' Laurids' father had once said to him, 'seeing how big you were when you were born. If the stork had dropped you, you'd have gone through the roof just like an English cannonball.'

'*Finggu,*' Laurids said, holding up his finger.

He wanted to teach the children the American language.

Fut meant foot. He pointed to his boot. *Maus* was mouth.

He rubbed his belly when they sat down to eat and bared his teeth.

'*Hanggre.*'

They all understood he was telling them he was hungry.

Ma was *misis*, pa was *papa tru*. When Laurids was away, they said 'Mother' and 'Father' like normal children, except for Albert. He had a special bond with his father.

The children had many names, *piccaninnies*, *bullies* and *hearties*.

'*Laihim tumas*,' Laurids said to Karoline, and pursed his lips as if he was about to kiss her.

She blushed and laughed, and then got angry.

'Don't be such a fool, Laurids,' she said.

IN 1848, WAR BROKE OUT BETWEEN THE DANISH CROWN AND THE rebellious Germans across the Baltic in Schleswig-Holstein, who wanted to cut their ties with Denmark. The old customs steward, de la Porte, was the first to know because the provisional insurgent government in Kiel sent him a 'proclamation', accompanied by a request to hand over the customs coffers.

All of Ærø was up in arms, and we immediately formed a home guard led by a young teacher from Rise, who from then on was known as the General. On the highest points of the island we erected beacons made of barrels filled with tar and old rope, attached to poles. If the German came by sea, we'd signal his approach by setting them alight and hoisting them up.

There were beacons at Knasterbjerg and on the hills by Vejsnæs, and all around our coastguards watched the horizon closely.

But all this war business soon became too much for Laurids, who never had much respect for anything to begin with. One evening, as he was on his way home from Eckernförde Fjord, he passed Vejsnæs where he neared the shore and yelled: 'The German is coming!' His voice ringing out across the water.

A few minutes later the barrel at the top of the hill was set alight, then the one on Knasterbjerg, and the others followed all the way down to Synneshøj, almost fifteen miles away, until the whole of Ærø was illuminated as on Bonfire Night.

As the flames rose, Laurids lay in his boat, laughing his head off at the mayhem he'd caused. But when he reached Marstal, he saw lights everywhere and the streets teeming with people, even though it was late evening. Some were shouting incomprehensible orders; others were whimpering and praying. A belligerent crowd was marching up Markgade armed with scythes, pitchforks and the odd gun, and terrified young mothers rushed around the streets, clutching wailing babies, sure that the German would skewer them on his bayonet. By the well on the corner of Markgade and Vestergade a skipper's wife was arguing with a servant girl. The woman had got it into her head that they should hide in the well and was ordering the girl to go first.

'After you, Madam,' the girl insisted.

We men were ordering each other about as well, but there are too many skippers in our town for anyone to heed anyone else, so all we could agree on was making a solemn vow to part with our lives only at the highest possible price.

The upheaval reached the vicarage in Kirkestrædet where Pastor Zachariassen was entertaining guests. One lady fainted, but the pastor's twelve-year-old son, Ludvig, grabbed a poker ready to defend his country against the advancing enemy. At the home of Mr Isager, the schoolteacher, who also doubled up as parish clerk, the family prepared for imminent attack. All twelve sons were on hand to celebrate the birthday of their mother, the portly Mrs Isager: she equipped them with clay pots filled with ashes and commanded them to throw the contents in the face of the German, should he dare to storm their house.

Our flock moved on through Markgade towards Reberbanen led by old Jeppe, who was waving a pitchfork and yelling that the German was welcome to come and get him if he dared. Laves Petersen, the little carpenter, was forced to return home. He had bravely slung his gun over his shoulder and filled his pockets to bursting with bullets, but halfway down the street, had suddenly remembered he'd left his gunpowder behind.

At Marstal Mill the miller's hefty wife, Madam Weber, already armed with a pitchfork, insisted on joining the fight, and because she appeared more intimidating than most of us men, we instantly welcomed her to our bloodthirsty ranks.

Laurids, who was an emotional man, was so fired up by the general fighting spirit that he too ran home to find a weapon. Karoline and the four children were hiding under the dining table in the parlour when he burst in and proclaimed cheerfully: 'Come along, kids, time to go to war!'

There was a hollow thud. It was Karoline banging her head against

7

the underside of the dining table. With effort, she crawled out from under the table, stood to her full height and screamed at her husband: 'Have you completely lost your mind, Madsen? Children don't go to war!'

Rasmus and Esben started jumping up and down.

'We want to go! We want to go!' they yelled in unison. 'Please, please, let us go.'

Little Albert had already started rolling his cannonball around.

'Have you all gone stark raving mad?' their mother shouted, boxing the ears of whichever child came near. 'You get back under that table right now!'

Laurids ran out into the kitchen to find a suitable weapon. 'Where do you keep the big frying pan?' he called into the parlour.

'You keep your hands off it!' Karoline shouted back.

'Well, I'll take the broom then,' he announced. 'The German will be sorry!'

They heard the front door slam behind him.

'Did you hear that?' whispered Rasmus, the eldest, to Albert. 'Father wasn't even speaking American.'

'The man's insane,' their mother said, shaking her head in the darkness underneath the dining table. 'Have you ever heard of anyone going to war with a broom?'

Laurids' arrival in our militant crowd stirred great delight. True, he had a reputation for being cocky, but he was big and strong and good to have on your side.

'Is that the only weapon you've got?'

We had spotted the broom.

'It's good enough for the German,' he replied, brandishing it aloft. 'We'll sweep him right out of here.'

Feeling invincible, we roared with laughter at his joke.

'Let's leave a few pitchforks behind,' Lars Bødker said. 'We'll need them for stacking the bodies.'

By now we'd reached the open fields. It was half an hour's march to Vejsnæs, but our pace was brisk and our blood was up. At Drejbakkerne, the sight of the flaming beacons further fuelled our fighting spirit. But at the sound of horses' hooves in the darkness we froze. The enemy was upon us!

* * *

8

We had hoped to surprise the German on the beach, but here on the hill the terrain still favoured us. Laurids positioned himself for battle with his broom and we followed suit.

'Wait for me!' a voice rang out behind us.

It was the little carpenter, who'd gone home for his gunpowder.

'Shhhh,' we warned. 'The German is closing in.'

The hoof beats grew louder – and it became clear that there was only one horse. When the rider appeared out of the darkness, Laves Petersen raised his gun and took aim. But Laurids pushed down on the barrel.

'It's Bülow, the controller,' he said.

The horse was dripping with sweat, its black flanks pumping in and out. Bülow raised his hand.

'You can go home. There's no German at Vejsnæs.'

'But the beacons were alight,' Laves called out.

'I've spoken to the coastguard,' Bülow said. 'It was a false alarm.'

'And we left our warm beds. For what? For nothing!'

Madam Weber folded her arms across her chest and fired us all a warning glance as though looking for a new enemy now that the German had failed to show.

'At least we've proved that we're ready for him,' the controller said soothingly. 'And surely it's good news that he's not coming after all.'

We mumbled in agreement. But although we saw his logic, we were sorely disappointed. We had been ready to stare the German in the face, and death, too – but neither had made it to Ærø.

'One day that German will be sorry,' Lars Bødker said.

Starting to tire, we decided to head home. A chilly shower had begun to fall. In silence we reached the mill, where Madam Weber parted company from us. Turning to face our miserable flock, she placed her pitchfork on the ground as though presenting a rifle.

'I wonder,' she said in an ominous voice, 'which one of you jokers got decent folks out of their beds in the middle of the night to go to war.'

We all stared at Laurids, towering there with his broom on his shoulder.

But Laurids neither flinched nor averted his eyes. Instead he looked straight at us. Then he threw his head back and started laughing into the rain.

SOON WAR BROKE OUT IN EARNEST AND WE WERE CALLED UP FOR the navy. The naval steamer, *Hekla*, anchored off the neighbouring town of Ærøskøbing to collect us. We lined up on the quay, and as our names were called one by one we jumped into the launch, which took us to the steamer. We'd felt cheated out of war that evening in November, but now the waiting was over and we were in high spirits.

'Make way for a Dane with his life, his soul and his seabag!' yelled Claus Jacob Clausen.

He was a small, sinewy man who liked to boast that a Copenhagen tattoo artist called Frederik the Spike had once told him he had the toughest arm he'd ever stuck a needle into. Clausen's father, Hans Clausen, had been a pilot, as had his grandfather, and Clausen wanted to follow in their footsteps; what's more, the night before we embarked he'd had a dream which told him he'd emerge from the war alive.

In Copenhagen we were inspected on board the frigate *Gefion*. Laurids was separated from the rest of us and was the only one to join the *Christian VIII*, the ship-of-the-line, whose mainmast was so tall that from top to the deck it stood one and a half times the height of the church tower in Marstal. We had to crane our necks to take it in, but the dizziness it induced filled us with pride about the great deeds we'd been summoned to perform.

Laurids watched us as we left. After a year on the American man-of-war *Neversink*, the *Christian VIII* suited him. He'd soon feel at home on her deck – though when he saw the rest of us disappear up the gangway to the *Gefion*, he must have felt briefly abandoned.

So off we went to war. On Palm Sunday we sailed along the coast of Ærø, past the hills at Vejsnæs, where Laurids had turned the island upside down with his cry 'The German is coming!' Now the Dane was coming, and it was the German's turn to light his tar barrels and take off like a headless chicken.

We moored off Als and waited. On the Wednesday we set course for Eckernförde Fjord and reached its mouth late that afternoon. There we followed the order to line up on the quarterdeck: in our homespun shirts and cloth trousers of blue, black or white, we were a motley crew. Only the ribbons on our caps emblazoned with the name *Gefion* and a red-and-white cockade announced that we were members of the King's navy. The captain, who was dressed in his finest uniform, complete with epaulettes and a sword, gave a speech in which he ordered us to fight like brave lads. He shouted three cheers for the King and waved his tricorn, and we joined in with all our might. Then he ordered the cannons to be fired so we raw recruits could hear how they'd sound in battle. A formidable roar rolled across the sea, accompanied by the acrid smell of gunpowder. A strong breeze was blowing, carrying the blue haze of cannon smoke off on the wind. For several minutes we couldn't hear a thing. The noise from the cannons had deafened us.

Two steamers arrived, and we recognised the *Hekla*, the ship we had sailed in from Ærøskøbing. We were now a full squadron. The next day we geared up for battle, settling the cannons in their ports, positioning the pumps and hoses where they could be put to immediate use if fire broke out on board, and placing case-shots, grapeshot and boxes of cartridges by each cannon. In the last few days we had practised this drill so many times that we knew most of the naval commands by heart. We were eleven men to each cannon, and from the moment the first command sounded: 'Get ready!' followed by 'Fuse powder and paper!' and 'Insert cartridge!' to the command 'Fire!' we scrambled around each other, terrified of making a mistake. We were used to working in threes or fours on our small boats and ketches but now suddenly we were to be masters of life and death.

All too often we'd stand there baffled while the gun captain screamed something like 'Tend the vent!' or 'Search the piece!' What the hell did that mean in plain Danish? Whenever we succeeded in performing a complicated routine without errors, the captain would congratulate us and we'd erupt in cheers. Upon which he'd look first at us, then at his cannon, and finally down at the deck, and shake his head.

'You bunch of puppies,' he said. 'Just do your best, damn you!'

We weren't entirely sure which German we were supposed to be shooting. It surely couldn't be old Ilse with the crooked hip who sold us our beloved schnapps when we moored our boats at Eckernförde's harbour. Nor Eckhart, the grain trader: we'd struck many a fine bargain with him. Then there was Hansen, the innkeeper at Der Rote Hahn. What could be more Danish than the name Hansen? And we'd never seen him anywhere near a gun. None of them could be the German; that much we understood. But the King knew who he was. As did the captain, who had been cheering with such bravado.

We approached the fjord. The enemy batteries on the coast started to thunder, but we were outside of their range and they soon grew quiet. We were given schnapps rather than the usual tea. At nine o'clock came the beating of the tattoo; it was time to turn in. Seven hours later we were roused from our slumbers. It was Maundy Thursday 5 April 1849. Again we got schnapps instead of tea, and a barrel of beer awaited us on the deck. We could drink as much as we wanted, so morale was high by the time we raised the anchor and headed into the fjord. We had no complaints about the victuals on board His Majesty's ships. Food had been scarce when we'd had to supply it for ourselves. They said you'd never see a seagull in the wake of a Marstal ship, and that was true enough: we never wasted a crumb. But on top of tea and beer, the navy gave us all the bread as we could eat and more. Lunch was a pound of fresh meat or half a pound of bacon, dried peas, porridge or soup; in the evening it was four weights of butter, and a schnapps to go with it. Long before we smelled our first whiff of gunpowder smoke, we loved the war.

Now we were inside Eckernförde Fjord, where the shores were closer and the cannons' positions clearly visible. Kresten Hansen leaned over to Ejnar Jensen and confided in him, yet again, his conviction that he wouldn't survive the battle.

'I've known it since the day the German demanded the duty coffers. I'm going to die today.'

'You know nothing,' Ejnar replied. 'You had no idea the battle would be on Maundy Thursday.'

'I've known a long time: the hour is upon us!'

'Shut your trap,' growled Ejnar. He'd suffered Kresten's bleating ever since they'd packed their seabags and laced their boots.

But Kresten was unstoppable. Breathing in rapid gasps, he placed a hand on his friend's arm.

'Promise me you'll bring my seabag back to Marstal.'

'You can bring it yourself. Now stop it, before you scare the living daylights out of me, too.'

Ejnar threw an anxious glance at Kresten. We'd never seen our friend in such a state before. Kresten was the son of the skipper Jochum Hansen, an official with the harbour authority. Kresten took after him, right down to the freckles, the strawberry-blond hair and the quiet manner.

'Here,' Ejnar said, handing him a pitcher of beer. 'Get that down your neck.'

He held it to Kresten's lips but the beer went down the wrong way: he spluttered and his eyes grew glassy. Ejnar slapped him on the back, and Kresten gasped and wheezed, the beer pouring from his nostrils.

'You dumb oaf,' Ejnar laughed. 'You won't drown if you're meant to hang. You nearly finished yourself off there. You're doing the German out of a job.'

But Kresten's eyes remained distant.

'The hour is upon us,' he repeated in a hollow voice.

'Well, I for one am not going to be shot.' Little Clausen had joined in the conversation. 'I know, because I dreamed it. I was walking down Møllevejen, going into town. There was a soldier on either side of me, ready to shoot. Then a voice called out: "You shall go!" And so I did. The bullets whizzed past my ears, but none of them hit me. So I'm not going to get shot today. I'm certain of it!'

We looked across the fjord: the surrounding fields were clad in spring green, and a thatched farmhouse lay snuggled in a small grove of lime trees in bud, with a road flanked by stone walls leading up to it. A cow grazing by the roadside turned her back to us and flicked her tail lazily, oblivious to the war approaching by water.

* * *

The cannon batteries to starboard were closing in; we saw the smoke, then heard their thunder roll across the water like a storm gathering from nowhere.

Kresten leaped up.

'The hour is upon us,' he said.

A tongue of fire flashed from the *Christian VIII*'s starboard stern. We exchanged puzzled glances. Had she been struck?

Being unfamiliar with warfare we did not know what a direct hit might entail. There was no reaction from the ship-of-the-line.

'Why don't they shoot back?' Ejnar asked.

'Because they're still not crosswise to the battery,' Clausen answered knowledgeably.

A moment later a cloud of pewter smoke on the starboard side of the *Christian VIII* announced that they were indeed responding. The battle had begun. Fire and earth exploded on the shore and tiny matchstick men rushed around. A good easterly wind was blowing and soon it was *Gefion*'s turn to deliver a broadside. The roar from the huge sixty-pound cannons made the whole ship shudder. Our stomachs lurched. We pressed our hands to our ears and screamed from a mixture of fear and elation, astounded by the force of the impact.

Now the German was getting a real hammering!

After some minutes, the firing from the battery on the point ceased. By now we had to rely solely on our eyes because we couldn't hear a thing. The shore looked like a desert landscape with sand shoved up in piles. The black barrel of a twenty-four-pounder stuck up in the air, flipped over as if by an earthquake. No one was moving.

We slapped one another's backs in mute victory. Even Kresten appeared to have forgotten his grim premonitions of doom and surrendered to the general ecstasy: war was a thrill, a rush of schnapps that fired up your blood – only the joy was wider and purer. The smoke drifted away and the air cleared. Never before had we seen the world with such clarity. We stared like newborn babies. Rigging, masts and sails formed a canopy above us like the foliage of a fresh-sprung beech forest. Everything bore an other-worldly sheen.

'Christ, I feel all solemn,' Little Clausen said, once our faculties had returned. 'Bloody hell, bloody hell.' He couldn't stop swearing. 'Bugger me if I've ever seen the like.'

We'd heard the thunder of cannons being tested the previous

evening, but actually witnessing their effect – that did something to a man.

'Yes,' Ejnar reflected. 'Those cannons make Pastor Zachariassen's hellfire seem tame. So what do you say, Kresten?'

Kresten's expression had turned almost pious. 'Fancy me living to see this,' he said quietly.

'So you've stopped thinking you're going to die?'

'Oh, I'm more certain of it than ever. But I've stopped being scared.'

We couldn't claim this incident as our personal baptism of fire, because the sixty-pound cannons that we manned were mounted on the top deck on the port side, and the fighting was to starboard. Our turn would come soon, when we sailed deeper along the fjord towards Eckernförde, where two more batteries awaited on either bank. But this was no great threat, as we saw it. It wasn't yet eight in the morning and the battle was already half won; we even began to fear the war would end before it had begun. We'd just had a taste of it, and now it looked as if the German might be beaten before lunch.

The *Gefion* continued towards the head of the fjord; the northern battery lay straight ahead. We were only two cable lengths from the southern battery when we shivered the topsails so they spilled the wind. We struck the jib and let go a drag anchor on the port side so that we lay facing the enemy with our broadside, and the *Christian VIII* did likewise. It was time to fire.

Our blood sang. We were like children waiting to see Chinese fireworks. Fear had melted away completely and only anticipation remained. We hadn't yet recovered from our first victory, and a second one awaited us.

Then the *Gefion* started to move. The drag anchor was failing to hold her and the strong current propelled us towards the southern battery. We looked across to the *Christian VIII*. The huge ship-of-the-line was adrift too and already coming under intense fire from the shore. Its sailors lowered the heavy anchor to stop her drifting and let off a violent salvo which burst from her side stem to stern. Cannon smoke erupted from the ports, floating across the fjord to form a rapidly growing cloud. But there hadn't been time to adjust the cannons before the ship's unexpected drift towards the shore, and they'd fired too high, hitting the fields behind the batteries.

A moment later it was our turn. We were now close enough to the coast to be within firing range of the German rifles. The current and the wind continued to torment us, and we were crossing the fjord with both broadsides facing the empty water. Only our four stern cannons had a chance to respond to the vicious fire from the battery onshore.

The first hit cleared our aft deck of eleven men. We'd been calling the cannonballs 'grey peas', but the thing that shot low across the deck, tearing rail, cannon ports and people apart in a shower of wooden splinters, was no pea. Ejnar saw its approach, and registered every metre of its journey as it swept across the deck, shearing the legs off one man and sending them flying in one direction while the rest of him went in another. It sliced off a shoulder here and smashed a skull there. It was hurtling towards Ejnar with bone splinters, blood and hair stuck to it. He let himself fall backwards and saw it shoot past. He later said that it took off his bootlaces in passing; that's how close it came before it tore out through the quarterdeck aft.

To Ejnar that cannonball was a monster with a will of its own. It showed him what war was: not a battery that exploded and sent matchstick soldiers fleeing, but a dragon that breathed hot fire on his naked heart.

The deck was in chaos; a wild-eyed officer screamed at him to go to the mast with the helmsman and a soldier. The order made no sense, but he did as he was told. The soldier collapsed straight away in a pool of blood. It looked as if something inside him had exploded: a hole had opened in his chest and blood gushed out. Ejnar saw a man's eye burst into a red mess and another man's skull torn off. That was a strange sight: pink brain matter exposed and splattered as if it were porridge, and someone had slammed a wooden spoon into it. Ejnar had not known that such things could happen to human beings. Then a second cannonball struck and killed the lieutenant. As he witnessed Armageddon, Ejnar went hot and cold and his nose started bleeding from the shock.

Another officer with blood pouring down his face ordered him to cannon number seven. Ejnar had originally been assigned to number ten, but that had taken a direct hit and now stood lopsided by the cannon port. Around it lay a roil of motionless bodies in a slowly spreading pool of blood. Small streams of urine formed deltas between their legs. He could not see if Kresten or Little Clausen was among them. A severed foot lay a short distance away. Like the dead men, Ejnar had wet himself. The roar of cannons had caused an earthquake in his intestines, and he'd filled his trousers, too. He knew that people emptied their bowels at the moment of death, but he hadn't imagined that it could happen to the living as well. The notion that war made a man of you vanished as he felt the stickiness slide down his thighs. He felt half-corpse, half-baby, but soon discovered that he was not the only one. The stench of upturned privy buckets wafted across the deck. It wasn't just coming from the slaughtered. Most of those still fighting had soiled trousers.

The gun captain at cannon number seven was still alive, bleeding from a cut above his eyebrow where he'd been hit by a flying splinter. He screamed at Ejnar, who could hear nothing, but when he pointed at the cannon, Ejnar understood that he wanted him to load it. His arms were too short to reach, so he had to climb halfway out of the cannon port in order to stuff the cannonball into the muzzle, exposing himself to the enemy battery. As he worked, there was only one thought in his head: when was the next round of schnapps?

Meanwhile, the *Gefion* had managed to reposition herself so her broadsides were aligned with both shores. But the steamer *Geiser*, which had tried to come to our aid with a hawser, had taken a hit to her engine and was being pulled out of the battle, and so was the *Hekla*, whose rudder was shot to pieces. The wind was due east and the loss of the two steamers, which were supposed to have towed us if necessary, meant that we were unable to retreat if things went wrong.

However, our luck was about to change. The northern battery took one direct hit after another, and we saw the matchstick soldiers on the beach run for cover. Their cannons were undamaged and new soldiers kept running to man them, so there was hardly any respite from their fire, but still, it was halfway to victory. The quartermaster came round with a pail of schnapps, and we accepted the outstretched mug as solemnly as if it were communion wine. Fortunately the beer barrel had survived intact and we paid it frequent visits. We felt utterly lost. The constant bombardment and the randomness with which death scythed us down had exhausted us, although the battle was only a few hours old. We kept skidding in sticky pools of blood and there was no avoiding the spectacle of all the horrifically maimed bodies. Only one sense was spared: our deafness prevented us from hearing the screams of the wounded.

We were afraid to look around for fear of staring straight into the face of a friend, snared by eyes that might plead for relief one moment and burn with hatred the next, as though the fallen blamed us for our luck and wanted nothing more in this world than to exchange fates with us. No one could offer a single word of comfort; it would pass unheard in the din from the cannons. A hand on the shoulder would have to do. But already those of us who were still uninjured were keeping to ourselves and avoiding the stricken, even though they were the ones in need of consolation. The living closed ranks against those marked for death.

We reloaded the cannons and aimed as the gun captains ordered us, but we'd stopped thinking in terms of victory or defeat. Our battle was to escape the sight of the wounded, and questions rang in our heads like an echo of the destruction around us: Why him, or him? Why not me? But we didn't want to heed them: we wanted to survive. Nothing existed beyond what we could see through the barrel of a gun.

The schnapps had worked its blessed magic. Drunk now, we surrendered to a blankness born of terror. We sailed on a black sea and we had only one goal: not to look down and drown in it.

Ejnar climbed in and out of the cannon port. It was a beautiful spring day and every time he appeared in the mild sunshine, he expected a bullet to his chest. He was muttering to himself, though he'd no idea what he was saying. He looked a sight, smeared in soot and blood, with a bleeding nose which from time to time he would wipe with his sleeve before tilting his head back to try and staunch the flow. There was an acrid taste in his mouth that only repeated swigs of schnapps could relieve. Eventually his tension loosened into lethargy and his movements became mechanical. But he was in no worse state than the rest of us, with his bloodstained appearance or his soiled trousers: none of us looked alive any more. We resembled ghosts from a battle fought long ago: corpses on a muddy battle-field where we'd lain for weeks, forgotten in the pouring rain.

*   *   *

Three times we saw the men on the northern battery relieved, and not one of the shots fired by the matchstick soldiers appeared to miss its target. It seemed that the batteries on both sides of the fjord had concentrated their fire on us.

At one o'clock a signal flag was hoisted on the mangled rigging of the *Gefion*. Its message was intended for the crew of the *Christian VIII*: we can do no more. Most of our cannons were now abandoned and the ones firing were undermanned. Those of us still standing were working amid piles of corpses and the dying, who reached out for us in their delirium, pleading for company in the mire of guts, blood and voided bowels.

The signal we sent was in code. The enemy on the shores of Eckernförde Fjord couldn't understand it, but the *Christian VIII* knew exactly what it meant.

On the ship-of-the-line there was no significant loss of life as yet. Early that morning a quartermaster from Nyborg had been killed and since then two men had been wounded, but the vessel had been spared any major hits. At the same time, Commander Paludan was forced to acknowledge that our squadron's bombardment of the batteries on the northern and southern shores had inflicted no significant damage. The battle had now been raging for more than six hours and there was no prospect of victory. Retreat was impossible; anyone could see that.

The two steamers, the *Hekla* and the *Geiser*, were out of action, and the wind was set against us. So when Commander Paludan decided to raise the flag of truce, it was not a surrender, not yet: merely a pause in the battle.

A lieutenant was rowed ashore with a letter and returned soon afterwards with the message that a reply would be forthcoming in an hour. *Christian VIII*'s top and lower sails were fastened and the crew given bread and beer. There was still order on deck, and though everyone had been deafened by the cannons, there was no mood of resignation. At most, the crew felt a vague unease at the course of the battle. They could see that the *Gefion* was in a bad way, but there was no way they could imagine the bloody chaos on our deck.

Laurids Madsen sat by himself with his bread, busy satisfying his hunger and as yet unaware of his fate.

By now thousands of people had spilled out of the town of Eckernförde and were crowding both shores. Watching them as he munched his bread, Laurids soon realised that it was not curiosity that had brought them out. They were lighting huge fires in the fields and collecting the cannonballs that lay scattered on the beach, then shoving them in the fires and heating them until the iron glowed red before transporting them to their own cannons. Horse-drawn land artillery appeared on the high road from Kiel and spread out behind the stone walls that bordered the surrounding fields.

Laurids recalled his father's account of the war against the English, when Marstal came under attack. Two English frigates had anchored south of the town; they had come to hijack the town's ships, of which there were roughly fifty in the harbour. The English sent out three launches crammed with armed soldiers, but the inhabitants of Marstal, together with some grenadiers from Jutland, managed to drive them off. They could scarcely believe their own eyes when the English started retreating.

'Well, I never did understand what that war was really about,' his father said afterwards. 'The English are good sailors, and I've no quarrel with them. But our livelihoods were at stake. If they took our ships, that would be the end of us. That's why we won. We had no choice.'

On the deck of the *Christian VIII* Laurids sat beneath the flag of truce, watching the teeming crowds on the shores. He wasn't sure he understood war any better than his father had done. They were defending the Danish flag against the Germans, and that had sufficed him up until a moment ago. War was like sailing. You could learn about clouds, wind direction and currents, but the sea remained forever unpredictable. All you could do was adapt to it and try to return home alive. Here the enemy was the cannonfire in Eckernförde Fjord. Once it had been silenced, the way home would lie clear. That was the war as far as he was concerned. He was no patriot, nor was he the opposite. He took life as it came. His horizon was one of mast tops, mill wings and the ridged turret on the church: the skyline of Marstal, viewed from the sea. Here were ordinary people throwing themselves into war: not just soldiers, but people from Eckernförde, a port where he'd often docked with cargoes of grain: the very place he'd sailed from on the evening he'd turned all of Ærø upside down.

Now the Eckernфördeners stood shoulder to shoulder on the beach, just as the Marstallers had once done. So what the hell was this war all about?

A boat was launched from the beach. In it sat the lieutenant from the *Christian VIII*, returning from a third round of negotiations. On each occasion the battle had been deferred. The ceasefire had lasted two and a half hours and it was now half past four. From the furious way the sailors were tugging at the oars, it was clear that something decisive had happened. Then out of nowhere the cannons on the beach burst into a roar. The flag of truce was still fluttering from the mast, but the war had resumed.

The *Christian VIII* returned fire immediately, while the *Gefion*, silent as a ghost ship, tried to get out of the way. We had given up and were using our last strength to inch ourselves forward with the kedge.

Now the enemy changed tactics, aiming the batteries on both sides of the fjord at the *Christian VIII* rather than us, in an attempt to set her alight. Many of the cannonballs that struck her were red hot from lying on the field fires half the afternoon. The Eckernfördeners had made good use of their time.

Within seconds, the deck was covered with fallen and wounded men. The attack had come out of the blue. Fires flared in several places, and we immediately deployed pumps and hoses to swill death off the deck, but the crackling flames had already taken hold.

Commander Paludan now saw that the battle was lost. The *Christian VIII* swayed to escape the line of fire, but the wind was still set against her and all she succeeded in doing was traversing the current, losing the advantage of facing the shores broadside-on. Second-guessing the commander's plan, the Germans immediately aimed at her sails and rigging. They weren't going to let us cut and run.

The heavy anchor was raised, but to huge losses. Firebombs landed on the bow; grenades exploded between the legs of the poor souls manning the capstan. They called for reinforcements and the new arrivals kicked aside the dead and the wounded with their boots. Then fresh grenades blew off the bars of the capstan, leaving ragged wood stumps, shattered bones and mangled fingers. Finally the anchor was pulled up, dripping with mud and seaweed. This feat alone cost the happiness of ten families. Their sons and fathers would never return home.

The jib was raised, the topsail sheets secured and the sails hoisted. As a topman, Laurids went up with the others and clambered onto the yardarm, from which he had an excellent view of the battle.

The sun was setting on the horizon, casting its soft light across the fjord and the landscape. Wisps of cloud fanned out across the blushing sky; only a few hundred metres from the fjord everything was peaceful and springlike. But the shores were black with armed people and the artillery was firing away from behind the shelter of the stone walls. From the beach, red-hot cannonballs flew in an endless cannonade, while civilians in their thousands raised their guns and took aim.

Once, Laurids had hung off the far end of a yardarm through a white-out south of Cape Horn, his hands freezing to lumps of ice. He'd had to crawl back to the rigging clinging to the yard with his arms and legs – but he hadn't been afraid. Now his hands were shaking so badly that he couldn't undo the simplest knot.

Sails, masts and rigging had been torn apart during the firing. Around him other topmen fell one by one, hit by grenades or fireballs or spear-like shards from the stricken masts, tumbling down between half-raised sails, ropes and halyards, plunging to the deck far below or plummeting into the water. Then he gave up and made his way back to the rigging.

On deck chaos reigned. The sails couldn't be hoisted because the halyards and braces were shot to pieces. Some of the crew were pulling like mad at the cross-sail and had almost managed to raise it when suddenly the blocks and tackle – heavy enough to crush any man in their path – came hurtling down.

Every attempt to rescue the *Christian VIII* had failed. Sailing her had become impossible and in any case the wind blew directly towards land. A severe gale was brewing and the mighty ship drifted helpless to the shore, where she foundered just east of the southern battery, which continued its ferocious shelling of the now defenceless ship. Only her stern cannons could have been used in this position, but she'd tilted so violently that nothing would hold in place.

Then the cry went up: 'Fire on board!'

The earliest shouts had been false alarms compared to this. A fireball had pierced the innermost battery and lodged in the starboard hold. The blaze spread quickly, threatening the powder magazines. Other areas had caught too. The men worked the pumps, but in vain. The flames had the upper hand.

At six o'clock the flag was lowered and the *Christian VIII* ceased firing, but the bombardment continued for another quarter of an hour before the enemy's lust for victory – over a battleship that only hours before seemed invincible – was assuaged.

Commander Paludan was rowed ashore as a sign of surrender, and it was at that point that the crew's courage finally plummeted. They gave up fighting the fire and shuffled around, filthy and foul-smelling. Their seamanship was of no use to them now. They had no experience of war or of defeat: they'd imagined the battle would be a laugh, and now their souls were drained of energy and their heads empty of all but the echo of cannons. This last shameful part of the battle had lasted one and a half hours, but it felt like one and a half lifetimes. They could see nothing beyond this. They were utterly spent.

Some sat down on the deck in the midst of the sea of flames, as if the clergymen's pulpit warnings about the fires of hell had become reality while others stood motionless, staring straight ahead, their inner mechanisms broken. Lieutenants Ulrik, Stjernholm and Corfitz rushed around screaming into their faces: they must act, they were needed more than ever, if complete disaster was to be prevented and the honour of Denmark saved after a battle that they could hardly pride themselves on. But they'd been deafened by the cannons, and only pushing, shoving and kicking would stir them.

Laurids let himself be herded to the powder magazine furthest astern, but it was slow work throwing the kegs into the water. They were only five men, and whenever a new crewman was forced into the chamber, he'd rush straight back out.

Suddenly came the cry 'All men up!'

They knew instantly what that meant. Exchanging looks of alarm, they dropped the bombs and the kegs and hurtled up the ladder to find sheep, calves, pigs, hens and ducks out of their enclosures running loose on deck among the terrified sailors. A pig rummaged about sticking its snout into bloody piles of guts, slurping.

The men raced about, each on his own urgent mission. Some

hunted for their clothes and seabags, while others climbed onto the rail as though contemplating jumping into the freezing water. No one paid heed to the wounded men, who got in everyone's way and were carelessly trampled. Their screams of agony went unheard: most of the crew were still deaf after the hours of intense shelling.

Laurids rushed below to the sick bay, concerned that the wounded might be abandoned. Smoke seeped up through the heavy oak planks. Covering his mouth with his hand, he stepped into the murky room, where an orderly with his face wrapped in a cloth came up to him.

'Is anyone coming?' Laurids realised his hearing had returned. 'We've got to get the wounded topside. We're choking down here!'

'I'll go get help!' Laurids shouted back.

On deck there was no sign of the officers who had kicked the crew and whacked them with the flat side of their blades; instead he saw a crowd of men flocking to an open gangway with a Jacob's ladder, and ran over to them. The evacuation was already in full force. He spotted a couple of the lieutenants slashing through the crowd with their swords as they tried to reach the gangway. The ship's second in command, Captain Krieger, stood to one side watching it all with an odd, distant gaze, his binoculars slung across his back, a gilt-framed portrait of his wife tucked under one arm and the other raised in salute.

'You have shown yourselves to be brave men,' he muttered over and over again, as if blessing his woeful flock. 'You have done your duty. You are all my brothers.'

No one took any notice of him; each man was focusing on the most important obstacle in his path to salvation: the back of the sailor ahead of him blocking his access to the open gangway. Laurids made his way to Krieger and screamed into his face:

'The wounded, Captain Krieger, the wounded!'

The captain turned to him, but his gaze remained distant. He placed a hand on Laurids' shoulder. Laurids felt it tremble, but the captain's voice was calm, almost sleepy.

'My brother, once we are ashore, we shall speak like brethren.'

'The wounded need help!' Laurids screamed once more. 'The whole ship is about to blow sky high.'

The captain's hand stayed on Laurids' shoulder.

24

'Yes, the wounded,' he said in the same monotonous, calm tone of voice. 'They too are my brothers. When we are ashore, we shall all speak like brethren.' His voice disintegrated into mumbling, and then he began again, reeling off the same phrases. 'You have shown yourselves to be brave men. You have done your duty. You are all my brethren.'

Giving up on the captain and turning to the men who were struggling to reach the open gangway, Laurids grabbed them by the shoulder one by one, shouting into their faces his message about helping the wounded. The first man reacted by punching him on the chin. The second shook his head in disbelief and then threw himself with renewed energy back into the brawl.

The evacuation had picked up pace. Fishing boats set off from the beach to rescue the crew from the battleship that only a few hours earlier had been bombarding them, while the ship's own main launch shuttled continuously between ship and beach. Laurids leaned over the rail and spotted the roaring fire leaping out of the stern cannon ports. It was only a matter of time.

Smoke was pouring out of every hatch, making it just as difficult to breathe above deck as below. Once again he rushed down to the sick bay but was soon forced to abandon the idea: the smoke was now so dense and suffocating that it seemed impossible that anyone might have survived.

'Is anyone here?' he called out, but there was no reply.

The smoke seared his lungs and a fit of coughing sent tears streaming down his cheeks. He hurtled back up to the deck, squeezing shut his burning eyes in pain, temporarily smoke-blinded. He slipped and fell on the deck, slick from human excretions and spilled organs. His hand touched something soft and wet, and he shot to his feet, rubbing his palm on his soiled trousers in terror. He couldn't bear the thought that he'd touched another human being's blood and guts. It felt as though his soul had been scalded.

He staggered to the rail, where the smoke was thinner, and tried to regain his vision. Through a mist of tears he made out the launch, which had run aground on a sandbank, forcing the crew to jump into the water and wade ashore, where the enemy soldiers were waiting for them. Then the launch came unstuck and immediately set course for the *Christian VIII,* while several of the fishing boats close to the ship started heading back to the shore. The launch, too, turned round. Howls of protest erupted from the open gangway.

Laurids stepped back from the rail into the billowing clouds of smoke.

'I SAW LAURIDS,' EJNAR WOULD ALWAYS SAY LATER. 'I SWEAR I SAW him.'

Ejnar was standing on the beach when the *Christian VIII* blew up. He'd been taken ashore from the *Gefion* under guard and grouped with the other survivors from the frigate, waiting to be led off. The German soldiers seemed almost taken aback by their own victory, and looked as if they had no idea what to do with us. Our numbers kept swelling as men from the two vanquished battleships filled the shore.

Then the warning cry rang out across the water.

Most of us, tired and disheartened, had been sitting on the beach with our eyes fixed on the sand as the soldiers pointed their bayonets at us with hands that trembled. But now we looked up. At the stern of the ship-of-the-line, a pillar of fire shot up with a deafening boom. Then more: column after column of flame broke through the deck as the powder magazines ignited. In seconds, the masts and yards were reduced to charcoal while the sails fluttered off in huge flakes of ash and the great oak hull became a weightless toy in the brutal hands of the blaze. But the worst was yet to come. The immense heat had set off the vanquished ship's cannons, which at the moment of capitulation had been loaded. Now, simultaneously, they discharged their deadly contents towards the shore.

Screams of horror rose from the crammed beach when the cannonballs started crashing down on us. Death was arbitrary. Burning debris rained from the heavens, wreaking destruction wherever it landed, so that the hour of victory was marked only by the sound of men screaming. This, then, was the dying ship's final salute to the victors and the vanquished: a murderous broadside that attacked both friend and foe alike. War showed its true face out there in the fire shower on Eckernförde Fjord.

* * *

For a moment it looked as if everyone on the beach had been killed. Bodies were strewn everywhere and not a single man was standing. Many were lying face down with their arms outstretched as if they were praying to the flames that leaped on the water. Here and there a piece of wreckage lay burning in the sand. Slowly, some of the prostrate figures got to their feet, anxiously eyeing the flaming ship. Cries came from the water. Several of the boats that had hurried to rescue the ship's crew had been struck and set ablaze. Lieutenant Stjernholm and four men had been heading for the beach with the ship's coffer, but their launch's stern had been blown off when the *Christian VIII* exploded. The coffer was lost, but the lieutenant managed to save himself. Only one of the men from the launch was with him when he staggered ashore, drenched through. The rest had drowned.

The beach was quiet except for the faint moaning of the wounded and the crackling of the still-burning wreckage, when suddenly a loud yell echoed across land and water.

'I've seen Laurids! I've seen Laurids!'

We raised our heads and looked around. We'd recognised Ejnar's voice, and most of us presumed the poor man had lost his mind. Then chaos erupted across the entire beach and everyone began shouting, as if the only way to feel alive was to kick up all the ruckus we could. In the confusion we could have escaped our captors, but we'd lost our nerve – and with it our ability to act. We had to content ourselves with having simply survived: we could muster nothing more.

Our captors weren't much better off. They led us away from the beach, their faces frozen, mute witnesses to the destruction they'd so closely avoided themselves. Our march looked more like a wholesale retreat from the theatre of war than an organised transportation of prisoners.

The Germans had routed us, but their faces showed no sign of triumph. Horror at the unthinkable forces that war had unleashed united both victors and vanquished.

THEY TOOK US TO ECKERNFÖRDE CHURCH. STRAW HAD BEEN SPREAD across the floor so we could collapse and rest our weary bodies. We were soaked through and shivering with cold. Once the sun had set, the April night grew chilly. Those of us who'd managed to save our seabags changed clothes and lent our less fortunate comrades what they needed. Soon food rations arrived: wholemeal bread, beer, and smoked bacon collected from the local grocers. No one in Eckernförde had expected to see the town filled with prisoners of war. On the contrary, they'd been expecting Danish soldiers to be patrolling their streets before the day was out. Now, instead of being under guard themselves, the town's citizens were playing host.

Old women appeared in the church to sell white bread and schnapps to those with money. One of them was Mother Ilse with the crooked hip. She stroked one prisoner's cheek with a sooty finger and muttered: 'You poor lad.'

She'd recognised him from his previous visits to the town. We'd all bought schnapps from her in our time. The man grabbed her hand.

'Don't you call me a poor lad. I'm alive.'

It was Ejnar.

In the long pause that had followed the hoisting of the signal flag, Ejnar had wandered the deck looking for Kresten, but he could find him among neither the living nor the wounded. Many of the dead were lying face down, and he'd had to turn them over. Others had had their faces shot off. Kresten wasn't among the bodies around cannon number seven.

Torvald Bønnelykke, who'd been standing by one of the other cannons, came up to him.

'Are you looking for Kresten?' he asked.

He was a Marstaller and had been party to Kresten's grim premonitions.

'He's lying over there,' he said, pointing. 'But you won't recognise him. A cannonball took off his head. I was standing next to him when it happened.'

'So he was right,' Ejnar said. 'Bloody awful way to die.'

'Death is death,' Bønnelykke said. 'I don't know if one way is better than another. The result's always the same.'

'I'd better go find his seabag. I promised him I would. Have you seen Little Clausen?'

Bønnelykke shook his head. They asked around, but no one knew where he was.

By now it was around ten o'clock. Exhausted, we were getting ready to sleep when the church door opened and yet another prisoner was led in, wrapped in a huge blanket. He sneezed incessantly, and his whole body shook.

'Bloody hell, I'm cold,' he said hoarsely, then gave another explosive sneeze.

'My God, if it isn't Little Clausen!'

Ejnar struggled to his feet and went over to his friend.

'So you're still alive.'

'Of course I bloody well am. I told you I would be. But this bastard cold will be the death of me instead: I'm sick as a dog.' He sneezed again.

Ejnar put his arm around him and led him to the straw bed he'd prepared for himself. He could feel Little Clausen shivering beneath the blanket, and his face was mottled with a feverish red.

'Do you have some dry clothes?'

'No, sod it, I didn't manage to save my seabag.'

'Take these. I hope you don't mind wearing Kresten's stuff.'

'So he . . .'

'Yes, it turned out he was right. But what happened to you? We looked everywhere. I thought you . . .'

'Don't they say that you don't drown if you're meant to hang? Seems the Lord has decided I'm to die from a cold, rather than in combat. I spent the whole battle suspended in an old bosun's chair along the side of the ship. I was supposed to be mending the holes with lead plates. They kept shooting at me, the bastards. But somehow they missed.'

'I didn't think you were a weakling,' Ejnar said. 'How come a bit of fresh air made you sick?'

'The rest of the crew bloody well forgot about me. I was stuck there the whole day with my legs in the water, freezing my arse off.' Little Clausen sneezed again. 'It wasn't until the ship was evacuated that I managed to flag down a boat. By then I was blue all over. I couldn't even walk when I got back onshore.' He'd put on the dry clothes and now slapped himself for warmth as he glanced around the church. 'How many were killed?'

'You mean how many Marstallers?'

'Yes, what else would I mean? I don't know the others.'

'I think we've lost seven.'

'Was Laurids one of them?'

Ejnar stared at the floor. Then he shrugged, as though embarrassed about something shameful. 'I can't answer that.'

'You don't mean he ran away?'

'No. Not exactly. I saw him shooting up into the sky. But then I saw him come down again.'

Little Clausen stared at him in disbelief, then shook his head.

'My eyes tell me that you've not been wounded,' he said. 'But my ears tell me that you've lost your mind.'

He gave another sneeze and sat down abruptly on the bed of straw. Ejnar sat next to him and stared into space with lost eyes. Perhaps he really had gone mad. Little Clausen leaned towards his friend and put his arm around his shoulder.

'There now,' he comforted him. 'It'll come back, you'll see.'

He lapsed into silence. Then added, softly, 'But I suppose we might as well write off Laurids.'

They sat for a while longer, saying nothing. Then they lay down and fell asleep, utterly spent.

At seven in the morning we were woken and treated to more bread, bacon and warm beer, and an hour later there was a headcount. When an officer arrived to take down our names and our home towns so that our families could be informed, we fell on him, yelling out our details so clamorously that by ten o'clock, when the order came to march us to the fortress in Rendsburg, he'd noted only half our names.

Outside the church they lined us up in ranks. The mood had

shifted: it seemed that Eckernförde was turning against its vanquished enemy, and our guards were losing patience with us. Many of us were still half deaf from yesterday's cannon fire and couldn't hear orders even when they were shouted right into our faces. So they shoved us around and beat us up. The town's citizens hustled around us, whooping at our humiliation, while a crowd of sailors with cutlasses swinging from their belts hurled out coarse oaths – which to our great irritation, we had to endure in silence.

The high road ran along the shoreline, affording us a final glimpse of our inexplicable defeat: the wreck of the *Christian VIII,* floating on the water. She was still smouldering, with smoke wafting from her charred hull, and the beach was littered with the debris of masts and yards flung ashore by the explosion. Like ants stripping the carcass of a lion, the Germans were already busy securing the flotsam from what had recently been one of the Danish Navy's proudest vessels. We passed the southern battery, which we'd spent a day bombarding and that in the end had sealed our fate. Not even the most unschooled among us needed to count fingers to calculate the enemy's firing power. Four cannons! That was all. A David had fought a Goliath. And the Goliath had been us.

Several vehicles overtook us, carrying officers from the *Christian VIII* and the *Gefion.* They, too, were heading for prison in Rendsburg. We exchanged salutes, and they were gone in a cloud of dust. Then came the rumbling of yet another cart and the sound of laughter. Some Holstein officers drove past us. Among them towered a bare-headed man.

Little Clausen and Ejnar looked at each other.

'The devil take me,' Little Clausen said. 'That was Laurids!'

'I told you so. He went shooting up into the sky and came back down again.'

Little Clausen's face split into a grin.

'Well, I don't care how he did it! The most important thing is he's alive.'

The cart stopped a short distance ahead, and the officers got out and shook hands with Laurids. One of them shoved a bottle of schnapps into his coat pocket, and another thrust a wad of banknotes at him. Then they raised their arms to salute him, and left. For a while Laurids just stood there dithering. Little Clausen called out his name. He looked in our direction and lifted his hand hesitantly. A soldier took hold of his arm and nudged him into the ranks next to his two fellow Marstallers.

'Laurids!' exclaimed Little Clausen. 'I thought you were dead.'

'And so I was,' Laurids said. 'I saw St Peter's bare arse.'

'St Peter's bare arse?'

'Yes, he pulled up his tunic and flashed his buttocks at me.'

Laurids fished the schnapps bottle out of his coat pocket and took a swig of the clear liquid. He handed the bottle to Little Clausen, who drank deeply before passing it on to Ejnar, who still hadn't said a word.

'Didn't you know,' Laurids said, 'that when St Peter shows you his arse, it means your time's not up yet?'

'And so you decided to return to earth.'

The explanation illuminated Ejnar's face, and he spoke with the relief of someone who has just been let off a criminal charge.

'I saw it,' he said. 'You were standing on the deck when the *Christian VIII* blew up. You were flung high into the air, ten metres at least, and then you came back down and landed on your feet. Little Clausen said I must have lost my mind. But I saw it. That's what happened, isn't it?'

'It was hot as hell,' Laurids said. 'But cooler higher up. I saw St Peter's arse and I knew I wasn't going to die.'

'But how did you get back ashore?' Little Clausen asked.

'I walked,' Laurids said.

'You walked? You're not telling me you walked on water?'

'No. I'm telling you I walked on the seabed.'

Laurids stopped and pointed at his boots. Somebody in the column behind him bumped into his broad back, and the ranks became muddled. A soldier rushed over and shoved Laurids with the butt of his gun.

Laurids turned round.

'Gently, gently,' he said with the tolerance of a drunk. He made a calming gesture, then fell back into the ranks and picked up the rhythm of the march.

The soldier kept pace alongside him.

'I didn't mean to hurt you,' he said in Danish. He had a South Jutland accent.

'No harm done,' Laurids replied.

'I've heard about you,' the soldier continued. 'You're the man who was blown up with the *Christian VIII* and landed right back on his feet, aren't you?'

'Yes, that's me,' Laurids replied with considerable dignity, straightening up. 'I landed on my feet, thanks be to God and my sea boots.'

'Your sea boots?'

Now it was Ejnar's turn to be mystified.

'Yes,' said Laurids in a tone of voice you'd use to explain something to a child. 'It's because of my sea boots that I landed on my feet. Have you ever tried wearing my sea boots? Damn heavy. No one wearing them could stay in heaven for long.'

'It's like the Resurrection.' The soldier gawped.

'Hogwash,' Laurids snorted brusquely. 'Jesus never wore sea boots.'

'And St Peter didn't flash his bare arse at him either,' Little Clausen added.

'Too right,' Laurids said, offering the bottle around.

The soldier, too, was offered a drop. Glancing quickly over his shoulder, he took a big swig.

But our merriment soon abated. It was thirty kilometres to Rendsburg and we had to walk all day to get there. When the farmers came out to stare at us, we didn't look back at them; our bravado had faded. As we staggered on, most of us just kept our eyes on the highway dust. A leaden weariness had us all in its grip, but whether it stemmed from our sore feet or from our sunken spirits we couldn't tell. Past caring, we jostled each other like drunken men, though only Laurids was enjoying the privilege of actual intoxication. He, for his part, was unmoved by our predicament. He marched along, humming tunes to himself – despite his visit to the Lord, none of the songs he chose were godly. Finally even he, too, fell silent and trudged on with his eyes turned inward, as if beginning to sleep off his inebriation while on foot.

From time to time we would stop at a pond for a drink of water. The soldiers would keep an eye on us, bayonets at the ready, while we filled our caps with water and passed them around. Then the marching resumed. Halfway to Rendsburg, our guards were relieved, and Ejnar and Little Clausen bade goodbye to the friendly soldier.

Laurids was still in a world of his own. The soldier took one last look at him and swapped a few words with his replacement, a Prussian. The Prussian threw Laurids a doubtful look and shook his head. But throughout the rest of the march, he kept eyeing him.

We reached Rendsburg at dusk. Rumours of the battle had preceded us, and the highway and ramparts were teeming with people who had come out to gawp at the prisoners. We passed through the town gate and crossed a bridge before going through the inner portal, then found ourselves in the narrow streets of the town centre. Here thousands more had gathered to stare, and our guards had to show their guns to make way for us and keep curious onlookers at bay. There were plenty of pretty girls among them, and it was galling to know that their eyes rested on us with contempt.

They held us in a spacious old church whose floor had been strewn with so much straw that it looked more like a barn than a house of God. We had eaten nothing all day, but now they distributed sacks of biscuits and warm beer. The biscuits must have been several years old; they turned to dust in our mouths, but the beer was welcome and soon we lay scattered across the broad church floor, fast asleep.

The next day, Holy Saturday, we milled about, assessing the accommodation and sleeping options, rediscovering some friends and noting the loss of others. There were men from both the *Gefion* and the *Christian VIII*. Some sections of the church had chairs, and curtains in the windows; these were quickly occupied, and their possession was considered a privilege. We men from Marstal gathered in a room by the chancel. The others stuck with those from their home towns too: men from Ærøskøbing here, men from the island of Funen there, men from Lolland, men from Langeland. There in the straw-carpeted church, we redrew the map.

We were strangers to discipline. We hadn't been in the navy long enough to value any formal systems of order beyond those we'd come up with ourselves. When our battleship had been set alight beneath our feet, we'd been separated from our officers, and now we obeyed only one command: that of the stomach. When the church door opened in the morning for the guards bringing bread, there was a stampede, with each man thinking only of his own hunger. In the end the soldiers just flung the bread into the air and we fought over it like wild animals. Someone tore Ejnar's loaf from his hands, and Little Clausen got kicked in the shin. It was a shameful episode, but whatever discipline the navy had instilled in us had vanished. In the new order we were forced to create, fighting was a useful skill. Only Laurids remained above it all, as though untouched by either hunger or thirst.

The next meal was distributed in the manner of a military exercise, with a major and a sergeant bellowing commands at us. They had brought the bosuns from the *Gefion* and *Christian VIII*, who divided us into the same groups of eight as on the warships, so we could be fed in an orderly way. We were each given a spoon and a metal bowl and made to line up by the altar. And it was, in its way, a form of communion, because it took every last scrap of imagination to transubstantiate what was in our metal bowls into something edible, and we consumed the sorry-looking mess of gruel and prunes only out of sheer necessity. Afterwards we lay down on the straw to sleep. The exhaustion that had overwhelmed us the day after the defeat still held sway.

Late in the afternoon the church door opened again, and a group of officers entered, along with some well-dressed men, doubtless prominent citizens of Rendsburg, and the Prussian soldier who had eyed our fellow townsman so suspiciously on the second leg of the march. While the guests waited by the door, the Prussian began walking around the church as if looking for someone. Finally spotting Laurids, he ordered him up from the straw and led him over to the party of officers and gentlemen. When they began talking, it became obvious they were questioning Laurids. Then after a while, they did the same thing that the departing Holstein officers had done on the way to Rendsburg: they handed Laurids banknotes before politely taking their leave. A few of the well-dressed folk even tipped their hats.

Laurids, the heavenly traveller, had become a celebrity.

The story was now circulating around the whole church. It turned out that Ejnar wasn't the only one who'd seen Laurids shoot up into the sky when the *Christian VIII* exploded, only to miraculously reappear on the burning deck once the column of fire had subsided. They'd all believed it to be a kind of mirage, an apparition brought on by the nervous strain of mortal danger during battle, and had mentioned it to no one – but now they came forward to bear witness to the rest of us, and soon a large crowd had gathered in front of Laurids.

We wanted to know why his clothes and hair weren't scorched.

'My boots are,' he said, sticking out a leg for inspection.

'And your feet?' We wanted to know.

'They stink,' said Laurids.

Ejnar couldn't take his eyes off Laurids. He looked at him the way you'd look at a total stranger – which was precisely what Laurids had become to him. He started treating him with a bashful subservience and couldn't seem to act normally around him. Little Clausen, meanwhile, accepted what had happened. Or rather, now that Laurids was standing in front of him as large as life, he accepted that others believed in his ascension. Personally he had been a sceptic right from the start, so when he became an official believer, it was mostly for the sake of comradeship, like joining in the laughter of a shared joke. In his eyes, Laurids was a born prankster. First he'd made the whole island believe that the German was coming. And now he'd made the German believe that he'd been to heaven and back. Little Clausen felt a jaw-dropping respect for this achievement. That Laurids was one hell of a guy!

While Laurids held forth on the subject, the church filled with women who'd been given permission to come daily with their baskets to hawk coffee, cakes, sour bread, eggs, butter, cheese, herring and paper. The men from the *Gefion* had money to spend: before throwing the ship's coffer overboard to prevent the enemy getting hold of it, the officers had opened it up and given each crew member a couple of coins, and most of us had managed to save our seabags.

We Marstallers considered ourselves privileged: we'd all, except for Laurids, been on board the *Gefion*. Laurids had recovered nothing from the *Christian VIII* except the clothes on his back and, of course, his reputation as an astral traveller. However, the latter was enough to secure him a considerable income. His pockets were stuffed full of five-mark coins given to him by curious Germans. When he saw that we had everything we needed, Laurids bought extra provisions and distributed them among the crew from the *Christian VIII*, who, like him, had been forced to abandon ship

37

without their possessions. They received his gifts with gratitude and this enhanced his reputation even further.

When we woke up, it was Easter Sunday – and we were to spend it locked up in a church without a clergyman in sight. We lay on our backs on the straw, gazing up at the soaring, pinnacled arches high above us. All around were dark paintings with heavy gilded frames, and carved wooden figures, and from the ceilings, which were as high as masts, hung chandeliers: all a far cry from Marstal's church, with its blue-painted pews and plain, whitewashed walls. But we weren't in any mood for worship, lying there in the straw. Straw was for farmyard animals, and we felt like pigs in a sty: the church's grandiose arches prompted not so much a feeling of religious contemplation as a sense of humiliation and mockery. For we were beaten men, robbed not only of our freedom but also – far worse – our pride. We hadn't fought with honour. Later we would probably be informed otherwise – and perhaps one day some of us might end up believing it. But right now, the events of Eckernförde Fjord were fresh in our minds, and they told the story straight. We'd been confused and panicky – and yes, even drunk too – and those of us who were skilled sailors weren't trained as soldiers, and those with military expertise knew nothing of seafaring.

Captain Krieger had been blown up together with his wife's portrait (and the Lord have mercy on his soul, the poor bewildered wretch) while Commander Paludan had been the first to board the lifeboat and be rowed ashore to safety. Was this conduct becoming of a commander? An act an honest seaman could respect?

Sitting there on the straw like the pathetic creatures we were, we gazed up at the arches. And from high above, they jeered back.

Pails of schnapps were to be found in several corners of the church, and we were offered all we could drink, for free. The hawkers didn't sell strong liquor, but from the very first day of our captivity, the German army doctor had decreed schnapps to be good for the health, and we headed for the buckets like pigs to the trough. Yes, we were indeed like pigs, sleeping and rolling around on the straw: pigs that had temporarily avoided the butcher's knife. We might be alive, but we were no longer human.

And we stank, too. We'd soiled our clothes during the battle, and we reeked of fear and uncontrolled bowels. For isn't it a secret common to all men that if you go to war, you'll fill your pants like a frightened child? As seamen, we'd all feared drowning, but none of us had ever crapped his pants when a gale ripped off the mast and rigging, or a wave crushed the rail and cleared the deck.

That was the difference: the sea respected our manhood. The cannons didn't.

'Hey, heavenly traveller,' we called out to Laurids, and pointed to the pulpit. 'It's Easter Sunday. Give us a sermon! Tell us about St Peter and his bare arse!'

Stumbling slightly, Laurids climbed the stairs to the pulpit. His elation had subsided and he was drunk again, like the rest of us. The pulpit was no mast top, but once up there he grew dizzy all the same. It was the schnapps. He'd been shipwrecked twice in his life. The second time he'd stood a whole night on a flat rock in the sea off Mandal, where his ship had gone down. There he'd felt both grief and terror, and he'd been within an inch of death. The water had slapped at his feet until dawn, when a pilot boat came and threw him a line. He'd felt no shame on that occasion, for it was no shame to be defeated by the sea. He wasn't a bad sailor. He knew that. The current, the wind and the dark had simply got the better of him. But in the battle on the fjord, where his seamanship had counted for nothing, a lesser enemy had defeated him, and that defeat and his commander's unmanly conduct had left him without honour.

When he stood on the pulpit, he found he had nothing to say. His gullet stung. Then he leaned forward and threw up.

We greeted this with cheering and applause.

Here was a sermon we could all appreciate.

Laurids remained silent the rest of the day. Once again, officers and local bigwigs turned up to visit him and hear the story of his ascension, but he turned his back to them in the straw, like a hibernating bear. They offered him money, but nothing could tempt him out of his retreat and in the end they had no choice but to leave. His fame dwindled in the days that followed. It would have been lucrative to put himself on display, press the flesh and expound his views of the hereafter. But he was in the grip of a foul mood.

He lay on the straw or paced up and down with his arms folded across his chest, frowning.

'He's thinking,' Ejnar said, filled with awe.

Ejnar was Laurids' only remaining disciple. But he could have spawned a whole sect if he'd wanted to.

As for the rest of us, our spirits had improved; we gathered in small groups, and soon music and singing echoed from various corners of the church. At first we'd congregated according to our home districts, islands or towns and looked at those from other places almost as enemies. But music united us. Here was a man from one of the islands next to a Jutlander, here a man from Lolland next to one from Seeland. As long as our voices were in harmony, it didn't matter that our accents were at war. That said, all the melodies came courtesy of the schnapps pail.

A few days later Little Clausen received a letter from home. It was from his mother, who gave him her version of the fateful Maundy Thursday when the battle took place. Ejnar and Laurids settled down beside him on the straw, and Torvald Bønnelykke joined them. We were all eager to hear news from home. Little Clausen read aloud in a stumbling voice, with long pauses.

His mother wrote that they'd heard the cannon fire in Marstal from early morning, and it was loud enough for you to think the battle was being fought at the end of the breakwater, rather than on the other side of the Baltic. The thundering had been especially fierce during Pastor Zachariassen's sermon in the church; the ground had literally trembled beneath their feet, and the vicar had been moved to tears.

Around noon it grew quiet, but no one could relax. Instead of going home for lunch, the citizens of Marstal wandered the streets discussing the course of the battle. A few men with combat experience, such as Petersen the carpenter and Old Jeppe, and even Madam Weber – all veterans of the great mobilisation, the night we thought the Germans were coming – had insisted that there was no way we Danes could lose. A ship-of-the-line could never be defeated by a coastal battery. The Germans must have got a good thrashing: what they'd been hearing all day was unquestionably the sweet music of victory.

Towards evening came a boom so gigantic that the cliffs at Voderup subsided. No one in Marstal got a wink of sleep all night, tormented by a creeping unease about the battle's outcome. News finally reached them well into the afternoon of Good Friday, a day which must have been as tough for them as it was for Our Saviour. For now their worst fears were confirmed.

'*I was completely beside myself with despair, though I should have put my trust in the Lord. I prayed to Him all night to keep you safe and He heard my prayers, though there were others He did not heed. Kresten's mother walks around with a tearful face and blames herself for not forcing him to stay behind. I tell her that Kresten foretold his own death and that no one cheats fate, but she says that Kresten had lost his wits, and it is a mother's duty to shield her son from his own lack of sense, and then she starts to cry again.*'

Little Clausen read all of this in a monotone. The strain of deciphering the letters required every ounce of his concentration; he had none left to understand the meaning of the words he was repeating.

'What does it say?' he suddenly asked.

We gave him a blank look.

'You're the one doing the reading,' Ejnar said.

Little Clausen looked helplessly at them, unable to explain his predicament.

'Well, it says that we lost,' Laurids snapped. 'But we don't need her to tell us that. And then it says that Kresten's mother has lost her wits from grief. And that your mother has been praying for you.'

'My mother has been praying for me?'

Little Clausen looked down and with some difficulty found the line where his mother described her sleepless night. Then he read it again, his lips moving silently as he did so.

'Read on,' Ejnar implored him. 'What else does she say?'

In a royal decree Marstal had been commanded to send all its large vessels to the navy immediately, in order to transport troops across the Great Belt. But although every sailor in town had gathered in the schoolroom to listen to the order, not one of them volunteered to comply with it. Eighteen vessels were then commandeered – but when the day of their departure dawned, the ships were gone. From the pulpit, Pastor Zachariassen lambasted the people of Marstal for their lack of self-sacrificial spirit, after which the townsfolk began to talk of replacing him. Everything was in confusion.

There was a war on, and times were harsh, but if only the good Lord would protect Little Clausen and the rest of Marstal, all this misery would surely have to end some day, and things could return to normal. Little Clausen's mother ended her letter by conveying her most fervent prayers and loving thoughts to her captive son, and expressing the hope that he was getting enough to eat and keeping his clothes neat and clean.

'Lack of self-sacrificial spirit!' Laurids fumed when Little Clausen had concluded his reading. 'That pastor's got a nerve! Seven men are dead and the rest of us are prisoners. We're prepared to give up our lives. But is that enough for him, the devil? No: he wants our ships, too. But he won't get them. Never!'

The others nodded their agreement.

The mornings began with warm beer, with bland gruel and prunes one day, split peas and meat the next. Our stomachs soon adapted to the pattern; they had no choice, and besides, we'd had worse at sea, working for stingy skippers, so we complained mainly for the sake of complaining. They'd confiscated our knives, leaving us to tear our bread or gnaw at it like horses. For one hour, morning and afternoon, we were allowed to stroll around the churchyard and smoke, while the sentries watched over us with loaded guns. There, we'd let our eyes wander from headstone to bayonet and back again, and if we fancied it, philosophise about the meaning of life. That was as much variety as our captivity afforded.

A FORTNIGHT LATER THEY WOKE US AT FIVE IN THE MORNING AND ordered us into the churchyard, where they lined us up in ranks. We were six hundred men in all, and we were joined by the junior officers, whom they'd been holding in a riding school. Our guards felt we were in need of discipline, and who better to knock it into our heads than our own cadets?

We marched out of Rendsburg with our seabags on our shoulders and our food bowls tucked under our arms. Our arrival in the small town of Glückstadt was met by thousands of onlookers. No longer covered in powder residue and at last wearing clean clothes, we almost resembled human beings, so it wasn't our appearance so much as our quantity that made an impact on the townsfolk.

We marched down to the harbour, where we were to be billeted in a grain warehouse. Inside there was a lower and an upper loft, with a separate room in each where the cadets were housed. In these vast spaces the men slept on the floor, 150 to a row; it seemed that one wall was to serve as our headboard while some planks hammered together would be our footboard. Our bedding, once again, was straw. But there were also tables and benches, and a yard at our disposal, so overall it was a change for the better.

A small pond lay between our warehouse and the one opposite; this made the fenced yard seem a complete landscape in itself. The eye rests easier on a fence than on a bayonet, and the pond fired our imagination much more than the headstones in Rendsburg, so outside, too, we found something new to enjoy: we built model ships, fixing scraps of fabric to masts made of sticks, and staging naval battles on the smooth surface of the pond. Half the ships sailed under the Danish flag, while the other half – which appeared to be stateless – represented German rebels, whom we could not bring ourselves to honour even with their own colours. During our battles we bombarded

43

the flagless German fleet with pebbles, and we Danes won every time, suffering losses only when one of our fleet took an accidental hit from a stray pebble.

We clustered in our hundreds around the ponds, cheering every time a pebble struck its target and a toy ship tipped over. This was our hour of restitution.

But Laurids turned his back on us, fuming with contempt.

'Yes, that's all we're good for. If only we could win when it really matters.'

Laurids spent most of his time in the straw, staring out of a window that faced the River Elbe, watching the ships sail to and from Hamburg. His eyes followed them as far as they could, and his heart went even further. He longed for the sea.

After his trip to heaven, he'd become a different man.

During the day we'd relax in the sunshine. Benches had been put out in the yard, and some of us played cards. We dictated our letters home to a literate seaman from Ærøskøbing, Hans Christian Svinding. He was never without a notebook in his hand and his eyes were always on the alert; he wrote everything down. But most of the men just stared vacantly into space, halfway to a schnapps-induced haze. In the evening there would be singing and dancing and the heavy floor planks would creak under our weight. The cadets made the most noise. They didn't mix with the crew but stayed behind the closed doors of their rooms, their drunken shouting drowning out even our music. They were mere boys and couldn't hold their drink. Not one of them was older than sixteen, and most were thirteen or fourteen. The youngest was twelve. Many of us had sons their age or older, yet as junior officers the cadets were our superiors, though they knew nothing and could do even less. We had to stand to attention to a bunch of cabin boys.

Speculation about Commander Paludan's desertion at the moment of greatest peril remained rife. Why had our commander got into the boat before everybody else? A soldier from Schleswig started the rumour that Paludan had claimed a German officer arrived on board the *Christian VIII* and commanded him off the ship before the wounded could be brought ashore. Paludan protested bravely but was told that if he disobeyed, the bombardment would resume.

However, no one on board the *Christian VIII* had known anything about this officer, whose name was supposed to be Preuszer, and the German rebel army denied any knowledge of him, too. The soldier from Schleswig said he thought that Commander Paludan had invented Preuszer as a cover for his own cowardice.

When Little Clausen heard this story, he opened his mouth to defend his commander: his own honour, as a Dane, was at stake. But he couldn't think of a single argument to make. In fact, the story sounded all too plausible. We'd been led by dishonourable men. Ejnar, too, stayed silent, but his eyes filled with tears of shame. Laurids swore.

Commander Paludan's treason didn't light the fire of rebellion in us; instead, it sent us more frequently to the schnapps pail. As our disgust at our captivity grew, our manners coarsened.

The cadets became a target for our anger. We'd already cracked plenty of jokes about their smooth chins, but only behind their backs. Now we told the little men to their faces: pull down your trousers so we can see if you're hairless there too.

The cadets' leader was a fourteen-year-old with the surname Wedel. He'd been the first cadet of the *Christian VIII* to board a rescue boat, and we'd all noted his triumphant expression as he sat next to Paludan – a close friend of his father – on the main launch. He led the drinking sessions the cadets held behind closed doors. But now he became the most frequent target of our increasingly aggressive bullying.

In response to a particularly cruel reference to the size of his manhood, Wedel slapped an able seaman, Jørgen Mærke from Nyborg, hard across his face. The fact that he had to stand on tiptoe to do so fuelled our mirth – but the slap was a proper one. The seaman stood dazed with shock before hesitantly putting his fingers to his stinging cheek, as though unsure that he'd really been struck.

'Stand to attention, God damn you!' little Wedel roared.

At this the seaman grabbed Wedel by the shoulders, flung him to the floor, and thrust a heavy sea boot into the boy's chest. A crowd quickly formed around them – not because anyone wanted to rescue the kid, but because here, finally, was a chance to vent our frustrated rage. Wedel was saved only by his screams. Two soldiers from

45

Schleswig-Holstein came charging up the stairs, brandishing their bayonets, but before they reached the boy, Laurids had dispersed the combative crowd, pulling the kid to his feet by the collar while holding off the bystanders with his free hand.

Wedel dangled limply, like a rag doll, fear buckling his legs.

'Now behave,' Laurids said in a calm voice.

He'd rediscovered the authority he'd lost on the deck of the ship. The menacing crowd dissolved, and the soldiers led the cadet away.

We heard Wedel sobbing all the way down the stairs.

Later the same evening the cadet recovered his courage. Another loud drinking session was held in the closed room, and from a corner of the loft someone began cursing the noise. It wasn't bedtime yet, but everything about the cadets was beginning to rile us.

We banged on their door, demanding silence. A brazen, high-pitched boy's voice immediately told us to shut up. 'Or we'll cut your prick off, you peasant oaf!'

'What did you say?' the seaman roared back.

The drunken men who sat clustered on benches around the sturdy central table staggered to their feet en masse. Hefting a bench, they swung it back and forth as if calculating its weight, then rammed it right into the cadets' door. On the other side, all went quiet.

'Right,' shouted one of the men. 'Bet you're not feeling quite so cocky now, are you?'

They stepped back for another salvo, then rammed the door again. This time it gave way and they poured into the room, knocking over a table and sending a bottle smashing to the floor. Someone screamed, and the crowd that was gathering outside started cheering the brawling men. Ejnar and Little Clausen stood at the back on tiptoe to catch a glimpse of the fight but could see nothing through the narrow doorway.

Then the German soldiers turned up, alerted by the uproar. Smashing their way through us with the butts of their guns, they broke up the fight.

The brawlers emerged one by one. From the way the cadets hung their heads, it was obvious who had borne the brunt. Wedel's nose was bleeding. Another boy had a swollen eye that had already begun to close up. A third spat out a tooth as he came through the door; blood streaming down his chin.

A cry rang out from the crowd. 'Someone's lost a milk tooth!'

Commandant Fleischer arrived shortly after. He was a sturdy man with a high forehead and soft curly hair on the back of his neck. His cheeks were flushed and his lips moist; he had gravy on one corner of his mouth, as if he had just left a dinner party and forgotten to wipe his face.

He was ranked a major, but he instantly disappointed us all with his jovial tone of voice.

'Listen, lads, this won't do. You've got to show your officers a bit of respect. Otherwise I'll have to be very strict with you and I don't really want to do that. So let's all try to get along. You'll be exchanged soon and there's really no need for us to fall out while we wait.'

We stared at one another, slack-jawed. Was this supposed to be the enemy? The German, who had blown the deck away from under our feet and was now holding us prisoner?

The next few days passed quietly. The pails of schnapps were kept full and we carried on drinking. Jørgen Mærke never missed an opportunity to needle the guards. Monkey arses, he called them. Dog shit. Snakes in the grass. Prickless pygmies. He insulted them with impunity, protected by his entourage who, if a guard approached, instantly formed a shield around him.

One day the soldiers finally decided they'd had enough. They'd been keeping an eye on Mærke, and two of them came up to the loft to nab him at the table where he was sitting with his gang. They were arresting him, they said, for drunkenness.

Jørgen Mærke's men laughed out loud at the charge and offered their wrists.

'Better arrest all six hundred of us, then.'

One guard grabbed Mærke by the shoulders. He clung to the edge of the table, yelling the usual insults and adding a few fresh ones for good measure. Leaping up, his men jostled the two soldiers, rendering their guns useless, then started pushing them towards the stairs. Scared, the soldiers made little resistance. One stumbled and fell backwards down the stairs, while the other got a shove that sent him flying. He lost his gun as he fell. It landed a few steps down.

The rebels looked at one another, then at the gun, then back at one another.

No one moved. It had all gone very quiet.

The soldier on the landing scrambled to his feet. He was too dazed from his fall to notice that he'd lost his gun. When he looked up there was no menace in his eyes, only confusion.

Jørgen Mærke took a step forward.

'Boo!' he shouted, tugging at his caveman beard.

The guard jumped, then turned and hurtled down the stairs. His companion got to his feet and followed him. The men laughed and slapped their thighs. Then their eyes rested on the gun and they fell silent. It was lying so near them! All they had to do was walk down a few steps and pick it up.

'Take me,' it seemed to beckon. 'Shoot, kill, be a man again!'

They stood spellbound, mute, listening to the gun's whisper.

Then one of them broke the silence.

'We could –' he began, taking a step towards it.

He looked at Jørgen Mærke. He was waiting for a nod, approval, an order: Yes, do it!

But Mærke's eyes were empty and the mouth behind the caveman beard stayed closed.

The man who'd spoken began to waver. The others took a step back, as if he were no longer one of them. Then he bent down and picked up the gun. He didn't look at anyone as he walked down the stairs, bearing the weapon in outstretched hands with the greatest of care, as it if were a sacrifice. When he reached the lowest landing, he leaned the gun up against the whitewashed wall. Then he turned round and walked back up.

We drank heavily that night and shouted 'Hurrah!' countless times. The cadets came out of their room and joined us. We were all brothers now.

The next day we made more model ships, decorated them with tiny paper flags in the Danish colours, and launched them. Bobbing there proudly on the scum of the pond, they reminded us of our nation's power.

We started doing drills in the yard, marching in closed ranks as though preparing for a major battle. Holding three fingers high, we swore that we would never retreat or desert, but preserve and defend

– puzzling phrases we barely understood. Nonetheless, they sounded impressive, and we proclaimed them out loud, there in the middle of the yard. Anxious-looking faces appeared above the wooden fence from time to time. They belonged to the townsfolk of Glückstadt, who were spying on us. It was in their honour that we staged these little dramas.

And sure enough, the rumour soon started spreading in Glückstadt that the Danish prisoners were gearing up to conquer the town, and the commandant informed us that from now on we were banned from equipping our model ships with the Danish colours. The people of Glückstadt were upset, it seemed, by the sight of the enemy flag.

We regarded that as a victory.

Now the German had learned to fear us!

There were many victories of this kind in the weeks to come, and we celebrated every one of them with large quantities of schnapps.

WE WERE MORE THAN FOUR MONTHS INTO OUR CAPTIVITY WHEN, at the end of August, it was decided that we would be exchanged for German prisoners of war. It took us ten days to get to Dybbøl, where the exchange was to take place. We suffered many delays and humiliations on the way, but we took them all in our stride because we'd regained our honour by alarming the people of Glückstadt. And when we saw the Danish ships anchored in Sønderborg harbour, we knew that we were free men. On board the *Schleswig*, the steamer bound for Copenhagen, they gave us white bread and butter, schnapps, and as much beer as we could drink.

We spent the night on the bare deck, with the ship rolling gently and the wheezing engine vibrating the planks we slept on. It was a cloudless night, and the starlit sky stretched high above us. 21 August 1849, was a good night for shooting stars, and the bright tails of the comets conjured a cannonade very different from the one that heralded our miserable captivity. Laurids breathed a deep sigh. Prison had cut him off from the stars.

When you can't see land, and when the wind, the current and the clouds tell you nothing, when your sextant has gone overboard and the compass won't work, you navigate by the constellations.

Now he was home.

'Hurrah' was the word we heard most often in the days that followed. On the Baltic Sea we passed a steamer filled with Swedish troops and from the deck of the *Schleswig* we shouted three cheers for the brave Swedes. At the Customs House in Copenhagen the crew of the frigate *Bellona* welcomed us with a triple cheer, to which we immediately responded; soon the entire harbour had erupted in answering hurrahs. Then it was the turn of the officers. They, too, were celebrated with applause. Commander Paludan took the lead as they walked ashore, just as he'd done when he abandoned the wounded on board the *Christian VIII*. Through his incompetence he was responsible for the loss of two ships, the deaths of one hundred and thirty-five men and the captivity of one thousand. But now he was being greeted with respect because he was a hero. We were all heroes. It seemed as if the applause would never end.

With our seabags in hand, we went our separate ways to look for lodgings for the night. Soon we were seated in the city's pubs, drinking and cheering. We missed the schnapps pails; since we were now footing the bill ourselves, our drunkenness didn't reach the extremes it might have.

The following morning we were due to meet at Holmen. The naval minister had announced that four months' captivity merited two weeks' wages. Afterwards we were to draw lots to decide who would return to the navy's ships and who would be sent home. Laurids, Little Clausen and Ejnar returned to Marstal two days later. Here, a celebration arch of spruce branches was constructed in Kirkestræde, where the homecoming men were applauded and the dead mourned.

A terribly deformed creature stood in the midst of the crowd that greeted us. One eye was missing, and the bones of his right cheek and his lower jaw protruded from his skin, which leaked constantly. Even those of us who had witnessed so much on that dreadful day on Eckernförde Fjord had to avert our eyes.

We didn't know who he was until he greeted us.

It was Kresten.

It emerged that not all of his head had been shot off, as Torvald Bønnelykke had told us: only half. He'd been in a hospital in Germany until recently and had been sent home some days before the rest of us. The army surgeon had tried patching him up, but his damaged jaw refused to heal. Now he was back home with his mother – who still hadn't recovered her senses and kept asking after her missing son. When poor Kresten assured her that he was standing right before her, she stuck her finger into the hole in his cheek, just as Doubting Thomas had stuck his into the Saviour's wounds. But unlike Thomas, she didn't turn into a believer. Her Kresten didn't look like this. It was a cruel thing for him to hear: he'd been expecting comfort and joy from the reunion with his mother despite his ruined face. Tears trickled from the one eye he had left. It would have been better, he said, if he really had died as he'd predicted.

Laurids temporarily regained his fame as a heavenly traveller because Ejnar had described the wondrous event in a letter, and now we all wanted to hear it from the horse's mouth – except for Karoline, who was convinced that it was just another of her husband's tall tales.

The children formed a circle around him calling out: '*Papa tru*, tell us a story, tell us a story!'

Albert, the youngest, yelled the loudest, and gazed at his father with shining eyes. The two of them were like peas in a pod.

But Laurids simply looked at them with the new, strange expression he'd acquired in captivity, as though they weren't even his children, and the notion of having ever produced them was unthinkable.

So Ejnar had to tell them the story instead, and he did it so well that everyone thought he must have been practising it for ages. The house filled with people who'd come to see Laurids. Karoline stood out in the kitchen boiling water to make coffee and turned her broad back to us, clattering the cups, as she was in the habit of doing whenever she was angry with her husband. But she finally succumbed and joined us in the parlour to listen to Ejnar.

'We will never forget how we fought for Denmark's glory,' Ejnar said.

Everyone nodded, suddenly consumed by ardent patriotism.

But what Ejnar said next startled us. 'We fought for Denmark's glory,' he repeated. 'But we found only disgrace. We willingly risked life and limb, and showed undaunted courage, to save the honour of our country. But thanks to a lousy leader, we lost it. I'll never forget how those cannonballs hailed down on us on Maundy Thursday. How we fought and fell and died in smoke and flames, and how that evening we were carted off to Eckernförde like slaves and locked up in God's house. How we lay there on the straw, exhausted and dazed. I won't forget how the *Christian VIII* was blown up and how so many poor souls died; how on Good Friday we were marched to Rendsburg, to another church, and how again we had to sleep on straw and eat stale bread for our Easter lunch. How the house of God became a cage for slaves, full of degradation and blasphemy, and how our captivity was a stretch of dark, miserable days. I'll never forget any of that, as long as I live.

'I saw Laurids,' Ejnar continued, 'and that became my only hope and comfort in captivity. I saw Laurids fly towards heaven from the deck of the burning ship, as high as the main, and I saw him come back down again and land on his feet. And that's how I knew we'd be seeing our loved ones again.'

'I've told you before, Ejnar, and I'll tell you again, it was the boots.'

Laurids stuck out his foot so everyone could see his sturdy leather sea boots.

'The boots saved me. That's all there is to it.'

'Didn't you see St Peter's bare arse?' asked Laves Petersen, the little carpenter, for this rumour was already spreading like wildfire. Little Clausen had been unable to keep his mouth shut.

'Yes, I saw the arse of St Peter,' Laurids said.

But his voice sounded weary and distant, as though he'd already forgotten the episode. We knew immediately that this was all we'd get from him. Most of us believed that just as each man has his own private hell, he also has his own private heaven. And it's his right to keep it to himself.

Those of us who'd been left behind in Marstal couldn't help noticing that Laurids was a changed man. We understood that the war had been a bad time for him and that he'd witnessed things that do a man no good. But he'd already been shipwrecked twice without it affecting him in the slightest. Little Clausen said that the fighting had been like a ship going down, only worse. But Ejnar retorted that Little Clausen had spent most of the battle with his feet in the water and had escaped with nothing more than a cold, while others'd got their heads blown off.

As none of the rest of us had experienced battle, we didn't know what to make of Laurids' attitude, and so we left him alone.

Karoline thought that her husband should find himself a job on land, so that both she and the children would get to see more of him. She worried about the change that had come over him and preferred to keep him close by.

Little Clausen and Ejnar were each called up several times during the war, but they always came home in one piece, and we soon grew tired of erecting celebration arches and applauding their return, and started treating them like any other sailors who made it back.

Laurids, too, was recalled, but by then he had already quit Marstal. He hadn't taken a land job, as Karoline had wanted, but had instead travelled to Hamburg along the Elbe, the same river he'd stared at every day during his imprisonment in Glückstadt. In Hamburg he was hired as third mate on a Dutch ship bearing emigrants bound for Australia; the other crew consisted of three Dutchmen and twenty-four Javanese. There were one hundred and sixty passengers on board and it was Laurids' task to hand out provisions and keep the accounts. After a six-month voyage the ship arrived at Hobart Town in Van Diemen's Land, where Laurids signed off. And that was the last we heard of him.

KAROLINE SAW NO REASON TO WORRY DURING THE FIRST TWO YEARS of Laurids' absence. He'd been away from home before, for two or three years at a stretch, and letters sent from the other side of the globe don't always reach their destination. Our women, who have no choice but to stay behind in Marstal, live in a state of permanent uncertainty. Even a letter is no proof that the sender is alive; it can be on its way for months, and the sea steals men without warning. We're all so used to enduring periods of anxious waiting that we never share our unease with one another. Which is why there was no visible change in Karoline for the first three years, until the day when her neighbour in Korsgade, Dorothea Hermansen, asked her, 'Isn't it about time Laurids came home?'

'Yes,' Karoline answered. And she said no more. She knew Dorothea had been working up to putting the question for a long time, and that she wouldn't have done it without first consulting the other women in Korsgade. It was in fact a statement, rather than a question: Laurids wasn't coming back.

That night, once she'd put the children to bed, Karoline wept. She'd cried before, but always tried to suppress it. Now she allowed the tears to flow freely.

The next morning the local women crowded into her parlour to ask if she needed help.

Laurids' demise was now official.

They sat around her dining table, each with a cup of coffee. At first their voices were pragmatic and matter-of-fact as they assessed Karoline's circumstances: when it came to help, she had little in the way of family, having already lost five brothers at sea, and with Laurids' father gone too. Then their voices softened and they started praising Laurids' qualities as a husband and provider.

Karoline started crying again. He came alive for her in these moments, resurrected through the words of others.

The oldest woman, Hansigne Ahrentzen, embraced her, and let her dampen her grey dress with her tears. They stayed until she was all cried out.

Thus ended the first meeting, which introduced Karoline to her new status as a widow.

A message was sent to the Dutch shipping company, but they reported no lost ships, nor did Laurids' name appear on any of their crew lists.

The merciful comfort of a grave where you can take your children and tell them about their father in front of the headstone that bears his name; the possibility of distracting yourself by clearing weeds or perhaps disappearing into a whispered conversation with the man who lies underground: a sailor's widow is denied all that. Instead, she'll receive an official document declaring that the ship her husband was working on, or perhaps skippered and owned, has been 'lost with all hands', gone down on this or that date, in this or that place, often at a depth beyond salvaging, with fish as the only witnesses. And she can put that piece of paper away in a drawer of the bureau. Such are the funeral rites awarded to the drowned.

She can hold her own memorial service in front of the bureau, which is the only grave she can visit. But at least she has the document and with it, certainty: a conclusion, but also a beginning. Life isn't like a book. There's never a final page.

But it wasn't like that for Karoline. No official message reached her. Laurids was gone, but how or where he'd disappeared no one could tell her. Hope can be like a plant that sprouts and grows and keeps people alive. But it can also be a wound that refuses to heal.

It's said that if the dead aren't buried in consecrated ground, they'll haunt us, and Laurids soon began to haunt Karoline. He became the ghost in her heart, and he never left her in peace, because he didn't know the difference between day and night, and finally neither did she. There was her yearning during the day when she should have been busy with domestic matters. There were the practical concerns at night, when she should have been sleeping or crying herself empty from loss. Without rest or relief, she grew gaunt and grey, as if she were made from the same substance as the ghost in her heart.

Only her hands never lost their strength. She'd draw water from the well, light the fire in the kitchen every morning, wash and mend clothes, weave, bake bread, bring up four children, and box their ears hard enough to remind them of the missing Laurids.

The Thrashing Rope

THE SUMMER HAD JUST ENDED, BUT THE SUN'S WARMTH WAS STILL in our blood, and we longed for the water. After school we'd run down to the harbour and jump right in, head first, or walk out to the long strip of beach known as the Tail. Once we'd swum, we'd lie on the warm sand to dry off and talk about Mr Isager, our teacher. The new pupils thought he wasn't all bad. Having your ears pulled or getting a slap on the side of the head was no big deal; it was no different from home.

But some of the older ones warned: 'Just you wait. He's in a good mood right now.'

'He said something nice about my pa,' said Albert Madsen.

'But what did your pa say about him?' Niels Peter asked.

'He said that Isager was a devil with the thrashing rope.'

His mother had then declared that they were not to call the school-teacher a devil and his father had retorted: 'Well, that's easy for you to say. You girls never had Isager.'

Remembering his father brought tears to Albert's eyes. He blinked and looked down. His nose thickened and he wiped it with an angry movement of his wrist. We saw his tears, but none of us teased him. Many of us Marstal boys had lost a father at sea. Our fathers were often away. But then sometimes, out of the blue, they'd be gone for ever. *Often away* and *gone for ever*: the two phrases marked the difference between having a living father and a dead one. It wasn't a big difference, but it was big enough to make us cry when no one was looking.

One of us slapped Albert on his shoulder and jumped up.

'Race you!'

And we tore across the sand and threw ourselves into the water.

Every summer we went to the beach, with its border of dried seaweed that crackled and pricked under our bare feet, its carpet of crushed mussel shells, its luminous green seabed and its swaying submerged forests of bladderwrack and eelgrass.

When we turned thirteen we went to sea. Some of us never returned. But every summer new boys came out to the Tail.

One day in August we lay on our stomachs in the warm sand, licking our salty skin, still tanned from the summer, and talked about Jens Holgersen Ulfstrand, who during the reign of King Hans had defeated the Lübecks in a naval battle; about Søren Norby, Peder Skram and Herluf Trolle, who had all fought on the sea we'd just emerged from; about Peder Jensen Bredal, who was killed at Als by a musket bullet to the chest; about King Christian IV, who boarded his own ship, the *Spes*, and chased the Hamburgers away from Glückstadt, a town that had been built on his orders. It was also where our fathers had once been held captive, but we never talked about that.

Our favourite naval hero was Tordenskjold, who spent a whole night off the shores of Ærø and Als chasing the *White Eagle*, a Swedish frigate equipped with thirty cannons, though his own ship, the *Løvendals Galej*, had only twenty. We knew all about his triumphs at the battles of Dynekilen, Marstrand, Gothenburg and Strömstad, where so many of his brave men perished, while he survived, safe and sound, though he always gave his utmost.

'Not this time!' we yelled, recalling the day when Tordenskjold found himself alone on Torekov beach in Scania, surrounded by three Swedish dragoons: he'd hacked his way past them and swum through the surf with his sharp rapier clenched between his teeth.

Then there was the story of how, having fought an English captain for nearly twenty-four hours, with just a brief pause between midnight and dawn, Tordenskjold announced to his wounded foe that he'd run out of gunpowder, and coolly asked for the loan of some more so the battle could continue. Upon which the English captain had appeared on deck, raised a glass of wine and saluted his Danish opponent with seven hurrahs. Then Tordenskjold, too, found a glass and they'd toasted each another.

Another story we liked was about the time he'd lost the foremast overboard on the *Løvendals Galej* in a howling storm, but managed to stoke fresh courage in his men by yelling 'We're winning, lads!' through the gale.

We walked home across the headland, on the other side of which lay the wide inlet we called the Little Ocean. In the distance you could see the ships tied to the black-tarred mooring posts in the harbour: a couple of old luggers, two cutters, a ketch and the fore-and-aft schooner *Johanne Karoline*, affectionately known as the *Incomparable*. Distinguishing one type of ship from another with the skill of an experienced sailor was something we'd learned long before Isager started drumming the alphabet into our heads. We often swam in the harbour, egging each other on to dive deeper and deeper, right down to the shell-encrusted ships' keels. Then we'd surface with our hands full of mussels.

Behind the harbour quay rose the town, where from the church rose the thin spire that reached skyward like the bare mast of a ship. Just then, the church bells started tolling a long-drawn-out farewell; a funeral procession was coming down Kirkestræde, led by girls strewing greenery across the cobbles. They were burying old Ermine Karlsen from Snaregade. She'd outlived her husband and both her sons. Death was a certainty for all of us, but whether the bells of Marstal would ever toll for us, there was no knowing. If we drowned at sea, there'd be only silence.

THE FIRST WEEK OF THE NEW SCHOOL TERM, ISAGER PAID US LITTLE attention. His movements and speech gave him the automatic, dazed, air of a man who has risen before truly waking and is floating in a pleasant dream. Still in dressing gown and slippers, he'd shuffle over to the school from his house, the thrashing rope coiled in his pocket like a viper drowsy from the heat. Isager had been a school-teacher for thirty years, so most of our fathers had felt the snake's lash, and many still bore the scars as marks of their initiation into manhood.

The good weather lasted well into September – and so did Isager's benign mood. He didn't bother us with revision questions and on the rare occasions when he hit us, it was never hard enough to draw tears or blood, and the infamous thrashing rope stayed in his pocket. He read aloud from *Balle's Textbook,* heedless that some of us had only just started school while others had been there five years. He'd concentrate on the first three chapters: 'God's Powers', 'God's Works', and 'Mankind's Corruption through the Fall', but'd stop at the fourth chapter, 'Mankind's Redemption through Jesus Christ'. There was no need for all that, he said. It was hogwash – as was every-thing that followed. Then he'd move on to the Old Testament. His favourite story was that of Jacob and his twelve sons, and it always made his eyes soften. 'I, too, have twelve sons, like Jacob,' he'd murmur.

We knew all about Jacob: we'd paid attention. We knew that he was an impostor who stole from his own brother, the hairy-armed Esau, and lied to his father, the blind Isaac, and sired children by four different women, Rachel, Leah, Bilhah and Zilpah, and that when one proved barren, he would simply move on to the next, and that he had a fight with an angel that left him with a limp, but that later, he was blessed by God. It was a peculiar story, but none of us dared point out its oddness to Isager.

61

Two of Isager's twelve sons were still at the school: Johan and Josef – the latter being the only one Isager had actually named after a son of Jacob. When we told the Isager brothers that their father's Bible hero was a liar, a thief and a fornicator, Johan burst into tears (he cried a lot anyway because Josef beat him up on a daily basis), and teardrops as greasy as candle wax dripped from his bizarrely huge eyes, while Josef, thumping his brother on the head with a clenched fist, merely retorted that their father was no fornicator: he was just a drunkard and a fool.

We never spoke about our own fathers that way. But from then on, we left the Isager boys in peace.

We knew that the mild weather was over one day in the middle of September, when an east wind brought looming clouds that covered the entire island with a lid of slate grey. The same day, we noticed that Isager's steel spectacles were sitting higher than usual on the bridge of his nose and pressing tightly against its flesh. Some of us had a theory that Isager's swings of mood related to the weather, so we'd developed the habit of glancing at the sky on our way to school, looking for indications in the cloud formations. But it wasn't an exact science, and even its most ardent proponents had to concede that Isager and the clouds weren't always in accord.

On this mid-September day, however, they were. Dressing gown abandoned, Isager appeared in a black tailcoat, commonly known as the Combat Uniform – and in his right hand he brandished the thrashing rope. His boots clacked on the cobbles as he crossed the yard that divided his house from the school. Then, positioning himself by the school door, he lashed each of us across the back of the neck as we entered, catapulting us over the threshold.

There were seventy of us in his class and we had to pass through the entrance one by one, tensing our scalps for the lash as we went. The older boys among us were used to violence and could take a beating, but no one could quell the fear in his heart as he waited for it. Pain that you anticipate is always worse than the kind that comes out of the blue. Before they even came close to Isager, the youngest lads' lips started quivering. A blow to the back of the head was their school baptism.

But worse awaited us in class.

* * *

We always started by singing 'Gone Is the Dark, Dark Night', with Isager leading in his braying voice. He doubled up as parish clerk, but he had to pay the assistant teacher, Mr Nothkier, to lead the hymns in church on Sundays because half the congregation had vowed that if Isager led, they'd march out as soon as he opened his mouth – and this was too much for his vanity. But we schoolboys had no such option, and indeed, we learned to appreciate his voice and to wish that the lengthy, turgid hymn would go on for ever, because as long as he was singing, he couldn't clobber us.

He'd pace restlessly up and down while in full flow; although he knew the hymn by heart, he held the open hymn book right up to his nose while his predator's eyes roamed the room over the top of the page. As he reached the last few lines, 'God grant us happiness and guidance, may He send us the Light of His Grace,' you'd usually catch the sound of someone crying. The hymn always served to drown our sobs – but only until it ended. It was the blow across the back of the head that brought on the tears. And it was fear that kept them welling.

Albert Madsen pressed his lips together firmly and fixed his eyes on Isager's spectacles, fighting his terror through concentration.

The teacher's face took on a vigilant expression as he scanned the room again, this time in an exaggerated manner, as though he were in a stage play. He went over to Albert and stared hard into his face. Albert was one of the younger ones, and they were always the first to crack. But Albert just stared ahead stiffly, and Isager let him off and moved on.

There were a lot of us. He never addressed us by name. He just called out: 'You there!' or hit us. His rope knew us better than he did.

The class grew silent. Those still crying covered their mouths, terrified of summoning a catastrophe with even the smallest squeak. Then from somewhere in our group a raucous sob emerged (clapping your hand over your mouth didn't always work) and Isager jumped, his eyes narrowing behind his spectacles as he looked around and roared: 'Shut up!'

'Mr Isager,' ventured Albert, 'it was wrong of you to hit us. We hadn't done anything.'

Isager paled. Even his red nose lost its colour. Then he unbuttoned his tailcoat. That was the sign we'd feared. All through the

63

hymn he'd been holding the rope: book in one hand, tool of punishment in the other. Just a moment ago he'd been singing about joy and good tidings and the light of grace; now he uncoiled the rope with a practised hand. If it were a whip, he'd have cracked it.

'You'll get your punishment now –' here his breath caught – 'upon my most sacred honour!' And with a single movement he yanked Albert up by the jumper, hauling him from his desk and ramming him down to the floor. Then, trapping him between both legs, he grabbed the lining of his trousers. He'd been saving his strength for this: for an entire long, leisurely summer, he'd had only Josef and Johan to thrash. His moment had come. Deploying skills he had honed over three decades of practice, Isager prepared to land his rope with full force.

Albert cried out in terror. He'd never been flogged before. Laurids had rarely hit him, and his mother mainly boxed his ears. He was used to that. But now he was being thrust down onto his knees. He squirmed to free himself from Isager's grip.

'So, you're being disobedient, eh?' Isager hissed and hefted him back to his feet by the hair. He looked Albert right in the face.

'Disobedient,' he muttered again, and whipped him across the cheek.

Then he moved on to his next victim.

By now, some boys had climbed up onto the windowsill at the back of the classroom and were struggling with the window catches. By the time Isager was aware of it, the window was gaping open and the boys had jumped out into the playground and escaped through the gate. Isager had the thrashing rope poised for the next flogging, but the boy between his legs wriggled loose and hurtled round the classroom in a blind panic. At this, Isager began storming across the room lashing out with the rope left, right and centre.

'Hurry up, hurry up! He's coming!' we screamed.

Another boy squeezed through the window just before Isager reached it, thrashing those who remained before hauling them down from the sill. The rope flayed our legs, our backs, our arms and our bare faces. One boy curled up in a ball on the floor, protecting his head with his hands, while Isager whipped his back and booted him in the ribs.

Hans Jørgen grabbed hold of Isager's arm. He was a big, strong lad who was due to be confirmed the following spring.

'How dare you lay a hand on your teacher, you lout!' Isager yelled as he struggled to free himself.

Even though there were enough of us to overpower Isager (and if all seventy of us had mobbed him, our sheer weight would have suffocated him) we simply didn't dare come to Hans Jørgen's aid. Indeed, it never crossed our minds. After all, Isager was our teacher. Most of us stayed in our seats, too frightened to move, even though we knew our turn was coming. But Albert approached the still-scuffling duo and looked our teacher up and down. Isager, busy freeing himself from Hans Jørgen's grip, was oblivious to him. Albert watched the two with the same scrutiny he had applied to Isager's spectacles earlier on. His cheek was red and swollen where the rope had landed. Suddenly, he kicked out with his wooden clog, catching Isager on the shin. The teacher howled in pain and Hans Jørgen seized the opportunity to twist his arm. Groaning, Isager sank to his knees.

That was the moment we should all have jumped him. But it was beyond contemplation. Isager was a monster you could never slay, even now, when he was on his knees, howling like a wounded animal. We all knew from our own skirmishes that the battle was over now. When you had someone kneeling with one arm twisted behind his back, you'd order him to plead for his life, or apologise, or otherwise humiliate himself. And since you'd never actually break anyone's arm deliberately, the unspoken rule was that the fight would end there. But with Isager the thing was murkier. There was nothing you wanted more than to break the hated arm he hit you with, but you couldn't do it. If an adult in our group had ordered us to finish him off then we'd have done it. But Isager was the only adult around. And so we let him go, without even forcing him to plead for mercy, however briefly.

Hans Jørgen took a step back. Isager didn't dare touch him now. Without looking at him, he brushed the dirt off his trousers, then lunged out at the nearest boy. It was Albert, who for the second time that day ended up trapped between the teacher's legs.

Isager was to experience a few more brawls because not everyone put up with his brutality. But the majority of us ended up, like Albert, in the vice of his legs, gritting our teeth and taking a flogging.

Isager returned to his desk, panting and short of breath; he was no longer a young man and flogging seventy boys was hard work. But he'd managed it. He put his left hand on the desk for support. The other still clutched the rope.

'You vile louts, you've just earned yourself another flogging,' he snorted.

But he was too exhausted to deliver it.

His spectacles were still in place. Not once during his skirmishes with the bigger boys did they abandon their position on the bridge of his nose.

It was Albert who deciphered the code of the spectacles. If they perched low towards the tip of Isager's nose, he announced, the day would be a calm one, with only minor, quick-healing injuries to faces and hands. If they were positioned halfway down, things could go either way. But if they were pressed against the bridge, that day's education would be provided by Mr Thrashing Rope, focusing on the tenderest parts of our bodies, which were also the ones least likely to learn anything.

This discovery, perceived as a tactical advantage in our ongoing war with Isager, earned Albert a certain amount of fame.

It was a war that left its mark on us. Our scalps were scarred from the sharp edge of Isager's ruler, and our fingers, which would get a lashing if our handwriting offended him, would often be so swollen we could barely hold our pens. He called this practice 'the distribution of ducats' – and it was currency he dealt out generously even on the days when his spectacles sat low. Limping and bleeding, our skin black and blue with livid bruises, we were always aching in some exposed place. But that wasn't the worst of what Isager did to us.

He left his mark in another, far more frightening way.

We became like him.

We committed appalling acts and only realised the horror of what we'd done when we stood gathered around the evidence of our atrocity. Violence was like a drug we couldn't relinquish.

He planted a thirst for blood in us. One that could never be quenched.

ONE AUTUMN DAY WHEN THE WIND HAD TORN THE LAST LEAVES OFF the trees, we stood, flogged and sore, in Kirkestræde, looking for something to distract us, when suddenly it waddled past us: Isager's dog, a stumpy-legged, bloated creature of indeterminate breed. Its short coat was white and grey, and its belly pink as a pig's. We'd seen Karo before, clasped in Mrs Isager's arms. She was as shapeless as her own dog and had eyes like a Chinaman's, squeezed to slits by the pressure of her fat cheeks.

We didn't know much about her, though we suspected she was the root cause of our woes. People said that she regularly pummelled Isager with her huge, ham-like fists and that it was this humiliation that sent his spectacles high up the bridge of his nose.

Now here was the dog trotting down the street with the easy air of a creature at home in its own drawing room, and perhaps that's where it thought it was, since none of us had ever seen it in town on its own before.

'Karo,' Hans Jørgen called, clicking his fingers.

The dog stopped. Its jaw hung and its tongue protruded between its teeth. We could feel the rage building inside us; suddenly we hated that dog. Fat Lorentz kicked out at it, but Hans Jørgen held up his hand and started singing the old nursery rhyme we'd chanted when we were little and wanted a snail to stick out its horns. Holding hands, we danced around Karo in a circle.

> Snaily, Snaily, show us your horn,
> Here we come to buy your corn.
> Are you a man or are you a mouse?
> Come outside or we'll burn down your house!

Karo jumped about, yapping.

'Come here, boy, come here,' Hans Jørgen enticed him and started running.

The obese animal lumbered after Hans Jørgen in happy anticipation. We circled him and started racing up Markgade. Anyone passing us would have seen nothing but a gang of boys on the move. We passed Vestergade. Ahead of us lay Reberbanen. Further out, the fields started, and it was here we'd roam when the town got too small for us and we needed to let off some steam. The road was flanked by ancient pollarded poplars, split by old age. We'd marked our ownership of them with wooden planks and nails, transforming them into tree houses with steps, rooms and attics. From these castles we lorded it over the fields. But we had to recapture them constantly because the farmers' sons claimed them too. They were children of the soil, sturdy and sullen, and they felt that the wide-open fields were their birthright. But we outnumbered them. We turned up here only in gangs, always ready to do battle, and we'd always leave the fields victorious. The farm boys were the natives and they defended their soil with the passion of savages. But we were stronger and we showed them no mercy.

'Can he run this far?' Niels Peter asked.

Saliva hung in strings from Karo's black lips as he pounded along, struggling to keep up with us. This was better than life as a lapdog with the teacher's fat missus.

'If Lorentz can do it, so can Karo,' Josef said and slapped Lorentz on his chubby shoulder. Lorentz was already puce from the strain of running: his shoulders and chest heaved, and he wheezed as though something inside him had punctured. His face was thick with fat and when you slapped his cheek hard, it would quiver hilariously: even his lips shook, and only his pudgy nose stayed still. His eyes would assume a pleading expression, as if to apologise for his shameful size.

'Look at him, he's disgusting,' said Little Anders, pointing at Karo. 'He's dribbling, yuk!'

'And he's got legs like a chest of drawers. What kind of a dog does he think he is?'

Karo responded by yapping merrily. He had company, and he had no idea of what lay in store for him. Why should he, the blameless creature? But in our eyes, Karo was no innocent. He was Isager's dog, and he couldn't escape the hatred we felt for our tormentor. As we ran alongside Karo, we pointed out the many similarities between the animal's ugly squashed face and our teacher's.

'All that's missing is the spectacles,' Albert said, and we all laughed.

We were heading for the high clay cliffs before Drejet, but Karo, only used to the short journey between his basket and his food bowl, was soon defeated: his stumpy little legs gave up and he collapsed on his belly, drooling from exhaustion.

But he was going to have to stick with it. What we had in mind wasn't something for the open fields.

Hans Jørgen picked him up and cradled him in his arms; Karo licked his face happily and Hans Jørgen grimaced.

'Eurk!' we shrieked in unison, and ran on, our excitement mounting. Down the first slope and up the next we ran, then along a field boundary and up the hillside. The cliff edge, with its dizzying drop to the beach below and the sea stretching in every direction, had always entranced us. As we stood there gazing out at the water it seemed that a great mystery lay before us: the mystery of our own lives, spread before our eyes. No matter how often we came here, it was a sight that always rendered us speechless.

The drop wasn't sheer everywhere. The cliff face was steep, but there were ledges where western marsh orchids, yarrow and golden buttons grew in the rich clay soil. You could hurl yourself off the edge and into the void, and land just a few metres below. You couldn't walk down the cliff, but you could conquer it ledge by ledge if you descended with care. Not always without injury – but then, cliff-climbing was all about putting yourself in mortal danger.

We reached the edge and surveyed the Baltic. Hans Jørgen was still carrying Karo, who yelped again. He probably thought we wanted to show him the whole wide world. We hadn't agreed on a plan. There was no need to. We all knew what was going to happen.

Hans Jørgen gripped Karo's front paws and began swinging him to and fro. Karo, in pain, tried to snap at him, but his thick neck was too short. He bared his tiny teeth and bit at the air, half whining, half growling, his hind legs flailing as if grappling for a foothold.

'Snaily, Snaily, show us your horn!' Hans Jørgen shouted, and we joined in. 'Here we come to buy your corn!'

Then he let go. Karo sailed up towards the overcast autumn sky, making a wide arc as he plummeted towards the stones on the beach far down below, his fat torso twisting and turning in mid-air. How funny he looked! We jostled right up to the edge so we could see him slam into the beach. At first he just lay motionless and silent, on his side, but then a sort of whine started up: the groan of someone losing strength. He twisted laboriously until he lay on his belly. Then he tried to stand up, but couldn't. His hindquarters wouldn't budge, although his front legs kept clawing. He tried again and again and all the time we could hear him. His cries sounded more like a child's than an animal's, a haunting, frail, yet penetrating sound.

Our triumph died instantly within us.

We didn't look at each other as we climbed down the hillside separately. Suddenly, we weren't a group any more. Most of us wanted to turn round, run home and forget all about Karo. But Hans Jørgen led the way and we followed, stumbling. Little Anders lost his footing and rolled down several metres before hitting a rock, then scrambled to his feet, crying. We were battered and bruised by the time we gathered around Karo, who was still whimpering in this scary way that we couldn't bear to listen to.

He gazed up at us and licked his nose with his tiny pink tongue. At that moment he almost looked happy, as if unaware that we were the cause of his plight, and was simply waiting for us to make everything all right again. His tail wasn't wagging, but that was only because his back was broken.

We gathered around him in a circle. None of us felt like kicking him now. He looked so innocent. He hadn't done anything wrong, and now there he lay, whining, with his spine snapped.

Albert squatted down beside him and started stroking his head.

'There, there.' He comforted the dog, and suddenly we all wanted to cuddle Karo.

If only he'd started wagging his stubby tail at this moment. But he didn't, and he never would again. We knew that.

Swiftly, Hans Jørgen moved across to Albert.

'Stop it,' he said, grabbing hold of Albert's arm to pull him away.

Albert got to his feet and faced him. Hans Jørgen was still holding onto him. He was the biggest of us and the most fair-minded. He was the one who bravely stood up to Isager when he paced up and down the classroom with the thrashing rope. He always defended the youngest children. Now he stood there, his shoulders sagging, just as lost as the rest of us.

'We can't leave Karo here,' Albert said.

'Well, cuddling him won't do him any good either,' Hans Jørgen snapped.

'Can't we take him back to Isager?'

'To Isager? Are you out of your mind? He'd kill us!'

'What are we going to do then?'

Hans Jørgen let go of Albert and shrugged. Then he started walking up and down the beach.

'Help me find a big rock,' he said.

None of us stirred. Anders was still crying. Karo had gone very quiet, as if Hans Jørgen's words had made him pensive.

'Listen,' Albert said. 'He's stopped whimpering. Perhaps he's feeling better.'

'Karo isn't going to get better,' Hans Jørgen said darkly. That's when we understood there was no other way.

'You can go if you want to,' he said.

He'd found a rock. He was clutching it in both hands.

We wanted to go, but we couldn't. We couldn't leave Hans Jørgen. If we did, it would be like being left alone with Isager.

Hans Jørgen kneeled in front of Karo. The dog looked up at him expectantly, as though he thought Hans Jørgen wanted to play.

'Turn him on his side,' Hans Jørgen said.

Niels Peter put a hand under the dog's hairless pink belly and turned him over. That's when Karo screamed. He didn't whine. He didn't moan. He screamed. We were all so terrified we started screaming with him, because it was all so sad: sad that he was so stupid, and sad that he couldn't understand a single thing about this world.

Afterwards, when we climbed back up the hillside, each of us carried a stone in his hand. We didn't really know why. We walked home without speaking, clasping our stones.

Lorentz met us, wheezing. He had given up on the first slope.

'What's happened?' he asked in his usual sucking-up way. Then he saw our faces.

'Where's Karo?'

'Shut your gob, you fat pig.'

Niels Peter walked right up to him and punched him in the stomach, and Lorentz sat down in the middle of the road, wearing that begging expression that we all loathed. No matter what you did to him, he always put up with it.

Later we met two boys from one of the farms in Midtmarken. They stank of cow shit, so we chased them, pelting them with our stones. They howled as they scampered home to their dungheap. We didn't care what they told their parents. Our mood hadn't improved. We had a feeling that, once again, Isager had won.

The next day we were sure that Isager would have vengeance on his mind. Sure enough, his spectacles sat high on the bridge of his nose, and he paced the schoolroom with the springy, elastic steps we had learned to fear. The thrashing rope, too, seemed to have acquired a life of its own. We sensed it twisting and turning in his hand, ready to lash out at its first victim. We were already cowering.

This was it.

Karo's failure to return home must have caused an upset in the schoolteacher's house, and whether or not Isager thought we were involved, we knew he'd make us pay the price, the way he'd made us pay for every other disappointment in his life.

Isager marched up and down muttering 'Bad boys, bad boys' as usual. But no one was ordered to kneel on the floor: when he struck, there was no warning. He started on Lorentz, who was sitting by his desk, taking up two spaces. He attacked him from behind, swiping him across his broad back. Then, quick as lightning, he whipped round to the front of the desk and hit him first across the chest and then the face. Lorentz squealed in a mixture of pain and fear and covered his head with his massive arms. Isager tugged at them to gain clear access for the rope, but Lorentz held fast, so Isager pulled him to the floor – he landed with a loud thud – and started kicking him. We'd all tried hitting Lorentz, even the smallest of us. His obesity had something fascinating and irritating to it, a feminine softness that attracted and provoked us at the same time. Word had it that he didn't have any balls and that his tiny white worm hung between the fatty masses of his thighs with an empty scrotum dangling behind. This feature made him a born clown in our eyes. We believed that his fat protected him, and even when he wailed from our blows, we thought he was crying because he was a sissy and not because it really hurt. So we hit him harder to make him stop whining.

Lorentz never hit back. He'd put up with anything to avoid being shunned. And we strung him along because we needed someone we could bully without the risk of punishment. Perhaps he thought we tolerated him. But we didn't; to us he was nothing but the thing we called him when we wanted him to do something: the fat pig.

Sticking together was the only thing Isager had taught us. He never, ever succeeded in turning us into snitches. We'd each rather take the blame than betray a comrade, and Isager knew it. That's why he regarded us all as equally guilty and beat us all equally hard.

Lorentz lay defenceless on the floor while Isager kicked at him. Of all of us, Lorentz was the least guilty, yet even so, not one of us raised his voice to protest the boy's innocence.

Was it solidarity that made us keep silent now, too?

Then we heard the familiar wheezing that usually accompanied our excursions when we ran faster and fat Lorentz began to lag behind, struggling for breath. Fighting to sit up, he forgot to shield himself – and Isager, who so far had relied on his boots, now raised the thrashing rope, ready to bring it down on his victim's unprotected face and his fat-girl chest. But something halted him in his tracks. Lorentz's arms were flapping, as though he were facing a new but invisible enemy. His face was turning blue and his eyes bulged in their sockets. He gurgled and gasped. He seemed to be choking.

Isager, at a loss, took a step back, then shoved the rope back in his rear pocket as though nothing had happened and headed for his desk.

By now Lorentz, shoulders still heaving in an agonising struggle for breath, had managed to sit up. Isager did nothing, but watched from the corner of his eye. We could tell that he was scared. Lorentz remained on the floor for the rest of the lesson, in a world of his own, his eyes sightless. Then slowly, his huge body began to relax and his wheezing died down. When he fully regained his breath, he looked around at the rest of us with eyes that seemed to beg that he might be one of us at last.

We looked away. None of us wanted to answer.

ISAGER HAD BEEN A SCHOOLTEACHER FOR THIRTY YEARS. HIS PRE-
decessor, Andrésen, had taught for fifty-one years, but only the old
folk remembered him. Isager had met two kings. The first was
Crown Prince Christian Frederik, who later became King Christian
VIII. Escorted by the schooner *Dolphin*, his ship had dropped anchor
at a stone bridge in the harbour – henceforth renamed Prinsebroen.
On his way to Kirkestræde he'd strolled up Markgade – which was
promptly rechristened Prinsegade. Whatever street Crown Prince
Christian Frederik put his feet on got a new name. The girls came
dressed in white frocks and the pastor gave a speech, but Isager
was the star attraction of the visit because the Crown prince had
come to inspect his pupils.

Twelve years later came another royal visit, this time from the
future King Frederik VII, who arrived by ferry in a northerly gale.
We were standing on the quay debating which passenger might be
the prince when a man in knitted gloves and a cap with earflaps
leaped ashore and secured the hawser, saying, 'Cold today, isn't it,
lads?' That was Crown Prince Frederik.

At school we sang 'We want to be sailors, as long as we live!'
(the words were supplied by Isager) and then we were subjected to
the teacher's grilling – upon which the Crown prince turned to his
adjutant and asked him if he could do sums as difficult as those
faced by the children of Marstal. The adjutant replied no, and the
man who would one day succeed to the throne as Frederik VII
announced, 'Neither can I.'

The calculation that had generated such admiration from the
Crown prince came from page forty-seven of *Cramer's Arithmetic*
and went as follows: 'The earth goes through its annual course of
129,626,823 geographical miles in $365 \frac{109}{450}$ days. Given that the
earth moves constantly at the same speed, how far does it travel in
one second?'

This question was enough to make anyone dizzy, especially since Isager had omitted to tell us that the earth circled the sun. However, he'd drilled the answer into us. It was at the back of the book: four geographical miles – plus a fraction that no one would have known how to pronounce had it not been for the thrashing rope. A boy called Svend gave the answer on this occasion. From that day on he was known as One-Second Svend, and he went on to take the famous fraction with him to his watery grave at the age of sixteen.

Isager bowed deeply in response to the Crown prince's compliment, and Frederik patted his shoulder. One-Second Svend had been ordered to keep his hands behind his back so that Frederik wouldn't catch sight of his damaged fingers.

That was all the wisdom Isager ever imparted to us: that the thrashing rope and the ruler could achieve what a teacher's skill could not. Isager's knowledge didn't extend far even with *Cramer's Arithmetic* in his hand. But the rope did its work. If we learned to count, it was only to keep track of the number of strokes we were dealt.

Marstal School was later named Frederik School in honour of the occasion.

But they might as well have named it Isager School. Crown Prince Frederik's pat on the back had turned the establishment – and our bruised limbs – into Isager's personal property. He'd bowed to two future kings, and two future kings had given him a pat on the back: that put him beyond criticism.

An education committee consisting of a wholesale grocer and two skippers had been set up, and our parents could complain to them if we came home looking worse than usual after an encounter with Isager's rope. But the committee members were simple people, who dumbly deferred to the learned schoolteacher. After all, he'd been praised by not one but two kings. So no complaint was ever upheld.

Besides, everyone remembered what it had been like in old Andrésen's time. There had been three hundred and fifty pupils at the school in those days, but only two classes, with a hundred and seventy-five pupils each. Andrésen couldn't possibly remember so many names, so he gave the boys numbers instead and directed them with the aid of a whistle. Pupils would sit wherever they could find space, including on the windowsills, in the kitchen and even out in the yard. This meant that the windows had to stay open until the weather grew too severe. But long before that happened, the pupils all caught colds and bronchitis from the draught. Then, once the windows had been closed for the winter, the atmosphere became suffocatingly close, and children fainted on a daily basis. And there were no blackboards or writing implements: the pupils stood in front of a tray of sand and scratched in it with a stick. A single gust of wind could blow their combined knowledge clean away.

With memories like that, the three members of the committee regarded the new school, with its inkwells and its blackboards and its headmaster who had been praised by two future kings, as progress. There was only one remedy for children's reluctance to learn, and that was more thrashing.

But then again, we rarely complained, because another aspect of the solidarity that Isager had taught us was that we couldn't even snitch on our tormentor. We'd return home with bald patches on our scalps where a furious Isager had ripped out clumps of hair; with black eyes; with fingers incapable of holding knife or fork. And we'd say we'd been in a fight, and when they asked who with, we said Nobody.

We swore that when we grew up, we'd give Isager what he'd been asking for. We couldn't fathom our fathers' tacit consent to our ill-treatment: they knew full well who Nobody was because they too had been victims of the rope. But they turned a blind eye to our sufferings.

Our mothers suspected that something was wrong, but they were always at a loss when it came to dealing with the authorities. It wasn't that they lacked strength: they had considerable supplies of it, with so many children and their husbands away at sea. But when faced by the vicar or the schoolteacher, they started doubting their own judgement.

'You're sure it wasn't Mr Isager?' they'd ask.

And we'd shake our heads. We hardly knew why, but we never pointed the finger at him as the cause of our daily injuries. Instead, we blamed ourselves.

'Well, perhaps this will teach you to stay out of trouble.'

And we would get a clip on the ear.

'Look at your sister, she comes homes neat and tidy every day.'

It was true. But then again, our sisters had Nothkier, the assistant teacher, and he never beat them.

This was another malign effect of Isager. He followed us home unseen and sowed discord.

WINTER ARRIVED, AND WITH IT THE FROST. THE BOATS WERE LAID
up in the harbour, the harbour froze over and an ice pack formed
on the beach. Island and sea became one; we inhabited a white
continent whose infinity both beckoned and terrified us. We could
walk as far as Ristinge Klint on the island of Langeland if we wanted
to, marching across frozen ships' channels between sandbanks that
lay like white hills, collecting snowdrifts fringed by ice packs. It
looked so wild, windswept and deserted.

This new landscape even forced its way into our streets, where a blizzard of snowflakes whirled and danced on the heavy drifts, then leaped
back into the air to obliterate the world once more. We were desperate
to get outside and join the dance, to take our skates down to the harbour
or trek out across the fields to the hills at Drejet to fight the farmers'
sons with snowballs and hurtle down the slopes on our toboggans.

Isager was an obstacle to this, but winter was on our side: without
a stove in the classroom, we couldn't cope with the cold – but a
stovepipe was easily obstructed, and once the room filled with smoke,
he had to send us home. On these occasions he'd stand in the doorway,
treating us to a clip on the ear by way of goodbye as we filed out.

'You rascal,' he would mutter to each of us. By that point he
could barely breathe and his eyes would be red behind his spectacles. But like the captain of a sinking ship, he was always the
last to leave the classroom: if he could still see well enough to
strike us, even though he was hacking and coughing, he'd stay on
to do it. He hated us so much that he'd rather choke than miss
out on a single blow.

So only on Sundays could we devote ourselves to the snow without
paying for it with a sore neck.

One day Niels Peter deftly dismantled the stovepipe and stuffed
his entire jumper inside, whereupon the stove duly started to smoke

as planned – but the jumper, too, caught fire. Isager stifled the blaze immediately. But the flames that burst briefly from the pipe wouldn't be forgotten in a hurry: even Isager was silenced by the episode.

If we could smoke him out, what else could we do?

On cold winter evenings Isager would go visiting. He frequently called on Christoffer Mathiesen, the grocer, his most fervent supporter on the education committee. A few other local people sat with him around the grocer's mahogany table, but not Pastor Zachariassen. Isager wasn't on good terms with the pastor, who was embarrassed by his poor teaching. Mr Mathiesen, on the other hand, was honoured to entertain the learned gentleman who had been patted on the back by royalty.

'And as the king said to me –' was Isager's most frequent remark in that company. He would sit there in his tailcoat with a two-finger toddy in front of him. Describing his royal encounters served as payment for the steaming brew, which he never raised to his lips without referring to it as 'the best medicine against the cold the good Lord ever created'.

As the medicine took effect, his lower lip would begin to sag and his spectacles slide towards the position Albert described as 'fair weather', revealing a face we never saw at school: not amiable exactly, but relaxed.

When Isager left Mathiesen's house in Møllegade one night he was unsteady on his feet. It had snowed all evening, and now there were drifts against the stone steps and across the street. There were no street lights in Marstal, so the town lay dark in the whirling snow. The wind was easterly, blowing up from the harbour straight into Møllegade.

We saw his face in the light from Mathiesen's window. For a brief moment his slack expression gave way to the same look of rage he wore on a punishment round, and we fully expected to hear him scream 'Rascal!' at the snowstorm. Instead his lower lip drooped and his eyes resumed their vacant look.

Now, outside, he was nothing but a shadow against the snow-drifts.

We followed him for a while to make sure that he was heading home via Kirkestræde. He made laborious progress, getting stuck in drifts and frantically shovelling himself free. This might have helped him warm up, but it didn't speed him on his way.

We could have got him right there and then.

Only the oldest of us were out that night. Niels Peter had sneaked downstairs from his attic room and left via the back door. Hans Jørgen had lied and said he was visiting a friend. His father was away on a long voyage that winter and his mother had started treating him like a grown-up. Josef and Johan Isager were not with us, obviously.

We all knew that our plan would mean trouble in some form or other the next day. But an extra beating made no difference to us.

Lorentz begged to be part of it.

'Please, please let me,' he said.

'Haaaaaaaaaa,' we said, imitating his wheezing when he was out of breath. 'We'll be running fast. You're no good.'

In fact, if we'd really loathed him, we would have let him join us. He had no idea what we were saving him from that night.

We waited for Isager on the corner of Kirkestræde and Korsgade, the crystals in the falling snow reflecting the starlight above us. Then we spotted him, a shadowy figure slowly growing in size among the glimmering snowflakes. The darkness protected us, and we had tied our scarves around our faces so that only our eyes were visible. Our breath felt hot behind the wool. We were shadows ourselves, a pack of wolves in the snowy night.

We started bombarding him with snowballs. We came up close, hitting him hard and with precision. But it was only fun and games. So far, at least. Just a gang of boys throwing snowballs.

One knocked his hat off. He staggered forward to pick it up. Then another, crusted hard with ice after being lovingly moulded in a hot and vengeful hand, slammed right into his ear, which already must have been burning in the severe cold. It might as well have been a stone. He touched his head.

'Rascals!' he screamed. 'I know who you are!'

He took a step towards us, and a snowball smashed him right in his face, blinding him. Then a direct hit to his neck. He raved in pain.

'Rascals!' he screamed again.

But the power was gone from his voice. He was moaning now – and he was scared.

That was what we wanted. We'd moved on from fun and games. Now he'd see us for what we really were. With every backward step he took, our fear shrank; we'd tasted our own strength and it had whetted our appetite. Outside the classroom he was nothing but an old drunk, alone in a winter storm. But we didn't see him like that. We had Satan himself in our grasp. And having captured the bringer of all evil, we'd show him no mercy – for if we did, we'd stay scared the rest of our lives. Hans Jørgen had once brought Isager to his knees and twisted his arm behind his back, but even then, he'd kept his power over us, and Hans Jørgen had let him go.

But this time there'd be no escape.

We backed off briefly and he cleared the snow from his eyes. Still he didn't see us. He seemed to think he was safe, but that was our plan. He gave up looking for his hat and stumbled on through the drifts, mumbling to himself. We knew he was cursing us. Then we attacked again. Harder snowballs this time. Pure lumps of ice. And there was no missing at such close range. It was like pounding him in the face, first one cheek, then the other, forcing his head to jerk from side to side. This was our thrashing rope. We stayed silent while he grunted and moaned. We would have loved to break every bone in that detested face, but we held off because we didn't want him to collapse here in Kirkestræde, where he might be found before the frost finished the job for us.

We let him get as far as the corner of Nygade before we surrounded him again, forcing him to flee down the street. We wanted to drive him out to the deserted area down by the harbour, where no one came at night. We'd almost got him down to Buegade: by now he was swaying and faltering. From time to time he'd fall into a snow-drift, head first. Then we'd wait until he got back on his feet and start again.

He was blubbering.

It was a dreadful thing to hear, but it stirred no pity in us. The snowstorm muffled all other noises, so the only sound was our tormentor's weeping. The tears ran down his cheeks, where they froze to ice. Snow hung in his sideburns, which made them seem longer and frayed. Sobs, mumblings: was he still cursing us, or was he pleading for his life? We weren't sure, but nor did we care. Finally, we had Satan under our thumb.

Isager sought shelter by the wall of one of the tall half-timbered houses at the bottom of Nygade. He tripped over the doorstep, collapsing onto some steps that were half buried by snow. When he pushed himself up with his hands, Hans Jørgen hit him on the nose with a rock-hard ball. The night was dark, but the snow lit everything up, and we saw the blood drip onto it, first a small stain, then a bigger one. Isager turned his head towards us and brayed with fear, blood dangling from his nose in a snotty strand.

Hans Jørgen launched yet another shot at him, but he missed, and the snowball smashed into the door instead.

A lamp was lit inside, and a light flickered behind the frost flowers on the icy window.

'Who's there?'

We heard scrambling in the hallway.

Then we legged it. In Buegade Kresten Hansen was coming along, swinging his lamp in the snowstorm. The glowing wick cast a flickering light across his mutilated face. He was a nightwatchman now. He slept during the day and worked at night to spare the town the sight of his face. He looked horrific. But he was the one who made way for us, and as we raced past he dropped his lamp in a snowdrift and darkness descended.

The next day, Isager wasn't there to greet us in the doorway of the school. Silently, we entered the empty, ice-cold classroom. But we felt no relief. It was so strange. We couldn't imagine a world without Isager. Was he dead?

Nothkier, the assistant teacher, arrived and told us Isager was ill. We were all to go home and come back tomorrow. The next day the classroom was empty again, but the stove had been lit. Nothkier arrived and informed us that 'Mr Isager's illness will be a long one' and that in the meantime he'd attend to our education, though our hours of instruction would be reduced, as he also had to teach the girls.

Nothkier was no better at teaching than Isager was: he, too, stuck to *Balle's Textbook*, which made very little sense to us, and *Cramer's Arithmetic*, which made no sense to anyone including him. But he never hit us. Sometimes he'd ask us whether we understood what he had just explained – and relieved, we'd answer that no, we didn't. He didn't get angry or call us donkeys or give out ducats: he just started again from the beginning.

It was still snowy, but we didn't block the stove or pour sand into the inkwells. Fewer of us played truant. It was as though we wanted to reward him.

Isager had pneumonia, it was said, and at home our parents talked about how he'd lost his way in the storm.

'He was probably pissed out of his head,' the men said. The women hushed them.

All the children knew what had happened, including those of us who hadn't been there. But we never said anything, not even to each other. As long as Isager didn't turn up for school, we were happy. Our failure to kill him the way we'd planned barely crossed our minds. Had anyone asked us if we really wanted him dead, we'd probably have replied that we didn't care, so long as we were rid of him.

Christmas came, and with it the holidays. Isager was still bedridden, and this year we spared him the torments we normally subjected him to on New Year's Eve in thanks for the year gone by. We didn't smash his garden fence or shoot the school's forty windows to bits or offer our trademark New Year's greeting in the form of clay pots full of ashes and stinking waste lobbed through his windows.

After New Year's Day, Isager returned, and everything was back to normal.

His skin was as white as the snow outside, and even his nose had lost its colour. But he wore his black tailcoat and his spectacles were high on the bridge of his nose, and the thrashing rope swung in his right hand like a viper roused from its winter hibernation, ready to attack. We stared at him as though he'd risen from the dead – not least because we'd already pictured him in his grave.

We sang 'The Dark Night Has Ended' as usual, but the words on our lips belied the feeling in our hearts. The dark night had begun anew, and a ghost walked among us.

After the hymn, Isager strode over to Little Anders and grabbed him by the ear. That was all it took for Anders to position himself obediently on his knees between the schoolteacher's legs. Isager raised the thrashing rope, ready to strike.

'Sinning is a disease of the soul. That's why it causes the soul to experience anxiety.' The calmness of his voice spooked us. Normally, even at this early stage of a punishment, he'd be in the grip of a mad rage. 'This anxiety we call conscience.' He looked up. 'Do you understand?'

The schoolroom fell silent. The only sound was the crackling of the flames in the stove. We nodded. When Isager finished with Anders he moved on to the next boy. Albert, too, kneeled obediently, and Isager gripped him by the lining of his trousers.

'The purpose of conscience is to judge and to punish.' Isager's lash made Albert jump: the stroke was unexpectedly painful on a backside that had toughened during the autumn but regained its normal sensitivity during the long break. 'Lie still,' Isager ordered him in the same calm voice as before, renewing his grip on the lining of Albert's trousers. 'But how does your conscience punish you? Through the inner unrest you experience when you have committed a misdeed. Does your conscience trouble you? Do you feel the punishment?'

He laid off Albert and looked around the schoolroom. Again we nodded. 'You're lying,' he said, without raising his voice, then moved on to his next victim, Hans Jørgen. We anticipated that one of their regular confrontations might erupt – but Hans Jørgen, too, kneeled to await his punishment. Oblivious to this unexpected triumph, Isager continued his lecture while raining down more blows. 'You know nothing of remorse. And do you know why? Because you have no purpose. Do you know what purpose is? Probably not. Purpose is God's plan for us. But God has no plan for you. You have no reason and you have no conscience. You don't know the difference between right and wrong.'

He straightened up and paced about the schoolroom. He made Niels Peter his next choice – but instead of thrashing him right away, he paused next to the boy's bowed back and brandished the rope.

'Take a good look at this,' he said, before laying into him. 'This is your conscience, and it's the only one you'll ever have. Only the rope can teach you about right and wrong.'

When school was over we walked across the snow-covered fields beyond town. None of us said anything. We were looking for some farmers' boys to start a fight with. Every now and then we'd steal a glance at Hans Jørgen. Had he let us down? We'd all presented our backs to Isager. But we hadn't expected him to.

Today the snow had none of the glittering surfaces and bluish shadows it took on when the sun shone. The dull weather cast everything in a uniform grey, and only the bare poplars provided any perspective. There wasn't a soul about.

'There's no one here,' Niels Peter grumbled.

We stole another glance at Hans Jørgen. He was walking slightly ahead of us, but suddenly he stopped and turned to face us.

'I don't want you to think that I'm afraid of Isager,' he said. 'Because I'm not.'

He sounded angry. We didn't say anything and looked down at the snow. A snowflake fell from the overcast sky, and then another. We expected him to add something, but he didn't.

'Why did you let him hit you?'

Niels Peter put the question without looking up, almost as if he were talking to himself. Hans Jørgen hesitated. Then he shrugged, as though defeated in advance.

'It doesn't matter now,' he said.

Albert looked up, squinting into the falling snow.

'I don't understand.'

Hans Jørgen paused. 'Well, we didn't get him,' he said. ' And now he's come back and he's worse than ever. It's all' – again he flung out his arms – 'hopeless.'

'But he was bleeding,' Albert protested. He hadn't seen it, but he'd heard detailed, almost painterly descriptions of Isager's dripping blood.

'Yes,' Niels Peter said. 'He did bleed.'

'And so what?'

Hans Jørgen turned round and started heading back to the town. The snowflakes came thicker now. We followed. For the first time, we disagreed with Hans Jørgen. He'd always been our leader. But now we had to answer for ourselves.

We'd killed the dog, but we'd failed to kill the master. He'd thrashed our fathers and he'd go on thrashing us. We did the maths on our fingers. We stayed at school for six years. Albert had five and a half years to go. Hans Jørgen had six months, the rest of us something in between. If Isager claimed six years of our lives, how many more would it take us to forget what he'd done? It sounded like a problem from *Cramer's Arithmetic*, but whether you solved it through addition, subtraction or multiplication, none of us knew.

We had seen Isager bleed one winter's night, and the sight of his blood on the snow had filled us with hope. We'd seen fire lick through Niels Peter's jumper in the schoolroom stove, and we weren't through with contemplating what those flames meant.

At which point we began to see the potential of fire.

HANS JØRGEN TOOK CONFIRMATION WITH PASTOR ZACHARIASSEN AND
went to sea. Eight months later he returned with the winter ice,
having saved up his wages and bought himself a tall hat like the
older sailors wore.

Now was the moment for taking his revenge on Isager, we told
him, because he was an adult, and no one could hurt him. But Hans
Jørgen said you got thrashed just as much on board ship, so nothing
had changed, and now that Isager was no longer his teacher, he'd
lost the urge to smash him to pieces. In fact he'd bumped into him
in the street, and Isager asked him about life at sea and they'd chatted
as though Hans Jørgen had never forced him to his knees by twisting
his arm, or lain on the floor being flayed: one adult to another.

'Do it for us, then,' Albert pleaded. 'You're big and strong. You're
stronger than last year. You can take him on.'

'I've already forgotten him,' Hans Jørgen said. 'He's of no interest.'

'You're full of it because you've just been paid.'

'You're not listening.'

Hans Jørgen squatted down so his face was level with Albert's.

'They thrash you on board ship too. It never ends. It goes on and
on. You might as well get used to it now.'

'It's not fair!' Niels Peter fumed.

'No –' the others joined in – 'It's not fair!'

'What's the point of teaching us to do sums, or to read and write,'
asked Hans Jørgen, 'when all we need to know is how to take a
beating, if we want to get ahead? And when it comes to that, there's
no better teacher than Isager.'

We looked at him uncertainly. Was he mocking us?

'Did the great Tordenskjold complain when a wave snapped off
the foremast? No. What did he say to his men?'

'We're winning, boys,' Niels Peter mumbled, and looked at his
feet.

87

'There you are. We're winning, boys! Just remember that and stop whining.'

'He's gone really strange,' Albert said afterwards.

We nodded. We felt more alone than ever. Hans Jørgen was no longer one of us. He'd become a grown-up and he knew more about the world. But we didn't like what he told us. We decided not to believe him.

However, from that day on, it seemed that we were more willing to put up with things. When Isager went on a thrashing round, there was less rebelliousness in the classroom, and fewer of us jumped out of the window to escape.

Christmas and New Year came round again. Isager had escaped our torments the previous year because he'd been bedridden, fighting for his life, but he'd won, and now it was time for more seasonal fun. We suspected we'd never be rid of Isager but we couldn't forget those classroom flames, the day Niels Peter used his jumper to obstruct the stovepipe, and it caught fire. Having seen the flames bursting out, we knew enough about fire to realise that once it had taken hold, nobody could stop it.

This, too, was Niels Peter's idea. How had the big fire of 1815 started? Had men with torches set fire to the thatched roofs at night? No: a candle had been knocked over in a house in Prinsegade. That was all it took! And the blaze had jumped from house to house, until a third of the town was reduced to ashes. The glow could be seen all the way from Odense.

Albert's grandmother, Kirstine, still spoke about the fire with terror in her voice.

'Granny, tell us about the Great Fire,' Albert pestered her, when she came to visit. So as she sat by the stove, Granny would recount the story of Barbara Pedersdatter, the maid who'd been hackling flax on Karlsen's threshing floor in Prinsegade with the tallow dip lit, but then taken it into her head, the silly girl, to read a letter from her sweetheart because he'd landed her in trouble and she was keen to know what he intended to do, given that it was all his fault. But in the process of opening the letter, the befuddled girl had knocked the candle over and the tow caught fire and soon it wasn't just Barbara Pedersdatter but the whole town that was in trouble. 'Whoosh,' Granny said, and flung her hands in the air to indicate how the hungry flames shot out through the thatched roof. She'd seen that fire and she'd never forget it.

'You pray to God that you'll never have to live through what we did,' she'd say, as she finished telling the tale.

But Albert prayed to God that fire would be unleashed again.

It was New Year's Eve and we did what we always did: we ate our traditional dinner of boiled cod with mustard sauce, and then ran out into the dark winter's night, banging on doors and wreaking havoc. We smashed fences and threw clay pots. We caught a dog and tied a bit of old rope around it and hung it upside down from a tree until its howls attracted the attention of its owner, who we then bombarded with more clay pots.

And now, having stuffed straw into our jumpers, we were waiting for it to get dark enough to surround Isager's house. There was still light coming from the inside, so we threw a couple of clay pots through the windows into the drawing room. We heard his fat wife squeal and, shortly afterwards, more noises came from the hallway.

Then Isager appeared in the doorway a stick in his hand.

'Louts,' he yelled.

'You can shout as much as you like,' we called back, and aimed a few more clay pots in his direction. One hit him on the shoulder and sent its foul, stinking contents running down his black tailcoat. His yelling ended in a strangled cough as if he was about to throw up. Another pot flew past him into the hallway. Josef and Johan stood looking out of the window, laughing at their father. They were never allowed to go out mischief-making on New Year's Eve, so this was their revenge. But they had no idea what was on its way, because we hadn't told them.

We legged it down Skolegade with Isager chasing after us, his stick raised, ready to attack. The sound of smashing glass now came from the other side of the house: Niels Peter and Albert Madsen had broken a bedroom window and thrown burning straw inside. The fire had started.

'Come out now or we'll burn your house down.'

We turned into Tværgade and raced up Prinsegade. We could still hear Isager shouting. We were back at the schoolhouse by this time; we'd tricked him by running in a circle. We felt the wind grow stronger. The day before it had begun to thaw, and most of the snow in the streets was melting, warmed by the mild western wind that always sucked winter away from us. You could hear it howling across town.

We'd broken the windows on both sides of the house, and Isager had left the door open behind him when he chased us, so now the wind rushed straight through the building, blowing through the burning straw in the bedroom. Flames began to lick the walls. We'd never seen fire like this before, and the sight of it sent shivers down our spines: so this was what a hungry fire looked like! Wilder and fiercer than we'd ever imagined, it shot straight through the roof and lit the house like a thousand tallow candles. Then it burst out of every opening.

Isager screamed, and we saw his wife stumble through the door. She slipped on the stairs and plonked down on her fat bottom. She stayed there, sobbing loudly and plaintively, like a child.

Isager ran over to her and thumped her with the stick, as if the calamity that had befallen them were her fault. Meanwhile Josef and Johan watched the scene as if it were no concern of theirs. Jørgen Albertsen from the house across the street came running.

Our group, which continued to grow, stood on the other side of Kirkestræde. We wanted to cheer loudly, but we knew it was definitely not a wise move, so we just whispered the Snaily Snaily rhyme, glancing furtively at each other and giggling.

Our tormentor had got his comeuppance.

The adults raced over with buckets full of water, but that made no difference at all, because the west wind was blowing in earnest now. And it wasn't just through Isager's house that it stormed like the devil, setting alight curtains, wallpaper, furniture and the loft; no, it carried on. Flames jumped on the wind's back and rode it from Isager's house to Mr Dreymann's house, from Mr Dreymann's house to Mr Kroman's.

Little Anders wasn't chanting the Snaily Snaily rhyme any more: he was screaming. It was his house that had caught fire. He watched his mother rush out with the soup tureen of tin-glazed English earthenware, which was the finest thing they owned. Soon all of one side of Skolegade was ablaze. The snow began to fall again, but this had to be Satan's snow, for it fell black rather than white.

The fire didn't stop until it reached the corner of Tværgade. Here the streets widened, and the houses on the other side had tiled roofs. But from the near side, glowing embers rained down on the cobbles, and anyone who ventured there came away with burn-holes in their clothing. Meanwhile, all along Skolegade, smoke and flames whipped up into the sky, like the lashing tail of a fiery dragon.

Finally, the fire engine arrived. The horses were neighing with fright; they'd never seen a real fire either. The heat prevented them from entering Skolegade, so the fire brigade left the engine on the corner by Tværgade and tried to stop the flames rampaging through the town. Meanwhile, efforts to extinguish the fire in Skolegade had ground to a halt, though Levin Kroman had shouted at us to join in, and we had. But the heat was too intense. We couldn't get near the Isager house and could only press ourselves against the houses on the opposite side of the street, clutching our buckets, while we watched the mighty sea of flames through stinging eyes.

It never crossed our minds that we were the cause of this unimaginable thing. No: the fire itself was the cause. It had a force, a consuming purpose, all its own. It had nothing to do with us.

Our hour had finally come. All our bitterness, fear and hatred – passions too huge to stay contained in the narrow chests of children – had fuelled this fire, whose flames had the awesome capacity to purge us of everything hateful or unnecessary. Entire houses had been turned into sooty carcasses by those flames, and tomorrow that would be a sad and terrible sight to see. But tonight it was a stupendous spectacle. That's what we felt: nothing more.

But a western wind always heralds rain. High above the flames the storm clouds burst, and a torrent of rain tipped down and drowned both the fire-dragon and our joyful excitement.

The next morning we wandered around and inspected the remains of the burned-down houses. Skolegade was one huge scene of devastation. The walls were still standing: the empty windows gaped darkly and the townsfolk gaped back. 1 January was a holiday. Men wore top hats and examined the damage expertly, with discerning expressions, as though they were assessors accustomed to major fires – even though almost forty years had passed since the last one. The women, including those who'd lost nothing, wore black shawls over their heads and wailed loudly. It seemed that fear had claimed the women of Marstal just as the fire had claimed the houses the night before. It was the same terror that the sea instilled in them, the fear of losing everything: brothers, fathers, and sons. But the fire had shown more mercy than the sea. It hadn't taken a single life.

In the midst of all this, we heard Mrs Isager calling out for Karo. She seemed to have forgotten that the dog was long gone. The other women spoke to her, but she shook her head and went on calling.

Though the lives of dogs and humans had been spared, many families had lost the things that help us through life, such as furniture and clothes and memories and kitchen utensils. The Albertsen family found a cast-iron pot that could still be used and the Svanes unearthed a frying pan. The handle had burned away, but Laves Petersen, the carpenter, said he could make a new one.

The fire had started while we were bombarding Isager's house with clay pots. We did this every year and we – even those who hadn't taken part – were all punished for it annually. Since we never snitched on each other, we were all regarded as equally guilty. But this year there was no punishment – because set against the scale of the inferno, our clay-pot larks seemed like small beer. They were forgotten, and so were we. Isager had been in the street when the fire broke out and simply didn't connect us with what had happened. By not being able to conceive that we might be responsible for such a disaster, he'd underestimated us. He was unaware of the wickedness he had sown in us, and his stupidity was our protection.

In the days that followed, we learned that his fat wife had lost her reason. She kept wandering around calling for Karo. She thought that the flames had scared him away and she put his bowl out every day to entice him out of hiding.

'She's improved,' Josef said. 'She keeps forgetting to thump us.'

THE FLAMES HADN'T TOUCHED THE SCHOOL, AND THE TEACHER'S home was rebuilt. Before long, new houses had appeared on Skolegade. But at school, nothing had changed. Isager had been bedridden and fought off death. His house had burned down. And we, his pupils, were behind it all. But he kept coming back. We'd lost. It was hopeless.

Again we counted the remaining years on our fingers. Sooner or later we would be old enough to leave the school. That was the only hope we had.

Lorentz was confirmed and became apprenticed to the baker in Tværgade. Appropriate, we thought, given his obese, unmanly body. As he grew older it had become increasingly feminine: he'd developed breasts, too, and the Isager boys had once taken him out to the Tail and made him strip so they could see what a girl looked like. Then Josef had held Lorentz in a vice-like grip while he twisted away at his fat, quivering flesh, and Johan, who was sensitive and cried greasy, waxy tears at every opportunity, had done things to Lorentz which afterwards made them both shoot us knowing glances, as if they were in possession of a secret which we could share if we begged them hard enough. But we didn't want to know what it was. No. We didn't.

Lorentz worked for the baker in Tværgade at night, kneading dough. But he lasted only a few months. The clouds of flour next to the hot oven got into his lungs, he said, and he couldn't breathe properly. But that was a load of rubbish. He'd always had breathing trouble because he was fat, and he and his mother were to blame for that. He was an only child and she was a widow and she fed him from morning till night like a goose she was fattening for Christmas. No: the baker didn't want Lorentz because Lorentz was useless; all he could do was hunch his shoulders and wheeze.

So Lorentz went to sea and came back that winter with a black eye. Hans Jørgen was right, he said. They hit you on board ship, too. And again he gave us the look which pleaded: can I be one of you now?

But we looked away, as we always did. Afterwards we thought that he'd never stand a chance if he looked that way at the crew of the *Anne Marie Elisabeth*.

No one respects a weakling who crawls.

Hans Jørgen wasn't around to say 'I told you so!' when Lorentz reported that they hit people on board ship, too. He'd gone down with the *Johanne Karoline*, affectionately known as the *Incomparable*, which vanished without trace one autumn day in the Gulf of Bothnia.

The future that lay ahead of us consisted of more thrashings and death by drowning, and yet we longed for the sea. What did child-hood mean to us? Being tied to life ashore and living in the shadow of Isager's rope. And life at sea? We had yet to learn the meaning of it. But a belief that nothing would ever change while we stayed on dry land took root in us. Isager was still Isager. His sons hated and feared him, and so did we. No one knew whether his wife hated and feared him too, but she'd stopped beating him up. She lived in a world of her own now. We'd robbed him of his dog, his house and his wife's reason, but he remained unchanged. He thrashed us as he'd always done, and taught us nothing. We battled back as we always had, and learned nothing. We no longer persecuted him when he walked home on a winter's night after his two-finger toddy with Mr Mathiesen, the grocer, or threw foul waste into his drawing room on New Year's Eve. But we still filled the inkwells with sand, blocked the stove, jumped out of the windows, played hooky and stole his books. Soon it would be Niels Peter scuffling with him on the floor, and one day it would be Albert.

Isager was immortal.

Justice

WE KNEW THE ROPE. BUT NOW IT WAS TIME TO MEET THE SEA.

Was it true, as Hans Jørgen had said, that the thrashing would never stop?

Laurids Madsen had once told Albert about punishment on board the *Neversink*, the naval frigate where any wretch who transgressed was tied to the mast and whipped till he bled. They beat seven kinds of shit out of him, Laurids said. It was not an expression we were familiar with, but Laurids told us it was American. 'Seven kinds of shit': we couldn't help thinking that was what the world beyond our island was like. What the great America was like. They had more of everything – shit included. We'd never noticed much variety when it came to our own shit. The colour might change and the texture might be either on the runny or the lumpy side, but shit was shit, wasn't it? We ate everything – cod, mackerel, herring, sweetened gruel, pork sausage and vegetable soup, cabbage – and we knew of only one basic type of shit. So this was what the wide world would do for us. It would change our diet, so we'd be eating deep-sea monsters that our local fishermen never caught: squid, shark, jolly jumpers, bright coral-reef fish; and fruits unknown to our farmers, like bananas, oranges, peaches, mangoes and papayas; curry from India, noodles from China, flying fish in coconut milk, snake meat and monkey brains. And when they thrashed us, we, too, would shit seven kinds of shit.

But in those days we mainly sailed grain to the German and Russian ports on the Baltic Sea, calling at Norway and Sweden for timber. No foreign spices, strange fish or new fruits for us: peas, porridge, salted cod and sweetened sago soup with barley dumplings and prunes were our daily fare. All our sauces and soups contained syrup as well as vinegar, the sweet with the sour, but we struggled to find the sweet side to life at sea. And when we were beaten, the same kind of shit still came out of us.

We said goodbye to our mothers. They'd been around all our lives, but we'd never properly seen them. They'd been bent over washing tubs or cooking pots, their faces red and swollen from heat and steam, holding everything together while our fathers were away at sea, and nodding off every night on the kitchen chair with a darning needle in their hand. It was their endurance and exhaustion we knew, rather than them. And we never asked them for anything because we didn't want to bother them.

That was how we showed our love: with silence.

Their eyes were always red. In the morning, when they woke us up, it was from stove smoke. And in the evening, when they said goodnight to us, still dressed, it was from exhaustion. And sometimes it was from crying over someone who would never come home again. Ask us about the colour of a mother's eyes, and we'd reply, 'They're not brown. They aren't green. They're neither blue nor grey. They're red.' That's what we'd say.

And now they've come down to the quayside to say goodbye. But between us, there's silence. Their eyes pierce us.

'Come back,' their stare pleads. 'Don't leave us.'

But we won't be coming back. We want out. We want to get away. Our mother sticks a knife in our heart when we say goodbye on the quay. And we stick a knife in hers when we go. And that's how we're connected: through the hurt we inflict on one another.

Some elements of our new life we'd already learned at home. We knew how to splice a rope's end and strike knots. We could climb the rigging, and the height of a mast didn't scare us. We knew our way round a ship. But we'd stood on the deck only in the harbour, in winter. We had yet to learn how big the ocean is, and how tiny a ship can feel.

We started out as cooks.

'Here,' the skipper said, shoving a tarnished copper pot at us.

This pot was the entire equipment of our galley and in those days the galley was nothing but a clay stove in the fo'c's'le, with a flue made of four boards nailed together, poking up through a hole in the deck. When it rained the water swept inside, and in stormy weather, when the waves washed over the deck, seawater would cascade down and put out the fire; at times we were up to our knees in water. The slightest wind caused the ship to pitch, and then we had to hold the pot in place to stop it sliding across the floor; we pulled down the cuffs of our sleeves to protect our fingers from the hot handles and watched the sago soup with smoke-stung eyes. Nothing we did was ever good enough. Someone had to be the whipping boy on a ship and if there wasn't a dog on board, then it was us.

We were roused at four in the morning and had to be ready with coffee at any point during the day. There'd be time only for a quick nap between any two cups, and then we'd be woken with a kick: 'Bloody hell, you sleeping again, boy?'

We never had a single hour ashore to visit the towns where we loaded and unloaded. After a year at sea we'd been to Trondheim, Stavanger, Kalmar, Varberg, Königsberg, Wismar and Lübeck, Antwerp, Grimsby and Hull. We saw rocky coastlines, fields and woods, towers and church spires – but we came no closer to them than to castles in the air. The only land we ever felt under our feet was the quayside, and the only buildings we entered were warehouses. The wide world we'd come to know consisted of the ship's deck, the smoky cabin and the permanently damp berths.

Every night when we were in port we had to wait up until after midnight for the skipper, just to pull his boots off.

'Are you there, boy?' he'd say in a thick voice as he sat down on the berth, blotchy and panting, with his legs outstretched.

It was not until then that we could turn in – only to be roused a few hours later.

We met every winter, when the ships came home to wait for spring and waters free of ice.

'Do you remember what Hans Jørgen said?' Niels Peter said. 'That the most important thing Isager taught us was to take a beating?'

'He should have taught us how to keep awake,' Josef said.

He was Isager's son, but he'd gone to sea anyway, while Johan had stayed home to take care of his mother – who since the fire had taken to wandering the fields dressed in rags and calling out for Karo. He was hoping to become a schoolteacher like his father.

We nodded in agreement. This was roughly the sum of our experiences during our first year at sea: beatings and the never-ending night vigils.

'The coffee ran out,' Albert said. He had sailed on the cutter *Catrine* for a year. 'I was given a quarter-pound. It was supposed to last three men for seven days, and the skipper said it had to be strong, and they were always shouting at me because it was too weak. But I got my own back in the end.'

'What did you do?' Niels Peter asked. He'd sailed a year longer than Albert and was still wrestling with the coffee problem.

'We've got plenty of dried peas, so I burned some and mixed them in with it, and the skipper said, "That's a fine cup of strong coffee; this will keep a man on his feet," but then he and the second mate got the bellyache, and that's how they found out. I used four measures of peas to one of coffee, but I never told them that. Anyway, then I had to come up with something else, so I burned a pot of rye instead. And now I'm getting praise for my strong coffee.'

'We always get the blame,' Josef said. 'When the porridge is burned or the peas won't soften or the rye bread goes mouldy.'

'My skipper thinks I should eat the food if it's spoiled. "Eat that mouldy bread," he goes to me one day. "Swallow those raw peas." And I said to him, "No, I'm not some pig that you can just throw any old swill at."'

Albert straightened his back. We could tell that he was proud of his reply, but we knew what it would have cost him.

'So what happened?'

'I got no breakfast or dinner for two days.'

Lorentz turned up. Johan stepped back and stared at the cobbles, but Josef sent him a challenging look, which Lorentz returned: his days of sucking up to us were gone. He was still huge, but a new strength infused his bulk. We had never fantasised about his fat white body the way we'd fantasise about women, but a warm tickling had gone through us when we thrashed his soft flesh. If you were to hit him now, you'd damage your knuckles.

He said nothing, and we retreated a step. Did his balls finally drop, once he'd climbed the rigging of the *Anne Marie Elisabeth*?

*　　*　　*

Albert sailed another two years on the *Catrine*. He landed at Flekkefjord, Tønsberg, Frederikstad, Gothenburg, Riga, Stralsund, Hamburg, Rotterdam, Hartlepool and Kirkcaldy – and saw nothing. So he signed off. He wanted to get away from the copper pot and the coffee war. The sea was ever-changing, and yet it left him with an impression of sameness. In the autumn he saw it congeal beneath low-hanging layers of stratocumulus cloud. The water moved sluggishly, like liquid mercury. The temperature fell, and when winter announced itself, he saw his own life reflected in the slowly freezing surface of the water.

The clouds above the frozen sea changed, but he was already familiar with them all. There was plenty for the eye to feast on, but nothing for the soul. He had a hunger for something that no sky could satisfy. Somewhere on the planet there had to be a different kind of light. A sea that mirrored new constellations. A bigger moon. A hotter sun.

The skipper offered to sign him on as an ordinary seaman.

'You're a sailor now,' he said one night in Stubbekøbing as Albert helped him pull off his boots. 'You can fix a flying jib and a topsail. You know the compass and you can sail by the wind and run before it.'

But instead, Albert did as his father before him: he went to Hamburg to find a ship that would take him further out into the world.

Before he left, he went up into the loft at home. Here, among the potato and grain sacks, sat the sea boots his father Laurids had abandoned when he left home for the last time. That had been an omen, they'd realised later. In stormy weather, when the roof shook and the gable quaked, Albert's mother thought she could hear the empty boots stomping about up there on their own. But no one ever dared go up and look.

Rasmus and Esben had never touched the boots. Out of fear, perhaps – or simply because they'd never matched their father's considerable height and their feet weren't big enough. Only Albert took after Laurids.

He came down the stairs holding the boots, their wooden soles still scorched from Laurids' famous trip to heaven.

'What are you doing with those?' his mother asked. Her eyes were anxious, as though she both hoped and dreaded he'd be throwing them out.

'I want to wear them,' said Albert.

'You mustn't!'

Her hand flew to her mouth. Did she fear that bad luck would follow him if he put them on? Was it superstition or premonition? It was hard to tell. There was a mother's worry, certainly. Perhaps she sensed that this time he would be going far, and would be gone many years. Which for her was the same as death.

'I'm going to' was all he said.

He had to stoop now to walk through the doorway, and his shoulders filled it.

'You promised my father to make them like new again,' he said, when he arrived at the workshop of Mr Jakobsen, the cobbler, in Kongegade.

'That was twelve years ago. You've got a good memory,' Jakobsen said. 'But a promise is a promise. You can pick them up on Saturday.'

Albert worked seven months as an ordinary seaman on board a Hamburg brig that sailed to the West Indies. He saw palm beaches and flying fish. He saw people whose skin was black and brown. He saw the cowed look in their eyes and their bowed backs and needed no one to tell him that that they knew the thrashing rope. Men like Isager weren't schoolteachers here. They were rulers of these sunny isles, including those where Danish was spoken, and they all ruled by the rope.

He drank coconut milk and ate alligator meat, which tasted like chicken. He shat seven kinds of shit, but none of it was beaten out of him.

He'd escaped.

'It never stops' was what Hans Jørgen had said. But it does. When you become an able seaman, when you're seventeen years old and big and strong enough to defend yourself, then it stops. Albert watched the black and brown men who loaded and unloaded the brig. They didn't have ownership of themselves, and they were forever in thrall to the rope. He wondered what would have happened if he'd been born one of them, to be flayed all the way to the grave. Would he have broken eventually? Or would he have looked for someone he could pass his humiliation on to, just so that he could feel vaguely human? Would he have found a dog to kill, a house to burn down, a woman to drive mad?

*　　*　　*

When we met every winter in Marstal we sized each other up. We were becoming men. Our eyes seemed deeper-set, and our cheekbones jutted: it was as if the beatings we'd suffered over time had led to something permanent. Our hands had grown big, our palms were tough, our biceps bulged, and sinews and veins fought for space on our forearms beneath the blue spiderwebs of tattoos. We'd grown bigger and stronger, to spite the rope.

Albert didn't come home. He returned to Hamburg and left again, this time for South America. On his return, he signed off in Antwerp and joined a Liverpudlian bark going to Cardiff to load coal. He wanted to learn English.

When the bosun yelled '*All hands up anchor!*' and '*Heave, my hearties, heave hard!*' he heard his father's voice, and felt his *papa tru* close by him once more. He remembered the American words that had so irritated his mother and so delighted him and his brothers.

'*Hanggre,*' he said in the mess.

They shook their heads and laughed at him.

'*Monki,*' they said.

It was a good while before he realised that his *papa tru* hadn't been speaking American but pidgin, the Chinese and Kanak version of English. That was what his *papa tru* had taught him. Pidgin English: the language of cannibals.

Albert crossed the equator and was baptised as his *papa tru* had been before him. They forced him to kiss the ochre-coloured Amphitrite, from whose pockmarked cheeks sharp nails protruded. They covered him in tallow and lamp soot, and mermaids and nigger boys held him underwater until his lungs were close to bursting. They shaved him with a rusty razor and gave him a scar which he hid under a beard from then on.

He learned a song that he sang to us for many years. He said it was the truest song ever written about the sea:

> *Shave him and bash him,*
> *Duck him and splash him,*
> *Torture him and smash him*
> *And don't let him go!*

He sailed south around Cape Horn, where he heard penguins

squawk in the pitch-black night and was finally made able seaman. He called at Callao and Lobus, the guano island, just south of the equator. He sailed back to Europe and signed on to a three-masted Nova Scotian full-rigged ship headed for New York. There he went ashore, looking for a job on an American vessel, where the wages would be higher. Perhaps *papa tru*'s dreams of America haunted him.

But it wasn't his *papa tru* he met on board the *Emma C. Leithfield*. It was something else: Isager and his rope all over again. And this time the battle would have to be settled.

Later, he told us that he would never forget the moment he first set foot on deck.

But, we asked him, had he really not heard about conditions on board American ships? Didn't he know that the crews would often mutiny, and that first mates were chosen not for their sea skills, but for their physical strength and their fighting prowess? And that the fist or the revolver gave the orders more often than the captain? Had he not known this?

Albert looked away and chuckled a little, as if deep down he had known, but couldn't bring himself to admit it.

He looked us in the eye.

'No,' he said, 'I didn't know it could be that bad. It was ten months in hell. I'd been there before. But finding the exit was one thing that blasted Isager never taught us.'

THERE WERE SEVENTEEN MEN BEFORE THE MAST OF THE *EMMA C. Leithfield,* of whom six were Scandinavians – and in Albert's opinion, the only decent sailors on board. It didn't seem odd to us that he felt this way because we always prefer our own. But he based his opinion on a single observation: they were the only ones who didn't keel over when they boarded the ship.

When the launch brought the newly shanghaied sailors alongside the *Emma,* a bunch of dead-drunk Frenchmen had to be forcibly shoved onto the deck, an operation performed by two brutal-looking crimps – land sharks in cahoots with a boarding house where the Frenchmen had already been relieved of their cash. A party of sozzled Italians and Greeks followed, while a third boat brought some drunken English and Welsh. Each sailor bore under his arm a small parcel of clothes. That was all he owned. Their hair was unkempt, their faces scarred and half-empty bottles of whisky poked out of their pockets. They may have jabbered and shouted in a chaos of languages, but they all came from the same place. They were the dregs of every port on God's earth.

They were all incapable of doing any work that day. They stared at the anchor chains but clearly hadn't the slightest idea where they led, and after gazing up at the rigging and grinning dizzily, they simply staggered to their quarters. Disappearing down the ladder to the fo'c's'le, they threw themselves on their berths or on the bare floor, where they fell asleep, snoring.

Captain Eagleton was a young man with bushy whiskers and shifty eyes. As soon as he ordered Albert down to the sleeping quarters to bring back the men's half-empty whisky bottles and throw them overboard, Albert knew he'd never gain the crew's respect. Eagleton should have thrown out the whisky himself, and in front of the whole crew, rather than behind their backs while they slept it off:

it was obvious. Albert eyed the bottles as they bobbed up and down on the waves. He'd already noticed the big solid armchair bolted to the deck like the throne of an absent king. Albert knew enough about seamen to recognise Eagleton as the type who'd stay clear of the deck and isolate himself from the crew, so it wouldn't be his. It might belong to the first mate, he speculated, but for now there was no way of telling, as the man had yet to make an appearance.

Meanwhile, a terrible racket had started in the fo'c's'le and the captain ordered Albert to investigate. From out of the darkness came angry shouting.

'You've nicked my whisky, you bloody dog,' yelled an English voice.

A reply came in Italian, followed by another in a language that could have been Greek. In between were sentences that contained a few words Albert recognised, but he couldn't work out their meaning. These men had lived in international crews for so many years that they now all spoke a tongue straight out of Babel.

One thing was clear: the row was over the missing whisky bottles. Albert heard the sound of a blow and then of a body crashing into a bulkhead. Glancing down the hatch he saw a knife flash in someone's hand; it was followed by groaning and the kind of laboured breathing you hear when men are raising the anchor. But it was something else they were hauling up. It was dark and terrifying and it came from the depths within.

Though Albert was still safe on the deck, he took a few steps backwards. There was nothing he could do down in that dark hole, and the brawl would eventually exhaust itself. He'd seen fights like that before, and they rarely ended in a killing. The men would emerge from the fo'c's'le the next day bruised and cut and severely hung-over, and begin work, mute and reluctant, with bloodshot eyes. Today they were animals. But tomorrow they'd be sailors again.

It wasn't the savagery down in the fo'c's'le that worried him. It was the captain's lack of authority.

'Out of the way!'

Someone grabbed Albert's shoulder and shoved him violently aside: he turned to see a monster of a man towering over him. His face was dominated by a bulbous red nose and disfigured by criss-crossed scars; his head looked like a pumpkin someone had slashed. Half drowned in this mass of battered flesh sat his eyes, their pupils like black stones on the bottom of a deep lake. Underneath a filthy, torn shirt, his vast muscular body, too, had been scored, as though someone had gone for the giant's heart with a sharp knife, but given up. It would be like trying to stab a steam train.

Albert instantly understood who was standing in front of him. This was the man to whom the throne belonged, the true ruler of the ship.

The first mate had made his appearance.

The giant didn't use the ladder but jumped straight down into the fo'c's'le, his huge body tumbling directly into the midst of the brawling men. There came another crash and some roaring from below, and the tumult intensified, with intermingled howls and groans of pain, the thudding of punches, and a strange whimpering that seemed quite unrelated to fighting. It went on for a while before starting to subside, until only one voice – that of the first mate – could be heard.

'Have you had enough? Have you had enough then?'

More of that whimpering sound. Then the thud of a few more blows – or were they kicks? And silence.

The first mate emerged from the fo'c's'le, panting. He'd acquired the makings of a few more scars down there in the darkness. There was a deep cut to his forehead, and blood ran from his neck, but he wiped his face absent-mindedly, as if the blood that welled in one dense eyebrow was no more inconvenient to him than sweat.

Albert hadn't shifted from the spot where the giant had first thrust him, but now he was swept aside once more, as the bleeding first mate shoved past him again to scrutinise the rest of the crew as if contemplating a continuation of the punishment he'd begun below decks.

'The name's O'Connor.'

At this, the men on deck nodded as if responding to an order.

O'Connor went over to his throne, sat down heavily, and belched. The blood that he'd smeared across his forehead gave him the look of a heathen idol that demands nothing but human sacrifices. Albert wondered if O'Connor would call for soap and water to clean his injuries, but he just sat there while the blood congealed, as though his scars were tattoos and he'd just added fresh details to the gruesome work of art that was his face and body.

Then he gave a sudden whistle, and a long-haired black monster of a dog that no one had seen before padded over with the skulking gait of a wolf and hunkered down at his feet. Pulling a heavy-calibre revolver out of the pocket of his nankeens, O'Connor started spinning the barrel pensively.

That night Albert ventured down to the fo'c's'le, but he soon came back up again. By the glimmer of his tallow dip he'd seen men lying on the floor in oddly contorted positions, while a few sat on benches, cradling their heads in their hands. He couldn't tell whether or not they were sleeping. But there was blood on the bulkhead and vomit covered the floor. He'd prefer to sleep on deck.

The next morning the men emerged, bearing the traces of yesterday's brawl. Some were limping, while others moved about slowly and deliberately, as if their bodies ached beneath their clothes. Their faces were bloated, with livid swellings around the eyes. One man had a broken nose – though its shape suggested it wasn't his first. These were tough men, used to beatings and the after-effects of prolonged drinking – men who could take practically any treatment without complaining. But they wore an expression you rarely see in a sailor. They looked cowed. They didn't so much as glance at one another and never lifted their eyes to O'Connor when he roared his orders. Instead they stared at their hands or let their eyes drift towards the rigging.

There was a proper cook on board the *Emma C. Leithfield* – and we understood Albert well when he pointed out the difference between a proper one and the kind we'd been on the Marstal cutters, when we'd all started out as galley boys, barely mastering any cooking skills beyond steadying the water pot in a storm to ensure the supply of hot coffee and satisfying the appetites of men more interested in filling their bellies than in the pleasures of the palate.

But Giovanni, said Albert, was nothing like that. He was an Italian and he made sure that every day, both fore and aft, there was freshly baked bread, a hot lunch and dinner, and plenty of pies and pastries. We ate better than at the best boarding house: not even Frau Palle in Kastanien Allée in Hamburg could compete with Giovanni.

All told, the *Emma C. Leithfield* was an odd ship. Despite the men's linguistic differences, they understood one another well enough to agree that of all the vessels of the American merchant navy, the *Emma* had the worst first mate and the best cook. The galley was heaven, and the deck was hell.

Giovanni was the last man to board, but he didn't arrive alone: with him came two suckling pigs, ten hens, and a small calf, for which he built a pen on the foredeck. O'Connor's dog grew restless and left his place at his master's feet to roam around, its huge jaw hanging open and a hungry look in its eyes. Spotting the dog, Giovanni went right up to the beast, which bared its teeth and growled menacingly: it seemed to think the whole ship was its territory. Giovanni stared straight into its eyes and slowly raised his hands – not to strike it, but as if to explain. Hypnotised, the dog lay down on its belly and whined pitifully, before starting to shuffle backwards. The sight of the ferocious monster, its belly to the floor, backing off from the small, agile man, was so funny that the sailors watching the incident started laughing.

O'Connor saw it, too. But he didn't laugh.

O'Connor never ate with the other officers. Instead, he sat on his throne on deck and had his food brought to him there. The weather never bothered him; his body seemed immune to everything. He never changed clothes, but always wore the same tattered shirt, barely covered by a waistcoat with no buttons and ripped buttonholes. By day, only a blizzard or a hailstorm could budge him out of the chair, while at night, they said he slept in another chair, bolted to the floor of a cabin that stank like a wild animal's lair. He was always on his guard. Word had it that he kept his muscles tensed even while he was asleep.

When Giovanni brought him his food the next day, instead of placing the plate on his own lap, O'Connor lay it on the deck and signalled to the dog, which immediately came and wolfed down the whole beautifully presented meal. All the while O'Connor kept his eyes fixed on Giovanni, and Giovanni met his stare. He was no more afraid of O'Connor than he was of the dog. He could control the animal with one simple gesture. But O'Connor was beyond his control – and he'd acquired a mortal enemy.

The next day Giovanni brought O'Connor his food in a dog bowl and placed it on the deck at the first mate's feet.

'Enjoy your food,' he said and turned to leave.

'Where's my dinner?'

O'Connor's voice was low and menacing.

'There.' Giovanni pointed to the bowl. 'If I were you I'd hurry up before the dog gets to it.'

In that moment, he sealed his fate.

Giovanni was far more than a mere cook. When a ship is at anchor in New York, it's not just tailors, shoemakers, butchers, ship's chandlers and fruiterers who come on board – all those practical men no ship can do without before she sets sail. No, along with them comes a motley crew of fences, offering false gold rings and pocket watches that stop at the slightest knock; tattoo artists with filthy needles whose every tattoo becomes a weeping infection; beggars and magicians; jugglers, fakirs and fortune-tellers; procurers, pimps and thieves. Giovanni, standing there on the deck with a red bandanna around his ink-black hair, juggling four eggs at a time without dropping a single one, seemed more at home with this crowd than with the crew of the *Emma C. Leithfield*. And that's how he first came among us.

No one had the faintest idea how he'd ended up at sea, but he'd begun as a circus performer. He'd been a knife-thrower as well as a juggler, and sometimes when we were off duty we'd linger in the doorway and watch him practise. He could juggle three or four sharpened knives until they whirled about in a deadly spinning wheel. He never dropped one, he never missed a catch and he never cut himself.

'Giovanni's setting the table,' someone would shout out on deck and the crew would rush to the mess to grab a front-row view of him laying the places without moving a single inch from where he stood. Knives, forks and tin plates would fly through the air – and land exactly in the right spot, right next to each other. It sent his audience dizzy with excitement. He never broke anything – but no one could understand how.

'How do you do it, Giovanni?'

He smiled and shook his head. There were no secrets. 'It's all in the wrists,' he said, flexing them.

The men winked at each other. They were proud of their cook.

With the whisky thrown overboard and the ship at sea, it was Giovanni who got them straightening their backs and going about their work feeling like a crew.

It was a fortnight since they'd left New York. The *Emma C. Leithfield* had just passed the equator, heading for Buenos Aires, and the men were admiring Giovanni as usual when O'Connor suddenly appeared. The cook was busy setting the table, and the plates were sailing accurately through the air en route to their destinations, when O'Connor stuck out his giant fist and intercepted one, sending it crashing to the floor. Tin plates don't break, but the effect of O'Connor's sabotage was greater than if it had smashed into a thousand pieces.

Giovanni's reaction was instant. When he performed, he was at once focused and dreamy. But now, they saw his expression switch to something new: wariness. When O'Connor's fist came at him, he dodged it with the same lightning agility they'd seen when he was throwing cutlery and plates, and O'Connor's fist, which would have turned Giovanni's narrow, delicate-featured face into a bloody mess, slammed into the bulkhead with an ugly crunch. When he regained his balance, his knuckles were bloody.

Giovanni stood his ground, his face showing not hostility, fear, anger or panic, but the concentration of an acrobat high in the circus tent, preparing for a tricky jump with no safety net. And when O'Connor lashed out again, he ducked with the same accuracy as before.

O'Connor stumbled forward as if he'd lost his balance. But those playing close attention sensed something was up. His eyes, narrowed to slits in his swollen, scarred face, bore a calm chill, which indicated the stumble was premeditated.

Giovanni leaped to one side and out of the path of the toppling giant. But instead of thrusting his hands out to break his fall, O'Connor flung out an arm and grabbed the little Italian, pulling him down to the deck. Guessing that O'Connor would straddle Giovanni and beat him up, the men began crowding in to pull him away. But the two fallen men just lay next to each other for a moment, motionless – until Giovanni uttered a sudden cry of pain and clasped his wrist. His hand was dangling from it in an odd way. It was all limp. O'Connor had snapped it with a single quick twist of his strong hand.

Calmly the first mate got up. Standing next to his victim, he fixed the men hard with his eyes. Then, without even looking down, he raised his foot and stomped his boot down on Giovanni's injured hand. They heard the sound of his fingers break.

When O'Connor walked away from the mess, the men stepped aside for him. But if they'd had one of Giovanni's sharp kitchen knives, they'd have buried it in his back deep enough to prick his rotten heart and extinguish the hellfire that burned inside.

They flocked around Giovanni and helped him to his feet. He was still clutching his ruined hand, and the tears rolled down his cheeks. It wasn't the pain that made him weep, but the loss of his ability. They looked at his broken fingers, which stuck out at unnatural angles. They'd seen enough accidents on board to know that he'd never use that hand again. Minutes earlier, he'd been an artist. Now he was barely a man.

They took him to Captain Eagleton, who had the hand bandaged. Much good that would do. Even a doctor couldn't have saved it. And when they protested about what had happened to Giovanni, Captain Eagleton looked the other way, as if it had nothing to do with him.

'O'Connor,' he said, 'has his reasons.'

And that was all he'd say on the matter.

Giovanni had turned the men into a united crew. But O'Connor wanted the opposite of solidarity: he wanted each one of them to face him alone. Not because he lacked the strength to beat up more than one of them at a time, but because he knew they feared him most when they had no one to share their fear with.

The captain had lied when he said that O'Connor always had his reasons. And the lie was a huge one. Nothing O'Connor did had a reason. He hit and punched and broke men's bones for pleasure, not as punishment for anything they'd done. He toyed with them as a god toys with its worshippers, leaving them to ponder the reasons for their own suffering. It was this unpredictability that made O'Connor such a monster. Whatever his dark motivation was, expressed in his hatred of everything that stirred on board, it lay deep within himself. The men ducked, or tried to make themselves small and invisible, in order to escape his motiveless malice – but even that wasn't always enough. His eye worked like a falcon's, searching for mice in the wheat.

They had nowhere to hide. What place of safety is there for those who live under the thumb of an all-powerful ruler? What choice but to do everything correctly and second-guess his slightest whim?

'What did Giovanni do wrong, apart from being the best cook who ever sailed, the best juggler who ever wasted his talent on a drunken and thickheaded crew? Apart from making each of us a better man than the Lord ever planned? What did he do to deserve a broken hand? What offence was he being punished for?' Albert asked.

A lad by the name of Isaiah had to take charge of the galley. He was from America and fourteen years old, with black skin that was so shiny and smooth it looked permanently wet. When he lit the fire in the morning, the glowing embers from the oven were reflected in his dark cheeks. He did his best. But gone were the fresh-baked bread, pies and cakes.

Giovanni had been sitting in the fo'c's'le for some days staring at his bandages in the half-light. Despite all that had happened, he'd not been broken. Soon he reappeared on deck, entered the galley and started bossing Isaiah around. Then his left hand woke up. It was, after all, the hand of a performer, and was just as deft as his right. He might be only half a man, but he was still more capable than most whole ones. Soon the plates were sailing across the table again. But there was a new air of defiance about him. He knew he was playing a dangerous game. His eyes shone. The crew guarded him, ready to defend him, though they were more terrified than he was.

But the falcon always spots his chance.

It was when Giovanni was briefly alone with Isaiah that O'Connor attacked him next. They came running at the sound of his screams – but it was too late. O'Connor had got hold of his left hand. Giovanni grabbed a knife with his right, but the pathetic bundle of broken fingers had lost all strength and precision and he could barely lift the blade. He knew he was fighting for his life, and all he could manage was a scratch across O'Connor's chest.

How desperate Giovanni must have been to use the knife like that. When the men in the fo'c's'le had encouraged him to take his revenge and promised to cover for him – and yes, even take the blame themselves – he'd replied, 'I'm a knife-thrower, not a murderer.'

The plates sailing across the table again, the reawakening of our taste buds: those had been Giovanni's revenge. Only now he'd gone for the knife. Isaiah said later that he'd seen tears in the artist's eyes as he clutched the weapon in his damaged hand – as if in that moment, forced to share the coarse tactics of his enemy, his honour was lost.

O'Connor laughed and offered up his chest.

'Come on,' he snarled.

But Giovanni put the knife down on the table.

When they got there it was too late. The killing blow had been struck.

Wrapped in sailcloth, Giovanni's body was swallowed by the sea the same day. Captain Eagleton wasn't present at the funeral. O'Connor represented him. The crew suspected he'd turned up only to relish his meaningless triumph.

Isaiah arrived with a shovelful of ash from the galley.

'Ashes to ashes, dust to dust,' the cook's boy said, and scattered the ashes over Giovanni's body as it lay on the deck in its sailor's shroud.

At that very moment, a gust of wind came like an avenging hand and flung the ash right into O'Connor's maimed face, where it settled into every line and crack, including the slits of his eyes. It burned and stung. He roared and thrashed about as if a real enemy had attacked him, and the men scattered: nobody wanted to be hit by the random flailing of his fists. From a distance they saw him commit a final act of sacrilege against the deceased as, cursing and shouting, he lifted Giovanni's frail corpse from the deck and tossed it over the rail like a piece of rubbish.

They were watching the funeral of a mutineer. That, at least, was the message that Captain Eagleton passed on to them.

But below decks, they plotted O'Connor's death.

EVERYONE VOLUNTEERED FOR THE JOB. NO ONE HAD ANY SCRUPLES when it came to killing O'Connor. If they hadn't all been hardened men when they signed on to the *Emma C. Leithfield*, they were now. They'd been abused on a daily basis, and there wasn't one of them who didn't bear the mark of the first mate's fist. He even beat his fellow officers. The second mate, a Swede by the name of Gustafsson, went around with a closed-up eye that might never regain its sight.

With no rule of law on board the *Emma C. Leithfield*, they'd have to create one themselves. It wasn't mutiny: it was justice.

Their only concern was technical. How to do it?

O'Connor was stronger than any of them: they'd learned that much. They'd never defeat him in an open fight. But the thought of their own weakness merely fuelled their anger.

'When he's asleep,' said a Greek who went by the name of Dimitros.

Could that be the answer? They exchanged glances. There were two problems. The first was the loaded gun that O'Connor always carried, and the second was the dog. When the first mate dozed in his chair on deck, the dog always lay at his feet, and the minute anyone approached, it raised its massive head and growled menacingly. No one could figure out how to get close to O'Connor without waking the dog first. At this point their rebellion began to crumble. They discussed the dog at length, but it wasn't really the dog they were scared of. The revolver, then?

No. It was simply O'Connor.

Even without his dog and his gun, he seemed invincible. What terrified them most was whatever went on inside that scarred, pumpkin-like head of his. They could never confess that openly, though. After all, they were seventeen against one. They sat in silence, some of them staring at the table, others at the bulkhead.

It was Albert who broke the silence. 'Anyway, isn't it wrong to kill another human being?'

113

They stared at him as though the idea had never crossed their minds. And perhaps in some cases it hadn't. They knew very little about one another's past, but they also knew that anything could happen in port or out at sea. A man's drowning wasn't always an accident – and O'Connor may not have been the only unpunished killer on board the *Emma C. Leithfield*.

'Would Giovanni have wanted to be avenged like that?' Albert continued.

'I don't care what Giovanni would have wanted,' said the Welsh seaman Rhys Llewellyn, surveying his hairy hands, which lay folded in his lap. The first mate had given him a bruise on one cheek – and it was a greeting he dreamed of returning. 'I'm speaking for myself,' he added, looking around the group. 'But I'm thinking about us, too. It's him or us. It's not revenge. It's survival.'

The others muttered their approval.

'Giovanni didn't want to pull the knife,' Isaiah said. 'I saw him put it down again.'

His voice was hesitant, and we could hear him breathing between the words. He was only fourteen, and it took courage to speak up in a gathering of men who were senior to him in rank and age. 'Do you remember that he said he was a knife-thrower and not a murderer? Are we murderers?'

'Shut up, you black dog!' retorted the Welshman.

'No, I won't!' The words erupted unexpectedly. Isaiah had found his courage now. He'd spoken out, and the damage was done. 'I get beaten by him just like you. So I've got a right to speak. And I don't think we should kill him.'

'The boy's right,' Albert said. 'We don't want to become like him. He's just waiting for us to become as desperate as Giovanni and pull a knife on him, because that's the game he plays. It's what he wants. Do you think he's stupid? At this very moment he's probably hoping that we're plotting to kill him because then he's got us. Do we really want to be like him?'

They mumbled and looked down again. Undoubtedly some of them did want to be like O'Connor. But they never could be. They'd have to find other ways of matching his power.

'I think I know how we can win, but it'll take patience,' Albert said. And he laid out his plan.

At first they didn't understand what he meant.

'It can't be done,' was the universal response – uttered in almost as many languages as there were men. No matter where they came from, none of the sailors had ever seen justice dealt in the way Albert proposed. The idea wasn't just unfamiliar; it flew in the face of all experience.

'But this is America,' Albert kept repeating.

'It's not America, it's a ship,' they said. 'And a ship has its own rules.'

But Albert dug in his heels and refused to back down. Every time he refuted one of their objections, they saw his certainty grow. And every time he spoke, he finished with the same question: 'Does anybody else have a better idea?'

No one did, apart from killing O'Connor – and in their hearts they knew they couldn't. They didn't have the courage, either individually or together.

So what was the strange, indefinable imperative that finally made them change their minds and agree to Albert's proposal? Might it be conscience? It was. But it was so mixed up with other things, like fear, and deviousness, and caution, and the clannishness of men in a pack, that in the end no one particular urge could be singled out. 'So for simplicity's sake we'll just call it conscience,' Albert always said when he told the story later.

They'd sailed for eight months with O'Connor by the time they called at St Iago in the West Indies to load sugar for New York. There'd been no shortage of opportunities to jump ship, but the crew had resisted; if they deserted, their plan would never bear fruit and their suffering would have been in vain. The real test of their strength would come here in St Iago. It would have nothing to do with muscle power – a commodity that had long been tried and tested, and the shortcomings of which were daily confirmed when they endured O'Connor's violence. But they stuck it out and began to look at O'Connor with an increasing boldness. For they'd discovered a force that the brutal first mate knew nothing of. Its name was fortitude.

The more experienced among them had already figured out that this was the place where Captain Eagleton would try to make them jump ship. They'd been through this before on other vessels. When a voyage nears its end, a bad captain will treat his crew so atrociously that they'll throw in the towel. And invariably, once they're branded as deserters, they'll forfeit their unpaid wages – thus increasing the profits of the trip. And so it was on the *Emma C. Leithfield*. First of all, O'Connor reduced their water rations while they sweated in the tropical heat. And then the provisions grew scarce too. Isaiah had picked up some cooking skills since Giovanni was murdered in his own galley, but now his limited knowledge was entirely superfluous: the crew's daily rations dwindled to three small ship's biscuits per man, while on Saturdays they were given rice and a single piece of salted meat. Their stomachs screamed for food. O'Connor's dog ate better than they did. The whole strategy was so damn clever. So devilishly, fiendishly cunning. You spend eight months with a brutal and malicious jailer, and then he opens the door to your cell.

Yet they refused to come out. They still had a score to settle with him. But, oh, how they longed to escape from his brooding presence and from their own terror.

They stayed because they had a plan. They stayed.

Faint with hunger and thirst, they scrubbed the deck and the deckhouse with sand and stones under the tropical sun. They were roused from bed a full hour before any of the crews of the other ships anchored in St Iago, and couldn't turn in until long after the rest of the port was asleep. Shaded by an outstretched sail, O'Connor sat in his chair with a loaded revolver in his hand and the huge hound at his feet. But he wasn't there to ensure they worked hard. Indeed, if one of the men had left the murderously hot deck, bolted for the gangway and rowed himself ashore, O'Connor wouldn't have lifted a finger to stop him. Instead he'd have grinned in raw triumph and wished him a fair wind.

When the washee-washee girls sailed by in their canoes with their pinned-up hair, bare shoulders and flared dresses, calling out flirtatiously, 'We're coming on board!' O'Connor rose and threatened them off with his revolver.

The battle of wills weighed the men down, and they became more exhausted, silent and emaciated with each day that passed. But by now, the sum total of their injuries constituted a victory. They saw O'Connor's gaze become evasive, and a puzzled expression began to disturb the restful calm of his mangled face.

* * *

On arriving at New York they did two things. First, they signed off from the ship on which their only consolation in the face of daily abuse and humiliation had been the limited triumph of passive endurance. Then, all together, they marched to the nearest police station and reported the first mate of the *Emma C. Leithfield*.

This had been their plan. It was Albert's idea, and it had helped them keep going. They'd discussed killing O'Connor, but something – perhaps their own terror more than anything – had held them back. Albert had realised that if a captain fails to intervene with someone as out of line as O'Connor, then his ship is lawless. The crew can't make the rules on a ship just because the captain fails to, unless through mutiny – which is no more than a cry for help and does nothing but add to the general lawlessness. So if justice can't be found on board, it must be found ashore.

And that was why they marched together to the police station: not to get revenge on O'Connor, but to seek justice.

They came to ask if there was any to be had.

And they received their answer.

They walked up the Lower East Side until they reached the police station on Twelfth Street. Grouped close together they filled the width of the pavement, and passers-by had to step aside to make way for them. Deep down they still felt ashamed that they'd failed to deal with O'Connor themselves. Here were seventeen large, broad-shouldered men, used to hard work, coming to beg others for justice – concerning just one man.

Was the law something only the weak resorted to?

They reached a grimy yellow building whose sign proclaimed it to be the home of the law. When they entered and saw men not unlike themselves being dragged in from the street by policemen, for a moment they weren't sure which side of the law they belonged on. But they approached a counter and stood there, nudging one another hesitantly. Albert ended up doing the talking. He told the police officer about the murder of Giovanni, and the Swedish second mate showed him his blinded eye.

The officer wrote a report. The moment they saw their words being committed to paper, something changed. They could look each other in the eye again, and stand up straight. They were no longer a group of frustrated men whose complaints merited no more than a disdainful shrug.

Two police officers accompanied them back to the ship. O'Connor was sitting in his chair on the deck, his dog lying at his feet. They knew he had a loaded revolver in his pocket – but you don't shoot the law. If you shoot a police officer, ten more will take his place.

They saw O'Connor's astonishment. He glared at the crew of the *Emma C. Leithfield* one by one. And when none of them looked away, he understood. They'd done the unthinkable. They hadn't beaten him up, or arranged a counter-attack, or tried to murder him – all of which would have met with his approval. Indeed, he'd have wanted it, because that was the language he spoke and understood. But now they'd acted in a way that was incomprehensible to him, in which *might* and *right* didn't mean the same thing.

For a moment he hesitated as he took head-to-toe measure first of them, and then of the policemen. The officers' faces betrayed no reaction on seeing the giant with the grotesquely scarred face, the tattered clothing, and the obvious bulge in his nankeens that revealed the presence of a revolver. But the crew saw them stiffen as their hands sought the butts of their own weapons.

O'Connor spotted it, too, and displaying a cunning they would not have credited him with, he asked the police officers what the problem was. They replied that he'd been accused of murder and assault and that the witnesses were the men standing next to them. They informed him that he was under arrest.

O'Connor handed over his revolver voluntarily. The men saw him trying hard to look smaller as he was led away between the two policemen. O'Connor!

They exchanged glances.

The law was so strong that a mere snapping of its fingers could reduce even the most bloodthirsty monster to a lamb.

They'd never have believed that O'Connor had the gift of the gab. He'd certainly never provided them with evidence of an extensive vocabulary. Grunting and roaring had been his favourite forms of expression. But now he revealed a completely new side of himself. They'd noted a flash of deviousness in his eyes when he agreed to come with the officers voluntarily. Now, in court, they began truly to understand what sort of calculating fiend was lurking within that brutal mass of flesh.

When the charge against him was read out in court, O'Connor grabbed the Bible and kissed it with a passion that he'd hitherto reserved for outbursts of rage. He held up his hand and swore that he'd never, in all his life, laid a finger on any man. Then he clasped his maimed head and turned it from side to side as if his neck were a socket and he was attempting to unscrew it.

'Look at this face,' he cried. 'Is this the face of a killer?'

He stared directly at the judge and then at the public gallery.

Had his latent violence not been visible in every bulging sinew, some members of the public might have burst out laughing, so grotesque was his claim to innocence. It was hard to imagine a more fitting face for a ruthless killer.

However, even the judge himself looked down when O'Connor stared hard at him, and they began to wonder who was stronger: the law or O'Connor.

Again O'Connor turned his head.

'Look,' he said. 'Look at my ruined face. This isn't the face of a man who fights back. It's the face of a man who turns the other cheek even when he's wrongly attacked.'

He looked directly at the witness box, and not one of the crew met his eyes. He showed the court first one scarred cheek, then the other. 'Do you really think that I would let anyone come near me if my blood was as bad as people say?' He ripped his tattered shirt, which he wore even here, with a theatrical movement, baring his scarred chest. 'This,' he said, his voice turning hollow with emotion, 'this is the body of a martyr. This is the body of the lamb.'

'He's going to win,' Gustafsson said, fingering his ruined eye as they sat in the nearest bar after the session. 'Did you see how scared of him the judge was?'

'But the law isn't scared of him,' Albert objected.

'What good's the law if the judge is small and weak and the criminal is big and strong?' asked Rhys Llewellyn.

Albert was the only one who still believed in the law. Every day they turned up in court, to be called as witnesses one by one. O'Connor contradicted them brazenly every time, looking at the judge, who averted his eyes. Their cuts began to heal, and their blue and yellow bruises were fading: only Gustafsson's eye stayed ruined, but even on his blind side he didn't have the courage to meet O'Connor's stare.

They'd had to put off looking for new work until the trial was over. They grew restless and lost faith. They drifted around the bars and drank their savings away.

'We should never have reported him,' they said to Albert.

'The law's stronger than O'Connor,' he replied.

'Look at the judge,' they retorted.

They didn't believe in shore justice. Albert had talked them into this. Soon O'Connor would be freed and he'd take his revenge. They should have swallowed their defeat and never sought the help of the law. It always sided with the strongest anyway.

'Look at the judge,' they repeated. 'He's small and he stoops. He's bald. He's barely bigger than a child.'

'So don't look at him,' Albert said. 'Listen instead.'

'So, what did you hear?' Albert asked them after the next session.

They mumbled something and looked away. Well, he had a point. When you listened to what the man actually said, you got a different impression. He sank his teeth in like a bull terrier. He was impossible to shake off: he kept asking questions until he discerned the heart of the matter, until the giant snapped and banged the counter in front of him with his fist as he roared across the courtroom, 'I'm a man of peace; everyone will testify to that!'

'Everyone except the crew of the *Emma C. Leithfield*,' the judge commented. He looked away again, but his voice stayed calm.

'It's the law that comes out of his mouth,' Albert said.

'No, he's speaking for himself,' Rhys Llewellyn said, 'but he does it well.'

After sixteen days of questioning, the judge convicted O'Connor, sentencing him to five years in jail for assault and manslaughter. Since it couldn't be proven that he'd intended to kill Giovanni, though no one doubted it, he wouldn't be branded a murderer and hang by his neck until he was dead. But they hadn't expected that. They'd expected him to walk free.

O'Connor roared like a wild animal when the sentence was pronounced.

'Serves you right, you brute!' Gustafsson shouted.

The judge turned and gave him an angry look, the first they'd seen from him throughout the whole trial.

They congratulated each other as they left the courtroom, but instead of triumph at the defeat of their enemy, they were filled with simple relief. It was as if they'd been on trial themselves. And now they'd been set free.

'I finally got rid of Isager,' Albert said many years later.

'But we don't want to hear about him,' we said. 'We want to hear about the boots.'

Voyage

I SIGNED ON FOR SINGAPORE AND FROM THERE TO VAN DIEMEN'S
Land, to Hobart Town, the last port where my father had been seen.
But it wasn't just his final port: it was everyone's dead end – and if
it wasn't yours, it soon would be, if you didn't get yourself out in
time. Picture the workhouse in Marstal: that's what Hobart was like.

The year was 1862. I met a man with one eye who'd been there
since 1822 and never had a day of freedom for the better part of
forty years. He'd counted every lash they'd given him during his
imprisonment: three thousand in total, he said. He was free now,
but his will was as broken as the skin of his back, which had more
ridges than a washboard. He wasn't the only one. He'd tell you his
story in exchange for a glass of gin, and with forty years on the
wagon to make up for, he'd happily tell it ten times a day. But in
Hobart Town there weren't many to listen. The place was full of
outcasts and ex-cons like him, who'd murder for the price of a drink.

Hobart had been a penal colony since the first house was built
there in 1803. Now they called it a town of free men, but since
everyone was either a former convict or a guard, the distinction
didn't mean much. They were all men used to either giving beatings
or receiving them. The option of living together like men with their
heads held high apparently hadn't occurred to anyone. No one there
ever looked me straight in the face. They'd keep their eyes on the
ground, and if they looked up, it was to judge the depth of your
pocket and whether what you had inside was worth killing for. People
said they'd steal the joey from a kangaroo's pouch. Kangaroos carry
their young in a pouch, did you know that?

There were plenty of old men in Hobart Town, but few young
ones. Anyone who had the strength or the slightest residue of hope
fled for greener pastures. Whole swarms of filthy children ran wild
with no sign of any fathers. The mothers were left in peace though
because they say convicts lose their appetite for women when they're

long in the clink and go for other men instead. Whether that's true or not I don't know and don't care to. But one thing's for sure: I wasted my wages on those scumbags.

I started my search at the police station, but they just said the same thing that all the other authorities I spoke to said: 'If a man wants to lie low and vanish without trace from the surface of the earth, then he'll pick Hobart Town.'

But *papa tru* hadn't had any reason to disappear, I knew that. The officers just shook their heads and said they couldn't help me.

So I walked up and down Liverpool Street. Every second pub was called the Bird-in-Hand. That made sense to me. In Hobart Town alcohol sang sweeter than any other bird, and if you've nothing else to believe in, then you'll believe in whatever you can grab hold of.

I bought gin for anyone who looked as if he might have a story to tell. And they all did. They'd start by asking me about *papa tru*: height, nationality, what he looked like. Then, oh yes, they remembered him well, they'd say, and they'd scratch their filthy hair until the dead lice dropped out, and look mournfully into their empty glass and tell you in this humble voice that another gin might just jog their memory. And sure enough, now they remembered him: the tall Dane with the big beard and the distant eyes! He'd stayed at the Hope and Anchor in Macquerie Street. Then he'd signed on to the . . .

Oh, but the name of the ship escaped them. They'd give their empty glass another wistful look and as soon as they'd had a refill, the name of the ship would come out.

Within a few weeks it was clear there'd been a thousand Laurids Madsens in Hobart Town, and my *papa tru* had signed on to a thousand ships sailing to a thousand destinations. I didn't have a single bird in my hand, but I had thousands in the bush. Laurids Madsen wasn't a man. He was an entire race.

Even so, I went to the Hope and Anchor to ask about the lost man. I'd come this far and I wasn't ready to give up. The man behind the bar was called Anthony Fox. He was an ex-con like the rest of them, but unlike them, he'd thrived – by making a profit from their misery. He stood behind his brass counter, rubbing it with a cloth until it shone. When I leaned over it to question him, I could see my face in it and I wondered if it had ever reflected my father's beard.

I ordered a gin – for myself this time – and mentioned my father's name. That was all I did mention, because by now I'd learned my lesson. I could have said that Laurids was a Hottentot with fiery red, woolly hair that stuck out on all sides and three legs instead of the usual two and they all would have said, yes, we remember that Dane well. So I left it at the name.

He stood there for a while. 'What was that name again?' he asked. 'And the year?'

'Fifty or fifty-one,' I said.

'Just a minute.'

He ordered a waiter to take over behind the bar and disappeared into a back room, returning with a large ledger tucked under his arm.

'I never remember a face,' he said, 'but I do remember a debt.'

He put the ledger on the counter and started leafing through it.

'There!' he exclaimed triumphantly and pushed the book across to me. 'I knew it.'

He pointed to a name. Laurids Madsen, it said.

I can't claim I recognised my father's signature. I still hadn't learned to read when he disappeared, and he wasn't a man to write his name down too often.

'What does he owe you for?' I asked.

'He owes me for two beers,' Anthony Fox said.

I found the money and paid him.

'We're quits now.'

'Don't tell me you travelled halfway around the world to pay Madsen's debt?'

I shook my head.

'He's disappeared. I'm looking for him.'

'Sailor or convict?'

He gave me a searching look.

'Sailor.'

'Then I suppose he must have drowned, like sailors do. Or jumped ship.'

He flung out his arm in a vague gesture that might encompass the Pacific Ocean with its tens of thousands of islands, as well as the ice-covered pole south of us, where no one had ever set foot.

'It's a big world. You'll never find him.'

'I found his debt,' I said.

'People who disappear don't always want to be found. Where does a sailor belong? On deck, or with his missus and kids? Sometimes he gets confused. Then he starts living like his life's a spinning top that he can spin again and again. He drowns ten times, and he comes back ten times – and each time he's got a new woman in his arms. Back home, his family's mourning him, while he's sitting next to a cradle on another continent, chuckling away. Until he gets fed up with that family too. Trust me. I've seen it happen.'

'I didn't know that sages tended bars here in Hobart Town.'

He grinned at me. 'You're his son. Am I right?'

'I thought you said you never remember a face. Do I look like Laurids Madsen?'

'I've no idea. I don't remember him. But I recognise an offended man when I see one. Only a son would pull a face like that when his father's accused of being a cheat.'

I turned to leave.

'Wait,' Anthony Fox said. 'I'm going to give you a name.'

'A name?'

I stopped in the doorway of the Hope and Anchor.

'Yes, a name. Jack Lewis. Remember it.'

'And who's Jack Lewis?'

'The man your father drank a beer with.'

'And you remember that man ten years on? I suppose he owes you for a beer, too.'

'He owes me for a lot more than a beer. Find him for me, and jog his memory about that debt.'

I turned back to the bar, where my half-empty glass of gin was still waiting. Fox hadn't cleared it away. He'd known he could pull me back.

It was early in the day and I was the only guest at the Hope and Anchor.

'Do you want something to eat?' he asked.

'Not if it's lamb.' I was sick of lamb. It was the only meat they ate in Hobart Town.

'I've got sea bass.' We sat down at a table. 'There's plenty of room here,' he said. 'Australia's bigger than Europe and it's still needing more citizens. The Pacific Ocean takes up half the globe. I call it the fatherland of the homeless.'

'Did you ever sail?'

'I've done everything. Farming, carpentry, sailing, being a con. Because that's a trade too. Two kinds of men come to the Pacific. The ones who just want to lie under a coconut palm and never do a day's work, and the ones who are following the money.'

'The money?'

'Jack Lewis was one of them. Opium from China, arms, human trafficking, name whatever vice you can think of – and I don't just mean cargo that can be weighed and measured – and Jack Lewis will step forward as your humble supplier. If you follow the money you need to stick to certain routes. On one of those routes you'll find Jack Lewis.'

'Give me the name of his ship.'

'The *Flying Scud*. But you need to make up your mind about something before you start. You need to decide what kind of man your father was. Was he the coconut-palm type, who wanted to spend his life lying on his back in the shade, or was he after money? If he was a coconut man you'll never find him. Melanesia, Gilbert Island, Society Islands, Sandwich Islands: ten lifetimes aren't long enough to visit them all. But if he's the other kind, you're in with a chance. Jack Lewis doesn't come here any more. But he's out there somewhere.'

'And how do I find him?'

'Not in any register. Jack Lewis is the kind of man the authorities don't know about. But he's lodged in a lot of men's memories. Including mine.'

'Tell me about his debt.'

'Just mention my name. Anthony Fox. And the sum of one thousand pounds.'

'One thousand pounds!' I exclaimed. 'But why did you give a thousand pounds to a notorious swindler?'

'Greed is the correct term, I believe,' Anthony Fox said without flinching. 'Besides, I hadn't acquired the money lawfully myself. Call it a loan between swindlers. Nowadays I wander the narrow path of virtue. But purely due to lack of means.'

'It's a topsy-turvy world,' I said. 'Most men become thieves out of necessity.'

'As did I once. Well, I was more than a thief. I'll leave you to guess what. Today I live an honest life. People keep their eye on an ex-con. The *Flying Scud*. Now you've got the man's name – and the ship's, too.'

'And if I find it?'

'I can't promise that you'll find your father. But you'll find Jack Lewis. I've no hope of seeing my money again. But now you know that Jack Lewis is a crook. Do whatever you want to him, and you'll have my blessing.'

That was how men in Hobart Town spoke to each other: as one con-man to another. I thought of the vast surface of the Pacific Ocean, which I'd already crossed once. Who could keep an eye on what happened on a deck thousands of miles from shore – or on an island no bigger than a ship?

The word *freedom* was something the world had taught me recently and I'd had to sail far to grasp its meaning. In Hobart Town I heard that word from men who'd chained themselves to their own greed. Freedom had a thousand faces. But so did crime. The thought of what a man might do made me dizzy.

'Honolulu,' Anthony Fox said. 'I suggest that you start your search in Honolulu.'

'If you know where I can find him, why don't you go there yourself and collect your money?'

'I've become an honest man. Only the stupid steal from the rich. The clever steal from the poor. The law usually protects the rich.'

'So you're not stealing from the poor?'

'No, I'm just exploiting their weakness.' He pointed to the bar and its battery of bottles. 'It's more profitable and less risky. A bottle in the hand is better than money in the bank. That's how the poor think.'

'Ah! So you own all those Bird-in-Hand pubs?'

'Indeed I do.' I got up to leave. 'One moment.' It was a trick he had, holding back information until the end. 'I do remember one thing about your father.' I looked at him. My heart was pounding in my chest. 'He looked like a man who'd lost something. Do you have any idea what that might be?'

'No,' I said, my heart still banging. 'I was only a child when he disappeared.'

I went out of the door and heard Anthony Fox's voice for the last time.

'You forgot to pay!' he called out. 'You're going in my book.'

I WAS ONLY TOO PLEASED TO BE LEAVING HOBART TOWN. I'D SLEPT with my head on my sea chest with the door locked, but even so, on more than one occasion I'd had unexpected visitors and had to fight someone off in the dark.

Now I was headed for Honolulu. It took me a year to get there. I had to sign on and sign off several times: no routes led directly from Hobart Town to Hawaii. I saw a lot on that journey, and there was more than one shore where I was tempted to settle. If Anthony Fox was right about there being two kinds of men who came to the Pacific Ocean, I knew which kind I was: the kind looking for the shade of a coconut palm and a view of a blue lagoon.

Yet I always moved on. I had nothing in my mind but the name Jack Lewis.

I had to wait fourteen days in Honolulu, and if I hadn't been looking for Jack Lewis, I would have stayed there for the rest of my life.

The women wore red ankle-length dresses that bared their shoulders, and they wriggled their hips in a way Marstallers would have called indecent. But their lives were governed by a different, more fertile kind of Nature than the one at home. The air was thick with perfume. At first I thought it was the ladies, tempting my nostrils in the same way they tempted the rest of me. But the scent came from the flowers. Jasmine and oleander were the only ones I knew the names of, but they grew everywhere – in front of the houses, in the shade of the trees and along the roads. Instead of gin, the drink of choice here was bourbon, and I'd down it on a shady terrace watching life go by on the promenade in front of me, listening to the surf.

The houses in the town were white with green shutters, and the roads were straight and wide. Instead of cobbles I walked on a carpet of crushed coral, shaded by tall trees with leaves that grew so thick no sunlight came through. The men wore the colour of the town:

white jackets, white waistcoats, white trousers. Even white shoes. They'd chalk the canvas every morning. And the women wore gypsy hats decorated with flowers.

The Micronesians have light skin, and they like to tattoo their faces. It was the men who struck you the most. They shave their heads and they're tattooed from the neck up, so their faces are just blue shadows, lit up by lightning-flashes of white from the glint of their eyes.

Hobart Town and Honolulu lie at opposite sides of the Pacific Ocean, and I've never been to two places more different. I'd first heard Jack Lewis's name in Hobart, but every time I mentioned it here, it was as if I'd brought some of its filth with me. People would eye me suspiciously and make me feel like undesirable company. One man even spat on the ground and turned his back on me altogether. It felt like the whole of Honolulu was shunning me.

An American missionary shot me a look of pity from beneath his broad-brimmed straw hat and addressed me in a fatherly tone. 'You look like an otherwise decent young man. Why do you want to talk to that dreadful person?'

I couldn't explain my business, so I just stood there mute. He misunderstood my silence, thought I had something to hide and walked away, shaking his head.

I felt unclean.

In the end, though, I got the information I was looking for. I learned that Jack Lewis was expected within the next few weeks. But I paid a price for my interest in the *Flying Scud*. I drank my bourbon alone.

The *Flying Scud* dropped anchor outside Honolulu, and I was waiting on the beach when Jack Lewis was rowed ashore by his crew, which consisted of four Kanaks. Their faces were covered in blue tattoos and I noticed one had an ear missing. I took the fact that Jack Lewis chose to surround himself exclusively with natives as a sign that he didn't trust anyone. I reckoned this was the kind of company a man preferred if he had a secret to keep. What did he talk to these blue-faced men about? Nothing, I guessed. They had their goals in life, and he had his – and their paths need never really cross.

Jack Lewis was a small, withered man with skin burned the colour of mahogany by the trade winds and the noonday equator sun. His face was wrinkled and his eyes were set deep, like an old monkey's. He wore a washed-out cotton suit with stripes that had all but faded away. A straw hat kept his face in shadow, except when he tilted his head back to look at whomever he was talking to, which he did with the air of a nabob holding court.

At first glance he seemed unremarkable. He didn't look like a captain: far from it. A modest merchant, maybe. And yet all sorts of rumours stuck to him. I'd already learned that just the mention of his name made you untouchable.

His crew pulled the boat up onto the beach, and he stood next to it, studying the sand, seemingly deep in thought. I went over to him and told him my name. He looked up at me. I watched his face, but it seemed my name rang no bells – or if it did, he wasn't letting on.

Then I mentioned Anthony Fox, and he turned his back to me. His men didn't seem to be listening to us, but they were clearly waiting for orders.

'I'm not here for the money,' I said. 'I'm here for something else.'

He swung round to look at me.

'Everyone comes here for money. What other reason is there?'

'I'm looking for someone.'

He sized me up with his close-set monkey eyes. 'Madsen,' he said. 'You're Laurids Madsen's son.'

'Is it that obvious?'

'It's easy to work out. Only a son would look for a man like Madsen.'

'What's that supposed to mean?'

I stepped up to him. I could feel my anger surge. But it was mixed with a fear of what I might discover. And when anger and fear get mixed up, anything can happen.

Jack Lewis didn't move. He kept staring me in the face. His eyes were inscrutable. I could tell this was a man who'd taught himself to control others with just a look.

'Listen to me,' he said. 'You're young. You're looking for your father. I've no idea why and it's not my business. Nor is morality. I'm not interested in good and evil and I judge no one. I'm only interested in whether a man is suited for work on board.'

'And my father wasn't?'

There was still anger in my voice: a ridiculous feeling of hurt pride on my father's behalf had swept through me. After all, the man passing judgement on him was no more than a criminal.

'The first time I met your father he seemed like a man who'd lost everything. As a rule, men like that are useful in my line of business. They have no illusions. They're survivors and life has taught them what really matters: money. I ask this out of curiosity, and you don't have to answer – what had he lost?'

I shook my head. 'I don't know.'

'His family? His fortune? Or some quaint notion of honour?'

'He had my mother. He had three sons and a daughter. He could get all the work he wanted. He was a respected sailor.'

Jack Lewis made a gesture of invitation. 'We're standing on a beach. Let's go into town and have a drink.'

When we parted a few hours later I discovered, to my astonishment, that I'd grown to like Jack Lewis. He reminded me of Anthony Fox. In Marstal I would probably have avoided him like the plague, but when you're far from home you learn to appreciate the strangest people. He was a man who considered things. He was direct and he never pretended to be anything he wasn't. He invited me on board the *Flying Scud* the following day, and I accepted his invitation.

Neither of us mentioned my father.

Sunshine filtered through a skylight onto the table in Jack Lewis's low-ceilinged cabin. At the centre sat the empty shell of a sea turtle, laden with a strange fruit – the Kanaks called it a pineapple – that I'd never seen before coming to Hawaii. A whale-oil lamp was burning, but it seemed that the real light came from the fruit. It was gold and it glowed like a slice of sun.

On the bulkhead a spear and shield shared space with two miniature portraits, which I studied closely. One was of a portly gent with sideburns and bushy eyebrows; the other showed a pale, weak-looking woman with a sharp nose, whom I took to be his wife.

'You're wasting your time,' Jack Lewis said. 'I've no idea who they are. I found them in a wrecked ship. I thought my cabin could do with a few ornaments. A couple of portraits like that give a man some respectability. Make him look as if he has ancestors and a family history. But I haven't and I don't want any, either. That would be stupid for a man in my position. Take a look at him,' he continued. 'A big man with a big appetite for life. And then take a good look at her: a misery guts. I bet that pointy nose of hers was always red from crying and whining. He can't have had much fun out of her. I look at them every now and again to remind myself why I'm here. Take the Pacific as your bride, and she'll bring you money and all the fun you could wish for.'

I pointed at the weapons.

'And those?'

'A gift from the Pacific. A healthy brawl with cannibals on a remote island that no one ever visits. A fight like that makes you feel alive. Especially afterwards, when you're wandering the beach looking at the enemies you've slain. Those weapons are trophies. They remind me why I'm here.'

He opened a wall cabinet and took out a bottle. It was an unusual shape and held a white liquid that seemed to whirl around like mist or boiling milk. I thought I saw something dark stir inside it. Jack Lewis shook his head and put the bottle back, then selected another one.

'Scotch?'

I nodded. We sat down facing each other.

'And my father?'

'He looked at things differently. He didn't share my view of a good time. He didn't want the same things as I did. But I didn't know what he was after, so we went our separate ways.' He raised his glass to me and we drank. 'Pity,' Jack Lewis said. 'He had it in him. He could have done well out here. I liked him.'

He got up and drew aside the curtain of the bottom berth. He was looking for something and a moment later he straightened up. In his hand he held a small parcel wrapped in a cloth that had once been white but had yellowed with age. He grinned at me.

'Now that we've got to know each other, there's something I want to show you. Initiate you into the inner sanctum, so to speak.'

He placed the parcel on the table and, with slow, careful movements, started to untie the string around the yellow cloth, almost as if he'd invited me to witness a ceremony. Then he whipped off the cloth with a quick tug.

Before me lay the most disgusting sight I've ever seen.

At first I couldn't even find a name for it, but my eyes were faster than my brain. Even before I'd understood what was on the table in front of me, my stomach started to go into spasm and my heart felt as if it had stopped. The thing wasn't much bigger than a clenched fist. The filthy, smoky hair, which must once have been white, was gathered in a pigtail at the back.

I clasped my mouth with my hand and staggered to my feet. Jack Lewis gave me a look of approval as if my reaction had lived up to his expectations.

'You've gone pale,' he said.

I grabbed the table for support, then withdrew my hand as if a scorpion had stung me: the revolting thing was still on it. A terrible thought struck me. I had only vague recollections of my father's face. We'd no pictures of him at home, and whenever I tried to recall his features, my imagination seemed to be conjuring something as shifting and unreliable as a cloud in the sky.

'My father?' I whispered.

I'd never have expected to see Jack Lewis erupt in laughter. But at this, his hard mask cracked and he guffawed – not a warm or hearty sound, but one as dry and harsh as his appearance. Still, he was laughing.

'For God's sake,' he hiccuped between fits. 'Of course it's not your father. What kind of a man d'you take me for?' Then he burst out laughing again. It was only when he'd finally stopped that it dawned on him that I was standing with my fists clenched. My fear had turned into rage. 'Don't be angry,' he said, holding up his palms to calm me. 'I'm only trying to contribute to your education.'

He picked up the head from the table.

'Do you know how to make a shrunken head like this? Clearly you have to start by scalping it. Now the redskins in America take only the scalp and the hair. For this, you have to slice off the whole face, because you can't shrink the skull. Then you dry it over the fire. Not much left by way of a resemblance. A shrunken head's hardly a fine example of portraiture.' He held up the head before my face and scrutinised it, turning it about so that I, too, could fully appreciate the sight. 'But still, something remains. His old ma would recognise him, don't you think?'

'It's a white man,' I said.

'Yes, of course it's a white man. Do you think I'd keep the head of a cannibal? No, a white man's head is a great rarity. I had to pay five rifles for it on Malaita. They're all headhunters there. It was a bargain. I handed over the guns and taught the cannibals how to shoot. Then they aimed them at me, so I shot all five of them before they had time to count to three. Which incidentally they wouldn't

133

have been capable of. I was a more experienced shot, of course. But I'd failed to mention they needed to release the safety catch before pulling the trigger. Sadly, I can't put the shrunken head of a white man on public display. But when I'm alone or in company I trust, I'll take it out and contemplate it.' He placed the thing back on the table. I stared at its horribly distorted features. They were still recognisably human, and that was the worst of it. 'If I have a religion, then it's him. He can't say a word, but he tells me everything I need to know about life. Look! What are we? A trophy for others? An enemy? Yes, that too – but above all, a commodity. There's nothing that can't be bought or sold. I paid with rifles. If those miserable cannibals had known about money, I'd have paid the right price and we could have avoided all that unfortunate shooting. Which, by the way, I don't regret. That, too, was a trade. In my favour. Another drink?'

I wanted to say no, but I needed another one. So we sat there drinking in Captain Jack Lewis's cabin with a shrunken head on the table between us. I glanced at it out of the corner of my eye until slowly I grew used to its presence.

'Who was he?' I asked.

'Even if I knew, I wouldn't tell you. Let's just say that I call him Jim and leave it at that. Do you ever look at yourself in the mirror?' Jack Lewis fixed his eye on me.

We had a small mirror at home, but it was hidden away in one of my mother's drawers and it rarely came out. I'd seen myself reflected in a windowpane more often than I'd stood before a mirror; none of the ships I had sailed kept one in the fo'c's'le.

'Not often,' I replied.

The question didn't interest me, nor could I grasp where Jack Lewis was going with it.

'A wise decision. You should never study yourself in a mirror. It tells you nothing but lies. When a man looks at his reflection, he starts getting all sorts of wrong notions about himself. I'm not talking about what a mirror does to a woman. A man doesn't look to find out how handsome he is. A man's vanity isn't in his face; it's found elsewhere. Still, the mirror gives him the idea that he's unique, totally different from everyone else. But it only looks that way. Do you know how we come across to others, in this mirror, here?'

He pointed to his eyes.

134

'Let me show you.'

He grabbed hold of Jim's pigtail with his claw-like hand and dangled him in front of my face. Startled, I jumped up.

Jack Lewis laughed triumphantly.

'That's you,' he said. 'That's how you look to me. And it's me. That's how I look to you. That's how we seem to each other. The first question we ask ourselves when we meet someone is this: what use is he to me? We're all shrunken heads to one another.' He sat down again and poured himself another drink. He gave me an encouraging look. 'Another one?'

I shook my head. All I wanted was to get away from this man as quickly as possible. But it wasn't an option. I'd travelled too far to meet him, and without him I'd never find my *papa tru*. I had yet to ask him where he was, but Jack Lewis beat me to it.

'I know where your father is,' he said. 'And I'm offering you a deal. I'll take you to him. But there's a price, of course.' He looked at Jim and laughed again. 'This is the deal. You don't get something for nothing. I'm bored with having only Kanaks for company, but it's difficult for me to hire crewmen of my own race. You'll be my first mate – which is a promotion, I'd imagine, for a man as young as you. You won't get paid, but you'll get free passage. Now here comes the most important bit.' He raised his index finger and stared at me with what seemed like an artificial gravity, though I didn't know him well enough to interpret his expression. 'I'm your captain and you'll obey my orders.'

'I obey only my conscience.'

'And what does your conscience bid you do?' he asked mockingly.

'My conscience doesn't care about the course we take, or wages, or time off. I'm not afraid of hard work. But there are some things it forbids me.'

'We'll see,' Jack Lewis said. 'It's your choice. Your father or your conscience.'

'Where is he?'

'I'm not going to tell you. The Pacific's a big place, and he's far away. The trade winds blow as they will, but I promise not to travel there the long way round. So, what shall it be? Yes or no?'

And I replied: 'Yes.'

WE SAILED A FORTNIGHT LATER. THE HOLD WAS FULL – BUT WHAT with I didn't know. Captain Jack Lewis had deliberately kept me away from the loading.

'The usual,' he replied, in answer to my question.

I knew it was pointless to ask again: I could see his urge to mock me was resurfacing.

'Remember your conscience. What you don't know won't hurt you.'

Our course was south-westerly, but that told me nothing. Hawaii was in the eastern Pacific, and the course merely confirmed what I already suspected: that my *papa tru* was somewhere across that vast expanse of water, on one of the thousands of islands.

I was at the helm and we were being carried along by a light breeze. Jack Lewis was standing next to me. He was a man of his word and he must have been serious when he told me how lonely it was with nothing but Kanaks for company, because now he rarely left my side.

'You may not be aware of this,' he said, 'but you're crossing the Pacific for the wrong reason.'

'How do you mean?'

He could always arouse my curiosity, though I rarely enjoyed his philosophy.

'If I ask someone like you where he's headed, do you know what you're meant to say if you're a young man with a zest for life? I'm headed for the whole world, you should say. For the oceans and all their islands. A young man goes to sea to escape from his father. But you're looking for him. That's the wrong way round. Is it because of your mother?'

'It would be better for her if he were dead, and she had a grave to visit. It would do her no good to know that he's still alive.'

'So you're not doing her a favour. Are you sure you're doing yourself one?'

'I need to know the truth.'

'What do you want from your father?'

'A man needs a yardstick.'

'A yardstick? Find another one. A ship, your own actions. Let the Pacific be your yardstick. Look at the swell. You'll not find a bigger swell anywhere. It has half the globe for its run-up. You're young. You have the whole world. Don't bother yourself with the past.'

I made no reply. What I wanted from my father was none of Jack Lewis's business, so why was he interfering? Besides, we'd struck a deal, and I wasn't questioning him about our course.

I thought about my *papa tru*. Once upon a time I missed him so much that my heart ached every day. Then I grew up and a feeling of bitterness crept in. I never doubted that he was alive – and I assumed he'd gone missing because he wanted to. I had to know why. That was all. What kind of life was he living? What would I say when I met him? I didn't know. I hadn't prepared a speech. I just had to see him. And then what?

I couldn't answer that either. I only knew that while I was searching for him, he'd changed into a different man. And that was the truth about him. He'd become a stranger. Perhaps that was what I wanted confirmed. I needed to find him so I could say goodbye.

It was a year since I'd left Hobart Town. I had been back and forth across the Pacific, but I hadn't seen it, because Jack Lewis was right: I'd been travelling with my back to it. But now I saw it for the first time. I saw its long swells, which were the remnants of storms past; I saw the dolphins leap and the sharks' fins cut through the water; I saw huge shoals of tuna churn the water to foam. Only rarely did I see a seagull; land was always far, far away – though I saw the albatross glide past on its massive wings. It didn't need to be near land.

They said the Pacific was just like any other ocean, only bigger. But I learned that was nonsense. It could be grey and rough like the North Sea, or calm like the South Funen archipelago, but I never saw the sky so blue or so vast over any other sea, and though the earth isn't flat and has no edge, I discovered that the Pacific was its centre.

On clear nights when I was at the helm on my own and even the constantly philosophising Jack Lewis had surrendered to the demands of sleep, the stars were the only geography. I felt like one of them, adrift in the centre of the universe.

The Kanaks sat on the deck, silently watching the constellations, and I knew that as a seafaring tribe who'd once navigated by the most remote suns of the universe, they too felt at home here. Suddenly I understood my *papa tru*. There comes a time in the life of a sailor when he no longer belongs ashore. It's then that he surrenders to the Pacific, where no land blocks the eye, where sky and ocean mirror each other until above and below have lost their meaning, and the Milky Way looks like the spume of a breaking wave and the globe itself rolls like a boat in the midst of the sinking and heaving surf of that starry sky, and even the sun is nothing but a tiny glowing dot of phosphorescence on the sea of the night.

I was filled with an impatient longing for the unknown, and there was a ruthlessness to it; perhaps this was what Jack Lewis had meant when he spoke about that need for adventure that makes young people yearn to see the whole world, the oceans and all their islands. Mystery emanated from the Pacific's vast surface. My *papa tru* must have felt it once. And when a man has felt it, he doesn't return.

I was reminded of a summer's evening on the beach back home. The wind had died down and the water was completely calm. In the dusk light, sea and sky had taken on a violet tinge and the horizon had melted clean away, leaving the beach as the only fixed point, its white sand marking the furthest edge of the world, beyond which lay endless violet space. When I took my first stroke I felt as though I were swimming straight into the immensity of the universe above me.

That night on the Pacific I had the same feeling.

The *Flying Scud* smelled of copra from stern to bow. There was nothing strange about that in itself. Dried coconut was the most important commodity in these parts. But given Jack Lewis's reputation, it occurred to me that the copra smell might be masking something else. It wasn't through dealing in copra that Jack Lewis had become notorious – though I couldn't work out what else he might be trading.

Anthony Fox had used the word *slavery*, and when I repeated it to Jack Lewis, for once he failed to reply in his usual direct way.

'I do what all sailors do,' he said. 'I take things to the places they're needed. That's the way of the world. I don't make it better and I don't make it worse.'

'Slave trading?' I asked.

'In case you don't already know, I can inform you that the slave trade's illegal in this part of the world. I'm a law-abiding man.'

He gave me a wry smile.

'Plantation workers?' I asked.

It was a well-known fact that there was widespread traffic in Kanak labourers, who were tricked into working on the large plantations, where instead of earning money, they ended up in bottomless debt. Their employers owned everything, including the houses the workers rented and the shops where they bought their food. A plantation worker's contract might be for two years, but he'd end up working ten before he returned to his native island, penniless and broken. If he ever found his way home across the sea, that is.

Jack Lewis shook his head.

'This is an amusing game we've started. But don't think that I'll provide you with the answer. You're not a practical man. And then there's that sensitive conscience of yours. With one of those, it's best to turn a blind eye.'

Jack Lewis always relieved me at midnight, precisely when the middle watch began. I wondered about it at first, then decided there had to be a secret side to him that forced him to be alone with the stars. One warm evening, when the sails hung limp and the calm surface of the sea mirrored the Milky Way, making its white starlight seem like surf breaking over a submerged reef, I fetched my bedding in order to sleep on deck.

Jack Lewis immediately ordered me below, his voice sharp.

'Kanaks sleep on deck. It's not appropriate for a white man.' I wavered. I felt no urge to return to the muggy cabin below. 'All right, stay here and get some fresh air.' His voice was conciliatory now, and I could tell he wanted to talk. I seated myself on the rail. It was very quiet, apart from the squeaking of the rigging. 'I've lied to you,' Jack Lewis said. I could hear him chuckling to himself in the darkness. 'I know very well who Jim is. But you won't believe me.'

'Out with it. I'll believe you. But tell me, why do you want to tell me the truth now?'

'Oh, so I've got your blessing, have I? Lucky me. Why do I suddenly feel like telling you the truth about Jim? Because the story's too good to keep to myself. That's the strange thing about a good story. No pleasure if you can't share it. So listen to this: Jim's real name is –' Here he paused for dramatic effect. 'James.'

I gave him a disappointed look. 'So what?'

Jack Lewis laughed. 'I'm guessing his surname will mean more to you than his first name. Cook. James Cook.'

I gasped. '*The* James Cook?'

'Yes, *the* James Cook. Captain of the *Resolution* and the *Discovery*. The man who discovered the Friendship Islands, the Sandwich Islands and the Society Islands. That James Cook.'

'But that's impossible!'

'Show me his grave, then. Go on, tell me where he's buried.' I shook my head. I didn't know. 'James Cook was killed on Hawaii. In Kealakekua Bay. He was strict but fair. You have to be if you're dealing with Kanaks. When one of them stole a sextant James Cook cut off his ear.' He fixed me with his eyes to make sure I'd understood what he'd just told me. I had. One of Jack Lewis's own Kanaks had an ear missing, thanks to this inspiring story, no doubt. 'James Cook shot a chief on Hawaii, who'd tried to steal a boat from him. Thousands of natives surrounded him and his men, but he could have been all right. The natives thought he was their missing god, Lono, making a return.'

'He shouldn't have shot their chief.'

'I thought you might say that. But the opposite's the case. Shooting the chief was vital. By making an example of him, Cook showed his strength. His mistake was that he revealed his weakness too. The natives were scared of attacking – though they had Cook and his men well outnumbered. But then one of them fired an arrow. Maybe it was an accident. No one knows. But the arrow hit James Cook. It didn't cause any serious injury. That wasn't what killed him. He died because he blundered.' Jack Lewis sent me the look he always used when he wanted to educate me. Though I couldn't see how James Cook had blundered, I guessed that some cynical remark about mankind's wretchedness was about to follow, and I wasn't mistaken. 'In the eyes of the Kanaks he was a god, and gods don't flinch. But Cook screamed when the arrow hit him. That gave them their signal to attack. Fifteen thousand men came at him and tore him to pieces. Literally. They roasted his flesh over an open fire – except for the nine pounds they sent back to the *Resolution*. They hung his heart inside a hut, where three children found it. They ate it, thinking it was a dog's. Some of his bones were discovered later by his officers, and they buried them at sea. But his head was lost.'

'So how did you find it?'

'It wasn't easy. The Kanaks kept it secret, you see. It became a trophy in their internal wars. Finally the head left Hawaii and started wandering the Pacific – almost as if it was copying its owner's voyage all those years before. At one time no fewer than five heads were rumoured to exist in the Pacific region, all attributed to James Cook. But I found the real one. I've got sources. I finally tracked it down on Malaita. The chief who sold it to me was an educated man. He spoke and read English. He'd been taught by a missionary. Whom he later ate with great relish, or so he claimed. He knew exactly who Cook was and what his head was worth. Besides, he saw nothing barbaric in headhunting. "I've read in your Bible," he said, "about David, the great warrior. After he defeated Goliath, didn't he cut off his head to show to King Saul?"'

Shortly after this conversation I returned below deck and soon I'd fallen into a restless sleep on my narrow berth, inhaling the sultry air and dreaming about Isager's house in flames that New Year's Eve, all those years ago. I was in the street looking through the window – and I saw the schoolmaster's severed head sitting on the dining-room table, staring back at me.

Then I heard the murmur of voices and the sound of bare feet against the deck. Confused about whether or not it was just a new dream taking over from the previous one, I woke with a tight feeling in my chest. I swung my legs out of the berth. The ship groaned and the waves heaved: the wind was no longer calm, and I decided to return to the deck to feel the fresh breeze on my face. I found the door to my cabin was closed – though I could have sworn that I'd left it open when I went to bed. I turned the handle, but the door was locked from the outside.

Something was going on that I wasn't allowed to see. And I now had a good idea what it might be.

I banged on the door and called Jack Lewis's name, but no one came. I couldn't break it down, so eventually I gave up and returned to my berth, where I surprised myself by falling asleep again.

When I woke, light was streaming in through the open door. I found Jack Lewis in his cabin with a cup of coffee. He looked as if he had been expecting me and smiled broadly when I entered.

'Coffee?' he offered, and gestured to a chair opposite him. I made no reply. 'Are we about to go another round? How about one of our Socratic dialogues about ethics? Trust me. Everything I do, I do purely to protect your delicate conscience.'

'An unused conscience is no conscience at all.'

'How philosophical we are this morning. Nothing makes a man more reflective than a locked door. If it weren't for this delicate conscience of yours, your door wouldn't be locked. But you're always welcome to come up on deck and enjoy the night. As long as you remember that I'm your captain and that my word is law on board.'

'So it is slaves? The *Flying Scud* is a blackbirder?'

'Certainly not. There are only free men on board the *Flying Scud*.'

'Who are locked in the hold during the day?'

'They can leave the ship whenever they want. Only I don't want them jumping overboard into the middle of the sea. They'll drown. Not even the strongest swimmer could ever get as far as any land. But the Kanaks are superstitious, and they're afraid to swim in the dark. So at night they're safe on deck.'

I understood nothing at all.

'Leave the ship whenever they want?'

My voice was thick with anger and disbelief. Jack Lewis was making a fool of me.

'Yes. Once we reach land, they're free to leave the ship.' He got up and held out his hand. 'The captain of the *Flying Scud* gives you his word.'

I remained standing with my hands at my sides.

'If they're free men, why have them on board? I presume there's a purpose?'

'Everything has a purpose.'

'Yours or theirs?'

I glanced at the cupboard behind him, which contained the Winchester rifles. I knew he had no need to give me an answer.

* * *

That same evening I was at the helm when he came on deck to relieve me.

'I'll do a couple of hours of the next watch,' I said.

'As you wish.'

In the moonlight his face looked like a carved wooden mask.

Nothing happened during the first hour. The Kanak crew were sleeping around the deck, for the nights were still warm. Then Jack Lewis roused them. They got to their feet without complaint, though it was the middle of the night and the moon was the only source of light. I could see that this was their routine. They disappeared into the galley and returned with jars of water and bowls of cooked rice, which they placed on deck before lifting the hatch. A black hole appeared in the centre of the deck and I wondered if all my questions would finally be answered. At last I was about to clap eyes on the 'free men' who spent their days locked in the hold.

One of the Kanaks hollered down the hole and a chorus of voices responded. Then one by one they emerged. I tried counting them, but it was hard in the dark. I don't know how many there were, but I think they were all male. Their skin was as dark as a moonless night, and their faces were hidden behind great clouds of woolly hair. In the moonlight they looked like Negroes from Africa, but I knew they had to be Melanesians from the eastern Pacific – the darkest of all the races spread across this vast sea, and notorious among white men for being not only the most bloodthirsty warriors but also the keenest of all headhunters.

Now they were wandering peacefully around the deck, where scenes soon unfolded that I imagine you'd experience in their villages. Some sat down around the bowls of rice. Others drank from the water jars or poured the water into their palms to wash their faces. Others went to the rail to relieve themselves. Soon they were all sitting on the deck in smaller groups and a monotonous murmuring spread among them.

One started singing, and others joined him until soon they were all singing a song that seemed to use the Pacific as a metronome, rising and falling with a slow dignity that matched the immense swelling rhythm of the waves. Then, as abruptly as it had begun, for no apparent reason the song ceased and silence descended over the deck again as the *Flying Scud* sailed across the sea towards a destination known only to Jack Lewis.

I looked around for him. He was leaning against the deckhouse with a Winchester rifle.

The same scene was repeated each evening. The hatch was opened and the black shadows, otherwise known as free men, moved around the deck going about their everyday business. Then they'd disappear. I had no idea what fate had in store for our free men. But Jack Lewis had told me too much about his philosophy for me to believe it would be anything good.

Why did he so adamantly refute the suggestion that they were going to be sold as slaves? After all, he was no hypocrite: I had to give him that. So what were they doing there?

'I've told you before, Madsen, and I'll tell you again: they're not slaves and they're not plantation workers. They're free men, like you and me.'

That was his answer the next time I pressed him on it. After that I gave up asking.

A few days later he sought me out. The look on his face told me I was in for a surprise.

'It'll do no harm to reveal it now, Madsen,' he said. 'We're heading for Samoa. That's where your father is.'

'So now I know,' I said, though I'll admit I felt no urge to thank him. Instead I said, 'So what's stopping us from going our separate ways? There's nothing to keep us together now.'

He laughed and flung out his arms as if to embrace me. 'Of course there is, my dear boy. Look around you. The sea! That's what binds us. How will you get to Samoa on your own? Swim? Get off on one of the desert islands that don't figure on any sea chart, and hope to obtain passage from there? No, you're tied to this ship. Just like the free men in the hold.'

Jack Lewis was right. Knowing where my father was – knowledge that I feared I'd paid for dearly even if I benefited from it – changed nothing.

'We'll make a single stop along the way,' Jack Lewis continued in the same triumphant tone. 'But I trust you won't feel the need to desert me.'

'And why wouldn't I?' I retorted.

'Don't be insubordinate, my boy. Because you're too smart to live out your days on a desert island.'

'If the island is deserted, what are we going to do there?'

'The same thing I always do wherever I go: trade.'

'Who with, if there's no one there?'

'A good question, my boy, more profound than you can imagine. Yes, who with? That question I can answer only with a new one. What's a human being? Yes, what?' He looked directly at me. 'Can you tell me that?'

Jack Lewis laughed in a way that signalled he had no interest in my answer and that our conversation was at an end.

TWO DAYS LATER WE SPOTTED A SEAGULL: OUR FIRST IN THREE WEEKS. But there was no land in sight. I took out my chart and found not a single island mapped in our vicinity.

Jack Lewis sent a man up the rigging. Shortly afterwards an affirmative shout came from above – and some hours later a palm-fringed coastline appeared on the horizon.

'Your desert island?' I asked Jack Lewis, who was standing alongside me by the rail.

He nodded but said nothing.

Once we got closer I could see that there was another ship off its coast. I pointed towards the island.

'Someone seems to have beaten us to it.'

'She's a wreck,' Lewis said. 'She's stuck on the reef. Been there for years. The *Morning Star.* That's where I got the portraits of the red-nosed lady and her husband.'

'And the crew?' I asked.

'The crew was long dead when I found the ship.'

'What happened?'

Jack Lewis shrugged. 'Only they know. And as they say, dead men don't tell tales.'

'Mutiny?'

He turned to give one of the Kanaks an order. I realised that I wouldn't learn more, but I couldn't tell from looking at him whether he was holding something back.

We crossed in front of the reef, looking for a way in. Jack Lewis steered towards the wreck. Just before we reached it, we saw a gap in the thundering surf – which the crew of the *Morning Star* had clearly been aiming for. They'd paid a high price for their lack of perfect accuracy. The ship sat high on the reef, as if she'd been flung there with great force. And her position explained why she still appeared undamaged, so that at first I'd assumed she was anchored off the lagoon. She barely heeled, and all three of her masts were intact. Her name was still legible on the stern. A weather-beaten figurehead in flowing white robes held out her hands beseechingly towards the shore, the sole, stiff survivor of that wreck.

The next minute we'd negotiated our way safely into the translucent water of the lagoon, where we could see every fish that darted across the seabed. Beyond the reef's white surf the water was a deep blue, as if in shadow, but in here it was emerald so dazzling you'd think the sand below contained a source of energy as strong as the sun. The beach was white and fringed by lush undergrowth, which melted into jungle. I sensed that this dense vegetation was the wall behind which Jack Lewis kept his secret.

My thoughts must have been drifting because I didn't notice we'd dropped anchor until Jack Lewis suddenly reappeared next to me, clutching a pair of binoculars. He was searching for something on the beach. I saw nothing – but he grunted in contentment.

'Now's the moment.'

'What moment?'

'The moment when I prove to you that I'm a man of my word. You didn't believe me when I told you that the men in the hold were free men and not slaves. Now you can judge for yourself.'

'You've got a gun in your hands.'

'A man needs to take precautions. But I don't plan to use it.'

He ordered the Kanaks to remove the hatch from the hold and then make themselves invisible in the fo'c's'le in front of the mast. It was a strange command, but they didn't look ready to question it, so I guessed it wasn't the first time they'd participated in the ritual, or whatever it was I was about to witness.

Jack Lewis signalled that we should hide behind the deckhouse and pressed a finger against his lips. He looked tense, and I noted that his other finger rested on the trigger of the rifle. Soon we heard voices and footsteps on the deck: the 'free men' were emerging from the hold. Lewis gestured at me to keep still, and for a while we just stood listening. Then I heard splashing, and his face lit up in a smile, as if everything was going according to plan. He nodded and grinned silently at me. A second splash followed and then a third.

I could see from the way Lewis moved his lips and fingers that he was taking some kind of tally. When he'd counted through all the fingers on one hand four times and reached twenty, he slapped me on the shoulder in high spirits.

'So, my boy,' he said, 'any questions?'

I glanced across the lagoon where the men, who until a few minutes ago had been trapped in the hold, were now making for the beach. They all reached it almost simultaneously – and then disappeared into the jungle. None of them looked back.

I didn't know what to say. I felt more baffled than ever. Jack Lewis cocked his head and studied me. 'Look,' he said. 'Free men. Did you see anyone trying to stop them running off?'

'You're a practical man, Mr Lewis,' I said. 'And I don't understand why you've fed these men for so many weeks only to see them disappear. What's in it for you? And what are the men doing on a desert island?'

'Surely that's their own business. I don't know what they're doing there and it's not my concern. All I know is that they had the choice. You saw with your own eyes that I ordered the hatch opened.'

'Who wouldn't have fled, if the alternative was to stay in a dark hole? Is that a real choice?'

'It's a choice,' Jack Lewis said. 'And I offered it to them. But that's enough talking. Let's get down to the real reason we're here.'

He went over to the fo'c's'le and shouted an order to the Kanaks, who immediately appeared on deck and started readying a boat.

'I think you should come ashore with us. You'll find it a worthwhile experience.'

Across his shoulder he slung an old-fashioned musket with a powder horn and a ramrod, and I gave him a puzzled look. In his hand, he held a Winchester rifle.

'Don't ask,' he grinned. 'I'm a superstitious man. This old gun is my talisman.'

I climbed down into the boat together with two Kanaks, who manned the oars. The beach was deserted. On a desert island, what else could it be?

We dragged the boat ashore, and Jack Lewis walked up and down the beach while he scanned the thicket as though in search of something. Then he waved at me. Behind a flowering hibiscus I spotted a row of calabashes. In the sand next to them lay a hide filled with something that looked like pebbles, but I was too far away to see it properly.

Jack Lewis went over to the hide and tied it into a parcel with some leather string while the Kanaks started carrying the calabashes to the boat. They made a sloshing sound and I realised that they were filled with supplies of fresh water. Jack Lewis weighed the parcel in the palm of his hand. I heard a rustling sound, and if his mask-like face had ever been capable of expressing an emotion like happiness, then that's what it was doing now.

Just then a gunshot rang out across the island.

Lewis froze.

'Bloody hell!' he exclaimed. 'Bloody, bastard hell!'

He clutched his leather parcel and turned to me.

'Quick!' he said. 'Take as many calabashes as you can carry!'

He yelled an order at the Kanaks, who immediately started pushing the boat back into the water. He gripped the packet tightly as he ran. I could tell from his face that our frantic flight was to save that, rather than our lives. Whatever it held was clearly his pirate treasure.

By now the boat was in the water, and I had to wade out thigh-deep before I could climb aboard. The Kanaks started rowing immediately, while Jack Lewis stood in the middle of the boat, cocking his rifle. He aimed at the shore and I heard a thundering crack. I turned towards the beach and saw it was teeming with natives. Several of them had guns and they were firing back, a whole salvo of bullets that hit the water around us. Jack Lewis returned fire, and I could see he was a good shot. One of the natives already lay outstretched in the sand. Soon another one tumbled.

'Ha,' he snorted. 'Fortunately for us those devils don't know how to aim.'

'I thought you said this was an uninhabited island.'

'I never said it was an uninhabited island. I said no humans lived here. If you call those devils humans once more, I'll order you off the boat. Then you can join your own species if that's what you want.'

He grinned cruelly at me and carried on shooting. Yet another native collapsed, but the rest kept firing.

'So, what's your decision?'

I shook my head.

'I think I'll stay here.'

I didn't understand any of this. Who were the natives, and why were they shooting at us? They couldn't be the free men from our hold. Where would they have got the guns? And the calabashes of water and the mysterious pebbles that had made Jack Lewis's rigid face crease with joy? What was their significance? He'd called it trading – but the deal appeared to go badly wrong.

No, I didn't understand anything. All I knew was that my heart was beating as it never had before and that the minutes I spent under this hail of bullets, with no task to distract me because the only oars in the boat were in the hands of the Kanak crew, felt like hours and days. The *Flying Scud*, which was probably a couple of cable lengths from the shore, seemed far away. Fortunately, the two Kanaks who'd remained on board ship had spotted our predicament and started to raise the anchor, but this didn't lessen the danger we were in: a second group of natives had pulled a long canoe across the beach and launched it not far from where the first group was positioned. They were still keeping up a heavy barrage of gunfire, though Jack Lewis's marksmanship had by now reduced them to half their original number, and the beach was strewn with bodies.

The canoe gained on us rapidly. Half of the men paddled while the rest stood shooting at us, so Lewis was forced to cover two targets at once. He fired a final shot towards the shore as a farewell and another native fell. Then he focused his attention on the canoe and I saw the foremost of the crewmen thrown sideways into the water just as our own boat suddenly slackened its speed.

Up till now I had watched the dreadful scene unfolding before me in mute fear, my role reduced to that of the spectator of a drama whose outcome had not yet been written. And if fate were cruel enough, the spectacle would cost me my life. Just then, one of the Kanaks collapsed over his oars with a howl of pain. I pushed him from the thwart to the bottom of the boat, where he stayed, clutching his wounded shoulder. The blood bubbled out of it in a glistening stream barely visible against his dark skin. With a part to play at last, I rowed as I'd never rowed before. As soon as my hands had found something to do, I felt I'd seized some control over my own fate: my dark thoughts vanished and time – which a moment earlier seemed to stand still – resumed. The *Flying Scud* quickly grew closer. Her mainsail and foresail were already raised, thanks to the nimble fingers of the Kanaks aboard. I thought we were saved. But then came a burst of obscenities from Lewis.

'Oh, bloody hell!'

I thought that for once he'd missed his target. Then I realised he'd stopped shooting. He'd run out of ammunition.

I looked up. He tore open the leather purse and started rummaging around in it. Then he fished out a small object and held it up to the light. As Jack Lewis twirled it in his fingers, the sun caught it, changing its colour from white to pink to purple to blue, and back again to white.

It was a pearl!

I can't say that it was the most beautiful pearl I'd ever seen because I hadn't seen many, let alone held one in my hand. But it was wondrously lovely, and for a moment I was completely floored by the sight of it. Somehow, it was an invitation to dream. And despite the dire situation we were in, I let myself be whisked away to somewhere entirely different from an undermanned launch pursued by a canoe of bloodthirsty natives who were swiftly gaining on us with brisk strokes.

Jack Lewis knocked me brutally out of my reverie.

'Row, damn you, row!'

I'd been sitting immobile, the oars in my hands, while I stared at the pearl. Now I watched as Lewis took the old musket from his shoulder, poured gunpowder into the barrel, shoved the pearl down after it, and tamped the whole thing tight with his ramrod. Then he raised the gun he'd called his talisman and took careful aim. Before the noise of the blast died down one of the natives flew backwards as if flung by a giant hand, and disappeared into the water.

'I'll send you the bill, you devil!' Jack Lewis screamed, his face distorted by rage.

He reloaded the gun. His fingers shook as he pushed yet another precious pearl into place. I could barely believe my own ears when I heard the strange sound that escaped his compressed lips: I could have sworn it was a sob. The gun went off with a bang.

The Kanak behind me jumped. I thought he'd been shot, but it turned out that his oar had taken a direct hit close to the oarlock and snapped in two. Now I was the only one rowing.

Our lives were riding on the pearls, Jack Lewis's aim, and the strength of my arms, and I rowed until they felt ready to drop. Desperation lent them a power I'd never known, and the gap between our pursuers and us began to widen. There were fewer of them now.

Lewis's precision with both bullets and pearls had taken every second man. Our enemy's victory song echoed in our minds just as menacingly as before – but its chorus had diminished. Finally we reached the *Flying Scud*, where a rope ladder awaited us. I slung the injured Kanak over my shoulder without feeling his weight, climbed the side of the ship and hefted us both over the rail, heedless of what kind of target we might present as I did so. Several shots rang out behind us, but neither one of us was hit.

The Kanaks on board had prepared everything for our departure: the anchor was hung from the bow, the sails were set, and if they'd had access to the captain's cabin and his stash of guns, they'd undoubtedly be handing him loaded rifles so he could continue shooting down our pursuers uninterrupted. But access to those guns was a taboo they dared not break.

We were barely back on deck before Jack Lewis had dashed to his cabin and reappeared with a box of cartridges and a new rifle. Then he kneeled behind the rail and resumed firing. His face was that of a man settling a personal score, rather than putting a dangerous enemy out of action. For every precious pearl that he'd lost, he was making the natives pay, not just with the life each pearl had ended, but with interest. He greeted every clean kill with a cry of triumph.

'Take this, you devil!'

He spat contemptuously over the rail.

I had to take the helm: the captain was too preoccupied with his bloodlust. It was up to me to get us across this lagoon and out through the opening in the reef. My success had nothing to do with seamanship, but with the fortunes of wind and tide, both of which were on our side. The wind had picked up and it filled our sails even before we were out of the lagoon. The tide was low and the current raced out through the gap in the reef. A believer would have said Our Lord was giving us a helping hand. But since I don't believe that the Lord, if He exists, would have been on Jack Lewis's side, all I'll say is that during one lucky hour, Nature ordered the sea and wind to side with him.

The feeling of being miraculously saved at the very last moment never quite left me, though I can't speculate who would have been worse off if Nature had decided to trap the *Flying Scud* in the lagoon, ourselves or the natives. There were many of them, but Jack Lewis's marksmanship was – to use a word that would undoubtedly have flattered his vanity – fiendish.

We sailed past the wreck of the *Morning Star* at a smart speed, at which point Jack Lewis took a break from shooting natives and turned his rifle on the wreck instead. I heard a bang and saw the face of the figurehead disappear in a cloud of splinters. It seemed that Lewis's rage could no longer be quenched by the blood of his enemies – and in that moment I sensed that we had not escaped danger. It had just changed shape. And now it was with us on board.

HAVING REACHED THE OPEN SEA, I MIGHT HAVE FELT IT WAS SAFE to breathe a sigh of relief – had I not seen that savagery in Jack Lewis's face. He'd finally put the gun down and left his position by the rail, and was now pacing up and down, muttering to himself.

'It's all ruined . . . Who is the bastard? . . . If only I could find that accursed bastard.'

He scowled at me as if I, too, were suspected of a crime, the nature of which I couldn't fathom. His plans, whatever they were, had been thwarted. He owed me an explanation for the nightmare we'd just lived through. But I realised that now was the wrong time to ask him. And if I valued my life, there might never be a right one.

I glanced over at him anxiously, trying to gauge the mood that accompanied his stream of muttered expletives. So when his face lit in a sudden smile, it caught me off guard.

'Well, I never,' he exclaimed, as though he'd just spotted a much-missed friend whom he'd soon be welcoming with open arms.

I turned to see what had caught his attention and there, half a cable's length astern, the natives' canoe was bobbing up and down in our gleaming wake. I could barely believe my eyes. How could they possibly think they had a chance of defeating us now?

They worked their paddles feverishly. They were all sitting down; not one of them stood to aim a gun. There were around seven or eight of them left: perhaps they wanted to be sure in advance they'd hit their target this time. They might even be planning to board us. Had they learned nothing?

I didn't for one moment worry about them attacking us. I simply pitied them and their naive folly, for it seemed they were not just dicing with death, but positively inviting it. Their daring filled me with deep sadness on their behalf.

No, I didn't fear the natives and their suicidal attack. I feared Jack Lewis's reawakened bloodlust.

'What a delightful surprise,' he declared. 'And I was just thinking that the fun was over.'

He grabbed his rifle and placed it on his shoulder. Then he lowered it.

'They're too far away,' he said, sounding disappointed. 'Let them catch up a bit. Sail closer to the wind.'

'But, Captain,' I objected, 'they've no chance of reaching us. Surely enough blood has been shed by now?'

He looked at me dispassionately. 'We were attacked and we defended ourselves. That's all.'

'But we're not being attacked now. And as long as we stick to our course, we won't be.'

'Sail closer!'

My hands still hesitated on the wheel. He stepped up close to me, and his small eyes widened with rage.

'Mr Madsen, I'm the captain of the *Flying Scud* and I have just given you an order. If it doesn't please the young gentleman to obey, he will be regarded as a mutineer, and mutineers get short shrift from me.'

He poked the barrel of the gun into my face and for a moment we stared into each other's eyes.

It wasn't his stare or the menacing closeness of the gun barrel that made me follow his order. The weapon was shaking in his hands, and I sensed that although his voice was calm, he was in an uncontrollable rage – not at me or the natives who had spoiled his plans, but at the entire world. And he didn't care who paid the price: the natives or his first mate. It was all the same to him.

'Aye aye, Captain,' I said and turned the wheel.

He lowered the rifle and returned to the stern. The ship dropped speed until we lay still with the sails flapping in the breeze. The natives' canoe came closer. Jack Lewis raised his rifle and began picking them off one by one. With each direct hit, he emitted a short, contented grunt.

The canoe kept gliding forward. One after another the natives stood up with their guns, aimed, fired and fell dead.

At last there was only one left – but he kept paddling towards us. Jack Lewis paused in his shooting, and his attention seemed to drift momentarily. It was clear that his rage had abated.

'Leave him be,' I said. 'It's enough.'

He looked up and gave me a small, sleepy smile, and in that moment his face had the strange gentleness of a newly woken child.

'You're right,' he said. 'It's enough.' He joined me.

'Aye aye, Captain, straight ahead.'

Once more the wind filled our sails and we raced ahead at the same speed as before. Neither of us spoke for a while. I'd escaped death only to have my life threatened by the very man who'd saved me – and now he was standing next to me, pretending that nothing had happened.

'Fine weather,' he said suddenly and inhaled deeply. 'Sea air! Nothing like it. Makes a sailor's life worth living.'

Of all the things I'd heard Jack Lewis say during the months I'd spent with him, this unremarkable comment seemed the strangest. I didn't believe for one moment that he meant what he said – and yet I welcomed his words. The terror I'd felt these past few hours had eased and we were once again a captain and his first mate on our way across the ocean.

'Yes,' I said, and imitated Jack Lewis by inhaling deeply. 'Sea air does a world of good.'

Our idyll was interrupted by an agitated Kanak who ran up, pointing backwards. We both turned. And there was the solitary native in his canoe, a black silhouette against our glittering wake. He wasn't far behind. How he'd managed to gain on us, on his own, in a canoe built for several oarsmen, was incomprehensible.

We watched him for a long time. The distance between our unequal craft remained constant. I glanced sideways at Jack Lewis but said nothing. I expected him to grab his rifle again and put an end to the life he'd spared in a moment of kindness. But he didn't.

Eventually he turned to the helm and ordered me to adjust our course. From time to time I'd look back across the water. The native was still there. The distance remained the same. He neither gained on us nor lagged behind.

A couple of hours passed in this manner, and as I watched our pursuer, my perception of him shifted. Now what I saw was a man all alone in a canoe on the sea. He wasn't a native any more, part of the savage group that had recently attacked us. I no longer knew who he was or what he wanted from us, whether he was a pursuer or someone in need. All I saw was the vast ocean and his lost figure at the centre of it. I felt he had to be some kind of messenger, but I had no idea what he was trying to tell us.

'This has got to stop,' Jack Lewis said at last.

I knew then that there was nothing I could do.

He went back to his rifle and picked it up. I didn't look at him but kept staring at the solitary oarsman in the middle of the sea. Somehow I wanted to say goodbye to him in the minutes he had left and make sure I wouldn't forget him. My memory would be his only tombstone.

He must have seen Jack Lewis aim his Winchester, because he suddenly stood up and flung his own gun onto his shoulder. A bang sounded from Lewis's rifle, and at the same time a red flash shot from the muzzle of the native's gun. They'd fired simultaneously. Our pursuer crashed backwards into the canoe, and it turned sideways in the wake, where it bobbed up and down. Quickly, the gap between us widened. Soon the canoe and the dead man would be gone from view.

So preoccupied had I been with the native's fate that I'd paid no attention at all to what was happening on the *Flying Scud*. But now I heard a loud groan. It came from Jack Lewis. When I turned around, he was sprawled on the deck, a red stain spreading across his shirt front. The native's bullet had also found its target.

Bewildered, the Kanaks kneeled around their captain, as if awaiting his orders. Could they not see that Jack Lewis lay dying right in front of them?

For a moment I wondered if they considered him immortal because his actions were guided by the same unpredictable cruelty shown by their own gods. He'd sliced an ear off one of them, and I'd never heard him address them in anything other than a tone of command. He'd used them as pawns in a game that brought them no profit yet might have cost them their lives, and he'd sacrificed them without explanation. So why not consider him a god? After all, this was how gods behaved, wasn't it? With an inscrutability that was indistinguishable from arbitrariness? Believers might offer prayers and even sacrifices, but none ever found a method of worship that ensured their prayers were answered.

When I saw Jack Lewis stretched out on the deck, with the bloodstain blossoming across his shirt front, I realised that he'd become my god too. He'd promised to deliver me to my *papa tru*. Instead, he'd taken me to an uncharted island where I witnessed mysterious transactions and a terrible massacre, on a ship with a cargo of human beings he insisted were free men.

I'd sailed with him to solve one puzzle, only to discover another.

I was just like one of his Kanaks. But I was also a white man, and I felt he owed me an answer to the riddle. He was about to die, and I wanted that explanation before it was too late.

I ordered one of the Kanaks to take the helm, and went over to Jack Lewis. Unlike my *papa tru*, who had been to war and seen men all around him blasted to pieces as the *Christian VIII* headed for disaster, I'd never seen a human being die. I'd seen men fall overboard and disappear into the sea, but that was different. Swallowed up by the waves, they were already lost from view by the time they began that lonely journey into the depths. They didn't die in front of your eyes. They just left your field of vision.

Jack Lewis was about to die, I was certain of it. Just as I was certain that now, as he lay on the deck like the statue of a deity toppled from its plinth, his stony facade would crack and reveal the naked human being inside. Bleeding from his wound, he'd soon be exposed as nothing more than a man, just like James Cook in Kealakekua Bay.

But as he stared at me, I realised that I'd been wrong to think that. Jack Lewis might be a toppled god, but he was still a god. There was no fear in his eyes and I didn't know why I ever thought I'd see it. Was there grief, then, at all he'd have to bid farewell to? Or regret, for all he wouldn't achieve? Or was there just pure rage?

I'd seen him lose his self-control when he was forced to use his precious pearls as bullets. Was that how he viewed his own death? As the waste of a pearl?

I was young and I'd never given my own death a second thought. Can the feelings prompted by another's death provide a forewarning of what you'll experience when you draw your own last breath? I was about to find out.

'Fetch the whisky.' He had to swallow between each word, but Jack Lewis's voice still retained its old authority. He patted the deck with a feeble hand as though inviting me for a final drink in his cabin. 'And Jim.' I stared at him. 'Are you deaf?'

Perplexed, I shook my head and went to his cabin to carry out his order. Unwrapping the ghastly head from its cloth, I placed it next to Lewis. Then I opened the whisky and poured some into my palm. I'd never treated a gunshot wound before, but I vaguely recalled that you cleaned them with alcohol.

'What do you think you're doing?' Jack Lewis snarled.

'I'm going to wash your wound.'

'My wound!' he exclaimed. 'My wound isn't thirsty. I am. Fetch two glasses.'

When I returned with the glasses, Jack Lewis was scrutinising Jim, as though he'd just asked him a question and was now awaiting the reply.

The Kanaks stood rooted to the spot in the middle of the deck. The helmsman, too, had let go of the wheel: I shouted at him and he returned to his post. But he kept turning round. It wasn't the dying captain his eyes kept roaming towards, but the shrunken head in his hands.

'Is this wise?' I said to Jack Lewis.

'That's none of your business.' His voice was thick with contempt. 'Of course, it's bloody stupid to show a shrunken head to a bunch of cannibals whose blood's just been roused. But I'll be gone in a moment. And then it's your problem, not mine.'

A gurgling noise came from his chest, and he bared his teeth in a grimace that might have been a smile.

'Fill up the glasses. Let's toast our onward journey. Mine's to the unknown. And yours will be as the newly fledged captain of a cannibal ship.'

I poured and passed him the glass, but he didn't have the strength to hold it: I had to support his head and raise the glass to his lips. He drained its contents with a groan, but it was impossible to tell whether it was from pleasure or pain.

'The free men,' I said. 'I want you to tell me about the free men.'

'The free men were just like Jim here.'

'So they were a commodity?'

'Yes,' Jack Lewis said, and his eyes took on a remote expression as though the conversation didn't interest him and his journey into the unknown had already started. I was going to have to hurry.

'But what was the deal about?'

'Grains of sand,' he whispered. 'Pebbles. Toys for children.'

His head slumped to one side and his eyes closed, as if he were falling asleep. For a moment I feared that he had died. Then he opened his eyes and looked at me.

'We despise the natives because they allow themselves to be mesmerised by glass baubles. I don't know what they must think of us. We'll kill over a grain of sand covered in oyster-scum.'

'What did you give them in return for the pearls?'

'I paid with the free men.'

'So they weren't free. They were your prisoners.'

'No,' Jack Lewis said and shook his head; again his shattered chest gurgled. 'You still haven't got it. They weren't my prisoners. They were my students.'

'You're right. I still haven't got it. I think you've been telling me a pack of lies.'

'Listen to me.' Jack Lewis was still lying with one cheek against the deck. When he glanced up at me again it was with a teasing look that was hard to associate with a dying man. 'The savages have no concept of freedom. They're free, but they don't know it. So before they can learn to value their freedom, they must first lose it.'

'And so you trapped them in the hold?'

Jack Lewis grimaced, but whether it was in response to my slow wits or because he was trying to smile again, I couldn't decide.

'No, I didn't trap them in the hold. I merely left them to their own fear. I made sure they never saw the light of day, and in the dark they conjured up all sorts of ideas about the terrible fate that was waiting for them. When I opened the hatch and allowed the daylight in, their education was complete. They understood instantly what freedom was, and they grabbed it.'

'What's that got to do with the pearls?'

'The answer lies with the *Morning Star*,' Jack Lewis said. 'She was a blackbirder, a slave ship. She foundered and the slaves in the hold rebelled, killed the crew and took over the island, which was uninhabited. There were women and children among them, so as far as they were concerned they weren't stranded on a desert island.

They'd been given a whole new world where they could start over. Their paradise was only missing one thing, and that's where I entered the scene.'

His face lit up in triumph, and it suddenly dawned on me why he was confiding all this to me. He was so proud of his cruelty that he couldn't bear the thought of dying with it unwitnessed. He'd turned his entire life into a mystery, but now he needed someone to know the full extent of a crime that he personally regarded as final proof – not of his cunning so much as his own unique insight into the human mind.

He turned ugly in his triumph, and I let my eyes slide towards James Cook, with his flared nostrils and stitched-up eyelids. In that moment, I preferred his horribly distorted face to Jack Lewis's. Yet I had to continue with my questioning. Even if I feared that by listening I might end up complicit in his crimes, I couldn't stop myself. I had to know the secret of the free men.

'So what were the savages missing in their paradise?' I asked.

'A change of diet,' Jack Lewis replied, and his face contorted in a terrible grimace, which I took to be the dying man's attempt at laughter. The sound quickly curdled into a hollow, gurgling cough. He seemed to be choking, and blood leaked from his cracked, narrow lips. Slowly I realised what he'd said. My disgust must have been obvious.

'They're cannibals, you see,' he explained, as though to a child.

'So you sell human flesh,' I said. Again I was looking at Jim.

'The world isn't a straightforward place,' Jack Lewis said. 'I don't sell human flesh. I sell the opportunity for victory. That's what's lacking in paradise, you understand. In every paradise. That's the flaw in its construction. The serpent isn't the enemy; he's just the tempter. I'm thinking of a real enemy, whom you have to fight or else be vanquished. I'm thinking of the chance to test yourself in battle, to win or die. That was the opportunity I gave those damned cannibals: not a shipload of human flesh, but a chance to prove their worth. For God's sake. They're savages. And they're men. They can't live unless they fight. I visited them once a year. I offered free men the opportunity to escape. And who won the battle once they'd swum ashore was none of my business.'

He fell silent, and again, for a moment I thought that he'd died. His eyes were closed.

'And then they discovered a new and better enemy,' I said out loud, but I was talking to myself as much as to him.

Jack Lewis opened up his eyes and gave me a reproachful look, as though I'd just reminded him of something unpleasant.

'Some idiot sold them guns and ruined my business.' He snarled and attempted to spit on the deck, but what came out was blood. 'I had a good operation running there. It could have carried on for years. They got someone they could fight, and kill, and eat. And I got the pearls. And then that bastard turns up.'

'Who?' I asked.

'None of your business.' He spat more blood. 'Get me another glass.'

I poured him another whisky and held it to his lips. He coughed and the liquid trickled down his lower lip and mingled with the blood, which was now flowing in a constant stream. He sighed.

'You'll inherit all this. A bag of pearls and a ship. A good start for a young sailor. More than you deserve.'

I didn't know what to say. I didn't want to take charge of this ship, which regardless of what her owner said was nothing but a blackbirder. Nor would I touch the pearls. Their pink sheen reminded me not of grains of sand but dried blood.

I said nothing. Though I had no respect for Jack Lewis, I respected the hole in his chest. He was dying, and you owe the dying your attention.

'Paradise,' he mumbled. 'A paradise complete with everything, including enemies, ready to kill you.' He glanced at the Kanaks and bared his yellow teeth. Blood was seeping out between them. 'The moment your back's turned, they'll stick a knife in it. They can see me lying here. And they've met Jim. If they didn't know it before, they know it now: white men can die, too.'

Jack Lewis closed his eyes again and sighed. He didn't move, and after a while I realised that he was never going to open them again. Despite those last words of warning, which echoed in my ears, there was no way that I could keep his death a secret from the Kanaks.

I couldn't keep him on board, so I went down to his cabin to look for something to wrap his body in before surrendering it to the sea. A flag was what I had in mind, but I couldn't find one, so I took an unused strip of canvas. His shirt front was soaked with blood, but I had no way of sending him overboard in clean clothes, and no urge to touch his body sticky with blood. So there he lay, wrapped in canvas bound by a piece of rope. A life had ended – though hardly a beautiful one, in my opinion. I didn't know much about Jack Lewis, but I knew enough not to mourn his passing.

I summoned the Kanaks, and together we eased Jack Lewis over the rail. He bobbed up and down in our wake for a while. And then he sank. No sharks circled his body before it went under. He'd regarded his fellow human beings as no more than meat on a butcher's slab, and I had no idea if he'd been a Christian, but I did him the honour of folding my hands and reciting the Lord's Prayer.

I said the words in Danish. The Kanaks watched in silence. When they saw me fold my hands, they folded theirs too. I interpreted this as a gesture of respect, towards me as much as the deceased. I was their captain now. What they thought beyond that, I had no clue. Their dark, blue-tattooed faces gave nothing away. Was this the start of another Kealakekua Bay? Would the fate that Jack Lewis escaped befall me instead? Would they tear me to pieces, eat my heart and smoke my head over an open fire? I wanted to hide in my cabin while I went through my options, but I felt that if I entered its protective darkness I'd never emerge again for fear they'd be waiting outside the door with their knives.

So instead I took the wheel.

I REALISED THAT THE FIRST THING I HAD TO DO WAS OVERCOME MY fear of the Kanaks, which Jack Lewis had planted so cleverly. As long as I was in thrall to it, Lewis was still on board and in control. I had to issue my own orders and assume they'd be executed. I needed to enter my cabin without dreading an ambush and go to sleep safe in the knowledge that I'd wake up again. In short, I had to do what men have done on ships for thousands of years: I had to be the captain.

But I was young and I'd never commanded a ship before. I was alone with four Kanaks, one of them out of action, and we were in the middle of the Pacific Ocean. I knew very little about the destination we'd been headed for, and I was aware that even if I skippered the *Flying Scud* to a safe haven, that wouldn't solve my problems. Who would believe my story?

I was still weighing up my prospects when I happened to look at the deck. There lay the shrunken head of James Cook, just where it had been when Jack Lewis bade it farewell. I steadied my voice and ordered one of the Kanaks to take the wheel. Then I picked up the shrunken head, carried it down to the cabin and settled it on Jack Lewis's berth.

I can't explain why I didn't throw it overboard immediately, because I had no desire to keep it or ever clap eyes on it again. But when I cupped it in my hands and gazed out over the shimmering sea, something held me back. I'd unwrapped the head for Jack Lewis when he'd asked to see it for the final time, but I'd been so preoccupied by his imminent death that I forgot I was handling the horrifying remains of a human being.

Now I became more conscious of the feel of James Cook's leathery skin and straw-dry hair, and the physical contact seemed to link me to the man he'd been before he'd been shrunk into a symbol of barbarism. I could ease my captain's dead body over the rail. But I couldn't do the same to James Cook.

It wasn't just because Jack Lewis had told me Jim's true identity. Did I believe him? Yes and no. But ultimately it made no difference: the whole thing seemed completely unreal anyway. If this was indeed the head of James Cook, it should probably be returned to England – though I had no idea what the people of England would do with it. Keep its existence a secret because the whole business was somehow embarrassing? Hold a ceremony to lay it to rest? Even provide it with its own coffin, perhaps? But how many times can you bury a man? What if a foot were to turn up some day? Would the funeral have to be staged a second time?

Naming this shrunken head Jim in the first place had seemed a malicious joke. But now the joke involved James Cook too. I thought it best to let him rest in peace, but his head was still here, the last vestige of a man who'd suffered a horrific death. I couldn't just toss it overboard like some broken object or a piece of meat that had started to smell.

It was at that point that I understood the difference between me and Jack Lewis. To Lewis, Jim was a shrunken head. To me, he was a human being.

I've often wondered whether Jim appeared more human to me than the Kanaks, whose individual features were hidden in the unfathomable darkness of the blue tattoos etched across their faces. I looked for something human in their gaze, but I found nothing but foreignness, as if their eyes were also tattoos. I never heard Jack Lewis talk to them, and I was never to do so either. I gave my orders and they carried them out. When I bandaged the wounded Kanak, I noticed he was the one with the missing ear. He looked away when I tried to clean his wound, and continued to look away while I bandaged it. A line lay between us and it was never crossed. But as the days passed, my fear of them faded. The ship told us who we were: I was the captain, they were the crew, and the trade wind that always came from the same direction and blew with the same strength assured us every day that all was as it should be.

It was under these circumstances that I started behaving in a way that I realised was strange. I started talking to Jim. I'd go down to the cabin, light the whale-oil lamp and unwrap him from his cloth.

Then I'd place him on the table in front of me, where the flickering light from the lamp lent his face an attentive expression. I could feel him concentrating, behind his stitched-up eyelids. But he never once talked back to me. And I was glad of that. It would have been ultimate proof that I had lost my mind.

I'd place the bag of pearls in front of him and take them out, one by one, to show him. Then I'd ask him if he thought I ought to keep them.

My first impulse had been to throw them into the sea after Jack Lewis's body. Indeed, at times I regretted that I hadn't done so right in front of him, while he still breathed. That missed moment might have represented some sort of victory over him and the amorality he clearly believed he'd infected me with. But I'd hesitated too long. One moment had turned into several, and now I kept the pearls hidden next to Jim. Before long I would probably tuck the bag under my shirt and start guarding it with my life, giving the Kanaks a good reason for taking both from me. Wouldn't they know the value of pearls and want some of what the money could buy – freedom especially?

I felt that I was holding my entire future in my hands when I felt the weight of the swollen bag. I didn't even need the *Flying Scud*. I could buy my own ship. I could buy three ships, become a shipowner and have my own house. Perhaps even the big, beautiful house built after the fire in Øvre Strandstræde, across from the vicarage. In my imagination I started peopling this house with a wife and children: yes, servants, even. I saw my future wife in a violet dress, picking roses in the garden.

I never described these fantasies to Jim. Instead, I asked him to be my judge. He must make the decision for me. It wasn't the suffering he had endured before he became a shrunken head that qualified him. Rather, it was his silence. I could put any reply I wanted into his mouth.

'So, Jim,' I'd say in the twilight of the cabin, 'should I keep the pearls? What do you think?'

Jim never said yes or no. He just looked at me through his stitched eyelids, and I felt that the answers to all my questions were hidden behind them.

* * *

I began thinking a lot about my *papa tru*. I'd never asked him for advice and he'd never given me any. We'd parted far too early for that. But now I was looking for him. That was my mission in the Pacific: to find my missing *papa tru*. But what did I want from him, and what would I do when I found him? Ask him for some good advice? Rebuild our lost relationship? The last time I saw him, I was a child. Now I was an adult and I couldn't turn the clock back. So what did I want to do? Show him that I could stand on my own two feet? Had I looked for him across half the world just to prove to him how easily I could manage without him?

I realised that I'd never thought past the moment when I stood face-to-face with him again. I was a skilled sailor. I'd crossed the great oceans, but when it came to this, I felt like a newcomer to the world – not because I didn't know its busy, overcrowded ports, its palm-fringed coasts and wind-lashed rocks, but because I understood so little of my own soul. I could navigate from a chart; I could determine my position using a sextant. I was in an unknown place in the Pacific on a ship with no captain and I could still find my way. But I had no way of mapping my own mind or the course of my life.

I emptied Jack Lewis's cupboard of bottles and went on deck to throw them overboard. I didn't open any of them – not even the mysterious one with the white fluid in which the outline of a dark shape could sometimes be seen – before chucking them into the water. The doors Jack Lewis had opened to me had led only to rooms filled with horrors. I watched the bottles fall astern and disappear beneath the waves.

I knew that I ought to have thrown out Jim as well. But he continued to keep me company. And so did the pearls.

The days passed. I fantasised about my future. I regarded the pearls at one moment as an unexpected stroke of good fortune, and at the next as a curse that would make me an accomplice in Jack Lewis's crimes, should I ever sell them.

All the while we held our course for Samoa.

As long as Jim didn't answer me, I felt I was still free. Nothing had been decided yet. I'd stopped time, and I caught myself wishing that I could remain for ever in this fuzzy inner world that I'd created with Jim in the twilit cabin, a world where dreams could come true and there was no price to pay for them. I forgot where I really was.

I spent most hours of the day alone, but my solitude was no burden. I took my meals in the cabin while the Kanaks ate on deck. They prepared the food: rice and steamed taro. From time to time they'd throw a line over the rail and catch a yellowfin tuna.

I appeared on deck only to correct the course and adjust the spread of the canvas.

After a week the trade wind died down. It disappeared one evening with the sun, which sank into the horizon like a red ball while the clouds fanned out on all sides.

I took that as a bad omen and prepared for a hurricane, but when the next day dawned, the opposite confronted us. The sea was dead calm, as if a heavy lid had been pressed on top of it. The overwhelming heat suggested that a thunderstorm was approaching, but the sky was as blue as a gas flame, and no menacing clouds loomed on the horizon.

I was still convinced that something was about to happen, but my imagination stretched no further than my fears of an imminent hurricane.

The days passed and we stayed put. The sails hung slack and we rigged an awning amidships to provide shade. For a while I had to part from Jim because it was too hot to sleep in the stagnant air of the cabin and I didn't want to bring him up on deck with me. Should I leave the pearls down there too?

The dark thoughts I'd nursed down in the cabin wouldn't leave me. I began carrying the leather purse – which contained my entire future – under my shirt, against my bare chest. But it clung to my body in the heat, which had grown so oppressive that I struggled to breathe; I felt as though a gauze bandage gagged my mouth. So I locked the pearls in the cabin with Jim and went barechested. From time to time I'd lower a bucket into the sea and pour lukewarm salt water over my body, but neither that nor the arrival of night brought any relief from the heat.

One night, unable to sleep, I headed for the deck. The Kanaks had attached hammocks to the rigging and were murmuring quietly. For the first time my loneliness felt like a burden, but I knew it would be a sign of weakness to approach them or try to strike up a conversation.

We'd secured the wheel. There was no course to stick to. With no current on which to hitch a ride, we weren't going anywhere. I gazed up at the sky. There were still no clouds, and the twinkling of the stars had grown faint, as if they'd given up signalling to us. I understood then how utterly cut off we were from the rest of the world. The *Flying Scud* was like a planet torn from its orbit and about to vanish into the deepest, darkest corner of the universe.

A groan came from one of the hammocks. I stepped closer. It was the Kanak with the bandaged shoulder. His wound had been healing over the past few days. Did his groaning mean that the fever had returned and that the wound had become infected? I knew what an infection looked like, but I had no idea how to treat it, apart from the primitive method of regularly pouring whisky over it. It was too dark to do anything, so I decided to wait until morning.

I didn't sleep that night; it was too hot, and I felt restless and irritable. Not because this dead calm had brought our voyage to an unexpected halt and cut us off from the world, but because it had severed me from something far more important: the interior world of the cabin, where I ran the pearls through my fingers and chatted to Jim on the table in front of me. That was where my life had been unfolding – and now it was closed to me.

I examined the Kanak's shoulder the following day. There were yellow stains on the white bandage and pus oozed from the gash. It had almost closed, but its edges were red and swollen. I cleansed it as well as I could. The Kanak's blue face stayed passive, but his shoulder twitched every time I touched the swollen wound. So I poured whisky over it and left it to his fellow Kanaks to change the bandage. I knew they fiddled with his wound, too. They had their own medicines, which I wasn't going to interfere with: I already doubted the value of my own methods.

The Kanak's infection gave me the frightening impression that the stagnant air around us was somehow poisoned. We were in the middle of the sea, yet it felt as though a dense jungle and the toxic breath of rotting plants surrounded us. Was I the only man here who felt that a giant hand was squeezing his chest?

I watched the Kanaks. Their movements, too, seemed to have

become more sluggish. Were they suffocating, like me? Did this calm, which had nailed us to the vast floor of the ocean, sit on them, too, like a dead weight? Were anxious questions beginning to surface in the dark eyes behind the blue masks? Were superstitious terrors rising in them like bubbles from the bottom of a stale swamp, demanding some explanation for our cursed immobility? And might their answer be me, the stranger, who didn't belong among them and who could therefore be used as ransom in the face of the inexplicable?

We cast lines, but no fish bit. Again I got the feeling that all life around us had vanished. The depths of the sea had become just as still as its surface. It wasn't the fear of sharks which prevented me from seeking refreshment in a swim. It was the notion that the sea would suck me down the moment I came into contact with it and I'd disappear into its darkness for ever.

On the fourth day I checked our provisions. We had half a sack of taro roots and a few kilos of rice left. I wasn't afraid we would starve, for I had enough common sense left to expect that the sea would, at some point, give up some of its riches and we would land a tuna. Our big problem was fresh water. We hadn't picked up sufficient supplies on the island and we were about to run out. A good rainfall would have fulfilled our needs, but the sky remained mercilessly blue. I had to ration the water, but I feared that this in itself might trigger a mutiny. So I decided that from now on we'd all eat our meals together on the deck: that way the Kanaks could see that everyone received the same amount of water.

We weren't equals, nor should we be. A ship's written and unwritten laws must be obeyed. But we had to be equal in our sufferings; otherwise we'd never get through them together. Slowly it began to dawn on me that, for a newly fledged captain, being becalmed like this could prove a far greater challenge than any storm.

Every day we continued to cast our lines but caught nothing. The fish shunned our ship, and I could see a perplexed look on the faces of the experienced Kanaks, who'd spent their entire lives on these waters. We were in the middle of the sea and there wasn't a single fish to be had! Were we cursed?

I handed out one mug of water to each man at every meal. One day I peered into the last water barrel and saw that it was close to empty: enough for two more days, at most. Our only hope was that the trade wind would start to blow and bring rain with it.

On the seventh day, the water ran out. Soft moans came from the hammock where the wounded Kanak was drifting in and out of his fever. No more relief came to his cracked lips, and his eyes rolled upward, as if he hoped to escape via the rigging. When he closed them again, he carried on whimpering. No other sound broke the silence on board. It was at once a sign of life and an omen of the fate that awaited us.

THE SECOND DAY AFTER THE WATER RAN OUT, WE WERE EATING OUR taro roots, which we'd boiled in salt water, when suddenly one of the Kanaks pointed at the horizon. I looked up and saw a cloud. It hung low above the water, and it was moving rapidly and oddly, like steam coming from a boiling pot, except that it didn't rise like steam, but spread in all directions at once, like the flocks of migrating starlings that gather in autumn above the fields outside Marstal. Sunlight shone right through this cloud, which was slowly approaching us, though there was still no wind. It seemed to pulsate, as if a whirlwind churned inside it, shaking the leaves of a dense forest.

Then the cloud was upon us, and fleetingly we felt as though we were being showered with the withered leaves of an autumn forest. Then I realised that it wasn't dead foliage, but living creatures whirling around us, fluttering silky yellow wings. We were at the centre of a vast swarm of butterflies.

There had to be millions of them. A storm, raging far away from the tyrannical calm in which we found ourselves, must have swept them off an island and out to sea. They must have been seeking land – and thought they'd found it on our doomed ship. They settled everywhere, on the ship's rigging and on every single one of its countless ropes, covering the slack sails and transforming them into bright tapestries of yellow. Within minutes this living breathing mass of exhausted insects had changed the *Flying Scud* beyond recognition.

And the butterflies settled on us, too, apparently unable to distinguish between wood, rope, canvas and human skin. Sharing our desperate thirst, they stuck their tiny prosboces all over our skin, to suck the sweat from it. It wasn't painful like a bee sting or a mosquito bite, but it was soon followed by an unbearable, prickling itch, which drove us out of our minds. The moment we relaxed, the creatures descended on us again in droves, seeking the moist corners of our lips and eyes, which we had to squeeze shut for protection. If we opened our mouths to scare them off with an angry roar, they instantly clung to our teeth, covering our tongues and tickling our palates with their fluttering wings.

We staggered around, blind and hacking, lashing out at them, but we were their last chance and nothing was going to keep them off. We smashed them against our cheeks, foreheads and eyebrows, but they kept coming at us, even though they were flying to their doom. I think we'd all willingly have jumped in the sea to escape them, had the water around the ship not been swarming with them. The *Flying Scud* sat like a coffin on a church floor littered with flowers.

When I briefly opened an eye just a crack to find my way to the rail, I caught sight of one of the Kanaks, his blue face and head half covered in butterflies. For a moment I forgot the danger and let myself be lulled by the lovely sight of his beautifully rounded blue skull clad in lemony insects slowly flapping their half-open wings, his dark eyes staring out from behind those shining fans. But unlike me, he seemed completely at ease. Whether this was simply because he'd accepted and surrendered to his fate, I never discovered, for the next moment I was hit in the face by a slosh of water: a quick-witted Kanak had lowered a bucket into the sea and started dousing himself and the rest of us. We followed suit and it was only then that we succeeded in ridding ourselves of the fluttering parasites.

For a while after that, the butterflies continued landing on our faces and naked torsos searching for moisture, until finally they gave up. We collapsed on the deck, which now was covered with a sticky mess of trampled and drowned butterflies. It was as if every living thing on board the ship had surrendered to the same lethargy.

I happened to glance at the hammock where the wounded Kanak lay. In his exhausted state he'd been defenceless, and now he was buried beneath a vibrating mountain of paper-thin wings. We took him the bucket, poured water over him and scraped handfuls of insects off his skin, not even knowing if he was alive underneath. He'd done the only sensible thing he could, which was to bury his face in his arms, and this was how we found him. His chest was heaving. He was still breathing.

We cleared a space for him on deck and lay him down. I fetched a sheet for him from my cabin, and brought clean shirts for the rest of us. On the ladder and the bulkhead and the floor of the tiny corridor in front of the cabin door, butterflies lay in heavy drifts: I had to brush them off the door handle to get in. As I did so, others immediately took off from the bulkhead to swarm into the new, unclaimed territory. Jim lay in the middle of the table just as I'd left him. They'd settled on his white hair, and it seemed, as they decked him with their beautiful wings, that they were paying some kind of tribute to him – though he was the one human here who could offer them nothing. But at least he was indifferent to their intrusion and didn't beat them off.

I left Jim and returned to the deck, where I rid myself of the new layer of butterflies that had settled on my face in the cabin. Then we – the captain and his crew – sat down together. We were all wearing shirts I'd taken from Lewis's drawers and my own sea chest.

We stayed on deck for the rest of the day and slept there the following night. The butterflies no longer stirred. There was no more water and we'd eaten the last taro roots. The world was exhausted not just of wind, but of everything. Only us and a million butter-flies were left. Everything else had died. The sea had stopped breathing and we were resting our heads on its lifeless breast. Soon our hearts would stop too.

I'm not superstitious, and I don't know whether the Kanaks are. Most likely they are, though what they'd call faith, we'd call super-stition. Yet I felt that the dead calm that smothered us was some kind of punishment – not for something Jack Lewis had done (because if there's a judge in the hereafter, which I doubt, then Jack Lewis was now facing him) but for a crime that was mine.

Chance had made me captain of the *Flying Scud*. I was unpre-pared and I was young, but that was no excuse. A captain is a captain, and I'd failed as one.

I'd sat in the cabin with Jim and a bag full of pearls, thinking about myself rather than my crew. If the Kanaks even crossed my mind, it was only because I feared that they'd stand in the way of my plans.

But what should I have done? I couldn't command the wind and make it obey my orders. So how could I be responsible for the calm that had descended on us like a curse?

It must have been fever, and thirst, and the oppressive heat, and the dying butterflies, and the sight of the leaden lid of the sea, and the gas-flame blue of the sky by day, and the growing remoteness of the stars at night, that had affected my brain and driven my thoughts down this mad path.

Does anyone fully understand nature? Why does the wind suddenly stop blowing?

Could it be that nature doesn't care whether we live or die?

It seems so much less frightening to blame yourself.

I stood up, went down to the cabin, grabbed the bag of pearls, returned to the deck and hurled it as far out to sea as my diminished strength allowed.

I believed this was the only way I could atone for my guilt and finally free myself from Jack Lewis, because I knew he was still on board. I'd been travelling with shadows and living in a world of ghosts. Superstitious as it was, I feel to this day that my action made complete sense. When my hands were finally empty of something I'd never had any claim to, and my mind was liberated from frivolous dreams, I'd earned the right to call myself a captain. Now I remembered a captain's honour and his only duty: to bring his crew back alive.

I'd thrown all my dreams of the future overboard, and I had only one wish left: that a storm would come and tear us loose from the becalmment we sat trapped in as if in hardened lava.

I stayed at the rail, scouting across the sea, and its surface stayed unchanged. I turned to look at the Kanaks, slumped on the deck with their wounded friend prone between them. They gazed at their hands and dozed in the oppressive heat.

I don't know if they saw me throw the pearls overboard, but if they did, they must have thought that I was making a sacrifice to a god not much different from theirs.

But I hadn't done it to appease any god. I'd done it for myself, to reaffirm my sense of duty.

The sun set just as it had every evening since the dead calm gripped us. That first night it had looked like a red bullet heading for my heart. Now it was even darker – not like blood, but like the bullet-hole itself. The whole world was prey, killed by an unknown hunter.

I was woken by a crackling sound. At first, still surfacing from sleep, I guessed fire had broken out on board, the heat having caused the

175

Flying Scud to ignite spontaneously. Then I realised that it wasn't the crackling of dry wood ablaze but something slamming hard on the awning stretched above us. I raised myself on my elbow and felt a puff of air on my face. The wind was rising. And it was bringing rain.

I stood by the rail and opened my mouth. Cold, heavy drops of water fell onto my face. They hit my shoulders and naked chest and a shudder passed through me, as if everything inside me was returning to life.

I heard movement behind me and turned round. The Kanaks came over, supporting their wounded comrade. Together we stood along the rail and let the rain soak us. I'd never known real thirst before, and I've never since felt grateful the way I did when those first drops of rain wetted my lips. I snapped at the air for more, and for a moment I forgot who I was.

The sea began to stir and when the first waves lapped tentatively against the side of the ship, she reacted with a slight swaying, as if she had been long awaiting an invitation to start moving again. The first wave broke, its top glowing white in the moonlight and the gaff above us flapped heavily in the wind. A storm was brewing.

We bustled about preparing the ship. The awning was sagging beneath the weight of the rainwater that had already collected in it: before we took it down, we filled our barrels. Our throats were no longer parched, but we hadn't eaten for days and as we worked it was clear how weak we'd become. But no matter: not even the prospect of facing a storm with no provisions could dampen our joy at the return of the wind and the rain. Every time I yelled my orders through the resurrected wind that howled in the rigging, the Kanaks replied with the only words I ever heard them say in English: 'Aye aye, Sir!' like a chorus responding to a soloist.

It might sound strange – even reckless – to say that we sailed into the storm with exhilaration, but there's no other word to describe our mood as, utterly drenched, we watched the waves toss around us, sending up huge sheets of flying foam that merged sea and sky. We'd double-roped the flying jib, but soon we had to drop all but the foresail to prevent the mast and rigging from going overboard. I lashed myself to the wheel as the vast waves thundered over us, clearing the deck from bow to stern of anything that wasn't strapped down. I stayed there for two days. I could have ordered one of the Kanaks to relieve me every four hours, but I didn't. Not because I didn't trust them, but because I had something to prove to myself. I think they understood that.

They'd stretched ropes across the deck to cling to when they moved around the ship, but most of the time they were lashed in place like me. They'd tied the wounded man to the rigging where the waves couldn't reach him, and from time to time they'd climb up with a mug of water to wet his lips. One of them brought me water too.

When a wave washed a tuna fish onto the deck, I took it as a sign. Before, the fish had stayed away; now they came to us. The sea was generous. In a brief break between two waves, one of the Kanaks hurled himself at the fish, slashed it with his knife, and brought me a hunk of live meat that still trembled in his hand.

During the two days the storm lasted, I remained in a state of undiminished rapture. I stayed on my feet with the wheel in my hands, tied to my post by the rope. If I was tired, I never noticed.

Finally, on the third day, the wind died down, so I untied the rope and allowed myself to be relieved. For a little while I just stood swaying on the deck – until suddenly exhaustion overwhelmed me. I thought I'd faint, and I had to return to the wheel to support myself, fixing my eyes on the deck as I tried to regain my balance.

When I looked up again, the Kanaks had formed a circle around me. The wounded Kanak had come down from the rigging and was standing unsupported, as if his stay up there had done him good. I held out my hand. They stared at it. Then they stuck out theirs too, and one by one we shook hands. They didn't speak, and no smiles lit the darkness of their faces. They just shook my hand. I don't know whether it was something they'd learned from white men or a gesture they also use among themselves. But I knew what it meant at that moment. We'd sealed a pact. These were sailors, not savages.

Below deck I lay down in Jack Lewis's berth. I felt I'd earned the right to it. It wasn't until the next morning that I discovered Jim was missing. I remembered that I'd left him on the table – but now he was gone. I looked for him in the bottom berth and the locked cabinet, but he was nowhere to be found. It wasn't until I crawled around on the floor that he reappeared. He'd rolled into a corner, and somehow finding him in that humble position on the not very clean floor stripped him of the horror that had both attracted and repelled me. I wiped the dust from his hair, wrapped him in his frayed cloth and locked him in the cabinet.

Not for one moment did I consider sending him off the same way as the pearls. He was no longer a threat. Jim was a witness to the darkness in Jack Lewis. But I'd been there, too, and I'd come back.

IT TOOK US A WEEK TO REACH SAMOA, BUT DURING THAT WHOLE time I never thought about the purpose of my journey: I was too busy with my duties as a captain. I measured the height of the sun, plotted our course, kept an eye on the sails and issued my orders. We had plenty of water and we lived on fish. We saw no other ships, and the trade wind blew constantly from the same direction.

When I stood in the bow and watched the never-ending break of waves and the white foam-flecks glinting like pearls spilling onto a stone floor, I remembered Jack Lewis's words: a young man should travel the whole sea and every island in it. But when my gaze slid astern towards the white stripe of the wake sparkling in the sunlight, it struck me that it was a kind of chain, and I knew that the moment I became captain of the *Flying Scud* I was free but at the same time bound.

The ocean was so infinitely vast. It could take you anywhere, and yet it shackled you.

The port of Apia is shaped like a bottleneck: a big bay encircled by two peninsulas. The western one is called Mulinuu, the eastern one Matautu. Beyond that lies a reef that looks a bit like the breakwater around Marstal. Here the thunder of the surf is so loud that it's difficult to hear yourself speak: even five kilometres away, high in the green mountains that soar up behind Apia, you can hear the waves roar. And no one in Apia will call a captain a bad sailor if he wrecks his ship trying to pass through the gap in the reef during a storm, because it's regarded as well-nigh impossible. Instead they'll call him irresponsible or ignorant, for everyone knows that in foul weather, the open ocean is a safer bet than their shelterless bay in an oncoming wind.

But I knew nothing of this when I bent over the chart in Captain Lewis's cabin. To me, Apia was no more than a name on a map.

But since that time, I've learned that a shipwreck can be a welcome thing, if the ship's loss saves a man's honour.

And as we neared Apia, my honour was very much on my mind. How could I ever explain the way I'd ended up as captain of the notorious *Flying Scud*? Who'd believe my story about the free men in the hold, the cannibals from the *Morning Star*, the death of Jack Lewis and the leather bag of pearls thrown overboard?

Yet I was bound to this ship, for I could not reach my destination without her. Jack Lewis and I were inseparable. He'd plotted the course and I could do nothing but follow it. From now on, regardless of whether people saw me as his killer or his accomplice, my reputation would be connected to his.

I'd considered changing course, but I wasn't responsible for myself alone. And where else would we go? We couldn't subsist on fish alone, trusting the weather gods for our supplies of water. I felt that my fate was already cast – and inescapable. I had only one thing left to hold on to: my duty as a captain. I had to guide the ship and its crew to safe harbour.

But in making my calculations, I'd forgotten one factor: the sea.

Every sailor knows this bitter feeling: the coast is near, but you know you'll never reach it. Is there anything more heartbreaking than drowning in sight of land? Is there a single one of us who hasn't at least once felt haunted by the fear of slipping away within sight of a safe haven?

I imagine that drowning is less devastating when a grey, raging sea has wiped out the horizon completely. But to close your eyes for the last time on something precious – a hope, a hand reaching out for you – that must be the worst. Even terror needs a yardstick, and surely the yardstick for the unknown is the known?

We could see land. The green mountains of Samoa appeared on the horizon just as the gale blew in at us – as though it had been lurking behind the island, awaiting our arrival. We held out for twenty-four hours. One moment we'd be flung to the top of a mountainous wave, and we'd get a view of Samoa; the next, another wave would plunge our bow underwater, and it would be just us and the sea again. We never came any closer to our destination, but nor were we dragged any further away. Then a huge wave came and knocked the ship onto her beam ends, and the shrouds and stays that had strained to support the mast gave way with a groan, sending both mast and the rigging tumbling down. It felt as if one of my own limbs had been partially severed and now dangled from my body by a few sinews.

And yet I still believe we could have ridden out the storm. I wasn't short of self-confidence on that deck. But I realised that the real threat to our survival came not from our crippled ship so much as our own fatigue. We were still weak and exhausted from our recent ordeal, and in that state, we were no match for the storm. We had to get to land.

Even though I'd never called at Apia and didn't know the dangers of trying to force the small gap in the reef during a storm, I was aware of exposing all of us to considerable risk. What if we struck the reef and sank? We'd lost our launch during the battle with the natives in the lagoon. Were we about to drown so close to our destination?

I told the Kanaks to chop the mast into pieces and lash them to the yards, to make a makeshift raft that could carry us the final distance across the bay into Apia, in case we failed in our attempt to pass the reef. Meanwhile I turned the *Flying Scud* so that she lay cross-wind – a manoeuvre fully as risky as anything else we were about to do. If a huge wave had crashed on top of us at that moment, that would have been it. We all knew our lives were at stake.

The Kanaks worked hard, concentrating on their axes, and soon the raft was secured to the deck. I'd long since packed my sea chest with my father's boots and Jim: ordering the Kanaks to tie it to the raft, I straightened up the ship and steered towards the reef.

From the crest of a wave I caught sight of Samoa again, beneath a stormy sky of poisonous purple. The sun had broken through above the island's emerald mountains, suddenly lighting them up – but I can't say this heartened me. Rather, it gave me the feeling that the elements were mocking us and jeering at our vain wish to survive.

As I clasped the helm, I felt the ocean's power as before: the wheel jerked in my hands as if it were arm-wrestling me, while the waves drove the ship in the direction opposite to its course. Suddenly I felt a new and violent force seize the vessel. It was the current, taking our side against the storm and sucking us straight into the bottleneck of the bay. The wheel shook again. And in that moment I lost control of it. Or of myself.

Had I let my guard down? Did I fail in my responsibility? I can't answer that question, and it haunts me still.

A massive wave seized us and flung us at the reef, making the entire ship shudder and flinging the last mast overboard. I found myself with my back against a rail, my shoulder and arm in such pain I thought I'd broken them. Then a second wave pounded the ship and nearly overturned her: a cascade of water flooded the deck before streaming back into the sea – and washing me overboard. I grabbed at a piece of the broken rigging, then screamed in pain as it tugged my arm, but I managed to hang on, so at least I knew it wasn't broken. The ship never righted herself. Each fresh wave hit her like a fist bashing a defenceless face, smashing everything to smithereens. Soon there'd be nothing left of us but a wreck on the reef. Clinging to the shreds of rigging, I crawled back up onto the skewed deck and saw that the Kanaks had cut the ropes to the raft – which now slid along the deck and vanished into the bubbling foam. The Kanaks jumped in after it.

I hesitated for a moment, then leaped. The sea was heaving across the reef in a continuous motion that sucked me right down: I felt sharp coral slash my feet before the water's pressure forced me upward again. When I broke the surface I spotted the raft a couple of metres away. Within a few strokes I'd reached it, and the Kanaks helped me clamber onto it.

We clung to our raft, hoping that the surf would carry us into the lagoon. The reef, which had snared the ship, allowed our flat-bottomed craft to pass, but I'd miscalculated when I'd thought we'd find safety in the bay. Here, too, the sea was in uproar. The reef broke the rhythm of the waves, but it didn't stop them. They were just as mighty within the bottleneck as they were outside it.

The raft and its makeshift lashings groaned.

And yet it wasn't fear that consumed me now; on the contrary, I was aware of a huge, spreading sense of relief. I'd got rid of the *Flying Scud*. When I reached land, I'd be leaving Jack Lewis behind. Trusting that the sea would erase all traces of the *Flying Scud*, I'd already set to work rechristening the splintered ship with a new, but for me familiar, name: the *Johanne Karoline*, after the old fore-and-aft-rigged Marstal schooner that we'd all dreamed of sailing in before she sank with Hans Jørgen in the Gulf of Bothnia. This was my new version of events – and who would be there to deny it? It wasn't that I wanted to avoid being answerable for my actions. It was just that I wasn't prepared to take the blame for misdeeds that weren't mine. It was a way of sidestepping Jack Lewis and his ugly taint.

We were still clinging to the raft, which shuddered from the the sea's pummelling blows, one whack after another. The green mountains loomed close now, but they'd darkened to shadows: the poisonous violet clouds had blocked out the sun, and the rain seemed to be lashing the mountainsides as violently as waves on a reef. The storm was at its peak, and though the coast was near, it offered no respite.

We could hear the thundering surf. Hoisting myself up on one elbow, I could see how close we were to the white beach. From my perch on the cresting waves I seemed to be level with the tops of the swaying coconut palms. That's when I saw the futility of my hopes just as clearly as if I were sitting on the roof of a collapsing house: the wave we rode was about to crush us all under a mass of water. When it broke with the roar of a thousand waterfalls, the raft shot away beneath me and I was in whirling free fall, with the sky below and the sea above.

I can't say everything went black: in fact, it went as green as the tropical sea itself. But I was off, in some place lost to memory: full of nothingness. When I came to, I was in the arms of one of the Kanaks. Behind us another giant wave crashed down, and I saw we were in the middle of the roiling spume, where the huge waves spent themselves before surrendering to the suck of the sandy shore. But we could gain no foothold. I was gulping and choking, while the blue face of my rescuer remained immobile, fixed on the job of dragging us both the last few metres to the shore. From his missing ear, I recognised him as the Kanak I'd borne back to the ship from the lagoon and later nursed. So now we were quits.

Another wave washed over us. Kicking out blindly in panic, I felt one of my feet touch bottom. I managed to stand but lost my footing again immediately, and tried instead to crawl on all fours through the raging foam. The surf had exhausted itself and the water retreated in a violent undertow, spraying my face and tearing at my limbs from beneath. I was just about to be dragged out to sea again when the Kanak grabbed hold of me. I walked the last few metres upright, leaning against him for support.

The beach was so deserted it seemed we'd arrived in an abandoned world. I wanted to throw myself on the sand from sheer exhaustion, but a prickling sandstorm was whipping at my half-naked body. Then I heard a loud crack and saw a palm tree snap in half. Its top tumbled through the air and landed on the roof of a hut, which promptly collapsed. We couldn't stay here: if we wanted shelter, we'd have to walk further inland.

A shout rang out behind us. I turned and saw two more Kanaks struggling in the surf and then staggering onto the beach. Then a third appeared. The entire crew was now safely ashore. Their blue faces made them look like mermen born of the boiling foam.

I felt enormous relief. I'd wrecked the *Flying Scud*, but I'd not lost a single man. True, they'd saved both themselves and me, so I couldn't claim the credit, but their survival made the loss of the ship easier to take.

The nearest huts were all empty, and as we passed them, the wind at our backs shoved us forward so we could barely walk upright. Soon we gave up running and stumbling, went down on all fours, and simply crawled. All around us we could hear the heavy thud of coconuts hitting the ground, and the storm howling through the wildly swaying palm trunks. I concentrated on my hands and knees, my only contact with the ground in this insane weather. It felt as if we'd all be blasted out into the endless universe.

Then at last our cries for help were answered, and someone let us into a hut. There was no fire burning, and the inhabitants sat silent and cowed, as if they hoped to avoid the rage of the storm by making themselves invisible. The hut quaked and the roof trembled ominously, but it was holding out. I was too exhausted to consider the impression I must have made on them. I was a ship-wrecked sailor seeking shelter. It made no difference to them that I was a white man. The storm had made equals of us all.

I fell asleep shortly afterwards. When I woke, it was quiet. It was night, and I heard the breathing of sleeping people around me. I stared into the darkness for a while, then drifted back to sleep.

*   *   *

The next morning I took my leave of the Kanaks, and for the second and final time we shook hands. My one-eared rescuer placed a hand on my shoulder and from the bottomless blue of his face, fixed me with his eye. As I returned his look, I felt a bond existed between us, though I don't suppose it could have been called friendship. We'd never exchanged a word. But now, as we parted, each of them said something, and I still remember what: 'Palea', 'Loa'a', 'Kauu'. The fourth word was longer. Something like 'Keli'ikea', but I'm not sure. At the time I assumed they all meant goodbye. Later it struck me that they had been telling me their names.

I went down to the beach. There was still a heavy swell, but the air was no longer filled with flying foam. Everywhere there were smashed palm trees and ruined huts torn apart by the wind and rain, and it struck me how lucky we'd been that the hut we'd sheltered in had withstood the storm. I went as close to the surf as I dared and scouted anxiously across the battlefield of the beach, terrified that I'd see wreckage from the *Flying Scud*, which might belie the story I'd prepared. A yard, a plank or a ship's wheel would be fine. A name board, though, would ruin everything. But when I scanned the horizon and the reef, I saw not a single trace of the ship. The sea had annihilated the *Flying Scud*, and wherever its wreckage might have ended up, it certainly wasn't here on the beach in Apia.

My sea chest had been on the raft, but I abandoned all hope of seeing it again. Its loss was the price I must pay for severing my connection with Jack Lewis.

I was in the western part of the bay, close to Mulinuu, which I'd seen on the map. I followed the shore eastward in the hope of coming across buildings that would indicate the presence of white men. Soon I spotted some brick houses with red-tiled roofs behind the palm trees and I headed for them. They, too, had not escaped storm damage: one house had a collapsed gable, and another's tiles were ripped off, exposing the bare rafters.

It was a sparsely built area, with houses scattered amid the palms rather than packed together in street formation. I got an impression of wealth and order: large airy compounds with whitewashed walls, covered verandas and broad eaves afforded their inhabitants the shade that people long for so keenly in the sun-baked tropics. Whites and natives were going about their business, with a well-organised clean-up operation already under way.

I wandered about aimlessly, feeling superfluous and alien, which, of course, was exactly what I was. No one paid me any attention or called to me. Many were merely passing through, too, I guessed: merchants, sailors and adventurers like me.

I stopped to look at a freshly polished brass plate that shone against the white wall of the house, hoping that within it there might be some kind of authority I could approach with my false report of the loss of the *Johanne Karoline*.

Deutsche Handels- und Plantagen-Gesellschaft, it said.

I had just finished reading the words when I heard someone behind me clear his throat. I turned to see a gentleman dressed all in white, his suit immaculately clean and newly pressed. He wore a fresh hibiscus in his buttonhole and looked as if he had spent the night of the storm preparing for a fancy dinner engagement. His pale eyes observed me from beneath the wide brim of his hat, while his hand stroked a moustache that unfurled in two impressive semicircles on either side of his suntanned, slightly lined cheeks.

'May I help you?' he asked, in English. Instantly recognising his accent, I replied in German.

'I'm a Danish sailor. I'm here to report the loss of my ship, the *Johanne Karoline* of Marstal, which ran aground on the reef outside Apia in the storm. Please can you tell me if there might be a consulate or another authority nearby, where I can go?'

'Ah, you're Danish. In that case we're almost compatriots. Obviously you won't find a Danish consulate here. And as far as any authorities go –' He shrugged as if the word didn't mean much in these parts. He let go of his moustache and surveyed the ground for a moment as though in search of something. Then he folded his hands behind his back and his face grew pensive. 'Well, *I'm* a consul of sorts; I mean, I'm the German consul. So I suppose I'd be the most appropriate person to deal with your case. I did hear that a ship had run aground on the reef, but the storm made any rescue mission impossible. Staying alive ourselves was challenge enough.' He held out his hand. 'Heinrich Krebs.'

'Albert Madsen.'

'Madsen? The name sounds familiar.' He took off his hat and wiped his brow with a handkerchief. 'But this heat does something to a man. Ruins his memory.'

'He's a fellow Dane,' I said. My mouth had gone dry, and my heart was pounding. 'There's supposed to be another Madsen here on Samoa,' I went on. 'I'd like to meet him.'

'Yes, I'm sure that's possible. I'll ask around. But I must warn you. Meeting a fellow countryman in these parts isn't always a pleasant surprise.'

He placed his hand on my shoulder and gave me a searching look. Then he smiled. 'Do come inside. You look exhausted. But you've had luck on your side, eh? Not many men emerge in one piece from an encounter with the reef at Apia. What about the rest of the crew?'

'Captain Hansen didn't make it,' I responded curtly, feeling a pang of conscience at my second lie.

'You could probably do with a bath and some lunch. You can make your report afterwards.'

A native servant dressed in whites as immaculate as his master's prepared me a bath. When I'd removed my filthy, torn clothes, I examined myself in the full-length gilded mirror. Its frame was far too elegant for the sight that greeted me. I'd grown lean and angular, and my body was covered in bruises. My face, too, bore witness to my recent trials: it was scored with half-healed cuts and scratches. One bisected my right eyebrow, while another made a blood-red line across my cheek. I looked like a drunken sailor fresh from a brawl rather than a man who'd been shipwrecked, and I wondered why the consul hadn't told me to clear off at once. I'd got the impression that my report on the shipwreck would be purely a matter of form: that no inquiry would be held, and no official authorities would become involved. It would have been easy enough for me to blend in with the other inhabitants of Apia, where no one would have noticed an extra vagrant on the beach.

The lie I was telling wasn't even necessary. Having told it, there was no withdrawing it now – but Heinrich Krebs was unlikely to unmask me, or even try to. I guessed that he simply wanted confirmation of his own importance. My role now was to enable him to play the benefactor and provide him with some distraction – for clearly a hurricane was not novel enough in these parts to count as excitement. That said, the impression he made on me was just like that of most white men I'd met in the Pacific: behind the facade of civilisation and order, you sensed they all had something to hide.

Not that Heinrich Krebs's secrets were of any interest to me. I'd made enough discoveries recently to last me a lifetime.

As I stepped out of the bath I noticed that a white suit had been laid out for me on a chair, and on the floor beside it was a pair of chalked white canvas shoes. Heinrich Krebs was lending me his own clothes – but as I was considerably taller than he was, both the trousers and the jacket were too short, and I couldn't even button the shirt. I had to forgo the shoes entirely and appear at lunch barefooted. I still looked like a vagrant – but a lucky one.

The dining room was pleasantly cool. Floor-length white curtains filtered the light from outside. The table had been set with a damask cloth, china, silver and crystal glasses. I've sat at many dining tables since, but never one that could match that of Heinrich Krebs.

Then he appeared. He'd taken off his hat, and his sandy hair was combed back and held firmly in place by a viscous pomade.

The table was set for two.

'You live alone?' I asked.

'I'm in the process of establishing myself. My wife and our three children will join me later.'

The food was brought in. 'A little surprise,' Heinrich Krebs said.

When the china serving dish was placed in front of me, I blinked in disbelief. Not knowing the name of the wonderful dish in German, I said it in Danish: '*Flæskesteg.*'

'Yes, *flæskesteg*,' my host said, in almost flawless imitation of my Danish. 'I have, of course, visited Denmark, and found that the Danes and the Germans share a fondness for pork. The crisp crackling, which I know you Danes value so highly, you'll have to do without, I'm afraid. The talents of my otherwise excellent cook do not extend that far.' Krebs was studying me. He gestured at the food. 'You can take many things with you. You can recreate your home, surround yourself with your treasured objects and your native culture, read familiar authors, eat the dishes of your childhood, and speak your own language, just as we're speaking mine now. And yet it isn't the same, because there's something you can never recreate. Perhaps even the very thing you once wanted to escape. Why does one leave in the first place? I often ask myself that question. Why are you here? You have been shipwrecked, endured all sorts of hardships. It's written in your face. But why?'

'I'm a sailor,' I replied.

'Indeed. But why did you become a sailor? Surely God didn't point His finger at you and command you to go to sea? It was your choice, I presume?'

I shook my head.

'My father was a sailor. My two brothers are sailors. My sister's married to a sailor. All my friends from school sail.'

'The Baltic wasn't big enough for you? It would suffice most men. Why the Pacific? What are you hoping to find here?'

I resented Krebs's curiosity, if that's what it was. Perhaps he just enjoyed the sound of his own voice. But he tried to get too close and I had no intention of confiding in anyone. I looked down at my plate again and concentrated on eating.

'This really is delicious,' I said.

'I'll pass your compliments on to the chef.'

I could tell from his tone that he was insulted. I'd rejected his invitation to confide in him, and a chasm had opened between us.

'This Madsen,' he said eventually. 'Is he a relative?'

I was already regretting having mentioned my father's name. But this was a big island, and I had to find him one way or another.

'No,' I lied. 'We're not related. We just happen to come from the same town.'

'And share the same surname?'

'A lot of Marstallers do. I promised his family I'd find out how he's doing. Since I'm here anyway.'

'Since you're here anyway. Since you happened to pass by Samoa.'

His voice was thick with contempt. He didn't believe me, but rather than saying so directly, he mocked my reply.

I didn't care. I'd had my bath and my hot meal. He could kick me out now if he wanted to, and I'd manage without his help. I wiped my mouth with my damask napkin.

'That was lovely, thank you,' I said, feigning politeness.

I could see that Krebs was reconsidering his position.

'There's dessert, too,' he said. 'Don't get up, please.'

Venetian blinds, made from thin bamboo, were swaying in the light breeze on the veranda. It was just as pleasant here as indoors, though the tropical sun blazed from its zenith. The natives were still busy clearing up after last night's destruction. The surf pounded the beach. In the distance I could see the foaming barrier of the reef where I'd nearly lost my life the day before.

Krebs questioned me about the circumstances of the shipwreck. I mentioned the raft and Captain Hansen, who'd gone down to his cabin to rescue the ship's papers and failed to reappear when the *Johanne Karoline* gave a last lurch and a wave washed us overboard. He asked about the Kanaks, and when I told him that they'd reached the shore alive with me but then disappeared, and that apart from that I knew nothing about them, he shrugged as though it were an insignificant detail.

He looked at me again and smiled the ambiguous smile that I'd quickly come to recognise.

'It's amazing what a good meal can achieve. Wouldn't you agree?' I nodded. 'Take me, for example,' he continued. 'My memory has returned. Madsen: yes, I recall him now. If you feel sufficiently rested, I can provide you with a native to show you the way. Then you can see him as early as this afternoon.'

'I really can't turn up looking like this,' I said. Even I could hear the panic in my voice.

'Of course not.' Krebs continued to smile. 'You're a stickler for etiquette, I see that now. Which attire would you prefer to wear when you meet this Madsen?'

'My own,' I said.

I could hear the falseness in my voice and it seemed to me that we were play-acting for each another. But truth be told, I could see nothing remotely funny about this comedy. In fact, I was afraid. I was afraid to meet my *papa tru* after all these years and I was afraid of Heinrich Krebs because he seemed to know something about my father that he didn't care to reveal. He'd sensed how eager I was to meet him – and he'd sensed my fear. He was toying with me, but I didn't know why. What was he after?

Krebs excused himself and left the veranda, and I spent the rest of the day wandering around the beach, looking out at the ocean and reflecting on my situation and all I'd been through. Should I have stayed away from *papa tru*? Should I have left him – as I would have left the dead – in peace? For if I had not gone looking for him, he would have been just as dead to me as any other man in Marstal's long list of drowned fathers, brothers and sons. What did I want from him, when he so clearly wanted nothing to do with me? He could easily have returned home to Marstal, but he hadn't. He'd rejected us. What do you say to a father who's stood with his back to you for fifteen years? You tap him on his shoulder. And what do you do when he turns round?

Punch him?

I returned to Heinrich Krebs's house towards the evening. He'd invited me to stay the night and I'd accepted his invitation because I didn't want to sleep on the beach. The dining table had been set for me, but Krebs was absent.

When I entered the room where I was to spend the night, I took it at first for a room that Krebs had furnished for himself and a wife whose arrival he longingly awaited. It was like entering a tent or being under the awning on a ship. Everything was in the same airy style as the dining room: the canopied bed was big enough for two or three people, and the huge mirror on one of the walls added a whole extra dimension.

It was the strangest place I'd ever slept in, and I hesitated before climbing into the bed. The floor seemed more appropriate for me – but then again, I'd never slept on a cloud before, and I felt I deserved some comfort after all I'd suffered, so in the end I threw myself into this paradise of goose down.

I woke up during the night when someone tentatively touched the door handle. It was pushed down, and then it went up again. Shortly afterwards I heard a plank squeak on the veranda. Then silence returned and I drifted back into my slumbers.

I was awakened the next morning by a knock at my door, to which I gave a drowsy reply. The servant had come with a pile of neatly folded clothes draped over his arm. In his hand he held a pair of high boots.

'Your clothes, *masta*,' he said, and disappeared.

I unfolded the clothes and gazed at them in wonder. They were indeed mine – but they weren't those I'd worn the previous day. These were my shore clothes: dark blue trousers and jacket, white linen shirt with a collar, and the grey wool socks that I'd darned myself. The boots, which I'd dragged around half the world, were *papa tru*'s. I'd been sure I'd lost my few belongings when the raft sank in the bay outside Apia. But now here they were, in my hands.

I dressed and pulled on the boots. I hadn't worn them for months. They felt heavy and uncomfortable in the heat, and my feet hurt as I walked to the dining room, where Heinrich Krebs was waiting for me with breakfast. As usual, he was immaculately dressed, with a fresh hibiscus in his buttonhole and pomade in his hair. My sea chest sat right there on the damask tablecloth. It looked like a large mouldy stain in the neat room. And there was my name on it. I'd painted it myself.

'It drifted ashore last night,' Krebs said. 'One of my men found it.' I said nothing. 'I presume the shrunken head isn't a member of your family?'

'No,' I replied. 'His name's Jim.'

'Well, that explains everything. Is he from Marstal, too?' I shook my head, having reached the conclusion that it was best not to answer. 'You're a very interesting young man, Albert Madsen,' Krebs said, and looked at me over the rim of his cup. 'Very interesting.'

'And you sneak a peek at another man's property without asking for permission.' I stared back at him without blinking. I was hoping he couldn't tell how outraged I was.

'If one doesn't, one never learns anything,' he said, without looking away.

'What is it you want to know?'

'Many things,' he said. 'You come crawling out of the surf like some merman, all alone in the world, with this story about where you come from and who you are. A story that no one can confirm or deny.'

'My name's on the sea chest.'

'Which contains a shrunken head. Of a white man.'

I reached for the silver coffee pot.

'That's another story. It doesn't concern you.'

'There's no need to get upset. You're quite right. It doesn't concern me. By the way, you'll be relieved to hear that your friend has suffered no damage from his time in the sea. Remarkable when you think about it, wouldn't you say?'

Krebs stirred his coffee. I couldn't make him out. He was toying with me and I hated it.

My host tilted his head and examined me. Then, without warning, he started whistling a tune I didn't know.

'So distant,' he said finally, sounding almost as though he were addressing himself. 'So young, so angry and so very unapproachable. How sad.' He shook his head. 'Tut, tut, tut.' Then he continued. 'By far the most bizarre thing about you is your interest in your namesake. You see, that interest – and you can trust me on this one – is shared by no one else here in Apia.' He got up abruptly. 'Right, let's get going.' He nodded in the direction of the sea chest, which was still on the table. 'You'd better take that. I presume you'll be staying with your –' he hesitated before tasting the word – 'friend.'

I nodded, but I was at a loss. I hadn't even thought that far ahead. But I supposed that Krebs was right. I would stay with my father. Fifteen years with his back to me, I tap him on the shoulder – and he turns round and invites me to stay? I could feel my earlier anxiety return. It was all so ill-considered. I really had no chart for this part of the voyage.

I got up and took the sea chest.

'Of course, you're always welcome to return here, should the stay with your friend fail to work out. I would be only too happy to renew our acquaintance.' Krebs bowed theatrically and gestured me towards the door with a sweeping movement. 'Do you ride?' he asked, as we stepped down from the veranda. Two horses, already saddled, awaited us.

'Well, I can try,' I replied, and stuck a foot in one stirrup with a movement that I hoped looked practised. Then I swung myself up onto the horse. For a moment I thought I might slide down the other side, and I could feel how bruised and battered I was. I secured the sea chest to the saddle.

'You're doing pretty well,' Krebs said, sizing me up.

With a light tap of his whip he got his horse moving at a walking pace, and I copied him as best I could. A white-clad servant trotted alongside me on foot: I presumed he was there to take charge if my horse decided to cause me any trouble. We followed the beach for a while. Here the pounding of the surf made conversation impossible, but when we turned towards the interior of the island and the ocean's din subsided, Krebs began a torrent of speech, which didn't end until we reached our destination. I was too preoccupied by my own thoughts to pay much attention to his words, but I recalled them later – along with the warning that lay buried in them.

'Take a look around,' he said. 'We have big plans for this area. We don't own much land at the moment. But that's going to change.' As he pointed his whip here and there, his posture straightened in a way I'd not seen before. 'Come back in ten years and you'll see the difference for yourself. Then all this chaos and lack of discipline will be gone.'

He snorted in contempt as he said this, and I recalled his house. Yes, it was light and airy – but it was also so neatly arranged that a sea chest on his dining table, and a man like me sitting next to it, looked like pieces of dirt. I followed the movements of his whip, and at first I thought that the chaos he was referring to was the mess left by the storm. Then I realised that it was nature itself that he saw as being out of control.

'Straight rows,' he said. 'In ten years there will be straight rows everywhere. Stone walls at right angles, and behind them, pineapple, coffee bushes and cocoa trees – in formation! Copra plantations, yes, but with the palms properly aligned. Areas for grazing, levelled out. Cattle. Horses. Avenues of palm trees, like soldiers on parade! Fountains!' His voice grew staccato as the list of future delights grew longer. Then he paused and became pensive. 'Of course, we'll have to import labour. The locals are utterly useless.'

'Why?' I asked – though mostly to demonstrate an interest in his impassioned words, because my thoughts were elsewhere.

'Oh, it's not because they're lazier here than anywhere else in the world. A native is a native. I can mention several individual examples of hard work, of course. But it never lasts.' He looked at me as if to signal that what he was about to say was of particular interest, before carrying on. 'Their families are their curse. When my servants go home for a visit, I make them leave their nice clothes behind. Take Adolf – yes, I give them German names, it makes it easier.' He pointed at the servant walking next to my horse. 'I gave Adolf permission to visit his family wearing his fine clothes. He was so proud of them. But he came back in rags. His family had taken over his uniform. I meet them, from time to time, prancing about. There's a cousin wearing the waistcoat, there's a brother in the jacket, an uncle with the shirt, and his pa's wearing the trousers. They'll wear one item of clothing at a time and nothing else – oh, it's a sight all right, eh, Adolf?' He poked the servant with his whip, but Adolf stared straight ahead as if he hadn't heard what Krebs had said, or didn't understand a word. The latter seemed the most likely. 'The Samoan doesn't work,' Krebs said. 'He goes visiting. He's not your industrious ant type. More of a grasshopper.'

'A grasshopper?'

'A grasshopper. You see, if a Samoan suddenly grows rich, whether through hard work, which is rather unlikely, or through luck, then his entire clan will instantly come and visit him. Even the most distant branches of the family tree will arrive. I've seen it. A whole village might move. And they'll behave like a swarm of locusts. They won't leave until they've stripped him of everything. Your Samoan has the same word for *visit* and *misfortune*: *malanga*. And you can figure out the consequences. It's a system that rewards the beggar and penalises graft. Hard work is nothing more than an invitation to be robbed. It's impossible to save. So what does the smart man do? He makes sure he earns enough to cover the bare necessities, so he can put food in his mouth and the mouths of those closest to him, and nothing more. A man like that's no use to me. No: imported labour. Single men who don't need much and, most important, don't have a big family.'

While Krebs had been speaking we had left the last houses behind, and only native huts surrounded us. The road had ended and we had to ride around a criss-cross of woven fences behind which black, hairy pigs grunted in the mud. A crowd of children encircled us. Adolf gave a warning whistle as though chasing away dogs and the children shrieked and retreated – but they soon reappeared, and every time they did, their chattering numbers had swelled. Women stared at us from the openings of their huts.

'Well, this is where Europe ends,' Krebs said. 'Now we're among the savages.'

* * *

A gust of wind swept through the tall coconut palms and set their tops rustling. I looked up. Their large leaves opened and closed like sea anemones, and I caught a brief glimpse of a man perched in one of them. He was white, with a naked torso and a large grey beard. Then the leaves closed again and hid him from view as if the palm tree were his home and he was now shutting its door against curious onlookers.

For a moment I doubted my own eyes. Most of all, I wanted to ignore the strange apparition, which seemed to belong to a dream world. Krebs had seen it, too. He stopped his horse and turned to me.

'We're here,' he said. 'So I'll be turning back.' He gestured to me to get off my horse. I took hold of my sea chest and dismounted, and he leaned down to shake my hand. 'I hope you won't regret it. You're always welcome at my house.' He squeezed my hand and turned his horse around. Then he looked back at me. A mocking smile appeared on his face. 'Good luck with your father.' Then he spurred his horse and galloped away.

I STOOD THERE WITH MY SEA CHEST UNDER MY ARM. THE CHILDREN gawped and gestured, but I ignored them until eventually they calmed down and squatted around me, looking curious and expectant. Women continued to stare at me from the surrounding huts. There were no men in sight.

I looked up at the palm tree where the hidden man, who might be my *papa tru,* had briefly appeared. I felt hot and uncomfortable standing there in my shore clothes and knee-high boots, not saying anything, so I shouted up at the tree.

'Laurids!'

I didn't call him *papa tru.* I couldn't bring myself to. The whole business seemed bizarre enough as it was. I didn't want to be the man standing on some remote Pacific island yelling for his pa. At first nothing happened.

'I've seen you,' I shouted. 'I know you're there!'

I grew annoyed, and then furious. But it was a form of rage that didn't know what to do with itself. 'Now come down! What do you think you are? A damned monkey?'

My own voice frightened me. I was addressing him as though I were the captain of the *Flying Scud* and he a primitive Kanak.

The palm leaves rustled, and then the man appeared between them. He was strong-limbed and bearded, with one of the natives' colourful cloths wrapped around his waist. Had it not been for his lighter skin and his grey beard, I'd have taken him for a Samoan. He grabbed the trunk with his large hands, planted his naked feet firmly against its rough surface, and came down, using a native climbing technique that made it look as if he almost walked down the tree. He landed with a bump and stood opposite me.

He stared at my feet.

I studied his face, with its dense beard. If I'd had a moment's doubt, it had vanished completely. I can't say that I recognised him after all these years, for what do the memories of a four-year-old count for? But I recognised myself. I don't often have an occasion to look in a mirror, and if someone were to ask me to describe myself, I'd lack not just the words, but the interest. Yet now I stood face-to-face with my mirror image. Time had drawn its marks across my father's face. Deep lines ran along his sunken cheeks, and wrinkles spread from his eyes like the marks a bird's claws leave in wet sand. But it was me. We were father and son, and now I saw how Heinrich Krebs had known what he'd known. All it took was one look at me.

I had no idea what to say or do; it was *papa tru* who broke the silence. Tearing his eyes away from my boots, he now fixed them on me.

'I see you've brought me my boots.'

'They're mine now.'

I gritted my teeth and made my voice as hard as his. But he held his gaze. The only thought going through my mind right now was that there wasn't a chance in hell of his getting my boots. Then he said a few words in a native language, and three of the boys in the circle around me stood up.

'Say hello to your brothers.'

Behind his beard his lips formed a vague smile. He pointed at the boys one by one. 'Rasmus. Esben.' He hesitated in front of the youngest one, whom I guessed to be about the same age I'd been when he left us. 'Albert.'

I don't know what he said next to the three boys, but none showed any sign of wanting to get to know me better, nor did their father encourage it. They just rejoined the circle of kids and started giggling.

To begin with I couldn't take in what he'd just said. He appeared to be living with a new family, just like his old one – and it included three sons he'd christened with our names. The whole thing felt like an idiotic and vicious dream. But if it was, it had gone on far too long. Fifteen years had passed since *papa tru* left us. The dream had swallowed up my whole life, turning night into day, until I no longer knew where I belonged, in the light or in the darkness.

I don't know what my face looked like just then – whether it was astonished, baffled, angry or blank. At any rate, *papa tru* made as if there was nothing remarkable about what he'd just said. And out of pride, I did the same. But I could feel resentment welling inside me, and I knew that it would keep growing until it changed into something far more dangerous.

I should have turned on my heel and left him at that moment. Made him call out after me, plead with me to stay, beg my forgiveness for all the years that had passed while he'd stayed away. But I already knew that he wasn't going to do that. He'd managed without me for all these years, and the only thing that interested him, when he finally saw me again, was his boots.

So instead, I stayed. I knew exactly why.

Because I wanted him to embrace me. Just the once.

'Right, let's go home and get a bite to eat in Korsgade,' he said.

Had he completely lost his mind? Korsgade! Rasmus, Esben – and Albert! And it followed that there would have to be a sister called Else, too, somewhere. It felt like staring into an abyss. Here, in the shade of the palm trees, my father had recreated the family he'd turned his back on. I might have been able to take the betrayal if he'd been living an entirely different life, if . . . I don't know. But this!

The small dark-skinned boy trotting alongside me was claiming to be Albert. So what did that make me? A first draft?

My heart was unmoved by the sight of the boys darting after *papa tru*. They were my half-brothers – but I felt no kinship to them. All I could feel was sudden, fierce bitterness. Now I understood Heinrich Krebs's warning. Hell, I even approved of his mockery. I watched my father's muscular back above his sarong. My father! No, he wasn't my father. He was the father of the little dark-skinned boys. Our blood tie was gone.

I watched the red dust beneath my feet; the hens, wandering freely; the woven fences with the snorting black pigs behind them; the airy huts. I heard the rustle of the palm tops. In the days when I'd dreamed of the Pacific that sound had called to me. Now here I was, reunited with my father, and it was no dream come true: it was a loss of hope. I'd rather have found his grave than the man himself.

'Papa tru,' I called out to his back.

He didn't even turn round.

'Papa tru,' I mocked. 'That's what you taught me to call you.

Do you actually know what that means? *Papa tru* – my true father. But what kind of father are you? One big lie – that's what you are!'

I should have turned and left at that point. But I followed him to his hut.

He shouted something and I understood that he was demanding food for his guest and himself. A woman appeared in the opening to the hut. I didn't look at her. I didn't want to know anything. I had no idea whether she knew about me. We sat there, waiting. The children formed a circle around us.

Laurids looked at my boots again.

'Give them to me,' he said.

'You're not getting them!' All of my disappointment was expressed in those words. 'You're not getting them!' I repeated.

He gave me a baffled look, as if he hadn't anticipated a refusal.

Then I looked him in the face and saw a peculiar lethargy in his eyes – and I knew that he was lost. He was no longer my father. Nor was he Laurids Madsen any more. He'd left everything behind, including a part of himself. I saw now that all the names from home that he'd strewn around him were nothing but a desperate attempt to grasp at something that was gone for ever. My rage gave way to horror. I wanted to get up and leave. I looked around for my sea chest, which I had set down, but it was nowhere to be seen.

'The boots,' Laurids said again.

He'd recovered his commanding tone, but I'd seen evidence of something else in his eyes. So I ignored him and began looking about for my sea chest, which I found over by the woven fence: the boys had dragged it there and were just opening it. They giggled in anticipation. The oldest one put his hand inside and rummaged around.

Then he froze. His eyes widened as though he'd discovered a poisonous snake, and he screamed. His brothers scattered. A word, whose significance I didn't know but could easily guess, echoed through the palm trees and across the whole village.

Laurids froze, too, and the lethargy in his eyes gave way to terror.

I can't explain how, but I knew instantly what was going on in his addled brain. The boy had found Jim – and Laurids now believed that I was a ruthless killer who wandered about with his victims' heads in his sea chest. Maybe he even thought I'd come to wreak revenge.

It was so ludicrous that I started laughing. If I hadn't, I'd have howled like a wounded animal.

My father gawped at me, paralysed with fear. Then he started to crawl backwards in the dust like a crab. He thought my laughter was triumphant, that I was about get my own back. He shook with fright, the poor shadowy creature.

In the hot midday sun the sight of him had stirred all sorts of feelings in me: anxiety and panic, bafflement and rage. For a brief moment I was even prepared to feel sorry for him. Now any compassion I might have felt turned into contempt. I got up and went over to my sea chest. A fiendish impulse made me grab Jim by his hair and dangle the shrunken head in the air. I took one menacing step towards the man who'd once been my father.

Papa tru was still crouched in the dust. A wet patch appeared on the sand between his legs. In his petrified state he'd lost control of his bladder. His children pressed themselves against him. Had I known their language, I'd have yelled at them that they shouldn't seek comfort in a father as miserable as this. The boys' mother, big and heavy, appeared in the doorway. Her eyes were wide with fear like her children's.

I put Jim back in my sea chest, tucked it under my arm, raised a finger to my cap in farewell and went on my way. The first few steps I took were measured. Then I started to run. As I ran, I felt the tears cascading down my face. The natives watched me cautiously. I'd interrupted their midday rest.

Laurids must have got his courage back at the sight of my retreat, because behind me I heard the sound of his voice one more time.

'My boots!' he shouted.

But I didn't turn back.

I never saw my father again.

I WENT BACK TO HOBART TOWN, WHERE THIS CURSED VOYAGE HAD begin. It was no happy return, for there was nothing in this wretched place that could inspire joy in anyone. But this was where it had all started, and so this was where it must end.

I went to the Hope and Anchor to say hello to Anthony Fox. When I left, he was black and blue. That was my conclusion to the story.

Fox hadn't been pleased to see me: he had no reason to rejoice at our reunion. But he did his best to conceal it. To him, I must have looked like someone back from the dead.

I told him that I was like him: I never forgot a debt. That wiped the fake welcoming smile from his face. He reached for his revolver, which he kept under the brass bar counter, the smartest in Hobart, but I'd anticipated that, and I was quicker than he was. We ended up in the back room. He fought well. He was an experienced fighter who knew plenty of dirty tricks from his prison days. But I was younger and bigger and I finally floored him. He stayed down for a long time. I kept pounding him even after he'd given up. My rage demanded it.

When I'd kicked and broken his last rib, I said, 'And Jack Lewis says hello.'

Not because I owed Jack Lewis anything, but to finally balance the books. We'd both been victims of the same fraudster. It was Anthony Fox who'd sold the guns to the natives on Jack Lewis's island, and when he told me his name, he must have calculated that I wouldn't be coming back alive.

I don't know what had happened between him and Jack Lewis. Nor do I give a hoot. Each was as bad as the other. If anything, Lewis was probably worse, and no doubt Fox had had much to avenge.

He'd played with my life. The idea of my death only added a

touch of spice to his game. So there was an outstanding debt between us. In fact, there were two. I owed him for the gin from our previous meeting, when he sent me on the voyage he expected would be my last. Before I left the Hope and Anchor, I tossed a coin at his pulped face.

There was once a time when I thought that I'd learn something if I found my *papa tru*. But I hadn't. I hadn't grown wiser.

I'd just grown harder.

Disaster

IT WAS MANY YEARS BEFORE WE HEARD FURTHER NEWS OF Laurids Madsen. Albert never told his mother anything and we all agreed that was the kindest thing to do. She'd died by the time Peter Clausen returned home, so Karoline Madsen never found out what had happened to the man she'd hopelessly yearned for all those years.

Peter Clausen was the last Marstaller to see Laurids. He was the son of Little Clausen, who had taken part in the battle at Eckernförde Fjord and been held captive with Laurids in Germany. After that, Little Clausen became a ship's pilot and moved to a house in Søndergade, in the southern part of the town. He built a wooden tower on its roof, so he could watch the comings and goings of ships that might need his expert knowledge of local waters.

Peter Clausen arrived on Samoa in 1876 when he and a fellow sailor jumped ship, and Peter took up with a native girl. In the beginning he lived by sponging, *malanga*-style. Then he bumped into Laurids and realised what could happen if you forgot who you were. Laurids had started to change after his German imprisonment, and he hadn't grown any more genial with age. On the contrary. Whatever the reason, he'd become even blunter and more closed off. He'd developed a fondness for the local palm wine – which was why you'd often find him in the treetops, where he'd use a machete to hack at the palm trunk to tap the sap. But he had to do it in secret, because palm wine was banned on Samoa during those years. Laurids had ended up a queer fish, respected neither by his fellow whites nor by the natives he'd chosen to live among.

Peter Clausen decided to become a merchant. He set up his own little trading station and ran the Danish flag up the pole outside. Around that time he took a native wife and and soon had children with her. He followed Laurids' example and gave them Danish names, but he never managed to teach them any Danish. Several years passed. He was just about making ends meet.

His Samoan family, as was the local way, considered his trading station to be a common source of income and settled on his lawn like a swarm of locusts, until he put them in their place. If there was one native habit that Marstallers never shook off, it was thrift. Peter Clausen didn't object to entertaining his relatives on festive occasions – that was entirely appropriate – but not daily. No bloody way. And so he chased them off. If they failed to get the message, he was happy to threaten them with his gun.

Their problem, he said, was that they didn't understand the meaning of 'daily'. They saw every day as one long party and never missed an opportunity to dress up or burst into song. An ordinary day was a concept you had to teach them.

His wife sulked, but when it came to imposing his will, Peter took after his father and eventually – according to him, at any rate – he ended up universally respected. He was no *mata-ainga* – that's a man who is weak and gives in to his family – nor was he a *noa*, which means 'beggar' or 'layabout'.

Then came 1889, the year that would turn Peter Clausen into a man of consequence and restore Laurids Madsen's reason.

One event changed both their lives.

By that time the English and the Americans had joined the Germans on Samoa. They'd all laid claim to the island, filled the bay outside Apia with their warships, taken sides among the Kanaks in their internal disputes, and given them all the guns they could carry on their broad, brown shoulders.

Heinrich Krebs was now an important man. All his plans had come to fruition, and envious competitors claimed he was the only plantation owner in the Pacific with his own private navy. And it was true that Germany indulged his every whim. He was a statesman and a plantation-owner rolled into one. His coconut palms were lined up as if on parade and the way his whip cracked, you'd think his land was a drill ground. People called his plantation simply the Company, as if there were nothing on Samoa but Heinrich Krebs and his dream of straight lines, though at this point Apia had both an American consul and an English-language newspaper.

There was going to be a war. The natives now had plenty of guns and enjoyed firing them – but they never worried much about taking aim first, so they seldom suffered great losses when they attacked each other.

Then the Flag War started. The great colonial powers had planted their flags around the island, where they had no business being in the first place. First, a shot was fired at a British flag. Then an American flag was burned, and the Germans were blamed for it. German troops came ashore to find themselves surrounded by Kanaks, who made short work of fifty of them. It was said that the house where the Germans held out had more holes in it than a fisherman's net by the time they'd finished. The Germans inside had been killed by American bullets, supplied by the British, and, all of a sudden, the bay outside Apia was packed with seven warships from three nations. Everyone was waiting for the first shot.

It was never fired, though, and that was the whole point of the story, Peter said. Because the sea attacked before the cannons had a chance.

The barometer fell to 29.11. Any sailor who knows the Bay of Apia knows what that means: get out to sea as quickly as you can. But the officers on board these naval ships hadn't a clue. They just wanted to challenge each other, and the poor fools didn't realise that their worst enemy was the ocean. The wind built to hurricane force and the waves in the bay grew big enough to frighten even those of us who'd witnessed an autumn storm in the Skagerrak or the North Atlantic.

The next morning revealed a sight to match any horrors of war. Three warships had run aground on the reef, two lay on the beach with their keels bared, and two had sunk to the bottom of the bay. The sea had swallowed cannons and ammunition and wrought its own destruction in their absence. Drowned sailors bobbed face down in the frothy surf before finally being washed ashore.

The sun rose and its glorious rays spread across a sky swept clear of clouds. But the beach was a different sight altogether. The recovered bodies were lined up, while mute survivors wandered up and down between the rows, trembling from either exhaustion or a lingering terror of the sea's power. These were troops, not seamen: they'd been destined for other forms of victory and defeat, death and survival than the kind we knew. They were soldiers who'd tasted a sailor's fate.

They never made history. No one would remember them. The Battle of Samoa was not won by the Americans, the British or the Germans. It was won by the Pacific.

Laurids walked among the water-logged bodies that had been placed face down in the sand. No one knew why they'd been arranged that way. Perhaps those who laid them out thought it too gruesome to look so many dead people in the face at once. The day before, these people had been ready to shoot each other. Now it was impossible to tell who was German, American or British. Laurids kept pointing at them as though taking a tally, and each body he counted seemed to cheer him.

'When I saw that, I thought he really had lost his mind,' Peter Clausen said later.

He, too, had come down to the beach that morning. But unlike Laurids, he wasn't counting the dead; he was counting the survivors. Every one of them was a potential customer, now that the fleets of three nations had been smashed to pieces and all provisions been lost along with a whole swathe of crew.

'Fortunately, there were more living than dead,' Peter Clausen said. Whether he meant fortunate for them or for his business wasn't clear, but at any rate, the disaster in the Bay of Apia proved to be a turning point in the fortunes of his trading station.

'All I know,' Clausen said, returning to the subject of Laurids, 'is that if he really had once lost his reason, he got it back that day. I can't say whether he became his old self again, since I've no idea what he was like before. But he turned up at my door asking if there was anything he could do. That was new. In the old days he showed up only when he wanted something – which he always did. Don't get me wrong. I was happy to help him within reason. I never refused him a meal and a cup of coffee. After all, we were both from Marstal. But he wasn't someone whose company I enjoyed. He never thanked me when he left with a full stomach. But if there was ever a different Laurids, it was the one I saw when he'd finished counting the dead on the beach. I couldn't help but remember that he'd been on the losing side in a naval battle too, and spent time in captivity. That must have given his pride a hard knock. Now it was as if he'd been redeemed.'

His father, Little Clausen, said: 'Laurids saw St Peter's bare arse. He went to heaven and stood at the Gates of Paradise. But then he came back down again, and his mind probably suffered some damage from that. Standing on the threshold of death and then turning back can't do a man any good.'

'Well, I wouldn't know about that,' said the son. 'I don't have a clue what mad people think. But the upshot was, he became almost human again. He'd been a palm-wine drunk who'd gone native. His life had been one big *malanga*. He wasn't exactly respected by the whites on Samoa. Not that they thought much of me either, because I had children by a native woman too. Even though they've got good Danish names, they're still called half-blood or half-caste and that's no compliment. The British are the worst when it comes to labels like that. But now I'm a rich man, and the American Navy is my customer, so I don't give a damn what they call us. My children will inherit the shop, so they'll be all right.

'The Germans are keeping a low profile these days. Heinrich Krebs has become a quiet man. Not much Bismarck in him now. He's a businessman again. While Laurids grew almost respectable. He trimmed his beard and stopped drinking. I even let him look after the shop from time to time. He built himself a smack and sewed his own sails. He'd sail through the surf and return with fish just like a local: no more twiddling his thumbs in a palm treetop for him. I only once asked him if he missed his family back home. Perhaps it was stupid of me. What's family, when you haven't seen them for forty years? He turned his back on me and disappeared with a face like a thundercloud. I thought he'd go off on another *malanga*. But he came back a few days later and he was still the new Laurids. The next day he sailed across the reef in his smack and never came back. The boat was never found. Most people would probably say that was the end of Laurids. But I had the strange notion that he'd set off to start a new life for himself.'

Albert hadn't wanted to listen to Peter Clausen's story. We told him anyway, once Clausen had left. He listened in silence and said nothing. He leaned forward and rubbed his boot with the sleeve of his jacket.

'I kept the boots,' he said. 'The rest is of no interest to me.'

He got up. He was still wearing the same boots, thirty years after his visit to Samoa.

II

The Breakwater

WE DIDN'T KNOW FOR SURE THAT HERMAN FRANDSEN WAS A MURDERER.
But if he was, we knew what drove him to it.

Impatience.

Our town has no such a thing as privacy. There's always an eye
watching, an ear cocked. Each and every one of us generates a whole
archive of talk. Your slightest offhand remark takes on the weight of
a lengthy newspaper commentary. A furtive glance is instantly returned
and pinned on its owner. We're always coming up with new names
for one another. A nickname's a way of stating that no one belongs
to himself. You're ours now, it says: we've rechristened you. We know
more about you than you know about yourself. We've looked at you
and seen more of you than you'll catch in the mirror.

Rasmus Arsewhipper, Cat Tormentor, Violin Butcher, Count of
the Dunghill, Klaus Bedchamber, Pissy Hans, Kamma Booze, how
can any of you imagine we don't know your secrets? Hey, Question
Mark: we call you that because you're a hunchback! And Masthead:
well, what better name for someone with a tiny head, a long body
and no shoulders?

Everyone in our town has a story – but it's not the one he tells
himself. Its author has a thousand eyes, a thousand ears and five
hundred pens that never stop scribbling.

No one saw what Herman Frandsen did. A moment came and went,
and with it went a human life, snuffed out for ever. There's no telling
what happened, or how. It's all guesswork. And because we don't
know for sure, we can't seem to let it go.

We know his motive, though. We found it within ourselves.

It was a summer's night in 1904, and Herman was twelve years old.
As he sneaked out the front door of his house in Skippergade, you

could hear the noises that emerged from within. His mother, Erna, and his stepfather, Holger Jepsen, were groaning and sniggering away on their creaking mahogany bed. Herman walked south until he left the last houses behind and then continued out towards the beach. Above him the Milky Way lit up. It was headed the same way as he was, spreading out of the night above the rooftops of Kongegade and disappearing somewhere on the other side of the Tail. In the endless universe there are no maps, yet the Milky Way still gives us Marstallers the impression of being a real road: a road that leads out to sea.

Herman did not stop until he'd reached the water. He took off his shoes and stood with his feet in the foaming surf and watched the Milky Way stretch away from him into the distance, and a feeling that could easily be mistaken for loneliness washed over him. It wasn't the kind of abandonment an orphaned child feels so much as the sense of loss you experience when the older boys go off on their adventures and leave you behind. You're full of anguish and you don't realise that it's a feeling born of impatience. You long to grow up, right there and then. You recognise that childhood is an unnatural state and that within you there's a much bigger person, one who you can't be right now but who'll come to life somewhere beyond the horizon.

Herman never spoke about that night to a single one of us.

But we knew: we've been there ourselves.

Herman lost his father early. That's something quite a few of us experience, but this loss was especially cruel. Frederik Frandsen from Sølvgade went down with his ship, the *Ofelia*, on the Newfoundland route in 1900. Herman's two brothers, Morten and Jakob, were on board too. Herman was only eight years old when he was left alone with his mother. Erna was a big woman, who'd matched her husband in height and in girth: he'd always had to bow his head and enter doors sideways, both in his modest captain's cabin on the *Ofelia* and at home in Sølvgade. The ceiling was so low there that if anyone in the family wanted to stand up straight, they had to go outside and do it in God's fresh air. Herman excepted, of course.

Erna soon remarried and this earned her a rather unfair reputation for cold-heartedness – though you could well argue she was the opposite. Was her swift remarriage due to the fact that she had no need to mourn – or that her heart was so frail in the face of loneliness that she had to seek comfort where she could? Her new husband was captain of the *Two Sisters*, Holger Jepsen from Skippergade, a quiet man who long since seemed to have settled into a bachelor's life. He was so sinewy that his bones looked as if they were bound in string, but he was small and slight of build, and standing next to big Erna he practically disappeared: it was almost comical. After their marriage he was nicknamed The Boy.

But you could see that Jepsen stirred something in Erna. She became a blusher, which she'd never been before. What's more, her moustache disappeared. Until Jepsen turned up she'd always had a shadow on her upper lip, though whether it was prickly no one could say, as she wasn't the type to go around kissing people, least of all her own sons. Frandsen had been a coarse man and everyone had agreed that the manly, broad-shouldered Erna had been a good match for him. But now she grew almost tender, if you can imagine tenderness in a woman with hands the size of shovels. It was as if Jepsen had discovered, within the giant woman, a wisp of a girl his own size, and lured her out.

But Herman was none too pleased. He'd already lost his father and two brothers, and perhaps he sensed that he was losing his mother as well. He must have felt homeless in Jepsen's house, as if he'd come to a strange country with a different language – though Jepsen treated him decently: it wasn't long before he presented his new stepson with his very own boat and taught him to scull, set sails, tie knots and everything else he needed to know to handle himself at sea. But in Herman's eyes, Jepsen had committed the unforgivable sin of turning Erna into a simpering fool. All that touching and holding hands is bad for your health, he'd tell anyone who'd listen. He behaved like Erna's rightful owner, watching his property as it was mismanaged. The way he puffed himself up and got all indignant like a right little man, you'd think he considered Erna's moustache her best feature.

Herman would also come to blame his stepfather for his mother's sudden death. Erna succumbed to blood poisoning after gutting a codfish. A hook buried in its flesh had pierced her middle finger, but she hadn't been concerned and simply pulled the hook out without so much as a wince. That was the old Erna, the one Herman liked. But two days later she was dead, even though Jepsen had fetched Dr Kroman, who'd done all he could.

Herman's view was that his mother wouldn't have died if his father had been alive. At home in Sølvgade she'd have survived, as the big, tough-as-nails woman she'd once been, not the quivering, blushing, moustacheless, lovesick jellyfish Jepsen reduced her to when he moved them to Skippergade. The fact that Herman still said 'at home in Sølvgade', long after his father's death, despite the fact that he lived in Skippergade for most of his childhood, should have served as a warning to his stepfather.

Erna and Jepsen never had children of their own. In the convivial company of Weber's Cafe, we told our favourite joke: Jepsen was too short to conquer Erna's majestic thighs, which were as tall and as thick as the mizzenmast on the *Two Sisters*. But when Erna was gone and Herman was left alone with no family in the world, Jepsen, who was more soft-hearted than was good for him, gave the boy all the affection he'd once given Erna, convinced that he needed a father's love and guidance more than anything in the world.

But Herman was of the opposite opinion. There was nothing he wanted more than to get rid of his stepfather.

And he did get rid of him, sooner than anyone had expected.

The way it happened both stirred our admiration and planted a strange, vague feeling of fear.

AS SOON AS HERMAN FRANDSEN WAS CONFIRMED, HE WAS OFF TO SEA. Holger Jepsen, who only wanted the best for the boy, made the mistake of signing him on to the *Two Sisters* rather than another ship. They had a fraught relationship, though their disagreements never actually ended in fisticuffs. Jepsen had more authority on the deck of a ship than he did on land. Although he was slight, he had a powerful voice, and he used it to order Herman up and down the ratlines and out on the foot ropes of the yards.

'Never trust your feet,' he shouted at the overgrown Herman, who was dangling up there like a seasick gorilla. 'Feet can slip and ropes can fail, and then you're falling sixty feet and learning the most useless lesson of your life. The sea won't spit you back up, and if you hit the deck we'll be scraping you off it with a shovel.'

Herman looked at his feet. If he couldn't trust them, what could he trust? Up on the yard, Herman stalled like a clockwork toy somebody had forgotten to wind. Not from fear or panic, but mistrust. He didn't understand what Jepsen meant.

Jepsen had to climb the rigging himself to get his stepson down. He clambered onto the yard and held out his hand.

'Come here,' he said, gently.

Herman scowled and tightened his grip on the ropes.

'Don't be scared,' Jepsen said, placing a hand on Herman's arm. But Herman wasn't scared. He was simply rigid with reluctance.

Jepsen had to prise open his fingers, one by one. It was a test of strength, but Jepsen was the stronger. 'There we go. Slowly. One step at a time. One hand at a time.'

He spoke to Herman as if he were a child learning to walk. Herman looked down at the deck. The able seaman and the first mate were staring up at him. They, too, thought he'd panicked.

'I can manage on my own. Leave me alone,' he hissed.

Jepsen pulled away, still facing him. 'Now remember,' he said.

'Hold on tight with your hands. And if you can't use your hands, use your teeth. And if your teeth fail you, use your eyelashes.' He gave Herman an encouraging grin and winked at him. Herman scowled back.

A year passed and we asked ourselves if it was time for Herman to sign off. There was bad blood between them now.

Then one spring day, shortly after Herman turned fifteen, the *Two Sisters* sailed out of the harbour with nobody on board but Holger Jepsen and his stepson. They were off to pick up a first mate and two able seamen who were signing on in Rudkøbing before the ship headed for Spain. It wasn't far to Rudkøbing, but we still thought Jepsen was running a risk sailing there with just a cabin boy on board. Perhaps Jepsen had pictured the crossing as a kind of initiation for his adolescent stepson? Or perhaps his tender-heartedness had worn off, and he felt the need to show Herman who was in charge on board, once and for all?

The trip did indeed turn out to be a test of manhood – but not the one Jepsen had in mind.

Jepsen and Herman set off early in the morning, and we didn't expect to see the *Two Sisters* again for another seven to eight months, when she would return via Newfoundland and dock in Marstal for the winter. But that very afternoon the ship reappeared with her course set straight for the harbour. A crowd quickly gathered on Dampskibsbroen. What was going on? Her sails were set and a brisk wind was blowing: we could tell even from this distance that she was going too fast. She was headed for collision – either with the breakwater at the harbour entrance or with one of the ships moored to the black-tarred posts just inside it.

There was only one man at the wheel, and he appeared to be the sole person on board. As the *Two Sisters* came nearer, we could make out that the lone helmsman was Herman, wearing yellow oilskins and a sou'wester. For a moment it looked as if the ship would crash straight into the quay. But just then, at the last minute, with a movement whose elegance none of us missed, Herman turned the wheel and the ship glided along the edge of the quay with only a few inches to spare. But she was still moving at top speed and in danger of colliding with another ship. If the situation hadn't been so unusual – not to mention desperate – we'd have believed that the boy was simply trying to show off.

Suddenly a broad figure shot out of the crowd on Dampskibsbroen and landed on the deck of the *Two Sisters*. It was Albert Madsen. He was in his sixties by then, but he was the one who did what the rest of us much younger men should have done. He'd spotted that something was terribly awry, with the boy alone on deck, all sails set, the ship on a collision course.

Albert may not have set sail in ten years, but the captain inside him was still alive.

He strode straight across the deck and landed a hand on Herman's shoulder. At this, Herman looked up, and then did something that made no sense. He tried to hit Albert. The big boy and the stout old man were about the same height and equal in bulk. But while the boy had the energy of youth, Madsen had the experience – and he responded instantly. His famous open-handed blow had the power to send a grown man flying several feet across the deck. And now was no exception.

Not a word had passed between them: there'd been no time for that. By the time Albert grabbed the wheel and turned the ship sideways, the *Eos,* moored to one of the posts in the middle of the harbour, was only feet away. When the stern of the *Two Sisters* hit the bow of the *Eos,* her speed had dropped enough to avoid any major damage.

Herman scrambled back to his feet, his hand clasped to his burning cheek. He'd lost his sou'wester. The way he glared at Albert Madsen you'd think the old captain had spoiled some game he had been playing, rather than averted a wrecking. As soon as we'd moored the *Two Sisters* to the quay and inspected the damage, it was clear to all that Herman felt humiliated. No one told him off. But no one praised him either, though he probably deserved it. He was only fifteen, and he'd steered a ship single-handed. Perhaps this was when things turned sour: when Albert hit him and we remained silent. But perhaps something had gone wrong with Herman long before. Perhaps he'd misunderstood the silence of the stars the night he stood staring at the Milky Way.

We don't know.

In any case, teenage sensitivities were not uppermost in our minds at this point: a ship had arrived at the port with only the cabin boy on board. Where was the captain? Had he gone ashore in Rudkøbing, and had Herman run off with the ship?

'What's happened to Captain Jepsen?' we asked him.

He was still nursing his sore cheek. 'He fell overboard.'

He sounded absent-minded, as though he needed time to recall who Captain Jepsen was.

'He fell overboard? No one falls overboard between Marstal and Rudkøbing in a light wind.'

'Maybe I didn't put it the right way,' Herman said. It was then that we first sensed a terrible arrogance in him. 'What I meant was, he jumped.'

'Jepsen? Jumped overboard?'

All we could do was stupidly repeat Herman's words like a bunch of parrots. It was that impossible for us to grasp what he'd said.

'Yes,' he said. 'He was always whining about missing Ma. In the end I suppose he couldn't take it any more.'

You could hear his arrogance grow with every word, and we felt like asking him whether he, too, hadn't 'whined' about Erna, and whether her death hadn't been a blow for him, as well as his stepfather. Then, finally, the truth dawned on us. Herman had lost his mother long ago, on the day she'd married Jepsen. By the time she died for real, he felt nothing but contempt for his stepfather's despair. Maybe he even had a morbid feeling that things had fallen into place. Had his stepfather's grief and anguish given him satisfaction? Did he feel avenged when Jepsen jumped overboard? Or – and here we hesitated, we never voiced it, but we thought it privately (and when enough Marstallers privately think the same thing, it's as good as spoken aloud) – when Jepsen was 'given a hand'?

'Where did he jump?' we asked – though we sensed that the way we phrased the question would take us further from the truth.

'I dunno,' the boy replied brazenly.

'You don't know? But you've got to. Was it in Mørkedybet? Outside of Strynø? Think. It's important.'

'Why?' He shot us a defiant look. 'Water's water. And when you're drowned, you stay drowned. Makes no difference where.'

We got nowhere with him.

Sooner or later Jepsen's body would drift ashore on one of the archipelago's many little islands, on Strynø, Tåsinge or the coast of Langeland, perhaps as far in as Lindelse Nor. And there it would lie, sloshing about in the seaweed, half eaten by fish and crabs. But it wouldn't be your regular washed-up body. Or so a lot of us reckoned. Because the forehead would be caved in by a marlinspike. Or a swinging boom. Or one of the many other weapons a would-be murderer might find on board ship.

But Jepsen was never found. Perhaps he sank to the bottom with a stone around his neck to keep him down. Or perhaps, a long-distance traveller to the very end, he drifted with the current and went south, deeper into the Baltic. Either way, he never came back to testify.

And that's why we never voiced our thoughts, though some of us would hint at them in a whisper: 'There's something not quite right about that Herman, isn't there? And Jepsen – could he really have jumped?'

A space grew around Herman. He was only a fifteen-year-old boy, but he was something else too, something different and alien. We slapped him on the shoulder and praised him, eventually, for having steered the *Two Sisters* safely back to Marstal. We had to, because he'd done something spectacular, something no other boy his age could have done. Another kid would have panicked or simply given up. Yes, Herman had the makings of a good sailor. But the toughness that we applauded in him also kept us at a distance.

Herman inherited the *Two Sisters* and Jepsen's house in Skippergade. He wasn't old enough to be the legal owner of either the ship or the house, so Jepsen's brother, Hans, was appointed his guardian. Hans Jepsen found a new captain and a crew for the ship, but when Herman demanded to be signed on it as an ordinary seaman, he refused.

'You haven't been at sea long enough,' he said.

'I sailed a whole bloody ship on my own,' Herman shouted. Red in the face, he took a menacing step towards Hans – who reacted by taking an equally menacing step towards the kid.

'You're only a boy and you'll sail as a boy.'

'It's my ship!' Herman roared.

Hans Jensen had been a first mate for many years so he was unimpressed by rebellious cabin boys, no matter how tall they were or how loudly they shouted.

'I don't give a damn who owns the ship,' he growled in a low, savage voice that was more terrifying that any yell. 'You'll be an ordinary seaman when you're old enough and no sooner, you upstart pup!' He jutted out his unshaven chin. He'd sailed on an American ship as a young man, and used threatening expressions like 'you're dead meat, buddy' and 'you're history'. We were never quite sure what they meant, but we got the gist when he ground his teeth and spat out more American cuss words as if they were gristle. Now he stared at Herman, his jaw working. 'I don't know what you did to my brother, but if you so much as look at me wrong, you can kiss your fat ass goodbye.'

Herman had his pride. If he wasn't allowed to sail as an ordinary seaman on a ship he regarded as his own, he didn't want to sail on her at all. He did the rounds of the harbour, but no one wanted to take him on as an ordinary seaman, or as anything else. So he went off to Copenhagen and signed on there.

For some years we heard nothing from him. Then he returned, and everything changed.

THERE ARE MANY WAYS TO TELL A MAN'S STORY. WHEN ALBERT MADSEN first began writing his diary, it contained very little personal information but concentrated instead on our town and its progress. He wrote about the school in Vestergade, which was now the biggest building in town; about the new post office in Havnegade; about improvements to street lighting and the removal of the open sewers; about the network of roads that extended in all directions and about the new streets that appeared in the south-west outskirts of the town and were named after Danish naval heroes: Tordenskjoldsgade, Niels Juelsgade, Willemoesgade, Hvidtfeldtsgade.

A sailor's often asked why he goes ashore. Whenever anyone put that question to Albert, he'd always reply that he hadn't gone ashore, he'd just swapped a small deck for a big one. The whole world was moving forward just like a ship at sea. And our island was just a ship on the endless ocean of time, heading for the future.

He always reminded us that the island's first inhabitants hadn't been islanders. Ærø had once been one of many hills in a rolling landscape. Then the huge northern glaciers had started melting. Rivers had ploughed their way through the country, and the vast freshwater lakes to the south had expanded. Then the sea had poured in, and what was once a range of hills became an archipelago. Which came first? Albert would ask. The wheel or the canoe? Which would we rather do, master the weight of burdens too heavy for us to carry or conquer the distant horizons of the ocean?

The harbour rang with the cries of seagulls, the banging of shipyard hammers and the rattle of ropes in the wind. The roar of the sea rose above it all, a noise so familiar it seemed to have been born in our ears. Those were the years when everyone was talking about America. And many left. We left, too, but not for good. In earlier days, we'd had to cram our houses right on the shoreline because there'd been no room anywhere else: the gentry and the peasants owned the fields. With no other choices open to us, we'd turned our gaze seaward. The oceans were our America: they reached further than any prairie, untamed as on the first day of Creation. Nobody owned them.

The orchestra outside our windows played the same tune every day: it was nameless, but it was everywhere. Even in bed, asleep, we'd dream of the water. But the women never heard its music. They couldn't – or they didn't want to. Outside the home, they never looked towards the harbour, but always inland, across the island. They stayed behind and filled the gaps we left. We heard the sirens' song while our wives and mothers blocked their ears and bent over the washtub. The women of Marstal didn't grow bitter. But they grew hard and practical.

Albert Madsen didn't miss the sea. How could he, living in a world capital like Marstal? He could sit on a harbour bench and chat with Christian Aaberg, the first Dane ever to walk right across Africa. Or with Knud Nielsen, who'd just returned after seventeen years on the coast of Japan. Half the male residents of the town had rounded Cape Horn, a perilous rite of passage for sailors the world over, and done it as casually as they'd take the steamer to Svendborg. Every street and lane in Marstal was a main road leading to the ocean. China was in our back garden, and through the windows of our low-ceilinged houses we could see the Moroccan shore.

There were a few cross streets in our town, but none of significance. Tværgade, Kirkestræde and Vestergade didn't lead to the sea, but ran parallel to it. At first we didn't even have a market square. Then a butcher's opened in Kirkestræde, followed by an ironmonger's, two drapers', a chemist, a savings bank, a watchmaker and a barber's. The sailors' hostel was torn down. We were to have a market square just like any other town. Suddenly we had a main street, but going the wrong way: instead of taking you to the harbour, it skirted the coast and then veered towards the heart of the island. Heading away from the dangers of the sea, it was a women's street.

Our streets all met and crossed. Some were men's and some were women's, and together they formed a network. The shipbroking and shipping companies were situated on Kongegade and Prinsegade, while the women did their shopping in Kirkestræde. But that balance was about to shift. At first no one paid much attention to it or saw what it might lead to.

The 1890s were Marstal's heyday. Our fleet expanded until only the one in Copenhagen could beat it: three hundred and forty-six ships! These were boom times, and we all caught investment fever. Everyone wanted a share in a ship, even cabin boys and housemaids. When a vessel returned from a voyage and was laid up for the winter, the streets teemed with children delivering sealed envelopes containing the dividends that were paid out to practically every household.

A shipbroker needs to know how the Japanese-Russian War will hit the freight market. He doesn't need to be interested in politics, but he has to pay attention to his skippers' finances, so a knowledge of international conflict is essential. Opening up a newspaper, he'll see a photograph of a head of state and if he's bright enough, he'll read his own future profits in the man's face. He might not be interested in socialism, in fact he'll swear he isn't: he's never heard such a load of starry-eyed nonsense. Until one day his crew lines up and demands higher wages, and he has to immerse himself in union issues and other newfangled notions about the future organisation of society. A broker must keep up to date with the names of foreign heads of state, the political currents of the time, the various enmities between nations and earthquakes in distant parts of the world. He makes money out of wars and disasters, but first and foremost he makes it because the world has become one big building site. Technology rearranges everything, and he needs to know its secrets, its latest inventions and discoveries. *Saltpeter, divi-divi, soy cakes, pit props, soda, dyer's broom* – these aren't just names to him. He's neither touched saltpeter nor seen a swatch of dyer's broom. He's never tasted soy cake (for which he can count himself lucky), but he knows what it's used for and where there's a demand for it. He doesn't want the world to stop changing. If it did, his office would have to close. He knows what a sailor is: an indispensable helper in the great workshop that technology has made of the world.

There was a time when all we ever carried was grain. We bought it in one place and sold it in another. Now we were circumnavigating the globe with a hold full of commodities whose names we had to learn to pronounce and whose use had to be explained to us. Our ships had become our schools.

They were still powered by the wind in their sails, as they had been for thousands of years past. But stacked in their holds lay the future.

Albert Madsen came ashore when he was about fifty, as most of us did. If you'd saved up 30,000 kroner by then you could put it in the savings bank, where they offered you 4 per cent interest per annum, and you'd get a monthly payment of 100 kroner: enough to live on. But Albert had earned much more than that, and he didn't put his money in the bank. Instead, he invested it in ships and became a shipowner and broker. Many of those who bought shares in ships in those days, including farmers from the interior of the island, knew nothing about shipping and needed advice from someone who himself had once sailed and understood the sea. This called for someone known as a corresponding shipowner, and Albert became a corresponding shipowner like no other. During his many travels he'd become acquainted with a Jewish tailor in Rotterdam who went on board ships docked there to make clothes for the sailors, and they'd become friends. Luis Presser was an astute businessman. After Rotterdam he'd settled in Le Havre and set up his own shipping company with a fleet of seven large ships. He had them registered in Marstal and made Albert, who'd just come ashore, their corresponding owner.

In Le Havre Albert had fallen in love with Presser's wife, a beautiful Chinese lady called Cheng Sumei. And she'd fallen in love with him. They'd looked at each other, realised that they'd met too late in life, and decided on friendship instead. When Luis Presser died suddenly of pneumonia, his widow took over the business and continued it with even greater success than her late husband. Perhaps she'd always been the woman behind the man. At any rate, she now became the woman behind Albert. It was she who advised him as he went from being captain on the brig *Princess* to managing ten ships.

Their two businesses eventually became so closely intertwined that Cheng Sumei's company in Le Havre was hard to distinguish from Albert's in Marstal. Albert, too, had a talent for making money. Once, when he was a young man, he'd stood on the deck of a ship in the Pacific with a bag of pearls in his hand that could have made all his dreams come true, and he'd flung it into the sea because he felt that the wealth they could buy him would bring a curse. Now a woman from China had placed a new bag of pearls in his outstretched hand. And this time he'd opened it.

We don't know whether Albert Madsen and Cheng Sumei were entwined as closely on a personal level as they were on a business one. Life had demanded so many changes from both of them: first they'd had to snuff out their growing love and replace it with friendship. Now the possibility of love was open to them once again. Did they grab the chance?

Cheng Sumei never had children of her own, but she always referred to the company's huge, elegant barks such as the *Claudia*, the *Suzanne* and the *Germaine* as her 'daughters'. She was now too old to bear a child, though you wouldn't know it from her strangely ageless features. The two held hands in public. They probably slept together, too, the slim Chinese lady with the smooth, polished skin stretched beautifully across her high cheekbones and the big, coarsely built Dane who could easily fill a double bed. But they never married.

She'd been born in Shanghai. She'd never known her parents and had survived on the street by selling flowers. Many of us had met her in Rotterdam when Presser was still alive and coming on board our ships to measure us up for clothes. But she'd also been seen in Sydney and in Bangkok, in Bahia and in Buenos Aires. Some claimed to have met her in a brothel; others had known her as the manageress of a boarding house. We all believed we knew something about her, but none of us knew anything for certain. She'd have needed nine lives, like a cat, to have appeared in all the places we thought we'd seen her. She was as well travelled as any long-haul sailor.

But she never came to Marstal; it was always Albert who went to Le Havre. Until one day he stopped. At first we thought they'd fallen out. But then we learned she'd died – quite unexpectedly. Albert didn't tell us any of this; we pieced it together ourselves. Why had they never married? Why hadn't they lived together? Had Albert not loved her enough? Had she not been enough in love with him?

If any of us got up the nerve to ask why he'd never married her or anyone else, he'd reply: 'I was in so much of a hurry that I clean forgot.' That made us laugh. He'd had plenty of opportunities.

When Albert first came ashore he bought the old merchant's house on the right-hand side of Prinsegade as you come up from the harbour.

Later, he moved across the street, into a brand-new house he had built for himself, with high ceilings and a first floor. From its large east-facing balcony he could see the breakwater and the archipelago. There was also a bay window that gave onto the street. On the small pane of glass above his front door he had his name painted in gilt letters: *Albert Madsen*.

Diagonally across from Albert's home was the house of Lorentz Jørgensen, who'd set up shop as a shipowner and broker many years before Albert. As a boy, Lorentz had been fat and wheezing, with a permanent pleading look in his eyes. Then the sea had hardened him until we forgot that we'd once thought of him as nothing but a flabby sissy with no balls. He hadn't stayed long at sea, and come ashore after sitting his navigation exam. Though he'd not been able to save up much from his modest wages, it turned out he had a talent for making money. He bought shares in ships and knew how to talk business with Marstal Savings Bank. He entered into a kind of partnership with the most successful shipowner in town, Sofus Boye, who was nicknamed Farmer Sofus because he came from Ommel, a village three kilometres inland from Marstal.

Lorentz Jørgensen hadn't yet turned thirty when he convinced us to have a telegraph cable laid from Langeland. He spoke of the *world market* and the *telegraph*. The words meant little to us, but he managed to convey that the world market was to the sailor what the soil was to the farmer, and that without a telegraph we'd never make contact with it.

The government turned us down when we applied for financial assistance for the telegraph. So Lorentz went to see Sofus Boye. Farmer Sofus was a modest man who despite owning the biggest shipping company in town could still sometimes be found waiting by the ferry dock hustling a few coins as a porter. He had no office as such: he'd just tap his forehead with his index finger and say he kept everything in there. But Farmer Sofus listened when Lorentz described the speaking cable that could shrink distances to nothing.

'It doesn't matter whether you live in a big town or a small one. Even if you live on the tiniest island in the middle of the ocean, as long as you have a telegraph, you're at the centre of the world.'

This kind of talk sounded fanciful to most people, but not to

Farmer Sofus, whose ears quite readily went deaf on other matters. He came along with Lorentz to Marstal Savings Bank and told him to repeat what he'd said about the telegraph to Rudolf Østermann, the manager.

'The centre of the world,' Lorentz insisted.

The bank manager, who considered himself something of a wag, was on the verge of asking if there was any chance of using this telegraph thing to contact the good Lord God – but one sharp look from Farmer Sofus wiped the grin right off his face. As it turned out, Rudolf Østermann soon became the most zealous of the invention's converts, frequently declaring, 'The telegraph office is the heart of a town, a pure blessing. They should have it in the church.' He'd completely forgotten the joke he'd been ready to crack the first time Lorentz told him about it.

Once Marstal Savings Bank and the biggest shipowner in town had backed the telegraph, other Marstal investors emerged. If the government wouldn't help us, we'd just have to help ourselves.

It was also Lorentz who came up with a scheme for the town's own mutual marine insurance. At first we insured only small ships and then as Marstal's prosperity increased, we took on big vessels too. In 1904 the Marine Insurance Company acquired its own building on the corner of Skolegade and Havnegade, a splendid red-brick house with a relief on its facade depicting a schooner in full sail. The building served the same function as the breakwater: it protected us.

Nothing escaped the attention of the meticulous and imaginative Lorentz. When he was appointed harbour master he ordered the construction of the 400-foot-long steamer quay, the Dampskibsbroen. He was also one of the co-founders of the whitewashed Marstal Dairy with its tall chimney, in Vestergade. He bought a horse, and he cut an impressive figure as he rode through town with the beast's iron-shod hooves ringing on the cobbles. He was the real master builder of the town – though the wall he built around Marstal was an invisible one, designed to shield us from all the unforeseen accidents of life at sea.

Lorentz married a woman two years his senior, Katrine Hermansen. It was a late marriage, but the couple managed to have three children. The eldest emigrated to America, the middle one he sent to England to learn the shipping trade, and the youngest, a girl, stayed at home and married a sailmaker called Møller, from Nygade. They had four children, who turned up at their grandfather's office in Prinsegade every day to sing to him in their gentle, clear voices. On Lorentz's desk lay telegrams from Algiers, Antwerp, Tangier, Bridgewater, Liverpool, Dunkirk, Riga, Kristiania, Stettin and Lisbon. In his later years he ran to fat and began to resemble his old self in the days before he went to sea. But no one teased him about his big body any more. As he sat in the swivel chair of his office, listening to his grandchildren singing, he reminded us of one of those chubby, contented Buddhas you see in Chinese temples.

The cemetery where Lorentz would one day be laid to rest was new, like so many other things in Marstal in those days. Previously we'd all been buried in the churchyard between Kirkestræde and Vestergade, in the shadow of the beech trees. But now we were put to rest in a completely new cemetery outside the town, one that sloped down towards the beach from Ommelsvejen and provided a view of the archipelago. In it we planted a long avenue of rowan trees that would last at least a hundred years. There was room there for many dead.

Certainly we were hoping to be just as numerous in the future as we were then. Perhaps we even thought there'd be more of us. We must also have hoped we'd no longer die in foreign ports or at sea, but instead draw our final breaths in familiar surroundings.

A cemetery that fills up slowly sends out a comforting message: you'll die in the place where you were born, the place you love, the place where you belong. You'll see your children grow up. You'll sit, bent with age, while your grandchildren sing to you and your life stretches out behind you like a slope that begins on the narrow, white edge of the beach and ends on a hill with a view of the archipelago.

When one of us was once asked why, when his ship was floundering in a storm, he'd refused to give up even though death seemed like a certainty, he'd given an answer that would seem strange to anyone but a Marstaller. It was Morten Seier, the first mate of the *Flora*, which was skippered by Anders Kroman. It was December 1901, and the ship was bound for Kiel with a load of English coal. A west wind rose and grew, and for six days the *Flora* was adrift in a hard gale, covered in frost, with only the reefed mainsail and the stay-sail set. Then the storm turned into a hurricane and swept off the longboat, the galley and the wheelhouse. The men could venture on deck only if secured to a line, while waves as big as houses crashed down on them from all directions. On the tenth day a huge wave took away the rigging and the cargo shifted. When the *Flora* rose out of the raging water again, she'd taken a severe list. Masts, rigging and all the superstructure had gone, and the wreckage floated on the waves, covered with white foam from the pressure of the hurricane.

They gathered in the cabin and Captain Kroman, who was a plain-speaking man, informed them that they shouldn't expect to see Christmas.

Then another huge wave crashed over the ship and flung them against the bulkhead. Now they were convinced that the *Flora* had been dealt her final blow. Knowing she would soon sink, they braced themselves for a watery grave.

But the badly damaged hull stayed afloat.

And that's when Morten Seier had the idea that saved them: to sling the entire cargo overboard so that the stern could lift above the waterline. They couldn't open the hatches for fear of flooding the ship with seawater, so instead they used their axes to chop through the bulkhead and into the hold. And from there they began heaving out the coal. None of them had got a wink of sleep since the rigging was swept overboard three nights before. Nevertheless, freezing in the howling snowstorm that swept the bare deck, and soaked by the icy water that washed over them incessantly, the six-man crew of the *Flora* used buckets and sacks to shift forty tonnes of coal and tip them into the sea. In one night: nearly seven tonnes per man.

Afterwards, according to Morten Seier, they were all dead on their feet. They soon fell into a deep sleep – the men in the now empty hold, Captain Kroman and Seier in the cabin.

When they woke it was early in the morning of 24 December, and the storm had died down. They calculated that they were approximately sixteen sea miles from the Orkney Islands, but as the storm had taken their lifeboat, the sight of land made doom just as likely as salvation. So they shackled the two anchor chains together to avoid drifting into the murderously rocky coast.

Finally help came. A Dutch fishing boat appeared on the horizon, and soon the crew of the *Flora* was on board.

'What made you keep going?' we asked Seier.

It was a stupid question, but we asked it anyway, though anyone could work out the answer. Morten Seier wanted to see his house in Buegade again. He didn't want to be parted from his wife, Gertrud, or his children, Jens and Ingrid, who needed him just as much as he needed them. He wanted to be back for Christmas. And like any other sailor, he wanted to end up captain of his own ship before he came ashore for good. To sum it up: it was too early for him to die.

But Morten Seier didn't offer any of those explanations. Instead he gave us something completely different: an intelligent answer to a stupid question.

'I kept going because I wanted to be buried in the new cemetery,' he said.

You might think this was a strange reply. Perhaps only a sailor could understand it. But our new cemetery represented hope.

It was something to come home to.

What would we have done if a stranger had told us that the burial ground would remain half empty, and that only a few gravestones would testify to the lives that were once lived here, or that the avenue of rowan trees we'd planted along the high road would one day be half buried by tall grass, so that only a trained eye could discern the landscape we'd planned in that wilderness?

What would we have done if a stranger had told us that the ancestral chains binding us to Marstal would soon be broken, and forces stronger than the sea would carry us away?

We'd have laughed at him, the fool.

ALBERT MADSEN DIDN'T BELIEVE IN GOD AND HE DIDN'T BELIEVE IN the devil either. He believed, a little, in mankind's capacity for good; as for evil, he'd seen it for himself on board the ships he'd sailed. He also believed in common sense, but even that wasn't his strongest belief. Above all else, Albert Madsen believed in fellowship. As far as he knew, those who believed in God had no proof that He existed. But Albert had proof of his own belief in fellowship – and it was a solid reality. He saw it every morning when he looked out of his gable window past the broker's office in Prinsegade, and he could see it from the bay window of his office below, too: in fact, it was the reason he'd added the window to the house. And when he descended the three stone steps at his front door and turned right down Prinsegade towards the harbour, there it was again, laid out before him.

The mighty breakwater had taken the town forty years to build. It lay in the middle of the bay, more than a thousand metres long and four metres high, built from boulders each weighing several tonnes. Like the Egyptians with their pyramids, we'd built a vast monument of stone. Ours, though, was not meant to preserve the memory of the dead, but to protect the living. Which made us wiser than them. The breakwater was the work of a pharaoh, Albert told us: a pharaoh with many faces. Together they represented what he called fellowship.

This was Albert's morning worship: his sailor's eyes would roam the sky and its cloud formations, full of messages for those who could read them, and then settle on the breakwater. It brought him a feeling of serenity. There it lay, a dormant power stronger than the sea, capable of calming the tides beyond it and providing shelter for the ships: living proof of human fellowship. We don't sail because the sea is there. We sail because there's a harbour. We don't start by heading for distant shores. We seek protection first.

Albert rarely went to church. But he attended services on festivals and special occasions, because the church, too, was part of man's fellowship, and he didn't want to be isolated from it. He had no particular respect for the ritual. But a church is like a ship. Certain rules apply and once you come on board, you have to adhere to them. And if you can't, you should stay away.

For years a succession of vicars had complained that the church was badly maintained. But when Pastor Abildgaard, with whom Albert was on otherwise good terms, went so far as to argue that money earmarked for the school should be spent on the church's facade, the pastor was given short shrift. When it came to choosing between education and religion, Albert said, he'd choose education every time. The school represented young people and the future – and the church didn't. If the school in Vestergade was bigger than the church, so much the better. Any town that believed in the future should take note.

'But what about issues of morality?' Abildgaard objected. 'Where will the child learn about those if not in the church?'

'On board his ship,' Albert replied tersely.

'And in foreign ports, perhaps?' the vicar retorted.

Albert said nothing.

Where life at sea was concerned, Albert had no illusions. He'd lived the unprotected life of a cabin boy, working like a dog and being treated worse, as he put it. However, times had changed. Living conditions on board ship had improved and become more humane. The children were better taught and in time they became better skippers. Albert believed in progress. He also believed in a sailor's sense of honour. Fellowship stemmed from that. On a ship, one man's negligence could have fatal consequences for everyone. A sailor was quick to see that. The vicar called it morality. Albert called it honour. In the church you were accountable to God. On a ship you were accountable to everyone. That made a ship a better place to learn.

In his experience, ultimately everything came down to the captain. The captain knew the function of everything on board, down to the last sail and rope, and so did the crew. By the same token, each man also had his function, and if the captain failed to make the role of each and every one clear from the start, the crew would settle it among themselves by fighting. And then the weakest –

though not necessarily the least able – would find himself at the bottom of the heap. He'd seen that happen on the *Emma C. Leithfield*, when Captain Eagleton let his brutal first mate, O'Connor, usurp his authority. The strongest isn't always the best suited to lead. A captain has to know the human mind as well as he knows the layout of his ship.

When Albert became a captain himself, he found that crew members would jump ship from time to time. But he'd never seen this as disobedience or evidence of the sailor's bad character, so much as a failure of his own insight into human nature. He hadn't paid enough attention to set the man on the right track. He believed there was good to be found in everyone. He knew that there was evil as well. But his basic view was that evil, too, could be disciplined and kept in check.

Once, in Laguna, Mexico, sometime in the 1880s, an able seaman pulled a knife on him. Albert, who was unarmed, had simply held out his hand for the weapon. He never thought for a moment that he was doing something unusual or courageous: he just did what he had to do in order to remain in charge. The seaman froze, frowning at Albert's outstretched hand, struggling to understand. Seizing the moment, Albert punched him in the jaw with all his strength, which floored him. Then Albert put his boot on the man's wrist, twisted the knife out of his grappling fingers, pulled the dazed man to his feet and calmly proceeded to beat the living daylights out of him – while taking care not to cause permanent injury. He was both inflicting punishment and enforcing his authority.

In the midst of all this, he was aware that he didn't represent good, any more than the seaman with the knife embodied evil. The two of them were simply opposing forces. Nobody sailed into a raging gale with all sails set. You didn't confront a storm head on. You adjusted the sails and found a balance. All genuine order depends on that kind of balance, not on one man's suppression of another. No rule deserving of the name is writ in stone.

When James Cook faced a band of furious natives at Kealakekua Bay in Hawaii, in the moment before a club struck the back of his head and a knife slashed his throat, he waved to his crew to come and help. But the boat that might have rescued him turned back to sea. And the men onshore who could have rushed to defend him threw down their muskets and fled into the surf. On his last voyage on board the *Resolution*, Captain Cook had had eleven out of seventeen of his able seamen flogged, giving them a total of two hundred and sixteen lashes. So when he needed their help, they simply turned their scarred backs on him. He'd pulled the wrong ropes.

Every sailing ship has miles of rope, scores of blocks, hundreds of square yards of canvas. Unless the ropes are constantly pulled and the sails endlessly adjusted, the ship becomes a helpless victim of the wind. Managing a crew is the same thing. The captain holds hundreds of invisible ropes in his hands. Allowing the crew to take charge is like letting the wind take the helm: the ship will be wrecked. But if the captain takes complete control, the ship will be becalmed and go nowhere: if he strips his men of all initiative, they'll no longer do their best, and they'll go about their work reluctantly. It's all a question of experience and knowledge. But first and foremost it's about authority.

When Albert had finished beating up the mutinous seaman, and the man lay battered on the deck, he helped him to his feet, then called the galley boy to fetch a basin of water so the man could wash the blood off his face. And that was the end of the matter. The man was again part of the crew.

Albert had once been beaten himself, with the thrashing rope. But he never became anything like Isager, who neither punished nor rewarded his pupils but hammered them repeatedly instead. Nor was he like O'Connor, the first mate who'd used his rank to indulge his murderous impulses. As for the captain who'd resorted to flogging to enforce his shaky authority, well, Albert was no James Cook either. Instead he was something which Captain Eagleton on the *Emma C. Leithfield* had never managed to be. It wasn't about obeying or disobeying rules. Life had taught him about something far more complicated than justice. Its name was balance.

IN 1913 ALBERT DECIDED TO CONSTRUCT A MONUMENT TO HIS personal doctrine in the form of a memorial stone to be erected close to the new Dampskibsbroen. He'd already picked out the stone and knew its provenance. It was about four metres long, three metres wide and two metres tall. It lay in the Baltic Sea out by the Tail, and in an offshore storm you could sometimes see it from land. In the summer boys would swim out to it and stand on it, their small blond heads just reaching above the surface of the glittering water.

The light would play on the waves and flicker across the stone's massive flank and sometimes Albert would sit in his boat, resting his oars, and simply contemplate it. It lay so solidly down there in the pale green, shifting waters. But even this boulder had arrived by way of a voyage, moving down from the north with the ice. Now it must be relocated again, this time to a permanent site, to remind Marstal of the construction of the breakwater, and man's power over nature.

He even came up with the inscription it would bear: *Strength in Fellowship*.

Then one sunny day in June, as he sat leaning over the rail, gazing into the lapping water, a severe bout of dizziness overcame him, and he got the sudden feeling that the world was losing its cohesion and that everything he believed in was doomed. He felt the shadow of a menace that went beyond the fury of the wind and the pounding of the waves: a foreboding of looming disasters from which even the unyielding boulders of the breakwater couldn't protect Marstal. The sensation was so vague and dreamlike that he thought he must have briefly nodded off in the afternoon sunshine. Then, fixing his eyes on the boulder in the water, he made out his own shadow on its scarred flank, and his sense of reality returned.

It was then that he got the idea. It came over him with a kind of urgent haste, in a flurry of inspiration. It was time to take stock, he decided: to make a big, strong, permanent mark to counterbalance his own sudden premonition of doom. The stone.

Only a few days after this epiphany, Albert called a meeting in the rooms of the Marine Insurance Company in Havnegade to present his idea to a circle of invited guests. His proposal for the memorial met with general support, and a committee was set up to carry out the preliminary work. The stone was to be put in place that very year, before autumn set in.

A week later Albert joined the chairmen of the harbour commission and the Marine Insurance Company to inspect it. A strong breeze was blowing from the west, baring the top of the rock as the waves broke against it.

On a mid-July morning, two crane barges were towed out to the boulder. On board were Albert Madsen, the chairman of the harbour commission, the harbour master, a fisherman and a rigger from one of the shipyards in town. A contingent of Marstal ladies brought sandwiches and refreshments to the white sandy beach, and these were ferried out to the sweating men on the two rocking decks. By two o'clock the stone had been lifted and secured between the barges. When the returning convoy passed Dampskibsbroen and sailed into the harbour with the stone tethered between them, the flag went up and the large crowd waiting on the quay cheered.

We were celebrating ourselves: ourselves and our flourishing town.

Two days later the boulder was hoisted ashore. Albert had telephoned Svendborg and asked them to send a flatbed trailer to transport it, and this arrived on the ferry the following day. A huge crowd turned up and everyone volunteered to pull. Shipyard owner and rigger, able seaman and shipowner, merchant and clerk: even the manager of the savings bank turned himself into a human mule and got hold of the rope, while schoolchildren ran around making a racket until they, too, found a place in the line. Even old, long-retired skippers interrupted their chatting on the benches by the harbour to offer a helping hand, their pipes still stuck firmly in their mouths. But Josef Isager, now known as the Congo Pilot, stuffed his hands in his pockets pointedly and scowled: he was way above this kind of work. Lorentz Jørgensen, too, kept to the sidelines, claiming age and bulk as his excuse. The marine artist's widow, Anna Egidia

Rasmussen, drawn to the harbour by the noise, which could be heard as far away as Teglgade, also looked on, clasping the hand of a grandchild. Anders Nørre, the village idiot, was jumping up and down in great excitement at the edge of the crowd. Spotting him, Albert nudged him into the flock. Once Anders had slung a rope over his shoulder, he grew strangely serene, and seemed to concentrate like the rest of the crowd.

Then Albert himself grabbed hold of a rope, raised his hand in the air and turned to the gathering.

'Right, let's pull!' he called out, thumping the air with his fist.

That was the starting signal. Albert put his whole weight into it. He was sixty-eight years old, but he didn't feel his age. It was as if his powerful body had been saving itself for this moment his whole life, as if anything he'd done up to now had just been preparation. His face reddened in the sun, and he felt a surge of happiness that seemed to come straight from his pulsing blood and tensed muscles.

Slowly the flatbed trailer shuddered to a start. They hauled it one metre at a time – until it stopped. The ground was too soft, and the weight of the stone had sunk the trailer's wheels into the gravel so it was impossible to move it. The legs of two hundred men strained in vain. They leaned forward into the ropes as though testing their combined weight against the stone. But it resisted them.

Albert straightened up and turned to the gathering.

'Come on, folks,' he called out, and punched the air a second time. 'One, two, three – pull!'

But the trailer wouldn't budge.

Somewhere in the sea of people, a sailor started up a shanty. The others joined in, and soon they were all singing, swaying rhythmically to the old working song that had rung across the sea for centuries. But it did no good.

Albert called out to a boy and asked him to run to the Navigation College in Tordenskjoldsgade and bring back some students. The boy raced off, and it wasn't long before thirty young seamen came marching together down Havnegade. They rolled up their sleeves to reveal their tattoos and shouldered the ropes. That's our youth and our future, Albert thought. That boulder doesn't stand a chance now.

And sure enough, the flatbed trailer started rolling again, its wheels groaning in protest, as if the whole vehicle were being torn apart by the enormous pressure. There was a tense moment when they rolled over a kerb; the stone wobbled, but it stayed put, and the shanty resumed. It wasn't until now that Albert had properly listened to its words.

> *I will drink whisky hot and strong.*
> *Whisky, Johnny!*
> *I will drink whisky all day long.*
> *Whisky for me, Johnny!*

Young boys sang along cheerfully at the top of their voice. The words held the promise of manhood. The trainee navigators led the singing. They'd sailed for long enough to feel like fully qualified seamen, and this song belonged to them: their years before the mast confirmed their right to it. For the old seamen, it was just a memory. It struck Albert that there were few men here who'd never hoisted a sail or heaved against a windlass to the tune of the whisky song – the national anthem of all sailors. It made no difference what language it was sung in; the message was in the rhythm, not the words. It didn't preach; it travelled to men's hearts via their muscles, reminding them what they were capable of, so that, forgetting their exhaustion, they'd toil in unison.

Strength in Fellowship would be the message on Albert's stone – but in the sweaty exhilaration of heaving it onto the trailer, he realised it could just as easily, though more crudely, be *Whisky, Johnny!* That, too spoke of fellowship.

He raised his red, sweating face to the sun and smiled.

The stone had reached its destination.

Albert had held several public meetings at Hotel Ærø about the memorial stone, or the Fellowship Stone, as he'd privately named it. It would be financed in the way that anything major and important in Marstal was always financed: through the collection of small contributions. Through fellowship. When he stood on the podium warming to his theme, he happily forgot that there was something important he'd never explained. What was the occasion for erecting the memorial stone? The seventy-fifth anniversary of the construction of the breakwater had been 1900, the year the century changed, but no one had organised anything back then. Its centenary was twelve years away. He couldn't count on being alive then; he'd be eighty-one years old, and he wasn't one of those arrogant men who assume they'll live for ever. But why now? Why in the year 1913?

Fortunately, no one ever put that question to him. 'Of course,' everyone had said, the first time he suggested it. Of course the town should have a memorial stone – and what better event to commemorate than the construction of the breakwater? So he was never called on to explain that, one day in June, he'd grown dizzy on the water south of the Tail and had premonitions whose meaning was unclear to him. He could hardly stand on a podium and talk about that. Indeed, he couldn't even have confided to a friend that this was his reason for having two hundred and thirty men drag a fourteen-tonne boulder around on a flatbed.

Why now, why in the year 1913?

Before it is too late, before we forget who we are, and why we do what we do.

Too late? What do you mean?

No. He could barely answer these questions himself. All he knew was that he'd been overwhelmed by a sense of doom, and to counter it, he'd thrown himself into organising the raising of the boulder.

Again and again, from the podium in the ballroom at Hotel Ærø, Albert recounted the history of Marstal's breakwater. He explained how the harbour had once been at the mercy of winds from the north and the east, and yes, from the south, too, where the sea often broke through the point that we call the Tail. How even ships in winter dock could get tossed ashore. And how, when we all faced ruin because our harbour was so vulnerable, one man had stepped forward. You could consider him the actual founder of our town as we know it today, Albert would say, even though he didn't build on land, but in the water. He was the creator of our fellowship, the force we're now erecting a stone to commemorate. Skipper Rasmus Jepsen was his name. He encouraged our town's residents to commit themselves in writing to the construction of a breakwater. Three hundred and fifty-nine people signed that document. Some provided their labour, some the stones, and some the money. But everyone gave something – all except one, who declined for the shameful reason that you should put your own needs first and not gamble on posterity.

'I will refrain from mentioning his name, for the sake of his living relatives,' Albert said from the podium.

At which point everyone turned and stared at Skipper Hans

Peter Levinsen, who was to become one of the keenest and most generous of the contributors to the memorial stone because it finally gave him the chance to erase his family's eighty-eight-year-old shame.

Continuing his speech, Albert recalled how, on 28 January 1825, which happened to be the birthday of King Frederik VI, a hundred men had gathered on the ice under the banner of fellowship to lay the first boulder of the massive building project. Even nature had been on their side, because if that year and the next few hadn't been ice winters, they'd never have been able to lay down the boulders. But they'd succeeded, and now here was Marstal's breakwater, an eternal symbol of what men can achieve through fellowship and hard graft.

'When you look at the breakwater,' he told the gathering, 'you see a line of boulders. But never forget the real building materials. Strong arms and unbreakable will.'

He concluded by reminding them that the pioneering Rasmus Jepsen had been awarded the Order of Dannebrog for his achievement. All sailors, regardless of how unruly and wayward they may appear, are monarchists, and any reference to the Dannebrog flag makes an impression on them. So sure enough, it was always at this point that the spontaneous applause erupted. Occasionally, Albert allowed himself to accept a little praise as the originator of the memorial stone, but in his heart he felt he hadn't earned it, since what he'd undertaken in these hectic, triumphant days had emerged from unstable mental territory, from visions as ephemeral as clouds.

On the morning of 19 July, the sculptor Johannes Simonsen arrived on the postal service steamer from Svendborg to inspect the boulder. He declared it fit for the purpose, made a series of drafts, and before he returned to Svendborg left instructions for cleaning off the moss and algae. The stone was dusted with chloride of lime and then washed with hydrochloric acid diluted in water. We dug a hole two metres deep for the base and filled it with concrete. At the beginning of August the plinth and iron fencing were cast. The stone was set in place in the middle of that same month. Albert Madsen himself joined in the work, together with several other committee members.

The day it was set on its plinth six torpedo ships entered the bay. Like the ships in the harbour, they were garlanded in bunting and they'd hoisted their flags. The quay was soon teeming with spectators. It was the first time that warships had called at Marstal, and even Albert's committee stopped its work to walk down to Dampskibsbroen to take a look. That same evening, a festive gathering for the officers from the warships was held at Hotel Ærø, and Albert attended the dinner. The sight of the narrow steel-grey hulls at Dampskibsbroen earlier had filled him with a strange unease, and now he succumbed to a dizzy spell similar to the one he'd experienced the first time he studied the boulder in the sea. He spent the entire meal in an odd state of absent-mindedness, which several of those present commented on, attributing his distraction to the huge pressure he was under during the final phase of the memorial's erection. At certain moments during the dinner he felt that the whole affair was taking place at sea. The tables seemed to be floating on the water, with the chairs bobbing around them on the waves. He saw black shadows dart across the blue-grey depths beneath him.

He was called back to reality by a voice addressing him directly. It was the commander of the six torpedo boats, Gustav Carstensen, who wanted to present his compliments.

'I heard about the memorial stone. I heard you're in charge of it and that you mobilised the whole town to shift it into place. Well, the young have the energy. It's just a question of coordinating it. As a captain, you know more than most about the importance of discipline.'

'I believe in balance between forces, and I believe in fellowship,' Albert said.

'Fellowship is certainly important,' the commander responded, looking pensively into the distance. Albert's remark had clearly provided him with a cue to proceed with his own thoughts on the matter. 'But fellowship must be created. That's why we need a great cause that people can rally round. Right now, people think only about themselves. We haven't had a war to unite and focus our young people for several generations. A war's what we need.'

Albert looked at him, his eyes still unfocused from the dizziness. 'But many perish in war, don't they?'

'Well, obviously, that's the price of it.'

A note of hesitation had entered the commander's voice. He gave Albert a searching look, as if he hadn't noticed the person he was talking to until now and was wondering if he'd been wrong about him.

'And anyway, the dead will have a grave and a headstone, won't they?' Albert continued, regardless.

'Of course, of course, that goes without saying.'

It was now clear to Carstensen that the conversation had taken a wrong turn.

'Go visit the cemetery here, Commander. You'll find many women and some children. You'll also find farmers, a merchant or two, and the odd shipowner, such as myself. But you won't find many sailors. They stay out there. They never get a headstone. They've no grave that their widow and their children can visit. They drown in distant seas. The sea's an enemy with no respect for its adversary. We fight our own war here in Marstal, Commander Carstensen. And that's enough for us.'

Someone proposed a toast to the navy, and the commander seized the opportunity to end his conversation with Albert, who, left alone, fell back into his brooding.

That same night the memorial stone worksite was vandalised. A gang of drunken shipyard workers knocked down the wooden fence that had been put up to protect it while the sculptor finished his inscription. Albert immediately reported the incident to Chief Constable Krabbe in Ærøskøbing and received a response within three days: the chief constable informed him that in the police court the vandals had been fined a total of 315 kroner for drunkenness and breach of the peace.

As the day of the unveiling approached, Albert's sense of discomfort grew. Fortunately, there was still plenty of work to be done. He'd already written a detailed history of the breakwater and had it sealed in a lead pipe, which was sunk into the cement foundation of the memorial stone. Now he began composing a speech to read aloud when the stone was unveiled. He portrayed the monument as though it were a human being with human disappointments and hopes and he referred to life as 'a place where joy, sorrow and failed hopes intertwine, and where the best-laid plans don't always bear fruit'.

He stopped.

What do you think you're writing? he asked himself. You were supposed to celebrate the breakwater and human fellowship. But you've written yourself into a corner.

He shook his head and switched off the desk lamp. Where had these doubts come from? He had no reason to question his life's work. The town was flourishing as never before, and that was precisely what the memorial stone was being erected to celebrate. This blasted dizziness was troubling him again. Premonitions, a swimming head, visions. Old wives' tales.

He got ready for bed. Sleep might offer some respite.

He stamped his foot angrily as if to scare off the unsettling spirits. The last thing he needed was to grow afraid of the dark, like a child.

Finally the day arrived: 26 September 1913. Hundreds of people had turned up, and Albert once more recounted the story of the breakwater's construction. A choir of young girls sang a song whose words Albert had written himself, and from which he'd succeeded in barring any hint of pessimism, to the tune of 'I Pledge to Guard my Country'. Then he pulled off the huge Danish flag that draped the stone; as he did so, the spectators flung bouquets. The chairman of the harbour commission gave a thank-you speech and the event concluded with three cheers for King Christian X, whose birthday it also was.

Afterwards a dinner commenced at Hotel Ærø for a hundred invited guests, including Chief Constable Krabbe from Ærøskøbing, whose wife Albert escorted in to dinner. The menu was roasted hare, cake and a selection of alcoholic beverages. Albert gave the main speech and finished by inviting the guests to stand and give His Majesty three cheers. Then they sang 'King Christian Stood by the Tall Mast', and Albert read out the birthday telegram that he'd written to the King, which he asked those present to endorse. Afterwards numerous toasts to Denmark and the Danish flag ensued, and several of the town dignitaries gave speeches in praise of one another. At eleven thirty a telegram arrived from His Majesty, thanking them. Dancing followed.

As far as Albert was concerned, the evening went off without a hitch. He was present the whole time and had no sense of foreboding. Nor did he suffer any visions of guests in their finery floating around in the sea among the flotsam of well-laid tables.

After saying goodnight to the last guests at about two in the morning, he walked round the corner to Prinsegade and returned home to a dreamless sleep.

When he awoke the next morning, he felt at peace with himself at last.

Albert Madsen was sixty-nine years old and he'd achieved what he wanted. Although he hadn't had children, which was a regret, the town he belonged to continued to prosper. The shipyards were busy as never before, and the town's leading shipyard would soon switch to building modern vessels, investing in the construction of steel ships instead of wooden ones. Last spring His Majesty the King had paid a visit to the town, which had been decked in bunting in his honour, and the navy's six torpedo ships had been there too. There were plans for a new post office and a copper spire on the church to replace the turreted section of the roof.

The memorial stone at the harbour commemorating the breakwater showed that the townsfolk remembered their history and acknowledged their debt to their ancestors. *Strength in Fellowship* ran the words carved in Johannes Simonsen's neat lettering. Now Albert Madsen's creed had become the town's too.

He knew that the reason for his sense of well-being that morning wasn't just the successful conclusion of his grand project, with the unveiling of the memorial stone and the party that followed. It was something much bigger: it was the harmony he felt between himself and the continuously prospering world he was part of. He opened the gable window and there in the soft sunlight of an early September morning, beyond the latticework of mast tops, it all lay: the breakwater and the archipelago. The cries of seagulls drifted up, mingling with the clang of hammers and the rasp of saws from the town's shipyards. He knew that these same sounds were heard in every port on every continent, and with a kind of triumph he felt himself to be a part of a much wider world.

Later he would think of this day as 'the end', though he never articulated exactly what had been concluded. Not his life, certainly, for he went on to live for several more years. But they were years spent half in reality and half in a world of dreams, and the two were linked by a bridge of terror, for in his dreams he acquired knowledge he couldn't bear alone and yet could share with no one. He ended up living in a town peopled by the dead, and he became death's silent witness.

Visions

WHAT DOES A SHIPBROKER WRITE ABOUT IN HIS LOG? HE'LL WRITE
about the ups and downs of the freight market, about cargo deals
he's made, about ships that never returned home, about crews that
were rescued, about insurance questions, about profit margins and
the fate of his company. But these days, Albert Madsen didn't write
about either business matters or his vessels at sea. Nor did he write
about his feelings, and he only rarely made a note of his thoughts.
It's true that he recorded certain things that were going on inside
his head. But mostly these were things he didn't understand.

A stranger lived inside his head, and he wrote about that stranger.

Albert wrote about his dreams.

But not all of them.

Like most people of a practical nature, he'd once regarded dreams
as things made possible only by the hibernation of the rational mind,
a confused summary of accidental and half-forgotten events that
might once have had a clear meaning but were now lost in a foggy
half-world. Like the rest of us, Albert could make little sense of most
of his dreams, and didn't try to.

Then one December night in 1877, when he was captain of the
brig *Princess*, he'd dreamed of a voice calling out to him, warning
that he was heading for danger. He'd leaped out of his berth and
run up to the deck: the ship was indeed about to run aground on a
large flat sandbank, where it would inevitably founder. The dream
had warned him. It seemed that his head contained knowledge he'd
been unaware of. A mysterious guest had moved in.

Two years later he had a similar experience, when he dreamed
that the *Princess* went down in a hard gale. But on this occasion,
even though he suspected that this dream, too, was a warning, he
decided to ignore it and left Grangemouth early the next morning
just as a south-westerly storm was gathering outside the harbour.
After sailing the ship along the coast the whole morning, he finally

had to drop anchor and chop down the masts to avoid being beached. As he clung to the tilting deck and watched the rigging fly overboard, it dawned on him that more than one kind of reality was possible.

Albert's gift was not one that everyone possessed. He also knew he must keep it to himself. We've read about that in the notes he left us, along with his other papers. He wrote that if the premonitions in his dreams were to become public knowledge, they would almost certainly harm him, or at least tarnish his reputation.

How often have we sat in a fo'c's'le listening to tales of the *Klabautermann*, the Grim Reaper who hangs in the mizzen shroud with his white face and his dripping oilskins? Or of the *Flying Dutchman,* or the ship's dog that howls in the night, searching for its lost ship? Albert, too, when he was a ship's boy, had listened, and been terrified and strangely fascinated, yet deep down he'd remained a sceptic. An explanation existed for every unusual event: science simply hadn't discovered it yet. That was always his conclusion, as we sat there in the dusk exchanging tales that illustrated how there was more between heaven and earth than we could dream of.

If he'd revealed his ability to see the future in his dreams, most of us wouldn't have hesitated to accept that he had supernatural powers. His reputation on board ship would have been strengthened, and possibly his authority too. But the awe would have been mixed with fear, and he didn't want that. Albert believed a captain's authority should be based on trust in his skills, not mumbo-jumbo.

In the period that followed the unveiling of the memorial stone, a grey emptiness opened up in front of Albert. He had dreams in which people he knew died, and the next day he'd be startled to see them walking around the streets as large as life. His dreams were full of riddles: he didn't know the times of the deaths he visualised, but the visions were always dramatic and terrifying. He saw people shot down on the deck, he saw ships burst into flames, he saw black shadows in the sea, and he understood nothing of what he saw.

But he never doubted that these dreams were telling the truth. He knew that all the people he'd just greeted, whose hands he'd shaken, to whom he had spoken recently but now increasingly tried to avoid, would die in horrifying and inexplicable circumstances. And they didn't have a clue.

He was walking around in a town of doomed men.

ALBERT'S FIRST DREAM ABOUT FUTURE DISASTERS OCCURRED DURING the night of the 27th of September, in 1913.

He saw a ship he knew, the *Peace*, a three-masted schooner from Marstal – and then he heard a shot. The crew appeared on the deck immediately, bracing the yards and lowering the topgallant sails; then they prepared to launch the lifeboat. For reasons he didn't understand, they seemed to attach huge importance to that one shot. But there was no visible damage to the ship.

Then more shots rang out and one of the men suddenly clasped his shoulder. His arm was dangling limp. The head of another was blown backwards as though an invisible hand had pulled his hair, sending a jet of blood gushing from his forehead as he collapsed on deck. The shooting was constant now. Several projectiles hit the descending lifeboat, and when it reached the sea's surface, it started to leak. The men were soon up to their waists in water as they worked to seal the leaks. Intense firing continued. Then one by one the masts went overboard, and the ship itself disappeared into the deep.

The weather was stormy and the sea was heavy. Clouds raced across the sky. The lifeboat lay low in the water. The men worked the oars hard. At first terror marked their faces, then exhaustion. The light was dimming. It grew dark, and a long time passed before the light returned. Albert realised that it had been night and now it was morning. It was still stormy and the waves ran high underneath the torn, racing clouds. Two of the men lay stretched out in the boat. The others lifted them up and eased them overboard. He caught a glimpse of a pale face, sunken in death. It was Captain Christensen. He'd clinked glasses with him at the party to celebrate the memorial stone just two nights ago.

The following night he saw the schooner *H. B. Linnemann* send out a distress signal. As in the previous dream, he saw the crew scrambling around on the deck trying to launch the lifeboat. Again he heard shots and was unable to tell where they were coming from. He instantly recognised the ship's captain, L. C. Hansen, standing on the half-deck right underneath a flapping Danish flag. Captain Hansen sank down as he pressed his hand to one thigh, where a large, dark patch was spreading. A moment later he was hit in the head and wiped from the ranks of the living. Afterwards three of the crew were shot in quick succession.

Finally it dawned on Albert what it all meant: the brutality, the mercilessness, the inexplicable killings of peaceful seamen and the sinking of ships.

He was foreseeing a war.

He thought about Commander Carstensen: he was about to get the war he wanted. And what would Albert get? He sensed darkly that in these dreams he was witnessing more than just the death of people he knew. He was witnessing the end of an entire world.

He couldn't explain this feeling in any more detail, only that it gripped him like a deep sorrow and sucked the light out of the panoramic view from his gable window. What use would the break-water be in a few years' time? Yes, the sailor was at war with the sea, but soon there would be another, crueller war that no amount of seamanship could win.

Albert had neither the imagination nor the political insight to envisage who might start this conflict, nor did his dreams tell him. But he thought about the battleships he'd encountered on the sea, and the torpedo boats in the harbour, and about the submarines which he'd read about but never seen. To what object on earth can you compare a sailing ship? None. A ship has her own wondrous architecture. But what about the new floating war machines? The submarine seemed to be made in the image of a shark; while the torpedo boats resembled armoured amphibians. It was as if the entire modern war industry had taken as its templates the prehistoric monsters that had lived on earth millions of years ago.

Albert had heard enough about the Englishman Darwin's theories on the origin of species to know that life evolved; it did not regress. But surely regression was precisely what mankind was aiming for with these war machines: a return to the brutal and simple life forms of bygone eras?

Was this what his dreams were showing him, a future in which humanity returned to its amphibian stage and became its own worst enemy?

The dreams continued. He saw schooners go up in flames. He saw them blown to pieces by sudden explosions at the bow, vanishing into the sea in minutes. He saw men drifting in sinking lifeboats. He saw the terror in the seamen's faces and heard their cries for help as they were sucked down into the deep. Finally, all he could see was the sea itself and its relentless waves. For a long time he felt as though he were floating on that iron-grey water, all alone beneath a clouded sky. He thought that the world must have looked like this soon after its creation, before life began.

He started keeping lists of the ships he saw go down in his dreams. He also wrote down the names of the dead, when he recognised a face. He wrote all this in the left-hand column in his office account ledger, leaving the right-hand column blank, reserved for the day when his dreams might start coming true. He reflected that these must be the strangest accounts ever kept and that he must be the oddest bookkeeper, because he was treating an imaginary world as if, like the real one, it must answer for its accuracy.

Albert was a strongly built man with a short beard and a head of hair that age had not managed to thin. For many years he'd remained unchanged, still exuding the same controlled strength. He didn't cut a youthful figure so much as a timeless one, as though he existed in a place where age didn't exercise its tyranny. But now he started to age visibly. He saw it himself, and he knew that people were talking. He still trimmed his beard and kept his thick hair neatly cut, but his broad shoulders began to droop and all of a sudden he seemed smaller. He kept himself to himself and made no excuses when he declined invitations. People could think what they liked. He found it especially difficult to be in the company of men whose deaths he'd seen in his visions. How could they live their lives so lightly when such a terrible fate awaited them?

How could Captain Eriksen stop Albert in Prinsegade, just as he left his office, and converse about nothing but freight markets and the dredger lying just outside the harbour as it scooped out Klørdybet channel? Didn't he realise his days were numbered?

Albert greeted him tersely and disappeared down towards

Havnegade. Then he regretted his brusqueness. Soon people would start saying he had grown strange. Well, never mind about that. What else could he do? Embrace Eriksen and weep for him? Warn him? Yes, but against what? Against the sea, the war?

'What war?' Eriksen would ask, and then decide – with reason – that Albert was deranged. An unbearable burden had settled on Albert's shoulders. He witnessed calamities and disasters whose origin and nature he could not understand. Would it have been easier if he'd been a man of faith? Would he have found comfort in Jesus? But it wasn't solace that a man needed. It was the chance to act. And that was why the dreams were like a disease. They attacked the core of his being. They sapped his energy and willpower. For the first time in his life, he perceived himself as helpless, and this sensation corroded his soul, draining him of strength.

As Christmas approached a severe snowstorm arrived from the north-east and the water in the harbour started to rise. Albert went down to watch the crews attach extra moorings. Over a hundred ships were docked in Marstal, and a howling concerto rose over the town from the many riggings raked by the north-easterly wind, the slapping and slamming of ropes against wood, and the bash of hulls against each other and the quayside as they waited to be re-moored by the crews. The water level continued to mount and the ships rose higher and higher, their menacing twilight shadows looming in the snowfall, like a fleet of *Flying Dutchmen* come to announce the destruction of the town. But then the water stopped. The only damage done was to Dampskibsbroen, where the waves had smashed up the paving.

In his notes, where he continued to keep accounts of the still-living, Albert remarked on the breakwater: 'the great achievement of our fathers still stood the test'. He wrote it in defiance, as if rebelling against all dreams. The breakwater had prevented the water from rising any further.

All the same, he knew that the age of the breakwater was over. Stronger enemies were coming, from whom the breakwater couldn't protect us.

SOMETIMES YOU'D SEE POOR ANDERS NØRRE HURRYING THROUGH THE streets, pursued by a gang of jeering boys. He walked in rigid strides which kept getting longer, as if he were desperate to escape but too afraid to run. He probably feared that an obvious attempt at flight would trigger some sort of alarming behaviour in his pursuers. In any case, he didn't stand a chance of outrunning a gang of boys.

The chase always ended with Anders forced up against a wall, where he'd cower, rubbing his cheek against the rough bricks and moaning softly. Then an impotent rage would take over and, roaring like an animal, he'd turn and chase after the boys, who scattered in all directions, like squirrels, shrieking with laughter.

Usually the adults would intervene, but not always. There were those who found these incidents amusing.

It was on one such occasion that Albert Madsen actually got to know Anders Nørre. Anders was older than he was, but apart from the white hair and beard, which bought him no respect from the badly behaved children, he was strangely unmarked by age.

The day Albert encountered him they'd chased Nørre all the way from the Market Square down Skolegade and Tværgade and had finally cornered him against the garden wall across from Weber's Cafe in Prinsegade. Albert raised his stick as though to strike them, and shouted menacingly. They fled.

'Let me walk you home,' he said to Anders Nørre.

Nørre had been standing with his hands covering his ears and his eyes tightly shut. Now he opened them and looked at Albert. He lived just outside the town, on Reberbanen, where he had a little hut. He'd sit there all day long, spinning rope on a wheel, and when the rope was finished, he'd make rope yarn. He'd followed this dreary occupation for as long as anyone could remember. The general opinion was that he was an imbecile.

Albert took him by the arm, and Anders succumbed willingly.

'Have you been to church recently, Anders?' Albert asked.

Anders Nørre nodded. 'I go there every Sunday.'

Anders Nørre's reputation for being slow-witted wasn't based on an inability to speak. On the contrary, he had a soft, pleasant voice and always expressed himself clearly and intelligibly, and engaging him in conversation was not a problem. No: it was more the blankness of his face, which seemed incapable of expressing any emotion, and the sad, tedious existence he led. He'd lived with his mother until her death, and it was said that, before that, he'd slept in her bed every night, long into adulthood. When she died, the women who laid out the body decided to leave her in her bed until she could be placed in her coffin the next day – and in the morning they'd found Anders Nørre sleeping right next to her, because when bedtime came he'd done what he always did and climbed in with her. At her funeral he showed no signs of grief. In fact, the only emotion he ever showed was an overwhelming stubbornness, if you can call that an emotion. If you contradicted him or stopped him from doing something he'd set his mind on, he'd leap up and start shouting nonsense words and waving his arms – not to hit anyone, that much was obvious – but in a kind of desperation. Then he'd storm out of his tiny hut and disappear across the fields. He might be gone for days before reappearing, worn out and bedraggled.

But there was sense somewhere inside him, and it wasn't just a little, but in fact quite a lot. The only problem was, it didn't seem to serve any useful purpose. If he was told a man's age and his date of birth, he could instantly calculate the number of days he'd lived, even making allowances for leap years. Someone once asked him how many days had passed since the baby Jesus was placed in his crib, and he'd answered promptly. When he left the church he could recite the vicar's sermon word for word, for the benefit of those sailors in town who preferred the bench by the harbour to the pew on Sunday mornings.

On the first day of spring he'd take off his shoes and socks and he'd walk around in bare feet until winter returned. In the cold season he'd root around in waste heaps and rubbish bins for food. No one would have let him starve, but he seemed to prefer this way of life, and for that reason we'd passed sentence on him and judged him an imbecile.

Albert had always greeted Anders Nørre, but there was nothing unusual in that. Village idiots were public property. We spoke to them in a good-natured and patronising way, were on first-name terms with them and patted them on the back. Not that they had the right to behave that way with us.

On this occasion Albert continued to question him about the Sunday service, and Anders Nørre answered all his questions willingly. His tone of voice didn't for one moment reveal what thoughts or emotions the service might have stirred in him. Even his ability to solve complex mathematical equations had a soullessness about it. Yet there was a soul somewhere inside him, Albert was convinced of it: the embryo of a human being whom no one had ever thought to nurture and develop. Now it was probably too late.

Anders Nørre had dropped Albert's arm, no longer in need of his support. He'd not been injured when the boys attacked him, and if he was upset, his passive features certainly gave no hint of it.

They passed Market Square, walked up through Markgade and continued up Reberbanen until they reached Anders Nørre's hut, close to the fields. On the last stretch Nørre entertained his companion with a word-for-word repetition of Pastor Abildgaard's Sunday sermon. Suddenly Albert froze: it seemed that the parrot by his side was addressing him directly with an urgent message.

He stared into Nørre's face. He didn't seem to have noticed anything. His voice was unchanged, continuing at the same pitch. The difference was in his words. They were unusual. Was Pastor Abildgaard really their author, or were these words coming from a completely different place, and if so, where? From Nørre's soul, which had finally awakened?

'You were at the height of your powers,' the man said. And because Nørre wasn't looking at anyone and his tone remained the same, the words really did seem to be coming from another place, gracing their speaker with the dignity and authority of an oracle.

'You sensed that the world needed your strength and you rejoiced in that. But then it changed. Your strength vanished and the world withdrew from you, and you felt alone. The world was like a big smile that enticed and beckoned you. But then it changed. Dark and hard times arrived and the smile of the world vanished behind menacing clouds. You were in the midst of a life filled with love. But then it changed. The treasure of your love was taken from you.'

Albert felt his throat tighten. The words affected him strangely. He felt that someone was talking directly to him, and to him alone. He thought: where there's a mouth, there'll be an ear too. At long last he could relieve himself of the burden of his loneliness. At long last he could share with someone all the things he'd been keeping to himself. Every word Nørre spoke was the truth. Albert's strength had indeed been taken away from him. And so had his enjoyment of life: a life in which he'd found things to love, and had lacked nothing. He could share his anguish with the author of these words. But who was he? Pastor Abildgaard? He refused to believe that. Nørre? That was even more unlikely. Or a third party? In which case, who might that be?

For a moment he was lost in his own contemplation. Then he became aware of Nørre's voice again. The Sunday sermon was reaching its conclusion. Old familiar themes now emerged, identical from one Sunday to the next: God's mysterious ways, the Crucifix on Golgotha, the love of Christ, and this Sunday the word *love* had been repeated over and over: Christ's thoughts of love, his loving help, redemption through his love. The same convenient trivialities that religion always peddled in response to life's hardship. So it was Abildgaard after all.

For a brief moment the vicar had succeeded in talking himself straight into Albert's soul. But it wasn't religion that Albert needed. It wasn't sugary words of comfort. What it might be instead he could not articulate. Perhaps it was just this: a listening ear. But not the vicar's.

What did Abildgaard know of Albert's predicament? Nothing, however much he might preach. How could he be aware of his banishment from the world of the living, his shipwreck on a dark and unknown shore of bones, peopled by the dead?

Albert shivered like a wet dog. He felt cold. Something inside him was trembling. He entered the hut along with its lone inhabitant. Nothing in Nørre's face revealed whether he welcomed his guest or would prefer to be left alone. As there was no other furniture, Albert sat down on the bed next to him. There was no heating in the hut, so the winter chill kept the most unpleasant smells at bay, but it was still hardly an inviting place.

'Do you ever dream, Anders?'

Albert looked at Nørre and tried to catch his eye. But as usual, he got nothing back. Albert leaned forward and looked at the floor. He began as if he were talking to himself or to the invisible ear he had searched for so long.

'The thing is,' he said, 'I've been having these strange dreams.'

His sense of relief was palpable. It was the first time he'd mentioned the dreams to anyone, and he could feel the pressure diminishing already.

'I keep dreaming about death. I see ships go down and men being shot or drowned. People from this town, people I know.'

There was no reaction. What had he been expecting? This was no confession, unless you regarded unburdening yourself to empty space or a blank wall a confession. How could he have hoped for a reaction from this halfwit? He already knew the answer: because it seemed to him that he, too, was entering the dark land of fools, an unknown territory where the mad moved with familiar ease, but where he was a new arrival. In a way, he was asking for help.

Albert was overcome by the other man's silence and had no idea how to go on. Yet he sensed that something had happened. Anders Nørre's hands were still lying quietly in his lap and his stare was blank as ever, but now something loomed behind that blankness, something other than endless mechanical calculations.

'Do you have dreams like that?'

Albert made his voice as gentle he could, as if trying to reach the hidden soul of Anders Nørre. But he knew that he was fumbling to find his own.

For a moment Anders Nørre sat frozen. Then he leaped up with a roar, a thick, inarticulate bellowing. He ran to the door and flung it open. He turned and gave Albert a wild look then disappeared into the twilight.

Albert stayed on the bed. Going after Nørre was pointless, he knew. Anders would be off on one of his long trips across the fields, and he wouldn't reappear for a couple of days. As for Albert, he couldn't even rise from the bed. Nørre's reaction had paralysed him. He really was in a bad way, he thought, if the village idiot ran away from him in horror. Even in the dark country so familiar to Anders Nørre, Albert was seen as a monster.

Does he dream the way I do, Albert wondered, or is he like the animals that sense an earthquake long before humans do and howl in fear the night before the earth splits open?

WHEN THE WAR STARTED, ALBERT WAS RELIEVED.

That's how it is, he told himself. If you dread something enough, even your worst fears coming true brings comfort.

He didn't know how he'd react once the town's sailors began dying. But for the moment he felt less lonely. Now he could discuss the war with others.

Denmark had declared herself neutral, but, nonetheless, the war had serious consequences for our town. All freight traffic was cancelled immediately, and Marstal's fleet went into winter harbour as early as August. It was strange to see the schooners filling the harbour with their forest of masts while the sun was still high in the sky and the children still splashed around in the water, playing among the laid-up ships. In recent years, prosperity had risen to ever great heights, so the seamen had plenty of money. You could see evidence of that in the bars. The restlessness caused by sudden unemployment and the uncertain future led to an increase in drunkenness.

Towards October, offers came in for grain freights to north German ports, but no one dared sail. Marine insurance didn't cover losses caused by war, and the Germans had peppered the Baltic Sea with floating mines. The smaller investors couldn't afford to risk their money.

'At least that's one good thing about this town,' Albert wrote. 'There are no ruthless shipping magnates who are prepared to risk the lives of their crew for a quick profit.'

His own ships were far from Europe when the war broke out and he kept them there for its duration.

Everyone feared the mines because everyone had shares in the ships. The North Sea, too, was filled with them.

Albert immediately began keeping accounts of ships blown up by mines. For a while the people of Marstal were safe, thanks to their caution, but just three weeks after Germany had declared war on France, two Danish steamers, the *Maryland* and the *Christian Boberg*, were sunk in the North Sea. Only two days later a trawler from Reykjavik was blown up. On 3 September, yet another Danish steamer disappeared.

Albert continued his list until the end of the year. Sometimes a ship's name matched a name from his dreams, and each time that happened, it had the same terrible impact on him. He'd been there and he'd seen it happen. The left-hand column recording his nightly visions was much longer than the right-hand one, but the war was still new. Many speculated that a quick breakthrough on all fronts would bring a swift end to the conflict – talk he dismissed with a shake of his head. For obvious reasons, he couldn't tell us the cause of his certainty.

'There's still much death to come,' he said.

This unexpected pessimism from a man who had put such faith in the future was seen as the weakness of old age. Albert Madsen had lost his nerve.

In the end, he kept his opinions to himself.

A few months after the war broke out we held a collection in aid of the suffering population of Belgium. It was a sign of how remote the war still felt: we had compassion to spare for the woes of others. Albert was persuaded to join a committee responsible for preparing a special public exhibition of items related to the town and its seafaring history; the entrance fees would go wholly to the Belgians.

The exhibition was a success, attracting a great many visitors. On display were old costumes from Ærø, intricate lace and embroidery work, brass candle-scissors and some beautifully carved cupboards and bureaus. We admired these things, but they didn't stir any nostalgia in us; on the contrary, they proved that the present was better than the past, and that the future would be better still. Our progress was especially evident in the display that documented the development of the shipping trade.

'Look,' we said to each other, pointing to the model of a Marstal cutter. 'Only twenty-four registered tonnes. And next to it, a three-masted schooner built at Sofus Boye's shipyard with a carrying capacity of five hundred tonnes. And it's already twenty-five years old.'

Albert was mainly interested in the collection of curiosities that the town's seamen had brought back from all parts of the world. The conches, the stuffed hummingbird and the set of teeth from a sawfish took him back to the days of his youth. But when he came to the telegrapher Olfert Blach's Chinese hoard of rugs, embroideries and a complete and very precious Mandarin costume he stopped to reflect.

'Yes,' he said to Pastor Abildgaard. 'A sailor knows from experience that there's no such thing as tradition. Or rather, that there are many kinds of tradition, not just his own. This is how we do it here, says the farmer on his ancestral land. Well, that's not how they do it there, says the sailor. He's the one who's seen more. The farmer provides his own yardstick. But the sailor knows that won't do for him. Right now the whole world is at war; it's not even two weeks since Russia, England and France declared war on Turkey because Turkey became an ally of Germany. Many millions of people are fighting each other, but does the world get any bigger because of it, or any smaller? The ships lie still. The sailors can't go to sea and come back with tales of new things. All we can do now is sit here on our little island and grow as stupid as the farmers.'

'You shouldn't say that. You're being unfair to them.'

The vicar wasn't from the island. He had an outsider's curiosity about anything local that he considered to be an amusing oddity, and he'd been responsible for that part of the exhibition. Albert knew that he was even writing an account of the town's local history because every now and then Abildgaard would ask for advice. A friendly, if not warm, relationship had developed between them. But Albert had often thought that the vicar would have been better suited to a rural parish than a shipping town like Marstal. Given his shackled life, the farmer, after all, fitted the basic Christian vision better than the sailor did. All those messages about bowing your head and throwing yourself on the mercy of fate were made for him. Of course a sailor was also subject to the whims of nature, but he challenged the weather and the sea; he was something of a rebel.

Still, no conflict festered between the vicar and the rest of us. The inner circle of his congregation was made up of old women who devoutly slept through his sermons, and no hint of rebellion touched its outer ranks either. We felt it was right and proper to have a vicar, and as Abildgaard never questioned our way of life, our relationship was characterised by mutual tolerance.

'You really shouldn't call the farmers stupid,' the vicar persisted. 'The farmers support the notion of public education, which I know you also favour. Just look at the adult schools. But sailors – well, is anyone more superstitious? And the new radical newspaper in the town – why isn't that prospering if the sailing profession is, as you say, so very enlightened and informed about international affairs? And at election time, haven't you noticed that people here inevitably vote conservative? How do you explain that?'

Pastor Abildgaard's tone had become teasing.

'It's the concept of ownership,' Albert said. 'If the cabin boy has a hundredth share in the ship, that's enough to make him feel like a captain. He believes that their interests are the same.'

'And what's wrong with that?' The vicar went on. 'Look at your own dictum. You've gone to the trouble of having it chiselled into fourteen tonnes of granite and unveiled to the sound of patriotic songs. Its message is precisely that there's strength in fellowship.'

'I meant that in a socialist sense.' Albert had grown irritated with the vicar and wanted to rile him. 'Where would this town be if its inhabitants didn't know how to unite? We have the second-largest fleet in the country, though the town itself, in terms of population size, is in hundredth place at best. We have mutual marine insurance, financed by the town's sailors. And we have the breakwater. No outsider built it for us. We did it ourselves. I'd call that socialism.'

'Which is something to mention in my next sermon. I'll inform the staunchly conservative citizens of Marstal that they are, in fact, socialists. I normally find laughter in church inappropriate; however, I'll make an exception next Sunday.'

Albert was aware that he wasn't acquitting himself well, but he refused to give up. For a moment it seemed as if his old fighting spirit had been rekindled.

'Take a sailor,' he said. 'He signs on to a new ship. He's surrounded by nothing but strangers. Not only do they come from other towns and parts of his own country, but often from completely different nations. He has to learn to work with them. His vocabulary's broadened, he learns new words and grammar, and he comes across new ways of thinking. He turns into a man different from the one who spends his life ploughing the same old furrow. These are the men the world needs, not nationalists and warmongers. I fear that this war will cut to the heart of a sailor's life.'

The vicar laughed again, ready with a new riposte.

'Yes, and then this cosmopolitan returns to Marstal, speaking in a broader Marstal dialect than ever, and claims that the farmer, simply because he lives a few field boundaries away, speaks a foreign language that no one understands. And therefore must be stupid. Yes, you've created a proper world citizen, Captain Madsen. I still prefer the nationalist. His sense of solidarity is more inclusive. It embraces high and low, farmer and sailor, as long as they share a language and a history. And I see no sign of this fellowship being destroyed in these unhappy war years. On the contrary, I think it's growing stronger.'

Such a long time passed before Albert spoke again that Pastor Abildgaard, with a little feeling of triumph that he did his best to conceal, assumed that the conversation was over and prepared to continue his inspection of the exhibits. But Albert, who'd been standing with his hands behind his back, contemplating his toecaps, finally cleared his throat and looked Abildgaard firmly in the eye.

'In the years before the war, you'd often take a walk to Dampskibsbroen to see the ferry leave, wouldn't you?'

'Yes,' Abildgaard said. 'Dare I say it, it's the only entertainment the town has to offer. Well, apart from the ferry's arrival, obviously. Which surpasses the excitement of its departure. So, yes, of course I did.'

'Did you notice anything in particular?'

The vicar shook his head. 'Not as far as I can remember.'

'The unusually large number of farmers, weighed down by baggage?'

'Ah, I see where you're going with this.'

Abildgaard smiled disarmingly, as though he knew he was about to be robbed of his earlier minor victory and was willing to be a good sport about it.

'Yes, I'm sure you do. But there's no harm in my pointing it out anyway. Those farmers were emigrating to America. There they were, the country's spiritual and cultural backbone, with ancient family farms whose soil their ancestors had cultivated for hundreds of years, saying a faithless farewell. Whereas the sailors, the rootless, restless, stateless freebooters –'

'I never said that,' Abildgaard tried to interrupt him.

'– brawlers and vandals, ruffians and half-criminals, drunkards and debauchers with a girl in every port, whose Danish is so mixed up with words from every continent that not even their own mothers can understand them when they come home, with their arms and chests as tattooed as a deck of cards – hearts, diamonds, spades, clubs –'

'I must protest,' the vicar said. 'My respect for the breadwinners of this town is too great to speak of the seafaring profession in such terms.'

'In that case you have good reason. Because you've never seen Marstal sailors queuing up on Dampskibsbroen with chests of valuables on their backs to emigrate to America. We might be gone for years. But we always come home again. Because we sailors, we stay.'

WHEN SPRING CAME THE HARBOUR EMPTIED BECAUSE A NEW INSURANCE policy had been established to prevent shipowners from suffering financially if a vessel were lost through war. After that the freight market went only one way, and that was up. We sailed like never before, not just to Norway and western Sweden and Iceland, but to Newfoundland, the West Indies and Venezuela, even right across the war zones to England and the French ports in the Channel. Everything was back to normal, only better, although we moaned about the English, who introduced endless complicated sailing restrictions and charged exorbitant prices for piloting and towing. In this respect the Germans were far more reasonable. Free piloting and towing assistance was available in German ports along the Baltic coast. So far, Marstal had yet to lose a single ship.

Then the submarine war began.

Our first loss was the schooner *Salvador*, which went down in flames on 2 June 1915, in the middle of a warm day. Albert made a note in the right-hand column in his account ledger. Now it would start to fill up.

No one had died. The crew returned home and behaved as if they'd achieved something important. Ha, they chuckled in the bars and streets, where curious onlookers crowded around them. It had been a picnic. All right, so they'd lost their ship, but the U-boat responsible had towed their lifeboat for a while. Their first mate, Hans Peter Kroman, had been presented with a pipe and some tobacco – Hamburg brand tobacco, very good quality, incidentally – and Captain Jens Olesen Sand received two bottles of cognac for the voyage home. The German U-boat crew? Very nice people, a bit on the pale side, perhaps, from being down deep for so long, but otherwise very respectable sailors.

'What a shame,' Sand had remarked to the U-boat captain, as they stood on the sub's deck watching the *Salvador* burn up.

'That's war for you,' replied the German, shrugging apologetically.

True, he was no Englishman, but a gentleman all the same. When the submarine crew finally unhitched the towrope, they asked politely whether the crew from the *Salvador* were sure they had sufficient provisions on the lifeboat. The cook who had lost his cap was given a sou'wester in its stead. Then, after exchanging mutual assurances that this really was nothing personal, the Danes and the Germans parted ways. The next day the lifeboat was picked up by an English trawler, whose crew also turned out to be nice people.

Some months later a letter arrived from the German government stating that the sinking of the *Salvador* had been unwarranted. Captain Sand received an apology from Kaiser Wilhelm himself, and 27,000 Danish kroner, the amount for which the ship had been insured.

A few months later, another schooner went up in smoke, and Albert wrote the name *Cocos* under *Salvador* in his right-hand column.

Again the crew returned home, speaking of the war as nothing but high jinks. The U-boat had sailed them to another Marstal schooner that happened to be in the vicinity, the *Karin Bak*, which was allowed to pass through unharmed after its captain, Albertsen, agreed to take the shipwrecked men on board. Then the U-boat sailed away, only to return with the crew's clothes, which in their hurry they'd left behind.

'Well, I must say! The level of service isn't bad when you're dealing with German U-boats!'

'Why didn't you ask them to wash your underpants while they were at it?' Ole Mathiesen joked, and laughter erupted once more.

Telegrams stuttered with news of terrible losses on all fronts. But in Marstal we all agreed that the war was a hoot.

Albert Madsen continued to keep his accounts, and as the war progressed they became his obsession. He believed they contained a message, as yet undeciphered. Convinced that figures had the power to prove things, he made lists of the price of life's necessities in Marstal: rye bread, butter, margarine, eggs, beef and pork. He knew the crews' wages, their war supplement, their bonus for European or overseas voyages and their accident insurance in case of death or disability. He kept an eye on the freight market and the price of ships, on exchange rates and quotations.

A shipowner must do all of these things to carry out his job properly. But does he also need to keep long lists of ships sunk by mines, of ships destroyed by torpedoes and fires, the number of fallen men from North Schleswig, and English losses as of 9 January 1916? Of the 24,122 officers dead and the 525,345 killed among the junior ranks? The numbers Albert jotted down are incomprehensible. And that's precisely why they make no impression. So why, then, did he write them down? Why did he constantly mention them in his conversations with us?

Why did a shipbroker and owner in a small coastal town in a country that wasn't taking part in the world war and was thus, in a sense, not taking part in the world, keep a two-column list of lost ships, a left-hand column enumerating those he saw sinking in his dreams and a right-hand column showing the same ships sunk on real seas? What was he trying to prove?

In the first year of the war, the town lost six ships, and in the second year only one. No Marstaller had been killed, though millions were dying elsewhere, beyond our field of vision. Within that field there were no dead; on the contrary, what we saw, and found so easy to understand, was that the freight market shot up so high that newly built ships earned back their start-up capital in a year, and sailors' wages trebled. The price of ships started to rise as early as 1915. Even older wooden vessels, battered from many years at sea, could be sold for almost double their pre-war value. By the end of the year prices had tripled; they continued to rise throughout the whole of the following year. The *Agent Petersen*, the most famous ship in Marstal, which in 1887 had completed the fastest voyage ever recorded between South America and Africa, was valued at 25,000 Danish kroner, but sold for 90,000.

Marstal had started to lose its fleet, but not to the U-boats.

Albert realised that between his right- and left-hand columns a third column was called for, one that his dreams had never warned him about: the list of ships that had been sold. It filled faster than the other two, and soon outstripped them. But there was no drama about this particular list. It contained neither dreams nor dead men but instead marked the strangely frantic wealth that flooded our town. Houses were repaired and painted, women who once dressed modestly now wore their Sunday best every day, and the shops stocked new, more expensive goods. The people of Marstal, once renowned for their thrift, were living as if there were no tomorrow.

This wasn't some frenzy brought on by the mortal fear of war. It was the dizziness that comes of having too much money.

THEN, FINALLY, THE WAR CAME TO MARSTAL WITH A FACE THAT WASN'T cheerful. 'Finally': that was the word Albert used in his notes. The wall between him and the rest of us was about to topple, and we'd all soon know what he knew. No longer did people perish at sea only in his lonely dreams. In real life they'd be shot down, drown, freeze to death, and die from exposure and thirst. Survivors came home and brought Albert's visions to life with their stories. Others vanished without trace.

A message came from the royal envoy in Berlin: the *Astræa* had been lost. There was no information about where or how. Seven men were missing, including two from Marstal, skipper Abraham Christian Svane and first mate Valdemar Holm. A man from the Faroe Islands and an able seaman from Cape Verde were among the others.

Albert had seen them die: they'd jumped for their lives through flying shards from a lifeboat under fire. It had been a calm, over-cast day. The sea had lain like grey silk. He'd watched the water close over them as their lungs gave up and the last air bubble burst.

Germany had declared unrestricted submarine war. Marstal, which had lost only seven ships in the previous two years, now lost sixteen in a single year, then four in a month. The returning survivors didn't get drunk and brag of their experiences; instead, they avoided atten-tion. The crew of the *Peace*, who'd seen their captain and their bosun shot down in front of them and afterwards drifted for days in a sinking lifeboat while two more men perished, stayed at home with their families. If an acquaintance approached them in the street they'd quickly veer down the nearest alley.

The *Hydra* disappeared without trace with six men on board. Not all of them were from Marstal, but the losses could be felt across the town.

Gaps began appearing in our ranks.

PASTOR ABILDGAARD WENT TO JØRGENSEN'S GROCERY SHOP IN Tværgade. The owner, whose full name was Kresten Minor Jørgensen, was a former first mate who'd come ashore and now sold groceries and ships' provisions. He manned the large wooden counter himself, a small, stooping man with a bald head that shone as if polished; on a summer's day when he strolled around in his short khaki jacket, his smooth head would reflect the sun, forcing passers-by to squint.

The small bell that hung above the door rang out, a noisy, irritating sound, as Abildgaard entered the shop. A couple of old skippers were chatting on a long wooden bench to the right of the door, but Abildgaard never learned what they were talking about, because the moment he closed the door behind him, a deathly silence descended.

Deathly was indeed the word, for death itself might have entered the shop with him. Jørgensen took a step back behind his wooden counter, his jaw dropping and his eyes widening. Abildgaard turned round, thinking that the grocer must have seen something shocking in the street through the open door. Meanwhile, the two skippers eyed the vicar and the grocer alternately, as if waiting for an incident of immense significance to unfold.

'Good morning,' Abildgaard stuttered, hesitating to utter such a pleasantry in this laden atmosphere.

Jørgensen didn't answer.

When the pastor approached the counter, ready to order his goods, Jørgensen took another step back and splayed his raised hands. His mouth was still open, and he looked like he'd stopped breathing. They stared at each other, the grocer seemingly on the verge of fainting, the sensitive Abildgaard paralysed.

Then one of the skippers on the bench shot a long blob of spittle into the polished brass pot in the corner and the sound snapped Jørgensen out of his trance.

'Just tell me, please, please just tell me!' he begged.

'A pound of coffee. But I want it freshly ground,' Abildgaard said, mechanically repeating his wife's instructions.

Jørgensen buried his face in his hands, and a strange snorting sound, halfway between laughter and tears, escaped him.

'Coffee, coffee, he only wants some coffee!' he choked from behind the lattice of his fingers.

Laughing uncontrollably, he went over to the coffee mill and began filling it with beans. His laughter made his hands shake, and he spilled beans all over the counter and the floor.

Then he pulled himself together.

'I won't be charging you for your coffee today, Pastor.'

But Abildgaard was by now outraged. 'Would someone kindly explain to me what is going on here?' he demanded, in the thunderous tone he employed in the pulpit.

'Jørgensen's just feeling lucky,' noted one of the skippers behind him.

Abildgaard glared at Jørgensen with all the authority he could muster. 'If this is some kind of joke, I can assure you that I don't find it in the least bit amusing.'

Jørgensen looked down, abashed, but at the same time a blissful smile spread across his face. He rubbed his bald head as though giving it an extra polish in honour of the vicar.

'I do beg your pardon, Pastor. You see, I thought you were here because of Jørgen.'

'Jørgen?'

'Jørgen, my son. He's an able seaman on board the *Seagull*. Well, I don't mind telling you, I was worried that you'd come to tell me the ship had been torpedoed and that Jørgen . . . Jørgen . . .' He gulped as if even now the fear still gripped him. 'Well, I thought that Jørgen had . . .' the grocer cleared his throat, '. . . had been lost.'

After that incident, Abildgaard grew afraid to show himself in the streets; it dawned on him that every time he left the vicarage in Kirkestræde, people thought he was coming to announce a death. He had a naturally sunny disposition, and he couldn't bear it. He'd become a harbinger of death, a black raven with a starched collar, imprisoned in the low-ceilinged vestibules of grief. He struggled to breathe normally, and when he talked to the bereaved about God's mercy and help and comfort through the love of Jesus Christ, he felt he'd choke. The words came out of him in a strangely helpless, hesitant way, as though they no longer contained real answers to the questions of the bereaved.

He'd often brought the consolation of faith to a family who'd lost a father or a son. What made it unbearable now was the sheer number of dead. Like a huge flock of migrant starlings, they hovered above the town, and one by one the announcements – the death of a father, a brother or a son – fell onto the roofs of Marstal in a downpour of wrecked hope.

Pastor Abildgaard became a recluse. He stayed indoors as much as he could, emerging only on Sundays, when he was forced to walk the hundred metres to the church, and to officiate at funerals. Fortunately, there were no more of those than usual. After all, the war dead did not return home.

Anna Egidia Rasmussen, widow of Carl Rasmussen, the marine painter who had decorated the altarpiece in the church, began visiting the stricken families when news of a death had to be broken. She was well acquainted with grieving homes. She'd lost her own husband under mysterious circumstances on a voyage from Greenland, and since then she'd had to part with seven of her eight children, all of whom had died as adults. Only one daughter, Augusta Kathinka, was still alive, but she was in America.

Anna Egidia Rasmussen lived in Teglgade, in a large house with tall windows, which her husband had designed and where he'd made his studio in the attic. For many years she'd been a source of help and comfort to neighbourhood families who'd been hit by losses at sea, who suddenly had to say goodbye to a father, a brother or a son. She had a strange skill. She could lead crying the way some people can lead singing. She'd made it her art. Contrary to what most people think, weeping isn't uncontrollable emotion that spills into tears. It's the opposite, a channel for feelings, a way to divert them in a healthy direction. Serenity was her life's mission. Anna Egidia had needed it to deal with her husband, a man of a nervous disposition and a sensitive mind, introverted and prone to brooding. Carl Rasmussen would stand on the beach for hours staring out to sea, indifferent to the weather and his own health. Finally she'd have to drag him back to their house, chilled to the bone, while between coughing fits, he begged her to leave him in peace. Afterwards he'd lie feverish in bed, his teeth chattering. At times like that her calm was essential, though it made him accuse her of lacking the imagination to understand his character and failing to share his enthusiasm and vision.

This widow became a second visitor to many houses. Death would be the first, and she would follow in its wake. She was a source of comfort not only to her own family, with its many grandchildren, but to a wide circle around Teglgade. When someone died, the family sent for Anna Egidia. She'd arrive in her worn black silk dress, sit down in the middle of the room, send the adults away and take the children by the hand. When a mother fell ill and was admitted to hospital while her husband was away at sea, Anna Egidia would care for the children in her own home. She was constantly invited to be a godmother to the newborn, as if she'd been charged with keeping watch at life's entrance as well as its exit.

Now the vicar, too, has foundered on the coast of bones, Albert thought, when he heard about Pastor Abildgaard's reclusiveness. He could preach about death in a way that moved even me. But he'd never met it. Now that he has, he's fallen silent.

Albert went to the vicarage to volunteer to assist the widow Rasmussen in her work. He felt his dreams obliged him to. He was shown into the vicar's study, where Abildgaard was sitting by the window staring out into the garden. There was a purple beech outside, dark and sombre, like a tree that knew neither spring nor summer but grew in an eternal autumn, its leaves burned black around the edges by the frost. Nearby, the rose beds, which were Mrs Abildgaard's pride and joy, were in bloom.

Abildgaard got up and shook Albert's hand, then returned to his position by the window. When Albert announced the purpose of his visit, the vicar didn't speak for a long time. Then all of a sudden he buried his face in his hands.

'My nerves!' he exclaimed.

His narrow shoulders trembled. He took off his steel spectacles and placed them on the desk in front of him. He dug his fists into the hollows of his eyes like a child surrendering to its crying, and the tears rolled down his smooth-shaven cheeks.

'Please, please forgive me,' he stammered. 'I didn't mean to . . .'

Albert rose and went over to him. He placed his hand on the vicar's shoulder.

'You've got nothing to apologise for.'

The vicar clasped Albert's hand with both of his and pressed it against his forehead as though he were seeking to ease a pain inside.

Neither of them spoke for a long time. Abildgaard cried himself dry, then put his steel spectacles back on his nose. As Albert rose to take his leave, he noticed a black object on the vicar's desk; it reminded him of a claw, but not a bird's. No, it looked more like the curled fingers of severed human hand, with nails as yellow as old bone.

'What's this?' he asked.

'That's the awful thing. I've no idea what to do with it.'

Abildgaard sounded as if he might break out in a fresh attack of tears. Albert took the object and peered at it closely.

'No, you mustn't touch it. It's vile.'

It was indeed a human hand. Albert was instantly put in mind of the shrunken head. But here the preservation technique was different: it seemed that the hand had been smoked and dried in the heat of a fire.

'Where does it come from?' he asked.

'You know Josef Isager? They call him the Congo Pilot, I believe.' Albert nodded. Josef Isager had been a pilot on the Congo River many years ago. He'd worked for the Belgian king, Leopold, and had returned home with a medal for faithful service. He was reluctant to speak about his years in Africa, but the neighbours said that they'd sometimes be woken in the night by screaming. It was Josef Isager. Once he'd kicked the headboard of his bed to pieces: a loud crack had sounded as the large mahogany frame fell apart. He'd leaped up and thrown pieces of furniture around as if it were an enemy and he was fighting for his life. His bedlinen, which fell in a messy heap on the floor, was soaked in sweat. It was malaria, so he told us.

Albert, who'd heard the stories about these nocturnal upheavals, had his own theory. These weren't malaria attacks, but nightmares. Josef Isager was dreaming about Africa.

'And then he comes to me with a severed hand. A hand – a human hand! "What do you want me to do with it?" I ask him once I've recovered from my shock. "Give it a Christian burial," he replies. "Who is it?" I ask. "I don't know," he says to me. "Some nigger

273

woman. Damn you, vicar!" he says. And he gives me a furious look. Perhaps I shouldn't burden you with such things, Captain Madsen, but the man scared me.'

Albert nodded. The Congo Pilot had the same effect on him. Josef Isager was a tough customer. But there were many of those. Life had kicked them around and they'd kicked back. The son of the old schoolteacher, he and Albert had been at school together, and Josef had been trapped in the war between the boys and their brutal tormentor, unable to take sides because he'd be a traitor no matter whom he supported. He'd vented his frustration with his fists, beating up his brother, the ever-whining Johan. Then he'd gone to sea and no one knew what he'd seen there: new abuses, with fresh victims, no doubt, where he himself had an outlet for his frustrations, for that was how things were. But perhaps he'd also found a way out. That, at least, was what Albert reckoned. The sea was a vast space where a boy could leave the ill-treatment of his childhood behind and rediscover himself.

After Josef shipped out we saw nothing of him for several years. We heard he'd gone to the Congo via Antwerp, and sailed on its great rivers. He returned to Denmark, but not to Marstal. Then he left again. Africa had got into his blood. We didn't know why. After many years the fever left him, and he came ashore and worked as a loss adjuster, first in Copenhagen and then in Marstal. His wife, Maren Kirstine, whom he'd married in his youth, was a Marstaller, and they'd settled down in Kongegade.

At first he didn't even mention his years in Africa. When we questioned him, he'd shake his head dismissively as though he couldn't find the strength to describe it and because we wouldn't understand anyway. But one day he'd asked Albert if he could see the shrunken head. For a while he sat holding James Cook in his hands, turning the head while he assessed it. He looked at it with expert eyes.

'Well, that's not how we used to make them,' he finally said.

'We?' Albert frowned.

'Yes,' Josef replied casually. 'We preferred to smoke them.'

He laughed – Albert couldn't determine whether from disgust or cynicism.

'They have put an effort into this one,' Josef went on. 'We only made sure they dried out. They looked like they were sleeping. Closed eyes, their lips rolled back a bit so you could see a thin white line of teeth.' He looked at Albert. His eyes grew distant, as though he were dwelling on the memory.

'Who are you talking about?' Albert asked.

The Congo Pilot snapped out of his trance.

'The niggers, who else?' He sounded disappointed. 'We had to show them who was boss, you see. There was this Belgian captain. He used Negro heads as decorations around his flower bed. Each to his own.'

He laughed again, and this time Albert thought he detected a hint of embarrassment. He sensed that the mention of the severed heads hadn't triggered it, but rather Josef's own ignorance. Perhaps he had taken Albert to be a fellow conspirator and was only just realising that he'd been mistaken. Albert stared at his old schoolmate and didn't know what to say.

'I know that look you're giving me.' Josef's voice was suddenly harsh. 'But it's the only language they understand. It was for their own good. Otherwise we'd have had to shoot the whole lot of them. They didn't want to work. They'd lie stretched out on a mat soaking up the sun like crocodiles in the sand. They could do that, all right. Proud and vain, they were. But otherwise they were just like animals.'

'I thought you worked as a pilot?'

'Yes, I was a pilot, port captain in Boma, *commissaire maritime*, I took the *Lualaba* all the way up to Matadi along a narrow and tricky branch of the river. Before I arrived, the ocean steamers could get only as far as Boma. Later they went all the way to Matadi, too. But I was the first.'

There was pride in his voice. He raised his head and looked Albert straight in the eye. For a moment it seemed as if Josef were observing him from a great height, though they were both sitting down and Albert was taller. Josef had deep-set eyes, a protruding, straight nose and a moustache whose ends reached all the way down to his strong jaw. His gaze became arrogant.

'I was the best pilot on the Congo River. I was the port captain in Boma. I did it all. But that wasn't what swung it. This is the most important thing . . .' He poked his cheek with his index finger. 'Your skin colour. That's what decides it. I was a white man. And I was master of all I surveyed. It's as hot as hell in Africa. But that's nothing compared to the fire you feel flare up inside you. That's Africa's gift: it finally teaches you your own strength. Only one man in four comes back. Fever takes the other three – the fever or the blacks. But it's all worth it.'

He leaned forward and fixed Albert with his gaze. His arrogance had gone. He seemed to appeal to Albert for understanding. His voice grew pleading. 'I've tried to explain it to people I meet at home. But they don't understand. No one can unless they've tried it themselves. Everything you've seen before – it's nothing. Everything that follows – nothing. See-through mirages. You bring only one thing back with you from the Congo, and it's not those trinkets that I've got lying about at home. We had this song. No, I'm not going to sing it to you.' He cleared his throat.

'Congo,' he recited. His voice suddenly quivered with emotion. 'Even the strongest man will shut his mouth and lie down for good. Even the hardest, wildest man soon ends up as rat food. They died like flies in the Congo.' His voice became more and more urgent, almost thick with passion. 'But I didn't die. I lived. Yes, I lived.' He slammed the table with the palm of his hand. 'Not like here! This is no life!'

Albert still hadn't spoken. He wanted to look away. But they kept staring at each other and Albert knew what he'd seen in Josef's eyes. The Congo Pilot had learned to view other people as only a god can: the look that asks, should this man be allowed to breathe, or does he deserve to die? This was the look that Josef Isager, the schoolteacher's son, had brought back from Africa.

Josef was getting on. He was as tough-minded as ever, but he was old, and in Africa they needed youth and vitality. So Josef had returned to Marstal, where he came from, and where he was now living like a king in exile. Nobody bowed before the threat in his eyes, apart from Maren Kirstine, who was a mute and terrified witness to his nightly rages.

'Did he say why he suddenly wanted the hand buried?'

Abildgaard shook his head. 'I asked him how he'd got hold of it. He said it was a kind of souvenir, like an elephant tusk, a necklace or a spear – he'd come back with quite a few of those sorts of things. It was common, he told me, as if it were something quite ordinary. Belgian soldiers would chop off the hands of natives they'd killed, so they could prove that they hadn't wasted their cartridges. It was on such an occasion that the hand had fallen into his possession. I didn't know what to say.' The vicar gave Albert a look of despair. 'I didn't want the hand. But he left it here. "You're a vicar," he said. "The dead are your field." I can't make myself throw it out. But I can't put it in a coffin and bury it in the cemetery either. There isn't even a name attached to it. I'm at my wits' end.'

'Pastor Abildgaard, in one of your sermons you spoke about feeling how the world withdraws and your strength disappears precisely when you need it the most.'

Abildgaard looked up with a smile of surprise.

'You were there, Captain Madsen? I'm delighted that you can remember my sermons. Yes, that was an excellent choice of words.'

Albert had intended to say something more, but now he fell silent, and Abildgaard lapsed into despondency once more.

'What am I going to do with that hand?' he wailed. Again he looked out of the window, as though the garden could provide him with an answer.

THE MONEY KEPT ROLLING INTO MARSTAL. THE FREIGHT MARKET
had never been so favourable, nor had seamen's wages. Ship prices,
too, continued their incomprehensible rise. Every other house in a
street might be grieving, yet the excitement of those families that
remained untouched couldn't be entirely suppressed. Women in their
Sunday best mingled with widows in black. Shop-fronts were decorated as if Christmas had already come. And no hearses drove to
the cemetery with girls strewing flowers before them: the dead sailors
politely kept away. They didn't disturb us, and the elderberry hung
low and blossomed over the streets that summer.

Every spring, before the fleet left the harbour, all Marstal smelled
of tar. Sailors armed with sticky brushes would coat the stone foundat-
ions of their houses as if they were ships whose bottoms needed
caulking in preparation for the summer's sailing. On the house gables
were numbers in cast iron, painted black, announcing the year each
house had been built. 1793, 1800, 1825. When we hammered away
at the tarred plinths, the black peeled off in layers like the rings of
a tree trunk. But the numbers never fitted. The layers of tar didn't
record years, so much as absences. The plinths were only tarred
when the men were home.

Now the men were disappearing, one by one, and the women
would have to take on this masculine job, along with many others.
Soon we'd see them in springtime, tarring away with brushes as
black as their fresh widow's weeds.

Excited students from the Navigation College cycled through the
town. They pretended to mow down children playing in the streets,
who squealed at them in mock terror. The young men were
returning to their boarding houses to eat their hot lunches. Albert
froze at the sight of some of them. He'd seen them, too. The

U-boats were waiting for them. They thought the future would bring them money and adventures. They had the fever of youth in their veins and feared nothing. Albert was the one who carried fear on their behalf.

He had odd thoughts about the war and its causes. He visited the church regularly these days. They were just laying the copper lining of the new spire, and the nave echoed all day with the sound of hammering, so Albert visited in the evening, when the day's work was done. He was looking for tranquillity. Behind the thick walls, in this cool, white room where dusk arrived early, almost as if the space had its own version of the rhythm of day and night, he felt he had time to think.

And what he contemplated was death. Some people complained when death came too early and claimed a child, a young mother or a sailor with a family to provide for. He'd never understood that. Of course it was a tragedy for those left behind and for the person who'd been robbed of the greater part of life. But it wasn't unfair. Death was beyond such notions. It seemed to him that the bereaved often gave short shrift to their grief in favour of railing fruitlessly against life's injustice. After all, no one would dream of saying that the wind was unfair to the trees and the flowers. True, you might feel uneasy when the sun switched off its light, or ice gave your ship a dangerous list. But indignant, outraged or angry, no. It was pointless. Nature was neither fair nor unfair. Those terms belonged to the world of men.

He was well aware of why he felt this way. He was thinking ahead and looking back at the same time, and he didn't focus on anyone in particular. He thought about the generations, living on from fathers and mothers to sons and daughters, who in turn grew up to be fathers and mothers who had sons and daughters. Life was like one big marching army. Death ran alongside and picked off a soldier here and there, but it didn't affect the fighting force. Its march continued, and its size didn't seem to diminish. On the contrary, it grew on into eternity, so that no one was alone in death. Someone else would always follow. That was what counted. Such was the chain of life: unbreakable.

But this war had altered everything. Albert would take a walk along the harbour and see how few ships were lying idle along the quays or moored to posts in the middle of the harbour entrance.

There were still shipowners who weren't prepared to risk lives, but most ships sailed. Despite mines and unrestricted submarine warfare, still they sailed. Six vessels might go down in one month, four the next. Never before had the sea demanded such sacrifices, but owners and captains who'd have kept their ships in the harbour while a storm raged sent them into the far greater storm of war.

Where did this contempt for death, this total heedlessness come from? Surely ten lost ships and two missing crews in two months was a lesson already dearly learned?

Along the one and a half kilometres of Marstal's harbour hundreds of ships were laid up for winter, bobbing on the water, waiting for their spring departures. That was our town. It was a sight no one would see again. The chain had been broken.

What had happened to fellowship and to what Albert thought of as kinship, in whose spirit he'd erected the stone only four years earlier? He'd thought at the time that he was establishing a monument to something living. Now he understood that it was a gravestone, marking the end of the spirit that had created the town. And the cause of death was in the third column in his account ledger: profit. The high prices, the increased wages, the freight that had risen tenfold, the premium on ships. Responsible owners who kept their vessels in the harbour had to watch their crews sign on elsewhere. Everybody wanted to take part in the spoils of war.

And so we sold our ships. What was the point of having them lie idle when they could be sold for three to four times their worth? The cost of building them could be recouped in a year, and so it wasn't just old, worn-out ships we disposed of, but also the freshly launched. We all spoke in pious terms about the dreadful war and vowed that this would be the last one. And dreadful it was for the millions who were killed in battle. But we, who were spared, benefited from it.

Denmark kept out of the war, taking no sides. But did we really think we'd be spared just because the Danish flag was painted on the side of our ships? A sailor needs a cool head. But this was recklessness. Marstal lay in the heart of the war zone. War fronts existed on dry land, but the sea had its fronts, too, and half the town's sailors faced them every day.

What drove us? Was the prospect of profit the heartbeat of this war? Was it bare greed that Albert now saw, even in people he'd thought he knew well? Had he simply grown old? Had something definitive changed? Or had it always been this way, without him realising it?

Albert suddenly felt ridiculous. He'd been worried about losing his mind because of dreams that contained information so terrible he dared not convey it to others. So what if he'd told us what he knew? Would we not have laughed at him and dismissed his words, even though we didn't doubt the truth of what he was telling us?

Die? Well, maybe.

Him and him, a first mate, an able seaman, a skipper. We might have pointed to others. But not to ourselves. Greed made us think we were immortal. Were we thinking about tomorrow? Our own, perhaps, but not that of others.

Skipper Levinsen had protested when the breakwater was going to be built, saying, 'You should provide only for yourself, not for posterity.' Once, the whole town had heaped shame on those words. But now the short-sighted Levinsen had become our role model.

HERMAN RETURNED HOME WITH A WALKING STICK OF WHITE BONE
in his hand, made from the vertebrae of a shark. He wasn't the first
man in Marstal to come back from the East Indies or the Pacific with
a shark's spine, but he was the first to stroll around with it in the
streets as though it were a sceptre, and he a king. Self-importantly
greeting old acquaintances, he'd use it to swipe the air with a fancy
flourish.

With the same stick that he knocked on the door of his guardian,
Hans Jepsen. As he did so, a group of boys watched him from a
safe distance, chanting: 'The Cannibal's loose! The Cannibal's
loose!'

When Hans opened the door, Herman waved his sailor's record
book in his face. He was an able seaman now, and he wanted to
show that he was entitled to respect. Without greeting Hans, he
announced his age: twenty-five. He spoke it like a punch. He'd come
of age, and he was announcing the dethronement of Hans Jepsen as
the official owner of the *Two Sisters* and the house in Skippergade.

But Hans Jepsen didn't seem to be listening. He observed the white
stick that Herman was waving.

'I see you staged an eating contest with the sharks,' he said. 'And
that you won. Shame it wasn't the other way round.'

Herman's stick sliced the air, but Hans had already slammed the
door. The shark's spine struck the green-painted wood and snapped,
its vertebrae flying in all directions. The boys shrieked with laughter,
scattering and yelling, 'The Cannibal's loose! The Cannibal's loose!'

Some time later they returned and picked up the remains of the
stick, which Herman had discarded. We didn't know why they called
him the Cannibal. Boys have their own reasons. They were probably scared of him and so they did what boys do around any object
of fear: they got up close, pointed a finger, gave it a nickname and
masked their terror with roaring laughter. They kept the salvaged

vertebrae in tins and boxes and brought them out to use in secret rituals or to decorate their hiding places inside the hollow poplars that bordered the high roads outside the town.

Every day for a whole week Herman bought a round at Weber's Cafe to celebrate his new status as a man of property. His cheeks were flushed and he wore a combative, I-dare-you look: he was constantly testing us, as if preparing to demand some oath of loyalty, a solemn agreement to submit to his whims or face the consequences. A quick glance at the way he impatiently clenched and unclenched his huge hands, as though eager for something to grab and crush, suggested what those consequences might be. He'd grown even bigger since the last time we'd seen him, with broader shoulders, impressive biceps and a chest like the front of a truck – but he'd also grown a belly. Although still young, he was already running to fat.

We asked him if he ate at Larsen's Chops or Nielsen's Pancakes, places we frequented for stew and mixed hash when we were looking for work in Copenhagen.

'I'm used to better things,' Herman said.

At Inky-Hans in Nyhavn, he'd had a crouching lion, ready to attack, tattooed on his right arm. The banner above it read *Smart and Powerfull*.

He ordered another round.

'Just you wait and see, damn it,' he said. 'Just you wait and see!'

Something about his voice made us think that he might surprise us the same way he'd surprised Holger Jepsen that day when, somewhere between Marstal and Rudkøbing, he fell, or jumped, or was helped overboard.

Herman had travelled far. We all had, but he'd been to one place we'd never gone: Børsen, the Copenhagen Stock Exchange. When he talked about that, the man we'd known as a boy, with his fixed scowl and a sullenness that possibly concealed a crime, burst into unfamiliar eloquence. But it seemed just as suspicious as his shiftiness over his stepfather's death a decade earlier.

Of course, we knew what Børsen was. It was a place frequented only by the rich and those skilled in arithmetic, where everything could be measured in money, which could grow or shrink; where people could be victorious one hour and vanquished the next; where life could shift from triumph to tragedy in the space of a second. Oh, we knew that. We also knew that we, too, were subject to the laws that governed money, that the rate of freight was not simply determined by weight and the number of nautical miles it had to travel, but also by supply and demand. And what we didn't know, Madsen, Boye, Kroman, Grube and Marstal's other shipbrokers and owners did. But though we knew laws existed to control this circus, we also knew that they were beyond us, and any one of us was more likely to survive a typhoon than to stroll out of Børsen with money in his pocket. Yet Herman seemed to have spent half the years he'd been away sailing through the maelstrom of money and bonds, where people and fortunes were swallowed up and spat out again. He called it the New America.

'You don't have to travel all the way to America to get rich. Just drop anchor in Copenhagen. Even the milk boys speculate on the Stock Exchange. You can deliver churns one day and be a millionaire the next.'

He spoke to us as though we were a bunch of illiterate, barearsed savages and he was a missionary come to enlighten us about the Promised Land. His voice was larded with a condescension that didn't suit him, and which annoyed us. Thorkild Folmer, first mate on the *Ludwig*, grimaced and retorted defiantly, 'Marstal housemaids have shares in ships, too.'

Herman laughed. 'Ha ha! Yes, a hundredth share. A hundredth of what? How much can one miserable old tub earn in one season? Who can become a millionaire from that? A tight-fisted man from Marstal, probably, if he lives to be two hundred and doesn't eat or drink in the meantime.'

And he renewed his unpleasant laughter, which he supposed proved he was smarter than the rest of us.

New words were forever on the man's lips. *Margin, bull, bear* – magic spells for those who understood their meaning, but to the rest of us pure, unfathomable gibberish. He mentioned the names of his friends at Børsen, who were visionary men of courage: indeed, pioneers in this new country. The Negro Thug, the Rolling Pavement, the Tooth Extractor, the Red Jew, the Track Changer: these men, as informal and straightforward as their happily worn nicknames implied, welcomed anyone into their club as long as he had the right attitude and wanted to get rich quick. Including an ordinary seaman. Or indeed a cabin boy.

'All I had to do was mention my inheritance and they lent me money. On the strength of my blue eyes. Me, a cabin boy.' Herman's face darkened briefly, and he looked around the circle at Weber's Cafe. 'Unlike others I could name.'

He hadn't forgotten that no one in Marstal had been prepared to sign him on as a cabin boy, let alone an ordinary seaman. But Børsen hadn't rejected him. He was good enough for the fine moneymen of Copenhagen, who included him in their circle. We'd shunned him. But now he was back.

'Just you wait and see,' he repeated for the umpteenth time, narrowing his eyes to slits. 'Just you wait and see, damn you!' He took a swig from his beer and spat it onto the floor. 'Beer – ha! No one drinks this dishwater in Copenhagen. We drink champagne for breakfast there.'

Weber's Cafe was packed, and Herman was the star attraction. He'd rolled up his sleeves and we stared at the lion on his right arm: *Smart and Poverfull*. Perhaps he was a murderer. Perhaps he was just a fool. But then again, perhaps everything he told us was the truth, and we were the fools, and he was the *smart and poverfull* one. We weren't like the boys who'd trail him through town, ridiculing someone they secretly feared. None of us grown-ups dared laugh at Herman; we were too scared of becoming the butt of his derision. Instead we nodded and looked knowing and hid our disgust. Champagne for breakfast! Bloody hell! Champagne was served on the patios of Buenos Aires whorehouses, the kind with palms, fountains and dirty paintings on the walls. It was the syrup of pleasure girls. No self-respecting man would choose to drink it except when he had a hard-on. It was the lubrication required to moisten a señorita. '*You nice. Please buy vun small bottle champagne.*' Champagne was part of the tariff.

We gazed at the bubbles rising from the bottom of our glasses. They looked like the last air squeezed from the lungs of a drowned man. We could have spat on the floor. But we didn't. We drained our glasses and thought the beer tasted strangely flat and bland.

A GROUP OF MEN, YOUNG AND OLD, WERE GATHERED ON
Dampskibsbroen one warm summer's evening when the water and
the sky were like a pastel drawing, all light blue and pink, and the
sea was as flat as a floor you could walk on all the way to Langeland.
The young men were the new breed who spoke boldly and frankly
in the presence of their elders. They'd only dipped their toes in the
ocean but they regarded themselves as experienced because of the
war and the money in their pockets. But today their attention was
fixed on a stranger in their midst.

For once even Herman was silenced. He stared intently at the
stranger: a tall, energetic man with a wide-brimmed straw hat and
a light-coloured summer jacket that hung loosely from his broad
shoulders. He had full lips and reddish-blond hair that flopped casually across his forehead. Only his bloodshot eyes told you that he
wasn't just another of the summer residents who came here for some
coastal relaxation. Ever-smiling, he flung out his arms, his voice rising
with excitement as he spoke, clearly delighted with the attention he
was receiving from his young audience. Meanwhile, the older skippers had withdrawn to the periphery: whether this was due to their
instinctive dislike of Herman, who stood within it, or the fact that
the stranger was so obviously Herman's ally (and indeed even resembled him in his large physique and bragging manner) was impossible
to tell.

Herman wore an expression we'd never seen on his face before:
admiration. Not only did he never take his eyes off the speaker's
lips, but his own started to move, as though silently echoing the
stranger's words and preparing to repeat them at the first possible
opportunity.

Herman wasn't in the habit of looking up to anyone. Albert Madsen
had once saved his ship from a serious collision, but the incident
had made Herman feel resentful rather than grateful, because on the

286

same occasion Albert had struck him, and he'd borne a grudge ever since. Spotting Albert now, out on his customary evening stroll along the harbour front, he invited him to join the circle, but his intentions weren't friendly. 'Good evening, Captain Madsen.' It was immediately clear that his politeness was only in honour of the outsider. 'Allow me to introduce Mr Henckel, the engineer.'

'Edvard Henckel,' said the stranger, offering Albert his hand with a broad smile.

Albert had never forgotten the look Herman gave him the day he'd jumped onto the deck of the *Two Sisters*. He hadn't expected the boy to lash out at him, but he'd easily dodged his blow and saved the ship. It wasn't the first time he'd made short work of a useless helmsman by landing him one. He might have believed that Herman, then fifteen, had tried to strike him in panic, but the boy's eyes had betrayed nothing but reckless fury, and Albert didn't doubt that Herman was capable of murder. There was a harshness about him. That in itself wasn't a bad thing, but beyond the harshness, something about Herman seemed dead to the core. Like fossilised wood, he would never sprout shoots, and his life wouldn't blossom in unexpected ways. There was no vitality there. Just brutality.

Albert was well aware that the young man saw him as an enemy. The feeling wasn't mutual. He felt an almost physical unease in the younger man's presence, but he felt pity too. Most of all though, he felt old and resigned. He approached Herman with the wariness he'd feel towards a dangerous animal with a bleeding paw stuck in a trap.

He shook Henckel's hand, then turned to Herman.

'You've sold the *Two Sisters*, I hear. What a shame; she was a good ship, a joy to behold, and she did the town proud.' He heard the pomposity in his own voice and felt annoyed with himself.

'Possibly,' Herman replied, 'but I made a good profit. That's the important thing.'

'To a businessman, yes, but not to a sailor. Surely other things bind us to our ships besides the prospect of short-term gain.'

'Now you listen . . .' A note of impatience entered the young man's voice, as though he were talking to someone hard of hearing. 'I could sail the *Two Sisters* to hell and back again, and even with the recent rise in the freight – tenfold – I'd never earn the same amount by sailing as I did by selling.'

'You're only thinking short-term,' Albert repeated.

They were clearly the principal players now, and their audience encircled them as if they were about to fight a duel. Henckel clasped his restless hands behind his back, an expectant smile playing on his lips.

'Who says I even want another ship? Oh, *shipowner* sounds grand as hell. But perhaps it'll soon be an empty title.'

The lack of respect wasn't lost on Albert. How dare this upstart tell him his time was over and his experience worthless? He felt a brief surge of anger as he eyed the young man who stood in front of him, his legs planted apart and a contemptuous look on his face. His shirtsleeves were casually rolled up in the warm summer evening, so you could see the lion getting ready to attack, and the words *Smart and Poverfull*.

'There are two spelling mistakes in your tattoo.'

Albert regretted it instantly. He'd allowed himself to get carried away. It was pointless rising to the bait. Herman was hard, callous. But his brutality simply reflected the era they lived in. And Albert? His time was over. But so was the town's. That was what no one seemed to realise.

Herman took a step forward. His huge fists were clenched, but Henckel placed a hand on his shoulder. He immediately froze, as if obeying a secret order. Albert was preparing to take his leave when the engineer spoke.

'There's a great deal of truth in what you said earlier. Am I right in thinking that these are the words of an old sailor? I grew up in Nyboder myself and my first apprenticeship was at the naval shipyard. I recognise a sailor when I see one and I know what it means to love the sea.'

Herman stiffened. A dangerous scowl appeared in his eyes, as if he'd been ambushed. Ignoring him, Henckel continued. 'It's true that Danish shipping is experiencing a renaissance. The war has brought us prosperity, and we need to maintain that growth.' He nodded towards Herman. 'More ships! Shipyards! That's what this country needs. Marstal is to have its own yard for building steel ships. You've heard of the Kalundborg steel shipyard and the Vulcan yard in Korsør? Well, allow me to inform you that I'm the man behind them. Now it's Marstal's turn. And it was Herman here who gave me the idea. He's already agreed to be the yard's joint owner. Of course, he's far too modest to mention that himself. But he's put in the considerable sum he raised from the sale of the *Two Sisters*. Which makes him our first investor. We're building Marstal's future, and the future of Danish shipping.' Henckel's large freckled hand with its dense cover of reddish-blond hair gave Herman's shoulder a comforting squeeze. 'Indeed, Herman, Marstal has reason to be proud of you. You're a true son of the town.'

Albert looked at Herman, who placidly allowed Henckel's hand to rest on his shoulder, and he understood that the engineer from Copenhagen had succeeded where everyone else had failed: he'd tamed Herman Frandsen. How had he done it? Perhaps, when the young dreamer had bragged about his grandiose schemes, he'd simply nodded his head instead of shaking it. But there was more to it than that, Albert reflected. Henckel had tamed Herman by appealing to his recklessness. Mentor and pupil were cut from the same cloth.

Albert raised his stick by way of goodbye. He wanted to be alone with the summer evening before returning home to his bed and his tormented dreams.

As he left, he heard the engineer invite the men to come and drink champagne at Hotel Ærø. They responded with enthusiastic laughter. Albert didn't turn round, but continued towards the memorial stone. He suddenly had the feeling that he'd lived too long.

He didn't believe Henckel's promises or Herman's boasts, but Henckel and Herman belonged to the land of the living.

Albert belonged with the dead.

ALBERT SAT IN THE CHURCH COMPOSING HIMSELF, PREPARING TO deliver more bad news because Pastor Abildgaard had cried again. In his days as a captain he'd often be called on to bear tidings of a sailor's death. Back then, he'd have been personally acquainted with the deceased and could speak of him knowledgeably, without ever resorting to empty generalities. And even though as a captain he kept his distance from his crew members, he knew enough about human nature to notice the men's quirks and tailor his words to the occasion. Albert knew that the captain's utterances mattered a great deal – even more than the pastor's. The vicar was closer to God, but he wasn't closer to life and death and the line that separates them. And that was what it was about. The captain's words, not the vicar's, were on the invisible gravestones people erected in their memories; as for funerals, the vicar was always underemployed in a town of sailors.

Marstal was a small town, so even when Albert hadn't known the dead man well, he'd know enough about him. When the war took a young man, he'd know the father, and could place him that way. If the man was older, he'd know him personally. He might even have had him as a crew-member. So Albert became a presence, a fixed point in the void that yawned open when death came. And in a way, he blocked death, standing in the doorway as a buffer that absorbed the initial shock and anguish of the bereaved, enabling them to face their loss the sooner, and in grieving begin to heal.

But there was one thing he knew about the dead that he couldn't share with anyone: their final moments, as he'd witnessed them in his dreams. He'd seen them surrender to the foaming waves. He'd seen them shot to shreds by bullets. He'd seen them with frostbitten faces, slumped lifeless across the thwart of an open lifeboat after a day on a winter-chilled sea. This knowledge he kept to himself, yet even as he concealed it, his words of comfort were informed by it.

He lied as only a man who knows the truth can lie. He lied away the horror and the pain, but he didn't lie away the death. He didn't speak of the hereafter, because he wasn't Pastor Abildgaard. And that was why they believed him. He was old and he'd been born in Marstal: he'd been one of the town's fixtures, with his broad shoulders and neat beard, ever since he came ashore. Even in the presence of death, he kept his captain's authority. He sat in a family's parlour, where he might never have sat before, and his presence gave death a meaning they might not otherwise have been aware of. He helped the mourners guard themselves against the darkness. They didn't feel alone, for it wasn't just Albert who sat with them, but the whole town and all it represented: fellowship, kin, the past and the future. Death was already half beaten, and life would go on.

No one asked to hear about Jesus when Captain Madsen was present, or about where the deceased was now, or whether he was happy. The captain's message was simple: this is the way things are. He taught us a vast, all-embracing acceptance which allowed life's realities to come at us directly. The sea takes us, but it has no message to convey when its waters close over our heads and fill our lungs. It may seem like strange consolation, but Albert's words offered us a foothold: things had always been this way, and these were conditions we all shared.

Albert knew that some couldn't get through their crisis without the Saviour and he left those to Carl Rasmussen's widow. He didn't regard their faith as a sign of weakness. He knew that people have different ways of coping, though personally he had none. His dreams were haunted. He felt alone, his faith in fellowship shattered. He walked tall when he left the grieving homes, but inside he'd shrunk.

He didn't know what he needed, so he sat in the church gathering his thoughts. Most of the time he studied his hands, but every now and then he'd look up at Rasmussen's altarpiece depicting Jesus calming the Sea of Galilee. Outside, the war raged on. More sailors were being killed than ever before and he noted the losses in his ledger. At times he thought he was just like Anders Nørre, an imbecile whose only hold on sanity was the endless list of numbers that flashed like lightning through the dark night of his mind. What would Jesus have done in the midst of a world war? One crucified man with a spear in his side seemed a trifle when millions were trapped in barbed wire dying with their intestines hanging out.

For his own part, Albert wrote down numbers. In what other way could he contain all this incomprehensible destruction? If anyone ever found his ledger, what would they think? That it had been written by a madman?

He got up from the hard blue-painted wooden pew, shivering. It was chilly inside the whitewashed church. He glanced again at the telegram in his hand, officially notifying the shipping company of the loss of the three-masted topgallant schooner, *Ruth*. Location: Atlantic Ocean. Travelling from St John's to Liverpool. Description of loss: Missing. Wind and weather conditions: Unknown. '*Since she left Newfoundland, the* Ruth *has not been seen. The ship is presumed lost with all hands.*'

Albert's job was to translate that terse verdict, made up of nothing but unknown factors into human speech. A ship had been sunk somewhere in the vast Atlantic, within a radius of a thousand nautical miles by ice, or a storm, or a freak wave. Or by an iron-clad prehistoric monster rising out of nowhere, spitting torpedoes, mercilessness incarnate: a reminder that the sea wasn't the only enemy. The result: a young Marstaller gone missing, never to be seen again, and this news about to be thrust in the face of Hansigne Koch, a sailor's widow who two years previously had lost another son, a seven-year-old, in a boating accident in the harbour. This was Albert's task: to guide the woman safely to port, ensure that she wasn't swallowed by the depths as she received the message.

Earlier, from his bay window, he'd watched Lorentz cross the street with the telegram in his hand. He'd let him in. Having hung his overcoat in the hall, Lorentz eased himself painfully onto the sofa. His many active years had taken their toll. He'd already had one heart attack, and his childhood frailty had returned. He was often short of breath, especially during the cold winter months. His shoulders heaved and he breathed in rasping, wheezing gasps, exhausted from crossing a single street in the stiff, sleet-laden wind. He'd forgotten to put on his hat: his wet thinning hair clung to his scalp and his Buddha face was flushed red. He'd brought his indispensable walking stick with him into the drawing room.

'This time it's the *Ruth*' was all he said.

Lorentz had lost two ships before her, and each time he'd informed the bereaved families personally. He probably intended to do so now, but in his condition a walk through town would be a feat of strength that might cost him dearly, and he'd become too old to mount his horse.

'You've forgotten your hat,' Albert said. 'Let me do it.'

So Albert had walked up Kirkestræde to inform Pastor Abildgaard, then gone to the church to compose himself. And now, finally, he stood in front of the house in Vinkelstræde. Hansigne Koch opened the door to him herself.

'I know why you're here,' she said, when she saw Albert's towering figure on her doorstep. 'It's Peter.' When she uttered her son's name, a shock seemed to run through her. The skin beneath her eyes paled and her lips began to tremble. 'Don't just stand there,' she said in a brusque tone, and Albert knew she behaved like this to keep from collapsing. She disappeared into the kitchen to make the coffee no visitor could escape, no matter how bad the news he bore. Albert entered the parlour and sat down. The room wasn't in daily use and the stove was cold, but he knew that this was where she'd wish to serve him. From the kitchen he heard the clatter of the coffee pot, the scritch of a match, the whoosh of the gas flame. But nothing from Hansigne. If she was crying, she was doing it silently.

She entered with the coffee cups. They were English tin-glazed earthenware, a gift from her husband, perhaps, or an heirloom. When she bent to light the stove, Albert didn't offer to help, nor beg her not to bother, nor suggest that they drink the coffee in a room that was already heated. He knew that the small household task was holding her together in this moment, just as other daily routines would help her survive the times to come. Coffee was a ritual, as significant as the funeral she'd never be able to give her son.

She sat down opposite Albert and poured the coffee. He accounted for the circumstances of the lost ship as well as he could. There wasn't much to say. 'Missing' meant only that it had failed to arrive at Liverpool, but it was important that she not draw hope from this uncertainty, for then her mourning would never end. Perhaps it never would, anyway. But hope stops time, and time only heals when its flow is not stopped. He knew that much.

He hadn't mentioned the war.

'Do you think it was a U-boat?' she asked.

He shook his head. 'No one knows, Mrs Koch.'

'I got a letter from him two days ago. Posted in St John's. He wrote that a lot of sailors had jumped ship. The *Ægir* couldn't even sail – there wasn't a single hand left. Men deserted from the *Nathalia* and the *Bonavista* too, even though they had rye bread on board. On the *Ruth* they had only ship's biscuits. "If only I had the crusts that Grandpa gives to his hens." That's what he wrote to me. Oh, I always worried that they weren't feeding him properly.'

She still wasn't crying.

'A mother never has peace of mind,' she went on. 'Sometimes I think I won't stop worrying till the day I die. I've been scared since his first minute at sea.' She fell silent. Then she said suddenly, 'Why does it have to be this way? Always the same fear. But a U-boat's the worst.'

Albert took her hand. He knew it had been a U-boat. He'd seen it himself, in his dreams. The crew had been shot down before they could leave the ship. Peter had been on deck preparing the lifeboat when a bullet ripped his chest open and he collapsed. Then the U-boat crew had boarded the ship, doused it with petrol and set it alight. The rigging and sails flared into a blazing pyre, and the *Ruth* had vanished into the waves with a hiss.

This was always the hardest moment. He had to stop his hand from trembling as he clasped hers. He was lonely. But his loneliness was nothing compared to hers; she'd lost her husband and two sons.

She looked directly at him. Still she held back her tears, as if subjecting herself to some terrible endurance test. 'Captain Madsen, I feel nothing.' There was disbelief in her voice, the disbelief of an accident victim who has been paralysed from the waist down and suddenly discovers that she can no longer feel her legs. 'I knew it,' she said to herself.

'What did you know, Mrs Koch?' His voice was gentle.

'When little Eigil drowned, I knew I'd never cry again. I'd never worried about him. What can happen to a child out playing? And then he drowns in the harbour. Oh, Captain Madsen, my heart stood still that day. I think I counted the seconds, and nothing happened in my heart. Not a beat, or a pounding – absolutely nothing. It was completely still inside my chest. Peter was at home. He hugged me and held me close the way I'd done with him all those years ago when he was little. "Ma, I'm so glad that I've still got you," he said, and though he couldn't take away my grief, my heart started beating again. He never, ever wrote without asking me to say hello to Eigil at the cemetery.' Still her eyes were dry. 'And now he's gone too,' she said. Her words came out disjointed. 'Now there's no one I can remember to little Eigil.'

She bowed her head, and her tears fell onto Albert's hand.

Time passed. Albert said nothing.

'Well, it turns out I haven't run out of tears after all,' she said eventually.

He could hear the relief in her voice. Her endurance test was over. She'd recovered feeling.

'There's something else you haven't run out of,' Albert said. 'Don't forget that there's still someone who needs you.'

Mrs Koch gave him a perplexed look, then jerked upright as if someone had just called her. 'Ida!'

Lorentz had told Albert something of the family; Ida was Mrs Koch's middle child, a girl of eleven. Today she'd be at school in Vestergade.

'Ida,' Mrs Koch said again, and rose with a bustling movement. 'I must go and get her.'

Quickly she put on her coat and was soon standing in the hall, ready to go out. They walked together up Vinkelstræde and along Lærkegade. Albert offered to accompany her to the school, but she declined.

'You said something very true a moment ago, Captain Madsen.' She shook his hand as they parted.

'There's always someone who needs us. We might forget it some-times. But it's what keeps us alive.'

Albert turned into Nygade and shuddered. The sleet blew directly into his face. Was he useful? Did anyone need him?

He stamped the slushy ground in irritation and wiped his wet face.

THE WIDOW OF THE MARINE PAINTER OFTEN VISITED THE CHURCH,
too. She sat alone on a pew, staring up at Jesus and the troubled
sea. Perhaps she was thinking about the Saviour, or about the children who had been taken from her, one after another, until only one
remained. Or perhaps she was pondering her late husband. It was
impossible to know. The first time Albert entered the church and
found her sitting there, with her back to him, he'd left quietly, not
wanting to intrude. He'd even checked the time – perhaps she had
regular habits – and started coming earlier in the day. If he stayed
long enough, she'd always turn up. She didn't leave when she saw
him; she simply sat some distance away and began her own quiet
worship. He could hear the rustling of her dress and the scraping of
her shoes. Once when he rose to go she looked up, and he nodded
briefly to her on his way out. After that he arrived every day at the
same time. Eventually, she too would appear. Two old people, sitting
quietly at opposite ends of the church.

Albert wasn't a man who knew how to seek solace. He knew how
to be useful to others, and sometimes the two things are one and
the same. But the burden he bore was something he couldn't discuss
with anyone, and since he didn't believe in God, it followed that he
couldn't talk about it at all. Yet he still came to church every day,
half an hour before Anna Egidia Rasmussen, and he sat there as
though waiting for her arrival.

If he didn't visit the church to find God, perhaps he went to find
a human being?

One day she came and sat down next to him. He wondered if that
was what he'd been waiting for. He looked up from his hands and
greeted her.

'So you're here again, Captain Madsen,' she said.

He nodded, not knowing what to say next. The *Hydra* had been reported missing and he'd another message of death to deliver, for the widow of Captain Eli Johannes Rasch. Mrs Rasmussen had one, too.

'Will this dreadful war never end?' she sighed, as she sank into her usual contemplation of her late husband's altarpiece.

'No. It'll never end.' He spoke in a burst of anger. Suddenly he was doing what he had sworn never to do in the presence of the bereaved: voicing his opinion about the war. 'It'll never end as long as someone profits from its continuation.'

'How could anyone profit from such horror and death?'

'Take a walk down Kirkestraede. Look at the shops. This town is flourishing as never before.'

'Are you seriously suggesting, Captain Madsen, that the inhabitants of a little town like Marstal are keeping the mighty engines of war in motion? Can't you see the grief it's caused this town? You must. Like me, you announce a death to someone almost every week.'

'Yes, Mrs Rasmussen, I see the grief. You and I see it because we visit the homes where death strikes. But the others are pressing their noses against the shop windows. It's human nature to worship the golden calf, and that's the main cause of the current war.'

'I know nothing of politics,' she said, looking down. 'I'm just an old woman who's lived too long.'

'You're eight years younger than I am, as far as I know.'

'I suppose I am. But as a widow . . .'

She stopped, too bashful to continue.

'Well?' he encouraged her.

'As a widow you no longer have your own life. You live through others. It's as though old age arrives in one fell swoop. I've felt old ever since Carl died, and that was twenty-four years ago.'

'I've noticed that you come here often. I suppose you're thinking about him.'

'I'm here for the same reason you are, Captain Madsen. To contemplate the Saviour.' She gave him a quick, critical glance. 'You are a believer, I presume.'

'I was,' he said, 'but not in the Saviour. I believed in other things. I believed in this town and the forces that built it. I believed in fellowship, in a community of people. I believed in being hard-working and diligent. But I've lapsed now, I'm sorry to say. And I, too, feel I've lived too long. I don't understand this world any more.'

'You sound like an unhappy man, Captain Madsen. I don't understand the world either. I don't think I ever did. Yet I have faith.'

'Perhaps that's precisely why you believe.'

'How do you mean?'

'You say yourself that you don't understand the world. Surely that's why you have to believe. Faith's a mystery. It's not a mystery I share. Whether or not that's a limitation, I can't say.' He gave her a questioning look, as if he expected an answer. He sensed that he was about to unmask himself to this woman, yet it didn't frighten him. There was an accepting gentleness in her and he felt that he no longer had anything to lose. 'I have these dreams,' he heard himself say. The urge to confide in her was overwhelming.

'What dreams?'

For a moment he hesitated. Then he made the leap.

'The drowned sailors,' he said. 'I see them drown. I see them almost every night. It's as though I'm there. I see it long before it happens. If you don't believe me, you can ask me the names of the people from Marstal who are going to die. I can give you their names, every single one of them.' She was staring at him as though she didn't understand what he was saying, but he could no longer hold back. 'For years I've been walking around this town like a stranger. I feel like a messenger from the land of the dead. The *Klabautermann* – that's me.'

He halted and gave her a pleading look. Did his words mean anything to her at all?

She was silent for a long time. Then she took his hand.

'It must be dreadful for you,' she said. 'It's more than a person can bear.'

For one moment he feared that she would start talking about the Saviour. But she didn't.

'So you believe me? You believe I have this special ability?'

'If you say it's so, Captain Madsen, then I do indeed believe it. You've never struck me as a man prone to fantasies, or one who needed to make himself appear interesting.'

'I've seen the war, Mrs Rasmussen.' He spread out his arms. 'All these deaths. I see the pleading in the widows' eyes. How did my Erik or my Peter die? And I know. I could give her the answer. And yet I can't. There's a terrible helplessness in that. Helpless, yes, that's how I feel. I'm a spectator both asleep and awake. Day and night

I witness suffering and grief, and I'm stuck. There's nothing I can do.'

Her hand was still resting on his. For a while they sat that way, without speaking. Then she withdrew her hand and stood up.

'Come, Captain Madsen, it's time for us to pay our visits.' On their way out of the church she turned to him. 'I believe in your dreams. But I don't wish to hear about them. I prefer to live in ignorance of God's plans for us.'

THEY BOTH CONTINUED TO VISIT THE CHURCH, BUT NOW THEY SAT next to each other. Sometimes they were silent, each lost in their own thoughts, but most of the time they conducted a whispered conversation. There was no physical contact. Her hand on his that day had been a sign of acceptance; there was no need for her to repeat it.

December came, and in the twilight the damp winter cold seemed to concentrate itself inside the unheated church.

'We're freezing here,' she said one day. 'Let's go to my house and have a cup of coffee.'

He looked around as they entered the drawing room of the house in Teglgade. A couple of Rasmussen's paintings hung on the walls. He knew she'd sold most of them, but clearly she'd kept a few as well. One was a portrait of a little girl from Greenland. Rasmussen had been one of the first Danish painters to travel to that icy wilderness, but the portrait wasn't typical of his work. His real subject was the sea and its ships; he'd made his name as a marine painter. The other painting showed a man wearing a gown, kneeling in prayer on the desert sand. In the background were a woman and a donkey. The man's face was strangely blurred, as if the painting were unfinished or Rasmussen's talent for human portrayal had fallen short.

'It's "The Flight into Egypt", the widow said, entering at that moment with the coffee pot. Albert nodded politely. There had been no need for her to tell him that. Though he was not a believer, he did know his Bible. 'It was rare for him to be inspired by stories from the Bible. Such a shame. I think it might have led him in a new direction. But towards the end it seemed as though nothing would come right for him. At any rate, he was very dissatisfied, very dissatisfied indeed. He was a tormented man. Please don't think that I was blind to his real character.'

Albert had first met the painter, who'd been a few years older than him, when he was just a boy. Back then Carl Rasmussen had made an indelible impression on him, not just because of his remarkable talent for drawing but also because of his peculiar innocence.

He was from the neighbouring town of Ærøskøbing, and the first time he showed up in Marstal a hostile gang of boys had instantly surrounded him: he was an outsider and he'd be made to feel it. But something about his attitude kept them at bay. He'd seemed so unaware that he was in danger of being beaten up. Instead of trouble, a friendship had developed between them, and they all spent one long summer roaming the island together. When Carl did his drawings, he'd be watched by a crowd of admiring boys. He'd also read aloud to them, awakening a hunger for a world beyond the dead rote-learning of Isager's lessons. Albert could still recall the impact *The Odyssey* had made on him, with the story of Telemachus who waited for his father for twenty years, never doubting that he was alive. Who knows, perhaps the path of Albert's own life was set that day.

But the idyll had ended with a confrontation. Albert no longer recalled what caused it, only that Carl had taken off with a bloody nose, and he didn't see him again until as an adult Carl came to settle in Marstal with his family. In the meantime Carl Rasmussen had made a name for himself as a painter and earned plenty of money, which he invested in the town's ships. He'd painted the altar-piece in the church and used local skippers as the models for Jesus' disciples. Jesus himself had the face of the carpenter who ran an illicit pub opposite the church. It was an audacious choice, but Rasmussen got away with it. There was no end to the town's enthusiasm for his talent. His likenesses were uncanny.

Carl had asked to paint Albert, too. But when Albert brought out James Cook and asked for a double portrait, the sight of the shrunken head had turned Rasmussen's stomach, and he'd had to lie down on the sofa.

Albert always had a feeling that the painter had come to Marstal in search of something he never found. Rasmussen's death was thought to be suicide. That wasn't malicious rumour, but a conclusion reached through basic sailing knowledge. It was inconceivable that anyone could fall overboard in fair weather. One moment Rasmussen had been standing on the deck, painting; the next he was gone.

* * *

Anna Egidia Rasmussen poured coffee into the blue-patterned china cup.

'Do have a biscuit,' she said, pushing a bowl towards Albert. 'I baked them myself. Well, I mostly do it for the grandchildren,' she added, smiling.

Albert took a biscuit and dipped it in his coffee.

'Your husband and I had many discussions about his paintings,' he said. 'But not about the religious ones.'

'Yes, I remember that well. You thought he was limiting himself by just painting life on Ærø and the other islands. I think in the end he agreed with you.'

'I'm no painter,' Albert said. 'I was probably the wrong person to be giving advice. I believe in progress. Or at least I used to. But how do you paint progress? I can't answer that one.'

'By painting steamers with smoke coming out of their funnels?'

He heard the irony in her voice and laughed.

'You're right, Mrs Rasmussen. We laymen should keep our noses right out of art. Once I believed the breakwater symbolised everything the people of this town were capable of achieving. But a big pile of stones like that would never have been much of a subject for a painter. And now I realise that there's one thing the breakwater can't protect us from, and that's our own greed. I must admit the way the town's livelihood is being sold off frightens me just as much as the war.'

'You mean the sale of the ships?'

'I do indeed. We make our living from the sea. If we cut our connection to it, then what will become of this town? It's as though the times have gone soft. Suddenly being a sailor isn't good enough any more. Better education plays its part too, I suppose. Children learn more and they begin to see options other than simply going to sea, like their fathers and grandfathers. But I think the mothers play their part in it too. They never miss the chance to tell their sons about their father's tough crossings, and all the sorrow and anxiety they put up with when he's away. That kind of whining kills a boy's desire to go to sea. And why hold on to the ships when the market's favourable? There's no one to carry on the tradition.'

'Have you ever considered what it's like to be the child of a sailor?'

'Yes, of course I have. I come from a family of seamen.'

'So let's imagine a fourteen-year-old boy who's off to sea. How much do you think he's actually seen of his father, when he leaves the home he grew up in?' He could hear the obstinacy in her voice and he knew she wasn't presenting it as a question. She was going somewhere with this, and his job was to follow her. 'I'll tell you, Captain Madsen. His father will probably have been at home roughly every other year, and never stayed more than a few months at a time. So when it's the boy's turn to go to sea at the age of fourteen, he'll have seen his father seven times. One and a half years in total, at the most. You call Marstal a sailors' town, but do you know what I call it? I call it a town of wives. It's the women who live here. The men are just visiting. Have you ever looked at the face of a two-year-old lad, toddling down the street holding his father's hand? He looks up at his pa, and it's all too clear what's going on inside his little head. He's asking himself, who is this man? And just when he's got used to this man he's just met, that man is off again. Two years later it's the same story all over again. The boy's four, and even his happiest memories of his father have faded. And the father has to reacquaint himself with a boy he hardly knows, too. Two years is an eternity in a child's life, Captain Madsen. And what sort of a life is it?'

Albert said nothing. He drank his coffee and ate another vanilla biscuit. His own father had failed him in a way he'd never been able to forgive. Yet he realised that he'd always regarded the absence of fathers as part of the natural order, even though men in other trades never left home for years at a time.

'Yes, what sort of life is it?' the widow repeated. 'For the father who barely knows his own children, and for the children who grow up as orphans even though their pa's alive somewhere on the other side of the globe. For the mother who's left alone with full responsibility for them, living in constant fear that the ship will be reported missing. Why wouldn't she try to talk her sons out of going to sea? We have electric light, the telegraph and coal-burning steamers; why should women and children be excluded from that kind of progress and live as they did in the last century? You believe in progress, Captain Madsen. So why don't you welcome this development? Because it changes the world you know so well? If I've understood it correctly, that's the nature of progress. It doesn't just make the world a better place, it makes it an unrecognisable one.'

Albert wasn't a parent himself. He'd never held a living child in his arms, a baby animal who, when it learned to speak, would call him Father. He was completely out of his depth here. At times he'd felt a void in his life, but he had no regrets. That was just the way things had turned out.

When he came ashore at fifty years of age, it had been too late to start a family. Besides, who could you get at fifty? Not even a spinster, unless she came equipped with a serious defect. A widow? Oh yes, there were plenty of those. They were keen to marry, too, though mostly for practical reasons. But they were hardly capable of having more children: their wombs were withered, their breasts were dry. And a young woman burdened with an old codger like him wouldn't have much of a future, would she?

That was how he'd explained it to us, in those casual, slightly contemptuous terms that can be so revealing for those who know how to listen. Now he told the widow, 'Well, I can't really comment. I never did have children of my own.' He took another biscuit. 'Strange, really. I was so absorbed by matters of kin that I forgot to ensure the continuation of my own.'

'I've never really understood that, Captain Madsen. You should have married.'

The widow knew nothing of the Chinese lady.

'Despite my long voyages?' he quipped.

'Those are the terms. You'd have made a good husband all the same. You have a sense of responsibility and you have vision. Those qualities aren't as common as we'd like to think. Children are a great gift. You declined that. You shouldn't have.'

'And you say that, even though you've had repeated experience of how that gift can be reclaimed?'

She looked down at her lap. 'More coffee?' she asked.

He nodded. He felt he might have gone too far by referring to all the children she'd lost. He lifted the china cup to his lips and looked at her through the steam.

She looked up and caught his eye.

'No, Captain Madsen, you don't regret having had a child simply because you lose it. Having a child isn't a deal you strike with life. As I said: a child is a gift. And what remains after a child is gone is the memory of the years it was allowed to live. Not its death.'

She stopped and he could see that she was moved. He wanted to do what she'd done for him that day on the pew: place his hand on hers. But in order to do so he would have to get up and walk round the table. He felt clumsy and shy, and the moment passed. He remained where he was, keeping a silence that might be interpreted as respectful but which he knew was caused by awkwardness.

'I've learned to bend.' Again she looked directly at him. 'I believe God has a purpose for everything that happens. If I didn't believe that, I could never have endured it. I have my Jesus.'

Again he was at a loss for words. There was something in her he couldn't fathom, a gulf between them. He wondered if their contrasting way of seeing the world was simply something to do with men and women and the differences between them. While he sought meaning in everything and became agitated if he couldn't find it, she accepted life – even when it struck in the hardest possible way, through the loss of a child. There was a fortitude in her that was beyond him. Perhaps he'd never had to be strong in the way she had, though he believed that his dreams gave him an intolerable burden. He'd always respected Carl Rasmussen's widow. Now he admired her as well, even though something in him rebelled against her outlook on life.

Silence had descended upon them once more, and again she was the one to break it.

'I still have many children around me. My grandchildren – and then there are the children from the neighbourhood.'

'Yes, I know you step in when a family's in need.'

'At times I look after a child for a while. I want to feel useful. If I didn't feel useful, I don't think I could go on living.'

Again she looked directly at him. 'Do you feel useful, Captain Madsen?'

'Useful?' he echoed. 'Do I feel useful? I don't know. I can't tell anyone about my dreams. Even you feel repelled . . .'

He hesitated for a moment. Once again he felt he'd gone too far. It was unfair to blame the widow. After all, she'd listened to him and not fled like Anders Nørre. He gave her an apologetic look. She looked calmly back at him.

'None of us is superfluous, Captain Madsen.'

'But, you just said –'

'I admit that I may sound pessimistic from time to time. When I think of this endless separation from my Carl, I feel I've lived too long. But when you've lived for too long and yet you can't die, then

305

you have to invent reasons to go on. You're of no use? Well, that may be so, but only in your own eyes. There's always someone who needs you. It's just a question of finding out who.'

Albert said nothing. He'd used almost exactly the same phrases when he told Mrs Koch of the loss of the *Ruth*, but he didn't feel that the words applied to him. He and Anna Egidia had different ways of looking at life. She'd found a purpose to it. He'd lost his, and in his opinion, that was that.

She leaned towards him.

'Listen,' she said. 'I happen to know a little boy in Snaregade. He lost his father not so long ago. He never knew his grandfather, who died at sea long before he was born. He hardly ever sees the other men in his family because they're all sailors. His mother's from the island of Birkholm. She's an orphan, by the way, so there's no family to help out on her side. Don't you think a little boy like that might need someone to take him for a walk along the harbour, even take him rowing in a boat and get him used to the sea?'

'Yes, I'm sure he might,' he replied, wondering what her point was.

Suddenly Anna Egidia smiled. It was a beautiful smile that made you forget her thin, bloodless lips. 'And then there's you, Captain Madsen, an older, experienced sailor who complains that he's of no use to anyone.' Her voice was teasing. She paused and gave him an encouraging look, as though expecting a reply.

'And then what?' he asked, slow on the uptake.

'You really have no idea what I'm talking about?'

Her sunken face grew almost round from smiling. Albert shook his head. He felt dim-witted. She was playing games with him.

'I imagine that you might be the man who would take a little boy by the hand and go rowing with him in your boat.'

'But I don't even know the family. I can't just turn up and impose.'

'I assure you that the boy's mother won't think you're imposing at all. She'll be both grateful and honoured.'

'I've absolutely no experience of children.'

He made his voice brusque to mask his confusion. He felt betrayed. She'd laid a trap for him and he'd walked right into it. In a moment of weakness, of unbearable loneliness, he'd opened up to another human being. He'd been under the impression that they were two old people talking about their lives. When old men met, they talked about the sea – but he had an inner life he couldn't share with anybody. He'd opened it to her. But behind what he had taken to be her sympathy, there'd been a hidden agenda, which she'd now revealed. He was just a pawn in her charity work.

As he stood up to take his leave, it wasn't the boy he was rejecting. It was her.

'Don't you want to know his name?' she asked, as she showed him out into the hall.

'No,' he said, 'it's of no interest to me.'

The Boy

THE NEXT DAY SHE TURNED UP OUTSIDE HIS FRONT DOOR HOLDING a boy by the hand. Albert stood in the doorway not knowing what to say. He was bad at estimating a child's age, but he supposed the lad to be six or seven years old. He had blond hair, and his ears, which stuck out, glowed red in the December frost.

'Aren't you going to ask us in, Captain Madsen?'

The widow smiled at him. Yesterday he'd loved the way her smile lit up her face and made it round and mild; now he was convinced it had been false. He stepped back, gestured them inside and helped the widow with her coat while the boy took off his own.

'Say hello to the captain,' the widow said.

The boy stuck out his hand and bowed stiffly.

'Aren't you going to tell the captain your name?'

'Knud Erik,' the boy said, frozen in mid-bow, staring at the floor in embarrassment. Albert was moved by his shyness.

'How old are you?' he asked.

'Six,' the boy said, turning scarlet.

'Let's not stay here in the cold hall.'

He escorted them into the drawing room and called his housekeeper.

'Coffee?'

The widow nodded.

'Yes, please.'

'And what would you like to drink?'

'I'm not thirsty,' the boy said, and blushed even more deeply.

'But I imagine you'd like a biscuit?'

The boy shook his head. 'No, thank you. I'm not hungry.' He shrugged and tried to make himself invisible. Albert took a large pink conch from the windowsill.

'Have you seen one of these before?'

'We've got one at home,' the boy said.

'And where does it come from?'

'My pa brought it back.'

The boy's hunched shoulders looked like the folded wings of a bird. He bit his lower lip and stared at the Persian rug as if he were deeply interested in its swirling arabesques. He was trembling slightly. Now Albert grew awkward; he looked at the widow. She shook her head silently. He felt like a fool.

'I might have something you haven't seen before,' he said to break the silence. 'Come here.' He took the boy by the hand and led him to his office next door. In the window was a wooden model of the *Princess*, over a metre long and almost as tall. Albert carefully carried it back into the drawing room and placed it on the carpet. 'I don't normally let anyone play with this. But you can, if you promise to be careful.'

'I promise.'

The housekeeper entered with the coffee and Albert sat down opposite the widow. The boy was busy examining the model's anchor. Then, very carefully, he turned its wheel. Slowly he pushed the *Princess* across the rug. With both hands on the hull he rocked the ship from side to side while imitating the sound of waves and the singing of the wind in the rigging.

Albert kept an eye on him. When he could see that the boy was completely absorbed in playing, he turned to the widow.

'I told you I don't know anything about children.'

Mrs Rasmussen laughed.

'Oh, don't you worry about that. Just treat him as one of your crew. The youngest member. And you just be the captain, like you used to.'

'He doesn't want to be with an old man like me.'

'Of course he does. You'll be like God to him. Just start telling him about your travels and your experiences, and you'll find you have an audience like you've never known. And now you must stop making a fuss because I'm not giving you any more compliments.'

The next day he went to Snaregade to fetch Knud Erik. The boy's mother, Klara Friis, was pregnant, and the time for her confinement couldn't be far off: her body was big and heavy underneath a black shawl. He couldn't remember seeing her before, which surprised him.

Marstal was a small town, and he had lived in it for a long time. Yet he no longer knew it.

She invited him in for coffee, but he declined, not wanting to inconvenience her. Besides, he wanted this visit over and done with. He felt he'd been tricked into it and he still felt resentful towards Mrs Rasmussen.

The boy walked silently beside him down to the harbour. It was a clear, sunny day. The boy had no mittens on and his hands were red with cold.

'What happened to your mittens?'

'I lost them.'

They walked along Havnegade to Dampskibsbroen and looked at the water. A thin layer of ice had formed during the night and the sun sparkled in the white frost around it. Albert felt he should speak but didn't know what to say. What did you talk about to children? His irritation with the widow increased.

'Come,' he said to the boy, who looked lost in thought at the sight of the frozen water. They walked on along the quay, past the coal depot and down towards Prinsebroen.

'What's it like to drown?' the boy asked.

'Your mouth fills up with water and then you can't breathe any more.'

'Have you tried drowning?'

'No,' Albert said. 'If you drown, you die. And I'm here.'

'Does everyone drown at the end?'

'Most people don't drown.'

'My pa drowned,' the boy said in a tone that implied that this kind of death gave him a sense of pride, and elevated his father. Then his voice grew more hesitant. 'If we drown, do we ever come back?'

'No, we never come back.'

'My ma says my pa's an angel now.'

'You must listen to what your mother says.'

Albert was feeling more and more uncomfortable. He dreaded that the boy might suddenly burst into tears. What would he do then? Take him back home? He couldn't return with a sobbing child. That would be like losing your cargo and letting the sea take your ship. He tried to distract the boy. The harbour was full of moored vessels, some kept back by their owners because of the war, others simply home for the winter. There was nothing to indicate that Marstal's days as a seafaring town were coming to an end. Albert pointed to the ships.

'Are you going to sea when you grow up?' he asked, and instantly regretted it.

'Will I drown then, like my pa?'

'Most sailors come home again. Then they grow old like me and die in their beds one day.'

'I want to be a sailor like my pa,' the boy said. 'But I don't want to drown and get eaten by a fish, and I don't want to die in my bed, either, because my bed is for sleeping in. Is there any way not to die?'

'No,' Albert said. 'There isn't. But you're very young. You have plenty of years left to live. That's almost the same as not dying.'

'Would you like to die?'

'I wouldn't mind now. I'm very old. So it doesn't matter if I do.'

'So you're not sad?'

'No, I'm not sad.'

'My ma's sad. She is always crying. Then I comfort her.'

'You're a good boy,' Albert said. He pointed across the water. 'Look, there's a steamer. When you go to sea, it'll probably be on a steamer.'

'Can steamers sink?' the boy asked.

Albert looked at the black-painted steel hull. *Memory* was written on the bow in white lettering.

'Yes,' he said. 'Yes, they can.'

He'd seen the *Memory* go down in a dream.

'A fire always burns at the bottom of a steamer and it's as hot as a wash house when the kettle's heating up. Men feed the fire. They feed it day and night, and only come out to sleep or eat. They never see the sun or the moon. But high up in the wheelhouse the first mate stands with his hands on the wheel, steering the steamer safely across the sea.'

'That's who I want to be,' the boy said.

'Yes, that's who you want to be. But then you need to pay attention at school. Otherwise you won't get a place at Navigation College.'

They had passed the boat harbour and walked on down to the shipyards. Rhythmical hammer strokes rang out through the red-painted plank walls of the buildings. The only quiet place was Marstal Steel Shipyard's newly constructed building near Buegade. Whenever

Mr Henckel visited, he would boast about all the orders he'd secured in Norway. But so far, nothing had been built.

The boy seemed lost in thought. He peered up at Albert.

'What does it look like when a steamer goes down?'

Albert scanned his memory. He had never seen it happen in his waking life, but his dreams had shown him every detail of the *Memory* being tossed about before vanishing into the depths.

'You can hear explosions from the core of the hull,' he said to the boy. 'That's the cold seawater seeping into the heart of the huge boilers. Then boiling hot steam bursts out through every opening of the ship. Big lumps of coal fly up through the funnel and the skylight. There, and there,' he said, pointing at the *Memory*. 'The ship keels over and lies bottom up for a moment.'

'Bottom up!' the boy exclaimed. 'Such a big steamer – with its bottom in the air!'

'Yes,' Albert said, astonished at the effect his story had on the boy.

'Tell me some more,' the boy said, looking at him expectantly.

'The steamer starts to sink stern first. Finally the stem stands almost vertically. The last thing you see before the waves close over the steamer is its name.'

Albert stopped. The boy tugged his sleeve.

'More.'

'There isn't any more.'

The boy looked at him, disappointed. Albert realised that he'd retold one of his dreams in detail for the first time: a closed door had unexpectedly opened. As far as the boy was concerned, the story was all one great big adventure. You could see it from the way his eyes lit up. Albert could tell him everything. He could even tell him about the source of his knowledge: his inexplicable nightly dreams. And the boy would accept it all as part of the same fantastic world, where nothing needed to be explained and no one would be branded as odd just because he could see the future.

No, he hadn't known anything about children, but now he'd learned something: a child's mind is open to everything. There was so much death in his dreams; there was practically nothing else. But he sensed that, to the boy, death in a story was one thing, while death in the real world another. He'd told him about a ship that had been sunk by a U-boat, and although Knud Erik's own father had disappeared at sea without trace, along with the rest of the *Hydra*'s crew, the boy had apparently failed to make the connection. As for himself, Albert didn't know precisely why he'd recounted one of his dreams for the first time, but he knew that it was important.

'There's no more,' he repeated, 'but I can tell you another story some other day.'

'Do you know lots of stories?'

'Yes, I do. When spring comes I'll teach you to row. Come on. Time to go home now.'

The boy's face glowed red from the cold. He skipped for a couple of paces, then stuck his icy hand into Albert's. Together they walked back down Havnegade.

ALBERT STARTED GOING REGULARLY TO KNUD ERIK'S HOUSE. ANNA
Egidia couldn't keep acting as their intermediary, so he fetched and
returned the boy himself. In fact, the boy could have made his own
way to Albert's house and back home again: the town was small
enough for that, though they lived at opposite ends of it. But he felt
that Knud Erik had been entrusted to him. With that came responsibility, so he stuck to formalities. He collected him from the front
door in Snaregade, and that was where he returned him.

When he came Knud Erik's mother answered the door, though
shyness rendered her almost mute. She'd given birth by now, and
when he appeared she clutched the baby in her arms as if to protect
herself from an unsettling presence. The first time he'd declined her
offer of coffee because he didn't want to inconvenience her, but the
second time he accepted out of concern that she'd interpret his refusal
as a sign of snobbery.

There were differences on board a ship. There was fore and aft,
and the captain's unbreachable preserve, which Albert privately
referred to as the island of loneliness. But these were practical necessities, enforcing rank and authority: he'd never regarded them as a
class divide. His eyes were opened in Knud Erik's home. Knud Erik's
father, Henning Friis, had been an ordinary seaman. He'd married
early and then hadn't been promoted. Most men waited to get married
until they were in their late twenties, when they could afford to,
once they'd finished Navigation College and owned a share in a ship.
But Henning Friis had been head over heels in love. Or possibly just
plain careless.

When someone hadn't got very far in life, Albert had always
regarded it as evidence of personal incompetence. Now he became
aware that there might be something else. The boy's mother came
from a social rank different from his own, one without expectations. He saw it in her almost mute self-effacement. Nothing but

half-strangled sentences came from her lips – 'There's no need', 'It's far too much', 'You shouldn't have'. Her eyes always sought the floor or the baby. This paralysis in the presence of 'posh people' was rooted in the behaviour of generations.

Her house was clean and tidy. Geraniums and wallflowers decorated the windowsill. But the furniture was a random collection from all sorts of places. No pictures hung on the walls, but the damp had left discoloured patches on the wallpaper. No amount of cleaning could keep those stains at bay. They came from within the walls and were due to the poor construction of the house, one built for poor people. Such a house did not become neglected. Neglect was its essence.

During winter it was either freezing inside or as humid as a greenhouse, depending on whether there was money for coal. On days when Albert showed up unexpectedly, his breath would linger like white clouds in the cold; on days when Klara Friis knew he was coming and invited him for coffee the overstuffed stove glowing in its corner turned the room into a steam bath. Heated or unheated, the atmosphere was equally unhealthy and unpleasant.

They'd never had a serious conversation. Her gratitude was expressed in her shy deference. She didn't look him in the eye or say anything that came from the heart. The divide between them remained.

When the water in the harbour froze, Albert took Knud Erik for a walk among the trapped ships. Between them stood wooden stalls where vendors sold apple pancakes and warm elderberry cordial. Business was brisk, thanks to the crowd of people who'd come out to test their skates, and the clear winter air echoed with cheerful voices. Albert taught the boy to recognise the various types of ships. There were small cutters and ketches with round, fat curves and flat sterns. There were all the different sorts of schooners: fore-and-aft schooners, topsail schooners, topgallant schooners and schooner-brig combinations and then the huge brigantines, which were the boy's favourite, undoubtedly because of their size. How the sails might be set was one big mystery to him, especially now, with all the canvas removed. Only the black lines of the yards and the rigging against the winter sky hinted at their secrets.

'It's just like learning to read at school. The layout of sails is the sailor's alphabet,' Albert told him.

'Tell me a story,' the boy would say.

So Albert did. He took one from his own life, or from his dreams. It made no difference to the boy and, eventually, to Albert either. He felt as though something inside him that had been violently forced apart had started to grow back together.

From time to time the boy's eyes drifted over to the skaters and Albert could tell that he was in another place.

'Do you know how to skate?' Albert asked. The boy shook his head. 'Well, we'd better teach you then.'

Their excursions always concluded with a visit to Albert's house in Prinsegade. Once Knud Erik had deposited his wooden-soled boots in the hall, he'd settle in front of the stove, where he'd take off his woollen socks and wriggle his toes in its heat. Albert would place his boots next to Knud Erik's. In winter he was still known to wear Laurids' old boots, which had plenty of room for an extra layer of woollen socks inside. There they stood, with their knee-high leather shafts and their metal caps, right next to the boy's.

The housekeeper would bring them hot chocolate with freshly whipped cream, and Albert would sit at the table, drawing. He was a good, meticulous draughtsman, and in his sketches he'd carefully detail the canvas and rigging of different types of ships. He added seagulls and a fair wind, so the ships would heel slightly, offering a view of the deck. Behind the wheel he'd put a man smoking a pipe. There was a galley, a hood and hatch. In front of the ship he always drew a spiral.

'What's that?' the boy asked one day.

'A maelstrom.'

'What's a maelstrom?'

'It's a whirlpool that sucks everything down. The ship will disappear in a moment.'

The boy looked up. Then he pointed to the matchstick man behind the wheel.

'The helmsman will save the ship. He'll just sail it somewhere else.'

'He can't,' Albert said. 'It's too late.'

The boy stared at the drawing of the doomed ship. Tears welled up in his eyes.

'That's not fair,' he burst out. He quickly snatched the drawing and started tearing it to pieces. Albert was about to grab hold of his arm, then stopped himself.

'I'm sorry,' he said.

'You always do that,' the boy said, 'you always draw that . . .' He couldn't get hold of the word. 'That thing. Why do you do that?'

'I don't know,' Albert replied, realising that he was telling the truth. He'd never wondered why he drew a maelstrom in front of the bow every time he drew a ship. The spiral simply pulled his pencil along like an irresistible force. He drew according to a secret command that only his pencil, but not he, could follow.

'I feel sorry for the ships,' the boy said.

'Yes,' Albert said. 'So do I. But their time is over. The age of sailing ships has gone.'

'But there are plenty in the harbour,' the boy objected.

'Yes, that's right. But no one wants to go to sea any more.'

'I do,' the boy said. 'I want to be a sailor.' He turned and gave Albert a look of defiance. 'Just like my pa.'

THE GRIEF NO LONGER SHOWED IN KLARA FRIIS'S FACE THESE DAYS,
and she seemed carefree: Albert thought that it was life calling her
back. Her husband had died, but she held a living child in her arms,
and as time went by, the balance of her feelings had to shift from
one to the other. The child, a girl christened Edith by Pastor
Abildgaard, needed her. And her grief had to surrender to that need.
She didn't grow any more talkative, but her eyes were no longer
fixed stubbornly on the floor.

Knud Erik had broken the ice between them. He'd long since lost
his shyness in Albert's company, though it returned somewhat when
his mother was present, as though she and Albert represented two
different worlds that he couldn't bridge. But now he would report
to her in a loud, clear voice the many adventures each day had
brought. In the beginning his mother would hush him. However, as
she had no conversation of her own to contribute, she eventually let
him speak.

At times Albert caught her glancing furtively at him, and then
she'd instantly look down again. But her face was no longer tear-
swollen, and the shine had returned to her hair. She also made an
effort to dress nicely for his visits. This, too, he thought had something to do with the difference in their social rank: she was smartening
up for the gentry.

'I can skate now, and Captain Madsen will teach me to row and
swim. Then I won't drown. And then I can become a good sailor.'

Knud Erik made this announcement one day as they sat in the
parlour drinking the obligatory coffee.

'I won't hear of such talk! You're not going to be a sailor!' His
mother's voice was sharp; her face tightened visibly under the soft curve
of her cheeks. Knud Erik looked down. 'Go to the kitchen right now!'

The boy disappeared, his head still bowed. Klara Friis turned to
Albert. He had stood up.

'I think it's time for me to get going.'

'Please don't go,' she said. Her voice was suddenly filled with anxiety.

Albert remained standing.

'Don't be too hard on him,' he said.

She got up from the chair and came over to him. 'Please don't misunderstand – I wasn't trying to . . .' She stopped, unable to continue; she did not know where to look. Then tears welled in her eyes. He placed a hand on her shoulder. She took a step forward and stood close to him. Then she rested her forehead against his chest. Her shoulder trembled under his hand. 'I'm sorry,' she choked. He could hear her swallow as if trying to suppress her sobbing. 'It's just so – difficult.'

He let his hand stay on her shoulder and hoped that the weight of it would calm her somehow. She remained standing as she gave in to her tears. He could feel the heat from her body. She held on to the lapels of his jacket as though she were afraid he'd push her away. He towered above her; she seemed to disappear between his huge shoulders. The forgotten feeling of being a man standing so close to a woman surged up in him.

He gave her an awkward pat on the back. 'There, there,' he said, 'sit down. Have some more coffee, you'll see it'll all . . .' He held her gently by the shoulders and steered her back to her chair. She slumped forward and buried her face in her hands. He poured a fresh cup of coffee and held it out to her; then, overcome by sudden tenderness, he stroked her hair. She looked up, but instead of taking the cup, she clasped his other hand in both of hers and gave him a beseeching look.

'Knud Erik needs you so much. You can't possibly know what it means to him – to us. I didn't mean to . . .' She stopped, and Albert seized the opportunity to free his hand. He sat down opposite her. 'Believe me, Mrs Friis,' he said, 'I do understand you. I know how hard your situation is. I'll do everything I can to help you.' The final words came as a surprise to him. He'd always drawn a clear distinction between the boy and his mother. He'd got involved with the boy. But now another barrier had fallen away.

She'd found her handkerchief and was wiping her eyes. Her voice was thick. 'No, that's not it,' she said. 'We can manage. It's just . . .' Again she struggled to stop herself from crying. 'It's so difficult . . .'

The tears slid down her cheeks. The hand holding the handkerchief lay in her lap. She had forgotten it was there.

Suddenly Knud Erik appeared in the doorway to the kitchen. His eyes were wide with fear.

'What's wrong, Ma?'

Incapable of speech, she gestured to him to let her recover. But he ran over and she pressed her face into his chest. He flung his arms around her.

'Don't be sad, Ma.'

There was an adult tone to his voice. Albert realised that Knud Erik was a child when he was with him, but at home with his mother, he was a grown man with a grown man's responsibility and duties.

'I'm going now,' Albert said quietly. Neither of them looked up. As he closed the door behind him, he heard Knud Erik's voice.

'I promise you, Ma, I promise. I promise I'll never be a sailor.'

IF THE WEATHER MADE GOING FOR WALKS OUT OF THE QUESTION, Albert and the boy would pay visits instead. Before Albert had been an eccentric who kept himself to himself. But now we saw him everywhere. One day he knocked on Christian Aaberg's door, and when the captain, who was in his mid-fifties, opened it, Albert introduced the boy.

'This is Knud Erik. He'd like to hear about Africa.'

The boy bowed and stuck out his hand, as he'd once done for Albert; this time he didn't stand staring at his shoes but rather followed the men cheerfully into the drawing room, where Captain Aaberg recalled the time he travelled right across Africa and was put in charge of twenty-two Negroes in a boat on Lake Tanganyika.

'D'you want to see my Negro spear?' he asked.

Knud Erik nodded.

Aaberg had two iron chests in his drawing room. 'They've travelled with me all the way to Africa and back home again,' he said, pointing to them.

'Did you carry them yourself?' Knud Erik asked.

Aaberg laughed. 'A white man doesn't carry anything himself in Africa,' he said. He opened one of the chests. 'Look, a Negro spear. And a shield. Why don't you try holding them?' He handed Knud Erik the spear and showed him how to grasp the shield. 'You're a proper Negro warrior now.'

Knud Erik straightened up and raised his arm as if to throw the spear.

'Watch out,' Christian Aaberg warned him. 'That spear can kill a man.'

Mr Blach, the telegrapher who had been to China, showed them Mandarin costumes and chopsticks. But they didn't visit Josef Isager: Albert was of the opinion that severed hands were unsuitable for children. Instead, they called on Emanuel Kroman, who'd rounded

Cape Horn and could do a terrifying imitation of the howling of a storm in the rigging in the world's most dangerous sea.

'I heard penguins squawk in the pitch-black night,' he said. 'We were at sea for two hundred days. The water ran out, and we drank melted ice in wine glasses. When we got to Valparaiso, we ate a whole sack of potatoes. We didn't even bother cooking them first. We were that hungry.'

'Really? You ate raw potatoes?' the boy gasped.

Everywhere they visited, there were sea chests filled with strange objects: shark jaws, porcupine fish, sawfish teeth, a lobster claw from the Barents Sea the size of a horse's head, poisoned arrows, lumps of lava and coral, antelope hides from Nubia, scimitars from West Africa, a harpoon from Tierra del Fuego, calabashes from Rio Hash, a boomerang from Australia, riding crops from Brazil, opium pipes, armadillos from La Plata and stuffed alligators.

Every single object told a story. Each time the boy left one of the low houses with its high roof, he was dizzy with excitement at the world's infinite variety. Everything whispered in his ear: a leather tom-tom from the Calabar River, amphorae from Cephalonia, an Indian amulet, a stuffed mongoose fighting a cobra, a Turkish hookah, a tooth from a hippopotamus, a mask from the Tonga Islands, a starfish with thirteen arms.

'Half a kilometre in that direction,' Albert said, pointing up Prinsegade towards the Market Square, 'that's where the countryside begins. The people who live there know only their own soil. They know nothing about the world beyond the boundaries of their fields. They'll grow old there, and when it's time for them to die, they'll have seen less than you already have.'

The boy looked up at him and smiled. Albert could feel how his longing stretched in all directions. Knud Erik was fatherless, but Albert was giving him new fathers: the town and the sea.

Spring came and Albert taught the boy to sail.

'What a good sound,' Knud Erik said as he sat on the thwart listening to the gurgling of water lapping against the side of the clinker-built boat, with its narrow planks layered one on top of the next. He'd heard it before, but only from the edge of the quay.

Now he was surrounded by it on all sides. That was something else.

Albert took the boy's hands and placed them on the oars.

Albert was well aware that he was encouraging the lad, but surely he was only promoting something that was natural for a Marstal boy? Things couldn't be otherwise. But he couldn't say this to Klara Friis's face. He saw how vulnerable and uncertain she was in the unfamiliar role of widow. Perhaps he was cowardly not to champion Knud Erik's cause, but he simply thought it was too soon. Life would have to be Klara Friis's teacher. She'd said goodbye to her husband. And then one day she'd have to bid her son good-bye too. It would be a different kind, though: not a farewell to a dead man, but a parting with a living one who was going out to stare death down.

So Knud Erik lived two lives. One was at home, where he had to promise his mother that he'd never go to sea. The other was with Albert, where he lost himself in dreams of following in his father's footsteps. The blue of the sea and the white of the sail were the only colours in the boy's mind. He was going to be a seaman. You might as well shorten that to 'man'. It was the promise of manhood that drove a boy seaward.

Why did a woman fall in love with a sailor? Because a sailor was lost, bound to something distant, unobtainable and ultimately unfathomable, even to himself? Because he went away? Because he came back home again?

In Marstal the answer was straightforward. There were few other men to fall in love with. For poorer people in Marstal, there was never any question about whether a son would go to sea. He belonged to it from the day he was born. The only question was which ship he'd first sign on to. That was all the choice there was.

Klara Friis came from Birkholm. It was a small island; we sailed past it when we left the harbour in springtime and went to sea through Mørkedybet. Albert remembered those spring days, when the sky was high and the wind brisk, when the ice broke up and a hundred ships left from Marstal. It was as if the whole town greeted the spring by setting its sails, as white as the scattered, rapidly thawing ice floes. It felt as if the sun rather than the wind filled the canvas: its bright, stirring warmth propelled us. We could fill half the archipelago with our spring parade. We sized each other up from deck to deck. We were on our way to a hundred different ports, but this moment united us. There was a sense of fellowship that swelled until it broke into a kind of joy.

Farmers on the small islands would come down to the beach and wave as we passed them. They stood there, tiny, rapidly dwindling specks on the white sand, tied to their own limited plots of earth, surrounded on all sides by the endless sea that beckoned them daily and whose invitation they daily declined, happy just to wave instead.

Was this how Klara Friis had found her sailor? Had she wanted to escape her little island, and so fallen in love with someone who wanted out even more than she did? Had she seen promise in those white sails, but failed to understand that the promise was for the men, not the women?

As they drank coffee, Albert asked Klara Friis about Birkholm. She hadn't been born on the island and it was unclear when her family had arrived there. He asked about her parents. Anna Egidia had told him they'd died, but she'd not said when.

She bit her lower lip. 'Our teacher was a real monster,' she said, sounding as if she'd felt pressed to tell him something about Birkholm and had found a way to stop him from getting too close. 'My ears were always aching. He loved to twist them.'

Albert nodded. He knew a bit about educational provisions on the island, which had to share a teacher with the neighbouring island of Hjortø. There'd be two weeks of school, then two weeks off. Precious little knowledge was imparted to Birkholm's young minds.

Klara Friis studied her hands for a while, brooding. She looked up and he saw darkness in her eyes: not her earlier grief, but something deeper, like the terror of an animal that fears for its life but doesn't know the nature of its enemy.

'Have you ever been to Birkholm?' she asked.

He shook his head. 'I've sailed past it. There's not much to see. I believe the island's very flat.'

'Yes, its highest point is just two metres above sea level.'

She smiled briefly, as if to apologise for this. Then her eyes darkened again.

'There was a storm surge,' she said, and shuddered. 'I'll never forget it. I was eight. The water kept on rising and rising. The land disappeared completely. We couldn't see it at all. Only the sea. Sea everywhere. I hid in the loft. But I got scared – it was so dark there. So I climbed onto the roof. The waves were crashing against the house. The spray soaked me right through. I got so wet. I felt so cold.'

She shivered as if she were still chilled to the bone. As she spoke, she curled up, and her voice faltered: she was a helpless, terrified child confiding in him. And although he was unaware of his own change of tone, it was that helpless child he addressed. In his mind, he didn't so much ask about her parents as summon them: where on earth were they in this story? Surely someone had been looking after her? He wanted a rescuing hand to appear, a father to clasp the girl in his strong arms, a mother to hold her tight and warm her with her body. But she spoke as if she'd been up there on the roof in the midst of a flood all alone.

'Wasn't there anyone else on the roof?'

'Yes, Karla was there.'

'Was Karla your sister, Mrs Friis?'

He still addressed her as Mrs Friis. Anything else would have been patronising. But at this moment it was like being formal with a child.

'No, Karla was my rag doll.'

'But what about your parents?' he finally asked.

'I sat on the ridge of the roof, clinging to the chimney. And it grew dark. I couldn't see anything at all. It was like someone had pulled an empty coal sack over my head. In the whole world there was just me and Karla. The wind was howling in the chimney something awful. The waves crashed against the house like it was a ship. I thought the walls would come down. But still, I must have fallen asleep. It could only have been for a minute. But when I woke up, Karla had gone. I must have let go of her and she must have slipped down the roof. I kept calling and calling. But she never came back.' Suddenly she smiled. 'What a chatterbox I am. You make me tell you the silliest things. It must sound like pure nonsense to you. All those years you've been at sea – I'm sure you've had far worse experiences.'

He looked at her solemnly. 'No, Mrs Friis, I haven't. Nothing has ever happened to me that comes even close to your night alone in that flood.'

She blushed. He'd seen the terror in her. And in that moment a bond was forged between them that he'd never be able to break. She'd given him something precious, told him a secret from the very heart of herself. He still knew very little about her, but the fear she'd shown him sufficed. It bound him to her.

'Karla,' he said, pondering, almost speaking to himself. 'That's very similar to your name. As if she were your twin.'

'Yes,' was all she answered. 'Almost like Klara.'

She gave him a look of gratitude. Now he would leave her in peace and intrude no further into her privacy. He knew about Karla and Klara; he didn't need to know more. She no longer had anything to prove, to explain or to answer. With him she could be something she'd never been before: a blank page. She got a fresh start.

He never asked about her parents again.

SUMMER CAME AND THE WAR CONTINUED. ALBERT HAD FEWER DREAMS these days, and those he had didn't affect him the way they used to. He had Knud Erik now.

'Have you had another dream?' the boy would ask him when they met.

'Not last night,' he would reply.

'Not last night,' the boy would repeat, sounding disappointed. 'I hope you start dreaming again soon.'

Knud Erik's own dreams were distorted and strange, as most dreams are. But he always told them with the same happy wonder in his voice.

One dream was different, though. He dreamed he was about to drown.

'I called for my pa. But he didn't come.' His eyes grew blank as he told it. For a moment, he sat just the way he had when Albert met him for the first time, with his shoulders hunched and his head hanging. 'And so I drowned,' he finished in a dull voice.

They sat facing each other in the boat. Albert took the boy's face in his hands and looked him straight in the eye. 'You're not going to drown. It was just a bad dream. If you're ever about to drown, then you'll call out for me. And I'll always come.'

The tension left the hunched shoulders. The boy's relief was palpable. A moment later he'd forgotten all about it. He pulled at the oars, not expertly yet, but with enthusiasm. His eyes sparkled.

'Where am I rowing us today?'

They were in the middle of the harbour, and they watched the *Memory* pass Dampskibsbroen, a black ribbon of smoke pouring from her tall, narrow funnel. Albert stared at the steamer long and hard. He knew she wouldn't return. The boy waved to the town's deaf sand digger as he rowed past.

'Keep your rhythm steady,' Albert ordered.

* * *

That night Albert had his final dream. He knew it was the last one because it began the same way as the first one, thirty years earlier. It was the same voice speaking. 'You're heading for danger.'

But this time he didn't wake. He wasn't on a ship, as he had been on the first occasion. It was years since he'd last been on one. He could have leaped out of his bed and run onto the balcony and stared into the darkness, but there'd be no shipwreck outside, no people needing to be rescued. He was on dry land, though he no longer knew if dry land was safe. It was an unsettling dream filled with terrifying episodes. And like those that had announced the coming of the war, he had no idea what it meant.

The next day he told the boy. 'Last night I had the strangest dream,' he began.

The boy looked up at him expectantly.

'Go on, tell me,' he urged when he saw that the old man was hesitating.

'I saw a phantom ship,' Albert said. 'Well, I saw lots of phantom ships. But that wasn't the oddest part of it.'

'What's a phantom ship?' the boy asked.

'It's a ghost ship.'

'How did you know?'

'Well, everything on the ship was grey. There were no other colours. Just grey.'

'Like a warship?' the boy asked, though he wasn't old enough to remember the day the torpedo boats called at the harbour.

'Yes, like a warship, only it wasn't one. It was a freighter, a steamer, a bit like the *Memory*, only grey all over.'

'And then what happened?'

'Well, now here's the odd thing. It was the middle of the night. But it was as bright as day. There were dazzling lights high up in the black sky. They didn't hang still like stars. They moved slowly down towards the water and when they hit the sea, they went out. But new ones kept coming. On the shore there were buildings on fire, but they weren't buildings like the ones we know. They were big and completely circular without windows. And the flames that shot out of them were even taller than the buildings themselves. Big guns were being fired all over the place. You can't imagine their thunder. And aeroplanes. Do you know what aeroplanes are?'

The boy nodded. 'What did the aeroplanes do?'

'They dropped bombs and the ships caught fire and sank.'

The boy sat very quietly. Then he asked, 'Was it the end of the world?'

'Yes, maybe.'

'Do you know something?' the boy said. 'That's the best story you've ever told.'

Albert smiled at him. Then he looked away, out across the sea. There was a part of the dream he hadn't told the boy. He hadn't been able to see the name of the phantom ship in the dark. But he knew with the strange certainty his prophetic dreams had taught him to recognise that the lad was on board. Knud Erik was there. Right at the end of the world.

ALBERT HAD THE FEELING THAT SOMETHING IN HIS LIFE WAS NEARING
a close. It wasn't just because of the war. He had accounts to settle.
The Negro hand on Pastor Abildgaard's desk kept haunting him.
Albert, too, had the remains of what had once been a human being
in his care, and it seemed to him that Josef Isager, who was so
contemptuous of his fellow men, had acted with more morality than
he had. After all, he'd requested a Christian burial for the hand, the
same hand he'd once packed in his suitcase like a cheap souvenir,
undisturbed that it had been brutally chopped from a human being.

A severed head in a box – was that any different? Surely he owed
James Cook a funeral, too?

He walked around to Josef Isager's house in Kongegade and knocked
on the door. He heard noises inside, but no one came to answer it.
Albert knocked again. The noise continued. It was muted by the
door, so he couldn't make out exactly what it was, but it sounded
like fighting. Someone was running. Then there was gasping, and
the sound of a body smashed heavily into a wall. Albert grabbed
hold of the knob, and the door opened instantly. He entered the
small, dark hall and knocked hard on the door to the drawing room.

'Is anyone there?'

The noise stopped. He pushed the door handle down. Josef was
in the middle of the room with his stick poised, ready to strike.
Maren Kirstine was standing on the sofa, looking like a little girl
who'd been caught doing something she shouldn't. She'd clearly
scrambled there out of fear. Her hair, which she normally kept under
a net, was dishevelled; grey strands hung down across her distorted
face. She was clasping her mouth with one hand as though trying
to suppress a scream.

Josef turned to his unexpected guest.

'Are you next?' he shouted, and stepped forward menacingly.

His face, with its heavy, drooping moustache and cold, arrogant eyes, was as formidable as ever, but his ageing body was bent and slumped. Albert snatched the stick from his hand and broke it in two across his thigh. A small feeling of triumph passed through him. He still had his strength.

'We don't hit women here,' he said, and forced Josef onto the sofa with one hand while holding out the other to the stunned Maren Kirstine. She took it and clambered off.

'Are you hurt?' he asked.

She shook her head, but her old red-rimmed eyes were brimming. Unsteadily, she dragged herself to the kitchen and closed the door behind her. The sight of her cowed back as she left made Albert incandescent with rage. Josef was too dazed to get up from the sofa, so Albert grabbed him by the lapels and started shaking him backwards and forwards.

'You beat your own wife?' he yelled.

Josef's hawklike head lolled. His eyes remained cold, but Albert could see how frail the former pilot had grown. If he had any strength left, it lay in his will, not in his hands.

'Ha!' Josef Isager snorted. 'I've grown too old, damn it. When I hit her these days, she can't even feel it.'

Behind them the door to the kitchen was cautiously opened.

'Please don't be hard on him,' Maren Kirstine begged in a pathetic voice.

Albert let go of Josef and straightened up, then stood there helplessly, not knowing what to do next. Josef collapsed on the sofa. He didn't look up. His face was drained, as though his confession of diminished muscle power had sapped the last of his strength and he was surrendering to old age without protest.

'Sit down, please, Captain Madsen. I'll make us some coffee.'

Maren Kirstine's voice had returned to its normal pitch, as if all visitors to the home roughed up their host before taking coffee.

Albert and Josef sat facing each other silently while Maren Kirstine moved about in the kitchen. Eventually she came in and set the dining table. Then she returned with the coffee and some pastries. She'd gathered her hair back under the net and wiped her eyes, though they were still red. Once she'd poured the coffee, she vanished back into the kitchen.

Josef's moustache dipped in the coffee as he slurped it. He stuffed a piece of pastry in his mouth and started chewing, spraying crumbs as he did so.

'Why are you here?' he asked. He was still eating. He wanted to show his contempt for the man who'd just put him in his place.

'The Negro hand –' Albert said.

'Yes, what about it?' Josef interrupted him.

'Why did you give it to Pastor Abildgaard?'

'None of your business.' Josef pressed his lips tightly shut and sucked them in. He was still chewing. Despite his drooping moustache, he suddenly looked like a toothless old crone, munching away on her sore gums.

'Is that all you have to say?'

'Yes, and you'd better bloody believe it!'

Josef had finished the pastry, and with his mouth empty, his speech became clearer. He stood up abruptly, pushing the table so hard that his coffee cup toppled, sending its contents flying across the embroidered tablecloth.

'Maren Kirstine!' roared the Congo Pilot. 'Maren Kirstine! Your coffee's as thin as piss! I want proper man's coffee!'

Holding the coffee cup in one hand, he flung open the door to the kitchen and slammed it shut behind him. The noise of the cup smashing onto the floor followed soon after.

Albert stared at the door, seemingly making his mind up. Then he rose from the table and left the house.

The next day he lowered the head of James Cook into the sea.

Mørkedybet seemed a fitting place of rest for the great explorer. So many voyages had started here, where the Marstal fleet set sail at the first sign of spring. A grave in the local cemetery would have been too complicated, and Albert didn't think Abildgaard's nerves could handle a funeral.

He decided to invite Knud Erik to come along for Cook's last voyage. He'd never shown him the shrunken head. It wasn't appropriate for a child, he'd thought. But now he brushed all such considerations aside. He'd filled the boy's head with horror stories about sinking and burning ships, and Knud Erik had loved it. He'd probably enjoy the ghastly head too.

However, the real reason for inviting the boy along was that he intended to give the shrunken head a proper send-off and wanted the boy as his witness. He suspected there was a moral linked to the story of James Cook – though the more he thought about it, the less certain he felt about what it might be.

On his first two voyages, James Cook had treated the natives he encountered with respect. He'd regarded them as his equals, but they'd reacted with scorn. So he learned from his mistakes and became brutal and callous instead. In a way, he'd ended up like Josef Isager and the white men in Africa.

Where was the balance in the life of James Cook?

On a ship it was the captain's job to find balance. But a ship wasn't the world: the world was far bigger. Where was the world's balance? Did Albert even know himself? Was there anything at all he could pass on to a seven-year-old boy?

James Cook had lived under enormous pressure, constantly having to prove his worth to himself and to others. Though Cook had been the great mapmaker of the Pacific, there'd been no chart to help him navigate his own life.

Albert had looked for a father and found none. He'd had to make his own way, and so would Knud Erik. Perhaps he could tell him that. Or perhaps he should say nothing at all. Perhaps it was all the same in the end.

Yet he brought the boy along.

He'd placed the bag with the shrunken head in a makeshift coffin, a wooden casket filled with stones. He positioned the casket on the thwart between himself and the boy.

'It's a surprise,' he told the boy. 'We'll open it once we get there.'

They took turns rowing. Albert did most of it. When it was Knud Erik's turn, he gave it his all. Soon they were in Mørkedybet, looking towards the flat island of Birkholm.

'That's where your mother's from.' Albert pointed to the shore. 'One spring day she was standing there when your father came sailing. And then she fell in love.'

He was making this up. Klara Friis had probably never told him about her first meeting with his father, but it wouldn't hurt the boy if Albert added some colour and scenery to his parents' love.

'So she knew he was a sailor?'

Albert nodded.

'Then why won't she let me go to sea?'

'She will one day. Your mother just needs some time. She's still upset about your father.'

The boy sat for a while. 'I want to see the surprise,' he said at last.

Albert opened the casket and took out the shrunken head. It looked just as it did when he'd inherited it from the captain of the *Flying Scud* fifty years before, and it was still wrapped in the same crumbling cloth. Removing the fabric, he held up the head.

Knud Erik stared at the dark face, as wrinkled and lined as a walnut.

'What is it?' There was no fear in his voice.

'It's the head of a man. He died many years ago.'

'Do you go that small when you're dead?'

Albert laughed and explained the technique of making shrunken heads.

'How did he die?'

'He died on a beach in Hawaii. He was fighting for his life, but the natives outnumbered him. In the end he was defeated.'

'And then they turned him into a shrunken head?'

Albert nodded. Knud Erik looked at James Cook for a while.

'Can I have him?' he asked.

'No, it's time for him to go to the bottom of the sea.'

'And he won't ever come back up again?'

'No. He was the greatest explorer in the world. But now he needs a rest.'

'Can I hold him?'

Without waiting for a reply, Knud Erik took the head of James Cook and cupped it in his hands. 'You died in the end,' he said to the shrunken head. 'But you fought first.' He patted the dry, faded hair of Captain Cook as if applauding his accomplishments.

They wrapped the head in the cloth again and put it back in the casket.

'I want to say a few words,' Albert said. And then he said the Lord's Prayer, as he'd done when Jack Lewis, captain of the *Flying Scud*, had been eased over the side of the ship wrapped in canvas, still wearing his blood-soaked shirt. He'd not prayed since then.

The casket bobbed briefly on the surface of the water. Then the weight of the stones dragged it down. A few air bubbles rose before it disappeared into the green-blue depths.

Albert contemplated the boy's words to the shrunken head. Knud

Erik had extracted his own moral from the little that Albert had told him. There was a kind of wisdom to it, perhaps the most basic: 'You died in the end, but you fought first.' As long as the boy held on to this, things couldn't get that bad. Life could throw in its own complexities later.

When they moored the boat at Prinsebroen, the boy tried to leap from the boat to the bridge, but miscalculated his jump and fell overboard. Albert stuck a hand into the water and pulled him out.

Knud Erik laughed. 'Let's do it again!'

'You've been baptised now,' Albert said. 'Once in the church and once in the sea. You're a sailor now.'

'Did I nearly drown?' the boy asked, trying to look important.

'Yes, you can boast about that. But not to your mother. Once underwater, twice underwater, but never three times. Remember that.'

'What happens the third time?' the boy asked.

'The third time's the shortest journey,' the old man said. 'The journey that leads to death. It only takes two minutes. Always take the longer journey when you become a sailor. Never the shorter. Remember that.'

The boy looked at him and nodded gravely. He hadn't understood any of this speech, but he sensed that something important had been said.

Albert pulled the boy's clothes off him and hung them out to dry on the front thwart. 'Come on,' he said. 'Let's do some more rowing. It'll warm you up.'

335

'IT CAN'T GO ON,' WE SAID ABOUT THE WAR. 'IT HAS TO END.'

We didn't know anything and we didn't understand politics.

'The good times will be over soon,' the old skippers said, as they sat in the summer sun on their benches by the harbour. Their lined faces, tanned to leather, gave nothing away. With their eyes hidden beneath the shiny brims of their caps, it was impossible to tell whether this was gallows humour or whether they really meant what they said.

Albert, too, sensed that the war would be over soon. The right-hand column was now nearly as long as the left-hand one. September came. The boy started school, but the two continued to meet in the afternoons, as they always had. Seven more ships were lost. The last to go down was the steamer *Memory*. Then it ended. Albert delivered his last messages to the bereaved. The war lasted a few more months, but as far as Marstal was concerned, it was finished.

Albert sat down next to the skippers who were soaking up the September sun beside the harbour, giving their old bones a last warm-up before the winter. The group shifted uneasily. They weren't used to his company.

'Yes, the good times are indeed over,' he said, and he didn't hide the sarcasm in his voice. They shifted again.

'Four hundred and forty-seven Danish sailors were lost,' he said. He knew his figures. 'Fifty-three of them came from Marstal. That means roughly one in every nine men who drowned came from this town.'

He paused to let them digest this fact. Then he continued with the figures.

'The number of Marstal inhabitants is only a thousandth of Denmark's total population. And what's the bottom line, gentlemen? Does our total amount to good times?'

He got up from the bench, touched his cap with his finger and left.

They looked after him as he walked up towards Havnegade, swinging his stick. Yes, he knew his maths, did Albert.

'Fifty-three hands lost,' Albert thought, as he continued along Havnegade. 'Perhaps I'm being unfair. A town quickly forgets. A mother, a brother, a wife or a daughter won't. But a town will. A town looks ahead.'

Mr Henckel still visited Marstal. Tall and broad, with his light coat-tails flapping behind him, he'd stride down Kirkestræde on his way to Hotel Ærø, where he kept a room permanently at his disposal. His arrival was celebrated with grand champagne galas for investors and other interested parties, of which there were always plenty. Herman, meanwhile, had sold both the *Two Sisters* and his house in Skippergade. This had left him homeless, and so he'd moved into Hotel Ærø, where he soon ran up an enormous bill. With his entire fortune sunk in Mr Henckel's engineering projects, he was unable to settle it right away. But that didn't matter, said Orla Egeskov, the proprietor; he was happy to extend credit to him and Mr Henckel. Orla Egeskov was an investor himself. He knew that every penny would come back tenfold; each bottle of champagne would be paid for out of future profits. And champagne was all Herman drank.

Henckel had built lodgings for the workers at the shipyard at the end of Reberbanen, where the village idiot, Anders Nørre, had once had his hut. Compared to the miniature proportions of most of the town's houses, it was an impressive structure with two stairwells, eight flats and a mansard roof. And instead of crouching in a narrow street as though sheltering from the wind, it stood on a bare field, open to all sides, with a view of the Baltic, as if the engineer meant to challenge both wind and sea. After the school in Vestergade and the stately post office in Havnegade, with its granite foundation and swirling cement garlands below each window, Henckel's workers' house was the biggest building in Marstal. Here, ordinary people would live one on top of another, with no back gardens or front doors leading directly to the street.

'It's for an army of working men,' said Mr Henckel, who was a fiery soul. 'It's just the beginning. The day will come when we'll tear down all the old rubbish in this town and make proper use of the space.' In addition to the shipyards in Marstal, Korsør and Kalundborg, he also owned a brickworks. 'I've enough bloody bricks to build a whole new Marstal if you want one. Just say the word,' he bragged in the bar at Hotel Ærø, as his eyes grew bloodshot and large patches of sweat formed on his shirt. Then he'd buy another round, and we'd toast the new era that was storming in. We'd grown accustomed to champagne. The bubbles rose to the surface and burst in little pops that tickled the lips. There was no end to them, just as there was no end to the engineer's ideas.

Herman raised his glass, too. He no longer went about with his sleeves rolled up, and he wore cufflinks on his shirt these days. We'd all heard about the two spelling mistakes on his tattoo.

All we'd had before in Marstal was a savings bank: now we got a proper one. The Commerce and Credit Bank from Svendborg, on the island of Funen, opened a branch. The building stood across from Albert's broker's office and it was even taller than the school, the post office and Henckel's workers' accommodation, with a large facade facing Prinsegade. Broad granite steps led up to a big varnished-oak door with a brass handle. It looked like the entrance to a castle.

From time to time you might hear the noise of a rivet hammer from Marstal Steel Shipyard, but no ships had been launched yet.

Albert nodded to Peter Raahauge, the boat builder, as he made his way home through Buegade at the end of the day. Raahauge raised a finger to his cap and stopped.

'When do we finally get to see one of your ships?'

Raahauge set his toolbox down on the cobbled street. He folded his strong arms across his chest, snorted contemptuously into his moustache, then shook his head. 'Damn strange way they do business,' he said. 'If laying down the keel is the same as building a whole ship, then I've built an awful lot of ships lately. I've yet to see any frames or shell-plating.'

'So how does that work?' Albert asked. 'It doesn't make any sense to me.'

'Or to the rest of us mere mortals. But that's because we're not as smart as Henckel. You see, Captain Madsen . . .' Raahauge leaned close to Albert. His voice became a confidential whisper. 'He's arranged it so that the Norwegians pay the first instalment as soon as the keel's been laid. Then he invites them down here, offers them champagne, and shows off the keel, and they think the ship's as good as built. How are they to know that the last set of customers were shown the same keel? It's the same one we show all of them.'

'So Henckel's taking large sums of money for ships he'll never deliver? But that's fraud!' Albert was outraged.

'You might say so, Captain Madsen. I couldn't possibly comment. Still, I'll be having to look for new work soon. Because there's no way in hell this can last.'

Peter Raahauge touched a finger to the brim of his cap once more and disappeared up the street.

FOR SOME YEARS NOW, ALBERT HAD GONE OUT FISHING FOR SHRIMPS. Many of us did that when we came ashore. Some did it out of necessity, but for Albert, it was a way of passing the time. The local waters belonged to boys and to old men. He'd learned his way around the archipelago as a child, exploring all its islands, bays, points, sandbanks and invisible currents. In between childhood and old age he'd sailed the world's oceans: now he'd returned to the smallest print of the sea chart, seeking out all the old familiar places. He'd begun in the good years before the First World War, and when his prophetic nightmares descended on him, he escaped their reign of terror by fishing for shrimps. Tending to his nets beneath the drifting clouds, he'd found, if not peace, then at least a ceasefire.

Albert was thinking about shrimps one evening after he'd left Knud Erik and his mother and was strolling along Nygade to his house in Prinsegade. Shrimps. He'd take Knud Erik with him the next time he went to check his nets. He'd teach the boy how to do it and give him a bucketful to take home to his mother. They could sell the rest at the harbour, and Knud Erik would get a bit of money in his pocket and bring in some earnings like a proper little man. It would be half play and half real help for the hard-up widow, who was unlikely to accept assistance in any other form. Normally he'd just give his shrimps away to anyone who happened to turn up at his office or to Lorentz across the street.

That summer he'd laid his nets along the coast of Langeland, starting at Sorekrogen and working his way towards Ristinge. In the light summer nights when he fished, the water's surface was like a mirror. The first glow of the sun blazed north-east as he rowed out through the entrance to the harbour, and the sound of the oars travelled far across the water.

Now he asked the boy if he wanted to come along.

*   *   *

The summer holidays had started. With school over, Knud Erik hung about during the long, empty days when the weather didn't tempt him to swim at the beach. After some hesitation, Knud Erik's mother consented to a shrimp outing. A bond had grown between Albert and Klara. He felt it keenly but he didn't explore its nature, though he found himself spending more and more time in front of his mirror, and sometimes a smile – one of recognition – would appear behind his dense, greying beard. It was an old friend he was greeting in the mirror, one he hadn't seen for many years: his own younger self.

He was to collect Knud Erik in the evening and take him home. The boy would sleep on the sofa in Albert's drawing room until three in the morning, and then he'd wake him and they'd head for the harbour. Klara was baking thick pancakes when he arrived. They were a local speciality; as she made them, she brought them directly out from the kitchen, so they could be eaten piping hot. He stood in the doorway watching her as she deftly poured batter into figures of eight in the hot pan, where they quickly rose into small compact mounds. When they turned golden, she placed them on brown paper to drain. Knud Erik stood next to her, eagerly awaiting the first pancake, which he immediately sprinkled with sugar.

No words passed between them as she worked on the pancakes, but the silence was a comfortable one. Standing in the doorway with his arms folded across his chest, Albert realised he felt at home in the presence of this young woman.

She'd tied a scarf around her hair to protect it from the greasy fumes: when a lock came loose and fell over her eyes, she blew it out of the way and shot him a cheerful glance. He smiled back at her.

She served gooseberry compote with the pancakes, and Albert asked if it was home-made. She nodded. There were gooseberry bushes in their little back garden. Even the most wretched hovels in the town had a garden. She'd made far more pancakes than they could eat, and she gave them the remaining ones, wrapped in a tea towel, along with a jar of compote.

'In case you get hungry tonight,' she said.

She turned to Knud Erik and handed him a woollen jumper.

'It can get cold out on the water.'

'I won't be cold,' Knud Erik said, in a tone that implied that his newly acquired manhood had been offended.

'Well, I'll be bringing my jumper,' said Albert. He placed his hand on the boy's shoulder. 'Say goodbye to your mother.'

Klara stood in the doorway waving after them as they walked up towards Kirkestræde.

When he roused Knud Erik at three and handed him a cup of warm coffee, the horizon was glowing, but the sky above was still dark, keeping the last stars alive.

'This will help you wake up.'

The boy scratched his head with one hand and took the cup with the other.

'Blow on it.'

The boy blew, and kept his lips tentatively pursed as he slurped his first mouthful. He made a face. Albert took the cup from him and added a teaspoon of sugar.

'Now try it.'

The boy took another sip and smiled. Albert pulled the woollen jumper over the boy's head. He'd already put on his own Icelandic one.

They slipped the mooring at Prinsebroen and started rowing out of the harbour entrance. The boy huddled on the thwart, shivering with tiredness and cold. Albert passed him an oar.

'Lend me a hand, will you?' he said.

The boy positioned himself on the aft thwart, then stuck the oar into the water and started moving it between his hands with a rolling motion, twisting it in the water like a screw. He was sculling, a technique Albert had taught him.

They passed Dampskibsbroen and headed for Ristinge. Knud Erik had warmed up and they made good speed across the bright, glassy water. Theirs was the only boat out this early. An hour later they reached Sorekrogen. The nets were brimming with shrimps.

'There'll be some for your mother, too,' Albert said.

They made themselves comfortable on the thwarts and ate the pancakes. The sun was now clear of the horizon, igniting a low-hanging stripe of cloud. Apart from that the sky was clear.

'It'll be beach weather today,' Albert declared.

'Tell me about the shrunken head,' Knud Erik said.

A few hours later they were back at the entrance to the harbour. The sun was higher in the sky and Albert could already feel its warmth, though it was still early in the morning. They passed Dampskibsbroen and approached Prinsebroen. Knud Erik went to the bow and readied the boat for mooring with accomplished ease. Albert filled a bucket with shrimps, then took the boy home to Snaregade. The lad raced through the door with the bucket in his hand.

His mother appeared in the doorway.

'Thank you for the shrimps, Captain Madsen. Now, why are you standing outside? Do come in, please.'

She stepped aside to allow him to enter through the narrow doorway. He tried making himself small, but he brushed her with his arm all the same. He knew his way round and walked to the sofa. A cup had already been put out for him. She disappeared into the kitchen and returned with the coffee pot.

'Shrimp fishing is a good business,' Albert said. 'Knud Erik will be a prosperous man.'

Her face tightened. 'We can't accept money.'

'It's not a gift, Mrs Friis. He's worked hard and it's only fair that he should get his share.'

Knud Erik started jumping up and down in excitement.

'Go find your swimming trunks and a towel. And then you can run over to the beach.'

'Really, can I, can I?' By now his jumping had built up a rhythm.

'Yes, of course. Now be off with you.'

He rushed to the kitchen and returned a moment later with a rolled-up towel. He was about to tear through the hall with his hand raised to bid Albert goodbye, when he stopped abruptly, went over to Albert and stuck out his hand. He bowed stiffly and thanked him for the day. Albert placed his hand on the boy's head and ruffled his hair gently. 'You're welcome.'

'He's a lovely lad,' he said, once Knud Erik was out of the door. 'Take good care of him.'

'You already do that for me.'

She smiled again and he looked up. Their eyes met and he couldn't decide if it had been by chance. He felt that he ought to look elsewhere, but seemed paralysed. He was aware of a smile spreading uncontrollably across his face. Klara Friis's cheeks slowly reddened. She, too, seemed unable to break away from the moment, which kept expanding from seconds to minutes to what felt like wondrous weightless hours. At last she looked down. He felt a sudden shame, as if he'd molested her. He had to stop himself from apologising, even though nothing had happened.

He cleared his throat. 'Thanks for the coffee.'

She gave him a confused look, as though he'd woken her from a reverie. Her cheeks were still red.

'You're going now?'

'Yes, I think I'd better,' he said, and hoped his words sounded neutral so that his leaving didn't seem to be a verdict on the awkward situation they'd just found themselves in.

'Oh,' she said, as if he'd surprised her.

He remained sitting and waited for her to continue. She stared at her hands.

'Well, I don't mean to impose on you. But would you like to come to dinner tonight? After all, we have the shrimps,' she said, looking up at him.

'I'd like that very much. I'll bring a bottle of wine.'

'Wine?' Her awkwardness grew.

'Ah, perhaps you don't drink wine?'

She wiped her forehead. Then she suddenly laughed behind her hand.

'I've never tasted it.'

'There's a first time for everything. And that time is tonight.'

When Albert left the house, he noticed the thickset figure of Herman striding briskly by towards the harbour with his flat cap pulled down over his forehead. Looking up, Herman gave the Friis house a quick once-over, glanced back at Albert and touched one finger nonchalantly to his cap. Albert returned the greeting, but there was no exchange of words.

Albert kept walking in the direction of Kirkestræde, pondering the look the young man had just given him. Was he checking up on him? Was he aware of something? Then he shrugged. What kind of nonsense was this? Nothing had happened between him and Knud Erik's mother. But the invitation for tonight? The wine? Not long ago he'd held a weeping widow in his arms. When they'd talked about the wine just now, her tone had turned almost coquettish. Her laughter behind her hand. Was she falling in love with him? Or was it the other way round? Was he interpreting everything in a certain light because he'd fallen for her?

He shook his head at himself. The mere thought was inappropriate. He didn't know the exact age difference between them, but it was huge. He could easily be her father – even her grandfather.

He had his own life and habits. He didn't want them disturbed. He'd seen and heard more than he needed to: his dreams had shaken him to the core. He'd experienced them as a cruel and vicious halting of his life, inflicted by a God whose savagery repelled him, who inspired in him neither the urge to believe nor the impulse to beg for mercy. His faith had been faith in mankind, and he'd lost it, ending up in the darkness, a badly injured, shipwrecked man on a shore of bones at the end of the world.

But, unexpectedly, his life had restarted. A seven-year-old boy had restored his faith. And now the boy's mother had become part of it, too, and the appeal of this new life grew stronger all the time. He couldn't deny that he felt strangely exhilarated in the presence of Klara Friis. Knud Erik had knocked the first hole in the wall of loneliness he'd lived behind. But now, when Klara was there, he felt the entire wall was on the brink of collapse.

Yes, it was inappropriate. And yet he couldn't stop smiling.

Late in the afternoon Albert was sitting in his bath in preparation for dinner when he felt something like a shooting pain in his mind. A man with a character less proud and stubborn would have called it anxiety. Once again, his thoughts were circling Klara Friis. Human beings are afflicted by a need to judge. So what might people think if they suddenly saw him in the company of a much younger woman? Some men, like the monstrous O'Connor, lash out with their fists, but there are other ways to do damage, and the tongue can be the most vicious weapon of all: in the courtroom of gossip, there's no appeal. But why should he care? He'd done his duty in life. He'd earned respect and built up a fleet of ships. His work was done, yet he carried on living. What was left? Might there be new, unexpected freedoms awaiting him in these closing years?

He got out of the bath and dried himself. He went over to the mirror and, with his towel, wiped a porthole shape on its steamy surface so he could inspect himself. He'd rarely viewed his body through the eyes of another. For him it was a tool. Strength and endurance were the yardsticks he measured it by, whether he was on deck fighting the sea or using his thick muscles to enforce his authority in front of an insubordinate crew. How long could he stay awake when a storm demanded his constant presence on the deck? How much power did he exude?

In the mirror he could see that his chest was sunken and long stretch marks ran from his shoulders down to his pectoral muscles, which sagged under their own weight. The curly hair that covered his chest had been grey for many years. Yet once he was dressed, his body seemed as impressive as it had ever been.

One summer evening long ago he'd made love with Cheng Sumei in her large suburban villa in Le Havre, not knowing that it would be for the last time. It had been an evening like many others. Wax candles, flames that stood straight up in the calm evening, the scent of incense. She'd leaned over him and let him loosen her silk kimono, which fell open to expose her naked body, as white as the petals of a tree peony, with a faint hint of something that was not yellow exactly, but more like cream. Her skin was as smooth as a polished jade figurine. He didn't understand it, the mystery of her ageless-ness, which he associated not with the Orient, but with her. In all the time he'd known her, only the few lines that appeared around her mouth betrayed her as the mature woman she was. They were like lines drawn on a picture. They only enhanced her beauty.

Cheng Sumei unbound her long hair and let it cascade over her shoulders, and he buried himself completely in its dense darkness. This was the unvarying prelude to their lovemaking. He closed his eyes and surrendered to her hands, which gently caressed his cheek-bones. Then her lips landed on his.

The next morning she didn't wake up. She just lay there with her black hair spread out across the embroidered white silk pillow. She'd died as though she'd merely turned her face away to look in a different direction. She'd never aged and was never struck down by illness. And yet her life had ended.

Cheng Sumei had passed away. That was exactly how he thought of it: she'd risen from the bed in the middle of the night and passed away, away from him. He looked at her dead body on the sheet as though it were a kimono she'd stepped out of. Every night for a long time afterwards, he expected to hear the familiar swish of silk as she undressed in front of him. He closed his eyes, though darkness already reigned in the room, and waited for the touch of her hands gliding across his face.

He worked hard during the day. But not even his daily activities provided distraction or escape. They'd worked together too closely for that. He'd accompany her to her office, and in the evenings they'd bring telegrams and newspapers home with them. Then they'd discuss freight rates and political events around the globe. He learned from her, and she learned from him. He had firsthand knowledge of the sea, and if there were problems with a crew, or if she was dissatisfied with a captain's decisions, she would consult him. If a new market was opening up, they'd make a joint decision, after extensive discussion, about how to respond. They discovered common ground in the brokerage business, and that was fundamentally the strongest bond between them.

He could still recall the moment he'd fallen in love with her. Luis Presser had invited him for the first time to dinner at the villa where he'd later spend so many nights. At table, he'd been mesmerised by her. He'd had to concentrate to prevent himself from staring: he forced himself to pay attention to the conversation, which was in English. After a while even he realised that it was embarrassing – odd almost – that he hadn't yet addressed her, or looked in her direction except furtively. If he felt anything, it was awe. There was something transparent about her beauty that in his eyes made her enigmatic, almost supernatural. He hadn't expected that she would deign to do something as profane as open her mouth to speak, and so when she addressed him, he was as startled as the devotee of some pagan god would have been, had the lips of the statue he was kneeling to suddenly parted to give him a jovial greeting.

'Monsieur Madsen, would you like me to tell you about the moment I fell in love with the West?' she asked.

She pronounced his name with a strong French accent, but otherwise her English was perfect. She sparkled, full of curiosity and playful teasing, as though she'd sensed his bashfulness and now wished to demystify herself. He hadn't noticed her eyes before. He'd only seen her long, dense eyelashes when she looked down, not the eyes behind them.

'It was the first time I saw a fire being put out,' she went on. 'You see, in China we believe fires are started by evil spirits. So when a house catches fire, we try to scare the spirits away.' She paused,

347

as if to emphasise the words that followed. 'With noise. Drums and cymbals. I've seen many houses burn to the ground to the beating of drums. We have a five-thousand-year-old culture, and in all those five thousand years it's never once occurred to us to put a fire out with water. The English had set up a fire brigade in Shanghai. A house opposite me caught fire. It started in the evening, and the English gentlemen, who were all volunteers, arrived straight from a dinner party, wearing top hats, tailcoats and starched white shirt collars, which quickly became filthy from the soot. They pointed large hoses at the flames. When the fire hissed and died away and most of the house was still standing – that was the moment I fell in love with the West. Do you understand what I'm saying, Monsieur Madsen? My philosophy is basically very simple. You put out fire with water. That's why I live here and not in China.'

She laughed. He laughed in response and nodded.

'Well, my philosophy tends to be that water's for sailing on. But I don't suppose that deep down we're so different.'

It was at that moment that his awe turned into love. Here was a woman whose attitude to life resembled his. Her cheerful directness liberated him. Her beauty suddenly became accessible. When Cheng Sumei took over her husband's business after his death and carried it on successfully, it came as no surprise to Albert. He'd already spotted that she had it in her.

He wasn't just one man with her. He was several. Any sailor, by necessity, must be one man at home, another on the deck and a third in a foreign port. But his inner selves are separated in time and space, always by vast distances: just like a ship, he has waterproof bulkheads inside, to prevent sinking. But with Cheng Sumei, Albert found he could be several men at once. He was first and foremost the man he considered his real self, the sailor and captain, and he often thought that the two of them, Cheng Sumei and Albert Madsen, were like two captains on the same vessel – an unlikely couple who nonetheless respected each other's authority and never risked the safety of their ship.

But he was also the man he remembered from the brothel visits of his youth. That self wasn't always rough. In the brothels of Bahai or Buenos Aires, a young seaman was a dumbstruck guest in marble palaces with fountains and palms, silk sheets and mirrored ceilings and walls. And the girl, yes, she was a compliant spirit put on this

348

earth to grant him his wishes in a brief, faithless moment, but though she was compliant she was also superior. How speechless, how blushing, how shy and ignorant and, at the same time, how infinitely grateful he'd felt in her skilful hands, which knew things about his body that he'd never even suspected – that battered body with its permanently aching muscles, sore from the rigging, covered with saltwater blisters and unhealed cuts, always on guard, always ready to fight back in the bitter necessity of self-assertion.

He'd never felt like anyone's master in those brothels. He didn't visit them to enjoy a master's dubious privileges: he'd felt like a guest and behaved with polite restraint. In them, his permanently clenched fists briefly opened up. But he learned nothing. He wasn't a better lover when he left. He remained the same clumsy, awkward man, made brutal by sheer uncertainty when it came to women.

With Cheng Sumei, it was like the brothel visits of his youth. In the bedroom she was a compliant and yet superior spirit. In their encounters he became his younger self. He didn't know whether he was a good lover. Desire had never been a demanding inhabitant of his body: it had never had the power to rearrange his life. It was not lovemaking he missed as he lay awake. It was a human being.

He finished drying himself and ran a hand through his short hair, which had begun to dry despite the humidity of the bathroom. He found a pair of scissors and started trimming his beard. He studied his face in the mirror and wondered what it was he'd awakened in Klara Friis. His age and position offered security. He presumed that was what she was looking for. And he'd seen gratitude in her eyes when he listened to her story about the flood on Birkholm.

What did he want from her? Was it just about gratified vanity? Though she wasn't exactly pretty, the traces of grief had vanished from her face, which, when they first met, had seemed both swollen and sunken. She dressed with more care nowadays: she'd lost the shapelessness of her pregnancy and he could see that she had a lovely figure. But it wasn't her looks that attracted him. Nor was it her personality. He didn't actually know her at all. Her words were few and reticent, stilted by the difference in social rank they were both only too well aware of. It was something impersonal that had stirred this feeling in him, which he still hesitated to acknowledge as desire.

No, it wasn't her. It wasn't even the woman in her. It was her youth, that fundamental force of nature, which had reawakened, with the summer, a last reflection of what she'd once been before childbirth and poverty started to grind her down and grief struck. It was his own doing, in a way. His attentions, which to begin with had been nothing but kindness, had rekindled her youthfulness.

The boy had come first. Then the three of them had sat down together and suddenly they'd resembled a family, the family he had never had, the family she'd lost. But unless he and Klara behaved like a man and a woman, could they be that family?

He was old. Again, he reminded himself of that. Old men had their regular orbits like planets that circle a sun. But the sun they circled was cooling down. He halted his reflections at this point. He ought to stay in his rightful orbit, around the fading sun. He was in the ice age of his life, and any open ground not yet covered by snow could only produce lichen.

But his hands spoke a different language when he tied the laces on his white canvas shoes and settled a straw hat on his head. As he passed through the dining room he stopped and took a white daisy from the bouquet his housekeeper had placed in the middle of the table. In front of the mirror in the hall he ran his hand through his hair once more, and put the daisy in the buttonhole of his summer jacket. Then he opened the front door and walked down the steps to Prinsegade, filled with the blind triumph that people sometimes experience when they've conquered their own better judgement.

WHEN ALBERT WAS ASKED TO STEP INSIDE THE HOUSE, KNUD ERIK
was there. Klara Friis had put up her long hair; he noticed that she'd
washed it. He rarely paid attention to the seasonal displays of changing
fashions in the shop window of I. C. Jensen in Kirkestræde, but he
could tell from the cut of her dress, which reached halfway down
her calves, that it wasn't new. She must have produced it for this
occasion: a garment set aside from the first years of her marriage,
perhaps, or an even earlier time, when she was full of youthfulness
and expectation.

The table was set for three, which both disappointed and re-
assured him. Knud Erik's presence ruled out any blunders occurring,
and yet Klara Friis blushed when she opened the door to him. She
stepped aside, just as she'd done this morning, and bowed her head
slightly. Her neck, exposed below her chignon, looked so delicate
that he had to suppress an urge to cross the line between protective-
ness and possessive desire, and put his hand on it.

Little Edith was nowhere to be seen, and Albert asked after her.
Klara told him that she'd already eaten and had been put to bed.

She invited them to sit down at the table. Knud Erik, whose sun-
bleached hair had been combed through wet, was the last to pull up
his chair. He sat down with an unnatural stiffness and stared into
the distance. A big bowl of freshly boiled shrimps stood in the middle
of the table. Albert had brought the wine in a basket, wrapped in
a damask napkin. He took it out and opened it with a little pop.
He'd had trouble deciding whether to pack wine glasses too. He
knew that she wouldn't have any but feared that if he brought his
own, she might take it as a slight, an underscoring of the poverty
of both her home and her life. In the end, it was his sense of tradition that won the argument. He didn't fancy drinking good wine
from an ordinary glass, so he took his best crystal. Old men and
their orbits indeed. He'd even brought a corkscrew.

He poured the wine into the glasses, glancing at Knud Erik, who was watching him attentively. 'I nearly forgot you,' he said, and pulled out a bottle of cordial and placed it in front of him. The boy laughed.

'Just like a picnic,' he said. He looked at the condensation on the wine bottle and touched it carefully. 'It's cold,' he said, and his voice was filled with wonder.

Albert Madsen and Klara Friis clinked glasses. She clutched hers as if afraid of dropping it. He glanced at her over the rim of his own. She blushed, unfamiliar with the rituals entailed in the consumption of wine. Her glance flickered confusedly away from the table, then she threw her head back and swigged from the glass as though its pale contents were medicine, best downed quickly. She grimaced, then reddened again.

'Please, may I taste it?' Knud Erik said.

'It's not for children.' His mother gave him a severe look. Albert could see that her rebuke was an attempt to hide her confusion at this meal, which was so unlike anything she'd ever taken part in.

'I'm not a child,' the boy retorted. 'I earn my own money.'

'Then you're allowed a taste.'

Albert winked at Knud Erik's mother and passed his glass to the boy, who took it carefully with both hands before raising it tentatively to his lips, as though already regretting his nerve.

'Just one small sip,' his mother ordered.

Knud Erik grimaced.

'Ugh,' he exclaimed. 'It tastes sour.'

Albert laughed. 'I think your mother agrees.'

'Yes,' she admitted. 'I don't think wine is for me.'

'It's always like that to start with. Later you'll learn to appreciate it.'

'Not me,' Knud Erik declared. 'I'll never learn to appreciate it.'

Albert wished that time could stop right then. He had a family. He was sitting at dinner with a boy who could be his grandchild and a woman who could be his daughter, and he wanted nothing more. He'd put the loneliness of the war years behind him. He almost felt as if he had a home that consisted of more than just himself and his memories.

He thought of his afternoon in the bath and his preening in front of the mirror. He'd dressed up, putting on a summer jacket and fixing a flower in his buttonhole. Perhaps there was a spark left in him. But if so, it was the last spark: the one that flares suddenly in the embers of a fire that has burned itself out overnight. Finding no nourishment in ashes, it soon fades. For a moment he'd given in to vanity, but it wasn't a woman he needed. It was this: two people he could be something to and who, by mere virtue of their presence, could be something to him.

He twirled the stem of the wine glass and chuckled to himself.

'What are you laughing at?'

'Oh, I'm not sure I even know. I just feel so comfortable here. Put it down to contentment.'

'That's good to hear.' Klara Friis got up. 'Time for dessert.'

She brought in a bowl of rhubarb compote and a jug of cream. Knud Erik followed her bearing three smaller bowls which he placed in front of them.

'You're good at helping your mother, I see.'

'Yes, he's a good boy.'

She sat down and served them.

'When you've finished you may go outside to play.'

Knud Erik wolfed down his compote, sending the cream splashing over the tablecloth. His mother frowned at him, but didn't speak. Then he disappeared out the door. She looked after him and laughed.

'Someone's got places to go.'

'It's summer,' Albert said.

The low-ceilinged room was semi-dark, but outside the street was bright as day. Albert pushed back his chair. 'Thank you, that was lovely. I suppose I'd better be off home now.'

She bowed her head as though he'd rejected her. 'Please stay a little longer,' she begged, and looked at him. 'See, I haven't even finished my wine. You did promise you'd teach me to enjoy it. So you can't abandon me now.' Her voice was coquettish, as if she were permitting herself greater freedom now that her son was absent.

'I'll stay a little longer, then. May I suggest that we go outside into the garden and enjoy the summer evening?' He could see that she was taken aback by this proposal. Her garden was small, a kitchen garden – more decorative than a bare yard, but not a place she'd invite guests or spend a spare hour.

'Allow me,' he said, picking up two of the high-backed, dark-varnished dining chairs. He carried them through the kitchen and set them next to each other in the garden while Klara disappeared into the bedroom to check on Edith, who had slept soundly through the entire meal. When she returned they clinked glasses once more, and this time when he tried to catch her eye across the rim, she responded. The soft evening light transformed her pale skin, giving it an enigmatic, intense glow. She smiled at him. He smiled back. For a moment they were both embarrassed.

He looked across the small garden. At the back he saw blackcurrant and gooseberry bushes. There were also potatoes and rhubarb. A small gravel path led to a flower bed bordered with conch shells bleached by salt water and sun; you'd find the same shells bordering most gardens in Marstal. Growing next to the house was a small rose bed. There was no terrace; he'd had to balance the chairs on the flagstones that had been laid here and there on the soil. No weeds between the stones, and he could see that the garden was neatly tended.

From the street came the sound of children's cries, while in the neighbouring gardens women were chatting quietly. An outsider wouldn't have noticed the absence of male voices, but Albert did. Summer was the women's season. At the first sign of spring, the ships began preparing to leave the shelter of the breakwater. Some would return at Christmas, but many, bound on longer voyages, would be gone for years. In the absence of the menfolk, it was the women who ran the town. Now he sat in the midst of this female life, surrounded by summer light and the scent of elderberries, and experienced a part of Marstal in a way he hadn't done in years.

He leaned forward and picked up one of the conches. He put it against his ear and listened to the rush coming from the spiral within.

'Listen,' he said, and handed it to her. 'They've invented the radio now. But when I was a child, we had these for radios.'

Instead of putting it to her ear, Klara replaced the shell in the border, with an expression that suggested he'd disturbed a secret harmony in her garden by picking it up.

The conch had a melody for everyone who listened to it. For the young, the conch sang of longing for distant shores; for the old it sang of absence and sorrow. It had a song for the young and another one for the old, one for the men and one for the women, and the women's song was always the same, as monotonous as the beating of the waves against the beach: loss, loss. The conch offered them no enchantment. When they put their ear to it, all they heard was the echo of their mourning.

They sat in the garden for half an hour. The sun went down behind a rooftop, and a grainy twilight filtered between the gooseberry and blackcurrant bushes as the sky turned an even deeper violet.

'Oh, it's way past his bedtime!'

Klara leaped to her feet. She'd just remembered her boy. It was time for Albert to leave, but before he managed to stand she'd disappeared through the door to the kitchen. He brought the chairs back inside and put them by the dining table, then waited in the parlour until she returned with Knud Erik.

'I've taken up far too much of your time,' he said apologetically.

'But you haven't even had your coffee!' She led him to the table and pushed him down in one of the chairs. Her movements had acquired a new freedom. 'Now you stay here while I make it.' She pulled some linens from a drawer and made up a bed for Knud Erik on the sofa and then left. The boy undressed and crept under the covers.

'Are we going fishing tomorrow morning?' he asked.

'No, not tomorrow. We can row to Langholm and swim there, if you like.'

But there was no reply. The boy was already asleep.

Klara appeared from the kitchen with a pot of coffee in her hand. 'It's been a long day.'

She sat down in front of him and filled his cup. The lamp in the parlour had not yet been lit, and in the dusk her pale skin shone above the neck of her dress. They sat for a while in silence as the dark intensified around them. They could hear Knud Erik breathing from the sofa in the undisturbed rhythm of sleep. Somewhere nearby a clock struck ten, deep and sonorous. In the growing darkness Klara's features grew indistinct and began to swim before his eyes, as if making strange grimaces.

'Thank you for a lovely evening,' he said, and got up.

She was as startled as if she'd been woken suddenly.

'Are you leaving now?'

Her face was a white spot in the dusk, and he couldn't read its expression. Was she tipsy? She'd drunk the first glass and he'd poured her a second. She'd had no more than that, but women have less tolerance than men. He felt a sudden misgiving about the whole situation. He wanted to get away.

Rising to her feet she accompanied him to the hall. But she didn't turn on the light and she closed the parlour door behind them. His heart was hammering at the wall of his chest like a prisoner begging for release. Again he felt the sharp shooting pain in his head. Then he felt her. Her hands fumbled on his chest, apparently unaware of his pounding heart. Then, abruptly, she flung her arms around his neck.

'I need to say goodbye to you properly,' she mumbled.

Her lips moved searchingly across his face until they found his mouth and pressed against it. The pounding of his heart grew stronger. A black wave surged inside him and rendered him helpless. He wanted to push her away, but he couldn't. She leaned into him with all her weight; he could feel the soft pressure of her breasts. Her hips rubbed against his. A moan escaped from her, like the prelude to a fit of tears.

'Ma,' came a voice from the parlour.

She froze and held her breath.

'Ma, where are you?'

Klara gasped, then flinched.

'I'm here, in the hall.'

'You sound so strange. Is anything wrong?'

'No, go back to sleep. It's late.'

'What are you doing, Ma?'

'I'm saying goodbye to Captain Madsen.'

'I want to say goodbye, too.'

They heard him shuffle across the floor. Then he stood in the doorway, a dark silhouette.

'Why isn't the light on?'

Klara found the switch and flicked it. Albert ran a hand through the boy's hair.

'Goodnight, lad. I think your mother is right, it's time to turn in.'

He turned to Klara but avoided looking at her face.

'Goodnight, Mrs Friis, and thank you for a lovely evening.'

He shook her hand. Her palm was hot and sweaty. Even this formal contact suddenly felt too intimate. He withdrew his hand and took his straw hat from the coat rack. Then he opened the door.

He heard it close behind him. Too agitated to go straight home, he headed towards the harbour. Turning into Havnegade, he saw a figure get up from the skippers' bench across from Sønderrenden.

'Good evening, Captain Madsen.'

Albert nodded under the straw hat. He had no desire to strike up a conversation. But the other man caught up with him and began walking beside him along Havnegade.

'You're out late.'

Albert recognised Herman's thickset shape.

'I don't believe I need to account to you for my movements,' he said curtly.

'Nice clothes,' said Herman, ignoring the hostility in Albert's voice. Albert increased his pace. Herman did the same. 'You seem quite youthful tonight,' he smirked, making no attempt to hide the falsity of this remark. Albert stopped abruptly and turned to face the young man.

'Tell me, what do you want from me?'

Herman flung out his hands. 'Want from you? What do you mean? I don't want anything from you. I just thought I'd keep you company for a while. But perhaps you prefer to be alone?'

Albert made no reply but turned and continued along Havnegade. He passed the slipways and the shipyard.

'Pleasant dreams!' Herman called out after him. 'You could probably do with a good night's sleep after this evening's exertions.'

Albert jumped, and tightened his grip on his walking stick. He briefly considered going back and punishing the scoundrel, but dropped the thought instantly. Those days were long gone. They were roughly the same height and breadth, he and Herman, but there was half a century between them. It wouldn't be an equal match. Not only would Albert lose the fight, he'd lose his dignity too. The realisation knocked him flat. He might as well already be lying on the ground, bleeding.

He walked up the stone steps to the house in Prinsegade and let himself in. He entered the drawing room without switching on the light and sat down heavily on the sofa. How could that rogue know what had occurred at the widow's? Had he been spying on them or was he just guessing? Was it so obvious what was going on? But the events of the evening had surprised even Albert. Had others seen things that he'd failed to spot himself?

Yes, he'd toyed with a few notions when he was getting ready for dinner, he'd admit that much. But he realised, too, that he hadn't really wanted it enough. He'd entertained the possibility that something might happen. But now that it had, he suddenly felt exposed. If Herman could see it, then the whole town could. He had to stop it now. He understood what he'd felt in the hall, when Klara Friis surrendered to him. It was fear, fear of his routine being knocked out of its orbit, fear of life's unpredictability, fear that everything he'd parted from in preparation for his twilight years would reclaim him. And Klara, he knew, had more strength than him. Just as Herman did. And for the same reason: they were young.

A panting embrace in a darkened hall, a street fight: those were the prerogatives of youth, not of age, and God help the old man who came too near youth and thought he could warm himself by its fire. The price for that was ridicule, and he'd have to pay.

The old should stick to their dying sun. This house, in which he'd built up and managed his business – this was the sun he circled. He shouldn't try to rebel against the laws of gravity that controlled life's end. During the war he'd earned a reputation for being strange. Now, perhaps he was stuck with that reputation; well, he could live with that. But he didn't want to be thought a fool. To walk around the town fully dressed and yet appear naked to the world was a shame he couldn't bear.

The next day he slept late and didn't venture out. The following day he rowed to Sorekrogen, alone, to tend to his shrimp nets. They were full, as always: almost ten pounds. He emptied the nets into the container of the boatwell and sat contemplating the myriad tiny creatures. He remembered how proudly Knud Erik had walked home to his mother in Snaregade with his bucket full of them. He heaved the container back onto the rail and tipped it into the water. For a brief moment the shrimps swarmed in a brown cloud, then vanished.

Being on the water brought him no peace. He missed the boy. But there was something else, something stronger, tearing at him: an inner pressure that swelled the more he refused to acknowledge it. He had felt not only fear when Klara had pressed herself against him in the hall. There'd been a physical stirring, too, that he hadn't felt in years. Now, the mere thought of that episode gave him an unexpected erection.

An old man in a boat on the sea on a summer's morning, with an erection. He was furious with himself. And he needed relief at the same time. He'd reached the critical stage of an illness. The only cure for it was time. And distance.

AFTER TWO WEEKS HE CAME HOME AND FOUND KLARA FRIIS IN HIS drawing room. She was sitting on the edge of the sofa when he entered, in the dress she'd worn on that fateful evening. He could see the contours of her body beneath the thin, loosely draped fabric.

'Your housekeeper let me in. I told her I had an important message.'

He remained in the doorway, looking at her guardedly. He knew his behaviour was rude, but he was held back by the fear that he might do something impulsive if he took another step. The urge he'd refused to name in his restless hours on the water took hold of him again, just as it had that night in the darkness of the hallway. Fear and excitement at the same time.

'It's Knud Erik,' she said. 'He doesn't understand why we don't see you any more. He asks after you every day, but he's afraid to visit you. Have you dropped him completely?' She directed her gaze at him. At the mention of Knud Erik Albert's fear seemed to evaporate.

'My dear Klara,' he said, and went over to her.

He took her hands in his. She looked at him, and her eyes suddenly reddened.

'There's something else. I miss you terribly, too!'

She freed her hands and flung her arms around him, pressing her lips against his. Suddenly he was overcome by rage. He grabbed hold of her waist to push her away, but his hands did the opposite. He pressed her to him as he kissed her hard, without tenderness. She buckled and he pushed her down onto the sofa. Landing heavily on top of her he tugged at her dress.

'Wait, wait,' she breathed.

She pulled her dress up around her waist and got herself ready for him. His anger hadn't left. When he entered her, gasping, he struck her hard across her face. In the excitement of the moment it seemed to him that he was hitting her in self-defence, in protest at her youth and what she'd lured him into. Then he collapsed, panting, already done, both with his own violence and with her surrendering body, which he'd barely seen or felt. She clung to him, apparently unaffected by the blow, which had left her cheek burning red.

Albert's head lay on her chest. He felt its softness and resented it. In her arms he was a defenceless child. He already knew that he was trapped. He'd come back to her and then he'd hit her again. He grew red with shame. He freed himself from her arms and started rearranging his clothes. She came up to him and rested her cheek on his shoulder. The mark of his hand was still visible.

'Are you fond of me?' she asked. 'Are you really fond of me?'

'Yes, yes,' he snapped. 'Now let me get my clothes in order.'

He didn't recognise himself. He felt no triumph in his conquest. Instead, the feeling that a disaster had occurred was slowly spreading through him.

Klara got up and went to fix her hair at the mirror hanging above a chest of drawers. When she'd finished, she turned to him.

'What do you want me to tell Knud Erik?' He shrugged and turned his head away. 'He knows I've been to see you. He'll be very disappointed if you drop him.'

'I'll be there to pick him up tomorrow. We'll go out and catch some shrimps.'

In the hall they grew formal again, shaking hands when she left. The small dark room was like an antechamber to the town outside, open to its ever-curious eyes. Albert remained in the doorway as she stepped into the street. Across the way Mrs Jensen, the draper's wife, was going up the granite steps to the bank. He nodded to her. She threw a critical glance at Klara from underneath the brim of her black lacquered straw hat and returned his greeting with a curt nod. His public undressing had begun.

When he turned up to collect Knud Erik the next day, the boy wasn't there. He'd been sent to fetch milk and was due to return soon, his mother said. Little Edith was having her midday nap. To his horror he saw that one side of Klara's face was swollen, and her cheek had turned yellow and blue.

'Don't look at me like that,' she said. She took his hand and held it against her cheek affectionately. 'It doesn't matter.'

Leaning against the kitchen table, she stretched her hands out to him as if to pull him towards her. He turned away, but his body gave in to her invitation. He felt it once again, his unmentionable old man's erection. He hated himself as he tore at her dress to get it up around her hips. He entered her again, but this time he quickly grew limp and slid out. He'd forgotten all about the boy, then suddenly remembered him and realised how rash and irresponsible their frantic coupling had been.

But she kept holding him close. He hadn't hit her this time, but he tore himself away with a violent movement. He didn't know what they wanted from each other and he told her so.

'Nothing good will come of this.' She didn't reply, but rested her head against his chest in a kind of deaf-and-dumb surrender which only increased his anger. 'Do you hear?' he said, shaking her.

Her head lolled as if she were barely conscious. Then they heard the boy at the door and quickly let go of each other. Knud Erik carried the milk pail into the kitchen and put it on the table.

It seemed to Albert that the boy's manner was guarded, but soon Albert realised that the awkwardness was his own. They'd walked down to the harbour and rowed the length of its entrance before he returned to his familiar ease. He'd imagined that he might need to explain his long absence, but Knud Erik didn't ask about it. Instead he sat on the thwart and showed off his rowing skills, his face red with eagerness and exertion.

Albert suspected that the mother had used her son's distress as a pretext for coming to see him. If only he could keep the two emotions separate – his love for the son and his fascination with the mother. But she wouldn't leave him alone. Who had started it? Should he be honest enough to admit that it wasn't her but something in him that had ruptured his tranquillity? And what was that? Desire? Or the memory of desire? Was it a longing for that part of life he'd failed to grasp before, which was now offering itself a final time, in the shape of Klara Friis?

Whatever it was made no difference now. He couldn't endanger his bond with the boy. But how was he to stop it?

Klara and Albert didn't speak much, and when they did it was mostly about everyday matters, as if they'd known each other a long time and all the important things had already been said. Albert thought that perhaps they had little to say to each other. In the beginning there'd been a cosiness to their silent companionship at the dining table or over a cup of coffee, just the four of them. Now their meetings were filled with a tense, electric impatience while they waited to be alone, without the boy.

Little Edith toddled around the floor and spoke her first words. Albert was always uncomfortable when she yanked at his trouser leg and looked up at him expectantly. He would lift her onto his knee and bounce her up and down. But his face stayed rigid and he didn't know what to say to her. *Bouncy, bouncy*, he supposed. But he remained silent.

'Papa,' she said one day.

He looked over at Klara, who smiled, embarrassed.

'I don't know where she got that from. It's not from me.'

Did language grow in a child like milk teeth? Was *Papa* a natural part of her budding vocabulary?

He stopped bouncing her. No more bouncy, bouncy. He looked sternly at the child in front of him. 'No,' he said. 'Not Papa. Albert.'

Edith began to cry.

No intimacy ever developed between Klara and Albert. They never spent a whole night in each other's company; indeed, they never even lay naked together, exhausted in a moment of tender calm after love-making. On the contrary, their encounters were always hectic and half hostile. Every time he held her, his chest became a battlefield: he was filled with reluctance, but his attraction won out, and the result was inevitably that he took her with a ruthlessness that he later regretted. When she moaned loudly as he thrust into her, he was never sure whether it was from ecstasy or pain. He would come with the sound of a man being punched in the stomach.

He hadn't hit her again, but he knew that this was only because his first blow had left evidence on her face which would be visible to the whole town. Only fear for his reputation stayed his hand when the urge to hurt her overwhelmed him. Oh yes, his stiff member could have the same effect as a punch, and be used to inflict pain, but here his age betrayed him. He didn't have the stamina he once had.

They made love like two people who are tied to others, and can only meet illicitly, briefly and breathlessly. And that was indeed their situation: he was married to his old age, and she to her youth. The bridge where they were supposed to meet had cracked the moment they had stepped on it. He didn't understand himself, he didn't understand her, and he knew that if he asked her to explain her feelings for him, he'd get no reply.

Knud Erik returned to school and a rainy autumn forced him and Albert to abandon their sea trips, but their meetings continued. They thought of other things to do. Knud Erik would visit him frequently in the afternoons, and they'd go through his homework together while the light faded outside. Sometimes Albert would go over to Snaregade, but Klara never came to his house. It hadn't been agreed on formally, but the understanding lay in the air between them. He could enter her world, but she couldn't enter his.

Albert stopped visiting the marine painter's widow, and it felt like final proof of his shame. Did the whole town know what was going on? He was sure it did. He couldn't put his finger on one thing in particular, but the signs were all about him. A passer-by would give him a stare, a conversation on a bench would suddenly stop when he passed, a shopkeeper who he'd long been familiar with would greet him with a new reserve.

Sometimes he'd run into Herman. After their confrontation, the young man no longer spoke to Albert, but wryly lifted a finger to his hat, or grinned coarsely, as though they were fellow conspirators. Albert ignored him, but worried at how often he encountered him on his way to or from Snaregade. Did that layabout have nothing better to do than spy on him?

We saw Albert sitting late at night in the bay window facing Prinsegade, with a book in his hand, trying to read. Most of the time, though, he simply stared into space.

What was he thinking about? He was old, but he hadn't found peace.

Had he realised that a long life didn't automatically bestow wisdom?

Albert and Klara did have one thing in common: their concern for Knud Erik. She trusted implicitly his insights about the boy, though he had no children of his own. His presence set Klara apart from most Marstal women who, with their husbands at sea, were forced into the role of father as well as mother. Any doubts about their own ability to achieve this they hid behind a strict, almost harsh manner. For many months of every year, and sometimes for years on end, they lived life like a dress rehearsal for widowhood.

Klara Friis was now experiencing the rare privilege of having a man around, an unexpected luxury which made her surrender to an inner weakness that she should have fought. She handed things over to him and stopped making her own decisions. She looked to Albert as though expecting that from now on he'd organise her life for her.

She stood firm on only one point: Knud Erik was not to follow in his father's footsteps. She'd listened to the conch and she'd heard the rush of death. Her son must never make a living at sea. When she talked about this, she abandoned the passivity that characterised her behaviour in Albert's presence: she straightened up in her chair and her voice took on an unwonted sharpness.

The boy flinched whenever Klara raised the subject. Albert had heard him promise his mother that he'd never be a sailor. But the boy's bad conscience was written all over his face. Albert almost felt guilty himself, though he'd long concluded, privately, that things could go no other way. Indeed, he'd been part of the boy's inspiration. His stories, the endless conversations about foreign countries and ships, the rowing and sculling, all these had pushed the impressionable boy in that direction. But there were other influences, too, which lay beyond the control of a mother or a father. The constant roar of the sea beyond the breakwater and the sight of topsail schooners, topgallant schooners and brigantines with the early-spring wind in their sails, ready for their big migration to the great ports of call: Rio de la Plata, Newfoundland, Oporto, Le Havre, Valparaiso, Callao and Sydney – legendary places that formed part of every boy's mental geography, and pulled at his young soul.

Klara Friis knew this. There was a hint of pleading in her sharpness, and it was directed at Albert. He had the power to wrench the boy in a different direction if he wanted to.

She looked from the boy to the old man and back again, and she sensed a conspiracy between them. 'How's your reading going?' she asked her son.

'Well,' the boy replied, as unforthcoming as any child questioned about school.

'He's only just started his second year, but he's already reading fluently,' Albert said approvingly.

Klara looked at him. 'So he's good at schoolwork,' she stated. 'Perhaps shipbroking would suit him?'

The question took Albert by surprise. He had to admit that he'd never imagined that path for the boy. In his view, the career of a good shipbroker didn't begin in an office. It began on deck, then spread into the more abstract world of freight rates. That was how he'd done it, and he'd expect all future shipbrokers to do likewise.

'It most definitely would,' Albert said, but his tone was evasive. He couldn't bring himself to explain his principles to her. Sensing his lack of enthusiasm, she took it to mean that he wouldn't be prepared to help the boy. Her mouth became a thin line and she slumped in silence. 'There are many things you can become if you get good marks. Surely it's a little early –'

'I know what you're going to say,' she interrupted him. 'You're going to say that a man with a good education can pass the navigation exam as well. But believe me, that's not the path my boy's going to take.' She turned to her son. 'Do you hear, Knud Erik?'

The boy nodded and lowered his head. A tear rolled down his cheek and he breathed in with a loud sob. Then he jumped up from the chair and ran out to the kitchen. Klara gave Albert an accusing look, as though it was he, rather than she, who'd prompted the boy's tears.

'There are several shipbrokers' offices in this town,' he said. 'I can easily get a place for him when the time comes.'

'That would be wonderful.' Her face softened and she blessed him with a smile. Then she went to the kitchen to bring the boy back. He could hear her voice through the wall. He sat alone, feeling the emptiness of his promise.

'When the time comes . . .' he repeated to himself, and did a quick mental calculation. 'When that time comes, I'll be dead.'

KLARA WAS EXPECTING A VISIT FROM ALBERT WHEN THERE WAS AN unfamiliar knock on the door. She went out to open it and found Herman on the steps. He was an acquaintance, dating back to the time when her husband was alive. Henning had sailed with Herman and talked to her about him. He'd heard the rumours about Herman murdering his stepfather all right, but he hadn't believed them. Henning always said Herman was a good mate. They'd shared a fondness for grandiose talk, and she suspected that, for the most part, their comradeship had been forged in sailors' bars.

When Herman reappeared in Marstal, he'd taken the time to stop by and offer his condolences. She'd never forgotten that, and it had disposed her more favourably towards him. She hadn't met him since then, but he always greeted her kindly when they passed each other in the street, and on one occasion he'd actually stopped to ask her if there was anything she needed.

Now he was standing at her door. She took a step back in surprise.

'I just wanted to see how you were getting on,' he said. Without waiting for an invitation, he strode over the threshold. For a moment they stood jammed in the small hallway, before continuing into the parlour. 'Hello,' he said jovially to Knud Erik, and ruffled the boy's blond hair as if they were old friends. Knud Erik, who didn't know him, took a step back, while Klara remained in the doorway.

'He's tired,' she said.

'I won't be staying long.' Herman sat down on the sofa and crossed his legs. 'I hear you're doing well.' Klara didn't reply. He looked at her. 'Old Madsen isn't a bad match.'

She stared harshly. 'What are you talking about?'

'What am I talking about? The same thing everyone in town's talking about. We're hearing wedding bells. You and the children provided for: good thinking.'

Klara blushed scarlet. She glanced down and chewed her lower lip. When she lifted her head, she avoided looking at her visitor.

'That's just people talking,' she said weakly.

Herman eased further into the sofa, as though he were in his own home. 'Now take it easy,' he said. 'A boy needs a father. I understand old men are good with children. All right, so he's not always very careful. But a bit of water never hurt anyone.'

'What do you mean?' Her question came out as a whisper. Knud Erik was watching both of them, but Klara had forgotten his presence.

'Well, the boy fell off the boat one day and nearly drowned. But I expect Madsen told you.'

Klara was shocked. She turned to Knud Erik. 'Is that true what Herman says? Did you nearly drown?'

Knud Erik looked at the floor and grew red. 'It was nothing. I just fell into the water.'

Klara opened the door to the hall. 'I think you'd better leave,' she said to Herman in a voice that had suddenly recovered its strength.

'By all means, if I'm not welcome.' Herman heaved his large body up from the sofa. When he reached the doorway he turned. 'I'll stop by another day.'

Klara slammed the front door behind him. Then she sat on a chair and folded her hands. Her knuckles grew white and her face assumed a look of concentration. The boy peered at her anxiously.

After a while she broke the silence. 'Why didn't you tell me that you'd fallen into the water?'

'But, Ma, it was nothing.'

'Nothing! You could have drowned. Why didn't you tell me?' Knud Erik pressed his lips together. 'Did Captain Madsen tell you not to tell me? Answer me!'

He blinked and looked away. A tear slid down his cheek. He swallowed. And then nodded.

When Albert turned up an hour later, Klara received him at the front door with Edith on her hip. 'What do you want?' she snapped, without returning his greeting.

She looked at him directly and the fury in her eyes gave her femininity a hint of something feral. A mother defending her young, he thought, and understood in that instant that he wasn't welcome inside. She'd answered the door only to deny him access to the house. He wouldn't be allowed in to assert his authority; no, he was to stand in the street and be made to feel small.

Knud Erik appeared by Klara's side. 'Go back inside,' she ordered him. The boy disappeared into the house. Again she turned to Albert and threw her head back as if she meant to butt him.

Albert instinctively took a step backwards. 'I don't understand . . .' he began.

'You don't understand what?' Her tone was commanding, as though she were still speaking to the boy.

'I understand that you're angry with me. But I don't understand why.'

'You don't understand why? Look at this child, take a good look. Look at me and my child. This child who's never known her father.' Her voice grew louder and angrier: taking fright, Edith started screaming, and squirmed in her mother's arms to be let down. Then she stretched out towards Albert. 'Papa,' she cried.

Klara's anger was undiminished. 'And you want to turn Knud Erik into a sailor. So he can drown like his father! That's what you want, isn't it?' she sneered. 'You want him to be like his father, like you, like the whole damned town, and drown like a real man!'

'But the war's over,' he said, trying to placate her. Her accusation was by now familiar, but he'd never heard her state it with such venom.

'So sailors don't drown any more? So ships don't get lost? So now everyone can survive a couple of days afloat after a winter storm in the North Atlantic – or even swim home to Marstal, if they're unlucky enough to lose their ship? So no one drowns in peacetime? Perhaps we've all grown gills? Is that what you're trying to tell me?'

He stood dumbstruck by this outburst from a woman whom he'd come to regard as half mute. He shrugged. Behind her he saw the boy's face at the window. But sensing Knud Erik's stare, his mother instantly shouted, 'Get away from that window!'

'Mrs Friis,' he began, with the formality he'd use to address a stranger.

'Be quiet,' she yelled. 'I haven't finished with you. And then I have to hear it from strangers that the boy nearly drowned. That he fell into the water and that you calmly pulled him out and forbade him to tell me! Well, that's a fine thing. His own mother gets to hear it from others. And all those stories you fill his head with: shipwrecks, destruction, shrunken heads, mad adventures! Do you think that's the way to help a child who's lost his father at sea? Do you?'

She stared him right in the eye. He looked away. He didn't know what to say to her. He supposed she was right. He said so. 'I suppose you're right. I don't know anything about children.'

'Don't know anything about children,' she snorted. 'No, you know nothing about children. You . . .' She looked him up and down as she searched for the right word. 'You bachelor.'

'I did my best,' he said. 'I was told that the boy needed some adult company and so I came.'

'Yes, you came. And now you can leave. *I want to be a sailor like my pa who drowned!* What a fine lesson Knud Erik learned in your company.'

The boy's face reappeared in the window. 'You get away!' she screamed.

'Papa,' Edith cried again.

Klara Friis turned her back on him and slammed the door behind her.

He lifted his cap to the closed door. Then he turned and walked down Snaregade. He thought he could feel the boy's eyes on his back.

A heavy November rain was falling. A cold drop hit his neck and ran down under his scarf.

ALBERT LET HIMSELF INTO HIS HOUSE AND WALKED AROUND SWITCHING the lights on. He was restless and didn't know what to do with himself. Still in his coat, he went upstairs and out onto the balcony. He was aware of the rain soaking his hair as he looked across to the breakwater. In the dusk the long line of boulders seemed to shimmer, as though it were made of fog.

He went back inside and asked his housekeeper to make him a pot of coffee. Then he sat down in the bay window. He watched the dark deepen outside and felt as if he were holding his breath, and that if he let it out, something violent and unpredictable would happen: he'd start shouting, or crying, or doing something that went beyond his own imagination.

He was gripped by a feeling that took him right back to childhood: the same feeling he'd experienced on the beach at Drejet as he stared in horror at Karo lying on the stones at the bottom of the cliff with a broken back. Albert had tried stroking the little dog's fur in the hope that a bit of tenderness might piece him back together. But in that moment, a notion that something irreparable had happened reverberated inside him with a long and terrifying echo. Now it reverberated again.

He took a sip of his hot sugarless coffee, and tried to calm himself. He had to clear his thoughts. He'd never lived in a marriage, never experienced a woman's emotional outbursts. His relationship with Cheng Sumei had been ruled by what he'd jokingly called a meeting of souls. It was a meeting that had never existed between himself and the young widow. How serious had Klara's anger been? Was her rage really caused by his conduct with Knud Erik? For heaven's sake, all boys fell into the water sooner or later. Someone pulled them out again and that was all there was to it.

No, he didn't believe the boy was the problem. Klara's anger was over something between the two of them, though for the life of him he didn't know what. Or perhaps Albert himself was the problem. He both wanted her and didn't. She was a disruptive force in his life. Either way, she'd now rejected him. So wouldn't the wisest course of action be to let this rejection, however hurtful, stand?

Then what about the boy?

If only the two things could be kept separate. But they were hopelessly entangled now and he was the one responsible. His thoughts ran in circles, taking him nowhere. He drank his coffee and stared into the darkness.

His housekeeper entered and asked him when he'd like his dinner served. He had no appetite and asked her to wait until eight o'clock. He put on his coat again and went back out into the November rain. A few minutes later he was standing opposite Mrs Rasmussen's house in Teglgade. It was an age since he'd last been there. What did she think of him now? They'd been close, but he couldn't go back to see her. She'd scrutinise him, and in that forthright way of hers, she'd target his sorest points. She'd do it with the best intentions, undoubtedly. But good intentions were of no use to him. He felt utterly lost.

He turned down Filosofgangen, then continued south along the harbour, and soon he found himself in front of Klara's house again. The light was on, but the windows were steamed up from the heating and he couldn't see inside. He continued his wandering. An hour later he was back there for the third time, furious with himself.

His longing kept drawing him back, but his fear drove him away again each time.

A period of waiting began. What was Albert waiting for? He didn't know. But he felt in his bones that his own death was drawing near. He looked at himself in the mirror, and where previously he'd found evidence of undiminished strength, he now saw only the ravages of time. He hadn't known what was lacking in his life until he met Knud Erik and Klara. Without them his old age was like Ithaca without Penelope and Telemachus. But with them? Could it even go on?

It seemed an unstoppable countdown had started.

He stopped going out in daylight, for fear of meeting Knud Erik. He did not know what to say to the boy. He'd be unable to handle seeing the lad's face light up. Or – far worse – watching him turn away in disappointment.

But in the evening, after a dinner which he left mostly untouched, his restlessness drove him out into the November darkness. We saw him wandering through the streets, icy drops of rain lashing his face.

He stood on Snaregade again, watching the lights glow in the windows of her house.

Then the waiting ended. One day Klara turned up at Albert's door and asked to come in. Her face displayed no joy at seeing him again; it remained hard and closed, as if she'd made an important decision and had come to inform him of it. He helped her off with her coat and escorted her into the drawing room. She didn't look at him as she spoke, but stared down at her lap. Her voice sounded neutral, almost flat, as though she were reeling off something she'd memorised.

'I think we need to find a solution to what's happened between us,' she began, then inhaled deeply. Only her uneven breathing betrayed any emotion. 'We can't go on like this. You always visit us, Captain Madsen – I mean Albert. That's not right. I hear things and people stare and I'm well aware of what they're thinking. They think that I'm a kept woman, and I don't want people to think that of me.'

She stopped. Her hands, which had lain unnaturally still in her lap during her speech, suddenly tightened into fists.

'But, Klara, dearest . . .' He put out his own hand to touch her. She froze, and then recoiled.

'Let me finish. It's no use saying they don't, because they do. I know more about what people think than you do, Captain Madsen.' Still she didn't look up; instead, she focused her attention on her knuckles. 'I can't live like that,' she went on. 'Henning's dead. I'm a widow. But Knud Erik and Edith need a father, and if it's not to be you, then it has to be someone else, Albert. That's how it is.'

He noticed she kept switching between his first name and his last. He couldn't follow her train of thought. 'I'm an old man,' he said helplessly.

'Not too old for us to – well, you know what I mean.' She looked away, then took another deep breath, as if about to deliver a message that was not only outrageous but also against her own nature. 'So I'm suggesting that Knud Erik, Edith and I move in here and that the two of us get married. So that – so that things can be put right.' Suddenly she slumped. Her clenched fists opened. She'd delivered her message. Now, exhausted, she awaited her fate.

373

Everything inside Albert contracted. This he hadn't expected. He sensed that the situation demanded an immediate and unequivocal answer, but nothing approaching it emerged. Instead, he asked, 'But do you love me?' He put the question in the dutifully polite tone he'd have used with a stranger; at this moment there was no trust between them.

'Do you love *me*?' she retorted sharply.

'I've missed you,' he said, and his voice grew thick. He couldn't come up with a declaration of love; nor was there any way he could express the chaos inside him more precisely. The way it came out, it sounded like a plea for mercy.

A moment of silence followed. A shiver ran through her, then she grabbed his hands and squeezed them between hers. 'I've missed you, too.' She leaned into him and gave way to tears. Unburdened now, she could surrender. He stroked her back mechanically. His own paralysis hadn't abated. He didn't share her relief. They'd reached a point where he felt he couldn't possibly deny her request. His answer had practically been dictated to him.

Did he want it himself? The question was as unanswerable as whether or not he loved her.

'That's how it'll be then,' he said eventually. He tried to give his words the ring of reassurance, but Klara couldn't have missed their undertone of resignation.

She'd won. But the victory came without joy for either of them.

The next day they appeared together in public. As they strolled down Kirkestræde, she held his arm and he bore himself tall and straight – not out of pride, but to avoid looking decrepit next to her. From then on, she regularly visited with Knud Erik and Edith, and all three dined together. She didn't stay the night. They'd never yet spent a night together and they weren't going to start now. The eyes of the town still rested on them. They both felt there was a line that shouldn't be crossed. They weren't married yet.

Knud Erik's attitude to Albert changed unexpectedly, as if now, for the first time, he realised that his father would never return. Someone else was going to take over the empty space at his mother's side. Before this, he'd felt magnetically drawn to Albert. Now the magnet had switched, and it repelled him.

He joined his mother reluctantly on their visits to Albert, and when Albert called on them in Snaregade he was introverted. It was as though he wanted each of them to himself, separately. When his mother's world and Albert's finally met, he seemed to lose ownership of both. His old ease with Albert re-emerged only when the two of them were alone together.

Albert didn't mention this to Klara. So much remained unuttered between them. Silence is sometimes the preferred language of lovers, but for him it was an unknown tongue for which he had no dictionary. He constantly felt an unfathomable pressure. He and Klara neither kissed nor embraced in Knud Erik's presence. They'd never done so before either, but in the past they'd had something to hide. Now that everything was out in the open, they didn't exchange so much as a hand-squeeze of reassurance.

Was there nothing between them except the raw passion that came only in sudden, illicit bursts? Ejaculation without relief – could that be it? He was unfamiliar with the conventions of marriage, and was unable to interpret what was happening between them.

When he'd stayed with Cheng Sumei, a certain measured respect characterised their behaviour towards each other, which he'd always attributed to the Chinese in her – and perhaps to the Dane in him. Yet when they sat at table, telegrams and documents covered with freight rates spread before them, they'd sometimes both look up and break into a sudden surprised smile, as though seeing each other for the first time. They'd never taken each other for granted.

They'd been intimate, but intimacy isn't the same as routine. There was always a spark that glowed.

He missed her.

'Was she beautiful, your Chinese lady?' Klara asked him once, out of the blue. The question startled Albert. He hadn't known that she'd heard the old rumours too. He shrugged. He didn't feel like talking about Cheng Sumei with Klara. 'Did she have tiny little Chinese feet?'

'No, her feet weren't bound. That was only for the daughters of rich men; poor girls escaped. She was already providing for herself from when she was very young.'

Klara stared into the distance. Apparently this piece of information had knocked her off course. 'So she was an orphan?' It was a word Klara had avoided when he'd asked about her childhood on Birkholm.

'You could say that.'

'So she was all alone in the world,' Klara said.

He'd expected more questions, not only about Cheng Sumei's appearance but also about their feelings for each other. He dreaded this minefield; each reply might trigger unfavourable comparisons and fits of jealousy. And he knew how he'd have replied: with icy distance in his voice. This was private territory.

Instead, Klara fell silent. Several days passed before she raised the subject again. Her questioning now pursued a new line, as though she'd been thinking something through.

'Was the Chinese lady very rich?' she asked.

Albert explained that she had become rich by marrying Presser and that she'd carried on his business very successfully after his death. 'She was an independent woman,' he said. 'A businesswoman.'

'All alone in the world,' Klara said. 'And then she became rich and independent.' She spoke thoughtfully, as though this brief account of Cheng Sumei was leading her to a conclusion about herself.

Christmas was coming. For Albert, the holiday was a pretext for postponing the wedding to a yet undecided date in the new year. Christmas had to be got out of the way first. Then they could get married and she could move in with him. She wouldn't be bringing much from Snaregade. Compared to his, her belongings were mostly junk. But perhaps they meant something to her?

He didn't ask, but he noticed that she looked at his home in a new light. She wandered about, assessing things; tentatively, she'd move an armchair or a table – just by a few inches – or shift a sofa when she thought he wasn't looking. But the look in her eyes announced changes that no ruler could measure.

His world stood on the brink of a great upheaval. It was the only world he had left, a reduced kingdom, but still a kingdom, built just as much on his habits as on furniture and floor space. Now he'd have to give up those habits too.

The distance between Albert and Klara grew. Every time she

mentioned a possible date for their wedding, he responded with an evasive reply. His reluctance was blatant. He'd given his overall 'I do', but it had been followed by a long series of small, unspoken 'I don'ts'.

When he thought about the moment he'd have to visit Pastor Abildgaard and ask him to read their banns in church, everything inside him cringed. The vicar with whom he'd shared so many discussions, the pastor whose duty to call on the bereaved he'd taken over in the dark years of the war because Abildgaard hadn't the strength to take care of his flock as a vicar should, the man he'd seen in tears: now Albert would have to stand before him with all his own weaknesses laid bare.

Abildgaard's approach was bound to be ironic, condescending even. He'd undoubtedly have the nerve to play the father figure: oh yes, he'd be unable to resist getting back at him by delivering some lecture to the far older and more experienced man who'd opposed him on countless issues in the past. And though Albert believed deep down that he'd long ago left the power struggles of Marstal behind him, he was still loath to turn up as a supplicant at the vicar's office.

He hadn't altered that much. He hadn't surrendered the last of his fighting spirit. He didn't want to sacrifice his own dignity. Yet he knew he had to do it, because the dignity of another was at stake. Klara would have to live longer with a ruined reputation than he would. She had a small boy and an even smaller girl to take care of. She'd still have a life to live, long after he was gone. This was what her visit to him that day was really about. Her reticence abandoned and her self-effacement put aside, she had indeed been a mother defending her young.

They spent Christmas Eve in Prinsegade. The dining-room table was set with a damask cloth, silver and china. The Christmas tree stood in the drawing room. Albert had asked Knud Erik to help him decorate it, and the boy had done so, but with his new sullenness. Albert had a hard time getting used to it: he didn't understand, and he caught himself interpreting it as ingratitude, a reaction that was entirely alien to him: he'd never before believed that the recipients of his gifts owed him anything. So now he grew irritated with both himself and Knud Erik, and he scolded the boy several times. He didn't notice that Knud Erik himself was actually ashamed of his own sulkiness, and wanted to snap out of it, but couldn't. Albert's sudden reprimands only made it worse.

They carried their bad mood with them to the dinner table. Knud Erik didn't utter a word during the entire meal. Klara had returned to her old, passive self, behaving like a servant who has found herself at the master's table and expects to be sent back to the kitchen at any moment. Albert was gloomy and tense, filled with dark premonitions. His housekeeper waited on them, her face tight with disapproval. When he saw Klara shooting her a furtive glance, Albert knew immediately that his first task as her husband would be to dismiss the servant who'd been with him fifteen years.

Edith climbed onto Albert's lap and started beating the rice pudding with her spoon. 'Papa,' she said, and pulled his beard with her other hand. He said nothing. He'd given up trying to correct her.

They rose from the table for the traditional dance around the Christmas tree, but its size prevented them from linking hands around it, and by tacit agreement they avoided trying to do so. Nor did they sing carols. We'll never be a family, Albert thought. We're just the wreckage of other families. She's a widow with two children, and I'm an eccentric hermit who should never have left his cave.

Few presents lay under the tree. Klara hadn't bought many, and their new situation had deprived Albert of the joy of giving. He'd bought Klara a pair of leather gloves and Knud Erik a box of tin soldiers. Edith got a doll. There was a tobacco pouch for him. They unwrapped these gifts in silence and thanked each other politely.

When she left to go home to Snaregade, Klara turned in the doorway. 'We need to agree on a date, and you have to talk to Pastor Abildgaard.'

They saw more of each other between Christmas and the new year. Albert's sister visited from Svendborg, and later they went to see his friend Emanuel Kroman. Everyone regarded them as a couple now. People took it for granted that a wedding was imminent, so no one was indiscreet enough to enquire about the date.

The oppressive atmosphere between Albert and Klara did not dissipate, but they eventually agreed on a Saturday in late January.

Once the new year was over, he'd have to pay a visit to the vicarage and make sure their banns were read.

January was relentlessly grey, with temperatures that hovered around freezing point. Showers of rain and sleet swept through the deserted streets, and the shops kept their lights on all day. The vicarage in Kirkestræde stayed lit, too. Albert often passed it in the rain, but he didn't knock on the door. As with Klara's house in Snaregade in the days of their estrangement, he could neither stay clear of it, nor enter. It wasn't just the meeting with Abildgaard that troubled him. Surely he could survive that, damn it. No, something different and more powerful held him back, but no matter how hard he tried, he was unable to articulate what it was. He felt as if he were standing on top of a steep cliff, waiting to step into the void. The mute instinct for survival: that was what prevented him from taking the fatal step. Nothing else.

'Why didn't you marry the Chinese lady?'

He didn't have to reply. He could see from her expression that she'd already decided on an explanation of her own. 'That's what you're like, isn't it?' she said. 'You never marry them.'

'Have you spoken to Pastor Abildgaard?' she asked the next time he came by Snaregade.

He looked away. 'Not yet.'

'Why not?'

He said nothing. A feeling of impotence overwhelmed him – shame, too. He had no idea how to reply. She bit her lower lip. She didn't know how to open him up. Unaware of his fear and resistance, she focused instead on her own sense of being jilted.

'I'm not good enough for you?' she asked. 'Is that it?' He didn't reply. 'You promised.' Her gaze hardened.

'I'll do it.' He was mumbling, a rare tone of voice for a man used to shouting orders on deck in high winds, and who'd not dropped the habit once he came ashore. But this answer was worse than none at all.

'I don't know what to believe,' she said, shaking her head. 'I don't suppose it matters, anyway. I thought that was what you wanted.'

'I'll do it,' he repeated.

He hated himself and hated her because she was addressing him like a child – and it was his own fault.

'So do it, then. Do it tomorrow.'

Unable to bear the humiliating situation any longer, he rose and left without saying goodbye.

'You're ashamed of me!' she screamed after him.

ON SHROVETIDE EVE THE LAMP ABOVE ALBERT'S DOOR WAS LIT. TO us this was an invitation: according to the traditional, unwritten law of Shrovetide Eve, every lit door was an open door. If you didn't want visits from revellers in fancy dress, you switched off the light.

The housekeeper answered our knocking and let us in. It looked as if she'd made preparations for our arrival. The punchbowl awaited us on a stand. We were just settling on the sofa and the chairs that had been set out for visitors when our host entered. We saw the surprise on his face – unpleasant surprise, disapproval even – and realised immediately that we'd made a mistake.

It could be that Albert and his housekeeper had misunderstood each other. But later we speculated that she'd let us in as an act of revenge. The prospect of another woman in the house couldn't have thrilled her, and this was her way of paying him back.

Obviously, we should have made our apologies and left. But we were full of a particular energy that night. We weren't that easy to control.

Was it our fault that Albert later forgot himself? No, it was mostly his own. The scandal was his, not ours. You have to be prepared to put up with a few jokes at Shrovetide. We meant no harm – well, not much. Besides, our host was welcome to give as good as he got, and join in the fun. It was all just high spirits. We certainly bore no responsibility for what followed.

We had nothing but sympathy for Albert Madsen. He'd been good to Marstal and we didn't begrudge him taking a young wife in his old age, if that was what he was up to, and not something worse. Which his procrastination over marrying Klara Friis certainly seemed to indicate.

When he opened the door and found us in his drawing room, one hell of a sight met his eyes. A cow was sitting on his sofa, yanking on a springy coil of yellow paper hanging from its tar-black nose.

Next to it, a Spanish señorita was brandishing a fan. Her red lips, painted on the silk stocking pulled over her head, were parted slightly, as though inviting a kiss. A heavy, thickset farmer's wife with a lampshade for a hat stood in the middle of the floor with hands – in man-sized gloves – planted on her hips. The room had filled with the smell of glue, naphthalene and other, stranger odours. A caveman was leaning his club against the wall, while a Chinese lady with slanted eyes painted in black on a yellow paper mask pulled a huge pair of knitting needles from a ball of wool on the top of her head and clashed them together. In a corner of the room a two-legged pink pig snorted contentedly, while the pirate beside it raised his sword as though proposing to slaughter the beast with one blow.

'Evening, Lil' Albert,' we yelled in unison.

Lil' Albert said nothing. A bad sign.

The housekeeper poured punch into glasses, which she passed round to us. We'd made holes in our masks and stockings where our mouths were, and we'd brought our own straws so that none of us would have to take off his mask and reveal his face.

After all, it was Shrovetide.

Most of us present that night were women: great broad-shouldered women with huge breasts. Their weight should have made us topple, but instead we pushed and battered them about like goose-down pillows. We wore woollen skirts with velvet ribbons, tight blouses, embroidered aprons and shawls long enough to cover head, chest and back – all from the bottom of the dressing-up box, mended and re-mended over the years, and brought out specially for this evening.

We swayed our hips and fluttered our hands with the giddy abandon that comes not just from emptying so many punchbowls in the course of an evening but from the odd feeling of freedom that floods a man when he dresses up in women's clothing. Hidden beneath capes, bonnets, caps, lampshades and wigs, with masks that were nothing but red-painted pouts and wide-open eyes with black lashes the size of fans, we snuggled up to the nearest manly chest while cooing like doves and delivering daring remarks – as close to outright obscenity as we could get away with in our character of virtuous ladies – in falsetto voices.

The crudest reveller of all that evening was the bride. She wore her petticoat outside her dress and a flesh-coloured suspender-belt circled her massive waist; two breasts swung in opposite directions behind her cream-coloured silk bodice, and every time she swirled coquettishly they collided with a loud slap. She wore a blonde wig with thick plaits sticking out, and her starched veil stood as stiff as a frozen snowstorm of lace.

She approached Captain Madsen and tweaked his ear lobe. He pulled back his head in irritation.

'How's your love life, Lil' Albert?' the bride asked in the high-pitched keening voice that countrywomen once used at funerals. 'When's the wedding?'

Captain Madsen's face seemed to indicate he'd decided this was some sort of endurance test, and that if he stood it long enough it would end of its own accord.

The bride placed a large gloved hand on his thigh, close to his groin.

'Trouble down there?' For a moment she forgot her part and burst into loud, braying laughter.

Then the pig tore itself away from the pirate and approached them, its two pointy udders sticking out from its pink belly, rigid and fixed as fingers of accusation. 'Have you lost your appetite, Lil' Albert?' asked the pig.

The bride made kissing noises and the pig offered him its snout. It was Shrovetide. Fun and games.

By now the housekeeper had left and the large punchbowl was almost empty. 'Lil' Albert,' intoned the pig. It must have had a poetic bent, because it started improvising on the subject of our host.

> Have you lost your appetite
> For the fun of the night?
> Is the girl too cold?
> Or are you too old?

Captain Madsen stared at the floor.

The pig raised its trotter like a conductor calling the orchestra to attention, and we repeated the crude verse in unison: we were in high spirits, and it came to us easily. Then Albert looked up and shot out his huge fist with a speed we'd never thought possible in a man whose old age we'd just mocked. He slammed the pig right on the snout, completely flattening it. Though cushioned by the mask, the blow was still hard enough to send the pig flying into the stand, and the punchbowl went crashing to the floor. The pig stayed down there amid the shattered glass, blood dribbling from its wrecked snout.

Then the bride, who was still standing right next to Captain Madsen, punched him in the face and the back of his head smacked against the wall. He staggered, then regained his balance. Tentatively he ran a finger across his split lower lip, staring straight ahead with empty eyes.

The bride looked ready to have a second go at him, but we restrained her and dragged her away. Things had got out of control and we had to put a stop to it, though we didn't understand what had gone wrong. Had we crossed a line? But surely the whole point of Shrovetide was that there were no lines. On this one evening, anything went. And after all we'd only done what we always did, which was to tell a few home truths in an entertaining fashion. There was no need for anyone to get violent.

We put the fallen table back in place. There was nothing we could do about the punchbowl. The housekeeper would have to see to that. Then we carried the unconscious pig into the hall and down the steps into Prinsegade.

There we turned and looked up at the bay window. Albert was looking down at us. Our masks were beginning to disintegrate in the cold February rain. The bride waved to the dark shadow in the pane.

'Is the girl too cold? Or are you too old?' she yelled.

One of her sleeves had slipped down to reveal a beefy forearm with a tattoo of a lion crouching to attack. In the dark, you couldn't make out the words.

North Star

IT RAINED IN THE MORNING, BUT THEN THE WEATHER CHANGED, AND the lid of grey clouds that had covered the island gave way to a high, blue sky that warned of frost.

Albert staggered about blindly, gripped by despair. 'You're ashamed of me!' Klara had screamed after him. No, he wasn't ashamed of her. He was ashamed of himself. He had to get away, take a walk to clear his head and decide on an unambiguous statement, a yes or a no, and then live with it. He wanted to say yes but couldn't bring himself to. He could have said no, but he didn't want to do that either. This wasn't a case of 'where there's a will there's a way'. There was nothing but will, but both ways led to a void. He was too old. They were right, these masked Shrovetide revellers who'd so humiliated him, and that was why he struck out at them. He couldn't handle such a big change in his life. He recognised this with savage indignation, a helpless rage that had nowhere to turn but inward.

Albert headed for the beach. Further out, a figure appeared. As it came closer, he recognised Herman, and he braced himself for a confrontation. It hadn't been difficult to figure out who'd played the bride that night, when he'd been ridiculed and struck in his own home.

Despite the cold Herman's shirt was unbuttoned down to his belt, where his hairy gut, which hadn't shrunk during his many months of the good life at Hotel Ærø, spilled over. His face glowed red from the cold and he was staring ahead with glazed eyes. He passed Albert without so much as glancing at him, walking as if he were set on a distant goal, somewhere beyond the houses of Marstal, and was prepared to walk though every wall in his path to get there.

Relieved to have avoided a clash, Albert walked on and was soon consumed by his thoughts again. He wanted to get away from the town, in the hope that out here, surrounded by nothing but sea and sky, a solution would reveal itself. 'Ha!' he snorted to himself. 'The only answer would be to stay out here for ever.' He strode forward, half expecting that some refuge really would present itself on the narrow strip of sand, in a limbo where no one could force a decision on him.

Walking on the wet sand was hard work. After some time it gave way to a carpet of pebbles left by the surf, which he stumbled across until he reached the dense shrubbery on the sandy crest of the spit, where well-trodden paths wound their way through the vegetation. Walking on, he came to the spot where the spit bends like a crooked elbow. Here, between spit and breakwater, the water lay heavy and oily, as if anticipating the arrival of frost and its own imminent crystallisation. It was dotted with tiny islands where rushes and bulrushes sprouted from thick, heavy mud. The breakwater lay between him and the town. He could see the masts of the ships in winter harbour. Behind them were the red-tiled roofs of Marstal and the newly constructed copper church spire.

He was staring at the town that spread panoramically along the coast, searching for a solution to the dilemma that tormented him, when he suddenly realised that he was stuck. He'd strayed from the sandy spit and into the shallow water by the shore of one of the little rush-covered islands.

The muddy ground tugged at him. He pulled back first one leg, then the other, so hard he nearly lost his balance, but he got nowhere. He felt the icy water seep into his boots. He stared down in disbelief. Then he laughed out loud, a brash artificial laughter to mock his own folly. He tightened the muscles of his right leg and tried again. With the shift of weight, his left leg suddenly sank deeper. This wasn't quicksand. He wasn't about to be sucked down. He was just stuck. It was nothing. He had to try again. He bent to haul himself up by his boots and nearly toppled over. He was a big man in a heavy winter coat, and he'd lost his suppleness long ago. He was aware that he was growing increasingly desperate, but he still refused to accept that he was in a risky situation. Ridiculous, yes, but not dangerous. What if he threw himself forward into the rushes? Would he find solid ground there and be able to drag his feet after him? But he didn't know what lay beneath their dense growth. Perhaps they were rooted in water and the same muddy ground he was now stuck in, in which case he'd only make matters worse.

The sun was approaching the horizon, and with the dark would come the frost. The thought didn't fill him with panic. He just felt like a fool, who'd carelessly landed himself in a tight spot. Soon it would be no more than an embarrassing memory. The highest price he'd have to pay for his stupidity would be a cold. Then he felt the icy chill creep from his feet to his legs. He shuddered for a moment, then slapped at his body to warm it up, but he was soon exhausted. Stopping, he let his arms hang limp by his sides. He couldn't stay here. He had to think of something. He tensed his leg muscles again, but it was no use. The mud wouldn't give.

Everything was casting long shadows now. The mast tops and the riggings threw a spider's web across the rushes. The church tower stretched over the sandy spit and reached the water behind him, and his own shadow seemed to straddle the rooftops. Then the sun disappeared behind a house, and the dark shape of the town swallowed him up. Marstal was nearby, but it might as well have been on another planet.

It struck him that for many years he'd observed the breakwater from within the harbour, where it lay like a protective wall. This was the first time he'd actually considered it from the outside. It no longer protected him. It was shutting him out.

He looked around. The darkness seemed to rise from the ground and the sea itself, and he thought of Homer's description of the twilight land of the dead, where all joy is frozen, and realised that this was where he was. He felt the frost as a sharpness against his skin. Soon it would reach all his limbs. For the first time it struck him that he might be about to die.

The stars appeared and the mud froze between his feet, until he was standing in a concrete block of cold. He looked up and saw the North Star and he thought about Klara Friis. In the last moments before old age closed in on him, he'd reached for youth. But youth was as unreachable to an old man as the North Star on a winter's night. Now he was certain. It was over. His life was about to end, as unexpectedly as a ship wrecked in a freak storm.

Numb with cold, he stood motionless in the mud. It was as if he was planning to die on his feet. He thought about Knud Erik and a sense of warmth filled him. That was his heart deploying its last resources.

Then the cold moved in and started its blockade of his flowing blood.

WE DON'T KNOW IF THAT'S HOW IT ACTUALLY HAPPENED. WE DON'T
know what Albert thought or did in his final hours. We weren't
there. We only have the notes he left us, together with the columns
of figures that spelled out what proved to be the beginning of the
end of our town. In telling this story, each of us has added something of his own. Our picture of him is made up of a thousand
thoughts, wishes and observations. He's entirely himself. And yet
he's one of us.

We've walked out to the Tail. We've visited the place where Albert
died. We've planted our boots in the mud and tried to pull ourselves
out of the sucking ground. Some of us say, yes, he was stuck. Others
say, no, he could have freed himself. Or he could have rolled out of
the trap the cold and the mud had set for him. A drenched winter
coat and soaked trousers are a small price to pay for an escape from
death. Even pneumonia is preferable to a sudden end to it all, and
he was a strong man.

We don't really know anything, and we each have our own version
of the story, because we're all looking for a little of ourselves in
Albert. Some of us would like to condemn him. Others regard him
as being above all petty-mindedness. We all have an opinion about
Albert. We followed him everywhere he went. We watched him
through our windows and passed on his words, not always for kind
reasons, and possibly they weren't the actual words he'd used, but
we attributed them to him because we thought it proper or likely
that he'd have said them.

We've gone over his life again and again, just as we always go
over each other's lives in our conversations – some whispered, some
spoken aloud. Albert is a monument we've all carved and erected.

We thought we knew everything about him. But that's not how
life is. When all's said and done, we can never truly know each other.

*   *   *

Albert was found the following day.

It had snowed through the night, and in the morning a couple of boys appeared on the breakwater. They'd half rowed, half crashed a boat through the new ice towards Kalkovnen, and they were in line for a major thrashing from their fathers, or anyone else who caught them doing something so blatantly dangerous. When it comes to boys who flaunt the rules that apply on the water, every single one of us has a father's rights and responsibilities.

But this time there was no thrashing.

They saw him from the top of the snow-powdered granite boulders of the breakwater where they were leaping about like mountain goats.

'A snowman!' shouted one, a boy called Anton. 'Who's built a snowman there?'

They ran through the stiff rushes, which rang in the frost like a forest of steel blades, across the rock-hard mud and solid puddles and frozen shallow creeks.

There he was.

They never forgot him. Such sights are rare. Some say unique.

Between Marstal and the sea, frozen to death in Laurids' boots, Albert stood upright.

III

The Widows

IN THE MONTHS THAT FOLLOWED ALBERT'S DEATH, KLARA SAT IN HER house in Snaregade staring blankly into space. We saw her when we walked past and glanced inside the lit parlour, where she'd neglected to draw the curtains. It looked as if her brain had stopped. At first we thought she was in mourning. It was a while before we recognised that Klara wasn't numb with grief, but rather in a state of profound contemplation.

Sometimes life unexpectedly throws up a wealth of possibilities – so many that the mere thought of having to choose between them can floor you. Was that Klara's problem? The sudden flood of freedom in which an ordinary person, unaccustomed to making her own decisions, might drown?

Then one day she ordered a horse and cart to collect her furniture. She called Edith and Knud Erik, and they all walked hand in hand to Prinsegade, where she took a key from her purse and let herself into Albert's empty house. She had her own furniture stored in the loft and left Albert's where it was. She sat on his sofa and slept in his bed as a guest in someone else's life. The housekeeper dismissed herself.

Klara sat in the bay window facing the street and stared into space again.

Klara Friis, a sailor's widow of modest birth, had inherited an imposing house, a broker's office and a fleet of ships. In one fell swoop she'd become one of the biggest shipowners in town. With the last glow of youth on her cheeks, she'd reached for the big prize and won it. Albert hadn't married her in life. But he'd delivered in death.

We wasted no time discussing how much she was worth, though we failed to understand that the most fascinating thing about Albert's legacy wasn't its size, but the power it bestowed. It was during these months, as Klara sat frozen in the bay window, that our town's fate was sealed.

One day Klara called a halt to her reflections and went to visit the widow of the marine painter in Teglgade. Wise as she was, Anna Egidia had once noted the fatherless Knud Erik's lack of confidence and spotted a child in need of a grown man's support. Since her introduction to Albert was all thanks to Anna Egidia, Klara Friis felt she owed the widow a favour. She now informed Mrs Rasmussen that she would like to be of assistance in her tireless charity work. But she offered more than that. As they sat in the drawing room with the tall windows and the paintings on the walls, she explained that her plan was to found an orphanage in Marstal.

'It will be an orphanage like no other,' she said. 'Where children will feel loved. They won't feel they're in the way – or at best, that they deserve to live only because they'll be of use to others. No. They'll feel they're entitled to be on this earth for their own sake. It'll be a place where the least wanted children will feel welcome.' Her voice ought to have been filled with light and energy as she described her plans to improve the existence and the future of those whom life had overlooked. But it trembled strangely.

Mrs Rasmussen observed her for a long time.

'You knew an orphanage from the inside once, didn't you?' she said gently.

Klara Friis nodded and began to weep. This was the unutterable part of her story, the part she'd been unable to tell Albert Madsen, even at their moment of deepest trust, when he'd guessed the secret of Karla, the rag doll lost to the dark waters of the flood.

Under the widow's maternal gaze, she finally felt able to confide her story. She'd grown up in Ryslinge Orphanage on the island of Funen. Then she'd been 'collected', as she put it. It wasn't an adoption: at least she'd never use that word for it, because the Birkholm farmer who'd taken her in at the age of five had no caring parental impulse. She wasn't a human being to him: just an extra pair of hands, cheap in terms of wages, food – and emotions. She laughed bitterly. No, when it came to feelings, she'd cost nothing at all. Love was a luxury that had been available to everybody except the orphaned girl.

On Birkholm there was no getting away from the sea. It ringed the small island like a wall enclosing her restricted life, but it also represented escape. She didn't dream about a knight riding in on a white charger so much as a knight blown in by a white sail. And every spring she imagined that he'd arrive. Hundreds of sailing ships passed the island – and then disappeared again. They came from Marstal, and the town became a place she yearned for. One day the sea came to her in the form of a flood. Doomsday was paying a visit. Instead of bringing a knight, the waves took away her doll. Now, at long last, with the help of Albert's fortune, she could stick her hand into the water and haul Karla out again.

'Do you want to know how I met Henning?' she asked the widow suddenly. The confidences were pouring out of her now, and before Anna Egidia had time to reply, Klara continued. 'I met him one winter night on the frozen sea.'

'On the ice?' The widow looked up in surprise.

'I was so young. Only sixteen. I wanted to go to a dance on Langeland.'

The sea had frozen, and it seemed as if tiny, flat Birkholm had started to expand, trying to meet and merge with the surrounding islands. On that moonlit Saturday night, snow crystals lit a path into the world, and her longing became irresistible. Having no party dress of her own, she borrowed one from a girl on the farm, then got hold of a bicycle and cycled across the ice towards Langeland. She wasn't running away. She'd just headed towards the lights of the houses on the distant island, hoping for a moment of happiness. Back then, she still dared to dream.

But she hadn't gone far before she reached black water. Suddenly, a rift appeared in the ice ahead of her, the massive steel hull of the *A.L.B.*, the ferry between Svendborg and Marstal, was ploughing through, breaking the ice. As it went past, sparks flew from its funnel. The ice under her feet shuddered. In the ship's wake came the *Hydra*, home-bound, her sails set to catch even the slightest wind that frosty night.

The *Hydra*'s crew crowded along the rail. A girl in a party dress in the middle of the ice was the last thing they'd expected to see.

'Where are you going?' they hailed her.

'To a dance on Langeland,' she replied.

They invited her to a dance in Marstal instead, and both she and her bicycle were pulled over the rail.

'You look frozen stiff,' said Henning Friis, the handsomest of them.

And she was indeed cold. Under her dress her legs were bare. He took her down to the fo'c's'le to warm her up in the top berth. And that was how she became his, with her blue lips trembling and cystitis lying in wait in the wretched block of ice that was her inadequately clothed body. She didn't get pregnant right away. Knud Erik came later. So did Henning's drinking and pub crawls and endless voyages.

One year Henning came home with a stuffed guenon monkey.

'The guenon is the most ungodly of all the animals,' he said. 'The son, grandson and great-grandson of Injustice.' An Arab had told him that.

'And what am I supposed to do with it?' she asked.

'You can look at it when you miss me,' he replied, his voice laden with contempt. That was how things had grown between them.

'The worst thing about the sailor isn't that he steals your virtue. The worst thing is that he steals your dreams,' she said to the marine painter's widow.

Now the *Hydra* was gone, and Henning with it.

'One day Marstal will be a good place to grow up,' she said, 'instead of a place where boys are raised to become fish food, and girls to be their widows.'

'Do you really think you can take the sailor out of a Marstaller?' asked the widow.

'Yes, I do. I have the means. And I know how to do it.' A new stubbornness had entered Klara Friis's voice, and her face grew ugly with defiance.

Wondering if the younger woman's mind might have become dislocated by grief or her vast inheritance, the widow quickly steered the conversation back to the orphanage, and to her relief Klara Friis became sensible and practical again.

But Klara never mentioned the most important part of her plan.

THE SAME DAY THAT ALBERT DIED MR HENCKEL WAS DECLARED
bankrupt.

At a general meeting of Kalundborg Shipyard Limited, of which he
owned 99 per cent of the shares, to everyone's astonishment he voted
in favour of liquidating his own company. It was subsequently revealed
that the shipyard owed Kalundborg Bank 12 million kroner. The bank
collapsed, dragging other businesses with it. Including, finally, Marstal
Steel Shipyard. Peter Raahauge the ship worker had warned Albert
there was no way in hell things could last. His prophecy had now
been fulfilled.

The nearly one million kroner that had been invested in the Marstal
enterprise was lost, and the yard was auctioned off for just 35,000
kroner. Mr Egeskov, owner of the *Ærø*, would survive. He had his
hotel to fall back on. But Herman had ransomed his house in
Skippergade, along with the *Two Sisters,* and he was left with nothing
but debts.

Court cases followed. Both Edvard Henckel and the manager of
Kalundborg Bank were arrested. Not even the devil could make head
or tail of their accounts. Henckel had been too smart for them. You
could argue that he was a kind of genius who happened to forget
the laws of the land and ended up on the wrong side of them. He
was quite open in admitting everything. He'd been irresponsible,
even thoughtless. But his intentions had been good.

We pictured him standing in the dock, broad and mighty in his
wide-brimmed hat, his coat tails flapping as though he'd brought
the fresh breeze of enterprise into the courtroom with him. His bloodshot eyes were bright with energy, and the way he flung out his arms
and confessed to all his mistakes, you'd think he was inviting the
judge, the journalists, the defence and the prosecutor to a champagne party.

It turned out he wasn't an engineer at all. Like everything else about him, the title was a fiction. Now he was off to prison. He took the announcement of his three-year sentence like a man, refusing to let it break him. He'd stormed through life bursting with grand plans for himself and for others; if he had to take a detour via a locked cell, it was only a temporary interruption. He'd come back out again eventually, and then he'd show us.

We no longer frequented Hotel Ærø. Our starched shirts stayed at home, once again reserved only for weddings, confirmations and funerals. Back in Weber's Cafe, we reacquainted ourselves with flat beer. We didn't gloat when we heard about the prison sentence. We couldn't even get properly angry with Henckel. Yes, he'd cheated us, but fraud takes two: we should have exercised better judgement. We certainly didn't regard him as evil. His enthusiasm and his spirit of enterprise were genuine. His problem was simply that he'd had too many ideas and he'd lost track of them until they became hopelessly entangled. But the man was willing to take a risk. We respected that. It was what we did all the time. We acknowledged something of ourselves in Henckel: not his fraudulence, but his get-up-and-go.

We toasted him the way we'd have toasted a ship that was lost with all hands.

Herman did the rounds of the shipping offices, looking for work. We'd expected him to run away from it all, just as he'd done when Hans Jepsen put him in his place and refused to sign him on as an ordinary seaman on the *Two Sisters*. Then he'd come back as a big shot: he'd talked big and had a wallet to match, but he'd lost it all and ended up where he'd begun. He'd been sold a pig in a poke. But then again, he wasn't alone. Quite a few of us had bought one. In that respect we were all in the same boat.

We never expected Herman to be humbled by his fall. It wasn't in his nature, which was stubborn-minded and arrogant. We just imagined that he'd flee the humiliation and reappear only when he had money in his pocket and was ready to start bragging again. Instead, he stayed in the town that had witnessed his downfall and signed on to the *Albatross*. We couldn't help but think that he must have finally learned his lesson and accepted that life had no plans to treat him differently from anybody else and that a certain amount of humility was therefore in order. Apart from that he was just the same Herman, as aggressive and unpredictable as ever. But he knew his way around a deck, so he had no problem finding a job.

He returned from his first voyage a war hero, though the war had ended long before. He'd fought in the defence of Denmark in a pub in Nyborg, together with two other men from Marstal, Ingolf Thomsen and Lennart Krull, fellow crewmen on the *Albatross*.

He sat in Weber's Cafe holding forth about his deeds, while Ingolf and Lennart nodded in affirmation. From time to time they'd interject. But under Herman's stern eye, it never amounted to more than 'Yes', 'No' or 'Exactly'.

So they'd been in this pub in Nyborg with the rest of the crew, and they'd started talking to this car mechanic, Ravn was his name, a greasy little bloke with a potato nose covered in blackheads, engine oil on his hands. When he learned they were sailors from Marstal, he pulled out his wallet and showed them a photo of a schooner in flames. It was the *Hydra*, which had vanished without trace in the Atlantic in September of 1917. So had the six hands aboard, including two from Marstal: the captain, and ordinary seaman Henning Friis, who left behind a widow, Klara, and a son, Knud Erik. Vanished without trace: that meant never seen by anyone, no bodies to recover and bury, no flotsam found afterwards, not even a lifebuoy with the name of the ship – nothing.

Ravn was from Sønderborg in South Jutland. He'd been drafted to fight for the Germans and had served on a U-boat. Photographs had been taken of all the ships the U-boats had sunk, and every man got a copy. He had a whole album of the pictures at home.

'I've got the photograph here,' Herman said. 'Do you want to have a look?'

He passed it across the table and turned to order a new round.

We instantly recognised the *Hydra,* and the sight of it in flames shifted a weight inside us. The black-and-white photograph echoed our own experiences of shipwreck.

'Anyway,' Herman said, 'Ravn won't be going around bragging about sinking Danish ships any more.'

'Perhaps we were a bit too rough with him,' Lennart said. We could hear the uncertainty in his voice.

'It was a fair fight. Ravn could have fought back. We've got nothing on our conscience.' Herman sounded like a priest offering absolution. 'He got what he deserved,' he added, turning to us. 'I beat him up for the men who died. And for the *Hydra*.'

Herman paid a visit to Klara Friis, intending to tell her the story of Ravn. We imagined he was hoping to profit from it. Only this time he'd say, 'I beat him up for Henning.'

Klara opened the door. 'What do you want?' she asked tersely, when she saw Herman on the doorstep. The last time he'd paid her a visit, his intentions hadn't been good. 'I've got news of Henning,' he said.

She listened to his story in silence. She'd paled when he informed her that he had news of Henning; now she reddened as he sat there boasting about having beaten to a pulp the man who sank the *Hydra*. When he concluded by claiming that he'd taken him on for Henning's sake, her face whitened again and her mouth became a thin line. She stared at him through narrowed eyes. Completely unable to interpret her expression, he felt temporarily at a loss.

'Perhaps you disapprove of fights, Mrs Friis?' His manner had suddenly become very formal. Still she didn't speak. He shifted in his chair and regretted having come.

Finally she broke her silence.

'I'd like you to accompany me to Copenhagen,' she said.

By now Klara Friis had hired a maid who could take care of the children in her absence. She'd been to I. C. Jensen and ordered new rugs and consulted Rosenbæk, the carpenter, about a new bed suitable to her status as a widow. She was filled with energy, but no one knew what she planned to do, apart from rearranging her life to suit her new financial circumstances.

She revealed nothing to Herman while they were on the ferry. He'd not expected her to be forthcoming, and nor had he speculated about what the trip to Copenhagen might involve. When she asked him to accompany her he'd sensed no definite promise on the horizon, so it was purely out of curiosity that he'd agreed. He was on the lookout for new opportunities in life, and although he couldn't determine the nature of this expedition, he felt it held possibilities.

'You know the money men in Copenhagen, Mr Frandsen,' she said to him.

She addressed him formally, and he preferred it that way.

It established a businesslike tone between them, and he was up for doing business.

'I want you to introduce me to them.'

He stared at her. Was she stupid or just hopelessly naive? Was she practically asking to be robbed? He hadn't given much thought to Klara Friis's intelligence, but there was no reason to assume she was a fool. Was this a test?

He decided to be honest with her – which in turn demanded a rare moment of honesty with himself.

'Are you referring to Henckel? But he was a fraud. Surely you know that he's in prison now?'

'I'm well aware of that. But you must have known others. You've been to the Stock Exchange. I need to speak with someone who understands finance.'

'You mean people like the Negro Thug or the Rolling Pavement? I'm afraid they're cut from the same cloth as Henckel. If you value your money, then don't entrust them with any of it.'

'They can't all be frauds.'

'Possibly not. But it's hard for ordinary people like us to tell the difference.'

He looked down at his big hands. For a moment he listened to his own voice. It sounded humble. He wasn't used to talking like this. He spoke about his own defeat in a frank, even regretful tone. Who could say if it was false or not. He was the shooting star who'd crashed and repented and learned from his mistakes.

'I've become wiser,' he pronounced, 'since I allowed myself to be robbed. Why don't you just leave your money where it is? I imagine it's well invested.'

'You don't understand,' she said. 'I have other plans.'

But by the time they arrived at Copenhagen Central Railway Station her confidence had deserted her. She took Herman's arm like a child grabbing its father's hand, terrified of becoming lost in the crowds. He'd sensed this fear when they boarded the train in Korsør: she'd tossed her head haughtily when she stepped onto the running board, but a shudder seemed to pass through her, hinting at a feral panic she couldn't control. She'd sat straight up on the seat opposite him and avoided looking out of the window. Later, as they passed Slagelse, she'd snapped out of her trance and turned to look at the scenery, but she'd had to shut her eyes right away. For most of her life, her only landscape had been the flat meadows of Birkholm. To her, Marstal was 'the city'. But you could fit its whole market square, church and high street beneath the vaulted roof of Copenhagen's station, where the buzz of countless travellers gathered into one great shouting echo.

The first place he took her was the vestibule of the Stock Exchange. He deliberately chose late afternoon, when the prices had been set for the day and the brutal circus known as the post-trading period had begun. His intention was quite simply to scare her off. He discovered he had a protective instinct, which, had he been at all interested in his own psychology, he might have described as selflessness. There was no need for her to be conned out of her money as he had been. Since he'd been unable to talk her out of the vague plans she was so hell-bent on carrying out, he'd make use of the deterrent power of example.

In the centre of the vestibule was a roped-off area resembling a boxing ring. Inside, stockbrokers roared out their offers all at once.

From one end of the vestibule a man with an odd, rolling swagger came walking towards them. Avoiding the swing of his bruising shoulders, the crowd parted to make way for him. He looked like an old sailor trying to keep his balance on a ship in a gale; his colleagues, who'd never stood on a deck, called him the Rolling Pavement.

He raised his bowler hat as he spotted Herman. They were old acquaintances. Herman returned the greeting with an inviting smile, and instantly the man stepped up to Herman and Klara.

'Ajax Hammerfeldt,' he said, and took Klara's hand with an elegant gesture, pursed his lips and planted a kiss on it.

The unfamiliar greeting startled her. She looked down and blushed, and forgot to introduce herself. So Herman did it for her, and added, 'Mrs Friis has just inherited a considerable fortune. She's in need of some good advice.'

'Then you've come to the right man, my dear Mrs Friis,' the Rolling Pavement said, and raised his hat a second time, as though they were about to become very well acquainted. He threw a quick glance at Herman to secure his consent to what was about to happen: when no reaction came, he took it as acceptance and continued.

'The shipping industry is enjoying enormous progress,' he said. 'Have you heard about the ship with no funnel, Mrs Friis?'

Klara shook her head, overwhelmed.

'The steamer succeeds the sailing ship. But the ship with no funnel will replace the steamer. That's the future, and you have the opportunity to be among the first to invest your money in it. You're young.' Here he threw her a flattering glance, then added, in a tone that suggested that he was now presenting his decisive argument. 'And the future belongs to our youth.'

Herman looked from one to the other. He couldn't help but admire the Rolling Pavement. He certainly knew his trade, even if it was a con man's, peddling a fraudulent blend of truth and lies. The ship with no funnel! It sounded made-up, but it wasn't: a ship with a diesel-powered motor, the *Selandia*, had been launched by B&W Shipyard some years ago. And she was undoubtedly a successor to the steamer. He waited patiently for Hammerfeldt to continue. The truthful part had been conveyed. Now for the lies.

'Kalundborg Shipyard,' the Rolling Pavement said. 'That's where the ship of the future will be launched. They've just issued the shares. The last one will be sold before the day's out. It's about striking while the iron's hot, don't you agree, sailor?' He winked at Herman, whom he still regarded as an accomplice.

Klara looked astonished, as if she couldn't believe her own ears. 'Kalundborg Shipyard! But that's Mr Henckel's company, isn't it? He's in jail!' She appealed to Herman, who nodded.

'Yes,' he said. 'That's correct.'

They both turned to the Rolling Pavement. But the cocksure hawker of future riches had already vanished into the shouting crowd.

Klara Friis had learned her lesson.

They crossed the Stock Exchange Bridge and continued down Slotsholmen. The quay was teeming with life: dockers were busy unloading fragrant cargoes of fresh-cut wood from bark- and brig-rigged ships from Finland. He glanced at her. The anxiety had returned to her face. All he'd wanted was to open her eyes a bit, but now it seemed she'd lost heart. That hadn't been his intention, though he kept asking himself what her true purpose was. What was it she really wanted here?

They crossed the square at the corner of Holbergsgade and

Havnegade. She looked up at the huge bronze statue of the naval hero, whose outstretched arm seemed to be directing the traffic.

'That's Niels Juel,' he said.

'Just like home?'

Marstal was her yardstick for everything, so she was probably thinking of Marstal's Niels Juelsgade. Perhaps she even believed this statue was named after a street in their own little backwater. There were no statues in Marstal, only the stone that Captain Madsen had erected in honour of fellowship. Now Klara could compare the two edifices and acquire a realistic sense of her benefactor's true stature. Copenhagen was the real world. Here, people didn't haul old boulders out of the sea and stick them up somewhere with a few lines carved into the granite. Here, people thought big and built big.

Suddenly Herman had an idea. He pointed to a foreign-looking building on the corner. It had tall, narrow windows with pointed oriental arches, and its roof sat like a heavy lid that was about to slide off into the street. A set of steps led up to a solid wooden door set in walls a metre thick. It was a house that looked as if it had turned its back on the rest of the city.

'The man who lives in there could give you some good advice.'

She gave him a puzzled look. Then she turned her head and scrutinised the sand-coloured building. 'Who is he?' she asked.

'He's a completely ordinary man. His name is Markussen. He was once an able seaman. Now he's a friend of the King. There are those who say his word is more powerful than His Majesty's. He'll help you.'

They crossed the square and stopped in front of the entrance. She gazed up at the facade. *The Far East Asia Corporation,* said the brass plate next to the door.

'It's a big house.'

'No smaller than his houses in Vladivostok and Bangkok.'

'Should I really go in?' she asked.

Herman nodded encouragingly, but he was already regretting his whim. Which was all it was, after all. He'd felt magnanimous when they left the Stock Exchange. Then he'd seen the sense of defeat spreading across her face, and felt obliged to do something more for her, to cheer her up. Magnanimity was a new and unfamiliar feeling for him. Finding it to his taste, he'd wanted to bathe in the sunshine of selflessness a little longer. But this was downright ridiculous. If she'd been disappointed earlier, her disappointment would only deepen with the rejection that awaited her. He cursed himself. Damn it all to hell! He should never have come with her on this doomed mission to Copenhagen; in a moment of weakness he'd once again succumbed to the temptation to look important.

'I'll wait for you out here,' he said, and smiled cheerfully.

This won't take long, he thought to himself as she disappeared behind the heavy door. But time passed, and she did not emerge from the building. Herman started pacing up and down the pavement. Why hadn't they seen her off? He went up the steps and opened the heavy door. A man in uniform blocked his path and asked him what his business was. Herman was taken aback; he hadn't prepared an answer. He looked over the doorman's shoulder, but there was no sign of Klara in the vast lobby. The doorman again demanded that he account for his intrusion. Herman shrugged and went back down the steps.

An hour later she reappeared.

'I'm meeting the commissioner again tonight,' she said. Herman's face became one big question mark. 'Markussen, I mean. He gave me some excellent advice. I'd like to thank you so very much for your help, Herman.'

His jaw dropped. Her tone of voice had changed. She was back to calling him by his first name. Before, she'd briefly addressed him as Mr Frandsen, and he'd taken it as a sign of respect. But since her audience with Markussen, he'd been demoted to the level of a servant.

She pulled her purse from her handbag. 'I'm delighted that you brought me here,' she said. 'I want to give you something for your trouble.'

Out came a hundred-krone note. His initial impulse was to reject the money. What did she take him for? Did she think he had no pride? Then he reconsidered. He'd done her a favour, after all. And wasted his own time, to boot. A hundred kroner wasn't to be sneezed at. He needed to get drunk. A roll in the hay wouldn't come amiss either. The good reasons for accepting the cash piled up until they tipped the balance. His precious pride forgotten, he stuck the note in the inside pocket of his jacket but didn't thank her.

'So, what did you and Markussen discuss?' he asked with forced casualness.

'The commissioner felt our conversation should remain confidential.'

Klara Friis pronounced the last word slowly and carefully, as if making sure that Herman caught every syllable. The word *confidential* was clearly a new one for her, too. Then, for the first time, she smiled.

When she'd entered the building, she'd found it just as forbidding inside as out. The heavy door had barely closed behind her when a uniformed man blocked her path, as if to inform her that she'd confused the front door with the tradesman's entrance. She'd sensed immediately that this was as far as she'd get.

A small man holding a black silk hat came over to her and asked her politely if he could be of assistance.

It was Markussen.

She'd been dreadfully confused. When she mentioned Albert's name and her inheritance, his expression changed from politeness to impatience. He was slim, with white eyebrows and a white, well-groomed moustache. His features were sharp, with a jutting nose and a firm chin, but a sunken cast to his face that bore witness to the first onslaughts of old age. His gaze grew inquisitorial. The doorman approached again, as if awaiting the signal to show her the way out.

The worst thing was that she seemed unable to stem her own nervous jabbering and take leave of her own accord, thereby preserving the last vestige of her dignity. Instead, she fumbled deeper and deeper into her story, which wasn't so much a story as a load of information that poured out helter-skelter. When you came right down to it, she had no actual business there. She just needed someone to listen.

Suddenly Markussen's expression changed. She could never afterwards describe the look that appeared on his face, though she'd often try, because she felt it contained the key to so much more than Markussen himself. A suddenly awakened curiosity? Yes, that was part of it. Darkness, pain, longing and regret? Perhaps.

At any rate, his impatience suddenly and swiftly evaporated. Bending down towards her, he looked searchingly into her eyes with an intensity that frightened her. She stopped talking. What did I say? she wondered. Why's he looking at me like that?

Then he took her by the hand. 'Come,' was all he said.

They took the lift to his office on the third floor. It was the first lift she'd ever been in. When the floor wobbled beneath her feet, her hand trembled in his.

He told a secretary to telephone to cancel the meeting he'd been en route to. He was still holding Klara's hand, as if afraid she'd vanish into thin air if he slackened his grip.

He gestured her into his office. 'I don't want to be disturbed,' he said to the secretary. He pulled a chair out for her and they sat opposite each other at a large desk of dark wood. Through the window Klara could see the statue of Niels Juel below.

'Chance is a strange force,' he said, stroking his white moustache. 'You came to me for reasons that seemed to me quite unclear, and I was close to asking you to leave. But in reality you and I have much more in common than you can imagine.'

'It was something I said,' she mumbled, and looked down.

'Very much so. But perhaps you don't realise what it was?'

She shook her head. Again she felt her inadequacy.

'I understand that you have some papers you wanted to show me. Let's get that out of the way first.'

He held out his hand. Obediently she delved into her spacious oilcloth bag and handed him the envelope containing Albert's will, together with the relevant deeds and share certificates.

For a while he sat bent over the documents, glancing up at her critically from time to time. She said nothing. Finally he gathered the papers into a pile on his desk. 'It's as I thought,' he said. 'The shipping company's just the tip of the iceberg. The actual fortune is invested in plantations in South-east Asia and factories in Shanghai. You're rich, Mrs Friis. Not quite as rich as I am. But still rich. Your assets in Asia actually constitute a kind of parallel enterprise to my own. It's not as strange as it may sound. The same person created both fortunes, you see.'

She looked at him, astounded.

'You mentioned her name yourself. I'm speaking of Cheng Sumei. I understand that she was Albert Madsen's mistress. She was mine once, too. She wasn't a woman who left her men empty-handed.'

He folded his hands on the desk. For a moment he looked lost in reverie. His gaze darkened. 'For many years I knew nothing of what became of her,' he murmured. Then he snapped out of his

407

trance and looked at Klara with new energy. 'Now tell me about your plans.'

She'd never described them completely to anyone before and as she gave an account of them, she felt unsure how they'd sound to a stranger. She felt she was breaking out of a shell of loneliness, one she'd been trapped in for months. When her flow of words finally ebbed, then ceased, he was silent for a long time.

'Have you heard of Xerxes, King of Persia?' he finally asked. 'Xerxes got it into his head to punish the sea because a sudden storm arose and destroyed his fleet before a decisive battle against the Greeks. His method was somewhat unusual. He had the sea whipped with iron chains. I'd say, Mrs Friis, that you're a modern-day successor to Xerxes.' He looked at her, but she didn't react. What he said had made no impression on her. 'I hope you understand that your plans will have fatal consequences for your little town.'

'On the contrary,' she said, mustering all her courage. 'I intend to save it.'

THAT SAME EVENING SHE DINED WITH MARKUSSEN IN A SUITE THAT he kept at his disposal in the Hotel d'Angleterre. He used it to meet with business associates and host important meetings. This evening it was reserved for the story of Cheng Sumei.

'Women,' he said, 'see themselves as conciliators. They're always diplomatic: not by nature, but by necessity. Women need to have a supple grip. Cheng Sumei did, too. But only until she'd found her real mission. Then that grip became as tough as steel.'

As he spoke, Klara understood instinctively that he was confiding something he'd never told another human being. He was like her. She, too, was unable to open her heart to anyone but a stranger.

She and Markussen needed each other.

He'd met Cheng Sumei in Shanghai. He'd been trying to break into the Chinese market, but being too inexperienced and ill-equipped to weather the losses that a beginner inevitably suffers, he was faring badly.

Cheng Sumei's background seemed unusual to him, as a Dane. But in fact it wasn't then extraordinary to meet a woman like her in a city like Shanghai. She'd been orphaned at an early age and had survived on the street by selling flowers. And flowers weren't all she sold. But that wasn't how he came across her. She'd been adopted by a benevolent Jewish businessman from Baghdad, a Mr Silas Hardoon, who would almost literally pluck urchins from the gutter and offer them a home, an upbringing and an education, teaching them English, Hebrew and Confucian ethics. He'd died relatively young and left a legacy to each of his twelve adopted children. This money had enabled Cheng Sumei to buy a share in a popular bar, the St Anna Ballroom. Markussen had first met her at a party there. Spotting the foreign guest who was clearly feeling like an outsider, she'd approached him.

Her beauty was all too apparent, but it was her intelligence that attracted him more than the perfect curves of her face. They spoke about nothing other than business. 'That's all I can talk about,' Markussen added coyly.

Klara Friis could tell it wasn't the first time he'd used this line.

He'd come to China to 'carve up the melon', the term used for foreign initiative in those days. But others had carved it up before him, and he found that Englishmen, Frenchmen, Americans and even Norwegians were in a more favourable position than Danes with no connections. He'd done quite well under the circumstances. He'd established himself on the Bund, chartered out ships for coastal sailings, built warehouses and founded a shipyard. But he hadn't made a profit from any of it yet.

'Fill your warehouses,' Cheng Sumei said.

He gave her a baffled look. What with? Yet more goods he couldn't shift?

She shook her head and laughed.

'Just do it on paper, *lao-yeh*. Fill your warehouses, but only in your account book.'

'And what if people find out that I forged them?'

'Stack your board with bigwigs from the cream of society. Then no one will know. That's the Shanghai way, *lao-yeh*.'

When that crisis was over, she suggested that he move the activities of his shipping company to Port Arthur. There, not Shanghai, was where the Russian expansionists had their headquarters.

'But there's a war coming.'

He was well informed about politics: he had to be. And he'd heard the Russian interior minister say that it was bayonets, not diplomats, that would make Russia great. The question of who had the right to plunder the defenceless giant that was China would be decided by weapons, and Markusson had no doubt as to who'd win.

'Exactly,' Cheng Sumei said. 'But there will come a time after the war that you can turn to your advantage.'

The war came, and Port Arthur was besieged. Following her advice he stayed on, rather than pull out his staff and dispose of his enterprises. Could he bear the loss if the town fell? It fell, and instead of loss he reaped an unexpected reward: Russian troops and refugees were evacuated on board his company's ships and he was paid handsomely for it. His fleet also transported war materials to the embattled Russians when the Japanese fleet blockaded Vladivostok; they needed neutral-looking ships that could be loaded and unloaded without arousing suspicion, and whose cargo would travel on to the Russian fortifications near Nikolayevsk, at the mouth of the Amur.

'Have you learned your lesson now?' Cheng Sumei asked him. The question was teasing. But as always with her, it was pointed too. 'Listen to your little sampan girlie. You succeeded in Port Arthur for the very same reason you failed in Shanghai, *lao-yeh*. You failed in Shanghai because the big powers had already carved up the melon. There was nothing left for a little Dane. An English businessman, or a French one, or an American can always support his claim with gunboats. A Dane can't. But that's why he's welcome in certain places. No one suspects he's got battleships to back up his merchant fleet. Being Danish, all you have is your supple grip and your light touch. There are plenty of places in the world where the guest who extends a weaponless hand is the most welcome. A man from a small and weak country is as good as stateless. Just wave your Danish flag. They won't see a white cross against a red background as a crusading banner; they'll just see it as a white cloth. So wrap yourself in its innocence, *lao-yeh*.'

He didn't take offence. He wasn't a patriot. His loyalty was to his ledgers, even if they were forged, and he recognised the wisdom of what she said. He used his Danish citizenship to signal his harmlessness before he struck. He acquired the supple grip and light touch of a woman.

'So why did the two of you part?' Klara asked.

The trust between them had already put them on a more familiar basis, without either of them thinking about it.

'I'll tell you one day. But not now. I've told you this story because I want you to learn something from it: not about me, but about what it's like when a woman runs a business. I've got three children, but my daughter's the only one who takes after me. My sons are complete write-offs. If I left the business to them it would sink immediately. My daughter's the one with the talent – but her sex works against her. So although she's going to be the real head of the entire company, she'll be working behind a frontman. She'll never get any recognition for her achievements. That'll be her tragedy. She'll operate through deceit, which in turn will be her strength. You must do the same thing. From now on, consider yourself a con artist.'

KLARA FRIIS RETURNED TO MARSTAL, WHERE SHE FOUND A NEW, unexpected ally.

Death.

The Spanish flu had arrived and was making a dent in our population, just as it was everywhere. Influenza was different from the sea, which took only men. This took everyone, but graciously, as they lay in their beds, and it left us graves to visit afterwards.

Pastor Abildgaard did his rounds, spoke to the bereaved and officiated at each graveside ceremony. The flu didn't scare him the way the war had. The cemetery acquired new headstones and flowers that needed watering every Sunday afternoon: the bereaved came along and mumbled to their dead, and from time to time they sobbed, but if they looked up and spotted a neighbour at the next grave, they'd soon strike up an animated discussion of the latest news. Forgetting where they were, children ran around noisily on the newly raked paths until somebody hushed them.

It was tough on the bereaved, but still, that was life. We had to bow our heads and accept it. No one lost control and raged at the heavenly powers or indeed the earthly ones. 'We'll manage. We have to,' we replied, when we met and asked one another how we did.

Though the Spanish flu struck without regard to age or sex, and made no distinction between rich and poor, it seemed to take a special fancy to the family of Farmer Sofus. Sofus Boye had died many years before, but his shipping company remained in the hands of his descendants. The year after Henckel's bankruptcy, they'd opened a new steel shipyard further north in the harbour. Every time we heard the boom of hammers knocking glowing rivets into a steel hull, the same thought went through our minds: *We can still do it*. The Boyes, a family from our own town, had created this shipyard. While all else, these past years, had proved fleeting or doomed to failure, what we created ourselves endured. Like the breakwater that shielded the harbour, we built things to last.

However, Poul Victor Boye, who was head of the shipyard, did not endure. He was a tall and dignified man with a wavy beard down to his chest. As a ship's carpenter and qualified ship's engineer, he'd been equally capable both in the office and at the slipway, where he'd always muck in if the yard was late with an order. But the flu came along with its sick breath and blew out his light.

A month later, his two sisters, Emma and Johanne, bade farewell to their husbands – both solid, sensible men who'd jointly run the Boye shipping company. They'd managed to maintain a precarious balance in their wartime account books; they'd lost men and ships, but never money, and when afterwards they felt the time had come to make the big change from sail to steam, they were ready to help launch that future.

But the flu had other plans.

For a second time and then a third, half the town accompanied a Boye coffin out onto Ommelsvej. Those who died at home rather than at sea got to have a bit of fuss made of them: in keeping with the old tradition, the funeral procession was led by girls who scattered greenery over the cobbles to prepare the deceased's path to paradise. Then came the hearse, drawn by a black horse.

Within weeks of each other, one by one, Farmer Sofus' heirs were laid to rest. The first time it didn't strike us that anything significant was happening, but by the third time we knew that we'd buried a lot more than three men.

'Well, that's the captain and the two first mates gone,' said Petersen, the stonemason, scratching his neck with the flat cap that rarely left his head. 'So it's only able seamen left now.'

We called Petersen the Collector of the Dead, because whenever anyone died, Petersen would carve a little statuette of them in wood. He was always sizing us up from beneath the brim of that cap: not in exactly the same way as the undertaker, but close enough. No sooner had a man been buried than his figurine would appear on a shelf in the Collector's workshop, which was right opposite the cemetery – convenient both for him and his customers, since the shiny stones with their crosses, doves, angels and anchors didn't have to travel far. The Collector's workshop was the cemetery in miniature – except that here you could view the dead themselves rather than their graves. The Collector never offered his carvings to the next of kin: when asked why, he'd reply that he didn't want to offend anyone. His little wooden figures always resembled their subjects, but in a crude way. In his hands, a big nose grew bigger, a bent back became more hunched, and the bow-legged seemed to carry an invisible barrel between their knees. Almost all of the deceased had had nicknames, and the Collector captured them in his likenesses. Smiling innocently, he said it was through sheer lack of skill, rather than ill will, that his figurines found themselves with slightly exaggerated peculiarities.

'Be patient with me,' he said. 'It's the best I can do.'

The Collector was busy during the influenza. By day he'd carve and polish his gravestones, while at night he'd sit with his pipe in his mouth and carve wood. More and more figures appeared on his shelf.

'Who'll sail the ship now?' he said to Captain Ludvigsen. The captain, nicknamed the Commander, had come to order a gravestone for his wife. Answering his own question, he continued. 'The women. Just you wait. Watch Klara Friis. Mark my words. The women will take over.'

Ludvigsen shook his head. 'Women don't know a bloody thing running a business.'

'I didn't say they did. All I said was that they're in charge now.'

IN THE NIGHT, WHEN HE WAS ALONE, KNUD ERIK CRIED. HE COULDN'T do it in front of his mother. After all, he was her little man. And men, both big and small, don't cry in front of women. When Albert died, Knud Erik had steeled himself for his mother's tears. He'd be the one to comfort her in her second mourning. He'd be the man at her side, whose job it was to shoulder her worries and her grief. He could do that: he'd prepared himself for it. And her red-rimmed eyes and joyless face always confirmed he was indispensable. He was the only one who understood her, the only one who listened with such attention.

He placed a hand on her arm one day as she sat staring into the distance.

'Ma, are you sad?' he asked, with the usual invitation in his voice. She could confide in her little man.

Her grief was a burden so heavy he came close to collapsing under it, and yet he couldn't lay it down. With that burden on his shoulders he was someone. Without it, he didn't know whether he'd be visible to her at all.

'No, I'm not sad,' his mother said. 'Leave me alone for a while. I'm thinking.'

He started playing with Edith. 'Where's Papa? Where's the man?' she asked.

But she wasn't really interested in the answer. She'd seen so little of Albert. Papa was just a word to her: she probably thought it was Albert's name. She was just a child.

Knud Erik himself no longer knew what he was. Just now, his mother had met his offer of consolation with a blank stare. This was new to him. Had their pact dissolved? Was he no longer her little man? If he wasn't, then what was he?

When he was very young, Knud Erik had learned that the world could disappear and reappear all by itself. A blind would be pulled down, and everything would vanish into darkness. Then a few hours later it would roll up again with a clatter, and the world would return. The bright blue canvas of the day would give way to the blackness of night, only to come back the next morning.

Loss was like the blind not rolling up again. Loss was a night that never ended.

His father had vanished in the night, but for a long time Knud Erik kept hoping that the blind he'd disappeared behind would roll back up with a clatter. He searched the horizon for a piece of string he could give a quick pull to, so the blind would roll up and his father – a man whose face had already dissolved in a mist – would reappear. He'd tried repeatedly to conjure his father's features, never certain if it was the same face as last time, until nothing was left but the word 'Pa'. He'd had one once. The certainty was like a gap in his mind, a white spot on the canvas of his memory.

Now he had to get over the loss of Albert.

He remembered him for all the good things he'd been. They'd been mates, friends, more. Albert was an entire universe that embraced him with arms strong enough to protect him from everything. And he knew that the old man had loved him, though he'd never said it aloud.

In death, Albert would help him one last time.

With his ginger hair, sinewy body and sprinkling of rust-coloured freckles, Anton was a figure so brim full of fighting spirit that far bigger boys respectfully made way for him. He kept a half-tamed seagull called Tordenskjold in a cramped bamboo cage in his parents' garden, and if you wanted to be on good terms with Anton, you popped a herring into Tordenskjold's hungry beak. He'd found the seagull as a chick at Langholms Head, where Anton rowed every spring to plunder the gulls' nests of eggs, which he sold to Tønnesen, the baker to the south. He put them in his sand cakes and his vanilla biscuits, which earned him the nickname Seagull Baker.

Anton's own nickname was the Terror of Marstal. He'd acquired it when he'd blown the porcelain insulator at the top of a lamp post to smithereens with an airgun and blacked out half the town. The gun, borrowed from a cousin, was one he normally used for shooting sparrows for a farmer in Midtmarken, who paid him four øre per bird. When the farmer tossed the dead birds onto the dunghill, Anton would simply retrieve them and resell them to his gullible client, presenting them as freshly killed – he often sold the same ones four or five times. As a result, the farmer had acquired an exaggerated impression of the size of the sparrow population plaguing his fields.

Anton was from Møllevejen, on the northern side of town; Knud Erik, who now lived in Prinsegade, belonged to the southern side. The invisible line that separated the two halves of Marstal was one that the boys took seriously, as if it were a front of the recent world war. Two factions, known as the North Gang and the South Gang, engaged in an unending and merciless war of their own. By rights Knud Erik and Anton should have been natural enemies. But while Anton was a respected member of North, Knud Erik, who kept to himself both in the school playground and on the streets to and from school, hadn't bothered to enlist.

One spring day when the wind clipped the crests of the waves beyond the breakwater, Anton sidled up to Knud Erik on his way home from school. Knowing Anton's reputation, Knud Erik braced his shoulders in anticipation of an attack: not being a thug himself, he was unaware that behaving defensively could provoke the very fight he was trying to avoid.

'It was me who found Captain Madsen,' Anton announced to him.

Knud Erik tried to make himself even smaller. Suddenly he wished the other boy would just hit him and get it over with.

'I wanted to tell you that I think he was quite something,' the older boy said. 'Dying like that with his boots on, standing up. I'd like to die like that.' Knud Erik didn't know what to say, but his tension started to dissolve. 'You knew him. He was like a grandpa to you, wasn't he?' His tone wasn't mocking.

'Yes,' Knud Erik said hesitantly. He paused, then asked 'How did he look?' He wanted to know if Albert had suffered in his final hours. If so, perhaps it had been written on his face. He was afraid the question made him look a sissy.

'He had frost in his beard and his hair. Over his whole head in fact. It looked really good,' Anton said.

Knud Erik summoned up his courage. 'What else?'

'What do you mean? He looked ordinary, I suppose. He was dead, wasn't he?'

They walked in silence for a while. The clouds gathering above their heads began to darken. They walked through Markgade and crossed Market Square. Knud Erik would soon be home and Anton might never seek him out again. He wanted to win the older boy's friendship. He racked his brains for something interesting to say. Then came sudden inspiration.

'Have you ever seen a shrunken head?' he asked.

Knud Erik no longer had an adult male in his life. But now he had Anton, who'd gained experience of the grown-up world through his countless clashes with it. Anton knew it in the same way an army spy knows the enemy's camp: with a view to capturing it.

One day after school Anton walked home to Prinsegade with Knud Erik. Under the guise of a visitor, in his secret role of observer, come to get the measure of his opponent. The maid, with her starched apron and pinned-up hair, received them. Anton looked her up and down as if he contemplated asking her out that evening, while she in turn glared at his clogs and sharply ordered him to remove them before entering the drawing room.

Anton's behaviour in front of Klara Friis was exemplary. He politely answered her questions about his parents and his school marks, though he failed to mention that he always signed his monthly report himself: indeed, his mother didn't even know such a thing existed. Klara was impressed by this model schoolboy whose friendship her son had won, and who'd clearly be an excellent mentor to him. She liked everything about Anton, in fact, except the restlessness of his eyes, which scanned the room as if registering every object it contained. And his legs kept swinging back and forth under the table. In the presence of mothers, Anton always found that the etiquette of keeping still required a monumental effort.

She asked about his plans for the future. Anton was only eleven, but in a couple of years he'd be confirmed and leave school, so it wasn't unlikely that he'd considered the matter. 'I'm going to sea.' His reply betrayed neither enthusiasm nor reluctance: just mild surprise that anyone would think to pose the question at all.

'Knud Erik isn't going to sea.' Klara said this with deliberateness, determined to distinguish her son from his friends. They should know who they had in their midst. Knud Erik was destined for other things.

Anton quickly glanced from mother to son, and then around the room. Again, it was as if he were taking an inventory. This left her with a feeling of unease.

'She's tough,' Anton said to Knud Erik, the next time they met. He sounded like a boxing coach sizing up his fighter's opponent. Seeing the defencelessness in Knud Erik's face he placed a hand on his shoulder. 'Don't worry, they're all bloody tough,' he said, by way of comfort. 'She wants you to end up in some shipbroker's office. You're to wear a starched collar and look ridiculous. No bloody way.'

'No, no bloody way.' Knud Erik hesitated as he repeated the words, trying to sound like Anton.

'There's a sure-fire way of avoiding this,' Anton advised him. 'You just need to do badly in school.'

Doing badly in school is harder than you think. Knud Erik was infinitely tempted to stick his hand up when he knew the answer. After all, he'd done his homework, and his instinct was to be a good boy.

Having always belonged in the middle stream of his class, he now deliberately sank to the bottom. This did no harm to his reputation among his friends, but he paid the price in punishment. Most of the teachers were spinsters. Some were fat and others were scrawny, but they all hit, scratched, pinched and otherwise disciplined the boys with an energy you'd never have guessed they had in them. Miss Junckersen would pull your ears; Miss Lærke would tweak the hairs at the back of your neck; Miss Reimer would slap you with the palm of her hand. Miss Katballe would put unruly children across her knees and smack their backsides, something that only Anton was sufficiently hardened not to dread. Rage would turn her face a terrifying blue-black. It was a colour we feared – along with her spluttering and her flying spittle – far more than the spanking itself. But the worst was Mr Kruse. There was no escape from him because he was a man, with a man's strength. He would dangle lazy pupils over the second-floor windowsill and threaten to let go: no one could withstand the all-consuming terror that breathed from the void below. In his lessons his every question was greeted by a forest of hands.

Knud Erik did his homework but kept his mouth shut in class. He didn't feel comfortable about it, but he trusted Anton's advice and hoped he'd get his reward in the hereafter that followed years of marking time at school.

In class Knud Erik sat next to Vilhjelm, who had a stutter. Whenever Vilhjelm tried to answer a question, the teachers lost patience with him – which in turn would make him lose patience with himself and give up before finishing his answer. Knud Erik took to whispering the right answers in his ear or writing them down on a scrap of paper. Soon he'd become a kind of ventriloquist, with Vilhjelm the dummy through which he channelled the knowledge he refused to show his teachers. Over time a friendship grew between the two of them.

Vilhjelm took home his best school report ever – and Knud Erik his worst.

His mother gave him an accusing look.

'What's happening to you at school?' she asked. In her voice he heard concern, budding panic and anger. But mostly anger. She was a different person now, and he was glad of the change. If she'd remained permanently close to tears, as before, he'd never have been able to pull this off; he'd have been too busy being her trusty little helper. Nowadays she lectured him, and he hardened himself to her just as he hardened himself to his teachers. She was a part of the regiment of women he had to endure before he was granted his freedom.

'You're a strange boy,' she said to him.

The words stung him; they felt like a rejection. For a moment he had the urge to throw himself into her arms and beg forgiveness. Part of him still desperately wanted to be reconciled with her, so he could be the big boy again, and she could be the poor little mother who needed him so badly. But she was no longer helpless, and her anger taught him to give as good as he got, and to stand firm.

Anton, meanwhile, remained guarded in his attitude to Vilhjelm. He wasn't keen to amass all the runts of the playground as his followers, and his interest in Knud Erik was mainly due to his connection with the late Captain Madsen, who in Anton's eyes grew into more and more of a hero as Knud Erik retold his tales. Anton had heard about shipwrecks and adventures in foreign ports – such yarns were daily fare in every boy's childhood – but he'd never heard of shrunken heads. Next to stories like that, what did the stuttering Vilhjelm, who could barely complete a sentence, have to offer him?

No, Vilhjelm couldn't compete with Knud Erik when it came to storytelling. But he had physical prowess. The proof of it came one winter day as they were climbing around a laid-up ship in the harbour, and Vilhjelm suddenly scrambled all the way up the rigging, going higher and higher until he reached the brightly polished acorn at the very top of the mast, twenty-five metres above the deck. Then he lay across it on his stomach and balanced there, stretching out his arms and legs as if in flight. The boys hadn't seen anything like it since the Dannebrog Circus visited the summer before. And even then no one had climbed as high as twenty-five metres.

None of the other boys dared to match Vilhjelm's feat. The bravest went as high as the acorn, then hesitated and backed down – even Anton. Some expected the Terror of Marstal to shrug and say it was nothing: if he didn't care to do it, it was because it wasn't worth doing. But Anton wasn't like that. On the contrary.

'Bloody hell, that was brave,' he said. 'Me, I just didn't have the guts when it came to it.'

He slapped Vilhjelm on the back in approval and Vilhjelm's fortune was made. He was no longer an outsider.

In fact, Vilhjelm was able to tell a story, but it took him a long time – and time was something we didn't have. Once, though, we heard him out, and he told us how he'd nearly died, and it was only luck that saved him.

It had happened on a Sunday morning, quite early. He'd gone with his father to the harbour to repair their boat. His father was a sand digger. He was also completely deaf, and it was his deafness that gave the story its excitement and set his experience apart from the usual kind of mishap that befell all of us: to explore the depths before you could swim was a rite of passage.

Vilhjelm was only three or four years old, and his father gave him instructions in his slow voice, which always made him sound like someone speaking into emptiness, concentrating on every word as if not quite sure of its meaning. 'Sit down there,' he told Vilhjelm. 'I want you to sit still, and if you need me you'll have to shake me.'

Then he turned his back and started mending a plank on the sail deck. Vilhjelm stared at the clear, calm water; he could still describe to us the impression it had made on him. The rocks on the wharf were green and slimy, and as the rays of the sun began to penetrate the water a wonderland of changing colours emerged, filled with starfish, scuttling crabs and shrimps that hung motionless, with only their antennae vibrating. Vilhjelm leaned forward, full of desire to explore further – and suddenly fell head first into the water. Most of us had done that. But none of us had a father who was deaf as a post as our only protection against drowning.

Vilhjelm bobbed to the surface like a cork, grabbed hold of the boat's rail and found a foothold on one of the slimy rocks of the wharf. Then he lost it and was left clinging there above the murky green depths until an icy undercurrent caught him and began dragging him under the boat.

His clogs had come off and he saw them floating nearby like the lifeboats of a sinking ship. His sodden clothes, so dry and comfortable a moment before, felt awkward and alien. His father was nothing but a huge, blue-clad back turned away from him. It was like the whole world giving up on him. He screamed in desperation, but his deaf father didn't hear a thing. He screamed a second time, so loudly his voice echoed around the deserted harbour.

'Help! Pa!'

Then his strength ran out. His fingers lost their grip on the rail and he disappeared into the water. He kicked it, he bit at it, he thrashed about in it as if he were fighting a wild animal, and yet it was only gentle, soft water, which pulled its duvet over his head as though it were bedtime and the water were bidding him goodnight.

And then – his father's huge arm came and dived in after him: a giant arm that could reach to the bottom of the sea if it had to, all the way down to death's door, to pull him back again. 'At the very, very, very last minute,' he said.

We knew that repetition wasn't related to his stammer. It really had been at the very, very, very last minute.

'And then he gave you a good thrashing, didn't he?' Anton asked, because that's how things were at his house.

But Vilhjelm hadn't been thrashed, not on this or any other occasion, and we didn't understand why until we met his father, who looked more like a grandfather. Vilhjelm had been an afterthought, and he behaved towards both his parents as we normally did towards our grandparents. He was kindly and devoted, and they all spoke to one another very carefully, as if the family's problem were not deafness, but rather sensitivity to any form of noise. By a strange coincidence his mother was deaf, too.

Anyone can work out that not much talking went on in this family. When his parents did speak, it was in an earnest, petitioning tone, as though they were making a humble plea. But they touched one another all the time, holding hands and stroking each other's hair and cheeks. Vilhjelm didn't just receive physical affection, he gave it to his parents too, all the time. No one ever hit anyone in Vilhjelm's family.

So Vilhjelm got something other than a good thrashing from his father the day he nearly drowned. We didn't realise what it was until Anton asked, as he always did on these occasions, 'What would you say was the worst thing about drowning?' and Vilhjelm gave a very strange answer.

Of course Anton, who knew an astonishing amount about the world outside Marstal, thought that the worst aspect of drowning would be missing out on all the adventures he imagined having later in life. He could reel off the names of the most famous red-light districts in the world. It certainly wasn't during our geography lessons in Vestergade that he'd learned about Oluf Samsons Gang in Flensburg, Schiedamsche Dijk in Rotterdam, Schipperstraat in Antwerp, Paradise Street in Liverpool, Tiger Bay in Cardiff, le Vieux Carré in New Orleans, the Barbary Coast in San Francisco or Foretop Street in Valparaiso. These were discussed in Weber's Cafe and, with the flinty expression of a connoisseur that was hardly appropriate for a boy of his age, he assured us that French girls were the best and Portuguese the worst because they were too pushy, and besides, they stank of garlic. If we asked what garlic was, he'd roll his eyes to indicate that our stupidity knew no bounds. He also knew the names of all the different kinds of booze he looked forward to tasting one day: Amer Picon, Pernod and absinthe – now *that*, he said, was something to really knock you flat. As for beer, he'd remain a loyal Hof drinker, no matter where on earth he might end up. Belgian beer, which many praised, was nothing but weak piss.

'You can list every red-light district in the world,' he concluded, 'and every brand of booze, and then you can add them all up and

424

you'll find the bottom line proves mathematically that drowning is a terrible waste.'

Knud Erik said that the worst thing about drowning was that he'd never see his mother again. He said this partly out of duty, because he felt he ought to say it, but also because he still longed for her.

Vilhjelm said the worst thing was that his parents would be sad.

'That means that you don't live for your own sake, but for your ma and pa's,' pronounced Anton. He elaborated on this theory. If you were obedient, good, polite, well behaved and dutiful, it meant that you lived for others and not for yourself.

'That's why I'm none of those things,' he said. 'Because I live for my own sake.'

When Vilhjelm had hung, soaked and wriggling, from his father's rescuing arm, he'd looked into the man's eyes and what he'd seen there was neither anger nor fear, but grief. What kind of grief it was or what had caused it he did not know, but he felt instantly that he had to make sure that his father never had reason to be sad again. He instinctively knew how to help him: by drawing as little attention to himself as possible. Being invisible would be best of all, but second best was to pass through life as inconspicuously as possible. So he'd turned into a quiet and dutiful child. Perhaps that was why he stammered: the effort of drawing attention to himself was beyond him.

Anton, on the other hand, lived for his own sake, and when Vilhjelm had balanced on the acorn at the top of the mast with his arms and legs outstretched twenty-five metres above the deck, he'd been living life the Anton way. For a moment, he'd forgotten to be invisible.

Of course, Anton had parents, too, though according to him he might as well not have. He could make his mother, Gudrun, believe almost anything. When she found out that he'd been lying about his school reports, she wept and said as soon as his pa came home he'd get a good thrashing – though she was quite big and heavy enough to dole one out herself. In the end his father just gave him a feeble slap: on the rare occasions he was home, he found that punishing his children for old, long-forgotten offences was hardly a priority. He could deliver a stinging blow, but it had to be cash on delivery, as he put it. He didn't want to mess with something stored in a bank.

'Spanking and banking! Do you get it?' his father roared, laughing idiotically.

At roughly the same time as Vilhjelm, Anton had made a discovery of equally far-reaching significance about his own father, Regnar, whose last name was Hay. Anton's last name was Hay, too, of course, but his middle name was Hansen. That was the mother's maiden name.

Regnar who had recently returned after several years' absence at sea, had just settled his son on his lap, having boxed his ears first, in compliance with his wife's demand that he punish the children for transgressions committed in his years of absence. He hadn't struck Anton very hard and didn't expect that Anton would hold it against him. Encouragingly, he asked the lad what his name was. Presumably Anton's willingness to affirm his paternity would assure him that harmony once more reigned between them. It's also possible that Regnar wanted to assure himself that he'd thrashed the right child, so that, having performed his fatherly duty, he could leave the house and head for Weber's Cafe.

'Anton Hansen Hay,' Anton said.

'What the hell did you say, boy?' his father shouted. His face grew fiery red, and he began shaking Anton, rocking him violently back and forth on the knee he'd sat him on only a moment earlier in a mood of father–son reconciliation. Then he hurled the bewildered Anton to the floor, where the boy skidded on its varnished surface until coming to a halt among the chair legs under the dining table.

'Would you believe it?' Anton said, as he told the story. 'The arsehole didn't even know his own kid's name.'

Anton had been christened while his father was away at sea, and Regnar had never troubled to look at his birth certificate or ask about the ceremony. Nor had he imagined that his wife would call the boy by her maiden name, Hansen, for he'd made no attempt to hide his loathing for her family. Anton's fat, compliant mother wasn't made for rebellion. She deferred to her husband just as she had always deferred to her own family and ended by trying to please them all; so she'd squeezed her family name between Anton's and his father's. *Anton Hansen Hay* became a three-word recipe for a family feud.

Anton himself couldn't care less. He never sided with anyone and described his father as a fool. Most of us called our fathers 'the old man'. It was a term of respect, because that's how sailors, among themselves, refer to their captain. But Anton respected no one. His nickname for his father was the Foreigner.

However, their relationship could have been worse. The Foreigner, after all, was the source of most of Anton's knowledge of the world, not because he confided in his son about his visits to brothels in foreign parts, but because he allowed him to listen in when the sailors on leave sat bragging in Weber's Cafe.

Deep down, Anton wanted to be like his father, but no one ever heard him say so, or indeed utter a single kind word about Regnar. Not since the day his father had hurled him to the floor for having the wrong middle name.

That was the day he started living for himself.

IN BOYE'S SHIPPING COMPANY ONLY THE WIDOWS REMAINED: THREE women stunned not just by grief at the sudden loss of their husbands but also by the task they'd inherited, a task as unfamiliar as it was titanic. Marstal's future lay in their hands. They alone had sufficient capital to switch the fleet to steam power, as the times demanded. The age of the sail was over; the men had known it and now it was up to them to turn their prematurely deceased husbands' vision into reality. The company owned five steamers already: the *Unity*, the *Energy*, the *Future*, the *Goal* and the *Dynamic* – names that spoke of a master plan.

In theory the widows knew what had to be done, but they didn't know how to put theory into practice. They'd turn up at the shipping office every morning and have coffee served to them while the day's documents were presented. Munching their home-baked vanilla biscuits, they brooded over freight offers, maintenance and crew costs, and proposals regarding acquisitions and sales. The whole world was clamouring for their attention, and every piece of information, every figure, every question mark felt like an insurmountable challenge.

No one ever saw them actually put their hands over their ears, but they might as well have. Every decision was discussed at such length that by the time they'd made it, it was too late. The fact that the *Unity*, the *Energy*, the *Future*, the *Goal* and the *Dynamic*, built to transport huge cargoes safely across the sea, were mostly laid up in port was due not just to unfavourable market conditions, but to the confusion of their owners.

Poul Victor's widow, Ellen, the oldest of the three, was tall and stately, just as he had been. But any willpower she might once have possessed she'd ceded to her enterprising husband, and he'd failed to return it when he went to his grave. His sisters, Emma and Johanne, were more confident. But despite being thorough matriarchs in their own homes, outside them they were at a loss. They looked to Ellen – and she looked to the cemetery. But the defaulting Poul sent her not the slightest hint.

The women owned a fair amount of land around the town, and they started selling it off. It was Klara Friis who bought it. She sat in Prinsegade and watched the three widows as a vulture watches some miserable animal about to collapse from thirst and exhaustion, and when three of the Boye lots came up for sale she took her first bite.

All three lots lay along Havnegade, the first on the corner of Sølvgade, the second at the corner of Strandstræde and the third, a large field enclosed by a fence, at the end of Havnegade, which was where the town ended, too. Farmer Sofus had once grazed sheep in the enclosure and raised hens and pigs there, ensuring a supply of live provisions for his ever growing fleet. But those days were long gone, and the field lay fallow. Everyone said Klara had been wise to buy the three lots: she could build on them.

But Klara Friis did no such thing. Stinging nettles still flourished there, and the apples and pears that grew on the trees Farmer Sofus had planted remained a target for birds and thieving boys. Marstal watched and wondered. What had Klara wanted with them, then? we asked ourselves. But we didn't ask hard enough. If we had, we'd have had an inkling of what lay in store for us.

Klara still dressed modestly, as if unaware of her change in status. This made a good impression on the three widows, who regarded thrift as a virtue. They weren't snobs and didn't look down on her, though their wealth was far more established than hers. They'd been surrounded by servants for several generations, but they still took part in the housework. They baked their own vanilla biscuits every Christmas, a generous batch that over the course of the year grew as rock-hard as the sea biscuits eaten every day on the company's ships – the only difference being that no maggots fell out of the vanilla ones if you tapped them against the table.

Farmer Sofus had been a man of the people, and his children and grandchildren were cut from the same cloth. They didn't make up a caste of their own; like everyone else, they belonged to the town. They knew that their money came from the hard toil of sailors: the boys had had to work their way up from the bottom of the ship's brutal hierarchy before reaching the broker's office or the board of the shipping company. Every word spoken in their daily meetings expressed a reality these men had personally experienced. But to their widows, who'd been brought into this new world with neither warning nor preparation, the language of shipping was a barrage of abstract terms that flew about their ears like lethal projectiles on a battlefield.

Sometimes Klara Friis would give them a piece of sound advice or display a sudden decisiveness that astonished them. Their good nature made them regard the young widow as a helpless creature who needed their charity. So they were baffled when the opposite frequently occurred: she was the one who rescued them from their difficulties. As they didn't have much faith in women's business acumen, they imagined that her good advice was pure serendipity, snatched out of thin air.

They weren't to know, of course, that Klara Friis was taking her own correspondence course in brokering, ship ownership and much more. Like the prince's kiss that breaks the witch's spell, the wealth that had come to her after Albert's death had aroused her slumbering intelligence. Before then, her mind had been imprisoned by her own humbleness, a humbleness imposed on her not only by her harrowing childhood but also by her position in adult life, which demanded that she work with her hands, not her head.

Now once more, there was a man in her life – but this one she didn't have to seduce with her already time-worn feminine charms. Unlike poor Albert, Markussen wasn't interested in kisses or cuddles, or what they might lead to. It was Cheng Sumei who bound him to her and to the task that, so late in his life, had fired his curiosity one last time: helping Xerxes find an apt way of punishing the sea.

They exchanged letters frequently and often spoke on the telephone. Every now and then Klara Friis would travel to Copenhagen. She could manage on her own now and didn't need Herman or anyone else to accompany her.

'You're not interested in taking over a shipping company on the verge of bankruptcy,' Markussen said, 'and you can soon straighten out the shipyard. Give them good advice, but not too good. They shouldn't get confident. You must make sure they keep thinking that disaster's only one wrong decision away. Tell them how dangerous the world is.' He wrote all this down on a piece of paper, so she'd remember it. Klara Friis was getting the support she needed.

But it was she who determined the course.

The three widows completely misread Klara Friis, both overestimating her character and underestimating her abilities. They thought her helpfulness was altruistic: they were wrong. They thought her often remarkably useful advice was pure luck: they were wrong there too. Deep down, they all thought they were doing her a favour by listening to her. They gave her their company and a little bit of attention – surely that was what a young woman in her situation, stricken by a dreadful loss and alone with two children, really needed?

They offered her home-baked bread to take with her.

'My dear,' Johanne would say to her, patting her cheek.

They recognised themselves in her. She was a woman – and by definition just as helpless as they were when it came to the ways of the world.

As they continued to puzzle over the mess in which their widow-hood had landed them, it finally dawned on them. They were in the jungle, and they needed what women had always needed to survive there: a man.

His name was Frederik Isaksen. He was the Danish consul in Casablanca, employed by a renowned French broker's firm. He'd started with Møller in Svendborg, then worked for Lloyds in London. A number of Boye's skippers who regularly called at Casablanca, including Captain Ludvigsen, had recommended him. 'Competent, and a man of vision', pronounced the Commander, who'd been elected spokesman by the other skippers.

'But does he do his job properly? Is he someone you can talk to?' Ellen asked.

'Not too pushy, I hope?' Johanne added anxiously, when the Commander mentioned that Isaksen had vision.

'Yes, I've heard about him,' Markussen told Klara over the tele-phone. 'I'd be happy to hire a man like him. He has drive. He wouldn't come to Marstal if he saw it as a provincial backwater. He's spotted an opportunity. Old Boye must have done better than we suspected. Capital in the bank, no debts. An enterprising man could go far with that. Isaksen could very well prove to be a spanner in your works.'

Isaksen was hired on the skippers' recommendation, and he arrived in the middle of August. Avoiding the complicated ferry and train transfers that made the journey from the capital to Marstal so onerous, he'd opted instead for a non-stop trip on the packet boat, which normally carried passengers of humbler origins. He stood on the deck, tossed the mooring line to the people on the quay with familiar ease, then waved his broad-brimmed straw hat as if he were greeting the whole town.

He was dressed in a white linen suit and wore a fresh carnation in his buttonhole, and when he raised his hat we saw that his skin was as dark and tanned as a sailor's. Or perhaps it was his natural colouring. His brown eyes were fringed by thick lashes that made him look both gentle and enigmatic.

A man of the world, we concluded as we returned his greeting. We didn't mind men of the world. That's what we were ourselves, and we had no need for any new arrival to go all meek and self-effacing just to suck up to us. He was welcome to show off a bit if he could back it up.

Isaksen could indeed back it up, and as the days went by, his popularity increased. The skipper of the packet boat, Asmus Nikolajsen, who'd chatted with him as they navigated the archipelago, reported him to be a straightforward and informed man, full of natural curiosity. Indeed, after answering all his questions, Nikolajsen reckoned the exotic-looking stranger probably knew more about packet sailing than he did himself. He clearly knew his way around a ship, and he'd very deftly lent a hand on board without once soiling his beautiful suit – something that further raised him in Nikolajsen's esteem: all sailors value cleanliness.

Of course, one big question remained. Would Isaksen know how to talk to the widows?

First he talked to us. He did a round of the harbour and sat down among the old skippers on the benches. He knocked on the doors of the brokers' firms, stepped inside, raised his hat and said immediately that he wasn't some rival come to spy on them. He'd come because he felt that this town was a community, one that could tackle the challenges of the future only if it set aside its own rivalries and grudges, pulled together and, to sum it up, dared to think big.

What he said reminded us of Albert and his speech about fellowship.

Only a few years had passed since we'd stood in front of the newly mounted memorial stone and heard those words, but it seemed a lifetime. It finally struck us: that day on the harbour in 1913 had marked the end of an era. And not a single one of us had realised.

Isaksen's words had a magic to them. He helped us see how things looked from the outside. Our shipping shares, owned by multiple members of the community, had helped us get this far, but the age of the small investor was over. The money now required was far more than a maid, a cabin boy or even a good captain could supply. Big investments demanded big money: the capital of a whole town. Marstal had that capital; it was just a question of knowing how to use it.

'My suggestion is that Marstal's capital should be in fewer hands. It's the only way that merchant shipping, and the control of it, can remain here.'

What was he hinting at? Some thought he seemed a bit too similar to the enterprising Mr Henckel, who'd promised us the world and ended up robbing us blind. But it was soon clear that Isaksen wanted something very different. He didn't want to take our money. He wanted to be our compass. He wanted to chart the course, not just for one shipping company but for the whole community.

He had only one hostile encounter and that was with Klara Friis. He'd done his homework, so he expressed no surprise at finding a youngish, modestly dressed woman at the helm of one of Marstal's most renowned shipping companies. He knew all about Albert Madsen and his alliance with the widow in Le Havre; he also knew that Denmark's last great ships, the beautiful *Suzanne*, *Germaine* and *Claudia*, were registered in Prinsegade. There was only one lesson he'd neglected when doing this homework. He hadn't looked into Klara Friis's heart, or her safe-deposit box. He had no idea of the size of her fortune, and more importantly, he knew nothing about what she planned to do with such a vast amount. She'd have welcomed him if he'd arrived like Genghis Khan, to lay waste to the entire town. Instead, he arrived like Alexander to found a city. So she received him as an enemy.

He wanted to build the new Marstal from the ruins of the sailing trade that had once made the town flourish. He was offering a renaissance, not a funeral. No swansong here: instead, a joyous salute to the future.

He touched something in us. Once before we'd seen progress arrive – sooner than most people – and we'd stood to salute it. Now he was asking us to rise and welcome it again.

Klara Friis had pondered what to wear when she received Frederik Isaksen. Finally she decided to dress in her usual modest fashion, so as not to draw attention to herself in any way. She wouldn't flaunt her wealth or her recently acquired self-confidence, or, for that matter, her femininity. She wouldn't have been able to seduce him anyway – not because she'd lost her bloom, but because she didn't have a sufficiently high opinion of her charms. She thought it safer to reprise the role she'd played so effectively for so much of her life that she, too, had believed in it: that of the poor, self-effacing woman who allowed herself no richer emotion than a barely articulated bitterness at the wicked stepmother treatment that life had given her. She wouldn't act downright dumb, but she'd let him think she was paralysed by anxiety and an inability to understand the great big world in which men moved; she'd feign the very helplessness that she encouraged in the three widows.

She responded to everything Isaksen said with a hesitant, mechanical smile and a nod contradicted by the blankness of her eyes, which clearly hinted that she hadn't understood a word of what he'd said but was merely acquiescing to it, with the timidity and submissiveness so typical of her sex.

But Isaksen didn't give up. He changed his wording, making his images simpler and more accessible. He even waxed lyrical about the sailor's uncertain existence to persuade her that his proposal actually involved a whole new style of life, one that would take the sailor's dependents into account and thereby free them from constant anxiety about his fate.

'Imagine the difference a big, well-managed shipping company could make to a sailor's job. Regular leave, safety on board, none of the poverty that currently forces smaller skippers to take risks in dangerous waters.'

He fixed her with his thick-lashed brown eyes, which she hadn't met until now. His voice grew urgent. He wasn't satisfied with the empty gaze that was her sole reaction to his words. She felt tempted to surrender but was immediately overwhelmed by a familiar terror: of darkness and flooding, of black waters rising up to reach the roof where she huddled; of Karla disappearing into the torrent; of the ridge of the roof pressing against her groin like an instrument of torture.

Cold sweat erupted on her forehead. She grew pale and had to ask him to leave, making excuses in a feeble voice about a sudden attack of migraine.

Isaksen left with a frown. He sensed that the performance he'd just witnessed was a peculiar mix of authenticity and pretence, but the point of it was beyond him. He had no reason to suspect that this woman – who reminded him of a timid servant girl – was his main opponent.

In between visits to the town's shipping companies, Isaksen worked on the three widows. He spoke of the sea and ships in a language he thought they would understand, using housekeeping as a metaphor. Shipping, too, had its shopping lists, expenses, accounts and servants. He knew these women were skilled housewives, and he tried to make them grasp that, viewed in a certain light, the shipping trade was not so very different from their own everyday experience.

It had just the effect he hoped for. The widows calmed down. They no longer felt that bullets were whizzing past their ears. Isaksen had done what they'd asked him to do: he'd released them from the war zone. The responsibility was out of their hands.

ISAKSEN CALLED A GRAND MEETING OF THE OWNERS OF THE BOYE
shipping company: its entire staff, all its skippers and first mates
who were currently ashore, and their spouses. He was smart enough
to have grasped that the wives were a force in maritime affairs as
well as in matters domestic. He booked the Marine Room at Hotel
Ærø, the grand salon hung with royal-blue Danish china plaques,
Danish flags and paintings of ships registered in Marstal, and he
planned a three-course meal. For the first course, he gave the hotel's
kitchen a recipe for bouillabaisse, which he knew most of the skippers
would be familiar with from their travels in the Mediterranean. For
the main course, he chose traditional roast beef with crispy fat. He
addressed the guests between the bouillabaisse and the roast.

It was a speech about the future.

He began by describing his years in Casablanca, the port he'd
been summoned from, and where he and so many of Marstal's skippers had become acquainted. Apparently he'd made a good impression on them, and he'd like to take this opportunity to thank them
for their support. But his heart sank, he said, whenever a Marstal
ship left Casablanca. Because he always feared it was the last time
he'd see it there. He wasn't referring to the risk that the ship might
be lost on her return voyage, although of course that was always
a tragic possibility. No, he was thinking of another, far more shocking
notion: the ship might simply vanish into thin air, never to be seen
again. However strange this might sound to the ears of his honoured
guests, this was more likely than a conventional shipwreck. They
might well be surprised to hear it, but the fact was, the ships' disappearance was as certain as the sun setting tonight and rising again
tomorrow.

By now he had his gawping audience's full attention. Not a single
one of us could imagine where he was going with this peculiar
statement.

'But listen,' he continued. 'I can explain this strange premonition of mine. What's more, I can help you make sure that it never comes true. The cause of my despondency whenever I see a Marstal schooner raise anchor in Casablanca' – and here he looked down so that his long eyelashes swept his tanned cheeks (visible all the way up the long table, this caused the bosom of more than one skipper's wife to heave and sink in a most unusual way, as if from shortness of breath) – 'The cause of my despondency' – he repeated the striking phrase – 'is' – and he suddenly assumed a most prosaic tone – 'that I happen to know the French authorities in Casablanca plan to build a new port. You'll all understand the consequences of this.'

Again he paused, but this time, instead of lowering his eyes, he looked around urgently, as if to remind us of some piece of knowledge we already possessed but had momentarily forgotten or suppressed. One or two women returned his gaze with flashing eyes, as if they'd received an invitation, and several of the skippers looked shamefacedly at the table, as if they knew only too well that they themselves should have said, or at least thought, what Isaksen was about to follow up with.

Resuming his speech, his words now came fast and sharp as whiplashes.

'It means that Marstal schooners will never again carry freight to Casablanca. The only reason that steamers have kept away from one of the most important ports in North Africa is the lack of a suitable harbour. Now the steamers will come, with their bigger cargo capacity and greater speed. You can time their arrival down to the minute. The compass plots a course, and the steamer follows it, without any deviations or delays. And I'm not just talking about Casablanca.'

Isaksen's voice, which had grown more and more forceful, now took on a doom-laden significance.

'I'm also talking about the freight to the French Channel ports, where the tide used to let in only sailing ships. The railways are taking over. I'm also talking about Rio Grande in Brazil and the Maracaibo Lagoon in Venezuela. In both those places, the shallow water over the sandbanks allowed only small vessels through. Now, with the railways, that obstacle to the steamers will be removed as well.'

At the mention of each port, the skippers and the first mates started visibly, as though he'd threatened them with his fist and they had no idea how to defend themselves.

'The sea was your America. But now America is closing her borders to you. There will be less and less demand for your services. The freight contracts will vanish into thin air. And that means that your ships will, too. You might decide to sell them. But think about it. Who's going to buy them? All that awaits them is the demolition crew. A funeral pyre to an era, *your* era, turned to woodsmoke and then thin air. But not all hope is lost . . .'

Isaksen's voice assumed a comforting tone, like the vicar who has just described hell and now offers heaven as an alternative open to anyone who sees the light.

'There are still places where nobody else sails. Harbours that can't be dredged or where dredging doesn't pay. Or where currents, rocks and frequent storms conspire to ban the steamer for ever. Newfoundland.' The comforting tone disappeared abruptly from his voice. 'The most inhospitable coast in the world, the most dangerous waters on earth. The Marstal schooner will still be able to load stinking dried cod there. You'll still be welcomed by places and cargoes nobody else will touch. You'll be reduced to living off the leftovers of the world markets. You'll be the pariahs of the seven seas, the rubbish collectors. You'll be those left behind.'

We'd thought he was going to give us encouragement. Instead, he had delivered our funeral oration. A deathly silence descended upon the table. Ellen Boye looked down. Her cheeks were burning bright red. Emma and Johanne looked to her for support, but her agonised face pained them so deeply they nearly burst into tears.

Then Isaksen started speaking again. He'd only paused for effect, but the hiatus had sounded like a full stop to us. What could possibly follow this annihilating verdict?

'Marstal has a great future,' he said, and again we raised our chins attentively, conscious now that we were nothing but puppets dangling from the strings of his artful words. 'Marstal has a great future because it has a great past. It's not always the case that one guarantees the other. Traditions can be a burden, too. If we believe a method will work for ever because it worked once, we get stuck in the past and miss out on the future. But it's different here in Marstal. You came up with your own design of ship – the hull with the heart-shaped stern and the rounded bow – and you named it after your town. You kept experimenting until you discovered what best suited your purpose. Your tradition is one of catching the wind. You may think that's an odd expression, and so it is in the mouth of a farmer, who thinks someone who blows with the wind has no roots and lacks stability because he doesn't do what his father did before him. But think of it like the sailors you are. Catching the wind: that's about seizing the moment, when the wind and the currents are on your side, and then hoisting the anchor and setting your sails. I'm sure you've heard of the Englishman Darwin and his famous theory about the survival of the fittest, and some people may have tried to make you believe that "the fittest" means "the strongest" and that Darwin is saying that only the strongest will survive. But that's not what he means. The fittest are those who catch the wind. And that's you. Your town's history reflects the way you sail: you've always known how to navigate your way through life's upheavals. That skill you can carry forward with you. But you'll have to abandon the ships whose decks you learned it on, because they're sinking. The age of sail is long gone, but the age of the sailor has just begun. Trust me, a town that's been the home of sailors for generations possesses a unique capital in a world where everything needs to be transported and the continents move ever closer to one another. The difference is that from now on, you'll put your skills to use on a deck that trembles from the vibrations of powerful engines working beneath it.'

He presented us with the same vision he'd given the town's various brokerage firms over the previous few days. But he went a step further. He confided secrets about the future of the shipping company that he'd kept from the others. He predicted that in time the Boye company would merge with all of the town's other shipping companies until only one big company remained. And this company would be rich not only in capital, but also, more importantly, in experience – centuries of accumulated experience, generated by the inventiveness, persistence, vision and will to survive that lay beneath the construction of the breakwater, the acquisition of the telegraph and the creation of one of the country's biggest merchant fleets – an experience which even now, at a time when Marstal was in a decline, inspired us to continue the fight to find new or forgotten corners of the globe where we could sail ships that should have become obsolete many years ago.

Isaksen held out his hand and counted on his fingers: inventiveness, persistence, vision, will to survive and, more than anything, the ability to unite in a common purpose to achieve what was impossible for the individual. Five fingers, one hand. The hand that blows with the wind, the hand of flexibility, the hand that seizes every opportunity that presents itself!

'It's the best kind of hand there is,' Isaksen said. 'With this hand you can shape the future to your own liking, and that's what you should be doing. The company already owns one shipyard. That's important because you need to control every link in the shipping trade chain, from the construction of the ship to the lading of the cargo. But the shipyard must switch over completely, not just to steel ships, but also to steam and motor vessels. That way we'll be able to control the price of every single ship we launch under the company's name. And here, too, the right conditions already exist. After all, the shipyard isn't short of skilled and experienced shipbuilders. It will require greater tonnage. We'll need to dredge channels so the new ships can pass through. We'll build our own Suez Canal, right across the archipelago, where it's shallow, and out into the open waters of the Baltic. We also need to move into the business of ship's provisions so we can supply not just our own ships but others too. In addition, one day we'll have to move into the fuel business. We'll own coal mines and, later, oil fields, because the motor ship will eventually replace the steamer. That way we can ensure a supply of fuel for our fleet at stable prices.'

Not only would we sail, but we'd manage half the world, and our town would be at the heart of it all. That was what Isaksen was telling us.

When he finally finished, our faces were flushed. We were exhausted, confused and reeling with the kind of giddiness you feel when you step off a merry-go-round. We rose to our feet and applauded him: brokers, office clerks, skippers, first mates and blushing wives. Even Ellen, Emma and Johanne got up to clap. This time they didn't need to glance at one another first for confirmation, as they almost always did. Their vacillation, which had been their defence against every final decision, had vanished. They rose along with the rest of us.

There was such power in Isaksen's enthusiasm that it spread through us like an inner weightlessness. If he'd spoken for much longer we'd have ended up floating out of the windows of Hotel Ærø.

ISAKSEN HAD CONSULTED THE COMPASS AND PLOTTED THE COURSE.
He'd spoken eloquently about our ability to navigate through life
even when it was at its hardest, but he'd overlooked one essential
thing about the art of steering a ship. You don't just keep your eye
on the compass: you also check the rigging, you read the clouds,
you observe the direction of the wind, the colour of the current and
the sea, and you look out for the sudden surf that warns of a rock
ahead. It may not be like that on board a steamer. But that's how
it is on a sailing ship, and in this respect its journey parallels that
of life: simply knowing where you want to go isn't enough, because
life is a wind-blown voyage, consisting mainly of the detours imposed
by alternating calm and storm.

We can debate till the cows come home whether Klara Friis caused
Isaksen to fail or whether it was the vanilla biscuits. His knowledge
of the female sex was certainly incomplete. He'd imagined that a
woman paralysed by anxiety needs to be rescued by a man bursting
with the urge to take action. That was how he saw the three widows,
the shipping company and in fact the whole town: we were the bride
and he was the groom. He would release us from our state of paralysis. But sometimes a whirlwind of energy can do just the opposite;
it can just whip up female anxiety.

When their husbands met with unexpected and pointless deaths
within three weeks of one another, the sailor's wife in each of them
left, along with what little courage and endurance she possessed, out
of the front door. And in through the back door came a woman
who, no matter how long ago her family abandoned the soil, was a
farmer's wife to the core. This woman was suspicious, brooding,
gloomy, passive and obstinate, and she clung tenaciously to her
ordained place in life.

*   *   *

Isaksen understood nothing of this. He believed he'd got the widows on his side. After all, hadn't they stood there cheering his speech, along with the entire staff of the shipping company? Of course, he'd heard of their indecisiveness even before he came. The skippers he'd been negotiating with in Casablanca had made no secret of the fact that the women were 'difficult' and 'tricky to deal with', but they'd concluded unanimously that 'all they needed was a firm hand' – and that he was the man to wield it.

Though Isaksen had previously regarded the women as the least of his problems, they were now proving themselves the greatest. They sat there with their coffee and their stale vanilla biscuits, dipping and munching endlessly, testing the hardness of the biscuits with their front teeth just like beavers. And that was what they were: a family of beavers, building dams around the flow of his ideas and blocking him from getting anywhere.

Out of sheer frustration he turned up for one meeting with a bag of fresh biscuits from Tønnesen, the baker in Kirkestræde. But this gesture had precisely the wrong effect. Emma and Johanne exchanged looks. So he was spurning their home-baked biscuits. That made him wasteful. And then to bring biscuits from the Seagull Baker! Did he really think they didn't know that Tønnesen bought seagull eggs from the boys in the town, who collected them on the little islands outside the harbour? What did he take them for!

The biscuits were a diplomatic disaster. Soon Isaksen noticed other signs of discontent.

'It's too risky,' Ellen Boye said, when he suggested building a new steamship at the steel shipyard.

He explained that the freight market was recovering and the investment would quickly pay for itself.

'Isn't that terribly uncertain?' Emma repeated, after a long pause, during which they all resumed munching. He could hear that it wasn't a question, but a no. In response he took a firm tone and said that if they wanted a reward for the trust they'd shown by hiring him, then they'd need to allow him free rein.

'But you do have free rein,' Ellen said authoritatively. 'Only the times are so uncertain.'

'I need power of attorney.'

Power of attorney? The three women looked at each other, not following. Again they were on shaky ground. Did he not trust them? 'Klara Friis says that –'

'Klara Friis?' Isaksen woke from the lethargy that often overpowered him these days in the company of the three widows. He'd suddenly spotted a connection.

'What does Klara Friis say?'

It wasn't clear precisely what Klara Friis had said, but she'd said something and it had left an impression: that much was evident. Words like *uncertain* and *risky* were much in her vocabulary. Words like that fed the farmer's wife in the widows, nurtured their suspicions and strengthened their simple philosophy: in this life you know what you have, but you don't know what you might get, and so it's better to stick with what you have.

'But that philosophy doesn't hold here,' he said in desperation. 'If you stick to what you have, you'll lose that too. Such are the times. Only by risking the unknown do you have a chance of achieving anything at all.'

'I don't understand,' said Ellen, the tall one, in a wounded tone. 'We haven't said anything about philosophy!'

He realised that he'd been thinking aloud, and that for a moment he had actually let them hear the inner dialogue he constantly had with them, trying to persuade them to let him get on with the job they'd hired him to do.

He stood up and made his excuses: he suddenly felt unwell. He needed fresh air. He knew they'd be staring after him as he left, and that the moment he was out the door they'd begin a discussion far livelier than any they'd ever let him be party to.

He went down Havnegade, turned on to Prinsegade and knocked on Klara Friis's door. A maid in a starched apron showed him into the drawing room. Klara Friis rose from her sofa, and he saw more than surprise in her eyes. He saw fear, as if he'd caught her redhanded being someone other than the person she'd pretended to be.

'What do you want?' she exclaimed involuntarily.

He watched her struggling to assume the vacant expression she'd worn the last time he visited her. But her face signalled vigilance and her eyes stayed alert, confirming his suspicions. So he came straight to the point.

'I want to know why you are working against me,' he said.

'I don't understand your motives. Do you think of us as rivals? As a shipowner you surely ought to have the town's best interests at heart.'

He spoke to her as to an equal and hoped this would make an impression and convince her to abandon her mysterious games.

'You talk like a mayor,' she said. 'But we've already got one of those.'

She gave him a defiant look. Her mask had fallen. Well, that's something, he thought. Now I don't have to put up with the usual feminine subterfuge. Now she can't get her own way simply by pretending not to understand mine.

Aloud he said, 'A mayor doesn't have much power. But I would, if you'd just allow me to get on with my work. And you would, too. I understand that you inherited a shipping company of your own and that you're managing it quite expertly.'

'I'm just minding my own business,' she said. 'You ought to do the same.'

Ah, there it is, the thought rushed through him. We're back where we started. If you won't fight openly, then obstinacy's your last defence.

'That's what I'm trying to do,' he retorted. 'But every time I try to get the widows to approve one of my proposals, I hear the same things. Times are too uncertain. It's too great a risk. Some say it would be wise to wait. And the same name keeps cropping up. Yours.'

He could feel himself growing angry. He thought about the plots of land that she'd bought along Havnegade, sitting unused. A vibrant harbour front could have been built there, buzzing with enterprise. Instead, the plots looked like a wasteland of ideas, destroyed before they'd had a chance to flourish.

'Every day I walk past the plots that you've bought, lying vacant. Shamefully so. Perhaps they reflect all too aptly what you have in mind: laying the whole town to waste. But let me tell you this, Mrs Friis.' His voice betrayed months of frustration. 'What you call minding your own business, I call neglecting the business of others. We're talking about a whole town. Its history and traditions.'

'I hate the sea,' she burst out.

If he'd been listening properly, he'd have understood she'd given him a vital clue and seized his chance. But anger had got the better of him: he now had no doubt that at last he'd come face to face with the cause of all his problems and the increasingly inevitable failure of his plans for Marstal. It would be the first failure of his career. And, he hoped, the last.

'What a strange thing to say,' he snapped at her. 'It's like hearing a farmer say he hates the soil. In that case I can only tell you that you're in the wrong place at the wrong time.'

'No, on the contrary. I'm in the right place at the right time.'

She was now just as angry as he was. But he heard something more than indignation in her voice: he heard his own wasted opportunity. He heard the bitterness of someone who feels rejected. He'd failed to listen properly.

'If I've accused you unfairly, I regret it,' he said, trying belatedly to rectify his mistake by striking a conciliatory tone. 'Please, can we try talking sensibly to each other? I think we have a great deal in common.'

'I must ask you to leave,' she said firmly.

He nodded briefly to her, turned and left the room. It wasn't until he was back on the street that he realised that she'd never even asked him to sit down. During the entire confrontation they'd been standing up, facing each other. She had a shocking lack of manners, he decided.

Isaksen went back to the widows a second time to request power of attorney, so he could finally carry out his plans for both company and shipyard.

'I must advise you that my demand for power of attorney is an ultimatum.'

They asked him what an ultimatum was. Relations between them were becoming so strained that he'd abandoned his much admired powers of persuasion and was increasingly resorting to the cold formalities of legal language. He explained that an ultimatum meant that if he did not get what he wanted, he would have to hand in his resignation and look for a post elsewhere.

'But good heavens! Aren't you happy here?'

He replied that yes, thank you, he was happy here, but no, he was at the same time most unhappy. He cared about the town. He could see that the shipping company possessed considerable and promising potential, but his work was being sabotaged on a daily basis. As he spoke, his anger resurfaced. 'I understand that you prefer to take the advice of Klara Friis. But I'm warning you. She does not want what is best for the company.'

Ellen shot him an outraged look, and he knew then that he was defeated.

'Klara Friis, that poor girl. If you only knew what she's been through. How dare you talk about her like that!'

The verdict had been pronounced. It was written all over their faces. He was a bad man. All right, he'd done his duty. Now he could leave. But actually, he'd failed to do his duty, and that was precisely what stung him. He'd spotted an opportunity and he hadn't been allowed to develop it. This was a challenge to his most deeply held values: he'd not carried out his task to the best of his abilities. He'd failed. He'd failed the shipping company, the town and himself. His persuasive skills had been inadequate. His psychological insight had been found wanting. He, the only one among them who knew which course to follow, had been prevented from taking the wheel and steering the ship, and he had no one to blame but himself. He wasn't the type to need scapegoats, though the town had offered him several.

The following day he submitted his resignation.

When Isaksen left town, he took the ferry, like any other traveller.

He didn't fit in – that was the general verdict.

But not all of us agreed. There were those who realised that the prophecy of doom he'd made in his appointment speech during the gala dinner at Hotel Ærø would now be fulfilled. The only person who could have prevented it was the one who'd made it – and he was leaving. It wasn't only Frederik Isaksen's back that was turned on us when he boarded the ferry. It was the world's.

He left on an autumn day of pouring rain. He was clutching an umbrella, but there was a fierce wind blowing from the west and the shoulders of his cotton raincoat had already darkened. A deputation of skippers and first mates had assembled on the quay to see him off. They'd all been there that night at Hotel Ærø when he gave his grand speech.

Their spokesman, Captain Ludvigsen, stepped forward. He'd been Isaksen's keenest supporter. Personally, he'd never have dreamed of setting foot on a steamship. But he regarded himself as a man of vision.

'A damn shame that it had to end like this,' the Commander said.

'Don't feel sorry for me,' Isaksen said with an encouraging smile, as though the Commander was the one who needed consoling. 'It was my own fault that it turned out like this. I should have been a better listener.'

The Commander wasn't sure he understood what Isaksen meant. 'Damn women' was all he said.

'You mustn't blame them,' Isaksen said. 'It's an unusual position for women to be in. They're just doing what they think best.'

The ferry gave a warning hoot. It was time to go.

'Where are you off to?' the Commander asked. He'd prepared a short speech, but he'd forgotten the words.

'New York. Møller's opening a new office. Drop by if you're ever in town. There'll always be work for a man from Marstal.'

Isaksen shook the Commander's hand. Then he went round and said goodbye to each of them individually. The ferry gave a last warning blast. He raised his umbrella, lifted his hat and disappeared up the gangway.

Now there was no longer anyone around to prevent us from becoming what Isaksen had predicted we would become: those left behind.

The Seagull Killer

'WHERE DID ALBERT BURY JAMES COOK?'

Anton was making big plans. He'd become the leader of North, but that wasn't enough for him. As far back as he could remember there'd been just the two gangs, North and South, and they'd divided the town between them. But now boys from Niels Juelsgade and Tordenskjoldsgade had started forming their own gangs. These had yet to split from South, but Kristian Stærk in Lærkestræde had already made the break. His surname, which means 'strong', had proved apt, and he named the gang after himself: The Strong Gang.

This trend worried Anton. He liked being at the forefront of everything, and now he feared being 'left astern', as he put it. He talked Knud Erik into stealing Albert's sea boots, which were waiting in the attic in Prinsegade until someone built the museum to which Albert had bequeathed them. Anton had the idea to form a new gang that would be named after Albert, and it would accept only those of us who were willing to swear that they were prepared to die, like Albert, with their boots on. Anton laid claim to the first trying on of the historic, rather battered Madsen footwear, but the boots were far too big for him. Still, he planned to don them whenever a new gang member swore his oath of allegiance, before ordering the initiate to kneel down and kiss each boot on the toe.

Knud Erik and Vilhjelm protested that he'd never get a real bloke to do that, and if the gang was to be worth joining, he'd need proper blokes in it. Personally, they'd both refuse. They surprised even themselves by this sudden defiance. Finally Anton gave in, and together they agreed that instead of the boot-kissing, new gang members would just wear them for the swearing-in. It was more dignified; even Anton could see that. The shrunken head of James Cook would be the group's mascot. Knowledge of its secret existence would cement them all as a gang.

449

There was just the one problem: James Cook's head lay at the bottom of the sea.

Helmer, who lived in Skovsgaden and belonged to North, got permission to borrow his grandfather's smack. Seven boys piled on board, but only Vilhjelm and Knud Erik knew what the mission was. Anton told the rest of us we were sailing to the part of the sea called Mørkedybet to go treasure hunting. He described the wooden casket but didn't say what it contained – only that it wasn't a sight for the faint-hearted.

Tordenskjold sat on the thwart next to him, surveying us with his beady, inscrutable eyes. From time to time the bird would take off, soar into the blue sky and dive into the water without warning. Returning to the boat, he'd settle on the thwart again and fling back his head, his sharp beak tilted skywards. We'd see his throat flex beneath the feathers, oblivious to our presence, as he swallowed the fish he'd caught.

'Well done, Tordenskjold,' Anton would say. He always addressed the gull as if it were a dog.

'Does the treasure have something to do with the English?' Olav asked. He was a big, burly boy whose hair hung low over his brow.

'In a way,' Anton said. 'That's all I'm going to tell you.'

Knud Erik and Vilhjelm exchanged a look.

We started diving in the Mørkedybet. It was a cloudless day in the first week of June. There were no waves, so you could see far down into the water, though not as far as the seabed, which lay hidden beneath an undulating canopy of green and dark blue. One after another we plunged off the side, but the deeper we dived the harder it became to see anything: the bottom was an impenetrable shadow. It was creepy to feel the seaweed caressing your stomach; it was as if the water had grown long, soft fingers and was tentatively reaching for you. A swaying colony of jellyfish kept us company, and at one point a plaice suddenly flipped out from its camouflage in the sand. But there was no sign of any treasure. We rowed from one place to another and kept diving, while our limbs got colder and colder. Anton held out longer than any of us, but every time he broke through the mirror of the water his lips trembled.

Tordenskjold took off and floated high in the blue sky, as if keeping an eye on us.

It was a hopeless enterprise, and soon it was hard to believe we'd ever imagined finding the head of James Cook at the bottom of the sea. We began to lose our enthusiasm along with our breath and our body heat. The sun was shining, but the sea was still tinged with the chill of winter.

The only one who wasn't shivering with cold was Helmer. He sat warm and dry on the stern thwart, picking at the places where his sunburned skin had started to peel and staring sceptically at the water. 'Well, the boat's mine,' he said. In his opinion, that was contribution enough.

'Chicken!' we yelled at him.

This offended his manly pride, and he swung himself out on the forestay. But when he realised how cold the water was, he forgot all about saving his honour. He grabbed hold of the stay and tried to scramble back into the empty boat, which promptly keeled over.

No one panicked and no one tried to climb on to the capsized vessel. It was too heavy to turn over, so we started pushing and dragging it towards Birkholm, where we'd be able to right it and bale it out in the shallow waters.

Knud Erik and Vilhjelm stayed behind to fish out everyone's clothes: shirts, jumpers and trousers that floated on the water like a blanket of algae. They hung some things up to dry on the perches that marked the channel; other items they brought ashore. Only Anton kept diving, determined to find Cook's head. It wasn't until the rest of us were lying naked on the sand on Birkholm, trying to warm up, that we saw him heading in towards the beach. He was swimming on his back and clasping something in one arm, as if he were rescuing a drowning man.

'He's found the treasure! He's found the treasure!' Helmer yelled.

Knud Erik and Vilhjelm looked at each other. Could he really have found the head of James Cook?

Anton staggered up onto the beach. His face was pale blue, and his teeth wouldn't stop chattering, so that for the first few minutes he was incapable of saying anything. He squatted down, breathing in a deep and gurgling way as if he'd swallowed a lot of water, hugging the treasure all the while. He exchanged a quick glance with Knud Erik and shook his head. Then he got up and stretched out his arms triumphantly. His torso was still shivering with cold, but his face was lit up by a grin.

'Look what I've found!' he shouted.

We all stared at the object he was holding in his hands. At first we couldn't make out what it was. Then Helmer gasped.

'It's a dead man!'

The others could see it now, too. Anton was holding a skull, green from long years in the water and covered with seaweed, which hung from the cranium like a drowned man's hair. The lower jaw was missing. Where the eyes used to be two gaping holes stared at them with the inscrutable glare of the dead. The bared teeth in the upper jaw grinned in malicious triumph, as though the head anticipated the fate that awaited us when we too became sad human remains.

'No,' Anton said. 'This isn't a dead man. It's much better. It's a man who was murdered.' He lowered his arms and held out the skull to us. 'See for yourself.'

We formed a circle around him. He turned the skull of the murdered man so we could view it from all angles. At the back of it we saw a big hole.

'It's a Stone Age man,' Knud Erik said. 'Someone whacked him with an axe.'

'No, this is no Stone Age man,' Anton declared. He looked around at all of us in turn, pausing between each of us to heighten the suspense. 'I know who it is.'

'Who is it?' we asked at once.

'I'm not going to tell you right now. But this was the treasure I asked you to find.'

Knud Erik and Vilhjelm were well aware that Anton was lying. We hadn't found the head of James Cook. But we'd found something, and Anton always knew how to turn the unexpected to his advantage. 'I want you to place your hand on the head of this murdered man,' he said, 'and swear not to breathe a word to anyone. Or I'll never tell you who it is.'

We all placed our hands on the skull. The slimy weed that sprouted on it was disgusting to the touch, and we shuddered. 'Swear,' Anton commanded. And we swore in unison that we'd never reveal the secret.

'Now tell us who it is.'

'Later,' Anton said, and made a calming gesture, as if asking us not to get too excited.

We rowed out to the perches and retrieved the rest of our clothes.

452

The sun and the wind had dried them, but none of us had remembered to gather up the clogs. We supposed that after Helmer capsized the boat the current had taken them.

Vilhjelm couldn't find his trousers either, and his embarrassment worsened his stammer.

'Give him yours,' Anton said to Knud Erik. 'That'll make your mother really cross.' This remained Anton's recipe for freedom: annoy your ma and pa as much as you possibly can.

People stared at the bunch of barefoot, trouserless boys walking home through the streets. We were clearly in for a thrashing.

But we didn't care.

Nothing could touch us the day we found the murdered man's skull. We had a secret. And a secret meant power.

A COUPLE OF DAYS LATER ANTON WENT TO SEE KRISTIAN STÆRK TO suggest they join forces to form a new gang which, he reckoned, would be the mightiest in town. Though 'the strongest' was the phrase he chose, quite deliberately, to flatter Strong's leader. He'd taken Knud Erik and Vilhjelm with him as deputies. Their most important task was to bear the wooden casket containing the murdered man's skull, which Anton considered to be vital leverage in the delicate negotiations ahead.

With Kristian Stærk, Anton's biggest disadvantage was his age and his height. Kristian was fifteen and much bigger than Anton. He had broad shoulders and a thick neck with a remarkably small head perched on top. The prominence of his ears once prompted Anton to remark that his head had 'unfolded its wings because it was planning to fly off and find a body that fitted better'. But no one came out with statements like that when Kristian Stærk was within earshot, because he loved nothing more than dealing out horse bites and Chinese burns, gripping the skin of your wrist between his clammy hands and twisting.

He was an apprentice at an ironmonger's, Samuelsen's in Kongegade, and no one understood why he still bothered running around with a gang of boys and getting into fights. The adults didn't think much of Kristian Stærk, but all the children were scared of him. Maybe that's why he carried on behaving like them. He preferred company that guaranteed his position as the biggest and the strongest.

In Anton's case, it was all the opposite. The adults were no fonder of him than they were of Kristian; the mothers, especially, looked askance at the boy who'd blacked out half of Marstal with a single shot. But we town boys idolised him. Anton never minded whether people were bigger or smaller than him because he was always more ingenious, and that was enough.

Kristian Stærk received him more favourably than he'd expected; his reputation preceded him. But Anton was well aware that his strongest card in their forthcoming talks was the contents of the wooden casket borne by his two deputies, Knud Erik and Vilhjelm. He was adamant that the name of the gang should be the Albert Gang, and he'd extended his plans for the initiation ritual: now, potential gang members would not only wear Albert's boots to pledge allegiance but also place a hand on the head of the murdered man. He'd scrubbed off the seaweed and polished the skull, hole and all, till it shone. Anton had decided that the name of its owner should remain a secret to all but the two leaders of the gang: Kristian Stærk and himself.

He asked Knud Erik to lift the lid of the casket, then solemnly took out the skull and handed it to Kristian Stærk. As he took it in his hands his protruding ears rocked back and forth: we could tell he was frightened of it, but we could also see the cunning boy's brain, trapped in its adult body, racing at full tilt. The head appealed irresistibly to his imagination and he knew instinctively that it would have the same effect on his peers. Whoever owned the head would have the biggest and strongest gang. He nodded wordlessly, signalling that he agreed to Anton's terms.

'And we're not talking about some Stone Age man clobbered with an axe here,' Anton said. He made Kristian squat down so their heads were level and whispered the name of the murder victim in his ear. Then they looked each other in the eye to seal their pact.

The first task awaiting the newly formed gang was to procure weapons and equipment for the new recruits. The Margarine Man, who sold butter and margarine from his horse-drawn cart, gave us lids from his empty barrels. We attached straps to them and they became our shields. Kristian Stærk proved himself especially useful by procuring bamboo canes from the ironmonger's, which we turned into bows. We used garden stakes as arrows, but they weren't really much use, though they could give you a bruise if you got hit on the forehead with the blunt end. We tried sharpening one with a knife, but the wood wasn't hard enough. It was Anton who thought of tying sail needles to them. They not only hurt more but pierced the skin, too: after a battle some of us looked like hedgehogs, especially in the summer, when we had less clothing to protect us, and the needles went straight into bare skin. This was the life. Our games were becoming dangerous, and danger was what we wanted. We had a name to honour and the skull of a murdered man as a mascot. Only the actual threat of death made fighting worthwhile.

We had certain rules. All members had to be more than ten years old. Knud Erik and Vilhjelm, who'd only just turned ten, were exceptions; other boys their age weren't admitted. The initiation test wasn't for the weak of spirit. You had to jump into the harbour clutching a big stone, sink to the bottom, walk under the keel of a ship and surface on the other side. If you dropped the stone while you were down there, you could wave goodbye to membership of the Albert Gang. Few adults would have been able to pass, but instead of scaring off applicants, the test attracted us in huge numbers. We all longed to prove our abilities, and we staggered around in the bottle-green darkness with bursting cheeks and bulging eyes from oxygen deprivation while the keel of a ship, alive with undulating seaweed, mussels and barnacles loomed above us like the overgrown abdomen of a sperm whale. We surfaced like bubbles popping from a bed of mud. As soon as we'd filled our lungs with air, we'd erupt in a yell of triumph while struggling not to sink again with the stone, which lost its weightlessness the moment we raised it above water.

Did we ever think that we'd just been down in the place where so many of our fathers had ended up? We swore that we'd die with our boots on. But then, you do that, too, when you drown.

We collected members from every street in town, including the half that had always been South's turf. But the test also meant saying goodbye to some of the old members of North. The most important thing was passing the test; it overrode where you were from. South had a hard core that refused to surrender, but this suited us just fine: we needed someone to fight. We gave them a hard time, and usually, they got thrashed. Sometimes we'd fight on rafts in the harbour or stage sea battles in stolen boats. But most of the time we met in a field in Vestergade where the adults never went. We didn't want to be disturbed while we inflicted cuts and bruises, black eyes and battered skulls on one another.

* * *

Until the terrible thing happened to Kristian Stærk, the leader of South, Henry Levinsen, was the only one of us to receive a permanent injury. He'd been wearing a copper flowerpot holder as a helmet, and Kristian Stærk gave it a whack with a stake from a fish trap, ramming it right down over his ears and breaking his nose on the way. Groth, the plumber in Vestergade, had to cut the pot free, and Henry's nose was crooked from that day on.

The adults called us piccaninnies. This meant 'children' in a language that wasn't English, German or French, but one they used in a faraway place. And that's just how the word made us feel: as foreign as savage natives from an undiscovered island.

If we'd ever bothered to count the members of our gang who were fatherless, we'd have realised just how many of us had at some point started blubbing in the street or the playground, suddenly remembering the father we'd lost when a ship went down. Whether in peacetime or in war, it was always the same: death by drowning and no funeral afterwards.

But we didn't bother ourselves with thoughts like that, even though there was undoubtedly a reason why some of us punched harder than others when we got into fights and why we didn't care how much it hurt when we got punched back. We clobbered each other the way a blacksmith clobbers red-hot iron. We did it to forge ourselves into some kind of shape.

Anton claimed that the murdered man appeared below his gable window every night and called out to him in a hollow voice that he wanted his head back. We didn't believe it though. How can you shout from the garden when your head's up in the attic?

Hadn't we noticed that his lower jaw was missing? Anton asked us. That was where the voice came from. He showed us the footprints in the potato bed at the end of the garden.

We reckoned he'd made them himself.

Anton sighed and said that being disbelieved by those nearest to him, even though he possessed great and burdensome knowledge, was a cross he'd have to bear. Not only did he know the identity of the murdered man: he knew the murderer too. He gave us a look that sent shivers down our spines. We didn't believe everything he said, but he had the power to unsettle us all the same.

We didn't know it at the time, but a night would come when a man in the garden really would call out for Anton. It wouldn't be the dead man wanting his head back, though.

It would be the murderer. Sent by Kristian Stærk.

IT ALL STARTED WHEN ANTON FOUND HE HAD LESS SPENDING MONEY than usual and had to cut down on his daily quota of Woodbines. Smoking them gave him a manly voice that made him sound much older. He said that the lack of money stemmed from a problem with Shooter, as he called his cousin's airgun. He'd been taking out fewer local sparrows than usual. He dismissed as pure nonsense the theory that he'd finally eliminated the population. Shooter was to blame.

As a result he decided to put the weapon to a conclusive test by bringing down a really big bird. Marstal's biggest, in fact. In our opinion this decision showed his true stature, but at the same time it worried us; indeed, it made us feel uneasy. Everyone in town was fond of this bird; it even had its own name. Of course, so did the many macaws, cockatoos, nymph parakeets, mynah birds and canaries that sailors had brought back to Marstal over the years. But those birds sat in cages begging for sugar lumps – and even Anton's Tordenskjold was half tame. This was different. This bird, whose life Anton planned to end, was a free and noble creature that flew just as far, every year, as the men of Marstal sailed. We were honoured that it had chosen to nest in our town. It was a stork, and it lived on the roof of Goldstein's house. We called it Frede.

Goldstein's roof was a strange place for a stork to pick for its nest. Storks like being high up, but Goldstein's house, which lay at the end of Markgade, was a low half-timbered building, painted yellow, with a red-tiled roof that looked set to skid right off the sunken walls. Abraham Goldstein was a white-bearded, mild-mannered shoemaker, who never looked at you. There was a reason for that: some said he could give you the evil eye. Any skipper who passed the shoemaker on the way to his waiting ship postponed his voyage until the next day. What's more, Goldstein had been sighted standing in Market Square early one spring morning, hypnotising sparrows. They'd flown onto his outstretched hands and hopped all the way up his arms and along his sloping shoulders, even settling on his hat. Others said this was all nonsense and that Goldstein was a completely ordinary man who should only be judged on his ability to resole a pair of boots. As far as that went, no one had any complaints.

We went over to Goldstein's house on a Sunday afternoon in July. The heat had driven everyone to the beach, so Anton could shoot the stork without worrying about witnesses. The whole thing felt infinitely sad. And yet we had to watch. We were sure we'd shut our eyes the moment the stork flapped its black-and-white wings for the last time and tumbled out of its big nest of twigs, its red legs in the air. We had a vague sense that great men and pointless sad events went together, and we saw the whole business in that light. Convinced that Anton was destined for greatness, we wanted to be there when it happened.

Anton raised the gun and narrowed one eye. He stood like that for a long time, as if unsure of his aim, and we thought we saw his hand shaking slightly. Looking at the stork, we understood. It felt as though we were bidding it farewell, and Anton surely felt the same. Then he pulled the trigger.

We all shut our eyes tight, as if on command, and kept them shut as the shot rang out. It seemed loud enough to carry all the way to the Tail. Absolute silence followed. Then Anton cursed. We opened our eyes and looked up at the ridge of the roof. The stork was still standing there motionless on its pile of twigs, as if it had fallen asleep.

Was that how storks behaved when they were shot? The bullet should have reduced the noble bird to a pathetic heap of feathers and long red legs; instead, it stood as upright as if it had been stuffed.

It took several minutes to figure out why. Anton had missed.

Furiously, he reloaded the airgun and fired again and again, until he had no pellets left. The stork didn't so much as twitch. It seemed deaf. But whether or not it could hear, one thing was sure. Despite Anton's cannonade with the airgun, Frede remained completely unharmed.

Suddenly the door to Goldstein's house flew open and a man appeared: not the little old shoemaker, but a giant who had to bend to exit the tiny door. Beneath his blue overalls his tanned torso was bare; we could see his massive biceps and the blue and red tattoos that snaked around his muscles. It was Goldstein's son-in-law, Bjørn

Karlsen, who worked as a rigger at the steel shipyard. He'd been enjoying his afternoon nap until Anton's shooting woke him.

'What the hell do you think you're doing, boy?' he shouted, threatening Anton and the rest of us with his clenched fist. 'Have you been shooting at the stork?'

But Anton seemed not to hear. He was staring at the gun in his hand with a look of intense hatred – a look we fervently hoped he'd never direct at one of us. We wanted to scarper, but we didn't feel we could desert him, so we just backed off a few steps. Which left Anton alone on the pavement when Bjørn Karlsen crossed the street with a couple of giant bounds and grabbed him by the neck. He lifted him up by the shirt collar so that his feet dangled in the air, as if he were nothing but a little kid. And perhaps, to a furious six-foot-five rigger, that's all he was. To us Anton was anything but that. Yet now we began to realise that there were several ways to see Anton. Bjørn Karlsen dragged Anton down Markgade, bawling him out.

'Is this gun yours?' he demanded, and Anton replied that it was. He couldn't be bothered to explain that it was really his cousin's: it was irrelevant now anyway.

'Let me show you what happens to the likes of you,' the rigger said.

He crossed the Market Square still holding Anton firmly. We followed at a safe distance. We couldn't understand why he didn't say anything. No one ever impressed him, and we'd never met an adult the fast-talking Anton couldn't get the better of. Now he seemed indifferent to everything. As for us, a strange, passive curiosity kept our mouths shut. We could have yelled words of encouragement or hurled abuse at Bjørn Karlsen, but we said nothing.

Bjørn Karlsen continued down Prinsegade and along Havnegade and all the way out onto Dampskibsbroen. We met no one on the way. The town was deserted, like a stage waiting for an important and sad event. Perhaps this would be the day we'd witness the fall of Anton.

The rigger stopped at the very edge of the quay.

'Here's all that this bloody gun's good for,' he said.

Grabbing Shooter from Anton he slammed it hard against the quayside, splintering the wooden handle. Anton said nothing; he just continued to stare into the distance. Then Bjørn Karlsen hurled the broken gun out into the water of the harbour, and with a small splash it disappeared below the surface. Karlsen was still holding Anton by his collar; now he grabbed hold of his trousers too, and with a forceful swing he sent Anton hurtling the same way as Shooter.

When Anton climbed back onto the quay, he pretended nothing had happened, even though he was soaking wet. He looked at us through narrowed eyes.

'Good riddance to that shitty gun,' he said.

There was something he wanted to prove, perhaps to us, but mainly to himself. It had to do with the accuracy of his shot. None of us could fathom how Anton, who'd always been capable of hitting a sparrow from a great distance or a hare running in panic, could miss a stationary stork. So the problem had to be Shooter.

As long as it was Shooter that had missed, and not Anton, his honour was intact. We could follow this line of thought, but we could see no further.

Next, Anton came up with the idea of shooting an apple off someone's head. He'd do it with a bow and arrow, like William Tell. Obviously, it would have to be done on a windless day. An arrow wouldn't let him down. Bows and arrows were ancient weapons and their accuracy depended on the skill of the archer and not, as in the case of the shitty gun that now lay at the bottom of the sea where it belonged, on some random technical issue. Kristian Stærk would provide the head that the apple would sit on. Who else? It wasn't Anton's style to command his gang members to risk their lives unless he, too, was in the danger zone. But he and Kristian Stærk were equals. All he had to do was drop the hint, and Kristian would volunteer. He was right. Kristian's ears rocked, as they always did when he was scared, but he didn't hesitate. He'd have been finished if he had.

Over and over we debated the possible outcomes. What if Kristian Stærk's courage failed at the last moment? Or what if Anton's aim deserted him again?

The big day came. We went to the field off Vestergade where we'd often met for battles against South. They turned up, too, with their leader Henry Levinsen, who stood there with his new nose, crooked

462

but healed, on show. They hadn't brought weapons. Like the rest of us, they were here to witness Anton's triumph or defeat. All in all we must have been about fifty boys.

It had just stopped raining, and the black mud made it heavy going.

Kristian Stærk positioned himself in the middle of the field, and Knud Erik tried to balance the apple on his head, but it kept rolling off. We hadn't held a dress rehearsal, and most of us considered this a bad omen. Kristian had to twist his longish, greasy hair into a kind of cushion before the apple would stay put. His ears kept rocking. We were reminded of Anton's joke about them: that they looked like wings getting ready to carry his head off to another body. Without doubt that was precisely what Kristian Stærk's ears wanted to do right now.

Anton faced him and their eyes met, like those of two duellists. Then Anton started walking backwards, narrowing his eyes as though in concentration – but he kept going until it was clear he'd have no earthly chance of hitting the apple: in fact we even doubted that an arrow could travel that far. Knud Erik yelled at him to stop and come back a bit. Anton refused, and it took a lot of arguing before he agreed to shoot from a distance of fifteen paces. Kristian, in the meantime, had grown so confused that he'd dislodged the apple again.

Finally, everything was ready. Anton put the shaft to the string and drew the bow, narrowing his eyes until they were almost shut. Quite a few of us thought the arrow would go as wide as the bullets he'd aimed at the stork, because Anton had lost his knack.

But this time, Anton didn't miss. It wasn't the apple he hit, though. It was Kristian Stærk.

We'd barely registered the twang of the bowstring before Kristian doubled up with a howl and buried his face in his hands. The undamaged apple hit the ground, but none of us saw it fall. We could see that the arrow was stuck into something behind Kristian's hands, but not exactly what. Then Kristian straightened up and roared up at the sky as if he'd lost his mind. It sounded scary; after all, he was almost a fully grown man. He threw back his head so he could scream even louder. The arrow stayed attached for a bit, then fell to the ground. Its tip was red.

Vilhjelm was the first to reach Kristian, a handkerchief at the ready. Anton didn't stir. It seemed he needed time to digest his defeat before he could even begin to take in that he'd shot Kristian Stærk. Later we often discussed which was worse: the damage to his reputation or the injury he'd inflicted.

Finally he snapped out of it. He ran towards Kristian but stopped a few feet away. 'He needs to go to Doctor Kroman,' he said, and he managed to make his voice sound completely matter-of-fact.

He was still our leader, and when he spoke we all calmed down, though several of the younger boys continued to shriek in fear when they saw how Vilhjelm's handkerchief had gone red from the pouring blood.

Anton went over to Kristian, who was still clutching his face and roaring. 'Let me see where I hit you,' Anton said, sweeping Kristian's hair back.

'Don't you touch me,' Kristian howled. Nevertheless he took his hands away from his face, and we could see that the blood was coming from his right eye, which was now a mess of red.

Anton took Kristian by the hand, just as he'd done with Henry Levinsen when the flowerpot holder got shoved over his ears. Henry would probably have been reminded of it too, if he'd still been present, but the members of South were long gone. 'We'll tell them that he got a twig in his eye,' Anton said, and looked around the gang with his old authority.

Together, with Kristian still screaming his head off, we walked through the town towards Doctor Kroman's. To everyone we encountered, we reported the same thing: 'He got a twig in his eye.' We didn't feel that we were covering up for Anton. We were covering up for ourselves. It was none of the adults' business how blood came to be pouring out of Kristian Stærk's eye. That was Doctor Kroman's business. He was the only one who could fix it. We'd leave Kristian's fate to him.

We didn't know then that Kristian's wasn't the only fate that would be decided that day in Doctor Kroman's surgery. Anton's would be, too. Soon we'd lose him as our leader for ever.

BY THE TIME WE REACHED THE SURGERY, A LARGE CROWD HAD gathered. The Albert Gang had been joined by twenty to thirty other people. It was outside normal surgery hours and Anton had to hammer on the door and call out for the doctor. Kroman opened up. When he saw Kristian he immediately put an arm around his shoulder and led him inside. Here Kristian quickly calmed down, as if recognising he was in safe hands – or perhaps he was just putting on a brave face.

'What do you think you're doing?' Doctor Kroman said, as the rest of us tried to follow them inside. 'Get out of here.'

He let in only Anton, Vilhjelm and Knud Erik. Then he asked what had happened, never once taking his eyes off Kristian.

'He got a twig in his eye,' Anton said.

'Can't you speak for yourself?' Kroman asked.

'I got a twig in my eye,' Kristian Stærk seconded Anton. In this moment we liked him enormously.

Meanwhile Kroman had got Kristian to lie on the couch and he'd started washing the blood off his face. Carefully he lifted up the eyelid to examine the eye fully. We turned away. We had no desire to look.

'Doctor Kroman,' Kristian said, and his voice was completely calm. 'Will I ever be able to see out of this eye again?'

'I'll be honest with you,' the doctor said. 'No.'

'Will I have to have a glass eye?'

Kristian's voice was still calm, as though the information Kroman had just given him was of no particular importance. Our awe of him soared to new heights.

'No, there's no need for that,' Doctor Kroman said.

'Good,' Kristian said. 'Because I'd prefer to wear a patch.'

Afterwards, when we talked it over, we realised what Kristian's game was. He'd worked out that Anton was finished and he'd spotted an opportunity. He could now become supreme leader of the Albert Gang. He'd have a patch over his eye and the murdered man's skull would pass to him. But in the surgery, the only thing we grasped was that Kristian Stærk had finally lived up to his name. Our admiration of the way he took the harsh blow fate had dealt him knew no bounds. We'd completely forgotten that Anton was present, too.

But Doctor Kroman hadn't. He stared hard at Anton. 'Every time someone gets hurt, you seem to be around,' he said. 'You brought Henry Levinsen here when he got a flowerpot holder stuck on his head, didn't you?'

'Yes,' Anton said. 'That's right. But I didn't do it.'

'And you didn't try to kill the stork either?' Doctor Kroman pursued his point.

Anton said nothing. He stared straight ahead, as if his thoughts were in a completely different place and he wasn't even listening. Again he narrowed his eyes in that irritating manner we'd noted so often recently, as if he were still taking aim with Shooter.

'And you've got nothing to do with this either?'

'He got a twig in his eye,' said Knud Erik.

'I got a twig in my eye,' Kristian confirmed from the couch.

'No. It was my fault,' Anton blurted out suddenly. 'I shot him.'

We couldn't believe our ears. First Anton had invented the lie about the twig. Now he was telling the whole story, just as it had happened.

'I shot at him with a bow and arrow,' he added. 'I didn't mean to hit him in the eye. I was aiming for the apple on his head. But it's my fault anyway. I'm the one who did it.' He looked straight at Doctor Kroman as he confessed.

A moment ago we'd forgotten all about him. Now we remembered him again, and we knew that no matter what happened, he'd always be our leader. There was only one Anton. And although he might not be the world's best shot, no one could beat him, not even the much bigger Kristian Stærk, three years his senior and sporting a pirate patch.

Doctor Kroman said nothing. We expected him to start scolding Anton, the way our teachers at school always did. We expected him to call him a rotten kid, a bad example, a thug and a habitual criminal; to reproach him for his latest irresponsible breach of conduct;

466

and to threaten him with the delinquents' home or even an adult prison. But the doctor was a practical man. He understood the body and its functions and he stuck to what he knew. He told us to get out so he could tend to Kristian's eye undisturbed. We headed for the door.

'Just a moment, William Tell,' Doctor Kroman called after Anton. 'I want you to come and see me tomorrow. There's something I want to take a closer look at.'

'Perhaps it's my brain,' Anton said afterwards. 'He wants to find out if I'm the dumbest guy in Marstal.' He looked utterly devastated, and no wonder. This was all his fault. He'd wrecked Kristian Stærk's eye. Although we'd lied when he'd asked us to, we were well aware that he'd done something so terrible that it was beyond apology.

The next time we saw Anton he was wearing glasses.

His face, which until now had looked so determined, hard even, appeared pale and defenceless behind the dark brown horn frames, which seemed to drag him downward. He looked as if he wished he were someone else entirely, and if there was a message in the eyes behind the lenses, it was this: 'Please pretend you haven't seen me.'

Not only did the spectacles mean that he was finished as leader of the Albert Gang, they meant he was finished entirely. He'd wanted to go to sea one day. That had been the whole point of his life: what else would he do? But a sailor can't wear glasses. It's simply forbidden. He needs to have the eyesight of an eagle. He's allowed to become long-sighted when he grows old, but if he's found to be short-sighted when he's young, it's all over. He won't even get his first job.

And over it was. Going to sea hadn't been Anton's plan, so much as what nature intended for him, the culmination of his growth into manhood. He was getting taller, bigger, stronger and older with every year, and one day all these changes, which no earthly power could stop, would result in him stepping onto the deck of a ship and staying there to the end of his days. The spectacles were a farewell to all that: to Schipperstraat in Antwerp, Paradise Street in Liverpool, Tiger Bay in Cardiff, Vieux Carré in New Orleans, Barbary Coast in San Francisco and Foretop Street in Valparaiso; they were a farewell to Amer Picon, absinthe and Pernod. It was as if someone had come and trampled on his destiny and utterly crushed it.

Doctor Kroman might as well have told him he'd never be a man. Anton with spectacles was no longer Anton.

Now we knew why he was always narrowing his eyes, and why he'd failed to hit the stork. It hadn't been Shooter's fault, but Anton's. He'd stopped being who we thought he was, and oddly enough, we felt sorrier for him than we did for Kristian Stærk. Perhaps that was because we'd all admired Anton and none of us had really liked Kristian, with his rocking ears and casual abuse of anyone younger and smaller. Besides, Kristian's life didn't change because he'd lost an eye. He kept his job as an apprentice ironmonger. But everything changed for Anton.

At first, our teachers interpreted the spectacles symbolically and thought that Anton had become bookish. Perhaps even turned into a swot. But they soon learned that he was as impossible as ever: the only difference was that they had to make him take off his glasses before they boxed his ears.

To us, Anton's lenses were like two locked doors. He hid behind them and he shut us out. He left the leadership of the Albert Gang to Kristian Stærk, but Kristian derived little benefit from his newly acquired power. The only advantage he had over us was his strength, and that was exclusively down to our age difference. Beyond that, there was nothing he could do that we couldn't do too; nor was there a single thing he could do that Anton couldn't do much better. He had no specific ideas about defending our position among the town's gangs and couldn't come up with an effective response when South, sensing our weakness following the loss of Anton, attacked us, and he was clueless about how to re-establish their respect for us. Kristian Stærk had run out of ideas. He lorded it over us and gave us horse bites and Chinese burns to cover up his anxiety, but his rocking ears told another story.

Not even the eyepatch, which made him look quite formidable, changed matters. Especially because Anton refused to hand over Albert's boots and the dead man's skull. Without them, Kristian was unable to perform the initiation rites of the Albert Gang, and he didn't have the imagination to come up with new ones.

Without the boots and the skull, the Albert Gang seemed to lose soul. In fact, Anton had been its soul, and Kristian Stærk had been nothing more than Anton's right arm. Now he was a right arm with no head, and that was the end of it.

The gang dissolved and new factions emerged. But things were never the same again. The truth is, Marstal became a more peaceful town once Anton got his spectacles. He sat alone in his attic bedroom in Møllevejen. When we learned about General Napoleon and his exile to St Helena, we were reminded of him. But we judged Anton's fate to be sadder than Napoleon's, because Napoleon got to create his own misfortune. He'd lost his final, decisive battle, but Anton hadn't lost anything. He'd just become short-sighted.

Kristian withdrew from gang life altogether and no longer needed to beat up smaller kids to prove his worth. Instead, he concentrated on his apprenticeship with Samuelsen. He regarded himself as a grown-up, and the ironmonger had come to share this opinion. He'd noticed that the chief effect of Kristian Stærk's conversion to adulthood was that the stock of canes, which Kristian had considered part of his armoury, stopped diminishing.

Initially, Kristian had felt that the score between him and Anton had been settled peacefully. Anton had said he was sorry, and Kristian had remarked that he almost pitied him, the poor short-sighted devil, for having to wear those ugly glasses. But when Anton refused to hand over the skull, Kristian realised that he had plenty of reasons to bear him a grudge. First and foremost there was the business of his eye. Second, Anton had always tried to outmanoeuvre him and make him look a fool. It was his fault that Kristian had lost control of the Albert Gang, a position of power he secretly missed every time he held a cane in his hand. His newly acquired adulthood went no deeper than that. All these factors added up to this conclusion: Kristian was entitled to revenge. And, vindictive as he was, he chose the most devious and cruel payback he could imagine.

Anton had entrusted him with the name of the murdered man. And in this case, or so we'd heard, if you knew who the victim was, you'd automatically know who'd killed him. So Kristian decided to tell the murderer that Anton could prove his guilt.

One day Herman entered the ironmonger's shop to buy a folding ruler. When the two of them were alone for a moment, Kristian blurted it out: 'Anton Hansen Hay knows that you killed Holger Jepsen.' He hadn't exactly thought through the wording in advance.

His ears were rocking madly. 'He has his skull as proof. And there's a big hole in it.'

If Herman hadn't been clever, he'd probably have grabbed Kristian Stærk by the collar there and then, and given him a thorough shaking until he revealed where Anton kept the skull. Instead, he wisely played the part of the injured innocent – which entailed whacking Kristian across the head and sending him flying into the tool drawers.

'What the hell do you think you're accusing me of, boy?' he shouted.

Samuelsen came rushing in from the back room.

'What's going on here?'

His voice sounded frightened. Like most people, Samuelsen was afraid of Herman.

'I'm teaching your apprentice some manners,' Herman said calmly.

Turning on his heel, he left the shop without buying the folding ruler. Kristian rubbed his sore cheek and tried to conceal a smile. His ears had returned to a state of peace. He'd seen Herman's hands shake. And he knew that he'd set something in motion.

ANTON HAD ONCE TRIED TO MAKE US BELIEVE THAT THE MURDERED
man stood in the potato bed every night, calling for his head, but
we'd never believed him. Then one night a black, stooping figure
really did appear in the dark garden below his window, and a voice
halfway between a whisper and a hoarse cry called out to Anton for
a head – not his own, but his victim's.

'Anton Hansen Hay!'

Anton, who was fast asleep, dreamed that he was being told off
either by a teacher or by his father, because they were the only ones
who ever used his full name. It took a while for him to wake up
and even longer to work out where the voice was coming from. He
looked out of the window and saw the figure, but couldn't make
out who it was. He wasn't scared; it had been ages since he'd thought
about the dead man's skull and at first he had no idea what the man
below was on about. He'd never believed in his own story about the
ghost haunting him at night, and besides, the black figure standing
there now wasn't headless.

Then he woke up properly, and though the man beneath the window
still hadn't identified himself, it didn't take Anton long to work out
who he was. And then he was scared, more scared than he'd ever
been of any ghost, more scared than he'd ever been in his entire life
– though that wasn't really saying much. If Herman could kill his
own stepfather, he could kill Anton too. It would be no problem for
him at all.

Having got this far in his reflections, Anton slammed the window
shut and hurried downstairs to make sure that all the doors in the
house were locked. They weren't, but fortunately the keys were in
the locks, and he frantically secured them all, one after another,
before running back to his room and hiding under the bed.

Eventually the voice outside the window stopped calling, but Anton
was too exhausted to climb back into bed. His last thought before

he fell asleep on the floor was that he was lucky no one was there to see him.

Anton's father wasn't at home: he'd gone to sea nine months before and he wouldn't be back for at least another year. He knew nothing about Anton's spectacles and Anton was convinced that the day he came home and saw his son's face, his greeting would include the term 'four-eyes'. No: Anton would never confide in The Foreigner, nor would he ever dream of confiding in his mother or any other adult. Anton was of the opinion that a boy should solve his own problems without expecting help from anyone else, least of all from adults, who were the natural enemies of children. If the adults had to choose between believing a child and one of their own, they'd never choose the child. Least of all the Terror of Marstal, who'd shot Kristian Stærk in the eye and kept a murdered man's head in his room for months without saying a word, even though he knew who the victim was and could have helped bring the murderer to justice. Anton had always been completely indifferent to the legal significance of his find. As far as he was concerned, Herman was free to go about his business as he wished. Now he realised what a foolish attitude that was. But he saw no way out of the fix he was in.

The morning after he'd heard the voice in the garden Anton found Tordenskjold dead in his cage; his neck had been wrung. His wings had been broken and nearly ripped from his body, as if by a person of unusual strength in an uncontrollable rage. Anton's hands started to shake at the sight and it was a long time before he was able to bury the dead seagull.

From then on, every night he locked all the doors of the house.

'What are you doing that for?' his mother said. 'You've grown very strange recently.' She was well aware that Anton had changed, but she didn't know whether or not it was cause to celebrate. She didn't ask him if something was wrong. Everything in Anton's life seemed so remote and alien to her that she sometimes caught herself wondering whether she really had given birth to the child known as the Terror of Marstal. Asking him if something was wrong was the same as asking him who he really was, and she knew from bitter experience that the only response he'd give her was a shrug.

'Do we have a chamber pot?' Anton asked.

'Are you ill?'

'Yes,' Anton said.

'This isn't about trying to get out of going to school tomorrow, is it?'

'I'll go to school all right. Now get me that chamber pot.'

With a puzzled look, his mother handed him the pot. In his room he emptied his bowels of their contents, which were impressive: he'd been holding out all day. When Herman returned that night and started calling out to him, Anton tipped the pot right over his head.

That worked. Herman didn't return, but Anton's victory didn't lift his mood. He started carrying a knife and he stopped eating. At night he slept with Albert's boots on. He didn't know why, but he felt safer with them than without. Perhaps he was preparing himself for death. His features grew stern and sunken, and his horn-rimmed spectacles, which had once made him look like a little boy, now turned him into an old man. Coal-black rings formed under his eyes. Once his head had been covered in bruises, cuts, bumps and even cheerfully blazing black eyes that turned purple and later faded to yellow. In a boy these were all signs of good health. But black rings weren't: they seemed more a mark of death, like the chalk stripe a forester puts on a tree he's going to fell. His mother started worrying about him in earnest, and for once she didn't threaten him with a punishment from his father when he returned home.

'Leave me alone,' he said, every time she came near him.

He was always fidgeting with his knife. He wanted to kill Herman, but he couldn't work out how to do it. He could run much faster than Herman, but what good would that do? You can't kill a man by outrunning him.

He went outside less and less, and when he did he was always looking over his shoulder. Before, he'd had a gang behind him. Now he was alone.

Not long after the incident with the chamber pot, he heard his name being called from the vegetable garden in broad daylight. He'd begun locking the doors of the house even in daytime, and now, as the rays of the afternoon sun came through the gable window and he heard a voice, he was pleased at his foresight. But it was calling out only his first name, and the voice wasn't the usual hoarse whisper: it was a boy's voice, like his. Deciding to risk it, he went to the window to look down and saw Knud Erik standing below.

'Is it you?' Anton asked stupidly.

Knud Erik said something he'd wanted to say for a long time. No matter how many times he'd rehearsed it, it always sounded wrong and hopeless, even desperately girly. But it was something he felt driven to say by his useless impulse to help and comfort, an urge that had no outlet now that his relationship with his mother had changed and his little sister Edith needed him less.

'I miss you,' he said.

He'd known in advance how pathetic this would sound. He was the younger boy, Anton was the older, and, of course, the one always missed the other. But why would the older boy care? The older ones were fine as they were. They certainly didn't need the little guys. Knud Erik hadn't dared to imagine Anton's response, and when it came it terrified him.

Anton started crying.

Anton wasn't like anyone else, and he didn't cry like anyone else. His tears were full of resistance. It sounded as though a ferret had crawled under his jumper and was ripping his stomach open, as though he suffered a terrible physical pain rather than unhappiness. More than anything he looked as if he wanted to stop the sobs, but they escaped him despite his own nature. He covered his mouth with both hands and wailed through his fingers. He cried away Herman, he cried away his fear and his loneliness: you might even think he was crying away his own belief in living only for himself, needing no one else. But that wasn't the case. When he eventually regained the power of speech, his voice was utterly matter-of-fact, even though the eyes behind the lenses were bloodshot.

'What the hell do you want?' he asked.

Knud Erik already felt defeated. He'd come out with it, and it had cost him, jeopardising his still shaky sense of manhood. 'I miss you.' Were those words so hard to understand? What else could he say? I want to help you, to be there for you, to hold out my hand to you? A fat lot of good it would do, saying that. So Knud Erik said nothing. He'd run out of courage as well as words. He didn't know what else to say, and that's in fact what saved him, because in the pause that followed Anton was able to compose himself and invite his friend up to his room.

There he blurted out the whole story. Knud Erik was too young to have heard about Jepsen's disappearance on that trip between Marstal and Rudkøbing, so he needed everything explained to him. The story was terrifying enough in itself, but it was more the way Anton told it that frightened Knud Erik. He heard a fresh sob hidden in every pause; Anton managed to hold back each one only through considerable cost and effort. The ferret was burying itself deeper and deeper in his intestines and soon he'd start to scream again.

'He killed Tordenskjold,' he said.

Knud Erik hadn't known Holger Jepsen, but he'd known Tordenskjold. He'd often joined in feeding the seagull fish and the sparrows Anton could no longer sell to the farmer from Midtmarken because they were too far gone. The horror started to take hold of him as well.

'He's definitely going to kill me, too.' Anton closed his eyes as if he expected the death blow at any moment.

'Why don't you just give him the skull?'

'I can't.' For a moment it was still there, that old stubbornness. Then his despondency returned. 'It's hopeless. He'll kill me anyway.'

'Nonsense,' Knud Erik said, summoning up more courage than he knew he had. 'But it's definitely Kristian who told Herman about the head. He was the only one, apart from you, who knew who it belonged to.'

Anton's anger flared up. 'I'm going to kill Kristian,' he hissed. 'I can't get Herman, but I can get him.'

'You've already shot his eye out. Don't you think that's enough?'

Knud Erik astonished himself. He'd never imagined himself talking to Anton like this. But Anton wasn't the boy he used to be. Which made Knud Erik free to change, too.

'I've got an idea,' Knud Erik said.

475

AS HERMAN LEFT WEBER'S CAFE A FEW DAYS LATER, HE SAW TWO boys hanging around on the other side of the road, staring at him. He walked up towards Kirkestræde and they followed him on the opposite pavement. At first he thought it was a coincidence, but when he turned the corner to head south, they were still there. He didn't know either of them. He stopped and turned round: he wanted them to see that he was on to them. As he'd expected, they paused too. But they kept staring. He stamped his foot on the cobbles. Startled, they retreated a step. But they continued to stare. When he reached the end of Kirkestræde, they disappeared. But then two more of them popped up in Snaregade, and when he started walking towards the seafront, they followed him, their eyes fixed on him in a persistent and mysterious manner.

'Do I look different from anybody else?' he roared at them. 'What are you staring at?'

They didn't reply. He could see them freeze, out of fear most likely. But they didn't run off. Nor did they taunt him. This baffled him more than anything. There was no point in chasing them. He was big and heavy and they were better runners than he was. He just had to control himself and pretend they weren't there.

He was used to the stares of the people in Marstal: he was a man who lived his life in full public view. He hadn't planned it that way, but he'd known how to exploit it when it happened. He had power, not over people's minds perhaps, but at least over the excursions their minds took. He was of the stuff that gossip and fear feed on, and in his case, both applied. They gloated when he fell, as he'd done when Henckel went to prison and the steel shipyard went bankrupt and he lost everything. But they did so only because they feared him. They'd thought, back then, he was finished. But Herman was never finished. He'd always bounce back. He recognised the things he saw in them: hate, fear, glee, envy and attraction. And he took nourishment from them all.

But he didn't comprehend the boys' staring. They were waiting for him outside the boarding house in Tværgade where he stayed when he was in Marstal. He could enter a shop and leave it, or take a stroll along the harbour, or hang out in Weber's Cafe and always they'd be there, waiting. More and more he began to feel the need for shelter and for places to hide. A door to something unknown was opening up inside him. He'd done something once, something on board the *Two Sisters*. At times the memory made him feel stronger. At other times he avoided it. Now he felt dread at the thought of being found out and the punishment that might ensue, and he understood instinctively that the boys' impenetrable stares held a power he couldn't fight. He'd believed he could scare off that damned Anton. But now every boy in Marstal was Anton's co-conspirator. And there seemed to be hundreds of them, with new faces all the time, an unpredictable people's court; he knew the charge but had no idea which laws operated there or the nature of the verdict. Their eyes persecuted him everywhere; eventually following him all the way into the darkness around his bed and into his dreams, like a madness that threatened to overpower him. He couldn't kill the whole bloody lot of them, though his fists began flexing as they used to in the old days, whenever something was revving up inside him. He drank more than before and got into fights more frequently at Weber's Cafe. That kept the fists busy.

Dutch gin was no longer to his taste; Riga Balsam, famous for a century among the skippers of Marstal, lost its power to cure; whisky, the greatest healer of them all, had no more effect on him than water. His hands started shaking when he raised his glass to his lips. Shunning the company of others, he drank alone.

Finally he gave in. One day he stomped down to the ferry with his seabag slung over his shoulder. His intention was to go to Copenhagen and sign on at Jepsen's Shipping Office. The boys knew it. It was as if they could read his thoughts. He didn't bother counting them all. But a farewell committee of at least twenty to thirty boys was waiting by the ferry to see him off.

In their usual inscrutable silence, their gaze followed him as he disappeared on board the ferry. He didn't go straight to the saloon to smoke a cigarette, which was his usual habit when saying goodbye to the town he hated but was linked to inextricably. Instead he stayed in the darkness of the enclosed deck, among the horse-drawn carts and trucks, breathing in engine oil and dung until he was certain he was no longer visible from land.

When he finally entered the saloon and lit the first cigarette of the crossing, he had trouble controlling his trembling hands.

Knud Erik had arrived at the idea through a very straightforward process. He'd tried to come up with the most unpleasant thing he could think of, and then he made the assumption that Herman would share the aversion. A good thrashing wouldn't work: it was beyond the boys' abilities, and besides, he wasn't sure Herman would mind a fight even if he bore the brunt of it. But burned into his soul was the memory of a worse persecution: the look his mother had fixed on him after his father's death. He couldn't call the look reproachful. It was just a silent searching, and it had followed him everywhere with a question he couldn't answer. What did she want?

He'd collapsed under the weight of that look, which seemed to challenge everything he did without suggesting an alternative. That was the worst thing: when someone looked at you constantly you had to guess what they meant by it while knowing that nothing you could say could ever lighten the burden. He imagined how you could put the same kind of burden on Herman, how the pressure of a silent stare might cause a hardened and unscrupulous murderer, who'd killed even as a boy, to crack.

And Herman would never guess what had hit him. That was the most satisfying part of all. Although he'd got the lads fired up about it, Knud Erik hadn't told them the real reason for their persecution of Herman. It was far too risky to tell them the secret of Holger Jepsen's murder. Who's Jepsen? they might well have asked, and been stupid enough to take their question to the adults, and then there'd have been trouble. No, he'd done something else. He'd taken them to Anton's home and dug up Tordenskjold, right in front of their eyes. He'd shown them the gull's limp neck, its dead eyes, its wide-open beak, the feathers that had lost their shine and the broken, dislocated wings. The body was crawling with maggots. 'Look,' he'd said. 'Herman did this.'

After that they'd itched to see the seagull killer lying at their feet, transformed into a mass of bloody pulp. His bones should be ground to meal, his skin should be flayed and hung from a tree, his guts should be dragged through the streets. But Knud Erik proposed something far better. They could make him shrink into something less than a man. They'd see his hands shake with fear.

The stares that had haunted and followed the terrifying killer everywhere he turned had been nothing but a boy's imitation of a mother's reproachful look.

No, Herman would never guess what had driven him out of town. We hadn't accused him of a man's murder.

We'd accused him of a seagull's.

HERMAN WAS GONE, BUT THE HORN-RIMMED SPECTACLES STILL SAT slap-bang in the middle of Anton's face, and he still had no future. The Foreigner wasn't due home until the summer, and in the meantime the boys' confirmation was coming up. Without discussing it with his mother, Anton went up to his teacher, Miss Katballe, and informed her that after seven years he was now leaving school. It was the best day of her life, she replied. With unexpected politeness he bowed, thanked her and said 'Likewise'.

He was confirmed and publicly swore to denounce the devil and all his works. He didn't know if hell meant the singe of fire or the gnawing of worms. All he knew was that he was already there, because, for him, hell was a life cut off from the sea and the world it offered. He'd never find out if French girls were the liveliest, or if Portuguese girls really did stink of garlic, or even what garlic was. During the service, he stood beneath the marine painter's altarpiece, which depicted Jesus saving his disciples from the raging storm. Yet Anton wasn't seeking salvation from the sea, but access to it.

When Pastor Abildgaard placed his hand on Anton's head, he shut his eyes tightly behind his glasses. He was in hell, and yet he didn't want to go to heaven. He felt homeless.

Regnar came home and threw a glance at his son. 'Why the hell are you still here?' he said. 'Why haven't you gone to sea? I even bought you a seabag.'

Anton said nothing. He just waited for the mockery to start.

'Is it because of your spectacles?' his father said. 'Runs in the family. I'm so near-sighted I can't see further than my own beer gut. Only no one's noticed.' He chuckled noisily.

'You can't go to sea if you're wearing spectacles,' Anton said patiently, as though talking to a child.

'No,' his father answered, unperturbed. 'Not if you want to waste your life on board some crock of a schooner. But you're going to be a proper sailor. You want to get yourself a job as a machine-man on a steamer. Nobody cares about spectacles there.'

So Anton was apprenticed to Hans Baldrian Ulriksen, the smith in Ommel. He learned to tell the difference between a sink hammer, a set hammer, a lock hammer and a shoeing hammer. He knew when a horse needed a wedge shoe and when it needed a ring shoe. He handled hoof irons, hoof jacks, files and rasps the way he used to handle the dead man's skull and Albert's boots. They started calling him the Horse Friend. He built his own bicycle so he could cycle the three kilometres to Marstal every evening to attend technical college. He found himself a girlfriend, a redhead just like him. Her name was Marie, and she cut her hair herself every week to stop it getting too long. One day he'd watched her give a boy a bloody nose for making fun of her red hair, and afterwards he'd chivalrously explained to her how to clench her fist when she hit, with her thumb on the outside, not the inside. Marie was a caring girl. When teasing Starry Jens, a filthy man who lived by Market Square, she'd throw a brick at his door like everyone else. But she'd wrap it in a rhubarb leaf beforehand, so as not to scratch the paintwork.

And Anton made a discovery. He found that the strange thrilling rush he used to get when, as leader of the Albert Gang, he left the battlefield with the usual bruises and cuts from arrows, clubs and spears, was available to him again, this time from shoeing a horse. He felt as if a great sail had filled with wind and unfurled with a snap inside the uncharted darkness of his head. When he first got his glasses, he thought he'd never again feel the triumph of having power over others. But now, power over people had been replaced by power over objects. When he saw the results of his handiwork, he felt a new kind of triumph. He felt like the upholder of the world.

'Precision is the soul of mechanics, and he who masters mechanics masters much more besides,' the blacksmith said. He was a well-read man and fond of expressing himself in philosophical terms.

Anton had found a new course to steer.

Finally it was Knud Erik and Vilhjelm's turn to stand in the church and be confirmed. As they opened their mouths to sing they stared at the model ships hanging from the ceiling with their black-painted hulls. That was their future up there. They sang, as generations had done before them, the old hymn dedicated to the sailing profession, which Pastor Abildgaard had loyally taught them: a hymn about their own fragility, and that of a ship's timbers, and the strength of God.

> *The cruel sea shall be our grave*
> *Be thou not by our side,*
> *Mid raging wind and crashing wave*
> *And lightning's flashing sword,*
> *Your word can calm the surging tide*
> *Be with us now on board!*

Knud Erik glanced furtively at Vilhjelm. He hadn't expected him to sing. He hadn't so much as opened his mouth during confirmation classes. But now he was singing, and his stammer had vanished, as if somehow the hymn carried him over even the hardest words. He didn't seem aware of it himself, but Knud Erik noticed it, and it changed his view of hymns.

But if God had worked a miracle, it wasn't a permanent one. On the way back from church Vilhjelm stammered just as badly as ever.

We didn't know it, but we were the last. Our children would never stand in the church and sing that hymn, or stand on the deck of a schooner at the mercy of the elements. They'd travel to every corner of the world, but they'd barely see a sail. Everything was happening for the last time these days. The sails would be set for the last time. The harbour would be packed with ships for the last time. And then Frederik Isaksen's predictions would come true: for us, there would only be the worst voyages, the most inhospitable coasts and the roughest seas.

But we were young. We didn't know that. For us, everything was happening for the first time.

The Sailor

THE FIRST MATE ON BOARD THE *ACTIVE* DIDN'T TOLERATE WEAKNESS, and when he beat you, he meant it. He'd use a clenched fist, and he'd hit you where it hurt most. But Anker Pinnerup wasn't a strong man. Ravaged by rheumatism and booze, he was a thug with no muscles. In his late forties, he was nearing the age when a sailor goes ashore.

Pinnerup was known as the Old Man, a nickname normally reserved for a ship's captain as a tribute to his skill and experience. In Pinnerup's case it wasn't a compliment, but a reference to his fast-approaching decrepitude. A sharp, clean-shaven chin protruded from his thick grey whiskers like the upended bow of a ship sinking in a sea of waste and dereliction, and this minimal shave was his only concession to personal hygiene. Beneath his filthy, greasy cap a few strands of colourless hair clung to his unwashed scalp. Clamped between his teeth, half concealed by his beard, was a broken meer-schaum pipe that he'd mended with a couple of wooden splints and a piece of twine. Behind his back the able seamen would joke that his patched jacket and trousers reminded them of a Red Indian wedding night: 'Apache on Apache'.

When, after serving him coffee for the first time, Knud Erik collected his cup and saucer to wash up, Pinnerup let out a roar and clocked him on the jaw. The cup and saucer were Pinnerup's personal posses-sions: no one else touched them. And to prove his attachment to his property, he spat in the cup and rubbed at it with his dirty thumb.

'Filthy swine,' he cursed. 'Monkey brain, snot-rag, devil's spawn!'

Every other morning when he was on duty and came to rouse Knud Erik, he'd appear in the fo'c's'le with a thick rope, and stand there, gathering his strength, before he began lashing out at the sleeping boy. He always went for his head, but the narrow berth hampered his swipe and diminished the force of his blows. Woken by the first stroke, Knud Erik would scramble to the bulkhead where the first mate couldn't reach him. He never uttered a sound: instinct told him that if he gave in to his fear, he'd have a hard job recovering.

One morning Olav, a crewman Knud Erik had known in the Albert Gang, arrived a few minutes before Pinnerup to warn him.

'Time to wake up,' he whispered, tapping his friend on the shoulder. Knud Erik arranged his duvet and pillow so that in the dull light of dawn they'd look like someone sleeping. The first mate lashed away as usual: when he realised the deception, he seemed to slump. His hand, still clutching the rope, fell limp to his side and he shuddered as though in a high fever.

'Spawn of the devil,' he hissed. 'One day I'll get you with the belaying pin.'

Then he stormed up the ladder and on to the deck.

When Pinnerup was at the wheel, Knud Erik would inevitably be woken during the night watch to make coffee or to climb up and rope a sail in the pouring rain. Down below the sea raged, and in the darkness he could dimly make out the foam. Freezing raindrops fell, mingling with the salt on his cheeks. It wasn't impotence or self-pity that made him weep. It was rage and defiance.

At the beginning of his first voyage he'd cried with his head buried in his bedclothes. He'd cried over his dead father and his indifferent mother, whose coldness he believed was his own fault, and he'd cried over his own nagging feeling of inadequacy. He wasn't sure he'd made the right choice in becoming a sailor. He was paying the price for it now. But he couldn't change his mind and go ashore. The loss of face would be unbearable.

Pinnerup used sleep deprivation as a form of torture. For whole days and nights Knud Erik might get no rest at all. He was called on incessantly, often in the deepest night, and at times he'd have to climb the rigging wearing only his underpants. He'd already heard stories about what it was like to be the youngest on board. The inexperienced were sent to work in the topgallant sails, twenty-five metres up. Able seamen never ventured that high. You were sent up to the mainmast to take in the vane sail, wobbling on the foot ropes, with one hand clutching the hand ropes and the other grasping the canvas. You did it even if you'd never been taught how, or if you suffered from vertigo, or if you were just a clumsy idiot who was a danger to himself. You just got yourself up there and hoped you'd get down again in one piece. Climbing around on the rigging of moored ships in the harbour, for fun, had been a kind of preparation for this, but out here the sea was high and the wind was screaming, for God's sake! Everyone took it for granted that you'd come back alive, but the way you saw it, you'd just become a survivor. Not that anybody noticed.

One time he'd hung up there, frightened out of his skin, with the narrow deck far, far below him. Every muscle was so cramped from the strain that he thought his hands would let go by themselves, just to be free of it. He'd been so terrified that he'd screamed. But no one heard him. Yet that scream into nothingness saved him. It forced the life back to his limbs, the strength to his hands and the composure to his dizzy head, and brought him safely down.

For Knud Erik, the man who'd sent him up there personified the rule of law at sea. But Pinnerup was also the sea itself: rapacious and dangerous. Unless you toughened up, you'd go under. Knud Erik stopped worrying about the injustices, the beatings and the insults. Instead, he allowed himself to be filled with a new sensation: hatred. He hated the first mate. He hated the ship. He hated the sea. It was hatred that kept him on his feet when he staggered across the see-sawing deck, in the pitch dark, carrying the coffee pot, which scalded his hands. It was hatred that helped him endure the saltwater blisters on his neck and wrists where his permanently wet woollen jumper chafed the unprotected skin, creating huge fluid-filled pustules. It was hatred that kept him silent and stoical when the first mate grabbed him by the neck and twisted his wrist, just where the worst boils were ready to burst.

Hatred was his apprenticeship, and in serving it, he grew up.

It was hard to become a man. But he wanted to. He dug in his heels and made himself stupid, pig-headed and tough. He became a human battering ram. He'd gain access to life, he realised, only if he bashed its door in.

The skipper of the *Active* was Hans Boutrop, who came from Søndergade. He was a jolly, rotund man whose considerable girth could not be attributed to the fare proposed by the Marstal ships' cookbook, which, had it existed, would have had *thrift* stamped all over it in giant letters. As cabin boy, Knud Erik had to help out in the galley where the captain taught him to make broth. His recipe, he said, was similar to pork broth but with a crucial difference: no pork was involved. Instead, you flavoured it generously with brown sugar and vinegar, which you flung into the boiling water along with a handful of rusks.

On Sundays, if the ship was in port, the galley served pot roast. This festive dish was made in its own special pot, whose wooden lid was blackened with age. The recipe followed the principle that governed all meat dishes: cook for a solid three hours. Full stop.

On rare occasions they had a pudding, which was left to set in coffee cups, then tipped out and served on plates in small, individual, wobbling domes that would fit in the palm of your hand. The crew called them nun's titties. The stringy tinned meat from Argentina they called cable yarn, while salt meat was known as Red Indian's arse, and salami was never referred to as anything but Roskilde High Road.

Often the smell of cooking and the enclosed atmosphere of the galley made Knud Erik seasick and he'd open the door and throw up on deck. In bad weather the waves usually washed the puke away, so no one knew about the half digested meals he routinely sacrificed. When he wasn't seasick, his appetite for his own food was good, and he continued to be amazed that he could cook.

The fo'c's'le was so small that only two men could get dressed at the same time. Below the floor was the coal for the galley oven, and behind the ladder was the potato crate: when its contents began to rot, it exuded a penetrating stench like fermenting shit. A strange smell also emanated from the box where the anchor chain was stored: it was the odour of dried mud and old anchor-weed that the broom couldn't dislodge. But from the rope berth came the good, strong smell of brown tar.

The crew relieved themselves into a beer barrel that had been cut in half. The seat was a rough iron ring that scratched the buttocks, and when the sea was bad and waves crashed onto the deck, you'd sometimes get knocked over as you sat on it. In fine weather Knud Erik would climb out on the bowsprit and shit directly into the bow splash. It reminded him of the flushing china bowl at home in Prinsegade.

Fresh water was for drinking only, so he never washed. The deck was cleaner than he was. Once a week, he and the crewmen would get down on their knees and scrub it with 'Marstal soda', a brick rubbed against crunchy wet sand.

As a parting gift, Vilhjelm's father had presented Knud Erik with two leather patches with straps attached. 'They're for your hands,' he'd said. Being a man of few words, he'd offered no further explanation – and it wasn't until the *Active* called at Egernsund to take on a cargo of bricks bound for Copenhagen that Knud Erik learned their purpose. Pinnerup showed him what they were for, strapping the leather patches to the boy's hands and then giving him a slap across the face by way of encouragement.

So he did have some compassion in him after all, Knud Erik thought.

The bricks were brought from the quayside to the ship, then passed down a chain of men until they reached the first mate in the hull, who transferred them into the stows. They came flying from man to man in packs of four, each bundle weighing somewhere between ten and fifteen kilos. The first one Knud Erik caught nearly knocked him over. If it hadn't been for the leather patches, his skin would have been flayed.

He stood panting for a moment, then took a couple of staggering steps towards the docker next to him in line.

'Listen, pal,' the docker warned. 'Don't break the chain. Your arms won't be able to stand it. If you don't keep the bricks moving, they get too heavy.'

He showed Knud Erik how to twist his body and send the bricks on in a single movement. Knud Erik kept the chain going the next time, but whenever a pack passed through his hands it felt as if his arms were being wrenched off. His limbs were lead weights, and he strained for breath. But he refused to give up. He found himself drawing on a violence he didn't even know he possessed, a force that came not from his paltry boyish muscles, but from some nameless inner place where it had lain dormant for years.

The docker glanced at him from time to time. 'You're doing all right,' he said, but the pity in his eyes belied his words. He was an older man who sweated profusely, but he knew the routine. He quickly forgot Knud Erik. There was a piecework rate to keep up.

Every time there was a hitch in the delivery, Pinnerup's hoarse voice would shout from the hull, 'Is it that bloody boy again?'

* * *

The crew of the *Active* had to help with the unloading in Copenhagen as well. They moored in Frederiksholm's Kanal; its high granite quays meant the loads had to be hoisted a long way up, so it was hard work. The first mate kept well away, sitting on the hatch coaming and watching Knud Erik fall out of rhythm again and again. The difficulty wasn't just in passing the heavy pack along, but throwing it upward too. Each time he pushed off, he had to squat deeper. 'Lazy swine, Sunday sailor,' Pinnerup snarled, and removed the broken meerschaum pipe from his mouth to spit on the deck.

Knud Erik was so used to this kind of thing that he hardly noticed. But one of the dockers put down his pack and went over to the first mate. 'We won't put up with this,' he said. He pointed to Knud Erik. 'The work's too heavy for a boy. Swap places with him and give him a rest.'

Pinnerup grinned and pulled his cap down. 'So you think you're in charge here?'

'No,' the docker said. 'I'm the one doing the unloading. But perhaps you'd rather do it yourself?' He turned to his mates. 'Bloke here thinks he doesn't need us.'

They swung themselves up on the quay and sat down. One of them took out a cigarette, lit it and passed it around. They didn't look in Pinnerup's direction, but started chatting among themselves, dangling their legs over the edge casually. Knud Erik stood there, confused. Something was happening that he didn't understand. These men didn't belong on the ship. They weren't familiar with its hierarchy or its unseen life-and-death struggles. They seemed to be a law unto themselves, with a strength of their own. They appeared to be their own masters.

'So when's break time over?' Pinnerup snorted sarcastically.

'When you take your hands out of your pockets,' retorted one of the dockers.

The others laughed in approval.

Pinnerup shrank. Here he was no one.

Suddenly Knud Erik could see him for what he was: a ridiculous, filthy man in patched clothes with a broken pipe in his mouth and a clean-shaven chin sticking out of a beard that looked as if it belonged on a greying orang-utan. He'd learned to suffer Pinnerup, yet the first mate had taken up his entire field of vision, like bad weather or a force of nature. Now he saw him as if from the top of the mast, a man the size of an ant on the deck. He saw him through the eyes of the dockers.

He climbed up on the quay, sat down next to them and dangled his legs just as they did.

That was Pinnerup's cue. He got up and went over to Knud Erik. The dockers sat up watchfully. One of them flicked his cigarette so that it landed at Pinnerup's feet, then jumped down onto the deck and looked him in the eye. Pinnerup's face tightened.

'Come on, what are you waiting for?' said Pinnerup, lifting up a pack from the deck. The dockers looked at each other and winked. One patted Knud Erik on the shoulder and offered him a cigarette. Then they took their places and the chain resumed.

Knud Erik stayed on the quay, smoking the first cigarette of his life. He inhaled without coughing. He studied the hand that held it. Every single finger bore a long, painful weal from where salt water and harsh ropes had split the tender skin open. Sea-gashes, they called them.

'Piss on them,' Boutrup had advised. 'It rinses them. And then bind them with a bit of wool. That'll close them up.'

The sun warmed Knud Erik's face and he felt good.

WHEN HE SIGNED OFF THE *ACTIVE*, HIS MOTHER ASKED HIM ABOUT the fountain pen. She'd given it to him as a confirmation present so he could write letters home.

'A lot of good that did,' Klara commented.

He'd also received a pillow and a duvet and eighty-five kroner. He'd spent forty-five on a pair of new wooden clogs which the shoemaker said would last him a lifetime. He bought his oilskins from Lohse's in Havnegade, where he also acquired a folding knife with a white bone handle. A seaweed mattress cost him two kroner and he'd bought himself a green-painted sea chest with a flat lid as well. He needed work clothes: a jumper and a pair of moleskin trousers. When he was fully equipped, every last øre of the eighty-five kroner was gone.

He'd written to his mother twice during his fifteen months at sea. Both letters basically amounted to the same thing: 'Dear Ma, I'm fine.'

He couldn't exactly write to her about the time he doubted his decision to go to sea. It would have been the same as agreeing with her view that a sailor's life was brutal misery. Nor could he write about how he'd overcome that doubt, because that meant the die was cast, and he was committed to being a sailor. So he hid himself in his letters: between the 'Dear' and the 'Love' there was silence.

She could see that he'd developed. But she saw more than that. The gulf between them had widened with every inch he'd grown, almost as if his growth were rooted in spite and disobedience. He'd come to look even more like his father: he had the same blond, curly hair and strong chin. But he had her brown eyes, and when she caught sight of him in an unguarded moment, she still felt she had a share in him. If he possessed an ounce of sense, he'd tire of life at sea in the end.

It was no use talking, or trying to pressure him. Instead, she served his favourite dishes in the months he spent at home waiting for his next job. An unexpected warmth emerged between them, but then she realised that he'd misinterpreted it, thinking she'd finally accepted his choice. He showed her the scars on his hands and the saltwater blisters and told her about the loathsome Pinnerup, proud to show off his newly acquired status as an experienced sailor.

But she was outraged when she saw what the sea had done to him.

'I hope you've learned your lesson now!' The words escaped her before she could stop them. She heard their sharp desperation.

He looked at her guardedly and said nothing. But she could read the message in his eyes: You don't understand.

No, she didn't. She felt her own impotence. The warmth that had briefly flared between them evaporated. Again they withdrew from each other and ate their meals in silence. Her handsome son. Yes, he had her eyes. But nothing else.

That autumn Klara bought the five steamers, the *Unity*, the *Energy*, the *Future*, the *Goal* and the *Dynamic*, from the widows.

We were pretty taken aback by this purchase, which would have required determination and willpower, not to mention the kind of capital we'd never have believed she had. We didn't know precisely how much she paid, but it had to be in the millions. For a long time we spoke of precious little else. She'd become an enigmatic force. We'd finally caught on that she was up to something. But what it was, we didn't know.

The widows had never found a replacement for Isaksen. There'd been several applicants for the post of managing director, but none of them was found to be suitable, and the company's skippers had shaken their heads. The rumours about why Isaksen resigned had travelled far and wide, so the qualified candidates stayed away, and the company was almost at a standstill. But there was still a chance that a man with the clout to sway the widows and revive their halting business might one day appear and make the town flourish again. This was a risk Klara Friis wasn't prepared to run.

'But, my dear, there's really no need for you to do that,' Ellen said when Klara put forward her proposal after lengthy discussions with Markussen. Ellen seemed to believe that Klara was buying the ships only out of gratitude for the coffee and vanilla biscuits they'd served her so frequently.

'It's the least I can do,' Klara said, making it sound as if the enormous purchase were a display of good neighbourliness, though she was fully aware that this conversation was absurd. Perhaps the widows had an inkling of this, too, for Ellen turned unusually pale, and Emma and Johanne's cheeks were scarlet. They glanced at each other, and Klara knew that despite their chronic indecisiveness, they'd cave in.

She hadn't exploited them. She'd offered them neither too much nor too little for the steamers, given the unfavourable state of the world market. Profit didn't motivate her. What drove her was the damage to Knud Erik's hands.

The sea-gashes had made her buy the steamers. The saltwater blisters on her poor son's fingers, wrists and neck had repelled her: they'd brought to mind the wounds of African slaves, chained and dragged across a continent before being stowed on ships and sold. They must have had scars like that, where raw iron had gnawed at bare skin.

This was Klara Friis's mission: to free the slaves. She wanted to release Knud Erik from the chains his mad and misconceived manhood had shackled him to. Sailors who had barely returned home, bruised and battered by their constant battle with the sea, would set off again as soon as they could, as if begging for more, unable to get enough of the lashings that came at them from all sides: the storms, the waves, the cold, the poor food, the dreadful hygiene, the brutality, the violence. And the weakest always bore the brunt. It had to stop.

A few days later Knud Erik informed her that he'd signed on to a new ship. He would get his seabag and sea chest ready himself.

THE *KRISTINA* WAS A TOPGALLANT 150-TONNE SAIL SCHOONER. HER captain, Teodor Bager, was a lean man with an anxious, sunken face, which neither the sun nor the wind seemed to touch. He remained equally pale in summer and winter, in northern hemisphere and southern. People said he had a weak heart and he should have retired, but he was too miserly to do so. His only love was his eighteen-year-old daughter, Kristina. He'd named his ship after her.

There were five men in his crew, including Knud Erik, who was now fifteen. He'd graduated from the galley to the deck as an ordinary seaman and regarded himself as an experienced sailor. He knew his compass. He'd mastered eye splices and short splices, and he could whip a rope. He could heave in the stays, veer and tack.

The boy in the galley, feeding the fire in the stove, was a pale little fellow, green-faced from seasickness. He was fourteen, as Knud Erik had also been once, an eternity ago. He recognised Helmer, who was scared of water and who'd once hung from the forestay of his grandfather's smack, capsizing it. And there was another Marstaller, an older man: Hermod Dreymann, the first mate on the *Kristina*.

The two able seamen, Rikard and Algot, were long-haul sailors from Copenhagen. They came from families with no seafaring tradition, as was clear from their kit. They had no sea chest or bedding. Apart from the seaman's classic canvas bag, with its cow horn of grease, sail needle, splicing fid, awl and sail gloves, neither owned anything but a blanket and a cigar box with shaving gear. Their shore clothes looked just like the clothes they worked in: blue dungarees and jumpers.

Rikard had a tattoo on his right arm of a naked mermaid bearing the Danish flag. Both Rikard and Algot used Polish cigarette holders, fitted with a flat bottom so you could set them upright when there was no ashtray.

The atmosphere on the *Kristina* was much more convivial than on the *Active*, but Knud Erik's old tormentor still haunted him. Fighting exhaustion at night, alone at the wheel with massive, ice-laden waves looming over the ship, he'd think of Pinnerup. He'd hear his curses in the wind's howl and see his face in the foam of a cresting wave. Yet even as he choked with weariness and felt the merciless torture of his saltwater boils, he knew, with a feeling of triumph, that he'd conquered him. He could still hate the sea with a child's defiance, but now it held no fear for him.

He'd seen the first mate humbled. He'd sat on the quay at Frederiksholm's Kanal dangling his legs with studied indifference, not really understanding what he was learning as he watched Pinnerup backing down in his clash with the dockers. Now he knew. Some things you had to pick up the hard way, but there was no need to humiliate someone just because they were new and green. The experienced man might even lend the inexperienced one a helping hand. And so when Helmer, exhausted and seasick, was ready to give up, Knud Erik helped him in the galley.

'Look,' he said. 'Your bread's too squishy and the crew keep complaining about it. The problem's in the rising. Shop-bought yeast doesn't work, see.'

He found a couple of large potatoes and told Helmer to peel them and chop them up into small pieces. 'Now get me a bottle,' he said.

He stuffed it three-quarters full with potato pieces and topped it up with water. Then he corked it and secured the cork with twine.

'Leave it somewhere warm and you'll have yeast in a couple of days. You strain it through a sieve into your dough. But be careful. Don't leave the bottle too long, or the cork will force the twine and explode. With an almighty bang.'

Helmer looked at him as if he'd just revealed the secret behind a magic trick. This must be what it was like to be an adult, Knud Erik thought. When people looked at you like that.

The *Kristina* plied the Newfoundland route. It wasn't the voyage Knud Erik had dreamed of, but it was the only work available, and the trip across the cold North Atlantic was a new initiation. They sailed timber from Oskarshamn in Sweden to Ørebakke in Iceland. During the twenty-two-day journey, his seasickness returned and eroded his sense of being an experienced sailor. It took fourteen days to unload the ship.

Afterwards they sailed on to Little Bay in Newfoundland with a ballast of volcanic sand from the Icelandic beaches. It was now November, and after a week at sea they hit dense fog. It lifted at noon and lay like a wall on the horizon while the sun shone brightly across the rest of the heavens. Then the fog returned, and the sails turned dark grey with moisture which dripped heavily onto the deck. One minute they could see far ahead, and the next they couldn't even make out the yardarm of the flying jib boom.

On the third day of the fog Knud Erik had just taken over the wheel when the grey mass lifted once more. To one side he saw high, ice-covered mountains. To his surprise, they weren't white, but blue, purple and a transparent sea green. One resembled a towering, massive cube; its right-angled corners and flat top made it look as if human hands had sculpted it. It seemed so unnatural to him that he began to feel uneasy. He knew only Scandinavia's low, flat, scoured rocky coasts and had certainly never seen anything remotely resembling this savage, alien world of ice and snow.

'Greenland to leeward, Greenland to leeward!' he yelled and could hear his own fright. The skipper and the first mate rushed up from the cabin. Bager stared briefly at the bizarre mountain landscape. 'It's not Greenland,' he said. 'Those are icebergs.'

He pointed to the horizon. More icebergs appeared to windward now, scattered so randomly that the illusion of a continuing coastline was shattered. Then the fog returned, and they were once more marooned on deck.

The skipper looked worried. His sunken face was paler than usual. 'We're in God's hands,' he said.

The fog bank remained with them for a fortnight. There was little wind, and the moist sails hung limp most of the time. The great Atlantic swells moved in a slow rhythm that left no ripples under the *Kristina*'s vulnerable hull. The water, smooth as oil, seemed to be thickening in the humid cold as if it were turning to ice. They were surrounded by silence, and at first Knud Erik thought that fog must dampen sound, just as it limited the view. It dawned on him that the crew had begun whispering, as if the icebergs crouched behind the wall of fog were evil spirits whose attention it was vital not to attract. The silence weighed on the men, and yet they dared not break it. Knud Erik wondered if even God Himself could keep an eye on them inside this dense grey shroud, as the skipper hoped He would.

When the fog lifted at last and they saw the sea around them free of ice, they started shouting. They could have cheered, but they didn't; they just yelled incoherently, wanting to hear the sound of their own voices. Each man had been isolated by the silence: now they were united again. No icebergs were stalking them. Shouting was permitted.

On the following day they spotted the coast of Newfoundland. They'd been at sea for twenty-four days since leaving Iceland.

They docked at Little Bay, and Knud Erik rowed the skipper ashore. He was going to speak to a broker and the port authorities, and he told Knud Erik to wait for him outside. When he returned, his face looked strange. Knud Erik positioned the oars and started rowing towards the *Kristina*.

'Knud Erik,' Bager said. His tone was confidential, which was unfamiliar to Knud Erik, for the skipper normally addressed him only to give orders. 'The *Ane Marie* hasn't arrived.' The *Ane Marie* was a Marstal schooner that had left Iceland eight days before the *Kristina*. The skipper sighed and looked across the water. 'So she's probably gone. I imagine she hit an iceberg.' The skipper kept looking across the water and said nothing else for the rest of the trip.

Vilhjelm. That was his first thought when the skipper told him the news. Vilhjelm was on board the *Ane Marie*. Knud Erik looked down at his hands: they were gripping the oars so tightly that his knuckles had gone white. He took huge strokes, as though shaking himself from a trance, and nearly fell off the thwart.

'Mind how you row,' Bager said. His voice sounded absent, almost gentle.

In the evening Knud Erik lay in his berth, grieving. Had Vilhjelm surfaced twice? Or had he gone straight to the bottom, pulled down by his clogs and heavy oilskins? What was the last thing he'd seen? The bubbles in the water? Or the frozen chaos of the icebergs? He remembered the unnaturally square iceberg he'd seen on the first day

496

of the *Kristina*'s voyage through the ice and the sinister feeling it had given him. Had the *Ane Marie* collided with it? What had Vilhjelm felt in that moment? Had he cried out for help? But why would he? There was no one to come to the rescue out there in the open North Atlantic.

He recalled their confirmation classes, marking the end of their childhood, where they'd sat in church every Sunday beneath the model ships suspended from the ceiling: symbols of Christian salvation. He'd looked up at the altarpiece, at Jesus calming the storm on Galilee with just a gesture. He'd joined in the old sailor's hymns that they'd all had to learn by heart.

> *Abide with us and turn away all evil,*
> *Send good winds and kind weather,*
> *To see us safely home!*

That's what they'd sung. Had that hymn been on Vilhjelm's lips in the final minutes before the ship went down? Or had he, like Knud Erik in front of the marine artist's Jesus on the Sea of Galilee, begun to doubt?

Where had God been when the *Hydra* vanished without trace with his father on board? Perhaps God was like Vilhjelm's father? Perhaps He was sitting with His back to us and just when it really mattered, had heard nothing?

It was pure luck who came home and who didn't. Knud Erik could find no meaning in any of it and he thought this must be how Vilhjelm had felt when he sank for the third time: God was deaf and hadn't heard him.

They had to clean the hold to prepare for the cargo of salt cod. They hosed it down and scrubbed it for five days, covered the bottom with a layer of spruce branches, layered birch bark on top and nailed more bark to the lining. The smell was pungent and fresh: it was the unfamiliar scent of mountains and woods. They were building a log cabin in the bottom of the ship. Salt cod was a demanding guest. Its lodgings must be ready and waiting.

Every day around mid-morning a curious event broke the monotonous routine of loading. A boat approached diagonally across the harbour, passing close to the *Kristina*. At the oars sat a young girl with black hair, cut short so that her neck was bared. She was tanned, with full lips, oriental eyes and strong brows. She rowed like a man, with long dogged strokes, and her skiff moved quickly. As she passed the *Kristina* she always glanced up. The crew would stand along the rail and stare back at her, but she never turned away: she seemed to be searching for a particular face.

After a couple of days Knud Erik grew convinced that she was looking at him in particular. One day their eyes met, and he blushed and had to look away himself.

Rikard and Algot talked about her afterwards. She always wore a baggy jumper and moleskin trousers, which made it difficult to comment on her body. She was slim, though, that much they could see, and this spurred their speculations. Judging by her dark eyes and generally oriental appearance, they were sure she was a descendant of 'the cunt ladder'.

'That's the ladder the hookers in Bangkok use to get on board the ships,' Rikard explained. Knud Erik said nothing. He pondered the look he'd exchanged with the girl and blushed every time he recalled the way her eyes had rested on him. Mostly, though, he thought about Vilhjelm. He couldn't sleep at night and during the day his head buzzed.

The next time the girl came by, Dreymann waved at her. She waved back, and this took the tension out of the situation. She always rowed the same stretch, out to a certain rock, behind which she disappeared. She'd reappear a couple of hours later, but on her return she didn't come close to the ship or look in its direction. Instead, she fixed her gaze straight ahead and rowed hard.

Where she was going and what she did when she got there formed another topic of discussion. Rikard puffed on the cigarette in its Polish holder and stated his opinion: she was visiting a lover. Dreymann dismissed that as nonsense.

'Look at her,' he protested. 'She's not a day over sixteen – seventeen at most.'

Rikard responded that the girls started early in Newfoundland, then looked around as if to say he wouldn't mind being interrogated on how he'd come by this special knowledge.

Dreymann said he thought that the girl was going to piano lessons.

'On a rock?' Rikard mocked him.

At least they knew who she was: the daughter of Mr Smith, a tall, broad man who went about dressed in plus fours and tartan socks. He lived in a large green-painted wood villa set on a small hill behind the town. Mr Smith shipped fish – which made him the most important man in Little Bay.

He'd come on board from time to time, and he talked to no one but Bager, though he glanced at Knud Erik occasionally.

Then one day, after Mr Smith's usual visit to the skipper's cabin and his typical departure without a word to the crew, Bager came on deck and approached Knud Erik. Clasping his hands behind his back, he leaned forward and spoke quietly to him, as if afraid of being overheard. 'Miss Smith would like a visit from you. Tomorrow at four. I'm granting you shore leave.'

Knud Erik said nothing.

Bager leaned even closer. 'Do you understand what I'm saying to you? A man from Mr Smith's office will come for you.' Knud Erik nodded. 'Good,' the skipper said, and turned to leave. Suddenly he stopped, as if he'd nearly forgotten to deliver another message. 'Watch that little madam.' He gave Knud Erik a warning look. Then he spun on his heel and left quickly, like a man who'd just got an unpleasant duty out of the way.

The others hadn't noticed the exchange, so no comments followed. Knud Erik was completely dumbstruck. He wasn't generally afraid of girls. After all, he'd often taken care of his little sister. It wasn't until Marie caught Anton's eye that he realised that a girl could be something other than a friend. Still, he couldn't imagine what this girl wanted and was worried that her interest in him would somehow brand him as 'girly'. He'd stand out from the rest of the crew, and if there was one thing he didn't want, it was that.

Knud Erik was collected the following day shortly before four o'clock. Rikard and Algot stared and called out after him. All the way up to the villa, his escort ignored him, as if he, too, found the whole business embarrassing and would prefer not to be involved with it at all. When they reached the house, he abandoned Knud Erik without a word.

Knud Erik stepped onto the veranda and knocked cautiously on the door. An elderly woman in a long, old-fashioned woollen dress opened the door and led him through a large hall into the drawing room. So far no one had spoken to him. She closed the door behind her and Knud Erik found himself alone. Tea was waiting on a small table set with a cloth by the window. Next to the cups and the silver teapot was a china plate with biscuits. He remained right inside the door, not sure whether he should sit down on one of the upholstered chairs. Still nothing happened, and he started to wander around the room. He took a biscuit from the plate, and at that very moment the door behind him sprang open. Flustered, he turned round and hid the biscuit behind his back. It was the girl from the rowing boat, but she was no longer wearing her jumper and men's trousers. Instead, she wore a dress. This instantly unsettled him. So did her face, which looked far more vivid than before. True, he'd watched her only from a distance, and now he was seeing her close up for the first time. But that didn't account for her eyes being so much darker and her wide mouth being so red, which made it look even bigger. He had to look down: the impression she made was almost too strong. As she came over to him he noticed that she was taller than he was. But then again, she was older.

She offered him her hand. 'Miss Sophie,' she said.

'Knud Erik Friis,' he said, unsure if he should have added a 'Mr' or if that title was exclusively reserved for men like her father, the mighty Mr Smith.

'Sit down, please,' she said in English, and gestured towards a chair.

Knud Erik obeyed. He was still hiding the biscuit. Sitting down with one hand behind his back was awkward, so he furtively placed it on the chair as he lowered himself into it, and felt it crunch underneath him. He was so embarrassed that he couldn't concentrate on a word Miss Sophie was saying to him. Not that he understood it: it was all in English. He felt completely out of place, sitting on a crushed biscuit and drinking tea with this girl, who was taller than he was and had strange colours on her face, while a flow of incomprehensible words poured from her mouth – words to which she apparently expected him to reply.

He stared at the amber-coloured tea, which he didn't like, nodding earnestly from time to time. Well, that would have to suffice as his contribution to the conversation. It was the best he could do. Suddenly he heard her laugh out loud.

'You're just sitting there, nodding. But you don't understand a word I'm saying.'

He gave her an amazed look.

'Yes, I can speak Danish.' She kept laughing with her big mouth. 'My mother was Danish. But she died a long time ago.' She said this in a casual tone, as if she didn't attribute much importance to it. She leaned towards him.

'Are you shy?' she asked.

'Of course not.'

He suddenly felt defiant, and without his being aware of it, this dissolved his bashfulness. He was angry now. She'd made him feel like a little boy. On the ship he felt like a man, and he wanted his newly acquired dignity acknowledged here, too. Besides, she spoke Danish. He was back on familiar territory. Miss Sophie simply needed to be treated like Marie.

'You know we talk about you on the *Kristina*,' he said. 'We don't know what you're doing. Some of us think you go to piano lessons. But one bloke says you have a boyfriend you visit every day on the rock.'

Miss Sophie gave him a teasing look. 'A boyfriend. Well, I might have. And what do you think?' Knud Erik didn't reply. 'No,' Miss Sophie went on. 'I don't have a boyfriend out on the rock. I have a dream place. Do you know what a dream place is?'

He shook his head.

'It's a place where you dream. There's a narrow sandy beach just beyond the harbour. That's where I sit and look out across the water. And then I dream. About passenger steamers, aeroplanes and zeppelins, about big cities and streets filled with cars and shopfronts along every pavement, about picture houses and restaurants.' She reeled off this list without taking a breath, as if she were releasing longings saved up over a long time. 'Do you have a dream?'

'Yes,' Knud Erik said. 'I dream of sailing south around Cape Horn.'

'Cape Horn,' Miss Sophie said, surprised, and then laughed. 'Of course, you're a sailor. But why Cape Horn? It's cold, it's always windy and ships sink there.'

'That may be,' Knud Erik said. 'But you're not a real sailor unless you've sailed south around Cape Horn.'

'Says who?'

'Everyone.'

'Are you scared of drowning?' Miss Sophie asked.

Knud Erik hesitated for a moment. Could this odd girl with the face that was at once so strange and so pretty really make him tell her everything?

'Yes,' he replied honestly. 'I'm very scared of drowning.'

'Have you ever come close?' Miss Sophie stared intensely at him with her deep, dark eyes: two lights beaming out of a mineshaft.

'Yes, once.'

'How was it?'

He didn't feel like replying to this. 'My best friend's just drowned. He went down with the *Ane Marie*, which was headed for here,' he said instead.

She looked down, as if she needed some time to compose herself. When she met his eyes again, she smiled encouragingly. 'You'll probably drown one day, too.'

She said this in a completely ordinary tone, as if she were announcing that dinner would be served shortly. It was a ridiculous thing to say. What did she mean? Did she think she could foresee the future? Again he felt her gaze on him. She was scrutinising him as if exploring the effect of her words.

Knud Erik looked away. The trust between them was broken. His grief at Vilhjelm's death overwhelmed him again, and his indignation flared up. 'Are you putting a curse on me?'

'Have you ever visited a big city?' she asked, and he detected hesitation in her voice.

'I've been to Copenhagen.'

'I don't believe that's a proper big city. Don't you ever dream about London and Paris, about Shanghai and New York?'

Knud Erik shook his head. 'I dream about Cape Horn,' he said stubbornly.

'What a shame. In that case we can't elope together. I don't want to go to Cape Horn, it's cold and horrible. Ugh, how boring you are.' She started laughing. Then she leaned forward and cradled his head in her hands. 'Still, you'll get a kiss before you leave.'

She looked into his eyes. For a moment he thought about freeing himself, but then he realised that it would be childish to resist. He had to take it like the man he'd turned into these last few months. He stared back and something strange happened to him. A shiver went through him, not of fear, but of something else, something unfamiliar. A quiet trembling ran through his body in expectation of something big and joyful. He closed his eyes to receive the kiss and be transported to some place where he instinctively knew no ship could bring him.

He felt her lips, their soft fullness pressing against his with a slightly sticky sensation that made him wish that they need never let go of each other again. His hands, which had been lying on the chair's armrests, slipped up her back, and as they did he felt a crackle of electricity. Then he got hold of her exposed neck beneath the short hair and gently caressed its soft curve. He opened his mouth slightly. He wished she would do the same so their breath could meet, and he could inhale her air into his lungs and breathe through the element that was her. It was like drowning while still being able to breathe. Now he opened himself to another element and let it fill him. He sensed how she followed him and let her lips part slightly. They breathed through each other's mouths and drew air from each other's lungs. Kissing Miss Sophie, he kissed the world. It kissed him back and he was filled with its sweet breath.

Then she pulled back from him, placed one hand on her chest and laughed. 'You really know how to kiss.' She handed him a napkin from the table. 'Here, you'd better wipe off the lipstick.'

He held up his hand to stop her as if she were about to take something valuable from him. 'No, come here.'

She laughed again. She took hold of his shoulder and wiped his mouth with the napkin. 'We can't have you leaving Mr Smith's house with lipstick all over your face.' She gave him a critical look. 'Has anyone ever told you how handsome you are?' Her voice was teasing. She got up and took his hand. Then she led him to the door to the hall. 'We'll say goodbye here.'

'Will we see each other again?' he asked, and realised instantly how this question had exposed him.

She held out her hand and winked at him. 'Have a good trip to Cape Horn.'

She didn't appear the next day. Late in the afternoon he kept going over to the rail to scout across the sea. Ever since he left Mr Smith's house he'd been agitated. He didn't think that he could be in love. This was different, more like when the *Kristina* heeled unexpectedly

503

and you had to grab hold of the nearest fixed point on the swaying deck.

He thought of her with irritation – no, with more than that: with anger and a fierce desire for vengeance. She'd humiliated him, wiping his mouth with a napkin as if he were a child. He barely dared recall their kiss. Words couldn't contain all the contradictory feelings the memory stirred in him. He'd felt both tiny and huge, as if he were being endlessly transformed. The kiss had sown a longing, and the longing hurt; it bruised his self-esteem.

The others noticed his restless pacing by the rail. 'Looking out for something in particular?' Dreymann asked. The other seamen laughed, even Helmer, the little shit. They'd been bursting with questions when he returned from the villa, but he'd been dismissive and kept his answers to the minimum.

'What was she like?' Rikard asked, wriggling the naked mermaid on his arm.

'She was nice enough' was all he said. 'We drank tea and ate biscuits.'

'Didn't you do anything else?' The crew studied his face. 'Look at those pretty brown eyes,' Rikard sneered at him. 'Do you know why your eyes are brown?'

Knud Erik shook his head defencelessly, sensing that a crude response was coming.

'It's because you were kicked so hard up the arse when you were a kid that the shit went the wrong way.'

They were making a fool of him, and it was her fault.

And then she didn't even show up!

One by one the days passed, all filled identically with the loading of the salt cod beneath a sky of unchanging grey cloud. Still she didn't appear. Knud Erik hung around on the deck, unable to stop thinking about her.

The others kept teasing him, and he blushed every time. They referred to her as 'Knud Erik's girlfriend'.

'Have you had your kiss today?' Rikard would ask.

Or, worse: 'Surely she's not bored with you already?'

By now the salt cod was piled almost as high as the hatch coaming: they'd nearly finished loading it, and soon they'd be off to Portugal and he'd never see Miss Sophie again. Out of sheer desperation

Knud Erik decided to do something rash. He'd return, alone, to the big green-painted villa. He'd stand outside the door on the veranda. And when she opened up, he'd turn his back on her. Or perhaps even spit on the ground. Or something, anything, to show that she meant nothing to him. That he had his own world, and she couldn't rock it.

It was the day before their departure and they were getting the sails ready. With no idea of how he might escape to visit her, his agitation was turning to full-blown panic. If he didn't get to see her one last time, his whole world would come crashing down. Unable to stand it any longer, he leaped over the rail and onto the quay, then started running towards the green villa. He heard Dreymann call out behind him, but he didn't turn.

Though the villa was visible from the *Kristina*, it was a long way to run and mostly uphill. He was out of breath when he got there, but he didn't stop until he reached the front door of the house. He knocked hard, then rested his hands on his thighs for support as he struggled to get his breath back.

He was still in that position when the door was opened.

He'd fantasised about this. With burning cheeks, he'd imagined their last meeting, the one that would set him free. But it wasn't Miss Sophie. It was the older woman who'd shown him into the house on his first visit.

She stared at him expectantly, as if she thought he must have an important message for the owner of the house, the mighty Mr Smith.

'Miss Sophie,' he gasped, still incapable of standing up and breathing normally after his long sprint.

Shaking her head, the woman said some words in English. He caught only the last two: '. . . not here.'

But the shake of her head conveyed her meaning. If he hadn't been in this wretched state he'd surely have attacked her, as if it were her fault that the object of his longing wasn't there.

'Where?' he panted, still breathless.

The woman gave him a disapproving look and seemed to consider whether she should even dignify the confused boy's question with an answer. 'St John's,' she said finally, and gave him another look, in which he thought he detected both malice and pity, though he couldn't see how the two could be combined in one expression.

His heart sank. St John's was the biggest town in Newfoundland, a frequent port of call for Marstal schooners. That much he knew. He also knew that the *Kristina* wasn't going there.

Miss Sophie had left. That was why she hadn't appeared for her daily rowing trips. She was somewhere else on this endless earth, and they'd never see each other again. Something that had hardly begun, heading in all directions, was already over.

Bager was waiting for him.

'What's the matter with you, boy?' he said and whacked Knud Erik across the back of his head.

'How far away is St John's?' Knud Erik asked, ignoring the blow.

'What the hell's got into you?' the skipper exclaimed, and whacked him again. 'One hundred and eighty miles, but we're not chasing skirt in St John's. We're going to Setubal with salt cod for the Catholics.'

The whacks weren't hard. Taps, really. An amused tone had crept into Bager's voice. He looked as if he was enjoying himself. 'Foolish lad,' he said. 'You think you're setting the course now? I told Mr Smith. Keep that girl under control, I said. She drives people mad. Spoiled little missy.'

The barometer had dropped the next morning when they left Little Bay and headed out through the Bay of Notre Dame. Showers of rain came and went, but the sea was calm. Late in the afternoon they came in sight of the lighthouse at Fogo. They'd follow the coast down towards St John's until they could put out into the Atlantic.

That night a south-easterly storm rose, and they started drifting towards the rocky shore. During the day Knud Erik had observed the tall, dark cliffs through the downpour. Now they moved closer, invisibly, in the impenetrable darkness of the night, and only the distant thunder of the surf warned of their proximity. Everyone below was roused and ordered to put on their oilskins so they could get up on deck immediately if needed.

The searching beam of the Cape Bonavista lighthouse swung across the turbulence, briefly ghosting the sails before sweeping across the shifting veil of densely falling rain. They were close to the coast and the ship was reefed until they were left with only the fore staysail. With all her power lost, the *Kristina* was reduced to pitching in the storm-lashed waves as she fought the gale.

The flicker from the lighthouse came and went like a star that has come too close to the sea, swallowed by waves one minute and struggling free the next. Clouds appeared through the darkness, big-bellied sharks chasing across the sky. Dawn broke and supplanted the beam of the lighthouse. But the storm continued to rage.

The skipper looked at the barometer. 'This is going to last a while,' he said darkly, and put a hand to his chest as if fearing his heart couldn't hold out that long.

Knud Erik never would have believed it, but mortal danger can bore a man stiff. The storm continued, day in and day out, ceaselessly battering the hull of the *Kristina*, howling in the rigging, tearing at the wheel, and putting them under constant strain. But paradoxically, the state of alarm anaesthetised their nerves, leaving them with a sense of infinite emptiness.

The deck was constantly flooded by the onslaught of the waves, giving the impression that only the stern and the bow remained afloat, like two severed pieces of wreckage that stayed inexplicably equidistant amid the chaos of breaking waves and raging foam.

The low-riding clouds chasing one another across the sky; the ranks of waves rolling endlessly towards the shore; the black, menacing barrier of a coast that represented death rather than salvation if they came too near: all this emptied his head of thought.

The storm endured, but so did the *Kristina*. Even his fear of drowning took a back seat, ceding to the tedious grind and the constant pain from the saltwater blisters, which spread furiously up his arms and around his neck. The only reason the open wounds didn't become infected was that they were permanently wet.

They pitched up and down like that for thirty days. Sometimes the black coastline sank into the horizon until it was nothing but a pencil line between sky and sea; at other times it would rise up and tower over them, an anvil on which the sea could hammer their frail hull.

It didn't make any difference whether the coast was near or far: to Knud Erik, the black cliffs represented neither destruction nor salvation. They weren't even land. They were just another aspect of the monotony, as real or unreal as the rain-laden clouds above their heads. Day and night came and went.

When he was off duty during the day he'd stagger, dazed, to the bow of the ship, clinging to the ropes the crew had suspended from the rigging for support as they crossed the flooded deck. He'd be waist-high in water already when a wave hit directly amidships and tugged at his legs, spume rampaging all around. He felt like a tightrope walker who has lost his footing and is hanging by his arms on a line suspended between two points in the sky. As if he weren't aboard a ship at all, but swinging himself across the empty sea.

He'd tumble down the ladder into the dark, foul-smelling fo'c's'le, with its flooded floor and its stove which remained unlit for fear of carbon monoxide poisoning. He'd climb into his berth fully clothed, because what was the point of undressing, and where would he dry his clothes? They were saturated with salt, which attracted moisture and spray. He'd curl up there like a baby and give way to unconsciousness until a hand shook him and he'd tumble out of his berth, barely awake. Splashing across the floor in his boots, he'd haul himself up the ladder again and meet either darkness or grey light. It was irrelevant which. He'd become a single-purpose being: a servant of the ship, its blind tool in the storm. He no longer considered the matter of his own survival. His only thoughts were of sails to be reefed or taken in, and ropes to be fastened.

Finally the wind died down. The sea still moved in heavy swells, but the rigging no longer shrieked and the ominous froth disappeared from the waves. The sun broke through the clouds; the big-bellied sharks were gone. The black coastline became land again, a place one could reach, the fulfilment of an impossible dream: firm ground underfoot, an amazing notion that it took time to get used to after thirty days on a convulsing sea.

Two black mountains with almost vertical sides appeared ahead of them. Between them was an opening.

'The Black Hole,' Bager said, paler than ever. 'The entrance to St John's.'

He turned to Knud Erik, who was at the wheel.

'Seems you'll get your way after all,' he grinned. 'We'll call at St John's to take in supplies.'

IT WASN'T MISS SOPHIE HE'D FORGOTTEN, SO MUCH AS HIMSELF. THE monotony of the storm had swallowed everything up. But the skipper's remark and the sight of the Black Hole brought her back. It was more important than ever to see her again. He'd been given a second chance, and it couldn't be a coincidence. Meaning returned to everything, and all the signs pointed in one direction: Miss Sophie.

He forgot about his blisters and his soaked clothes. The tension that had stiffened his body for thirty days and nights, making it ache more than any physical exertion could, disappeared. The storm had passed, only to make way for a new, internal one. The skipper's words had prompted more cursed blushing. An impatient wind whipped his blood and made his heart race.

Bager took the wheel and they passed through the Black Hole. Behind it the narrow entrance to St John's opened up, teeming with fishing boats, schooners and small steamers. Wooden houses stood on the rocky slopes, and along the harbour front dense rows of buildings faced the water, with warehouses and ship's chandlers packed cheek by jowl. The quays were crowded with people and horse carts. The din from the street mingled with the screeching of seagulls, and the stench of fish and fish oil pervaded everything.

Knud Erik could tell right away that St John's wasn't a major city. Copenhagen was bigger, but compared to the life here, the quays along Frederiksholm's Kanal seemed deserted. Knud Erik had imagined St John's as a slightly bigger version of Little Bay: somewhere behind the town Mr Smith would have a house much like his other one. He could simply stroll up to it, knock on its door and meet Miss Sophie again. Looking around now, his heart sank. He'd never find her here. There were sure to be hundreds of other Mr Smiths. And – the thought almost paralysed him – perhaps hundreds of other Miss Sophies too.

* * *

They lit a fire in the fo'c's'le stove to dry out their clothes, washed in buckets of warm water and put on clean garments from their seabags. For a while they sat around the table at the centre of the fo'c's'le like something on display, before one by one they began to nod off.

'I feel like a damn spatchcock. Not a single bone left in my body,' Rikard said.

The next morning the skipper announced shore leave that same evening, and they all headed into town together. Even Helmer was allowed to join them. The storm had been his baptism; the punctual coffee service he'd provided throughout its duration had earned him membership of the group. They made for Water Street, right behind the harbour front.

Dreymann winked at Knud Erik.

'You'll probably find Miss Sophie there.'

They went into a pub and ordered beer. The place was full of women; one of them came over to their table. Her face was painted and she laughed at them with a big red mouth.

Algot put his arm around her thick waist. 'You're better off with this one,' he said to Knud Erik. 'You'll get more for your money than with that skinny Miss Sophie. Isn't that right, Sally, or whatever the hell your name is.'

'Julia. My name's Julia,' the woman said in English.

She was used to Scandinavian sailors and understood a little of what was being said. She leaned provocatively towards Knud Erik. She smelled of perfume and sweat: close up he could see that the floury powder on her face had cracked, revealing the wrinkles underneath. She made as if to kiss him: he instinctively turned away but she grabbed hold of his neck and tried to shove his face deep into her cleavage.

'A pretty boy like you shouldn't sleep alone.'

He squirmed free and turned his back on her while the others roared with laughter. He took a swig of beer to cover his embarrassment: its bitterness made him wince. He took another, hoping it would taste better the second time. It didn't. Did he really have to drink this stuff?

He turned to the others. The woman was now sitting on Algot's lap, a bottle to her lips. The rest of the crew were deep in a discussion about something or other.

'Wait till we get to Setubal; this is nothing,' Rikard said.

'Setubal!' Algot snorted. 'Give me Martinique any day. The girls there dance on the tables naked.'

'And give you syphilis,' Rikard retorted. 'We had this bosun once. Spends one night with one of them: three months later he's a goner. Priciest cunt in the world, that one. So no nigger bitches for me, mate.'

'I suggest you enjoy it while it lasts, lads,' Dreymann said indulgently. 'When we get to England, we pick up the skipper's daughter. Once Miss Kristina's on board, you'll need to start watching your language.'

Knud Erik looked across to Helmer, who sat clasping his bottle in silence. He hadn't drunk much of his beer, either.

'Don't you have something else to drink here?' Knud Erik said, trying to sound like a man of the world.

'You mean lemonade?' Rikard called out, laughing at his own wit.

'Gin,' the woman said. 'Give him some gin.'

Dreymann sent Knud Erik a warning look. 'Watch out,' he said. 'It's as strong as schnapps.'

'Rubbish,' Algot shouted. 'Looks like water, tastes like water, even has the same damn kick as water.' He pushed a glass of clear liquid towards Knud Erik. 'Down the hatch.'

Relieved to escape the bitter taste of beer, Knud Erik took a large gulp. The others looked at him expectantly. The taste was strong, but it wasn't sharp. Tentatively he took another swig. The gin filled his mouth with a pleasant softness, but rather than sliding down his throat the sensation seemed to run the other way and creep into the walls of his skull. It felt like someone was stroking the inside of his head.

Algot nodded in approval. The woman grinned and presented her lips to him again, then turned to concentrate on Algot, who had one hand up her skirt.

Knud Erik looked at the others: pleasure was nudging at him. His gaiety needed an outlet. He laughed in the direction of Helmer, who returned his smile, glad of the attention. 'You should try gin,' he said knowledgeably. 'It's much better than beer.'

Helmer shook his head. 'I'm not thirsty.'

'It's not about being thirsty. It's about getting drunk!'

Helmer shook his head again, and Knud Erik decided to ignore him. 'Well, what the hell. Cheers!' He raised his glass with a flourish and spotted his reflection in a large mirror with a gilded frame. A blond lock fell across his forehead. His eyes were brown. His mother's eyes. Perhaps he really was a *pretty boy*.

The world seemed to be in motion, but unlike the rolling of a ship, its movements were unpredictable. The floor kept finding new and surprising angles of tilt, and though he quickly learned that his chair was the safest place to be, he kept wanting to get up and stagger about on the floor. There was a playfulness in him that was too big for the company around the table: he wanted to watch the dancers, perhaps steady himself against a table and rock a bit to the music himself, or fling his arms out to embrace them. From time to time a woman's hand would glide tentatively across his chest or touch the seat of his trousers. But the look on his face soon told them that he wasn't heading in that direction tonight, and they'd push deeper into the crowd, their hips swaying.

He surrendered to the pushing and shoving: the sheer pressure of the bodies around him prevented him from falling flat on his face. Suddenly, through the blissful tickle of the gin, the thought struck him that Miss Sophie was out there waiting for him. All he had to do was walk out of the door. He'd definitely find her. He contrived to get himself jostled towards the entrance, found the door and disappeared into Water Street.

He had no idea how late it was, but the street was still teeming with people. Most of them were men swaggering heavily and unsteadily across the pavement or in the middle of the street, with whinnying horses and hooting cars navigating around them. But there were also a few women who sized him up with kohl-rimmed eyes.

At the end of Water Street the crowd thinned. He backtracked a few steps and turned into a side street. Then, on the corner of Duckworth Street, he recognised her neck. She was walking ahead of him, dressed in a winter coat with her boots just visible beneath, and carrying a handbag. He could be wrong about anything else, but not her neck. That bare, exposed neck, suntanned against the winter fur collar: it was hers!

He ran after her, and then lost her. He got tangled in the crowds on the pavement and when he and a hefty woman attempted a mutual sidestep, they bumped together instead. Stumbling again, he felt her sharp alcoholic breath on his face, and darted back onto the street, where a coachman cursed at him and lashed out with his whip. He started running along the gutter, and when he reached the crossing at King's Road he spotted Miss Sophie again, on the opposite side of the street. He soon lost sight of her, but now he was convinced that he was on the right track. He stopped running. It was part of the game. He didn't want to reach her too soon.

They'd kiss again. And afterwards? Nothing. The kiss would be enough. Inhaling the air from her lungs into his just one more time.

He started jogging to test the steadiness of his feet on the pavement. His body had a floating feeling of lightness. Never before had he had such faith in himself.

The street ahead was now completely empty. Signal Hill Road started its long, slow ascent, crowned by Cabot Tower, a black silhouette against the swirling belt of the Milky Way. The whole starry sky seemed to be moving in the same direction he was, like a shimmering flock of birds migrating south through the night.

He spotted her some distance up the slope, a black figure against a road white with frost. She seemed almost to glide, as if pulled by an invisible string.

He started running again but ran out of steam and had to stop to catch his breath. Then he sprinted on past a lake and some trees. Everything was silver, covered with crystals of ice that shone like the stars high in the frosted sky. Below he could see the black forest of masts in the harbour and the illuminated pubs along Water Street.

By the time he caught up with her, she'd reached Cabot Tower. Her back was turned to him, and she was staring out across the Atlantic, which stretched beyond the harbour in all directions, a matt black surface that sucked up all light. For a moment he stood, too, completely lost in the sight of its vast expanse.

'Sophie,' he called out, then suddenly felt a prick of doubt. When she turned round, she showed no surprise. 'Yes, Knud Erik,' was all she said. Her lips were black in the faint starlight. 'What do you want from me?' His drunkenness restored his courage. He flung out his arms and prepared to embrace her.

'Are you drunk? Have you been pub-crawling on Water Street?'

He was mortified. 'I'm not drunk. I just want a kiss.' A smile spread across his face. He'd already forgotten his resentment. He was in a place where the only thing that mattered was the joyful song in his head.

Grabbing her with unexpected force, he leaned forward and found her lips. She didn't move. He'd closed his eyes, but now he opened them again. She was staring straight ahead and didn't appear to see him. Carefully he pressed his lips against hers, hoping to rekindle the magic of their first kiss. But nothing happened.

Then she pushed him away. 'Leave me alone,' she said. 'Do you hear me! Go away!'

Knud Erik stood open-mouthed and uncomprehending.

'Leave me alone!'

She was shouting now, and her eyes glittered. She stamped the frozen ground with her boot. 'Stop chasing after me like some dog!'

He was overcome by a sudden anger as intense as his infatuation had been. 'Don't you dare call me a dog!' he shouted.

He clasped her shoulders and started shaking her. She was taller than him, but he was stronger. Even with her head jolting, she kept up her defiant glare.

'Dog!' she said again.

All at once he let go of her. He was panting angrily.

'Bitch!' He spat on the ground between her boots, then turned on his heel and started running down Signal Hill.

'Knud Erik!' she called out after him.

He didn't stop. Sprinting wildly over the frozen ground he nearly crashed several times, but his drunkenness made him strangely light-footed. The cold slapped his face.

At the foot of the hill he found a changed town. The pubs along the harbour front had closed and the dense, heaving crowd that had filled Water Street had vanished. A fine layer of hoar frost covered the street, and its cold sheen underscored the unnatural silence that replaced the din. The masts along the quays were plated with silver and stood like a forest burned to white charcoal: ghost trees that at the slightest gust of wind might turn to dust.

He found the *Kristina* and stumbled down the ladder to the fo'c's'le where his drunkenness finally overcame him. Collapsing dizzily onto his berth, his eyes closed instantly.

*　*　*

The next morning he was woken by Rikard's swearing.

'Where the hell did you get to, boy? What makes you think you can run off like that?'

But the men's grins told him that they'd been too drunk themselves to be seriously worried. He remembered the maelstrom of people in the pub, but his hunt for Miss Sophie through the streets of St John's came back to him only in fragments. Their encounter on Signal Hill was equally blurred. If a door exists between dream and reality, that episode had occurred on the wrong side of it.

He was still stung by a sense of having been jilted. He vaguely recalled the vertiginous feeling that a void had suddenly opened up, but he didn't know why. The memory kept churning away, but he remained none the wiser.

The frost had set in. It was ten below zero, and a thin crust of ice was already forming on the water in the harbour. In the afternoon the skipper came over to him. He was expecting a beating, but instead Bager asked him to join him on a visit to town the next day.

'Find a clean sack,' he said. 'We're going to the butcher's in Queen's Road tomorrow to get fresh meat.'

As they walked through town the next day they noticed clusters of people talking together in the street. There was a strange, electric atmosphere, a kind of rippling unease. Strangers stopped to address one another, then peeled away towards the next agitated group. Bager, who spoke some English, asked the butcher what was going on. He was a giant of a man in a bloodstained rubber apron, busily chopping his way through heaps of red meat on a white-scoured block. He took his time before answering. Finally, putting down his cleaver, he spoke, throwing his arms about and shaking his red-veined head sadly. Knud Erik didn't understand the words, but he recognised the name Mr Smith.

Bager's face darkened, and he glanced sideways at Knud Erik. 'I knew it,' he muttered. 'I told you so. That girl will come to a bad end. But it's a terrible thing all the same.'

'What did he say?' Knud Erik asked after they'd left. Bager didn't reply but increased his pace until he was some distance ahead. They didn't speak all the way back to the harbour, where the skipper kept him at a distance.

The blood seeped through the sack of meat and left large dark stains on the grey sackcloth: Knud Erik felt people must be staring and got it into his head that he looked like a murderer carrying the remains of his mutilated victim through the town in broad daylight.

When they were back on board, Bager asked Knud Erik to come to his cabin.

'Sit down,' he said, seating himself opposite the young man. Then he leaned forward, hands folded on the table. 'Miss Sophie,' he started, and then he stopped. He gazed down at the table and gave a deep sigh. 'Miss Sophie,' he repeated, 'has gone missing.' Then he slammed his hand down hard. 'Damn it all!'

Knud Erik said nothing. The room didn't grow black in front of his eyes, but in his head, a kind of night began. He could see everything vividly, but he was incapable of thought.

'She's been gone two days now. No one knows where she is. An accident maybe. Or a crime. Personally I think she's eloped with some sailor. That girl's disturbed. I probably shouldn't be saying this, but she's not quite right in the head. Her mother died a long time ago – she probably told you that – and Mr Smith was too busy to take care of her properly. She always got her own way. That's never healthy in a girl that age. All this nonsense about inviting crewmen to tea. Dressing up like a lady and turning their heads. You weren't the first, I'm afraid.' Bager looked directly at Knud Erik. 'And dear Lord, you fell for her, too. And yes, I blame myself. I shouldn't have let you go. But Mr Smith charters us, so it's no easy thing to say no. I didn't see the harm in it. But look what it's led to.'

Knud Erik didn't speak. Now he knew what had happened to him in his drunkenness. Or did he? He saw Miss Sophie's slender coat-clad figure glide up Signal Hill where Cabot Tower stood, a dark silhouette against the Milky Way. He saw her face and her lips, black in the pale starlight. And he finally traced the source of the helpless, jilted feeling which had haunted him these past days. He recalled his wild race down Signal Hill and the silent town shrouded in frost. He'd left Miss Sophie up there under the cold stars. Was whatever happened to her afterwards his fault, because he'd run off? But she'd told him to go. She'd stamped her foot and called him a dog.

The whole thing seemed like a dream. Could he trust his own memories? What if something completely different had happened? Had he hit her? Suddenly he wasn't sure.

'I'm sorry,' the skipper murmured, still looking at the table. It sounded like he was talking to himself. 'I'm sorry you met her. I know it's my fault.' Then he looked up and noticed the vacancy in Knud Erik's eyes. 'Are you even listening to me, boy?'

When Knud Erik came up on deck, he could tell right away that the others had heard the news too: it must have made its way from town to deck, via the harbour. They eyed him gravely, but said nothing. Only Rikard's mouth twitched, as if it were about to burst with its stock of malicious remarks.

What was going through their minds? Did they suspect him of anything? What would they think if they knew the truth about his night on Signal Hill?

Well, what did *he* think?

Did you always know what you did when you got drunk?

The question stumped him. When it came to drunkenness, he had no experience whatsoever. He had no knowledge of himself either. He sensed that something fateful had happened that night on Signal Hill. It wasn't just his confusion that kept him silent: the whole event was too intimate. He couldn't speak about it without revealing his defeat. He desperately needed to confide in somebody, but an instinct for survival made him keep his mouth shut. If he didn't, he knew all too well that the others would fall on him instantly.

That night he climbed into his berth without exchanging a word with a soul.

By now the temperature was between twelve and fourteen degrees below zero every day, and the next morning the deck was covered in snow. A snowball came flying through the air and turned to powder as it collided with the rigging; soon a full-scale snowball fight had erupted between the ships that lay close together in the narrow port of St John's.

But Knud Erik didn't join in. He stood with his hands in the pockets of his fleecy moleskin trousers and shuddered in the cold.

THEY SAILED FOUR DAYS AFTER THE FROST SET IN. A TUGBOAT LED them out through the Black Hole. A brisk wind was blowing from the north and the Labrador Current was with them. They sailed through pancake ice but made good speed nonetheless. Around eleven in the morning the skipper ordered Knud Erik up the foremast to look for open water. He climbed the rigging until he reached the topgallant yard; below him the sails were rigid with frost. To the south the ice extended as far as the horizon. The vast unbroken surface, gleaming white in the sun, gave him a mild feeling of nausea, which stayed with him back on the deck.

There was pot roast for lunch, but Knud Erik thought of the butcher's chopping block and the dark patches on the sack where the blood from the meat had seeped through. He had no appetite but didn't want to leave his plate untouched either. He put a piece of meat in his mouth and left it there. It seemed to swell. Then he rushed onto the deck and puked over the rail.

On the second day they spied open water. The wind was rising and the sea began to shift. With the temperature still low, the *Kristina* had started to freeze over. During the night and the following day the ship became encased in a thick armour of ice. The halyards froze together in lumps. The bulwark became a frigid wall, and on the main deck the ice stood a foot deep. The bowsprit was a single compact block that reached as far as the martingale.

The fully laden ship now lay even lower in the water, her weight increased by several tonnes. The bow was already dangerously sunken, and the deck was level with the sea on the other side of the frozen bulwark. The sails looked like heavy sheets of wood that inscrutably had been hoisted from the mast.

It was like being on board a giant block of ice that a sculptor was trying his best to carve into a ship. But he was hampered by the block's continual growth, which returned the shapes he carved to formlessness: the elegant rigging, the beautifully curved lines of bulwark and bowsprit – everything that gives a ship her definition and her advantage over the sea – had become a jumble of lumps and cubes. No longer a ship, nor even a reasonable imitation of one, the *Kristina* became a death sentence signed by the frost, stripped of her last remnant of seaworthiness, transformed into a deadweight of ice and salt cod doomed to sink.

The crew knew their lives depended on a successful battle against the relentless freeze. Opening up the tool chest, each man grabbed a maul and attacked the glittering castle that was building itself around them. Ice chunks clattered brightly down from the rigging and the halyards before hitting the deck. But the deck itself resisted all their efforts. They hammered themselves sweaty and red-faced, producing a crack here and a crack there, but the heavy sheet of ice wouldn't shift, and the slope of the bulwark remained imprisoned inside. They couldn't even get close to the frozen lump that was the bowsprit. You risked your life venturing onto it.

At first the challenge excited them, and they yelled out to one another. But after a while they fell silent. In the end their hammer strokes stopped, too. Bager was the first to give up. He put a hand to his chest and his eyes turned glassy as he gasped for breath. Then Dreymann called it a day. They slumped, exhausted, where they'd stopped, each wrapped in his own loneliness, as though absorbed by the growing masses of ice all around.

Icicles hung from Dreymann's moustache. He had hoar frost in his eyebrows and under his nostrils. On Rikard's and Algot's cheeks, where day-old stubble grew, the frost was sprinkled like white powder, giving the men's faces a deathly pallor.

Would their lashes freeze their eyes shut too? Would that be the cold's last gesture, to close their lids so they didn't freeze to death staring up at the grey sky?

BUT IN THE END, THE ICE THAT THREATENED TO KILL THEM WAS THEIR salvation. They'd reached new sub-zero waters: not pancake ice this time, but a compact layer that in the course of a few hours enclosed them, lifting the *Kristina*'s laden hull half out of the water. For the moment the danger of sinking had passed. The ship's heavy timbers groaned in the ice's powerful grip. If the *Kristina* had been made of steel, the hull would have cracked from the pressure and they'd have been doomed. Now, while the ice toyed with them, they were granted a stay of execution.

For days they'd been so caught up in struggling to survive that they'd barely glanced at the horizon. Now they spotted another ship far off, also stuck in the ice: a badly damaged schooner with a broken mainmast and sagging rigging.

Dreymann fetched his binoculars and directed them at the distressed ship, trying to read the name on her bow. 'Bloody hell. It's the *Ane Marie*.'

'Anyone on board?' Bager sounded hopeful. Knud Erik's heart started pounding. He was thinking about Vilhjelm.

'Not that I can see.'

'Let me take a look.' Bager snatched the binoculars and began scanning the ice. 'Am I seeing things or what?' he exclaimed. 'Penguins live at the *South* Pole, don't they?'

'Yes,' Dreymann said. 'Penguins live at the South Pole. There aren't any around here.'

'That's what I thought. Call me crazy or whatever you want. But there's an emperor penguin out there on the ice, right in front of the *Ane Marie*.'

The binoculars were passed round. Sure enough, an emperor penguin was rocking back and forth on the vast icy plain in front of the battered schooner.

'It's coming this way,' Knud Erik said.

They crowded together by the rail. The penguin approached them slowly with that bird's unique waddle, dragging and swaying as though pulling a heavy burden across the ice.

'Poor little bastard, you're going to be disappointed,' Dreymann said. 'What grub we've got left we'll be keeping for ourselves. You won't get a crumb.'

Knud Erik stood completely silent, not listening to the others. He was squinting. 'That's not a penguin,' he said.

Dreymann raised the binoculars again. 'Boy's right. If that's a penguin, it's grown old and grey.' He scratched his head under his cap. 'God only knows what it is then.'

'Penguins have a white chest,' Algot said. He'd once visited the Zoological Gardens in Copenhagen.

'It's a human being!' shouted Knud Erik. He leaped over the rail and landed with a thud on the ice below, then started racing in the direction of the strange creature, which continued its awkward waddle towards the ship without seeming to notice him. Bager shouted for him to come back, but he didn't hear. He ran like the wind. He could see that what they'd taken for a penguin was a man wearing a winter coat that reached all the way to his feet, completely concealing his legs. He must have been wearing several layers of clothing underneath because the buttons barely held. The sleeves stuck out to the sides like two flippers. A scarf was wrapped around his head, and an oversized flat cap was pulled deep down over his wool Elsinore hood so the brim almost hid his face. From a distance it had looked like a beak.

Knud Erik was closer now, and the man in the coat, attempted to wave his arms up and down, which reinforced the penguin impression. Then the two men stood in front of each other. He couldn't make out the face; it was buried in clothing. The man had stopped moving and stood as if he had a key in his back and was waiting to be wound up. Knud Erik's hand shook as he removed the flat cap, whether from impatience or fear of what he might find, he barely knew. A small face with sunken cheeks and deep-set eyes appeared. The skin, red-veined from the cold, was marked by frostbite. On the chin grew a fine blanket of down – not a big manly brush, but enough to be called a beard. The hoar frost hung from it just as it hung from everything else.

'Knud Erik,' the face said.

'You've grown a beard.'

Tears rushed to Knud Erik's eyes, and he began to sob at a volume that surprised him. Vilhjelm's smile was careful: his lips were badly cracked. Then he rolled his eyes and his penguin-like shape collapsed on the ice. Behind him Knud Erik could hear Rikard and Algot approaching. They'd finally caught up.

They were sitting in Bager's cabin staring at the small figure wrapped in blankets and duvets and lying in the berth. Vilhjelm slept peacefully, his sunken face resting on the white pillowcase. They were waiting for him to wake up.

Rikard and Algot had gone on to the *Ane Marie*, where they'd discovered the skipper, Ejvind Hansen, and the first mate, Peter Eriksen, both from Marstal, lying dead in their separate cabins, both looking as if they'd passed on in their sleep. There was no sign of the crew, and they assumed the men must have been washed overboard in the storm before the ice trapped the ship. The waves had cleared the deck and taken both foremast and mainmast. The crew had tried to rig an emergency mast, lashing the ship's derrick to the stump of the foremast. Through the layer of clear ice that covered the deck of the *Ane Marie* they could make out a tangle of rigging, spars and sails. More wreckage was frozen to the side of the ship.

When Rikard and Algot had delivered this account they both fell silent. They kept shivering as though they were cold, though the narrow cabin was well heated.

When they'd undressed the unconscious Vilhjelm they'd counted four layers of clothing. He'd probably been the smallest person on board the *Ane Marie*: he must have taken outfits of different sizes from the sea chests of the lost men and put one on top of the other.

'How did he manage to take a shit?' Algot asked.

'I don't think shitting was his biggest problem. It was more getting something down the other way.' Dreymann lifted the covers gently and pointed to the boy's emaciated ribs. 'Taking his clothes off was like opening a can of sardines and finding nothing but fish bones.'

They'd rubbed his naked body with rum, then dressed him in clean clothes, wrapped a blanket around him and settled him in the berth. Over the thirty-six hours he slept, they took turns watching over him. Knud Erik sat with him the whole time, and Bager let him. Rikard and Algot went to the front to turn in, and Bager and

Dreymann swapped shifts sleeping in the first mate's cabin. All rules were ignored. The frost had brought them together, and the *Ane Marie*'s broken silhouette against the grey sky was a fixed reminder of the fate they'd all share unless luck was on their side.

It was in the middle of the second night that Vilhjelm opened his eyes. The only light in the cabin came from the petroleum lamp that was bolted to the bulkhead.

'I'm hungry' was all he said. He sounded like a small child.

Bager, who'd been snoozing next to Knud Erik, bolted up from his couch. 'Bloody hell,' he said drowsily. 'The sand digger's boy is awake.'

He stumbled towards the berth with a bottle of rum in his hand. Supporting Vilhjelm's head with his other hand, he lifted the bottle to his lips. 'That's it, lad, have a swig. It'll do you good.' Vilhjelm drank but began to splutter when the acrid taste of undiluted rum filled his mouth.

Bager straightened up. 'Dreymann!' he roared, so his voice could be heard across the whole of the rear of the ship. 'The lad's awake. Let's have roast beef.' The first mate came stumbling into the cabin.

'Ay, ay, Captain.' He stood to attention and made a mock salute.

'Dreymann will cook you a Sunday roast you'll never forget.' He winked at Vilhjelm, who gave him a faint smile in return.

'But I think the boy needs a few biscuits to start with, Captain.'

Bager found the biscuit tin and handed a couple of biscuits to Vilhjelm. He munched them with stiff jaws, as though the movement of chewing had become unfamiliar. Bager, Dreymann and Knud Erik all watched him as if they'd never seen anyone eat before. 'What did you eat before we found you?' Knud Erik asked.

Vilhjelm had survived on sea biscuits, but they'd run out some days before. During the storm a freak wave had cleared the deck and the galley and taken the rest of the provisions with it. The galley boy was already dead: the lifeboat had torn itself loose and crushed him against the bulwark. He didn't know what had happened to the other seamen. He assumed they'd been washed overboard. He had no concept of time any more and had no idea how long the *Ane Marie* had been trapped in the ice.

He spoke in a very weak voice, and long pauses fell between the sentences. He didn't sound like Vilhjelm at all.

523

'The sea biscuits were disgusting,' he said. 'They were frozen solid and I had to keep them in my mouth for ages to thaw them. I was really scared that the maggots would start wriggling around in my mouth when they warmed up. But they'd died from the cold. So I ate them too.'

'You probably owe your life to those maggots,' Dreymann remarked drily.

Knud Erik stared at Vilhjelm. He realised suddenly why the emaciated boy in the skipper's berth didn't sound like his friend from Marstal.

'You're not stammering any more!' he exclaimed.

'Aren't I?'

Rikard and Algot had arrived. They all stared at Vilhjelm as if he were the most wondrous sight they'd ever clapped eyes on. Here lay a boy who couldn't just munch a biscuit: he could articulate his words properly too.

'Well, would you believe it,' Dreymann said. 'Seems that keeping your mouth shut can cure a stammer.'

'I didn't keep it shut,' Vilhjelm said with his new voice.

'So who did you talk to, if I may ask?'

'I read the skipper's copy of the Merchant Navy's *Book of Sermons*. Every day for hours. I walked up and down the deck and read it aloud. Everyone else was dead. And it was so quiet.'

'Helmer!' Bager roared. 'Where's that blasted boy? We need to get that roast in the oven.'

They all looked towards the door and then back at Vilhjelm. He'd turned his head on the pillow and closed his eyes. He'd fallen asleep again.

Rikard and Algot collected the dead first mate and captain from the *Ane Marie*, carried them across the ice on laths, and laid them out on the deck of the *Kristina*. Dreymann wrapped the bodies in canvas and left them there, face up, waiting for the ice to break so they could be buried at sea. Captain Hansen had once been a hefty man, and his body still looked big under the canvas. Cold and hunger alone couldn't have finished him off; age and the physical weakness it entailed must have played a part too. He'd been in his late fifties, far too old for the North Atlantic.

The first mate, twenty-seven-year-old Peter Eriksen, didn't take up much room next to his skipper. He had a wife and two little girls back in Marstal, and there they were, not knowing what had happened to him. Why had he succumbed and Vilhjelm survived? The first mate of the *Ane Marie* lay on the deck like a great unanswerable question. Knud Erik looked at the contours of his face, which you could faintly make out through the canvas, and thought of his father.

Bager also stood there contemplating the dead. He'd known Captain Hansen well and was probably asking himself a similar question. Why him? Why not me? The two ships had left Iceland roughly a week apart. It could just as easily have been Bager brought to rest on Captain Hansen's deck. As he gazed at his friend he held the *Book of Sermons* in his hand, and from time to time he read it. Vilhjelm had given it to him and he was presumably rehearsing the ceremony for burial at sea.

By now Vilhjelm had recovered enough to leave the berth and take a walk on the deck. He even asked if he could help out in the galley. For the time being there were sufficient provisions and when Vilhjelm and Knud Erik wanted some time alone, they'd give Helmer a break and send him to the fo'c's'le. But he was reluctant to leave: apart from the skipper's cabin the galley was the warmest place on the ship. Besides, he was convinced that the two older boys would begin to share secrets the moment he was gone, and he had a young boy's appetite for tales of experience.

However, little was said about Vilhjelm's time alone on the *Ane Marie*. Whenever Knud Erik asked about it, Vilhjelm fell silent and looked down at the floor. Knud Erik feared he might even start stammering again.

Vilhjelm, who was keen to change the subject, noticed that something was troubling his friend and made Knud Erik tell him about Miss Sophie. What bothered him, Knud Erik admitted, wasn't her rejection of him, or the stinging contempt in her voice that night on Signal Hill when she told him to stop chasing her like a dog, but the mystery of her fate and his own part in her disappearance. He was haunted by a vague, nagging feeling of guilt.

When he'd finished telling the story, Vilhjelm looked at him directly. 'You think everything's about you,' he said in his new, clear voice. 'She was just crazy. That's all.'

'But –' Knud Erik objected.

'I know what you're about to say. You can't remember what

happened that night, so you think you might've done something bad. But that's rubbish. She's run off with someone, that's all.'

Vilhjelm didn't have a mind superior to Knud Erik's, but in the matter of Miss Sophie he was more open. He wasn't the one in love with her, so he could see things objectively – which put him in a better position to judge what had happened.

Knud Erik was greatly relieved.

Having got this far, Vilhjelm started asking in detail about the kiss and its effect.

'I've never tried that,' he pondered, his curiosity finally satisfied.

'You will.' Their roles had been reversed. Knud Erik suddenly felt like the wise, experienced one.

'Well, I nearly missed out on it altogether.' It was the closest Vilhjelm ever came to admitting that his life had been in danger.

They kept on waiting for the ice to break. Finally, the current turned south, the thaw arrived, and with it the promise of the first open water. Soon they could say goodbye to their dead passengers. Water started raining down from the rigging: huge icicles came loose and crashed onto the deck. The sails, which had been too rigid to take in, dripped constantly, soaking everything on deck, as if the *Kristina* were an island with its own climate.

A sudden wind began to blow: a sure warning that the ice would soon break. Then a shower came, and they donned their oilskins. A huge crack split the ice close to the hull, followed by another. It was time to bury the dead.

Bager stayed in his cabin and refused to join them. He mumbled through the closed door that he was feeling ill and that they should leave him alone.

Dreymann went to fetch the *Book of Sermons*. They used boards to build a ramp against the rail and placed the bodies on top so they could glide over the side and disappear into the sea. Soberly the men lined up, clasping their sou'westers in their hands.

Dreymann turned to the final pages of the book. The lines were set in old Gothic type and he had to squint to see them. The rain was pouring down his cheeks. 'Damn it,' he muttered. 'I'm too old. I can't read those tiny letters. Could one of you young lads do it?' He held the book out towards Rikard and Algot.

'Let me, please,' Vilhjelm said. 'I know it by heart anyway.'

Dreymann stared at him. 'Are you telling me that you read aloud the rite for burial at sea on the *Ane Marie*?'

'Yes,' Vilhjelm said. 'I know the entire *Book of Sermons* by heart.' Without waiting for Dreymann's reaction, he started reciting. 'Our Lord Jesus Christ says: The hour shall come when everyone in their graves shall hear the voice of the Son of God and they shall go forth – those who have done well, to their resurrection, but those who have done ill, to their judgement.'

Helmer stepped forward. In his hand he held a small shovel with ashes from the oven in the galley. This had to serve as the soil, to be scattered over the wrapped bodies before they were surrendered to the sea.

'Earth to earth,' Vilhjelm said in his new voice, which Knud Erik still hadn't grown accustomed to. Helmer scattered ashes over the deceased. The rain was falling hard now, and the ashes dissolved and spread in a huge stain across the grey canvas.

'Ashes to ashes.'

Another shovelful. The ashes landed in a new place; the canvas grew dirtier.

'Dust to dust.'

Rikard and Algot stepped up to the boards and raised them, one after the other. The laced-up canvas bundle that contained the mortal remains of Skipper Hansen fell vertically into the water and disappeared with a splash, muted by the falling rain. Peter Eriksen followed.

The sea was black beneath the gathering storm clouds and the surrounding ice had taken on a yellow glare. Then suddenly, as if the sea had finally lost patience with its forced burden, it shook its enormous back with irritation: the ice sheet shattered into infinite pieces, which shot out sideways and smashed against each other. In the distance, the *Ane Marie* slowly keeled over and sank down on her side: the ice had supported her damaged hull, but now the sea reclaimed her from its grip to wreck her fully.

Dreymann ordered them on deck immediately. Overhead they saw a nimbus cloud like a huge granite fist, clenched and ready to strike. They were being freed from the ice, but now that very liberty posed a new threat to their survival. They took in the reefs until they were using only the forestay and a close-reefed gaff. A hailstorm hammered them, and the sea raged, with waves mounting on all sides and ice

527

floes riding atop their foaming crests. When they broke across the deck, the huge shards collided with everything in their path, and the crashing sound fought against the devils' chorus that howled up in the rigging.

The men watched the pattern of the waves as they swept the deck: three huge ones were usually followed by several smaller ones, and they chose those quieter moments to slosh their way across the flooded deck to the fo'c's'le.

Bager was still lying down in his cabin. Dreymann took the first shift together with Knud Erik. Rikard and Algot were sent below to get some sleep. In the galley Helmer clung on as tenaciously as a monkey on a falling tree: he'd already proved himself able to provide coffee even if the ship were on her head. Dreymann had ordered Vilhjelm down to his own cabin.

'How hard's it blowing?' Knud Erik shouted. He was clinging to the wheel next to Dreymann, who was practised enough to keep his balance on the madly veering deck.

At intervals the stern would be lifted by a mountain of water while the bow dove into the foaming sea. Then the bow would rise until the entire ship appeared aimed at some distant point high in the sky. Knud Erik's stomach lurched horribly each time. It was as if the sea, which had so often challenged and not yet conquered them, now demanded one final, decisive rematch.

He'd already learned that in a North Atlantic storm, expert seamanship went a long way, but not the whole way. No sailor could guard against the freak wave that cleared the deck and wiped off the masts. So much depended on luck. Some called it Providence, others God, but luck and God had one thing in common when it came to these waters: their intervention was always arbitrary. Peter Eriksen and Skipper Hansen, whose bodies they'd just given to the sea, were probably no better and no worse seamen than those who'd survived the worst storms. There was no point in trying to make sense of it all. Nor were prayers of any use, except to calm and encourage the person praying. He didn't believe they influenced whether a ship reached her port safely or not. He understood very well what Vilhjelm had been doing when he'd read aloud from the *Book of Sermons,* all alone on the *Ane Marie.* It was his inner stammer he'd wanted to overcome: that stammer of the soul that sapped his will to survive. But Knud Erik didn't have Vilhjelm's ability to let the word of God work for him.

'How much is it blowing?' Knud Erik shouted again.

'Gale force twelve,' Dreymann said.

They reached Newcastle ten days later. Bager reappeared from his cabin, sullen and withdrawn. The fear in his eyes had nothing to do with the hurricane.

Together with Dreymann he surveyed the damage to the ship. They'd lost the lifeboat, the cabin door had been smashed to pieces, the collar on the mizzenmast had snapped, two water barrels had gone overboard, a gaff had broken, the sails were torn, one hundred and ninety feet of bulwark had been warped, the name board aft on the starboard side had been smashed, and so had the starboard lantern board.

The damage had to be repaired, but that wasn't the only reason they'd called at Newcastle. Bager's daughter, Kristina, was expected on board. She'd sail with them to Setubal in warm and sunny Portugal.

Knud Erik found his fountain pen and wrote a letter to his mother. He asked her to give his best to everyone before describing the fair weather that had followed them right across the Atlantic. There was no need to worry her unnecessarily. He also wrote that he was looking forward to the voyage to Portugal.

Later he admitted that if he'd known what lay ahead, he'd have signed off in Newcastle.

WHEN HERMAN HAD RECOUNTED THE STORY BEFORE, IT HAD ALWAYS gone down well. But with Miss Kristina it had the completely opposite effect. Something about it frightened her. Well, that had been his intention, but it had frightened her too much and she'd got up, turned her back on him and gone to the cabin. With a slight sway of her hips. Damn it, that woman confused him!

Women should never get what they ask for, he thought. Ideally they should be weeping and pleading in front of a locked door. Never be nice to them, even though you might be tempted. That's what made it all so damned difficult. You had to scare them a bit. Not too much and not too little. Too much and they'd panic, and you wouldn't get what you wanted. Too little and they'd wipe their dainty little feet all over you. It took experience to get the balance right. You had to feel your way.

Women liked a man who could make them laugh. But they loved a man who made them cry. They respected only what they didn't understand. Respect was what it was all about. He'd seen enough of the world to know that it wasn't a woman's love that made life bearable for a man. It was her respect, and respect always contains an element of fear.

Knud Erik and Vilhjelm had been there on the hatch listening to him tell the story about Ravn, the car mechanic who'd sailed with a German U-boat during the war and sunk Danish ships, and who late one night in a doorway in Nyborg had got what was coming to him. Miss Kristina had listened with interest, too, until he got to the part about the punishment in the doorway. Then she had got up and left without saying a word.

Afterwards Herman had sounded off to Knud Erik and Vilhjelm about the awkward and fundamentally incomprehensible nature of women. They'd laughed at his remarks, but remained guarded as they always were when he was around. When he'd first come on board, he'd scrutinised them as though trying to retrieve something from his memory. They'd both looked away and he'd brushed it aside.

'There's the Seagull Killer,' Vilhjelm had said, when he saw Herman board the *Kristina*.

Everything had gone wrong in Newcastle. Dreymann received a telegram from home informing him that his wife was gravely ill and might not have long to live.

'I hate to leave my post before the job's done,' he said. 'I've got four children. Three of them were christened and I wasn't there. Two were confirmed, and one was married – and I wasn't there either. I can't bear the thought that Gertrud might kick the bucket when I'm not around to hold her hand.'

Rikard and Algot signed off and made no effort to hide the reason why. They'd had their fill of ships from Marstal that did nothing but sail into one storm after another, and if they'd wanted to be undertakers, they'd have sought a different apprenticeship. The *Kristina* could get along without them, and good luck to her.

They grabbed their kits and half-empty seabags, stuck their Polish cigarette holders in their mouths and left.

Bager offered Knud Erik the job of ordinary seaman. He hadn't sailed for quite long enough to merit it, but he knew the job, broadly speaking. And the sail-mending that was part of a crewman's duties he could surely pick up. He couldn't increase his wages, though.

'What about me?' Vilhjelm asked.

He and Knud Erik had agreed that they wouldn't be parted.

Bager thought for a long time.

'You'll get your food,' he said.

They still needed a first mate. There was none to be had, but Herman, who'd fallen out with the skipper of the *Uranus*, happened to be in Newcastle and was broke. He had the experience and plenty of sailing time, but not the exams: he'd never pulled himself together enough to attend Navigation College. Bager offered him the job.

When Herman demanded the same wages as a qualified first mate, Bager did the mental arithmetic. He'd already saved the wages of two seamen and had some money to spare. 'Your papers aren't in order,' he said. 'So I'm actually doing you a favour. But I'll add twenty-five kroner to what you usually get as an able seaman.'

'Forty kroner,' Herman said.

They agreed on thirty-five.

In fact it was Bager, not Herman, whose papers weren't in order – something which Mr Mattheson at the shipping office in Waterloo Street pointed out to him. All right, they were prepared to overlook the situation with Herman. After all, they'd failed to find him a first mate for the *Kristina* and they wouldn't want to stand in the way of a man trying to make his living. But he couldn't have two boys running around pretending to be seamen. Bager would need to sign on at least one qualified man. If he didn't, they'd report him.

That was how Ivar joined them.

The *Kristina* had barely left Newcastle before the first clash occurred.

Knud Erik and Vilhjelm had instantly warmed to Ivar. He came on board wearing his shore clothes, a tailor-made, double-breasted cheviot suit, with French cufflinks, white collar and a silk tie that he'd bought in Buenos Aires. Ivar was a man of the world. He didn't need to tell them all the places he'd been, from South America to Shanghai: they could tell just by looking at him. He'd gained his experience on steamers and had signed on to a sailing ship only out of curiosity. He was the son of a captain from Hellerup and had yet to decide if the sea life was for him. He was tall and well built, with a mass of raven hair, and he carried himself with the assurance of a man who's left more than one fight victorious.

Ivar had a talent for things mechanical. He brought along a radio that he'd built himself and could take apart and reassemble any way he wanted. He settled it on the hatch when they were in port and attached the antenna to the rigging.

'You'll never get that thing to work,' Herman said, the first time Ivar set it up. Which made Herman look a fool because of course the radio had worked. They heard fragments of foreign languages, voices from different parts of the globe, and dance music, the kind you normally got to hear only in the French Channel ports.

Even Herman couldn't stay away when Ivar hooked up the radio. Ivar glanced over and smiled at him. 'Right, the first mate's come to join us,' he said.

Herman spun on his heel and left.

When they were sure he was out of earshot, they laughed at him.

Knud Erik and Vilhjelm always referred to Herman as the Seagull Killer, though Vilhjelm had learned the true extent of Herman's crimes long ago. One day Ivar, overhearing the odd nickname, asked about it, but they immediately deflected his queries. It was just a name. Anyway, didn't he look just like someone likely to strangle seagulls with his bare hands? Ivar shrugged. Their explanation didn't really make sense, but he didn't probe further.

Later they regretted not telling him the truth. They knew what Herman had done: they'd held the skull of his victim in their hands. They used the nickname like a counter spell, to dampen the terror they constantly felt in his presence.

They sought out Ivar's company because they knew they needed protection.

Ivar hadn't been on board long before he expressed indignation at the food. He found their evening meals, in particular, entirely inadequate. Twice a week, on Wednesdays and Saturdays, they were given a cheese, a salami sausage, a tin of liver pâté and a tin of sardines: this was to be shared among four men. They'd always wolf down the cold meats, cheese and sardines the first evening and survive on rye bread until the next handout.

'But it's not my fault,' Helmer said, spreading his arms helplessly.

Ivar went to the captain on behalf of the crew and complained about the small portions. By the crew he meant the three lads he shared the fo'c's'le with.

Miss Kristina was in the cabin when Ivar arrived. She was tall and slim, with a mane of chestnut hair, and she had the frank, energetic nature typical of most girls from Marstal. It was in their upbringing; they knew that one day they'd have absolute rule of the home. She also had dimples and a beauty spot by her right nostril, which always made her look as if she'd just dressed up for a party.

At first Bager said nothing. He glanced furtively at his daughter, as if he wanted to ask her opinion. He was clearly caught between his own meanness and the desire to make a good impression on her.

'Just because you've worked on a steamer,' Herman snarled. He was present as well and considered himself the captain's spokesman.

'I know maritime law,' Ivar said calmly. 'We're not getting the food we're entitled to. In future I insist on seeing the food weighed out.' He turned and smiled at Miss Kristina. 'You might think it strange to attach such importance to a few grams of food, Miss?'

She shook her head and returned his smile, unaffected by the tense atmosphere in the cabin. Herman looked from one to the other with a watchful eye. It was obvious what he thought. Ivar was trying to influence the captain through his daughter.

'Please don't think that we're afraid of hard work, Miss,' Ivar continued. 'We work hard, but most of us have yet to turn twenty. Just take a look at the cook and the two crewmen: they're only fifteen, not even fully grown. And then we work in the fresh air all day. You've probably noticed yourself that the sea air gives you an appetite.'

Herman cleared his throat menacingly. Ivar's eloquence had paralysed him, and he needed to gain time. But Ivar wasn't even looking in his direction. He was still smiling at Miss Kristina, and she was returning his smile as though they had a secret bond.

Bager didn't seem to notice any of this. But now he spoke – and what he said was so striking that it should have been clear even then that something was bound to go wrong on board the *Kristina*.

'Five loaves and two fishes,' he said. He seemed to be trying to make his voice sound firm, but it was strangely insubstantial, as though his thoughts were somewhere far away.

'Sorry?' Ivar made an effort to be polite. 'I don't think I understood you.'

Bager raised his voice. 'I said five loaves and two fishes. That was all Our Lord Jesus Christ needed to feed five thousand people. Are one cheese, one salami, a tin of liver pâté, and a tin of sardines not enough for you, though you are only four?'

'We're not talking about Bible history. We're on board the *Kristina* of Marstal, and maritime law states –'

'Do you deny the Lord your God?' Bager said in a sharp tone, giving Ivar an accusing stare. 'How is it possible, after God has borne you, clothed you and kept you for so many days, for you to doubt that He can and will continue to do so?'

Even the articulate Ivar was left speechless by this outburst from the normally taciturn Captain Bager. He gave Kristina a questioning look. She spread her hands, at a loss. You could expect just about anything from a Marstal skipper. He could be unyielding and harsh, unreasonable in his demands, unfair at times. First and foremost he could be stingy. Thrift was essential for his survival. But no one had ever heard a captain back his actions with religious quotations, and certainly not in such foggy terms.

Herman suppressed a brutal laugh. This was promising to be truly entertaining.

'I'm talking about maritime law,' Ivar said again, firmly.

Miss Kristina leaned towards Bager and placed her hand on his. 'Be reasonable, Father. It's no skin off your nose if the crew gets a bit more to eat.'

Bager clutched his chest, like a man suffering some deep inner turmoil. 'As you wish,' he said finally, in a weak voice.

'Father, are you feeling unwell?' Miss Kristina asked anxiously.

Back in the fo'c's'le Ivar told the story to the crew. Then he looked at Knud Erik. 'You've sailed with him the longest. Is he normally like this?'

'Stingy, yes,' Knud Erik said. 'But speaking like Pastor Abildgaard?' He shook his head.

'What did he say again?' Vilhjelm asked.

'It was that bit from the Bible about the five loaves and the two fishes.' Ivar thought a moment. 'Then he asked me how we could doubt the Lord who'd clothed and kept us.'

'It's from the *Book of Sermons*,' Vilhjelm said. 'Seventh Sunday after Trinity. A sermon for the poor and for the rich. By Jonas Dahl, a seamen's priest in Bergen. Bager seems to have memorised it. He must be in a really bad way.'

From time to time Miss Kristina invited the whole crew for pancakes or went around the deck with the coffee pot. In the galley Helmer was constantly beaming. She came in often to help with the cooking. It was so narrow there that they had to stand close to each other, and the rustling of her dress and her female presence intoxicated him. She praised his skills and he made an extra effort. They all did. It was good to have a woman on board.

Miss Kristina would often sit down next to the helmsman and chat to him while he kept one eye on the rigging and the other on her.

One evening as they approached the coast of Portugal she strolled the deck in the moonlight with Ivar. Herman stood by the rail, trying without success to eavesdrop on their muted conversation. She'd turned her back on him after he'd told the story about Ravn in Nyborg and kept him at a distance, though she wasn't generally reserved. Since the confrontation about the food, his stock had been lower than ever.

He felt Miss Kristina's presence like something poisonous and something infinitely sweet mixing together in his blood. Inside him, a lack of willpower and a colossal tension battled it out. He felt both weak and furious at the same time. He went around with his fists clenched, ready to fight, yet what he wanted most of all was to hold and be held.

The *Kristina* cut up against the south wind that always blew along the Portuguese coast. When Ivar was on duty, Miss Kristina would sit at the helm next to him. Herman went over to them, stiff and haughty, relishing his role as the first mate. 'The helmsman is not to be distracted,' he said curtly, and remained there with his hands folded behind his back until she got up and left.

Yes, she had to yield to him there. However, he was uncertain whether her yielding had been a victory or a defeat. He got no closer to her and was beginning to think of her and Ivar as 'the couple'. After all, that was what they were becoming.

One afternoon a shoal of dolphins broke the monotony. 'Springers!' the helmsman cried out, and the crew bustled to arm themselves. Ivar led the way. He jumped out on the bowsprit and hurled the harpoon into the water just as the ship dived, shortening the distance to the nearest leaping creature. The dolphin struggled powerfully as Ivar pulled in the line. Then Knud Erik came over and managed to get a hawser around its tail.

Herman disappeared down to his cabin and reappeared on deck with a revolver in his hand. The crew formed a circle around the dolphin, which arched its smooth, elegant body in dying spasms while its strong tail beat the deck rhythmically, the blood pouring out and flowing in a greasy stream across the planks. Miss Kristina watched from a distance with her hands over her mouth. Someone had to deliver the death blow to the convulsing animal.

'Move!' Herman shouted.

They turned to look at him. He waved the revolver at the circle of men as if he'd not yet decided on his target. They stepped back. He walked up close to the dolphin, aimed carefully, then fired twice. The dolphin's eye exploded in blood. Its tail slammed against the deck a final time, and then it lay still.

He looked up and saw Miss Kristina huddling against Ivar. Both were staring at him. He grinned at them. Then he stuck the revolver into his belt and returned to his cabin.

He sat on the edge of his berth. He was still smiling. This had been a perfect moment. No one had known he had a revolver. They were surprised when he came up holding it, and he'd seen the fear in their eyes. They'd turned from the dolphin to stare at him. He'd been in control. That was how he wanted it.

Early one morning the wind fell, and after that their progress was slow. Around noon they saw Setubal ahead of them: large white-washed villas sitting atop steep cliffs; lush, green vegetation hanging like a veil over the rocks. When the sails were down, Miss Kristina served each man on deck a glass of wine. It was an old custom.

Her eyes lingered on Ivar, but when she reached Herman, she turned her face half away, as if she couldn't wait to move on to the next man in line.

There was already one Marstal schooner in the port. Over the next few days, more arrived and soon there was a small flock: the *Eagle*, the *Galathea* and the *Atlantic*, all veterans of the route, loading salt in Setubal for Newfoundland, then sailing back across the Atlantic with salt cod for Setubal.

Not that they were short of fish here. The port teemed with fisher-men who caught sardines as big as herrings. The men were small and sinewy and their chests were bared to the sun, the muscles clearly defined beneath their tanned skin. Spotting Miss Kristina they called out and waved, their white teeth gleaming beneath their black mous-taches; she waved back to them and they raised their huge baskets of glittering fish as though offering a joyful tribute to her sex, so rarely sighted on the deck of a sailing ship.

Bager was rowed ashore to buy provisions, but he came back empty-handed. There were neither potatoes nor bread to be had. Setubal was in the grip of a strike – or was it a lockout? At any rate, some sort of uprising or revolution. A nine o'clock curfew had been imposed, and anyone found in the street after dark would be shot.

'Why is there a revolution?' Miss Kristina asked, her eyes lighting up with excitement.

Her father shrugged. 'I suppose people are starving,' he said. 'There's a lot of poverty here.'

'But that's awful,' Miss Kristina said. 'Those poor, poor people.'

'Don't fret about it,' Herman interjected. 'It's nothing unusual. There's always some fuss going on here. They create havoc and shoot at each other. They say they want change, but the next time you visit, everything's the same as it always was. It's the way they are. They can't control their tempers and they never get anything done.'

The word *revolution* went around the deck. Everyone wanted to taste it, like an exotic fruit bursting with a strange, tantalising flavour. Revolutions were a part of the south. Now they'd be able to return home and say that they'd witnessed one – though as far as they could see there was nothing to witness. The sardine fishermen seemed unperturbed by the revolution – if that's what it was – and heavily laden ships arrived every day. Then the uprising spread further and it was rumoured that the sardine factories were striking, too.

For the next few days the fishermen stayed in port, and the docks around the *Kristina* fell silent. The *Nauta* and the *Rosenhjem* showed up and soon a tiny floating Marstal was established, with plenty of traffic between the ships. Visits were paid, coffee was drunk. Miss Kristina stopped strolling around with Ivar in order to meet the other skippers, who were all friends of her father and used to visit their home in Marstal. One day she went with them to see the town, which seemed peaceful enough despite its revolution. Like the proper skipper's daughter she was, she rowed the boat that ferried them all to shore.

She returned with a bunch of flowers that a park gardener had given her, and treated the crew to a lively description of the large cafe in the town square where a military band had been playing. 'Lovely to hear a brass band again,' she said.

Herman shrugged. A woman of the world probably spoke like that, but he couldn't recall a brass band ever playing in Marstal. She'd been to the cinema too, where the film had been accompanied by a string orchestra. Twenty men at least, she said, and her eyes sparkled.

Several of the crewmen on the Marstal ships had brought instruments with them: two accordions, three mouth organs and a violin. Off duty, they made up an entire orchestra themselves. That night there was music and singing. Ivar had a very fine voice, but it was his radio, in particular, that made him popular among the other crews. They were proud of him on the *Kristina*. He was theirs; no other ship had a man like Ivar. He'd switch on the radio and voices came zooming in from all over the world, and music too, including the Portuguese *fado*. Ivar was the only one who knew that word, and he explained the mournful music to them. But even stranger sounds came from the radio – such as Arabic music from a station in Casablanca. Ivar had to admit defeat there. He couldn't put a name to it or tell them anything about it.

When Ivar turned on his radio, even the skippers couldn't resist, and came out of the cabin where they'd been enjoying their Dutch gin and Riga Balsam. Miss Kristina did her round with the coffee pot and asked if anyone fancied pancakes, and a chorus of 'Aye aye!' rose from the men.

IN SETUBAL HERMAN FOUND HIMSELF AMONG HIS PEERS AGAIN. THEY
were sailors, and they were from Marstal. He'd beaten up a man in
a doorway in Nyborg and claimed he'd done it for the sake of his
town – but now he felt like an outsider. The trouble wasn't simply
his jealousy. Perhaps it wasn't jealousy at all, but the fact that he
didn't know where he belonged: he only really felt at home when
he was in charge, treated with respect and fear.

The wind and the waves had a lawlessness and unpredictability
that felt familiar to him. He sensed it the moment he embarked. On
land, life became lilliputian again and he stumbled around like an
awkward, homeless giant unable to squeeze through the doorways
that bid others welcome.

There was a gentle feel to the evening, an intimacy that flowed
from the warm air of the south – the way the stars were mirrored
in the calm sea, the enigmatic quiet of the town and the caress of
music and voices. The skippers broke their habit and turned up
together to mingle with the crew, amid the smell of pancakes that
spread from the galley.

Herman was with his own, but he didn't belong among them.
It stung him suddenly, a terrifying feeling of being not whole, but
crippled. In one horrifying flash he observed himself from the
outside and saw a monster. He wanted to hide, to flee this world
he couldn't cope with, where he was on a lonely track that led him
nowhere.

He felt no urge to drink or fight. He just had to get away.

He went down to his cabin to get his revolver. Then he climbed over
the rail and into the lifeboat that was moored to the side of the ship.
He pushed off and began rowing.

Where was he going? He didn't know. He stopped and rested on
the oars, at a loss. The port was deserted. No lights were lit, and

the silence of the empty town seemed to fall from the night sky, as though Setubal had been sucked into the vast vacuum of the universe the moment the curfew descended.

Suddenly he realised what he wanted. He wanted to walk the darkened streets. This was his territory: a forbidden zone where being spotted could cost you your life.

A moment ago a storm had raged within him. Now the tide in his veins turned, giving way to the dangerous silence of the ebb.

Making his strokes as noiseless as possible, he rowed slowly towards the nearest quay. Only the faintest splashes were audible, and they were instantly swallowed by the dense darkness. The music and voices coming from the *Kristina* were now so far away that they seemed the echoes of another world, a world he'd left behind and could never return to.

He didn't know what awaited him in the abandoned streets, nor did he care. A magnet was pulling him: he abandoned his will and obeyed. It was there, in the magnet's powerful stillness, in its deadly metallic cold, that he belonged. He felt the weight of the revolver in his pocket and readied himself.

He moored the boat and climbed up onto the quay. There was no moon, yet the town hadn't been completely absorbed by the dark. Here and there, light streamed from a window or slid through the slats of a shutter. He could hear voices, then the sound of a piano – a delicate music protesting against the silence, only to be engulfed by it again.

He stood between two rows of houses and tilted his head back. He could see the Milky Way running parallel with the street, a celestial track of shining pebbles forging through the wasteland of the night. He recalled the first time he'd seen it. He had been a boy then, alone in the night. He'd stood on the beach and cocked his head the same way, bursting with impatient hope. But now, tonight, he turned his back on everything. He was alone with the Milky Way and a gun.

Did he want to survive this night? Was this a test he had designed for himself, or was it something else he was after? He didn't know. He didn't understand the language of the stars well enough for that.

He stood in the middle of the street, looking upward. The white walls of the houses glowed blue as if reflecting the starlight. Gates and doorways pulsated black. Was it wise to be standing in the middle of the street?

His peculiar intoxication, which had been generated not by drink but by his loneliness beneath the night sky, evaporated. He ran across the pavement and pressed himself against a wall. Here he was likely to be just as visible: a dense black mass against its glowing blue.

He hadn't come here to hide. He returned to the middle of the pavement and started walking.

Suddenly he heard steps. He stopped. They sounded measured. Was it one or more men who were approaching? He listened again. It certainly wasn't a group, he decided. Perhaps there were only two of them? Soldiers on night patrol? Who else would be out and about after dark in a town with a curfew? He looked behind him, then ahead. It was a wide street, and palm trees blocked the starlight: he had to be on a boulevard. He ought to head for the narrow, winding lanes where it would be easier to escape. He wavered, but stayed put. Then he raised his gun and turned round slowly. Darkness: nothing but darkness. He could still hear the measured footsteps. Were they coming closer or moving away?

He walked on cautiously, gun in hand. If they were to meet, it would be them or him. He knew that.

The footsteps continued.

Yes, they were definitely approaching, but he couldn't decide which direction they were coming from. He might just as easily be walking towards them as away from them.

He'd been going for a while when he spotted them. They were standing still, just three or four metres in front of him, as if they'd been waiting. He stopped at once. One of them called out.

The cry was drowned out by a deafening explosion. Herman looked around to determine the origin of the blast and saw the revolver in his hand. He must have fired it.

He had no idea if he'd hit anyone. He started running. No shots or footsteps rang out behind him. At one point he was tempted to stop and look back, but the pulse of his blood gave his flight a momentum he couldn't fight. His head felt completely clear. But his legs pounded like pistons; they seemed to have a will of their own.

He rounded a corner and kept going until finally he regained control of his muscles. Stopping, he pressed himself against a wall and listened to the night. At first he heard nothing. Then, far away, he made out the sound of running feet, coming first from one direction and then another. A shot was fired, then several more in quick succession, drowned out by the long stutter of a machine gun. He heard orders being shouted and the stomping of boots, as if a whole army had started marching. Somewhere a car engine revved up.

Firing the gun had broken the silence and now it sounded as if his shot had detonated a mine, and that mine, now exploding, was the entire town.

He was surrounded by darkness and the noise of salvos. One moment an intense fusillade, the next a loaded silence. Who was shooting whom? Was the army firing on the strikers, and were they responding? Was it just a chaos of feral predators lurking in the dark, hissing and lashing out with their claws before withdrawing again into the shadows? Was this what revolution meant: guns rebelling and overpowering their owners under cover of darkness, wooing men's blood, and luring it out to flood the streets?

Were they shooting at each other to celebrate that there was no longer good or evil, order or disorder, only untamed life, a town of stones splashed red with life's essence?

Herman started running again. His breathing was laborious, but he didn't stop; his heavy body stampeded like a raging rhinoceros through the lanes. At some point he was fired at: he heard the bullet slam into the wall behind him. Later he surprised two men hiding in a gateway. He shot at them and resumed his manic race. Who were they? Had he hit them?

He didn't care.

He spotted a division of soldiers marching towards him and found a doorway to crouch in. They'd barely gone past when he emerged, turning in mid-run to fire a shot in their direction.

Someone had built a barricade across the street, and he saw shadows moving behind it. The dark was too intense to make out what was going on, but he knew instinctively that this was revolution: an uprising of guns, here to drain blood. There was a brotherhood between rebels and soldiers. They were united by a common urge to kill.

They called out to him, and he answered in his sailor's broken Spanish. They invited him to join them on the barricade, and when they saw his revolver they slapped him on the shoulder and called him *compañero,* a word he well understood, a gesture based on an assumption as naive as they were. He didn't care about their cause. They needed an excuse to shoot their guns. He didn't.

Shots were fired at the barricade, and they fired back into the darkness. He saw the flames at the muzzles of the revolvers and felt something warm on his cheek. Had he been hit? The man next to him slumped against Herman's shoulder, his head resting there for a moment as if he'd fallen asleep. Then he slid gradually to the ground, his shirtsleeve soaked in blood.

The shooting intensified, the flames from the gun muzzles at the end of the street erupting into fireworks. The din was deafening. Herman felt a wild, dry heat burst through his skin as if his heart were on fire. He was alive!

The firing was coming closer: the soldiers had launched their attack. The men around him abandoned the barricade. As their footsteps retreated into darkness, he set off afresh, in a wild sprint. He heard a man's laugh, then realised it was his own. A prostrate body lay in front of him in the street. He leaped over it. Someone grabbed his arm and pulled him into a side street and under an archway. Together they scaled one wall, then another. Herman muttered *gracias,* though he felt indifferent. His whole body screamed with the ecstasy of immortality. He still had the gun in his hand.

It felt as if he'd been in this darkened town for ever, as if all that had gone before had faded to insignificance. He felt it suddenly: tonight he was liberated. Out here in the dark where the only street lights were flames from the mouths of guns and the gutters flowed red, he could exist without feeling incomplete. He was simply blood, body, instincts and reflexes. He was his revolver, and, through it, he belonged with all those like him, who moved, armed, through the night. He was at one with all men, with life and death.

From the hills behind the town the huge red ball of the sun came rolling down the boulevard towards him, and all around the colours lit up, weak at first, then vivid. He met the dawn with a mixture of disappointment and relief. The sunlight seemed to tidy the chaos of the night, and within the space of an instant it put the houses and their inhabitants back in their rightful places.

He looked down and saw that his shirt was bloodstained. He ripped it off and hurled it into the street. He felt the heft of the revolver in his hand. He hesitated for a moment. Then he let it drop and walked on.

He reached a large square where upturned chairs and tables lay scattered about and men in uniform were carrying bodies away. Soon the tiles would be washed clean of blood. Day had returned.

As he crossed the square, a soldier called out to him and approached, followed by two others. They looked him up and down. He stood there, bare-chested and smelling pungently of sweat, the face beneath his short blond hair reddened by wind, drink and sun. What was he? A sailor who'd forgotten time, place and curfew in the excitement of the moment?

He stank – but they assumed it was from bedlinen and women: he could see it in their faces. He grinned at them, and they grinned back. The tallest of the soldiers pointed to Herman's cheek. Herman touched it and felt a scab where a bullet had brushed past him.

'*Mujer*,' he said. Woman.

'*Mujer*,' they laughed. One of them made a cat's paw of his hand, with its claws out.

He'd shot at them in the night and they'd shot back at him. Shadows firing at shadows. Now they were simply men in the first light of dawn. They let him go.

He went down to the harbour and found the boat. He loosened the mooring and began rowing slowly back to the *Kristina*.

THE NEXT DAY HERMAN WAS QUIET. THE CREW SHOT HIM FURTIVE glances. They'd noticed his absence, but no one said anything. From time to time he'd smile an odd smile that seemed to be directed at no one in particular. They exchanged warning looks. What would follow this calm? Ivar gazed thoughtfully at Herman's massive back. Only Bager seemed not to notice anything.

Herman was aware of their glances. What were they thinking about him? What did they surmise he'd been up to during the curfew in Setubal? If they thought he'd merely been whoring, why didn't they just say so? Were they afraid of the answer?

With the strike broken, the *Kristina* could dock. A couple of barges arrived and the dockers began unloading the salt cod. Bager had gone into town to buy provisions, taking Miss Kristina with him. She came back in a state of excitement and told them that the chandler had invited them to lunch: they'd eaten fish with fried olives.

'But imagine, all the windows in the restaurant had been smashed. I wonder if there was fighting last night?'

Herman smiled but said nothing. He watched the dockers working in the hull and on the quay; he watched the fishermen rowing out to sea with empty vessels and returning with full nets; he watched the soldiers standing with their bayonets at the ready; he watched the people of Setubal. His gaze took in the whole world. Time stood still, and in its silence he solved all the riddles of the earth.

Was that the moment he was struck by the fatal certainty that Miss Kristina would be his?

The *Kristina* was readied, and they left Setubal. For the first two days a southerly wind was behind them. Then calm set in. They lay-to with the fore staysail and topsail: the helm looked after itself.

The sea was still heaving with lingering swells and the water rose all the way up to the bulwark. High overhead the midday sun leached the colour from sea and sky until everything melted into a white mist of heat. The *Kristina* heaved and dipped with the slow breathing of the sea. Their world had fallen into a deep slumber. They wandered around the deck like sleepwalkers and breathed in the rhythm of the waves.

Miss Kristina sat on the deck, embroidering. No one spoke. Bager sat next to his daughter with the *Book of Sermons*. They didn't converse, and they looked as if their closeness didn't require conversation. He turned a page, then looked absent-mindedly across the sea before returning to his book. She concentrated on her stitches. Her skin had tanned, and she let her hair hang loose. Helmer served the coffee.

These were the last warm days before they approached the Bay of Biscay.

The calm continued through the following afternoon. Then around seven in the evening a brisk wind set up, and Ivar and Knud Erik climbed up to set the sails. During the night the wind freshened. When Miss Kristina appeared on deck the next morning, a wave hit her in the face. She wiped the salt water off and laughed at Ivar, who was at the helm, then threw an expert glance at the sails. The gaffs had been reefed during the night and of the squares, only the foresail and the lower topsail were left. The flying jib was taut and would soon be taken in.

'The canvas is taking a beating,' she said, still laughing and wiping her wet face.

She had put on her father's wooden clogs and an oilskin jacket that was far too big for her. She had tied a scarf around her hair, and now it was soaked. She wrung it out and stuffed it in her pocket, leaving her thick brown curls exposed to the gale.

We passed two small fishing boats heading south. Miss Kristina positioned herself next to Ivar and watched them as they dipped violently and vanished into the trough of one wave, only to reappear a moment later riding the next. Her eyes followed them as if searching for a fixed point. Then a strained look came over her, and she suddenly clapped a hand over her mouth and ran to the rail. Ivar looked away discreetly.

She returned to him. 'I think I'll go to the cabin,' she said.

He nodded.

At noon the wind turned. Wind and current were now working in opposite directions, and the *Kristina* plunged hard in the waves, her bow repeatedly disappearing into the swell.

Herman was at the helm.

'We need to take in the flying jib,' he said to Ivar.

Ivar stared at him. 'Are you telling me to climb out on the bowsprit?'

'Are you thick in the head or something?'

'Are you seeing what I'm seeing?' Ivar was openly defying him now.

'I can see that the flying jib needs to be taken in.'

'I can see that the bowsprit's under water half the time.'

'Scared of getting wet?' Herman made no effort to hide his contempt.

'Unless you run her into the wind and slow her down, I'm not going out there.' They glared at each other.

'Are you giving me orders?'

'You're the first mate, and I'm an able seaman. I'm simply urging you to do what anyone with the faintest knowledge of sailing would do. Or the flying jib can stay where it is.'

Herman looked away. He knew that Ivar was right. It would be irresponsible to send a man out on the bowsprit with the bow plunging so deep. He eased his grip on the wheel and the ship ran into the wind. At that moment Miss Kristina came up from the cabin. She was clasping her mouth again, as if preparing another sacrifice to the sea. But the two men facing off caught her attention. She looked from one to the other, her hand still covering her mouth.

Ivar crossed the deck. The ship had stopped plunging, and the flying jib was flapping in the wind. The dripping bowsprit pointed up at the slate-coloured sky. Ivar climbed out on the bowsprit and started rolling up the sail.

Herman watched his tall straight figure, which held itself so confidently out there on the smooth bowsprit, poised over the raging deep below.

Time contracted and stood still.

It wasn't just a man's strength that made Ivar strong. It was also his knowledge of others' weaknesses. Herman had despised Ivar from the moment he met him, but found his own contempt strangely unfocused with nothing firm to fix on. Did Ivar have an Achilles heel? Could he perform under pressure?

Gripping the wheel, Herman felt the pull and strain of the eternal arm-wrestle between helmsman and sea: he had to shift it continually to keep up the steering speed. He slackened, just for a moment – and with an explosive boom, the wind instantly refilled the sails. The bow shot skywards on the rolling crest of a wave, and the whole ship plunged and kept plunging, plummeting through the air before hitting the surface of the water and sending fountains of spray flying to both sides. The *Kristina* cut through the spume like a knife, and her entire stem dived down as if heading for the seabed.

Time slowed right down, as though the sun had shifted to an invisible point in the galaxy. And yet the whole thing had happened so quickly that no one had time to react; Miss Kristina was still clasping her mouth, her eyes wide open. Then the ship rose slowly once again and the water raced sternward across the deck. The bowsprit pointed triumphantly towards the sky. And there was Ivar, clinging like a baby monkey, white-faced.

Even in this brief instant, Herman could see that Ivar was frozen. He'd have to fling himself onto the fo'c's'le right away: if he didn't and the ship plunged again, he'd never make it. This was Ivar's decisive moment like Herman's in Setubal.

But Ivar kept clutching the bowsprit, his brain and body paralysed. His fingertips dug into the bowsprit as though his terror had turned him into an animal that could sink its claws into the hard wood. On impulse, Herman cupped his hands to his mouth and shouted out to him. 'Jump, sailor, jump, damn you!'

He didn't know himself whether he intended to snap Ivar out of his trance or just taunt him. Then the ship dipped again. When she came back up, Ivar was gone. The bare bowsprit pointed briefly at the clouds as if that was where he'd disappeared to, rather than down into the foam around the bow. Herman turned the wheel and let the ship run into the wind, halting the upward movement of the stem.

At this point everything happened very quickly. Miss Kristina ran up to him. 'You bastard,' she choked. 'I saw what you –' Suddenly overcome with nausea, she vomited in a stream that hit Herman in the middle of the chest. She buckled over from stomach cramps; this time the stream hit the deck. When she straightened up, gasping, a half-digested yellow-white substance dripped from her chin. She stared wide-eyed, her face distorted. 'You swine, you monster, you disgusting . . . you . . . you . . .' She collapsed in convulsive sobbing.

She'd seen what had happened, and as a skipper's daughter, Miss Kristina understood what it meant. She'd seen Herman change course. And she knew what that entailed, when there was a crewman on the bowsprit.

And it was true. He couldn't deny what he'd done. Yet he'd always claim she was mistaken. It wasn't he who'd taken Ivar's life. It was the sea. The sea had swallowed Ivar because he'd failed at the crucial moment. The sea took him because he didn't belong on it. Herman had just been its tool.

There was a second witness: Helmer. The galley boy had been ready and waiting by the downhauler while Ivar took in the flying jib. But he understood nothing of what he'd seen, and even if he'd formed the opinion that something was wrong, Herman had the means to shut him up. He couldn't be accused of anything, and for a very good reason. He hadn't done anything.

'Man overboard!' Helmer yelled.

At once Miss Kristina stopped screaming and regained her senses. She tore the lifebuoy from its housing and flung it into the sea to mark the spot where Ivar had disappeared. Knud Erik and Vilhjelm appeared from the fo'c's'le.

'Who? Who?' they yelled anxiously.

'Ivar,' Helmer screamed, with panic in his voice.

Herman ordered him up the rigging to be on the lookout for Ivar in case he resurfaced. Then he gave the order to brace aback. Miss Kristina was standing by the rail, vomiting again. From shock this time, he thought.

Bager came rushing up from his cabin and Herman gave him a brief report. He made his voice deliberately calm and matter-of-fact. 'Ivar went overboard from the bowsprit. He'd gone out to take in the flying jib.'

'How could that happen? Didn't you sail into the wind?'

'Of course. But suddenly he wasn't there.' Herman shrugged, a gesture that suggested the accident was Ivar's own fault.

Knud Erik and Vilhjelm were busy lowering the lifeboat into the water. Bager ran over and took command, jumping in himself. Herman watched as Miss Kristina, too, climbed up on the rail, then pushed off and disappeared over the side.

A moment later the boat appeared. Miss Kristina was standing at the stem, her hair whipping madly. Strings of vomit were still visible on her chin, but she kept her balance with ease. Bager sat slumped on the thwart. Knud Erik and Vilhjelm rowed. Herman stayed at the *Kristina*'s helm. He had a soaring feeling that now he was in charge of the ship.

They rowed around in circles, not knowing what else to do. One moment they were on the crest of a wave, the next they'd disappeared behind one. The *Kristina* drifted in the wind, and so did the life-buoy. Where exactly was it that Ivar had disappeared? There were no signposts on the sea. They drifted further and further away until the lifeboat was nothing but a white-painted nutshell in the middle of the changing landscape of turbulent waves that eternally reared and ran themselves out, tired from chasing the distant horizon.

Then something seemed to be happening out there. The tiny figures stood up in the boat, waving their arms. They bent forward, as if they were struggling with something. Had they found him?

Herman called out to Helmer in the rigging. 'Do you see anything?'

'I think they've got him!' Helmer began waving with one hand, as if welcoming Ivar back to the land of the living.

It was unclear what happened next. The figures bent forward even more, almost disappearing over the side, and the lifeboat rocked perilously from the sudden imbalance. Then they straightened up again. Only one of them remained crouched. Again Herman called out to Helmer. 'What's happening now? Have they got him?'

While he waited for the reply he felt neither fear nor its opposite. If Ivar made it, he made it. Life went on regardless of what happened out there on the water. Herman was calm and openly indifferent.

'I think . . .' Helmer hesitated and narrowed his eyes. 'I think they've lost him again . . . at any rate, I can't see him.' They were still lying against the wind. The sails flapped in the storm.

The lifeboat started circling again. It did so for a while before heading back to the ship. Bager was the first to climb on board. He held his hand to his chest and he was pale. Miss Kristina followed him. She buried her face in her father's shoulder. She was shaking all over and sobbing loudly. Bager held her tight. He put his arm around her shoulder and led her down to his cabin, a clenched fist pressed to his chest, his mouth a thin line that cut across his anguished face.

Herman called Knud Erik over. 'What happened?' he asked.

'We found him. He'd managed to stay afloat, but he was half drowned and his eyes were strange.'

'Strange?'

'Well, I don't know what to call it. As though it wasn't him. Like he'd gone mad. When we tried to pull him on board he just thrashed about. We couldn't get a proper grip under his arms. So we started pulling at him – well, and then it just happened.'

'What happened?'

'Well, his oilskins must have opened up. He slipped out of them. Suddenly all we were holding were the empty sleeves.' Knud Erik's voice grew thick and he struggled to carry on. 'He went right down. We never saw him again. But we'd just held him. We'd looked into his face. I was closer to him than I am to you now. He was saved. And then . . .' He stopped and gave Herman a peculiar look. 'But that's what you wanted, wasn't it?' He shook his head and turned away.

Herman looked long and hard after him. Then his attention was caught by a loud slamming noise. It was the flying jib, still flapping in the storm. He called out across the deck. 'We still have a flying jib that needs taking in. Any volunteers?'

Helmer was hanging in the rigging. Herman ordered him down and told him to get lunch going. There was a ship to be sailed and life had to go on.

Herman started thinking about what Knud Erik had said, and the peculiar look he'd given him. He had a feeling that the boy had looked straight through him. He remembered Kristian Stærk's warning about Anton Hansen Hay, who'd found the skull of his stepfather. The boy might know something. Those blasted kids had stared at him until he was driven half crazy and had to leave town. But nothing had ever come out. Surely that story was long forgotten?

He took his lunch with the three boys. The mood was edgy and they ate in silence. He made a mental note to put them back on their old rations, since Ivar was no longer around to speak up for them. 'Does anyone here have something to say?' he asked.

Helmer cowered and concentrated on his food. Herman looked at Knud Erik and Vilhjelm. They both shook their heads.

'We lost a mate today,' Herman said. 'It's happened before and it'll happen again. That's life at sea. There are good sailors and then there are those who aren't so good . . .' He let the last sentence hang in the air.

'Ivar was a good sailor,' Knud Erik said.

Herman felt like lashing out at the boy, but he controlled himself. 'It was the sea,' he said soothingly. 'When the sea's in that mood, there's nothing to be done.' Even he could hear the hollowness of his words. 'But you'd got hold of Ivar. What happened? Did he panic?' Knud Erik shook his head, unwilling to reply. Herman knew that he'd hit a weak spot. After all, they'd found Ivar. He could have been saved – but he'd sabotaged his own rescue. A good sailor, yes. But was this how a good sailor behaved when his life was at stake? Knud Erik might suspect a murderer in Herman, but the boy had also seen the coward in Ivar, and this made him less certain of his accusation. Herman repeated the question. 'Did he panic?' The silence that followed the question was an answer in itself.

When Helmer got up to take coffee to Bager's cabin, Knud Erik looked up, his eyes dangerously defiant. 'I'm going to tell the skipper everything,' he said.

'Tell him what? You were asleep in the fo'c's'le.' Herman's voice was calm.

'Vilhjelm knows it too. We'll tell Bager.'

'That old story?' Herman laughed. 'All of Marstal has spent the last fifteen years wondering if I killed Holger Jepsen.' He flung out his arms and laughed again. 'And look! I'm still here!'

Helmer returned with the plates from the skipper's cabin. Neither Bager nor Miss Kristina had touched their food. 'Skipper wants a word with you,' he said.

Herman stood up from the bench. Once on deck he breathed in deeply. He had to focus and direct his energy. He had no idea what he was going to say. The survival instinct that he depended on was about to be tested again. He saw Miss Kristina standing by the helm next to Vilhjelm. He'd be alone with Bager. That was probably for the best.

He opened the door to Bager's cabin and stepped over the high threshold. He'd been there before, but it felt as if he were seeing it for the first time. His eyes scanned the framed family photographs screwed to the bulkhead. Above the leather-covered couch was a bolted-on shelf filled with books. Finally his eyes rested on the skipper. Bager had undergone a dramatic change. He was still clutching his chest with one hand; with the other he gripped the table as if to keep himself from sliding off the couch. He'd grown even paler, and his eyes had sunk deep into his head. His thin hair was damp and tiny beads of sweat had formed on his hairline. He blinked nervously.

Herman remained standing right inside the door. Straightening his back, he made his tone as formal as possible. When it came to willpower, he was stronger than Bager. He had never doubted that, and at this moment it was clearer than ever. But the captain outranked him. He had to impress and intimidate, but he couldn't show disrespect for the hierarchy he was bound to uphold, no matter how much he despised its chief representative. He was no mutineer.

'You wanted to speak to me,' he said.

Bager looked down at the table as though he'd forgotten what he'd wanted to say and was now looking for it in the grain of the lacquered wood. Then he loosened his grip on the edge of the table and let the palm of his hand glide across the surface. Suddenly he slammed the table hard, as if signalling to himself that now was the time to talk. He looked up and fixed his eyes on Herman, but the nervous blinking continued.

'A serious accusation has been made against you,' he said, and stopped, as though awaiting a reaction from Herman. Herman simply looked at him. It would be funny if he suddenly started quoting from the *Book of Sermons*, he thought.

Bager looked away before focusing again on Herman, clearly overcoming his reluctance. 'Someone . . .' He hesitated as he struggled to find the right word. 'Someone . . . someone whose word I have no reason to doubt claims that you deliberately endangered Ivar's life when he went out on the bowsprit to take in the flying jib.'

He stopped, exhausted, and waited for a reply. Herman didn't react but remained standing, as calm as before. Bager wiped his forehead with a handkerchief, sweeping a few strands of sweat-soaked hair so they stood upright. His lost face took on a comical resemblance to a big question mark.

Herman said nothing, and Bager had to break the silence again.

'You were at the helm, and the moment Ivar was out on the bowsprit, you changed course so the ship fell off and the stem dived under.'

Herman took a step forward. Bager jumped. 'Who says so?'

'That's none of your concern. Besides, it's not for you to ask the questions. I'm holding this inquiry. Remember your place!' Again Bager wiped his forehead with the handkerchief. For a moment he seemed to listen to something that was going on elsewhere. Herman began to wonder if it was this situation that was scaring him or something else altogether. Then Bager spoke again.

'Not only have you acted irresponsibly and contrary to all good seamanship, but everything suggests that you changed course on purpose.'

'What are you trying to imply?' Herman could no longer control himself. Positioning his hands on the table, he leaned menacingly towards his captain.

Bager pressed one hand against his chest. He was panting now, and had completely given up on mopping the perspiration from his forehead. His hair was still standing up. But his voice was calm. 'I'm not implying anything. No, I'm putting it to you directly that you killed Ivar.' He stopped to catch his breath, which was coming in long, wheezing gasps. Herman stood frozen, still pressing his weight on the table.

Bager got his breath back. 'There will be a maritime inquiry in Copenhagen. The truth will come out there, I can promise you that.'

'It's Miss Kristina, isn't it? She's been telling you a pack of lies! Fucking bitch. He panicked. That's why he drowned. He was a weakling. There's no room for his sort at sea. That's all there is to it. That's all I've got to say on the matter.' Herman had thrust his face dangerously close to the captain's. He had to suppress the urge to grab hold of him and throw the skinny old man's body against the bulkhead.

Bager was looking at him, but his eyes seemed distant. The sweat was streaming down his pallid forehead. Again he seemed to be listening to something far, far away and was barely aware of Herman's presence.

'Are you even listening to what I'm saying?' Herman roared. 'It was that bitch. She'd got the hots for him!' He didn't care what he said. He'd lost his head but still kept control of his hands, though the effort made his whole body shake. Surely the old fool knew he was playing with fire? How much more would he have to put up with? 'Are you saying I'm a murderer?' he thundered, and it felt liberating to say the words out loud. A feeling of righteous indignation welled up in him, and he regained his self-control.

The captain's face remained unchanged. His gaze was still intensively fixed on some distant point: it seemed to preoccupy him. Suddenly he inhaled deeply and something like a hiccup or the beginning of a belch escaped him. His facial muscles tensed, his eyes widened and his lower lip went slack. Then he slumped forward and his head thumped onto the table right between Herman's hands.

Herman leaped back. He stared down at the captain's hair, which fell in thin strands across a scalp as grey as parched earth. He stuck out his hand and checked Bager's pulse. He felt it fade and stop. Then he ran up the ladder and out onto the deck.

Vilhjelm was at the helm, with Knud Erik standing next to him. There was no sign of Miss Kristina. She was probably in the galley with Helmer. He went over to the two boys. 'Do you have a problem with dead bodies?'

They stared at him, baffled. He pointed to Knud Erik. 'You're coming with me.' He led him back to Bager's cabin. Knud Erik froze when he saw the figure slumped across the table.

'What happened?'

'What do you think?'

'Is he dead?'

'I've looked for his pulse. I couldn't find one, so I suppose he is.' Knud Erik's shoulders started to shake. 'We need to put him in his berth,' Herman said. He took hold of Bager under the arms while Knud Erik slid an arm under his legs: together they pulled him sideways off the couch and carefully laid the skinny body in the berth. The eyes were still wide open. So was the mouth. Herman closed the dead man's eyes and pressed his jaw shut. 'This was an accident.' Aware that Knud Erik was staring at him, he shot him a challenging look. Knud Erik looked away. 'Trouble always comes in twos,' he added. He said it to placate him. He could speak only in platitudes now: meaningless phrases, tired expressions. Yet there was something soothing about uttering them, as if he wanted to console not just Knud Erik but himself. Bager's death had scared him: it was as if the captain had suddenly shouted 'Boo!' in his face. Not that he'd miss him. He'd instantly realised that Bager's death was nothing but an advantage for him. He'd avoid a lot of unpleasant accusations. 'I need to speak to Miss Kristina,' he said, and went up the ladder.

Knud Erik followed. Herman opened the door to the galley. She was there, huddled on the little bench. Helmer was standing by the stove with his back to her. She looked up at them. Her face was pale, grimy and red-eyed. The salt water had flattened her hair, and it stuck to her head in messy clumps.

'Miss Kristina,' he said. 'I need to speak to you. It's about your father.'

'My father?' she asked, uncomprehending.

'Let's go outside.' He moved so she could pass through the galley door. She obeyed without asking further questions. There was a somnambular quality to her movements. He led her to the rail on the lee side. Facing each other, they gripped the rail while the ship heaved and dipped on the heavy sea. He didn't know what would happen next, but he was aware of his own tension. Would she break down? Or would she fly into a wild rage and hurl fresh accusations at him? The uncertainty he always felt in her presence was back, but magnified a thousandfold. Could he handle this?

With great effort he made his voice sound matter-of-fact. 'Miss Kristina,' he heard himself say. 'I'm terribly sorry to be the one to deliver this sad message to you, but your father has just died. He had a heart attack.'

He didn't look at her as he spoke but cast his eyes downward, hoping she'd interpret it as a sign of sympathy and respect for her grief. But he knew deep down it was uncertainty that stopped him meeting her eye. He felt that he'd already lost the game and that something terrible was about to blow up in his face, a chain reaction of unstoppable events that would sweep him to his doom.

He'd spoken. He awaited her reaction. But nothing happened. Unable to bear the wait, he looked up. She was still facing him. Her expression remained unchanged, as if she hadn't heard a word he'd said.

What happened next came as a total surprise to him. She took a step forward and bowed her head. Then she rested her forehead on his shoulder and started to cry. For a few seconds he stood stock-still, his arms dangling at his sides. Then he embraced her, swaying steadily to the ship's roll, so they wouldn't lose their balance and fall onto the wet deck. Everything in him opened up all at once, and the uncertainty that had gripped him a minute earlier was transformed into a feeling of triumph that surged like an erupting geyser.

They stood like that for a while. He could have stayed there for ever. He felt his own strength, and the light pressure of her forehead. He stroked her wet, tangled hair and muttered a stream of comforting, meaningless sounds. An unexpected bond had been created between them. He had no idea how. But it was there. He felt it so strongly that he responded with a wash of tenderness. It was like embracing a child.

'Come,' he said. 'It's time for you to see your father.' He escorted her to the door of the cabin before opening it for her. 'I think it's best if you have some time alone with him,' he said gently.

Then he relieved Vilhjelm at the helm.

He ordered more sails to be set. He sailed hard. The ship tilted from the pressure of the wind till the rail was nearly level with the sea. He could see the boys' unease, but nobody said anything. He called them over. 'Bager's dead. I'm the captain now.'

Then he was alone at the helm again. He felt the power of the sea travel through the wheel into his hands. The tenderness he'd felt settled and became a certainty. She was his. It was irrevocable.

He thought about the dead man in the cabin. Most of all he wanted to wrap the body in canvas and ease it overboard without too much ceremony, but he knew he wouldn't get away with that. St Malo wasn't the nearest port, but if the wind lasted and he continued to sail hard, they could get there in two days. Obviously Bager couldn't stay in his cabin. And Miss Kristina couldn't sleep in the room with her dead father. The fo'c's'le was an option. After all, there was a spare berth there. He chortled. That would serve them right, the little brats. They could sleep with a corpse.

Herman stayed at the helm for the rest of the day. He had no desire to be anywhere else. The ship was his. He shot across the sea with a dead captain and a woman waiting in the cabin. He hummed the old shanty about the drunken sailor: *Put him in the bed with the capn's daughter*. A dream. And now it was coming true.

That evening he took Miss Kristina a plate of soup. The cabin was dark: he struck a match and lit the petroleum lamp that was screwed onto the bulkhead.

'You need to eat,' he said, handing her the bowl.

She raised the spoon to her lips obediently. He stayed there and waited silently for her to finish. Then he took the bowl back to the galley.

At midnight he was still at the helm. He'd done three shifts in a row. Now the middle watch started. He secured the wheel and crossed the deck to the fo'c's'le entrance, then climbed down the ladder and woke Vilhjelm. The boy tumbled out of his berth. He'd been sleeping with his clothes on. In his hand he held a jackknife that he'd probably been given as a confirmation present. Knud Erik leaped down from the other berth. He, too, was armed.

The *Kristina* was still sailing hard against the wind and the fo'c's'le boomed every time the stem hit a wave. Herman glanced at the knives and shook his head. 'That's some pretty impressive manicure equipment you've got there,' he said jovially. 'You'd better stick those in your belt. Or I might start thinking you're mutineers.'

Every word he spoke made them flinch. They were so scared they were on the verge of tears. Herman told Vilhjelm the course and climbed back up the ladder. He crossed the deck and tried the handle of the door to the captain's cabin. It was unlocked, and a moment later he was in the darkness on the tilting floor. He listened. He couldn't hear Miss Kristina breathing, but he knew he had to act now. The certainty of it had been growing in him up there in the stormy darkness.

He stuck his hand into the berth, fumbling in the duvet. He felt her hair: she must be lying with her back to him. He'd dreamed of her back. He stroked her hair, which was still stiff from the salt water. She didn't react: he was sure she was asleep. He allowed his hand to wander across her neck, which felt warm and soft. His grip enclosed it. Feeling her delicate spine, he was flooded with tenderness. Still she didn't react. He couldn't hear her breathing, and he had to suppress the urge to take her pulse. Was she still asleep? Was she holding her breath out of fear? No, he was certain of it: she'd been waiting for him. His whole body was telling him so. He flung her duvet aside, grabbed hold of her nightdress and yanked it up to her shoulders.

He hesitated for a moment. I don't know her, he thought, perhaps she's stronger than I am. He was overcome by a sudden fear. Then he unbuttoned his trousers and clambered into the berth next to her. He didn't speak. He felt awkward with his clothes on; he should have taken them off first. Now it was too late. He put an arm around her and pressed her to him. His woollen pullover must be scratching her naked skin. At this point he felt he was exploiting her vulnerability rather than protecting it. The contact made him grow hard, but the heat of passion had deserted him, leaving him coolly detached. He observed himself from the outside, and his self-observation made him hesitate; but his erection was still there, like an animal's, responding to the heat of another body and blindly seeking release. He continued to watch himself from a distance. A big, clumsy man in sea boots and a pullover fumbling with an immobile woman in a narrow berth.

Suddenly she stirred. She mumbled something as if half asleep, and tried to turn over. Instinctively he tightened his grip around her neck and shoved her face into the bed. She screamed, but the pillow muffled it. Her body arched in protest and her arms flailed about.

As he entered her she let out a sigh, as though he'd dislodged the air inside her: an exhalation without emotion, the noise of lungs emptying themselves. After that she was silent, as if it were a spear he was impaling her with.

He paused, and strained to make out if she was still breathing; seconds later he ejaculated in an involuntary surrender that made him feel he'd stepped off the edge of an abyss and was falling in the dark. His hips kept shaking for a long time. She continued to lie there, completely passive. He hugged her motionless body tight. A swarm of words buzzed through his brain: he wanted to say something, but nothing came out. To him she was Miss Kristina. But he couldn't call her that in this moment, when he'd finally become one with her. Thinking about this, he fell asleep.

He woke up, perhaps only a few seconds later: she was shaking herself free. He managed to sit up, but before he'd had time to react she'd kicked out at him. He was flung out of the narrow berth and landed heavily on the floor. He got to his feet and tried to button his trousers. His groin felt damp.

She screamed and screamed.

He felt nothing, apart from irritation at the endless screaming, which filled the narrow cabin and forced him to the door with an almost palpable pressure.

He stumbled out onto the deck. It was blowing harder, and the sails were taut. For a moment he looked across the sea. The foaming crests glowed in the dark. The only sounds were the howling of the wind in the rigging and the thud of the waves as they crashed across the deck. He went over to relieve Vilhjelm at the helm. He decided not to take in any sails, though he knew the risks of driving the ship so hard. Heavy rain pelted his face.

He wasn't a man to weigh up the pros and cons of things. Totally emptied of thoughts, he welcomed his inner blankness just as he'd recently welcomed sleep.

When he asked the boys to relieve him at the next shift, they refused.

'Do you want a shipwreck?' he asked them.

They didn't reply. They just stood there waving their ridiculous confirmation presents, which they considered deadly weapons. The wind had fallen, and the ship lay calmer on the sea. Having secured the wheel again, he strode towards the captain's cabin. But the boys ran ahead of him and blocked the door, still holding their knives. Miss Kristina must have told them everything. Now they thought they were her protectors. He'd outraged their childish sense of justice. The worst thing about a sense of justice is that it makes people wild and crazy. In giving them courage, it robs them of their caution and their instinct to survive.

'If you come closer, we'll kill you,' Knud Erik said, and his voice trembled.

Helmer was sobbing loudly, but he held on to his knife. They were blind with fear and in their blindness they had only one point of reference, the jackknives in their hands. Herman didn't doubt that they were capable of stabbing him. Perhaps it was the only way they could cope with the terror he'd provoked. They were unpredictable, and for this reason alone they suddenly presented a danger.

He realised that nothing would ever come of his plans, whatever they'd been, exactly. Miss Kristina was lost to him. He was alone with three boys who might do just about anything out of panic, and who didn't care whether they lived or died. He could snap their spines one by one, but what good would that do?

Disgust welled up in him. It was time to move on and do what he always did in these situations, when all other exits were closed: show the world that he didn't care and that he could leave it all behind. His life heaved and collapsed like the ocean swell.

He returned to the wheel. From now on it was an endurance test. He'd get no more sleep. The French Atlantic coast stretched to the east. In harsh weather like this, its surf could mean ruin for a schooner, especially one without skilled mates.

It was sometime later that day that he changed their course.

Homecoming

MONSIEUR CLUBIN WAS THE FIRST PERSON TO NOTICE THAT THE topgallant sail schooner pitching in the sea by Pointe de Grave was in distress. At first he wasn't sure there was anyone on board, but after watching the ship through his binoculars for a few minutes, he realised that some desperate will was fighting to keep the ship clear of the dangerous beach. No distress signals were being sent, but Monsieur Clubin's sense of duty, forged over the course of thirty years as a ship's pilot in Royan, demanded that he investigate.

On board the *Kristina* he found three boys and a young woman, all of whom seemed bewildered. The captain lay dead in the fo'c's'le. There were no able seamen and no first mate, and the lifeboat was missing.

The boys' explanation, as presented to the port authorities and subsequently to the police in Royan, was that the first mate had murdered an able seaman and the captain, and then assaulted the captain's daughter. Precisely what they meant by assault, the boys either could not or would not specify, and the young lady herself refused to open her mouth: during her entire stay in Royan, the young woman uttered not a single word.

They further claimed that the first mate had committed a murder in his home town, the same town they came from, though he'd never been punished for it. He'd jumped ship earlier that morning when Monsieur Clubin came on board, and used the lifeboat to make his escape.

After a thorough examination the police found no cause to charge the missing first mate. The captain's body showed no signs of violence, and the subsequent autopsy established that he'd died of heart failure. The circumstances surrounding the drowning of the able seaman were not sufficiently well documented to bring charges, and his death was ascribed then, and later, in the maritime inquiry that followed in Copenhagen, to one of those unfortunate incidents that occur at sea, though it was acknowledged that the first mate's disappearance might justify any number of suspicions. However, none of them could be proven.

Ultimately the unfortunate chain of events that culminated in the *Kristina*'s perilous drift around Pointe de Grave was her captain's lack of judgement: he'd signed on a first mate of notorious character without proper papers. Nor did the alleged assault on the young woman lead to an indictment. The lack of evidence was down to her stubborn and persistent silence, along with the boys' unclear description of the nature of her assault.

The captain was buried in the town cemetery. Because the local newspaper, *La Dépêche de l'Ouest*, had written about the ill-fated ship – *'le navire maudit'* – a number of curious onlookers turned up for his funeral.

Monsieur Clubin's compact figure was also to be seen there, but it was duty, rather than curiosity, that made him attend. After all, he had come to the ship's rescue, led her to a safe port and looked after the crew, who in his eyes were mere children. He'd welcomed them into his home, and Madame Clubin had provided the young lady with a room and lent her a black hat and veil so she could be suitably dressed for the funeral.

The young woman put up with it all and allowed the pilot's helpful wife to treat her like a doll. She didn't express gratitude nor did any sign of grief mark the pale, rigid mask she showed the world. Madame Clubin attached no importance to outward appearances, and made no attempt to coax emotion from her young, stricken guest. She was firm only when it came to meals. Madame Clubin was a French Basque, and in a voice that tolerated no contradiction she ordered her guest to finish the platefuls of *ttoro, gabure, camot* and *couston* that she placed before her every day. The young lady obeyed without thanking her for the food or expressing any opinion on it. But she ate it, and Madame Clubin announced to her husband, as she was in the habit of doing, that the sum total of her life's experience was that what an unhappy person needs most is maternal care and good food.

After receiving orders from the shipping company back in Denmark, one of the young men stayed on board the *Kristina* to await the arrival of a new crew. The other two left Royan with the young woman, who retained her silence to the last.

When she stepped onto the train, her two escorts bore her luggage with brotherly care. She carried only a seabag, said to have belonged to the drowned seaman.

ONE DAY KLARA FRIIS RETURNED HOME TO FIND KRISTINA WAITING
in her drawing room. Klara was well aware of her story. We all
were. Vilhjelm and Helmer reported only that Herman had
assaulted her, but it was obvious to everyone that it had been a
case of rape. Whenever the boys said the word *assault* we nodded
knowingly in a way that must have irritated them. Of course they
knew what had happened to her. Boys know that sort of thing.
But they chose their words carefully because they wanted to protect
her.

We referred to Kristina Bager as 'the poor little thing', but Klara
was the first to learn that she had a secret. When she came in,
Kristina rose from the sofa and stared at her. She didn't speak: she
hadn't uttered a word since her homecoming. Then she pointed to
her belly with one hand and made an arc in the air in front of it
with the other. Klara understood right away, and her eyes welled in
compassion. She felt so helpless. Not only had the poor little thing
been raped, but she was carrying her rapist's child. It couldn't have
been any worse, and how money could help her now was beyond
Klara – though she imagined that was why Kristina had come.

Immediately, she took the young girl's hand and said, 'Come with
me.' Together they went to Teglgade, to Mrs Rasmussen. Anna Egidia
settled Kristina on the sofa. She served coffee and placed a bowl of
home-baked biscuits in front of her while making a range of
comforting noises, which, like the cosy, everyday domesticities she
performed around her distressed guest, were aimed at calming her
down. It was a ritual Klara had observed many times before, and,
as always, it seemed to work. Anna Egidia placed her hand on the
girl's belly and stroked it. And, as if her touch had activated some
sort of inner mechanism, Kristina opened her mouth and spoke for
the first time in several weeks.

'I want to go to America,' she said.

The two women looked at each other.

'I don't want to have this baby in Marstal,' she said. 'And I don't want to be sent away to have him in secret and then give him up for adoption. I want to go to America and build a new life for me and my son.'

'Your son?' Klara was stunned.

But Anna Egidia, who knew more about matters of the heart than did Klara, refrained from asking her what made her think that the child was a boy. Hearing the tenderness in Kristina's voice when she spoke about her unborn child, she realised immediately that there was more to this story than rape.

'So Herman isn't the baby's father?' she asked.

Kristina shook her head. Her face was lit up by a sudden happiness that quickly turned to grief, the grief she'd hidden behind her silence and stiff features. She started crying hard, and the two women sat down on either side of her and held her.

The father, she told them, was Ivar, an able seaman to whom she'd given her heart and much more: the heart's natural companion, her virtue, which in a moment of such great and true love was not worth keeping, because he was the most wonderful man, the most handsome, the wisest she'd ever met, not like that animal, that heartless swine Herman, the monster who had murdered the best man in the world.

'My husband,' she said. 'He was my darling, darling husband. We would have been married. I'm sure of that. There was no one else in the world for me.'

They understood then that when she spoke of Ivar as the baby's father she wasn't talking about a fact, so much as a hope.

'America isn't such a bad idea,' said Klara. Anna Egidia nodded. One of her daughters had been there during the war.

Anna Egidia spoke to Kristina's mother, and Klara organised the ticket for the boat to America, making sure there would be someone to meet Kristina in New York. Now all they had to do was wait for the baby. Who would it look like when its head popped into the world? Would it be born with the signature of crime or of love?

A jubilant new mother telephoned from New York.

'If I'd had a boy, I'd have called him Ivar,' Kristina said. 'But it's a girl and her name will be Klara. Need I say more?'

A small face, too small to smile but big enough to bear witness to its origins, had confirmed her faith in the conquering power of love. Nature had delivered her gift and the baby's true father had signed it. Ivar had sent his last greeting from the hereafter in the form of a strong chin, a straight nose, a clear forehead, dark brows and black hair.

Klara shared her joy. At least Kristina had cheated fate. And yet something inside Klara wept too, as if she'd been abandoned yet again. When we're wretched, we long for the company of others who also mourn: for the bittersweet confirmation that we aren't suffering because we've been unlucky or made the wrong choices, but because it's the law of life. When Kristina cheated her fate, Klara found hers all the harder to bear.

Her own child had been on that ill-fated ship, alone with a man no one in Marstal now doubted was a murderer. Knud Erik could have been killed, and she knew that she'd have experienced his death – as she'd experienced Henning's and Albert's – as a stinging rebuff. No one wanted her. They turned their backs on her and disappeared into the darkness. Or they went to sea. And that was the same as dying.

Helmer and Vilhjelm had returned with Kristina. Vilhjelm was still weak from his ordeal in the Atlantic. Helmer sobbed like a baby when he saw his parents. Now he was apprenticed to Minor Jørgensen, the grocer.

And Knud Erik? He'd stayed in France to look after the ship until a new crew could be found. Klara assumed he'd been ordered to do this. She went to visit the owner of the *Kristina*, the late Captain Bager's brother, Herluf Bager. She'd imagined it as a meeting between two shipowners. Man to man: that was how she described it to herself before entering the shipping company's office in Kongegade.

'Of course I realise that the boy has been through a great deal,' Bager said, after getting up to welcome her and then sitting down again in his leather office chair, which seemed to absorb him until chair and man melded into a single mass of unperturbed and – she could not help thinking – manly authority. 'But someone had to stay on to watch the ship.'

'He's only fifteen,' she exclaimed.

'He's a robust boy. I hear only good things about him. Of course he's welcome to sign off, though it would make things difficult for us. However, he hasn't expressed the wish to do so.'

He looked her up and down, and in that moment she knew he was not going to order Knud Erik home as she'd asked. And she knew the reason: a reason that until now she'd failed to understand. This was not a meeting between two shipowners. This was a meeting between a woman and a man. And a worried mother knew nothing about the business of seafaring.

She stamped her heel on the floor and left without saying goodbye. He could tell the whole world about this if he wanted to. Her impotence made her burn with rage. Who did he think he was, the fat, smug little so-and-so? It would require no effort at all to ruin him, to crush him under the heel she'd just stamped his floor with.

Then she calmed down. Her agitation gave way to common sense. No wonder she couldn't get through to Knud Erik. The whole town was in the grip of this delusion that the future lay at sea, when in reality the sea promised nothing but brutalisation and an ice-cold death by drowning.

THE DAY CAME WHEN SHE THOUGHT KNUD ERIK WAS DEAD.

But when it turned out he was still alive, she decided she'd have to kill him herself. It was time. He was twenty when he told her, in his usual monosyllabic way, that he'd signed on to the *Copenhagen*. A couple of months later, the big bark had disappeared en route from Buenos Aires to Melbourne. They looked for her everywhere: Tristan da Cunha, the Prince Edward Islands, the New Amsterdam Islands. But nothing turned up. No name board no capsized lifeboats, not so much as a single lifebelt.

When the list of the sixty-four crewmen was published, Knud Erik's name wasn't there. It turned out he'd been sailing on one of Klara's own barks, the *Claudia*. He'd repeatedly asked her for permission to do this, and Klara had always refused. But she hadn't checked the crew register, and the captain had signed on Knud Erik behind her back.

During the dreadful days and nights when she believed he'd disappeared with the *Copenhagen*, she'd gone over their last conversation again and again. He'd asked her if he could sign on to the *Claudia*. It was one of the few times he'd opened up to her, and she'd rejected him. Now he was gone. Her obstinacy had sent him to his death.

'Do you realise,' he'd said to her, 'that the barks you inherited from Albert are the last big sailing ships in the world?' They weren't just the last, they were also the most beautiful, and the final vestiges of an entire era. With their thin summer sails set, they'd ply the north-east trade wind right across the Atlantic to the West Indies to fetch dyer's broom. Every sailor, just once in his lifetime, had to experience what it was like to stand under those towering white sail-cloths, with the trade wind behind him and the hot sun above, or to sit on the yardarm of the main sixty feet above the deck, king of the whole world. His eyes lit up as he spoke. He'd let her see inside him.

He was a man now. Long-limbed, but no longer gangly. Muscular and straight-backed. She could see Henning in him. She'd always been able to, but now she could see something more, something better and stronger.

'No' was all she'd said.

She couldn't even be sure that he *had* died, because his name was missing from the list of those lost when the *Copenhagen* went down. So where was he? She walked past the Collector's workshop. She was afraid to look in. What if he was carving her drowned boy right at this very moment?

There were nights when she paced the rooms restlessly, screaming out her loneliness and the loss for which she felt so cruelly responsible, while Edith lay in her room with a pillow over her head. She, too, was weeping for the brother they both thought was lost, but her mother's uninhibited grief terrified the girl.

Those of us who passed by in the street didn't label Klara insane. We're all familiar with the line that separates grief from madness, and we know that sometimes the only way to stay on the right side of it is to scream.

Then a letter arrived from Knud Erik postmarked Haiti. Klara's hands trembled. She waited a long time before opening it. She thought it was a missive from the hereafter: that the devil himself had written her a letter, mocking her hubris for thinking she could prevent the sea from taking her son.

But from the letter it was clear that Knud Erik knew nothing of the loss of the *Copenhagen* – and consequently nothing of what she'd gone through. He was simply writing to apologise for telling her he had signed on to the *Copenhagen* when he hadn't: for the past few months he'd been sailing on the *Claudia*. He closed his letter as he always did, with a line that always upset her because she knew how many unspoken things it must hide: 'I am doing fine.'

Her response was instant. She wiped her remorseful night vigils from her mind completely and sold the deck right from under his feet. When the *Claudia* called at St Louis du Rhône, she'd offloaded the bark to Gustaf Erikson from Mariehamn on the Åland Islands. The remaining barks followed shortly afterwards.

Having practically destroyed all seafaring in Marstal, she now decided to kill her son too. It would put an end to her constant fear of losing him.

For several tortured months she'd believed him dead and reproached herself for it. Then she'd found her agony was based on a lie. When Knud Erik returned to Marstal to pass his first mate's exam at the Navigation College in Tordenskjoldsgade, and she spotted him from the bay window coming to pay her a visit, she immediately ordered the maid to turn him away.

'Tell him he's dead,' she said.

'I won't say that,' the girl answered.

'Do it!' screamed Klara, losing control.

The girl went to open the door, but instead of remaining in the doorway and delivering Klara's message, she stepped out and closed the door behind her. 'She doesn't want to see you,' she told Knud Erik. 'I don't know what's the matter with her. You'd best come back another day when she's in a better mood.'

From her bay window Klara watched her dead son as he walked back to the harbour.

Was she a good person? Or a bad one? Was she someone who'd wanted to do good but ended up doing the opposite? She'd ask herself these questions during her night vigils when she believed Knud Erik was dead and blamed herself. The doubts lingered, and her only way of suppressing them was to shut Knud Erik out of her life completely.

She'd founded her orphanage, and according to the school, its children were among the best in the class and always full of confidence. That had to be a good deed. She'd donated a library to the town and created a financial base for the Maritime Museum. She'd even done it anonymously. She'd given money to the Østersøhjemmet, the big old people's home that lay to the south with a view over the meadow and the beach huts on the Tail. She'd donated funds to purchase equipment for the hospital in the neighbouring town of Ærøskøbing.

Kristina wasn't the only young girl she'd helped get to America. Sometimes she thought she ought to send every young woman in Marstal across the Atlantic, so the men could learn their lesson. She kept in touch with the teachers at the school, and if a girl showed academic promise, she'd step in and pay for her education off the island. This was the future she'd planned for Edith. She wanted to make women independent. They had to help themselves and provide their own counterbalance to the tyranny of the sea.

In the old days, in the criss-cross grid of Marstal, the main streets had always been those that led to the harbour and the sea. Then along came Kirkestræde, full of shops with women bustling in and out. It was around their lives that she wanted to build a new town on the ruins of the old one. The orphanage, the old people's home, the library, the museum. Women would leave the island and return home stronger and wiser. And that was just the beginning.

It was a secret conspiracy and she was heading it.

'THIS IS YOUR BIG CHANCE,' MARKUSSEN SAID IN HIS DRY, DETACHED
manner. 'War in Asia, civil war in Spain, crop failure in Europe.
Things are looking up. Freight prices will rise again.' He scrutinised
her with that look of his, which she could never quite fathom and
which made her feel both safe and uncertain. He took care of her.
She never doubted that. Not once during all these years had he given
bad advice. He'd trained her and she was an apt pupil, and every
time she made the right decision, she received a look of approval
that assured her that she'd not yet exhausted all her options. But
there was also a cool curiosity in him, and she sensed that if she
were to fail and go under, it wouldn't disturb him unduly. He'd
regard her downfall as merely another chapter in the endless textbook of life; he might even feel enriched by the new knowledge that
the study of her ruin might afford him.

It was like walking a tightrope. He was a father to her. She'd
never known what it was to have one, and had always longed for
one. But because she had never been able to satisfy her longing with
a real person, she didn't know that a father had limitations. Now
at last she was learning them. Yes, he was a rock she could cling to.
But she also might be smashed to pieces against it. She learned to
keep her distance and this distance lay at the heart of their relationship. Distance was his element.

Markussen was old now. Rheumatism had bent him so that it
looked as if he was growing in the wrong direction. He walked
beside her, hunched over his cane, taking tiny, cautious steps, as if
doubting the solidity of the ground beneath his feet. His helplessness filled her with maternal tenderness, an emotion she hadn't felt
in a long time. But she knew she should keep those feelings to
herself. Not because he'd be offended if she recognised his increasing
decrepitude: indeed, he made a joke of it, laying bare his own weakness with the confidence of the powerful. That's the luxury of power,

and power was what he was all about; she could see that clearly. He was surrounded by people who depended on him, and in their attentiveness and helpfulness he recognised nothing but rational self-interest. Of course they'd want to keep on the good side of him. It benefited them personally.

She took him for a stroll through Marstal; Markussen himself had insisted on it. His photograph was never in the newspapers, so no one recognised him. She was obviously entertaining a distinguished visitor, but people knew no more than that.

They walked past the vacant plots, and as he cast his glance across the nettles growing high behind the tarred fences, she was aware that the sight intrigued him. He eyed her sideways and smiled, acknowledging her willpower. Money could have been growing in there instead of weeds.

'What do they think of you?' he asked.

'That I'm a bit odd, maybe. But they don't think ill of me.'

'They should.' He laughed conspiratorially. He saw the destroyer in her. The avenger. The punishing fury who operated underground. This was what attracted him, and this was the pact they'd entered into: he'd make all his experience available to her, and then let her do the opposite of what he'd have done himself. He created; she demolished. What she wanted to do besides that, he didn't understand.

They turned towards the harbour. Moored to the black-tarred posts lay the true evidence of her efforts – a sight that made him point out, not for the first time, that her big chance was now.

There they lay with their huge black hulls and their tall narrow funnels, towering as high as the smaller masts, which were there only because of the derricks. Two-thirds of the town's tonnage was distributed among those five steamers, the *Unity*, the *Energy*, the *Future*, the *Goal* and the *Dynamic*. The rest were smaller ships, including the last three or four Newfoundland schooners; the others had been converted to motor-powered vessels, which sailed only local routes. The hope of progress had foundered on a rock. And the rock was Klara.

'My steamers will stay where they are,' she said. 'I won't allow them to sail again.'

Markussen nodded. Klara Friis was an apt pupil. She was strangling Marstal. The town needed to get back on its feet after the long depression that followed the 1929 crash, sentencing large parts of the merchant fleet to idleness.

Instead, she made sure that nothing happened.

The laid-up steamers represented an era that, thanks to Klara Friis, was gone for ever.

People talked about it. She was well aware of that. But she hadn't been lying when she told Markussen they spoke no ill of her. They saw the steamers idling in the harbour as evidence of female indecisiveness and lack of skill in running the affairs of men. They forgave her for her impossible gender. They were tolerant, almost condescending. Women included. And although Klara Friis received no thanks either for the things she *had* achieved, she enjoyed the secret satisfaction of having done the right thing. She saw herself as a breakwater, shielding the land from the ocean's destructive force.

It wasn't until that evening, when they were sitting down to the dinner her housekeeper had served, that Markussen aired an objection that made her temporarily doubt her own wisdom.

'What if,' he said, smiling, as if merely testing her intelligence, 'what if the men run off to sea anyway? There are no longer any significant shipping companies in Marstal, so they might just decide to sign on elsewhere. They won't find it hard to get work. They've proved their skill over the course of several centuries.'

For a moment he reminded her of Frederik Isaksen. 'They won't do that,' she retorted sharply. 'Every year the Navigation College admits fewer and fewer students from Marstal.'

'Congratulations,' he said, and raised his glass. 'Then you've almost completed your mission.' She couldn't avoid noting the sarcasm in his voice, but nodded to him all the same over the rim of her glass.

'You don't understand me,' she said.

'You're right. I don't understand what your goal is. You pretend to do one thing while simultaneously doing the exact opposite. A library, an orphanage, a museum, a home for old people: you act like the town's benefactor, while pulling its means of living right out from under its feet.'

'The sea was never a real way to make a living.'

'I built up this country's greatest shipping firm. I'm a shipowner.'

They both fell silent. They'd reached the point they always reached.

'Your son's a sailor,' he said, out of nowhere.

She looked down. 'And his father was lost at sea. You don't need to remind me of that. Can't you understand what I want?'

'Yes,' he said. 'You want the impossible. You want to whip the sea until it begs you for mercy.'

That was the last time they saw each other. She'd known it would be. Their conversation had come to an end. She'd learned what she needed to learn, and he'd conveyed what he'd wanted to convey. He'd built a monument to Cheng Sumei and even though that monument existed only inside Klara Friis's head, at least he'd shared the story. It was up to her to extract meaning from it. He'd never managed to fathom it himself.

Klara Friis had put herself in Cheng Sumei's place. Like her, she was a player who never revealed her hand, and they both had an excuse for their subterfuge. Cheng Sumei's was love. She'd wanted to make herself irreplaceable to a man who'd never previously needed one particular human being any more than another, and then she'd built an empire around him. True, he hadn't needed her heart, her sex or her lips. But he couldn't do without her talent for business, and the cynical methods she'd learned in a lawless town. And these became her gift of love.

Klara, too, had a gift of love to offer. Not to a man, but to Marstal. She wanted to save it from the sea. She wanted to return its lost sons – boys to mothers, husbands to wives, fathers to children.

Oh, she knew well enough that the night of the flood would never really end. She'd still keep plunging her hand into the waves over and over again, trying to save Karla. Every time she sold a ship or laid it up, every time Marstal was ruled out as the possible home for yet another ship, every time the shipyard received one order fewer from one of the town's shipowners, every time a young man found a livelihood on land, every time the number of students from Marstal at the Navigation College declined – then her hand grasped Karla and pulled her upward through the dark water. The flood would abate, and for a while the pressure would ease. She dreamed of a globe on which the seas retreated and the land masses merged, offering people a home where they could all live together. Fathers, mothers and children united for ever.

*   *   *

'This is your big chance,' Markussen had told her, when they said goodbye for the last time. He'd been referring to the wars in Spain and Asia. Thousands of people killing each other was good news. The freight market would go up and his ships would be busier than ever.

Unlike her steamers. They lay still, their boilers cold.

Now was the time to act. Here was the moment to seize. But she wouldn't be sending them out to take part in orgies of profit while drowned men floated in their wake.

She went to her office and enquired about the prices of ships. And she heard what she expected to hear: it was time to sell. She'd bought the steamers from the widows ten years ago when the freight market was in a slump and everyone was suffering losses. Now the freight prices had increased, she could resell at a huge profit. She knew what the town's businessmen would say.

'Bloody hell,' one would exclaim. The others would nod in agreement. They'd be reluctant to acknowledge her good move with anything more than a curse. But that, at least, would be a tribute to her skill. They'd thought her female brain was short-circuited when it came to profit, and that her ships were laid up simply because she couldn't make up her mind what to do with them. Now they'd realise that every step she'd taken, or failed to take, had a basis in cold calculation.

Others would take a different view. They'd think that she'd sold off not just the ships, but Marstal's livelihood. They'd be closer to the truth.

Was she taking more than she was giving?

What would be left of Marstal once she'd sold off her steamers? A tiny fleet of schooners with auxiliary engines, many of them rigged down to ketches and reduced to plying the local Baltic routes, with perhaps an occasional venture into the North Sea. The circle was complete. The town would end up where it had begun more than a hundred years before.

The sea would be the loser, because there'd be no more human sacrifices to His Merciless Majesty. And the winner? That would be the women.

Or would things go the way Markussen had hinted? Would the men sign on elsewhere and settle at the ends of the earth?

Would the flood never end?

IV

The End of the World

IT WAS THE END OF THE WORLD.

He was on an alien planet or somewhere in the future. Whatever it was, it was heading for destruction. Convinced he was about to die, Knud Erik closed his eyes. Then suddenly he realised where he was.

He was in the middle of a dream. But it wasn't his own.

He was seven years old, sitting on the thwart of Albert Madsen's boat as they rowed through Marstal's harbour. The old man's voice came back to him, talking about a phantom ship painted grey, huge tubular buildings on fire, a night sky lit by a blinding phosphorescent white light, and air that quivered from the pressure of exploding bombs and collapsing houses.

Yes, that's where he was: in a dream that had visited the old man more than twenty years before. He opened his eyes and saw what Albert had seen, and for the first time he understood that the old man's dreams had been prophetic and that what he'd presented to a child as tales of adventure had actually been his own visions of horror.

'That's the best story you've ever told me,' Knud Erik had said back then. And now here he was, right in the middle of it. He'd never heard the ending. But it was on its way, and he sensed it would involve his own death.

Just then, a Stuka dived towards the ship and dropped a bomb. As he watched the missile falling, time stood still: he realised it would plummet right through the grey-painted funnel and detonate in the engine room with devastating consequences. Preparing himself for death, he tensed his muscles.

Now!

The bomb disappeared with a splash into the water a few metres from the side of the ship. He'd mistaken its trajectory. His muscles were still locked rigid. He waited for the column of water and the sudden keeling of the ship, for the water pressure to burst her steel plates and come flooding in. But nothing happened. The bomb was a dud.

He waited for the next one.

The noise was deafening. Two oil tanks on the north side of the Thames had caught fire, and a frustrated roar sounded from the sea of flames, like the great mythical wolf of Ragnarök straining on its chain at the end of time, howling to be unleashed on the whole world. The black smoke was a clenched fist headed for the distant stars, extinguished one by one in the roil of darkness and toxic fumes. Beneath its black lid everything was ablaze, as though the sun itself had been shot down and was flaring for the last time in the midst of the ruined oil tanks.

The whole of Southend was on fire. The windows in the tenement blocks glowed in the blaze; flames leaped from the roofs like strange vegetation growing at explosive speed, determined to consume the very soil it grew in, and the docks shuddered in convulsions of destruction. Flashes of fire spurted from the anti-aircraft batteries on the roofs that were still intact. The ships on the river were firing, too. Knud Erik could hear the sputter of the old Lewis machine gun that had been mounted on board the *Dannevang* some months earlier: four of the crew had been trained in the use of weapons by the British Navy. He was one of them. The machine gun, which dated from the First World War, they'd soon discovered to be useless when it came to defending the ship, but it had another, more important function. It beat whisky, and if anyone still remembered to pray these days, it beat praying, too. Clutching and firing it gave you a blissful feeling of calm – though at a price. Its overheated metal stock burned your palms and its explosive coughing deafened you. But for a moment, the waiting stopped.

You were responding. You were taking action.

In a strange way the machine-gun position was the best place to be during an attack even though you were clearly visible on deck, which made you the perfect target for a hail of enemy bullets and bombs. But at least out there, your helplessness didn't drive you insane.

When the air-raid warning sounded, the crew would instantly release the mooring and head for the buoys in the middle of the Thames. It was standard procedure for all ships to leave the quay during air raids because it took weeks to clear the wreckage of a bombed ship and in the meantime it blocked the quay to other vessels. So, resigned, they'd head out for open water, where they couldn't just jump onto land if the ship took a hit. 'We're off to the cemetery,' they'd joke.

So it was good to have your hands on a Lewis.

Several of the ships around them were on fire now. One capsized slowly and began to sink. The crew in the lifeboats rowed haphazardly: the whole harbour was ablaze and a crane had fallen halfway into the basin. High up above them one parachute after another unfurled and floated down towards the river, swaying calmly. As they drew nearer, Knud Erik was able to see that what was suspended from them wasn't human. The parachutes hit the water and their vast fabric canopies crumpled langorously before settling on the river. They looked like flowers scattered across a grave.

An hour later the air-raid alarm sounded the all-clear. Fires were still blazing on the quays, and the oil tanks were belching black fumes into the night sky. An acrid smell of oil, soot and brick dust hung over the river, along with a faint trace of sulphur whose origin Knud Erik couldn't identify. His eyes stung from exhaustion.

Knud Erik had been through the same scenario in Liverpool, Birkenhead, Cardiff, Swansea and Bristol. Sometimes it seemed that they were sailing in an ocean of flames, and the sky was filled not with cumulus, stratus and cirrus clouds, but a whole weather system made up of Junker 87s and 88s and Messerschmitt 110s. When their ship passed into the Channel they came within reach of the German batteries at Calais; in the North Sea U-boats awaited them. It was everywhere and it was constant. The whole world had contracted and turned as black as a cannon mouth. They didn't call it fear: it manifested itself as sleeplessness. At sea, they always worked double watches, and when they were attacked, nobody slept. While in port, the whole crew frequently had to move the ship to another mooring point, so their sleep was constantly interrupted. Did they sleep at all? Well, they closed their eyes and they were gone in a moment, free of memories, until death yelled 'Boo!' in their ear again and they tumbled out of their berths, wide-eyed, as though dreaming of an exit. But there was no exit, no hatch in the sky, no trapdoor in the deck, no horizon to escape behind. They lived surrounded by three elements – not sea, sky and earth, but what they concealed – U-boats, bombers and artillery. They were on a planet that was about to explode.

Albert Madsen had been right. He'd seen the end of the world. But the old man hadn't told Knud Erik he'd be trapped in the middle of it.

Tonight, he'd manage two hours' sleep before rousing the crew. They were going further up the Thames with the tide and for him, it was a matter of honour to be ready before any of the other ships. He prayed for a dreamless sleep.

He didn't know that the next day he'd get to learn a new word. He'd expanded his vocabulary over the past few months, with technical expressions that bore witness to mankind's endless ingenuity. This ingenuity was so convoluted and contradictory that he found it impossible to follow, but he knew its mission well enough. A newer and even fancier way had been found to destroy him.

Yes, he got the sleep he'd asked for. Darkness descended and contained him – that rare, longed-for darkness in which, for a moment, he could renew his strength. This time it held him for so long that when it finally released him, he stumbled out of his berth with those wide, dazed eyes that are the normal reaction to an attack. He'd neglected his duty. He'd overslept.

He rushed out of his cabin. Many of the other ships already had smoke emerging from their funnels. Then, within the space of a second, more than just smoke was pouring out. A massive explosion that recalled last night's bombardment rolled across the river without warning. Another followed. Nearby, the bow of the *Svava* rose into the air, then snapped off. The ship started sinking immediately while smoke and flames devoured their way towards the wheelhouse. He saw several men jump into the river, one with his back in flames. Then the bow of the *Skagerrak* exploded. Two Norwegian steamers blew up next, and then a Dutch one.

His first thought was to get away. But what were they fleeing from? Where was the enemy? The sky was clear and it couldn't possibly be a U-boat.

A dinghy approached from one of the British escort ships. At its front a man with a megaphone hailed him with the day's new word: '*Vibration mines!*'

Knud Erik needed no further explanation. The mines were triggered when a ship's screw started turning. The objects he'd seen last night falling gently through the air suspended from parachutes were vibration mines.

A couple more ships exploded. Those that remained lay still, their boilers cold. Around them flaming ships were reduced to sinking wrecks in seconds. A grim regatta of burned bodies floated between the wrecks.

Later, they were ordered to drift upriver with the tide, without using the engine. The only sound they heard was the lapping of waves against the side of the ship. It was as quiet as if they'd returned to the age of the sail.

THEY WERE ON THEIR WAY TO ENGLAND IN A CONVOY FROM BERGEN
on the west coast of Norway when the radio announced Germany's
occupation of Denmark. Their captain, Daniel Boye, immediately
called a ship's counsel and presented the choice: to continue to an
English port or reverse course and return to Denmark or Norway.

In a way, they felt the decision had already made itself. They were
sailing in a convoy under the protection of British warships. Didn't
that mean that they, too, were at war with Germany, like the ships
escorting them?

The answer was clear. Thanks to a war that wasn't their own,
freight rates were high. So were wages, which now came with a
300 per cent war supplement. With overtime and various allowances
this meant a quadrupling, sometimes a quintupling of a man's
income. The reason they'd sailed was money. Now they were being
asked to join this war and to be in its front line. Danish neutrality
was no protection: seventy-nine Danish sailors had been killed last
Easter and more than three hundred had lost their lives since the
outbreak of war, despite having sailed on ships with the Danish
flag painted on the side. The torpedoes on the U-boats couldn't
tell the difference. A ship on her way to an enemy port was a
ship on her way to an enemy port, regardless of the stripe of those
on deck.

All of the seventeen crewmen on board the *Dannevang* agreed to
continue on to England, out of sheer defiance more than anything
else. They'd made the decision to go to sea. And now no one was
going to frighten them off deck.

They sensed that this same defiance – not patriotism nor love
of the motherland nor ideology, nor indeed any understanding of
what the war was about – would pull them through and keep them
alive. Doubtless these other motives played some part, whether
large or small, in each crewman's decision, but the men weren't

being asked to offer their opinion on the war. They were being asked to make a choice that would have unforeseen but crucial consequences for the rest of their lives. In what way they couldn't know, but their sailor's instinct told them it was a matter of life and death. They felt all of the sailor's stubbornness when faced by an overpowering force – a hurricane or a Messerschmitt 110 – and they said yes, not to the war that raged this year, but to one which had raged for aeons; not to England, but to the road to England: to the sea, and to a challenge that made them feel like men.

They arrived at Methil, in Scotland, on 10 April and were immediately ordered to sail to Tyne Dock in Newcastle, where their ship would be assigned to the British Admiralty. There was no ceremony to mark the transfer. An officer from the British Navy stuck a note to the aft mast: a brief text stating that the ship had been requisitioned by the British in the name of King George VI. The Dannebrog was lowered, and the Red Duster, a scarlet cloth with a Union Jack in one corner, was raised in its place.

They'd never taken very good care of their Danish flag. It was frayed around the edges, and its white cross was blackened by soot from the funnel. But it was theirs. Among strangers, it was half of their identity. Now they'd lost the right to display it. Their country had surrendered to the Germans without a fight, and so their flag was taken away. From now on, they counted only if they no longer considered themselves Danes. They'd be fighting the war stark naked: their stripping had just begun.

The second engineer asked what wages they'd get under the British flag.

'Three pounds, eighteen shillings a week and one pound, ten shillings for victuals,' the officer replied.

The second engineer did a quick mental calculation. He glanced around at the rest of the crew and shrugged. They could do the maths too. The pay was a quarter of what they'd been getting. That said, they wouldn't be providing for their families any more: they'd been severed from them indefinitely.

'Don't worry, you'll be home for Christmas,' the officer said. He'd observed their faces closely.

They forgot to ask which Christmas.

*   *   *

587

They were ordered to paint the *Dannevang* grey, as grey as a winter's day on the North Sea. Not even the varnished oak doors and window frames around the wheelhouse escaped. This was their ship. That winter they'd scraped off the rust and painted every square centimetre of her: the black hull, red below the waterline, the white superstructure, the red-and-white stripe that ran like a ribbon around the funnel. They'd lovingly traced the white letters on the bow, and they'd kept the *Dannevang* so clean you could walk about on her in shore clothes even after loading coal. They'd maintained the steamer in the old sailing ship style, as they called it, with a scrubbed deck and washed-down bulkheads. It was miserable and hard work, but it gave them pride. Now the *Dannevang* they'd cherished had slipped through their fingers, almost as if she'd sunk into the wintry sea from which she'd borrowed her new colour.

The *Dannevang* had once been registered in Marstal. The steamer had been owned by Klara Friis and had been laid up for years before being sold to a shipowner in Nakskov. The captain and the first and second mates were from Marstal, the seafaring town that no longer had its own ships, but whose men had become the aristocracy of the Danish merchant fleet. Marstallers were everywhere, most commonly on the bridge as first mates or captains: the only ones who sailed as seamen were those still too young to be anything else. Daniel Boye, a distant relative of Farmer Sofus, had been captain of the *Dannevang* when she still belonged to the family and sailed under her old name, the *Energy*.

He'd been among Frederik Isaksen's supporters and he'd stood on the quayside when Isaksen caught the ferry to Svendborg after his defeat.

'You won't remember Isaksen,' he'd said to Knud Erik, 'but he remembers your mother.' Knud Erik had shuddered slightly. His mother was a sore point. He'd neither seen nor spoken to her in a decade. However, he knew Isaksen well. Isaksen had retained his affection for the people of Marstal and never closed his door to a Marstaller if a voyage brought him to New York. He'd even married a Marstal girl: Miss Kristina.

Always the gentleman, he'd been waiting for her on the pier in New York when she arrived. Klara Friis had written to him, 'I know that you do not owe me anything. But I do believe that you are a man with a strong sense of responsibility.'

Isaksen certainly was. He'd not only taken Kristina Bager under his wing but also ended up marrying her. Knud Erik had visited them from time to time. Isaksen was a wonderful father to Ivar's child, but he and Kristina never had children of their own, and Knud Erik couldn't work out whether they were happy together: he had his doubts about Isaksen's relationship with women. He was fond of the vivacious Kristina and he had good reason to be, but as far as Knud Erik could see he wasn't fond of her in quite the way a man should be of a woman. Although Knud Erik and Kristina Isaksen confided in each other, on this matter he never enquired.

'My little knight,' she'd call him. She used a sisterly tone, though he'd outstripped her in size a long time ago.

Knud Erik had been in New York when Kristina's daughter was confirmed. It had been a strange experience to sit in a Protestant church on the Upper East Side watching the fourteen-year-old Klara, a girl named after the mother he hadn't seen since the day she'd declared he might as well be dead. Her kindness to Kristina Bager was a side of his mother he'd never seen himself.

Whenever anyone tried to talk to him about why his mother had renounced him, Knud Erik always turned away in silence.

Captain Boye had received two telegrams on the morning of 9 April. One was from the ship's owner, Severinsen, in Nakskov, ordering the *Dannevang* to return to Denmark. The other was from Isaksen.

Boye read it aloud and looked at his first mate. 'Isaksen suggests we go to a British port,' he said. 'It's actually none of his business, as he doesn't own the ship. But I happen to agree with him.'

'Isaksen's a man of honour,' Knud Erik said.

The majority of Danish shipowners had done what Severinsen had done. Møller, who appeared to be well informed, had stayed up with his son the night before the Germans invaded Denmark, telegraphing his ships with orders to seek a neutral port. The crew of the *Jessica Mærsk* had mutinied, tying up the first mate and locking him in the chart room: the ship had been bound for Ireland, which was staying out of the war. The crew had forced the captain to sail to Cardiff instead. Rumour had it that the *Jessica Mærsk*, too, had received a telegram from Isaksen. From his New York office he'd been just as busy as his former boss. As Boye remarked, Isaksen had stuck his nose into something that was none of his business. But this was how a man of honour sometimes behaved.

On the other hand, it was hard to feel honourable on board the *Dannevang*. You'd behaved honourably, all right, but you'd been stripped of dignity for your pains.

They might be in a pub in Liverpool, Cardiff or Newcastle downing as much Guinness as they could manage between two air-raid alarms. And always there'd be someone who noticed their accent and asked them, 'Where are you from, sailor?' That was the killer moment.

They learned quickly. The one thing you never did in that situation was tell the truth. If you said you were from Denmark, the information was received with cold silence or open contempt. You'd be called a 'half-German'.

In the Sally Brown, a pub by Brewer's Wharf, a girl with a low-cut blouse and remarkably red lips had approached Knud Erik, and he'd bought her a drink. They'd raised their glasses and she'd looked deep into his eyes across the rim of hers. He knew the routine and how the evening would end. That was all right with him. He needed it.

Then she'd asked. Back then he hadn't heard the question often enough to know the effect the word Denmark would have.

'Why aren't you in Berlin with your best friend Adolf?'

He was bloody furious. Hell, because he was here, in a pub where half the windows were broken, in a bombed-out city, risking his life for measly wages, cut off from his family and friends! He could have been lying under his duvet back in Denmark. Instead, by way of payment for his willingness to face an abrupt end to his miserable life, he confronted, on a daily basis, every kind of explosive devilry ever invented. She wiggled her arse as she walked off in her tight skirt, determined he should know what he was missing out on because of having the wrong nationality.

When news came of Denmark's fall, Danish shipowners and the government had encouraged Danish sailors to seek neutral ports right away. But the crew of the *Dannevang* had done the opposite, risking homes, families, safety, everything. It didn't help. There was no free Guinness from the barman, no sympathy pussy from women with low-cut blouses and red lips.

Instead, they were reduced to watching the good fortune of others from a distance. Down there, at the other end of the bar, for instance:

the underage boy with blue eyes and a lock of blond hair falling across his forehead. For him there was no end to the back-slapping, the flirtatious looks, the free beer, the invitations to an all-expenses-paid night in a room where a mattress with broken springs would squeak the night away. The kid didn't even speak English, apart from the crucial words 'I'm from Norway.'

They were fighting the Germans in Norway; the king and the government were in exile in London; thirty thousand Norwegians sailed in the service of the Allies and they sailed under their own flag. The Norwegian merchant fleet had been assigned to the state, and the king was now its official owner.

Scandinavians were popular wherever they went. But to English ears Scandinavian meant Norwegian. Denmark had dropped off the map, and if a sailor mentioned that was where he came from, it sounded as if he was offering a shameful reminder of the past. On 9 April 1940, the crew of the *Dannevang* had become stateless. They were in the line of fire, but they were stark-naked.

They downed their Guinness in silence.

The end came the following January, one day at around four o'clock in the morning. The *Dannevang* was on her way from Blyth to Rochester with coal. Afterwards they were unable to decide whether it had been a vibration mine, an acoustics mine, a magnetic mine or just an old-fashioned horn mine – but her bow was ripped apart. The ship started to take in water immediately, but she didn't sink right away. They'd been blacked out during their voyage, and when they climbed into the lifeboats Captain Boye ordered the lights turned on. They rested on their oars as they bid farewell to their ship, and a bottle of rum was passed round. They'd rarely drunk on board. On New Year's Eve Boye had held long discussions with his officers before he decided to give each man a glass of cherry brandy. When the bottle of rum came back to him, it hadn't even been emptied. Seventeen men! He gave them a look of approval.

The *Dannevang* keeled over. The sound of explosions came from the engine room as the water reached the hot boilers, and lumps of coal flew out of the shattered skylight. The stern rose up in the water and the screw gave a brief screech as it spun round for the last time. Then it stopped, and all over the ship the lights went out.

Knud Erik closed his eyes. Albert had dreamed something like this. He'd seen a sinking steamer and he'd described everything; just as it was happening now.

When he opened them again, the sea had closed over the *Dannevang*.

The men sat in the lifeboat and watched, their wool-lined Elsinore caps in their hands. No one spoke. Knud Erik felt the captain ought to say a prayer, or recite the funeral text from the *Book of Sermons*. How the hell were you supposed to send off a ship?

The steward was puffing on a cigarette; its tip glowed red in the night.

'A cig would be welcome right now.'

It was Boye who broke the silence. He looked at the steward. 'Hammerslev, did you remember the cigarette cartons?' The steward nudged the mess boy, who looked miserable. 'The cigs, Niels.'

The mess boy dived under the stern thwart and triumphantly pulled out a carton of cigarettes. They got a packet each. They'd been forced to leave their ship's chests and seabags on board – there wasn't room for them in the lifeboat. Now all they owned were the clothes they were wearing, their discharge books, and their passports, which proved that they belonged to a nation that no longer existed because the war had swallowed it up. And a packet of ciggies.

It was all right. They'd manage. They were alive, and soon their lungs would be filled with smoke.

'The matches,' Boye said. 'Where are the bloody matches?' He looked sternly at the mess boy. 'I'm throwing you overboard if you've forgotten them.'

The mess boy flung out his hands in desperation. 'It all happened so fast,' he said. So the steward passed his lit cigarette around, and soon seventeen tiny red dots glowed in the winter darkness. Dawn was still a few hours away.

'Niels,' the captain said to the mess boy, 'it's your job to make sure that at least one cig's always lit, even if you have to smoke in your sleep. Is that clear?'

The mess boy nodded gravely and puffed away as if his life depended on the orange spark in front of his nose.

Knud Erik looked around. It had been a good crew. He'd been first mate on the *Dannevang* for three years. On board were seven men from Marstal and one from Ommel. The rest were from Lolland and Falster. Now they'd be scattered all over the place.

A couple of years later he would return to this moment and do the maths. Of the seventeen survivors of the *Dannevang*, eight were dead: the captain, the second mate, the steward, an able seaman, two ordinary seamen, a junior ordinary seaman and the chief engineer. Five were Marstallers. Captain Boye was run down by an American convoy ship. The junior ordinary seaman was on board a munitions ship when she was torpedoed. There'd been only three survivors out of a crew of forty-nine, and he wasn't one of them.

But right now they were all together, waiting for dawn. They were close to the English coast and they knew they'd be spotted soon. Death was the last thing on their minds. Their only concern was keeping the red glow of the ciggies going until they were picked up.

THE CREW OF THE *DANNEVANG* REMAINED UNEMPLOYED FOR A FEW weeks in Newcastle, where they spent most of the time at the newly opened Danish Seamen's Club, honing their pool skills. It wasn't exactly that they missed the air raids, mines and U-boats: any nostalgia for bombs could be easily satisfied by taking a stroll around the docks. It wasn't as bad as London, but almost. No: the fact was they'd made a choice, and it seemed ludicrous to spend a world war playing pool. Besides, the food ashore was disgusting. Powdered egg, Spam, and grey bread smeared with a reeking, oily substance known as Bovril. Meat inevitably meant corned beef. The British diet wasn't dictated by meanness, but by the war, and it showed on the British. Their patched-up, pre-war clothes were a fair measure of how much weight they'd lost. The food on the *Dannevang* had been better: from time to time they'd had real eggs or a piece of fresh beef. 'The English eat the way we did on the old Newfoundland schooners,' Knud Erik commented.

He hadn't sailed the Newfoundland route since the fatal voyage on the *Kristina,* and the *Claudia* had been his last sailing ship. Once he'd passed his navigation exam he'd decided to crew on a motor ship. He'd applied to the *Birma* and the *Selandia,* vessels belonging to the Far East Asia Corporation, but they'd both turned him down. Knowing nothing of the connection between his mother and the owner of the company, old Markussen, he'd never understood why. So he'd taken jobs on steamers.

Helge Fabricius, second engineer of the lost *Dannevang,* laughed at what Knud Erik said about the food. He was in his mid-twenties and not old enough to have sailed the Newfoundland route. Knud Erik was thirty, less than ten years older, but they'd been born on either side of the great divide between the age of sail and the age of steam. They weren't even separated by a generation and yet they were children of two different worlds.

Behind the pool table hung a blackboard with VACANCIES written on it in chalk. Under this was scrawled *Nimbus of Svendborg*. Nothing else. What were they looking for, a first mate, a steward, a chief engineer? Knud Erik and Helge went to see the Danish consul, Frederik Nielsen, to find out. To their surprise, he offered them the whole vessel: its crew had jumped ship. The *Nimbus* was theirs if they wanted her. Knud Erik would be promoted to captain.

This was the other side of the war. It imposed restrictions, but it also offered opportunities. They went to inspect the ship. On the bow you could make out the letters that had once spelled *Nimbus* and more marks on her stern that had probably said *Svendborg*. But you had to apply your imagination.

As they walked up and down the quay inspecting the vessel, Helge Fabricius started counting. Knud Erik didn't need to ask him what he was up to. 'There's no way that crew jumped ship,' he said. 'They're all dead.'

'One hundred and fourteen . . .' Helge intoned.

'The only cheese they ever got on that ship must have been Swiss.'

'I'd like to see them make a cup of coffee,' Helge said, abandoning his numerical litany.

They both laughed and walked up the gangway. They'd seen ships with half the bulwark ripped away, with the superstructure blown off, with craters in their sides, which had nevertheless managed to stay afloat. But they'd never seen anything like this. The *Nimbus* had received not one direct hit but a thousand. The steamer was riddled with bullet holes. She was intact, yet utterly destroyed. Waves and waves of Messerschmitts must have strafed her. Not one of the Germans' aircraft bombs or torpedoes had struck her; if they had, the *Nimbus* would be at the bottom of the sea. But their machine guns certainly hadn't missed. There was something awe-inspiring about the sight of the ship's perforated superstructure: it exuded a defiance that seemed almost human.

They entered the galley, where a blue enamel coffee pot still sat on the stove. As if to give the lie to Helge's joke, it was still in one piece.

'I'll be damned,' said Helge.

They found some English coffee substitute, made from acorns, in a cupboard, and sat down at the table while they waited for the water to boil.

'We'll take this ship,' Knud Erik said. Helge poured the boiling water and shot him a questioning look. 'She's a lucky one.'

'You mean her coffee pot was lucky. It's the only thing on board that doesn't have holes in all the wrong places.'

Knud Erik shook his head. 'No, the whole ship's lucky. Have you ever seen so many direct hits? But the *Nimbus* is still here. She's still afloat. And she'll share her luck with us.'

They were both well aware that this was pure superstition. On the battlefield – and the sea was a battlefield – there are no rules that govern who will be spared and who will fall. Whatever decides your fate is unfathomable and random, so you might as well call it luck and trust it as such. On the *Dannevang* they'd had a Lewis. On the *Nimbus,* they'd have the more effective Lady Luck.

They returned to Consul Nielsen and told him that they'd take over the ship. He looked relieved.

'These are our terms,' Knud Erik said. 'We won't be needing all that ventilation on the Atlantic, so we want the holes mended. We want some decent tackle on board so we can defend ourselves. And we'll be in charge of the hiring. We want to decide whom we sail with.'

The *Nimbus* was taken to the shipyard to be repaired, and Knud Erik and Helge returned to the Danish Seamen's Club to find her a crew. On the chalkboard under VACANCIES they wrote a list of the crewmen they needed. Then they settled themselves in a corner near the pool table and waited.

Within a few days they'd hired a first mate, a mess boy, a donkeyman and a couple of able seamen. They were still looking for a second mate, a steward, a chief engineer and a few more able and ordinary seamen. It would be a crew of twenty-two.

Knud Erik hadn't expected to become a captain this early in his career. He didn't doubt his abilities, but he wasn't sure he had the necessary authority. Could he judge a man well enough to make the most of his strengths and help him forget his weaknesses? And what about twenty-two men all at once?

On the fourth day Vilhjelm stepped through the door and asked to sign on as second mate. It was two years since he and Knud Erik had last seen each other, and that had been in Marstal. Vilhjelm had a family now: a son and a daughter with a woman of his own age, who was the daughter of a fisherman from Brøndstræde. His stammer had never come back, and whenever he was in Marstal he went to church every Sunday. He kept the *Book of Sermons* from the *Ane Marie* at home. He didn't need it with him on board. He still knew it by heart.

'How's your father?' Knud Erik asked.

Vilhjelm's father had stopped his hard job as a sand digger a long time ago. Now he fished instead, though he was actually too old for that as well. But he persisted doggedly, trapped in his own deaf world.

'He was fishing over at Ristinge when the Germans came. He couldn't hear the sound from the aircraft, of course. He looked up because shadows were crossing the water, one after the other, too fast for clouds. Apart from that, he didn't give it a second thought. He was more interested in how many shrimps he'd caught. That's the war as far as he's concerned.'

The next man to turn up was also from Marstal: Anton. He was appointed chief engineer on the spot and he wanted to know everything about the engine.

When he heard that the *Nimbus* had only eight hundred horse-power, he said, 'I have my doubts,' and fiddled with his black horn-rimmed glasses. 'Don't think there's much top steam in that old tub.' He wanted to know what type of coal they'd be using. 'I'd like it to be Welsh coal,' he said. 'Coal from Newcastle gives off too much soot.'

'You'll get all the coal you want,' said Knud Erik.

It was a joke, of course: he didn't know the first thing about coal, and he had no idea what they'd be able to get hold of.

Anton sulked over this for a while, and Knud Erik suspected he'd get up and leave. They'd been friends once and they still were, though they were often on opposite sides of the globe. But Anton wasn't sentimental; he was a professional and wanted a decent vessel on which to exercise his talent for mechanics. So his answer took Knud Erik completely by surprise. 'Well, what the hell,' he said. 'We Marstallers should stick together. I'll take the job. I'll get this old tub to shift.'

The third man to approach the corner table that day had applied for the job of able seaman. Under his open shirt he wore a white

T-shirt that emphasised his gleaming black skin. They assumed he must be an American.

'Fritz says hello,' he said in Danish.

Knud Erik's jaw dropped. Fritz! He didn't even notice that the man had addressed him in his own language. 'I thought Fritz was in Dakar?'

'He is,' said the man. 'Or at least he was the last time I saw him.' He stuck out his hand. 'I'd better introduce myself. Absalon Andersen from Stubbekøbing. Yes, I've heard it all before. I'm a Negro. Black Sambo and all that. But I grew up in Stubbekøbing and if you promise not to ask me where I learned Danish, then I promise not to ask you where you did.'

He smiled at them as if pleased that introductions were now out of the way and they could get down to business. 'I was in Dakar with Fritz,' he went on. He pulled out a chair and made himself comfortable. Knud Erik offered him a cigarette. 'Well, that bit of the story you're familiar with, I suppose?'

Knud Erik nodded. Dakar, in French West Africa, was every sailor's nightmare. There was nothing wrong with the town itself. But when France fell to Germany, the governor of Dakar proclaimed, initially, that he was on the side of the Allies. A few days later he changed his mind, and the many ships that had come to the port to enter Allied service were interned instead, dooming the sailors who had been willing to sacrifice themselves in battle to months of idleness on their own sun-baked decks. Vital engine parts were confiscated to prevent them from escaping. And when the British bombarded the port, these sailors suddenly found themselves on the wrong side. It was one hell of a situation. One Norwegian ship managed to escape: the crew claimed that the ship's engines would rust unless they were run from time to time, so the idiot French handed over the missing engine parts and the crew gave them back replicas, then made their getaway in the middle of the night. The other ships – six Danish ones among them – were still rotting there. The war was calling out for them and they couldn't go. They must be feeling absolutely and utterly useless.

'But you're not Norwegian,' Knud Erik said. 'So how did you get out?'

'I'm something even better than Norwegian,' Absalon Andersen said with a self-assured grin. 'I'm black. I just walked out of Dakar.

No one tried to stop me. I looked like all the other Negroes. After various detours I ended up in Casablanca. By the way, Captain Grønne says hello, too. You boys from Marstal, you're just about everywhere.'

'How did you manage to get here?'

'I have beer to thank for that.'

'Beer,' Helge said. 'You're telling me you paddled from Casablanca to Gibraltar in a beer crate?'

'That's not the whole story,' Absalon said. 'But almost. Many try to escape, but only a few succeed. The French don't miss a trick. A few of us found this rotten old dinghy upriver. The French knew about it, but they never suspected a thing. It would have been sheer madness to try to go to sea in a tub like that. The problem was water for the crossing. We couldn't just stroll through town with a whole water cask. The French would have seen what we were up to right away. So Grønne gave us a couple of crates of beer. The French just grinned when they saw us carting them along. They thought we were off on a picnic. We rigged a mast and some sails and set off late at night. We had to bail the craft for the whole voyage. That tub took in water like a herring crate. We reached Gibraltar after four days. The dinghy sank right under our feet as we sailed into harbour.'

'So you made it at the very last minute.' Knud Erik said. He was impressed.

'Damn right we did,' Absalon said, nodding gravely. 'Damn right it was at the last minute. We'd just run out of beer.'

When the next man appeared, Knud Erik gave him a curious look and raised a hand before the man could open his mouth.

'Let me guess your name. It's Svend, Knud or Valdemar.'

'Valdemar,' the man said, without batting an eye.

'How can a Chinese end up being called Valdemar?' Helge asked, looking him up and down. The man was young and slender, with the high cheekbones and narrow eyes of the East. A mocking smile played on his well-formed lips. He was handsome, in a surprisingly gentle, almost feminine way.

'I'm not Chinese,' he said, in a patient tone of voice. 'My mother's from Siam. And my father's surname is Jørgensen.'

'You have a Danish passport, I hope?' Helge needled him. The young man's reply had unsettled him, and he wanted to recover his authority.

'Don't worry about that, as long as your discharge book is in order,' Knud Erik said, to smooth it over.

A harsh glint appeared in Valdemar Jørgensen's dark eyes. 'I was born in Siam,' he said. 'I have a Siamese passport and a Danish passport. The Danish one I cheated to get. I'm a member of the Seamen's Union of the Pacific. Is that good enough for you lads?' He gave them a combative look.

Knud Erik laughed. 'The job's yours, if you want it.'

'I want to know if we're going to America.'

'Ask the British. If I were you I'd prepare myself for the North Atlantic.'

'I want to give you a piece of advice. Just the one. Don't marry an American girl.'

'And what's wrong with American girls?'

'They're up for anything. Real hot chicks. But then they want to get married. I've been on ships where the lads were boasting of their conquests: wedding rings, wedding photos, true love, happily ever after – the whole shebang. And then two of them discover they've married the same girl. Know why? Those broads get ten thousand dollars in widow's pension if a sailor's lost in Allied service. Pain in the arse. Get my drift?'

'Sure do.' Knud Erik was finding it hard to keep a straight face. But the lad didn't appear to notice.

'You should, because you're not married, are you? You old guys are easy pickings for them. Take care, pal!'

The kid really didn't miss a thing. He'd noticed Knud Erik wasn't wearing a wedding ring. Knud Erik leaned forward. 'Listen to me,' he said. 'I'm not your pal. I'm the captain of the *Nimbus*, and if you want to go to sea on my ship, you'll have to change your tone. Is that clear?'

'Aye aye, Captain,' he said. He was halfway across the room when he turned and addressed Helge. 'Listen. If you've got a problem with Valdemar, then just call me Wally.'

THEY SAILED IN CONVOY, FIRST FROM LIVERPOOL TO HALIFAX, NOVA
Scotia, and back, and then to New York via Gibraltar. They sailed
ballast westward and returned with timber, steel and iron ore. They
had mounted four 20-mm machine cannons, one fore and one aft.
The remaining two, placed on the bridge wings, pointed menacingly
out to sea. These weren't manned by the crew but by four British
gunners who sailed with them.

The *Nimbus* wasn't built for the North Atlantic. In fact, it was
hard to identify what she *was* built for. Anton did his best in the
engine room, but he could never get her above nine knots. When
they sailed in convoy and the U-boat alert sounded, they had orders
to zigzag to avoid the torpedoes. The forty ships in the convoy left
Liverpool in a straight line, then regrouped into a square, four by
four. It was hard to maintain position, as the *Nimbus* wasn't sufficiently manoeuvrable: they inevitably fell astern.

Captain Boye had once told Knud Erik that in any situation that
threatened the ship's destruction, the captain must forget rules, regu-
lations and ship's insurance, and follow a single unwritten law: treat
people they way you'd like them to treat you.

Boye's words summarised Knud Erik's experience as a sailor. Later
he heard that Boye drowned after giving his life jacket to a stoker
who'd panicked and left his own behind. More than once he'd
witnessed a captain risk his ship to come to the aid of another vessel.
And he'd seen ordinary sailors in the navy do the same for one another.

Sailors were neither better nor worse than other people. It was
the situation they found themselves in that encouraged loyalty. In
the finite world of the ship, mutual dependency overrode individual
survival instinct. Every man knew he'd never make it alone.

Back then Knud Erik believed, naively, that the war had turned
the whole world into a ship's deck and that the enemy they were
united against resembled the sea in its brutal, uncontrolled power.

He didn't know that war had different rules, or that those rules would break his loyalty and the strong sense of fellowship that the years at sea had rooted in his soul. He sailed ballast one way across the North Atlantic and timber and steel the other way, under armed escort, and he risked his life, and he did it because he'd learned on deck that no human being can turn his back on the fate of another. Yet the day would come when his commitment to the war would reduce him to a lesser human being, and he wouldn't realise it until it was too late. A time would come when he'd feel his existence was dictated by the little red lights, rather than the torpedoes that sought to end it. And the impact of the lights would be far worse.

There were rules for sailing in a convoy. A meeting was held ashore before departure, and each time the order from the convoy's commodore was the same: maintain speed and course. Every ship had her position, which she must stick to at all costs. And there was another order, which would come to balloon in their consciousness like a tumour: never go to the aid of a stricken ship; do not stop to pick up survivors. A ship that was stationary even for a moment would become a target for U-boats and bombers, and risk losing cargo essential to the war effort. The convoy sailed to deliver that cargo, not to rescue drowning sailors.

This rule sprang from bitter necessity. Although Knud Erik recognised this, he still felt it was an assault on his whole identity. It wouldn't be a torpedo that destroyed him, he suspected, but an order that forced him to ignore drowning men who were crying out for help.

Escort vessels sailing at the rear of the convoy were tasked with picking up survivors, but they were often prevented from doing so by the wrath of the bombers or forced to divert their course to avoid torpedoes. Then the shipwrecked men would drift behind and disappear on the vast sea. The last trace of them would be the red distress lights on their life jackets.

They were the lucky ones. As their body temperature dropped, they'd drift into sleep, and then death. Or they'd give up, undo their life jackets and let themselves slip into the darkness that was awaiting them. The red lights glowed on for a while longer. Then they, too, went out one by one.

When a ship was torpedoed, the destroyers would speed over to the attacking submarine and drop their depth charges. Any survivors in the water would implode from the enormous pressure of the explosion, strong enough to rip away the U-boat's armoured steel plates, or the men would be propelled into the air on a powerful geyser of water, their lungs forced out through their mouths: tattered human shreds of which not even a scream remained.

He'd seen it happen on the voyage back to Halifax.

They had orders not to deviate from their course because the danger of colliding with the other ships in the convoy was greatest when they sailed at top steam while attempting to flee the U-boats. Knud Erik stood on the bridge, his hands on the wheel, and sailed right into a whole poppy field of red distress lights in front of the *Nimbus*'s bow. He'd heard the frantic pummelling against the ship when the life-jacketed survivors drifted alongside and desperately tried to push off so as not to be caught by the screw propeller. The ship's wake foamed red with blood from the severed body parts being churned around, while he stood on the bridge wing, looking back.

Don't look back was the rule for moments like this. Having done it once, he never did it again. But something inside him still watched what a moment ago had been men, and this part of him kept watching until it turned to stone. No one, *no one* willingly did this to another human being. And yet he'd done it. Treat other people the way you'd like them to treat you. If he couldn't believe in that, what was he left with?

Nothing. Absolutely nothing.

He counted the little red lights from his captain's cabin. Their glow stripped him bare. He'd lost his last point of reference. He'd got his cargo to its destination. Yet he was doing the wrong thing. He'd done damage to others, and in doing so, did damage to himself. He felt that close to the men in the water screaming out for help.

When the convoy was attacked, he appeared on the bridge with a face that was frozen and hard. He didn't think about the U-boats. Nor did he think that the ships taking a direct hit might just as easily be the *Nimbus*. He simply braced himself for the little red lights. If they came, he'd push the helmsman aside without a word and take the wheel himself. He had the bridge cleared. He wanted to be alone, not only when he tried to avoid the bobbing distress lights ahead, but also when he ploughed straight into them because there was nothing else he could do. He was the captain. He set the course. It was his responsibility.

He shielded his crew from it, determined that their hands, at least, would stay clean. If they wanted to, they could point him out as the guilty one.

He didn't know what they thought. He never discussed it with them.

When it was over, he'd go to his cabin, open a bottle of whisky and drink himself unconscious. It was his substitute for penance; he knew no real penance was possible. He'd done something irreparable. There on the bridge he'd forfeited the right to his own happiness. Any thoughts about the purpose of his life faded away. He watched himself from the outside, but he could no longer make anything out. His soul had turned to dust, pulverised on the grindstone of war.

He isolated himself. He never went to the mess. Nor did he fraternise with the first or second mates. He didn't even speak to his boyhood friends from Marstal any more. He took his meals alone and opened his mouth only to give orders.

No one tried to coax him out of his solitude. No one addressed him with jocular remarks or asked him a question that didn't relate directly to daily duties on board. And yet they helped him. They helped him maintain his solitude, as if they knew that the price he was paying was on their behalf too.

An outsider might have thought that the crew was behaving coldly – ungratefully, even – in responding to his wilful isolation by keeping their distance. But the contrary was true. They knew that the smallest sign of sympathy – a pat on the shoulder, a kind word, a glance – would have made him break down. Instead, they kept him going. They shielded him so he could get on with the job of shielding them. They needed a captain and they gave him the chance to be that man.

Dear Knud Erik,
I am writing to tell you about a dream I had last night.

I was standing on the beach, staring across the sea, as I used to do when I was a child. I felt the same mixture of fear of the sea and longing to sail on it that I used to feel back then. Then suddenly the sea started to withdraw. The pebbles on the beach rattled as they were sucked out by the pull. The water lay flat as though a huge wind were passing across it. This went on for a long time, and finally there was nothing left but bare seabed all the way to the horizon.

If you knew how I have longed for a moment like that! You know how much I hate the sea. It has taken so much from us. But I felt no triumph, though I saw my most ardent wish come true at long last.

Instead, I was filled with a premonition of something terrible.

I heard a roaring. Far out a wall of white foaming water had risen and it was approaching at speed. I made no attempt to escape, even though I knew that I would be swept away in a moment.

There was nowhere to escape to.

What have I done? What have I done?

This question screamed inside me when I woke up.

You might think this sounds insane, but I feel a terrible guilt when I wander the streets. I see boys and girls, I see people out shopping, I see the women – and there are many women – I see the old people. But I see so few men, and I feel that I am the one who chased them away when I deliberately ruined the seafaring business here.

Marstal is not in the habit of counting the missing. But I am. Somewhere between five and six hundred men are no longer among us – sons, fathers, brothers. You are on the other side of the wall that the war has built around Denmark. You sail in the service of the Allies, and the outcome of the war will determine whether you can ever return home. But even victory is no guarantee that you will survive.

The flood of my nightmare is upon us, and I was the one who provoked it.

I wanted to banish the sea from men's hearts, but I achieved the opposite. You looked for work elsewhere because there were hardly any ships registered in Marstal. You sailed further away. The time you were home with us became even shorter than it used to be. Now you are all gone indefinitely. Some of you, many, I fear, for ever. The only proof we have that you are still alive is the letters we receive. There are long intervals between them. When letters fail to arrive, we are left guessing.

Dear Knud Erik, I once said that you were dead to me, and this is the most dreadful thing a mother can do to herself. I know so little about you, only what I hear from other people, and they fall silent in my presence. I feel they regard me as something unnatural. I do not know if they have forgiven me for what I have done to this town. Maybe they do not even realise that I was behind what has happened. But no one has forgiven me for disowning you, and I have grown even lonelier than I was to begin with.

You will not get to read this letter. I will not send it. When the war is over and you have returned, I will give it to you.

I ask for nothing more than that you read it then.

Your mother

KNUD ERIK DIDN'T GO ASHORE IN NEW YORK. THE LAND SCARED HIM more than the sea did. He suspected that once his feet touched the pier, he'd never be able to walk up the gangway again. And that would be a failure of duty. He'd no longer be part of the war – but men who stayed on in it were failing in their duty, too. The red lights had taught him that. So the choice the war offered him was a choice between two failures. Alone on the bridge, he honoured his duty to the Allies, to the war, to the victory to come, to the convoy and to the cargo. But he didn't honour his duty to the men who screamed for his help. It felt as if every single one of them was calling out his name.

When Vilhjelm went to the Upper East Side to visit Isaksen and Kristina, Knud Erik was briefly tempted to accompany him. The last time he'd seen them had been at Klara's confirmation, and he'd been invited to dinner afterwards. But he shook his head. He preferred the solitude in the cabin. He huddled inside it as though it were an air-raid shelter.

There were men who, when they feared they were losing their nerve, started counting women, as though recalling their conquests in foreign ports made them feel stronger: women on one side of the scale, death on the other. It gave them a sense of balance.

Knud Erik could have gone ashore and tipped his own balance. He was thirty-one and unmarried. It wasn't too late, but – as he often told himself – neither was it too early. He was restless, and he'd known many women. It wasn't immature lust that prevented him from making a final choice. His indecisiveness was caused by something he could neither pin down nor articulate. At times he still thought of Miss Sophie, the crazy girl who'd turned his head at the age of fifteen. Surely she couldn't be what was stopping him? He'd barely known her. And her behaviour, which he'd found enigmatic and compelling at the time, had been nothing but youthful pretentiousness. And yet it seemed she'd laid a curse on him. By suddenly vanishing into thin air – a disappearance that might have been anything from an amorous adventure to death by foul play – she'd tied him to her. It wasn't her he was seeking in the harbour bars or in Marstal's down-to-earth girls. But he was missing something, and every time he reached out for it, it vanished.

He'd managed one engagement in Marstal, to Karin Weber, who'd later broken it off. 'You're always so distant,' she'd said, and she wasn't referring to the normal absences of a sailor. He was well aware of that.

Something inside him longed desperately for a family. He needed to have a human being to miss. He needed a counterbalance to the terrible things the war had done to him, and he couldn't find that in port bars. He was a ship with no moorings.

He sat in his captain's cabin like a monk in his cell, but there was nothing edifying about his solitude. He counted the red lights. He counted his soul into tiny pieces. His dreams about the life he could have had crumbled like a child's sandcastle.

IN LIVERPOOL HE DESERTED. HE WAS RUNNING AWAY FROM HIS SENSE of duty. The same whisky that had helped him maintain a balance could also make him lose it. And in Liverpool he lost it.

Even shaving every day had become an ordeal. How do you shave without looking in the mirror? Shaving was the last struggle before the final rot set in. He knew this was an unwritten law for prisoners of war in the German internment camps. And that was how he felt: like a prisoner of war. He'd fallen into enemy hands. Only the enemy was inside him.

On the last voyage they'd sailed with ammunition in the hold. A hit would have meant total annihilation: no men in the water with their pleading little red lights. Not even the captain's cap would have survived if the *Nimbus* had disappeared in a gigantic spurt of flame. He'd caught himself fantasising about the relief that death would bring. But no torpedoes struck them. Nor did any bombs drop through the deck and hit the cargo.

Yes: the *Nimbus* was a lucky ship. She kept a steady course through the drowning men and he cursed it all.

The ship's radio could pick up the frequency of the Royal Air Force and when the crew approached the English coast after crossing the Atlantic, they'd gather on the bridge to listen to the conversations between flight command and the RAF pilots. They heard the words 'Good luck and good hunting', which signalled the start of the radio transmission of a life-or-death battle. They cheered and shouted in support of their team. They cursed the enemy whom they could not hear but sometimes saw, because the fights took place in the sky right over their heads. They clenched their fists; the veins bulged in their foreheads. They rooted for the pilots, who shouted their warnings or triumphs out into the ether. And then sometimes suddenly slumped in their seat, shot to pieces. These men sacrificed themselves for the ships, and yet the sailors all wished they could swap their eternal waiting position on the deck for the pilot's exposed cockpit. There wasn't one of them who didn't long to deliver death, instead of waiting for it. They got so worked up during these transmissions that if someone had handed them revolvers, they'd have been hard pressed not to gun each other down like dogs.

Knud Erik was the only one who didn't fantasise about firing a gun. He'd have preferred to be the target of one. They were welcome to pull the trigger on him. He'd be happy to oblige.

He stopped Wally as he made his way down the gangway, suitcase in hand. He'd heard the lad boasting about its contents, which he'd acquired in New York: nylon stockings, salmon-pink satin brassieres and lace panties.

Knud Erik made an effort not to sway. 'Take me with you,' he said in a thick voice. 'I want to see what your underwear buys you.' It was a plea, but he made it sound like a command. Not that it was the kind of order a captain would give to a crew member if he wanted to maintain respect. Show me the way to the gutter, let us be companions in degradation!

He'd left his cell to commit weaponless suicide.

Anton and Vilhjelm weren't there. If they had been, they'd have stopped him. Wally didn't have the maturity or the experience to do that. Knud Erik saw the boy's eyes flicker, but he knew he wouldn't dare raise any objections.

'Aye aye, Captain' was all he said.

Absalon aproached. 'But, Captain . . .' he said.

Knud Erik could hear it was the start of a protest. After all, leaving the ship was tantamount to deserting it. The Liverpool docks were bombarded incessantly. They had to keep re-mooring. A captain couldn't just walk off in circumstances like that. It would be an unforgivable dereliction of duty. Never mind, he'd just have to add that one to the list. He shrugged. 'Vilhjelm will look after her.'

Absalon looked away.

He and Wally kept their distance from Knud Erik on the road to the railway station, which ran between rows of bombed-out houses, where lean men and women were sifting through the bricks. There was no hostility in that distance. He was the captain, and they were just trying to uphold what remained of his dignity.

He'd once told Wally that he wasn't his pal – but this was what he was trying to become now. He felt the poison of self-loathing spread. He hoped that it would kill him.

Knud Erik fell asleep on the train to London, and Wally woke him when it stopped at the platform. Dazed, he looked around the compartment. Moving between New York and England always felt like time travelling: the Americans existed in a permanent pre-war state, with well-nourished bodies and faces that exuded rude health, while the English, with their skin drained of colour, looked like blurred, yellowing photographs of half-remembered people in an old album kept in a dusty attic, vegetating in a shadowland of ever decreasing rations.

They'd just left the station building when the air-raid alarm sounded. It was night, and a dense darkness lay between the houses. They stopped short, not knowing what to do. Spotting some people running, they took off in the same direction. Somewhere a faint red light glowed, marking the entrance to an air-raid shelter. The irony wasn't lost on him. At sea, a red light meant yet another life on his conscience. Here it meant salvation. For a moment he had the urge simply to stand there and wait for the bombs to rain down on him. Seeing his hesitation, Absalon grabbed him by the arm.

'This way, Captain.'

He let his legs take charge and followed the others.

There was no light in the shelter. They sat tightly packed together surrounded by pitch-black darkness. Knud Erik could hear whispers, a cough, a child crying. He'd lost track of Wally and Absalon, and it was a relief to be among total strangers. There was a powerful smell of unwashed bodies and musty clothes. An anti-aircraft battery right above the bunker started firing, making the air tremble. Then the bombs started falling. Chalk and dirt dropped from the ceiling; it felt as though death had grown hands and was tentatively feeling their faces before it grabbed them. He heard gasping and whispering. Someone began sobbing uncontrollably and someone else murmured words of comfort, then broke into a panicked 'Shut up for Christ's sake!'

'Leave her alone,' another voice interrupted.

'Please can we go home?' a child's voice begged.

A little girl screamed for her mother, and the voice of an old woman responded with the Lord's Prayer. A bomb exploded nearby and the whole floor shook. For a moment Knud Erik expected the shelter to collapse on top of them. Everyone fell silent, as if death itself had hushed them.

Then he felt a hand on his. It was a woman's: small and delicate, but with a work-hardened palm. He stroked it reassuringly. He felt her head rest on his shoulder, and he held the unknown woman to him in the darkness. Another bomb fell, and the concrete walls of the shelter groaned from the pressure. Someone started screaming. More screams followed, and soon the darkness vibrated with panicked shrieking as the confined people surrendered to hysteria, while the bombs drummed an accompaniment.

The woman put her hands around Knud Erik's neck and started kissing his mouth greedily, then fumbled at his groin. He slid his hand inside her coat and felt the contour of her breast. Her burning hot sex welcomed him. The screaming surrounded them like a wall as they took each other in blind, brutal lust, with the bombs dictating the rhythm of their thrusts. Yet there was selfless tenderness in the soft, anonymous body that united with his own. She offered him the warmth of life itself, and he offered it back until their moans of pleasure mingled with the cacophony of terrified voices.

And for a moment he escaped the little red lights.

Some hours later the anti-aircraft battery above the air-raid shelter stopped rattling, and the sirens sounded the all-clear. The door opened onto a dark street. It had to be the middle of the night.

Knud Erik lost her in the crowd heading for the exit. Or perhaps he'd let her go deliberately. And perhaps she'd let him go, too. Fires burned outside. He scanned the faces in the flickering light. Her? Or her? The young girl with the scarf around her head and her eyes fixed on the ground? Or the middle-aged woman with the hard face, trying to fix her smeared lipstick in the glow of burning houses? He didn't want to know. Both he and the unknown woman had found what they were looking for. Faces and names were irrelevant.

He stayed in London for three days.

He did it in backyards, in pub toilets, in hotel beds; he did it to the thunder of bombs and he did it without any accompaniment other than his own panting and that of his arbitrary partner; he did it until he reached a place where silence and darkness met and took him. He drank with men and he had sex with women who felt just the same way he did. When the bombs dropped nobody knew who would shortly be joining the rapidly growing toll of the dead, or whose workplace had been reduced to rubble, or whose family was buried under a collapsed house. They all lived so steeped in fear that the losses they had yet to suffer had already consumed them. Every single second was a rebirth, every kiss a stay of execution, every shuddering breath in the arms of a stranger a declaration of love to life. Every drunken stupor – the permanent stupor Knud Erik had sought and found – was a gift, because just like a bullet to the brain, it eradicated all he was, his face, his name and his past, and unleashed all the hunger in his body. For three days he was his own ruthless appetite for life and nothing more.

On their last night they gathered up the remaining contents of their suitcases: underwear, nylon stockings, coffee, cigarettes and dollars. Dollars especially. They behaved like Yanks and paid for a night in a hotel suite that took up an entire floor. They brought in the girls themselves and tipped the waiters generously. The porter kept an eye on their tab to warn them when their money was running out. They ate, drank, danced and whored through yet another night of bombing. Wally was in charge of the gramophone. They danced to Lena Horne and knocked back beer, whisky, gin and cognac.

The air-raid alarm went off at eleven o'clock. The waiters hammered on the door and called out to them to go to the basement.

'I suggest we stay here,' Knud Erik said. He'd dropped the commando tone. He wasn't the captain now, but a pal among pals.

'Aye aye, Captain,' Wally saluted him and poured himself another cognac.

They switched off the light and opened the curtains. Outside, searchlights were strafing the night sky. The first bombs fell, far away to begin with, then closer. It sounded like a drummer testing his kit before his great solo. The building shook, and they dived under the beds. They knew that a mattress was no protection. But the intimacy of another body was. Their instincts took over: sex made them invincible.

The bombs came closer and closer. Outside a purple light flickered sporadically and a fiery glow dappled the ceiling. Every time common sense wormed its way into their muddled brains with the message that they should leave this minute and head for the safety of the basement, they grabbed their women tighter and thrust deeper, lust and fear driving them to ecstatic heights. Then they collapsed together, limp and exhausted, flung out their arms, and dozed briefly but blissfully, as if they'd already made it safely through the night.

But they hadn't. The bombs wouldn't let go of them. The fear returned, with its constant companion, ally and friend: desire. From the darkness beneath a bed, someone would suggest, 'Change? – Who wants to swap?' And then a scramble would start, and they'd shuffle across the floor on their stomachs to a fresh, uncharted love nest, where new arms, a new greedy mouth and new moist openings awaited, while the German bombers beat their kettledrums on the roofs of London.

At last all went quiet. They crawled out from under the beds, closed the curtains and lay down next to each other on the untouched beds.

They'd won.

KNUD ERIK WAS THERE WHEN THE *MARY LUCKENBACH* WAS BLOWN up.

The *Nimbus* was sailing in a convoy north of the Arctic Circle, on its way to Russia with supplies for the Red Army. The weather was fine and visibility good. They were half a nautical mile behind the *Mary Luckenbach*.

The men on the bridge of the *Nimbus* watched in total silence. They'd seen tankers take a direct hit before; they'd seen the two-hundred-metre flames. But they'd never seen anything like this. Neither had Knud Erik. It wasn't terror that silenced him, though. It was relief.

The German Junker flew in so low over the water that it seemed to skim the waves. Just three hundred metres from the *Luckenbach*, it dropped its torpedoes, then roared across the ship's deck and got caught in the machine cannon fire. Small flames darted from one of its engines.

Then the torpedoes reached their target.

One moment the *Mary Luckenbach* was there. The next, nothing but a stillness as terrifying as the explosion itself. There was no sign of fire, no wreckage floating on the sea: just a black cloud of smoke that rose with majestic slowness, as if it had the power to lift thousands of tonnes of steel and carry them off.

The smoke rose unbroken to the clouds, several kilometres up, where it slowly spread out until it covered half the sky. Black soot fell silently as snow over the sea, as if the explosion had come from a volcano rather than this war.

There would be no little red lights: that was Knud Erik's only thought. Fifty people had just been wiped out, right in front of his eyes. A minute ago, through his binoculars, he'd seen gunners crouched behind the machine cannons, and a black mess boy calmly crossing the deck with a tray. Now they were gone and all he felt was relief: he'd been spared. Not his miserable life, which he no longer valued, but his wrecked conscience.

They attacked in waves of thirty to forty aircraft, flying only six or seven metres above the water, swarming blackly over the grey sea. The sirens mounted on their wings let off a terrifying howl designed to drive the enemy mad and short-circuit his ability to react. Their 20 mm machine cannons pounded the ships, and white and red tracer bullets sprayed the deck as the planes dropped their torpedoes one by one. The inexperienced gunners on the decks panicked and aimed wildly, their bullets hitting lifeboats and the wheelhouses of surrounding ships.

It made the crew shudder reluctantly, but they were forced to admire the German pilots' courage. With suicidal determination, they flew into a wall of fire intensified by the four-inch cannons aimed at them from the escorting destroyers.

The *Wacosta* and the *Empire Stevenson* were hit next, then the *Macbeth* and the *Oregonian*.

It was all over in five minutes. Then a Heinkel made an emergency landing on the water at the centre of the convoy. The aircraft stayed afloat and the crew crawled out onto one of the wings and held up their hands in surrender. They were no longer enemies. Without their machines they were just defenceless human beings. They kept looking around as if they wanted to catch the eye of every single one of the sailors crowding the rails of the surrounding ships. Then they meekly lowered their heads, awaiting sentence.

A shot rang out. One of the men clasped his shoulder and turned halfway round before sinking to his knees. A second shot finished him off. He slumped forward into the water, but his lower body stayed on the wing. The three remaining crew started running around him in a panic, looking for cover. One of them tried to crawl back into the cockpit. He was shot in the back. He fell and rolled into the water. The two survivors threw themselves to their knees and clasped their hands beseechingly.

They'd realised what was happening. They hadn't been transformed: they hadn't become human beings. They were still the enemy, and the proof hung over their heads in the shape of the black cloud that had been the *Mary Luckenbach*. The *Oregonian* was lying close by, capsized and sinking slowly after being hit by three torpedoes on her starboard side. Half her crew had mercifully drowned. The rest had been rescued by the *St Kenan*, where they lay on the deck vomiting oil, their limbs so frostbitten they'd probably have to be amputated.

Knud Erik remembered the nights on the *Nimbus* when they'd tuned in to the RAF frequency. Every one of them had longed to come face to face with a German he could empty his revolver into. At last the enemy was standing before them, not in the form of a war machine, but as a living, vulnerable human being whom they could hurt and take revenge on. Finally they had a chance to redress the massive imbalance of their lives. In those days, Knud Erik had desperately wanted to be on the receiving end of an enemy bullet. Now he felt the same bloodlust as the others. It was urgent and strong. The imbalance in him was greater than in any of his crew.

He saw the two men kneeling on the wing of the shot-down aircraft and the sailors in their hundreds, teeming along the rails of the surrounding ships, some with rifles in their hands, and the gunners in their positions behind the machine cannons. They fired light-heartedly, as if at the shooting gallery of a summer fairground. They probably felt that they were men again, because men aren't cut out to take a pounding and not fight back. They were fighting back.

The bullets whipped at the water around the aircraft. One of the two remaining airmen shot backwards from the wing, as if a mighty hand had come to sweep him off and, in doing so, prove just how pointless his life was, how futile his prayers to preserve it. The shot must have come from one of the heavy-calibre machine cannons. He landed in the water and vanished instantly.

The survivor slumped. He unclasped his hands and settled them on his thighs, leaning forward and baring his neck as if awaiting the mercy shot.

The rattle of bullets stopped: the men lowered their rifles, and the moment became a solemn one, as if they were all holding their breath before completing the execution. Slowly it began to dawn on them what they'd just done. Even before the enemy had been annihilated, their thirst for blood was quenched.

Knud Erik pushed the *Nimbus*'s gunner aside. He was an untrained shot. At first the machine cannon spat its bullets straight into the sea, drawing a long stripe of foam across the water, before starting to strike the aircraft wing. Then they hit their target.

Now Knud Erik had killed another human being, and everything inside him collapsed. He fell on the machine cannon sobbing, oblivious to the hot metal burning the skin of his palms.

THEY'D SAILED NORTH AROUND BEAR ISLAND, ON THE SEVENTY-fourth parallel, when a new order came from the British Admiralty: spread out. From the briefing Knud Erik had received in Hvalfjörður in Iceland, where the convoy had set out, and from his experience of every other convoy he'd been with, he knew the order was a death sentence. Many rules applied to convoy sailing, but one overrode them all: stick together. You'll only get through if you're united. On your own, you're lost, easy prey for the U-boats, with no protection and no one to pick you up if you're sunk.

How often had his crew heard that message over the megaphone from a passing destroyer, when, despite Anton's efforts in the engine room, the *Nimbus* lagged behind: 'Stragglers will be sunk.' This wasn't so much a warning as a sentence, a farewell unaccompanied by the usual encouraging assurance of *we'll meet again*.

They knew one thing for certain: the cargo had to arrive. The tanks, vehicles and ammunition in their hull would continue via some complex route and end up on a distant front where the fighting between the Germans and the Russians would determine the outcome of the war – and ultimately their own fate. They knew it because that's what they'd been told, but they'd never been sure about the actual mechanics of it. The only part they were familiar with was the sea, the Junkers and the Heinkels attacking them, the wake of the torpedoes, the ships exploding and sinking, and the men fighting for their lives in the icy water.

Their contribution to the war effort was important. They needed to keep faith in that. But the moment they received the order to give up their place in the convoy and fight their way to Molotovsk on their own, they realised such faith had been pointless and supplanted it with speculation about the reason for the fatal order. And as always, in a shaky situation involving immense pressure, their guesses hardened to suspicion and they recalled the rumour that had dogged every single convoy they'd ever sailed with to Russia, a rumour that clung with the persistence of smoke to a funnel, a wake to a propeller and a torpedo to precious cargo: they were bait.

In one of the Norwegian fjords a 45,000-tonne German battleship, the *Tirpitz*, lay in ambush. She was the biggest battleship in the world, a threat to everything that moved in the North Atlantic and a symbol of the Nazi dream of world domination. Probably the battleship's greatest value lay in simply being that symbol: certainly she rarely ventured out of her hiding place in the fjord, with its protective mountainsides, to make an onslaught. Instead she lay chained there like the great wolf of myth, threatening a Ragnarök that never came. But now that Ragnarök was imminent: the wolf at the end of the world was going to snap its chain at last and grab the bait.

Hard experience, the same experience that had lined their faces and tortured their bodies with frostbite, convinced them of this. When the thirty-six ships of the convoy abandoned sailing in formation and tried limping on their own to Murmansk, to Molotovsk or to Archangel on the White Sea, the Germans wouldn't require the overwhelming firepower of the *Tirpitz* 15-inch guns to sink them: the U-boats could manage it with ease. Now that the British destroyers and the corvettes that had escorted them had been called off to go chasing after the *Tirpitz*, the convoy's thirty-six ships were left defenceless. No, they were doomed. Their own protectors had tricked them into an ambush.

With bitterness they realised their insignificance. They were expendable.

But what about their cargo? In Hvalfjörður they'd been told that in total they were carrying 297 aircraft, 594 tanks, 4,246 military vehicles and 150,000 tonnes of ammunition and explosives to Russia. Were the British Navy's officers prepared to sacrifice all that, simply to boast that they'd sent the *Tirpitz* to the bottom of the ocean?

They didn't get it. The only thing they understood about this whole business was that they couldn't trust anyone but themselves if they wanted to stay alive. If they didn't survive, they'd die without a soldier's sense of duty fulfilled or the comfort of knowing that their sacrifice made sense. If they were sunk, they'd disappear not just without honour, but without any acknowledgement that they'd so much as existed.

The defiance that flooded them wasn't directed solely at the enemy, but at friend and foe alike. As if they'd lost all notion of the difference.

The order came as a relief to Knud Erik. It meant that he could stop worrying about the drowning men. From now on, it was all about him and his crew. He could finally allow himself to surrender to the cynicism that comes when a crisis of conscience has exhausted itself. His sole priority was survival. They'd be alone in the middle of the ocean, and that was where he wanted to be. Alone, with no little red lights.

He changed course and headed north for Hope Island, sailing as close as he dared to the rim of the ice. Dense freezing fog covered the whole area. He ordered the crew to paint the entire ship white. They lay still for a couple of days, with the boilers switched off so the funnel smoke wouldn't give them away. The pack ice grated against the sides of the ship, and her steel plates protested in an ominous bass growl that from time to time shrilled to a treble scream. The message from the hull was clear: with a little more pressure from the pack ice, the *Nimbus*'s luck might just run out.

Knud Erik thought back to the time when the *Kristina* had been trapped in ice. The heavy timber of the sailing ship had been pliable; it didn't need to prove its strength the way steel did but instead let the ice push the vessel about until the weight that threatened to crush her ended up supporting her.

He ignored the *Nimbus*'s screaming hull. Better ice than U-boats. He dreamed about letting the *Nimbus* freeze and stay frozen until the whole world began to thaw and the weapons fell silent. He'd fought the sea his whole life. Now he embraced the dangerous ice as a friend.

He switched on the radio and invited the crew to gather round it as they'd done when they listened to the RAF frequencies. They heard nothing but distress signals: one SOS after another, and each cry for help a funeral service. There were only minutes between a ship's being attacked and its sinking. No one came to its rescue. Their crews went down alone in the icy cold sea. The *Carlton*, the *Daniel Morgan*, the *Honomu*, the *Washington*, the *Paulus Potter*. They counted twenty ships. There was nowhere to hide, not even here in the freezing fog at the end of the world.

They got going again and the *Nimbus* followed the ice edge north of the seventy-fifth parallel until she reached Novaja Zemlja, then headed south towards the White Sea. The ship encountered four lifeboats containing survivors from the *Washington* and the *Paulus Potter*. Both ships had been sunk by a formation of Junker 88s. The planes had flown over them as they climbed into their lifeboats, and the airmen had waved to them cheerfully while a cameraman filmed them for the German weekly newsreels. They hadn't waved back.

Captain Richter from the *Washington* came on board to consult a chart. After a while bent over it, he asked if they could spare a compass. His crew were still crouching in the lifeboats.

'Why d'you want a compass?' Knud Erik asked. 'We'll take you.'

Richter shook his head. 'We'd prefer to sail on alone.'

'In an open boat? The nearest coast is four hundred nautical miles away.'

'We'd prefer to get there in one piece,' Richter said, eyeing him calmly.

Wondering if the captain was suffering from shell shock, Knud Erik addressed him in the kind of tone he might use to persuade a wayward child.

'We can't offer you berths, but of course we'll find you a warm place to sleep. We've enough provisions, and in this weather we can manage nine knots. We'll be there in a couple of days.'

'You do realise what's happened to the rest of the convoy?' Richter said, in the same calm tone. Knud Erik nodded. 'A lifeboat's the safest place to be. The Germans won't waste their bullets on men in a boat. They're only interested in ships. They'll get you too. I'm grateful for the offer, but we'd prefer to go it alone.'

He climbed down the ladder with the compass. In the boat, his men were slapping themselves to keep warm. If the wind rose, they'd get splashed and become encased in an armour of ice. But still they preferred their lifeboats.

The men pulled their oars while Knud Erik ordered the ship full speed ahead. He stood on the bridge and watched the boats as they disappeared.

The next day a solitary Junker appeared on the horizon and headed straight for them. You could hear its machine guns rasping from a great distance. The gunners on the bridge answered back. The wheelhouse took several direct hits, but no one on the bridge was wounded. Then the Junker dropped its bomb. The plane was so close it almost collided with the mast. The bomb exploded in the water near to starboard, not near enough to tear up the side of the ship, but enough for the detonation to lift the *Nimbus* half out of the water and land her again with a force that snapped a steam pipe in the engine room, which made the engine cut out. They were no longer manoeuvrable.

The Junker turned round and came back with a howl. The machine cannons on the *Nimbus* were firing at maximum capacity. The wheelhouse was pierced again, and the crew all threw themselves to the floor. Only the gunner on the bridge wing was left standing. They waited for the explosion that would signal the ship's deathblow. She was loaded with British Valentine tanks, lorries and TNT. If they received a direct hit there'd be no time to climb into the lifeboats. They all knew that.

'Do it then, goddammit!' Knud Erik cursed.

Outside the gunner kept firing as if his hands had frozen fast to the trigger. Then, through the rasping of the cannon, they heard the noise of the Junker's engine die away. Had the pilot decided to spare them after all? They remained on the floor, unable to believe that the danger had passed. Surely any minute now the plane's engine would roar over them again, and they'd be finished.

Total silence. The machine cannon on the bridge wing was quiet, too.

'It's over,' the gunner said.

They were still shaking as they scrambled to their feet. The Junker was now a tiny dot on the horizon. The pilot must have been on his way home after an expedition when he spotted them. He must have had only one bomb left, and chanced it.

Once again, the *Nimbus* had proved herself to be a lucky ship.

Dear Knud Erik,
Grind a man into the dirt and observe him beneath your heel.
Is he fighting to get up? Does he cry out against the injustice
he has suffered? No, he stays there, proud of all the punish-
ment he can take. His manhood lies in his foolish endurance.

What does such a man do when he is held underwater? Does
he fight to get up?

No, his pride lies in his ability to hold his breath.

You let the waves wash over you, you saw the bulwark
smashed in, you saw the masts go overboard, you saw the
ship take her final plunge. You held your breath for ten
years, twenty years, one hundred years. In the 1890s you
had three hundred and forty ships, in 1925 you had one
hundred and twenty, a decade later half that. Where did they
go? The Uranus, *the* Swallow, *the* Smart, *the* Star, *the* Crown,
the Laura, *the* Forward, *the* Saturn, *the* Ami, *the* Denmark,
the Eliezer, *the* Ane Marie, *the* Felix, *the* Gertrud, *the*
Industry *and the* Harriet: *vanished without a trace, crushed*
by the ice, rammed by trawlers and steamers, lost, smashed
to pieces, stranded by Sandø, Bonavista, Waterville Bay, Sun's
Rock.

Did you know that one in four ships that sailed the
Newfoundland route never returned? What would it take to
make you stop? Fewer cargoes? But freight rates kept falling:
they halved in a decade. You simply lowered your wages, ate
even worse food, gritted your teeth. You practised holding your
breath underwater.

You sailed where no one else dared or wanted to. You were
the last.

You didn't have chronometers on board. You'd stopped
being able to afford them. You could no longer work out the

*longitude, and when a steamer passed you, you would signal
'Where am I?'*

Indeed, where were you?

In despair,

Your mother

WALLY WAS THE FIRST TO NOTICE IT. THE OTHERS WERE ON THE bridge supervising the unloading when he turned to them and remarked enthusiastically, 'Can't you see what a great place this is?'

They shrugged in their duffel coats and looked out over Molotovsk. Half-sunken, battered ships languished in the port, while along the quay stood vast piles of rubble which were the remains of warehouses. Further off in the low, rocky landscape loomed sooty barrack-like buildings roofed with tarpaulins. It was the height of summer and although the sun was in the sky twenty-four hours a day, it did little to warm the air. In the perpetual light they felt as if their eyelids had been cut off and they lived in a world where sleep had been abolished. The rocky grey landscape, the sunlight and the knowledge that they were one hell of a distance from civilised society, filled them with a creeping, woolly-headed lethargy.

'Fetch the straitjacket,' Anton snarled. 'The boy's gone mad. He thinks he's in New York.'

'This is better than New York. The chief engineer may have gone blind as a mole down in the machine room, but surely the rest of you can see what I mean.'

And then they did. The workers unloading and placing tackles around the ammunition crates in their hull weren't men: they were women. Women with machine guns, patrolling the quay where emaciated, thinly clad German prisoners of war stacked the crates onto the waiting transport trucks. And behind the wheel of each, a woman, preparing to drive the freight to the front line.

'Take a look at her arse,' Helge said, pointing.

Not that you could see much: they wore felt boots and baggy boiler suits that concealed their curves. All the men could do was guess at the bodies hidden under the shapeless clothing, speculating whether they were slim or thickset. Some of the women were young, though most seemed to be over thirty. It was to hard work out their ages. They had broad faces and grey, unhealthy complexions. Their hair was hidden under caps, though a few wore headscarves.

Not that any of that mattered. It had been three months since the men's last shore leave, and the sight of women in the hold or on deck was enough to stimulate the most important component of sexual desire: imagination. They started talking animatedly about their favourite parts of female anatomy, while mentally stripping the dockers and guards in the insane hope that beneath the coarse, filthy uniforms every single one of them was a pin-up girl: a butterfly trapped in a grubby grey cocoon.

Knud Erik was wearing his captain's uniform. Normally he never put it on, but it was universally acknowledged that the Communists respected uniforms and nothing else, so when you negotiated with the Soviet authorities, it was smart diplomacy to look as official as possible if you wanted to get anything done. He noticed that one soldier kept staring at him, and he imagined it was his uniform that attracted her. He met her gaze and held it. As far as he could tell, she was slim and about the same age as him; she had ash-blonde hair fixed in a tight bun at the nape of her neck. He didn't know why he looked back at her. It was a reflex he couldn't control, though he realised that it could be taken as a provocation. She didn't turn away but stared straight back, as if testing him. He couldn't interpret her look any other way, though he had no idea what the point of it was.

His concentration was broken by a loud bang. A crate of ammunition had slipped out of its tackle and crashed onto the quay, where it had sprung open. One of the German prisoners immediately began rummaging around inside it, probably hoping to find something edible. Two female dockers grabbed hold of him and pulled him away. He struggled briefly, then gave up and let himself be dragged along the quay. The unloading had stopped.

The soldier who'd been staring at Knud Erik the moment before shouted a brief command, and the dockers released the prisoner. The soldier stepped up to him, released the safety catch of the machine gun strapped across her shoulder and fired from a short distance. She glanced briefly at the skinny figure lying prostrate before her, as if to make sure he was dead, then looked up at Knud Erik. This time he was in no doubt what she was up to. It was a challenge.

*　　*　　*

That evening, as he sat alone in his cabin slowly numbing his brain with the bottle of whisky that he never touched during the day, he had no doubt who the woman was. She was an angel of death come to claim him. This crazy – even revolting – notion, which he didn't have the strength to resist, filled him with desire, and for the first time since the nights of bombardment in London he got an erection.

The town, which lay a couple of kilometres from the port, was nothing but a handful of wooden houses arranged around a square. The streets radiated from it like wheel spokes that led nowhere: a few hundred metres away, the wilderness began.

The town had an International Club, and that's where they headed that night. The first sight that greeted them was a badly stuffed, scrawny-looking bear standing on its hind legs with its mouth open, baring a row of yellow teeth. The two fangs were broken, as if snapped off by someone afraid that the creature might spring to life and attack the customers.

Behind a table in a corner sat a bald man wearing a white shirt and red braces and guarding a money box, a crutch at his side. An accordionist had placed himself on a chair on a makeshift stage made of roughly sawn timber. He, too, was unable to walk without the help of a crutch. Both men were around fifty and each had a row of medals on his chest. They were the only other men the crew of the *Nimbus* ever saw in the club.

They'd got a general picture of the losses the convoy had suffered. Only twelve out of thirty-six ships had reached their destinations. Most had been bound for Murmansk or Archangel, and only the *Nimbus* had managed to reach Molotovsk, which meant that in this town of women, they had no rivals. They saw other men in the streets, but like the cashier and accordionist in the International Club, they were crippled or white-haired.

The few children begged the foreign sailors for cigarettes and chocolate. Their faces, which seemed wise beyond their years, would light up with an inviting smile as they approached.

'Fuck you, Jack,' they said. British sailors had taught them this greeting.

'Fuck you, Jack,' Wally answered, and passed out cigarettes.

The beer in the club tasted of onions, so they drank Russian vodka, which tasted like meths and most likely was. Every time they sat down on the red velvet sofas, the only furniture apart from bare tables, they raised clouds of dust. The floor was filthy, too. Anton's explanation was that once a woman had wielded a machine gun, a mop did nothing for her.

The crew from the *Nimbus* sat at one end of the club, and the Molotovsk women at the other. In the evening the women changed out of their work clothes and into dresses that looked like altered smocks. They put up their hair, too, but their broad, heart-shaped faces were as colourless as before; they didn't own any make-up. Rumour had it that they were all spies who seduced foreign sailors in order to wangle secrets out of them, and this added to their fascination. Not that the crew of the *Nimbus* had any secrets.

'They're welcome to have a go,' Wally said. 'They can spy on me all they like.' He crossed the dance floor and pulled a lipstick out of his pocket. The women looked at him with bright eyes and started giggling. He handed the lipstick to a hefty blonde in a faded blue dress, who immediately started painting the lips of the woman closest to her. The lipstick was passed around, and a bevy of red lips turned to him, united in a huge smile. He pursed his own lips at them, and another wave of giggling rolled through the room.

He walked up to the stage where the accordionist had yet to start the evening's entertainment, and handed him some cigarettes: the musician stuck them behind his ear and began playing. A moan sounded from his instrument as he squeezed the air out of it in a heavy, stomping rhythm.

Wally went back to the women and bowed to one of them. She leaped up with surprising agility and led him to the centre of the dance floor, where she placed her hand on his shoulder. He responded by putting his arm around her generous waist. She was older than he was and didn't hesitate to guide him through the unfamiliar steps. When the dance was over she curtsied and returned to her seat.

'That didn't get you very far, did it?'

It was Anton. Wally turned to him.

'That was merely the preliminary discussion. I start by showing them a small selection of my wares. Then I give them time to think about it.'

'You can't have much faith in yourself if you have to buy them.'

Helge gave him a scornful look, and howls of protest erupted from the others.

'Stop that sanctimonious shit,' Absalon said. 'We all do it from time to time. You wouldn't stand a chance with that potato face of yours unless you left a few notes on the chest of drawers.' The others laughed.

'They're just like us,' Wally said. There was an unaccustomed tenderness in his voice. 'They're in need. So are we. Yes, we probably *could* get some Commie pussy for free. But where's the harm in spoiling them a bit? I mean, they don't look as if their life's all that much fun as it is.'

Knud Erik didn't join in this conversation: he sat alone, scanning the women at the opposite end of the hall. Was his angel of death among them? He wasn't sure he'd recognise her out of uniform. He knew now that it was the unexpected sight of a machine gun in female hands that had attracted his attention. They'd stared into each other's eyes. And he felt oddly convinced that if she were here tonight, she'd try to catch his attention again. He didn't need to look for her. She'd find him.

Nevertheless, he continued studying the women's faces. Most were fleshy and worn, with a bottomless exhaustion that seemed close to resignation. It provoked tenderness in him, but it wasn't a human being he was searching for. It was the most extreme kind of self-obliteration.

They visited the club three nights in a row but not once did he feel the unease of that penetrating gaze on him, though women did look at him. He wore his captain's uniform to make it easier for her to recognise him, but the gold stripes on his sleeve and cap attracted women other than the one he sought. A young one in a green dress that matched her eyes kept staring at him, but he turned away and ignored her clear interest.

The dancing was well under way. Men and women settled down at each other's tables. The barrier between the Russian women and the foreign sailors had fallen. Wally, the experienced boy-man with the big appetite for women, was – as ever – at the centre of it all. As for Knud Erik, he stayed on the red velvet sofa and avoided the dance floor.

That same evening Molotovsk was attacked from the air. The German Junkers were aiming for the harbour. The midnight sun glowed on the horizon when the air-raid alarm sounded. The *Nimbus* was the only ship in the port and an obvious target. The half-drunk crew jumped from the deck onto the quay and started running around in panic. There were no shelters in the area and the first bombs were already falling. The anti-aircraft guns around the harbour were responding furiously. They, too, were operated by women.

A little distance away lay some huge cement pipes that could serve as shelters: the men ran inside them. They were big enough to stand upright in. One of the already destroyed warehouses took a direct hit. Further away a transport truck exploded. Hard cracking noises resounded in the pipes, and the men jumped. It was the heavy-calibre shells from the anti-aircraft guns; they hadn't made it to their target and were showering down from the sky like iron rain. Then they heard the shrill sound of a Junker spinning, followed by the hollow boom of a bomb, or a stricken aircraft colliding with the ground.

The anti-aircraft guns kept on firing. An unfolded parachute floated towards the ground with the pilot dangling from the cords: the man hit the ground flat and the chute settled on top of him. He didn't reappear and nothing stirred under the thin material.

The alarm was called off shortly afterwards. The *Nimbus* was still lying by the quay where they'd left her. She didn't appear to have been hit, but a bomb crater on the quay showed that it had been a close call.

A sudden impulse made Knud Erik head for the parachute. Anton came with him. He lifted the fabric and pulled it away to reveal the pilot's face. His blue eyes were wide open, and so was his mouth, as though his own death had surprised him. He lay in a dark red pool of guts. His lower body and legs were twisted at an odd angle; looking closely, they could see that he'd been torn almost in half. He couldn't have received the injury when his aircraft was hit; he'd never have been able to leave the cockpit. The women who manned the anti-aircraft guns must have used him for target practice as he drifted down. The heavy cartridges designed to bring down an aircraft had shredded his body, and dark stains soaked the fabric of the parachute. He must have landed with the blood squirting from his exposed intestines. Something in them came to a standstill.

'It's no use, Skipper,' Anton said eventually.

Knud Erik looked up. Anton had never called him skipper. Yet he felt as if it were the first time in months that another human being had addressed him. 'What do you mean?' he asked.

'I know what you're thinking. It's no use you trying to make any kind of sense of what you go through in this war. No use blaming yourself, either. The only thing that helps is forgetting. Forget what you've done, and forget what others have done. If you want to live, then forget.'

'I can't.'

'You'll have to. It's the same for all of us. Talking about it does nobody any good. It only makes it worse. One day the war will be over. Then you'll be back to who you were.'

'I don't believe that.'

'We have to believe it,' Anton said. 'Or I don't know what'll become of us.' He placed his hand on Knud Erik's shoulder and shook him gently. 'Come on, Skipper. Time for us to turn in.'

The next day, he saw her. She was standing on the quay in her uniform with the machine gun hanging from the strap. Even before he looked up, he felt her gaze resting on him, as if they had a secret connection, a kind of sensitivity to each other's presence that created a bond between them. He didn't understand its nature; her look never developed into a smile or a nod that might betray her real intentions. He held back, too. Only their eyes connected. In her rigid face, unapproachable as any other soldier's, he saw no sign to suggest that this exchange was anything but a test of strength; its only possible outcome would be one of them finally falling on their knees in surrender.

A sudden thought filled him with terror: she'd execute another German prisoner working in the harbour. And she'd do it for him, as if a dead body might provide a new link in some secret connection that strengthened by the day. To his relief, nothing happened.

The unloading was proceeding slowly, and they supposed that it would be some months before they'd be able to leave. By now most of the crew had found themselves girlfriends, and all of the women appeared at the club with red lips. Several had eyes lined with kohl, and in the breaks between the dances, there was unashamed hand-holding.

It was another seven days before she appeared in the club.

He was disappointed when he saw her. Had it not been for those eyes, which, as usual, stirred a tickling sensation at the nape of his neck, he wouldn't have recognised her. Her thick ash-blonde hair was parted at the side and fell heavily across her forehead. She'd put on red lipstick like the others, and she stared continuously at him from the table where she sat alone. The other women seemed to keep their distance from her. He immediately stood up and went over to ask her to dance. The others, both men and women, were staring at him now. It was the first time the captain of the *Nimbus* had joined them on the dance floor.

She was wearing a white, freshly ironed shirt. Lines around her mouth hinted that she was probably in her mid-thirties. Life had left its mark on her, but she wasn't unattractive.

It wasn't those aspects of her appearance that disappointed him. But now that she'd taken off her uniform and laid down her machine gun, she was just a woman like the others. She was no longer his angel of death. He'd been mistaken about that. She'd simply looked at him the way any woman looks at a man and there'd been nothing else to it. He'd been so affected by all the destruction he saw and participated in, that his normal sense of things had evaporated. All he sought was oblivion and he sought it with such intensity that it was indistinguishable from a desire for obliteration.

He put his arms around her and she pressed herself against him. She was a good dancer and they stayed on the dance floor for a long time. She never took her eyes off him, and he could see the longing in them. She wanted something that he felt he no longer was: a human being. She wanted his tenderness and his embrace. But he had nothing to give to anyone, just a brutal, urgent lust that sought only its own relief.

How could she hope for anything, she who'd shot down a defenceless human being before his eyes and made herself a part of the horror that surrounded him? How could she feel tenderness, love, longings, or even infatuation? Did she see something in him that he couldn't see in himself? Did she think she could find salvation in him, that one night of love could give her back what she had lost for ever when she killed another human being? Where did such optimism come from?

Or was she simply so callous that she could inhabit two separate worlds at once, that of killing and that of love? He couldn't. He knew it for certain, but his body reacted when she pressed herself against him, as though a part of him still possessed a hope that the rest of him had lost.

They left the club together some hours later. They hadn't spoken. Unlike the others on board, he hadn't bothered learning the Russian for those few words that pave the way. Yes, no, thank you, hello, goodnight, goodbye, you beautiful, we make love, I never forget. She'd tried exchanging a few words with him, but each time he'd shaken his head.

It was light outside: the smouldering, dying, yet powerful light that fills the summer nights north of the Arctic Circle. She rested her head on his shoulder. All he knew about her was her name, Irina, though he'd have preferred to go without even this elementary information. He wondered if Irina was the equivalent of Irene. He'd never met a girl with that name, in Russian or Danish, but he'd always thought it embodied feminine refinement and fragility. Now he was walking beside one, and she was a cold-blooded murderess.

They walked in the direction of the sooty, tarpaulin-roofed huts. He supposed that they must be barracks, but there were no guards or blockades. He'd heard a story about a sailor smuggled into such a barrack by a girl. They'd lain down on a bed in a large dark dormitory, and he'd just got his trousers off and was ready for action when the lights came on. And there he lay with a proud erection and a circle of women standing around the bed, gawping.

These barracks turned out to be empty. They stopped in front of a cubbyhole with a padlocked door. She found a key and unlocked it. Then she rolled down the blackout blind and lit a petroleum lamp. A bed and a table were all she had. On the table stood a photograph of a woman he thought must be her. She stood in a clearing among some trees with a man in uniform; they held the hands of a girl of about five. The sunlight dappled the ground, and the man and woman were smiling. The soldier had taken off his cap and put his free arm around Irina's shoulder. She was wearing a white shirt just like the one she was wearing tonight.

Where were they now? The man had to be at the front or dead. God only knew where the girl was. She certainly wasn't in Molotovsk. Perhaps she'd been evacuated to a safer place, deep in this vast country?

Irina looked away when she saw his eyes linger on the photograph. Her averted face gave him the feeling that both the man and the child had died. She lay down on the bed and waited for him.

633

He slipped in and put his arm around her. He touched her breasts with his hands. How soft and warm her skin felt. He wanted nothing but this softness and warmth. It was need, more than desire, that welled up in him – bestial but without violence. All he wanted was to touch living, breathing skin, even if its warmth came from a woman who was used to killing and did so without so much as blinking.

What had she thought when she'd looked at him after firing her machine gun? Had she sought forgiveness, understanding? Had she asked herself, and perhaps him too, if he could still look at her and see a human being?

He felt the warmth of her skin under his palm, its infinitely pliable softness, and he placed his cheek against her naked breast like a shipwrecked man who has got himself out of icy waters and presses his face against the beach and feels solid ground. He wanted to lie like this for ever, never stir again, merely exist on a continent of naked, warm female skin that stretched endlessly in every direction.

Then she started to cry. She hugged him tightly while her hands ran through his hair, and she repeated his name in a pleading voice. Nothing but his name, over and over. She was drowning, just like him. Everything in him contracted. Two drowning people can't save each other. All they can do is drag each other down.

He struggled to free himself from her embrace. He couldn't do this. He'd been alone all along, even when he lay with his cheek against her naked breast. And he was doomed to be alone. He'd sought an angel of death and found a human being, and he couldn't cope with that.

He sat up in bed with a jerk, leaped out and ran through the empty barracks, where his footsteps echoed as if all the soldiers who'd once filled the building and were now dead had come back.

KNUD ERIK WAS SENT FOR JUST AFTER LUNCH. SENT FOR: THAT WAS how he thought of the summonses to meetings with the local Soviet authorities. A soldier and an English-speaking official turned up, both in uniform and both female. The official was young, and confident in a way that suggested she regarded herself as a representative of something great. The Soviet state spoke through her, in an English superior to his and in phrases that took the form of commands.

She wore a faint trace of eyeshadow and he couldn't work out where it had come from. He'd never seen her in the club and he was certain she didn't mix with any of the sailors who called at Molotovsk. If there was any truth in the men's rumour that some of the women were spies, then she was an obvious candidate.

These meetings generally concerned cargo. Endless discussions were sparked by small details that didn't add up, and he always attended them in the same resigned mood. He knew that he'd be wasting yet another day on bureaucratic squabbling and be forced to listen to insulting comments about the Allies' inadequate war effort.

On one occasion, however, he'd been pleasantly surprised: they'd handed him an envelope filled with cheques for the crew. It was a war supplement. The Russians were paying a hundred dollars to each man; Joseph Stalin had personally signed the cheques.

'You'd have to be stupid to walk into a bank with this and get your hundred dollars,' Wally said, when he was handed his cheque.

'Anyway, they might be fake,' Helge said. 'And then we'd get arrested.'

'One of my friends, a guy called Stan, got one of these cheques and went to a bank on the Upper East Side to get his hundred dollars from Uncle Joe. The cashier kept turning it over. "Do you have a moment?" he said, and took him up to the fourth floor to see the manager. He started staring at it too. Like Helge, my pal thought something was wrong. "I'll give you two hundred dollars for it," the bank manager says. "What?" my friend says, gasping. He doesn't understand. "OK, OK," the bank manager says. "Three hundred dollars."

'I don't get it,' Helge frowned.

'It was the signature. Stalin's personal signature. It's worth way more than the cheque.'

But this time the meeting wasn't about cheques or cargo. The official told him he was going to the hospital.

'I'm not ill,' he snorted. It had to be some kind of mistake.

'It's not about you,' the official said sharply. 'It's about a patient we want you to take back to England.'

'The *Nimbus* isn't a hospital ship.'

'The patient is as well as he'll ever be. He can take care of himself. We can't continue to look after him.'

'So can he work on board?'

'That depends on what you want him to do. By the way, he's Danish. Like you.' He'd never told her he was Danish. She was well informed.

'Let's go,' he said brusquely.

He'd expected the hospital in Molotovsk to be located near the harbour, but it turned out to be some distance outside town, along one of those roads that seemed to lose itself in the wilderness. The hospital was a long low building, and there were no signs to suggest that medical work took place behind its crude wooden walls. A heavy woman in a dirty overall had turned the floor into a pool of mud and water, which she stirred with a mop in a doomed bid to give the impression of cleaning. Their footsteps splashed loudly as they turned down a long, murky corridor filled with beds of patients who, judging by the sounds that escaped them, were all dying.

In a ward where you could barely have squeezed in one more bed, a figure sat slumped in a high-backed wheelchair by the window. He appeared to have nodded off, but he woke when the official greeted him, and looked up drowsily. He was wrapped in a blanket that concealed most of his body, but Knud Erik could see that his left arm was missing. His face was swollen and flushed scarlet.

According to the information Knud Erik had received, the man had been in the hospital for four months, so the stark colour of his face wasn't due to excessive sunbathing. This was Russia, where the vodka doubtless flowed freely even in the hospitals.

The man's red face broke into an ingratiating smirk when he spotted Knud Erik in his captain's uniform. He was keen to sell himself, and Knud Erik could see why. He was desperate to get away from this backwater and return to civilisation, no matter how bombed out civilisation was at the moment.

'I understand you're Danish,' the man said in a cracking voice, as though it had been a long time since he'd spoken.

Knud Erik nodded. He held out his hand and said his name. The other man clasped his hand enthusiastically, then appeared to hesitate, as if he couldn't remember his own, or was considering giving a false one. Then he came out with it.

Knud Erik turned to the official, who was standing behind them with her normally pursed lips relaxed in a friendly smile, as if congratulating two long-lost relatives on their reunion.

'You can do what you like with this creature,' said Knud Erik. 'You can take him to the basement and shoot him on the spot for all I care. Or you can send him to Siberia or wherever the hell it is you send unwanted people here in Russia. But there's one place he most definitely won't be going, and that's my ship.'

He marched out of the ward without looking back, splashing his way up the corridor where the cleaner had resumed her efforts with the apparently inexhaustible bucket.

'Captain Friis,' the official called out after him. Yet again he had to admire her pronunciation. Her English accent was perfect, and when she said his surname, so was her Danish one.

He left the hospital and started walking towards Molotovsk. He'd gone a fair distance and could already make out the low wooden houses of the town when a car pulled up in front of him. The official stepped out onto the road. It wasn't until then that he noticed that she had a black holster attached to her belt.

'I don't think you understand how serious this is, Captain Friis. I gave you an order. You don't have a choice.'

'You're welcome to shoot me,' he said calmly and nodded at the holster. 'And make that freak an honorary citizen of the Soviet Union afterwards. I really don't care. But he's not coming on board my ship.'

'Watch your words, Captain.'

She spun on her heel and got into the car, which turned round and drove back to the hospital.

He returned to the *Nimbus* and issued orders to sail immediately.

The first mate gave him a startled look. 'We can't do that, Captain. We need to light up the boiler first. And our papers aren't ready. They'll come after us and make us turn round.'

'For Christ's sake!' He started pacing up and down the bridge, awaiting the inevitable. Sure enough, in just half an hour a truck pulled up on the quay in front of the *Nimbus*. On the back of it sat the man in the high-backed wheelchair, with a seabag on his lap. The official stepped out of the cab. The crew crowded around the rail to stare at the man, who raised his one arm and waved to them.

'Hello, lads!'

The official ordered two men to lift the man off the bed of the truck and carry him up the gangway. Once he was settled on the deck, she saluted Knud Erik with irony.

'Over to you, Captain.'

'He's going over the side as soon as we leave the harbour.'

'That's entirely up to you.'

She turned round and got back into the cab of the truck. The engine revved and the truck drove off.

The man in the wheelchair waited. Knud Erik crossed the deck and placed himself next to him, then turned to face the crew, who were standing in a semicircle, eyeing the new arrival curiously.

'I'd like to introduce our guest,' Knud Erik said. 'His name is Herman Frandsen.'

Vilhjelm and Anton looked shocked. In the eighteen years since they'd last seen him, Herman had changed into something so ravaged and burnt-out that they hadn't recognised him until his name was uttered.

'He's known to several of us on board. But not for good reasons. He's a murderer and a rapist, and if any of you accidentally push him overboard, you'll be rewarded with a bottle of whisky.'

Herman stared into the distance, seemingly unaffected by the speech with which Knud Erik had honoured him.

'In the meantime we'd better find you some work to do,' Knud Erik said. 'You've rested long enough. Get up.'

'I can't.'

With his remaining arm Herman calmly flipped the blanket aside. His trousers were empty from the knees down. It was more than an arm he'd lost. Both his legs had been amputated.

HERMAN WASN'T THROWN OVERBOARD WHEN THEY LEFT MOLOTOVSK, and nobody tried to win the whisky bottle on offer to whoever sent him to the resting place he deserved at the bottom of the sea.

'I've still got the most important thing,' Herman said to the crowd that had gathered around him in the mess. 'My right hand. A sailor's best friend in those long off-duty hours. And I can still raise a glass,' he said. 'What more can a man ask for?' His wanking hand, he called it. 'Shake,' he said, offering a big paw. 'I've washed it.' He wriggled the tattoo on his arm. 'The old lion still roars.'

They lined up to greet him.

Herman spent most of his days in the mess. He helped out at mealtimes, setting the table and clearing it afterwards. He could just about manage that with one arm. It was degrading work, but that didn't seem to bother Herman. There was always someone ready to go for a stroll with him on deck when the weather permitted. Someone, Knud Erik didn't know who, had rigged up a pulley so they could lift him onto the bridge. One day he found him sitting on a high chair in front of the wheel, which he controlled with his one strong fist.

He'd given strict orders that Herman was not to be given alcohol, knowing full well that at the heart of the command lay a secret desire to make Herman's life unbearable. Yet again and again he came across him obviously under the influence. There was a secret cache of vodka somewhere on board, and the crew were supplying him with it. They treated him as if he were a mascot rather than a murderer.

There were three people on board who wouldn't have been alive if Herman had had his way: Vilhjelm, Anton and Knud Erik himself. Miss Kristina's life would have taken a different and happier path without him. Ivar would still be among the living. And so would Holger Jepsen. God only knew how many people around the world

639

Herman had killed since then because they'd been in his way for one reason or another.

And yet here he was, calm, relaxed, jovial and sociable, making himself popular with the crew, who seemed unaware that he was a monster who'd only been rendered harmless through amputation. The younger men seemed especially fascinated by him. When the mess boy brought coffee to the bridge, he described Herman as 'an amazing bloke who's had lots of adventures'.

'He's got some incredible stories,' Duncan said. He was seventeen and from Newcastle.

'Did he tell you the one about smashing his stepfather's skull till his brains spilled out? When he wasn't even as old as you are now?'

He glanced furtively at the boy to see if the words had any effect. They hadn't. Stubbornly, the boy looked straight ahead. He had his own view of Herman and there was no way the captain was going to change that.

Knud Erik knew perfectly well why. Before the war, everyone would have avoided Herman if they'd known the truth about him. They'd all have shunned his company, and whoever had the guts to would have treated him with open contempt. But the war had destroyed their moral defences. They'd seen too much and perhaps done too much as well. Why should a mess boy take his captain's strictures seriously when only a few months ago he'd seen him shoot a pilot who was kneeling on the wing of a wrecked plane pleading for his life? Where was the difference between Herman and Knud Erik?

The war had made equals of them, and Knud Erik could only hope that Herman would never find out what he himself had done. He could imagine his reaction. 'I wouldn't have thought you had it in you,' he'd say, bursting with malicious joy at knowing that Knud Erik, too, had succumbed to the worst in himself.

Herman was made for war. He was the type of man who felt naturally at home in it. He had that ability which Anton had said was essential to survival: he could forget. The big, brutal muscleman had been reduced to a helpless, barely human lump of meat, and yet he didn't give up. He didn't brood on the past but adapted to the present. Once he'd had four limbs. That was one kind of life. Now he had one. That was another kind of life, but it was still a life. He was like the worm you can cut in half without injury. A pioneer, in fact. In war, everyone had to become like him or go under.

'He took part in the battle for Guadalcanal in the Pacific, Sir.'

The mess boy was still standing there.

'Is that what he told you?'

'Yes, Sir. His ship was sunk and he was in the water for an hour fighting a shark. He says you have to punch them on the nose or in the eye. Those are their weakest points. But the shark kept coming back. Their skin's like sandpaper, it scrapes you.'

'So he knocked out the shark in round three and got away with a scrape?' Knud Erik couldn't control the sarcasm in his voice.

'No, Sir,' the mess boy said. The naivety in the boy's voice made him feel ashamed. 'The shark was shot by someone on the ship who came to his rescue. It took a chunk out of his legs and some of his lower arm.'

'Has he shown you the scars, perhaps?'

'No, Sir. He says they were on the parts that were amputated.'

'So it wasn't the shark that took his arm and his legs?'

'No, Sir. That wasn't until later. That was frostbite.'

The core of the crew came from Marstal: Knud Erik himself, Anton, Vilhjelm and Helge. Then there was Wally, who was half-Siamese, and Absalon, who, though he'd grown up in Stubbekøbing, must have had roots in the West Indies from the days when a few of its islands belonged to Denmark. They made up the Danes on board the *Nimbus*. The rest of the crew were from all over the place. There were two Norwegians, a Spaniard and an Italian; the gunners were all British, as was the mess boy; there were two Indians, a Chinese, three Americans and a Canadian. They were a floating Babel, at war with a god intent on ruining the Tower.

What united them?

The captain did. He was its fragile core. Though worn down by his own inner strife, he embodied the law of the ship and issued the commands they had to follow if they wanted to reach the next port alive.

Did they ever wonder why they sailed? Was it duty, conviction, or something deeper that kept propelling them into the danger zone?

At the start of the war, Knud Erik had believed that behind their willingness to risk their lives fighting was the same moral attitude that kept them united and determined to rescue fellow crewmen in a storm. He'd stopped believing that. But his old belief hadn't been supplanted by a new one.

At times he agreed with Anton: they were united by their silence. If they began articulating their thoughts, they'd feed one another's insanity and everything would fall apart. This was merely a cease-fire, and he knew it couldn't last.

'What's he been telling you now?'

Knud Erik never entered the mess, so whenever Duncan appeared on the bridge with coffee, he questioned him, with the excuse that, as captain, he needed to know what was happening on board.

'He told us about the time they were torpedoed and climbed into the lifeboats. The water was as clear as gin. He could see the two red-and-white bands on the torpedoes before they hit. The cook had taken an axe with him and started chopping at the rail. "What the hell do you think you're doing, chef?" the captain asked. "I'm making a notch for every day we're on the lifeboat." "If you keep hacking away like that, there won't be many more."'

Duncan stopped and looked at Knud Erik. He was clearly expecting the reaction that Herman had got in the mess for this tale: a roar of laughter.

Knud Erik didn't laugh. He took a sip of his hot coffee. 'What else did he say?'

'Well, a few days after that they spotted a cork bobbing up and down. They couldn't see any land. But it cheered them up because the cork meant it couldn't be far off. Then a few hours later another cork floated by. Still no sign of land, and they started thinking it was strange, all these corks floating about in the middle of the sea. And that's when they discovered that some of the crew had a stash of whisky in the bow and they were emptying one bottle after another on the sly. That's when Herman got his frostbite.'

'And how did that happen?'

'Well, you see, Sir. They started fighting about the whisky. And he was pushed into the water. Herman said that it took them a hell of a long time to pull him back on board.'

Herman turned every tragedy in this war, including his own, into a joke. Through the stories he told them, he came as close to conveying

642

the unspeakable as you could get without saying the words out loud. That was why they listened to him.

When he heard that their nickname for him was Old Funny, Knud Erik realised that it was no longer silence that united the crew.

It was Herman.

The latest tale to come from the mess was that Herman could drink scientifically. During surgery, the doctors had removed some of Old Funny's surplus guts, which meant he had plenty of extra space inside. There was skill involved, he explained; it was like packing a hull with the maximum cargo. You had to have a method based on scientific fact, and he'd found it. To be perfectly frank, they couldn't see that his drinking was so special. He just knocked it back in the same way they did – the only difference being that he could keep at it longer. But this, he argued, was surely proof that he was drinking scientifically. He never needed to stop. As far as that went, they had to agree with him. They'd retire one by one to their cabins, and he'd stay on in the mess, downing more.

The only time Old Funny had met his match was when a young Salvation Army officer had come on board in Bristol to convert the crew to the Lord Jesus Christ. Old Funny had proposed a bet. If the evangelist could drink him under the table, he'd become a believer. But if Old Funny was the winner, the youngster would have to leave the Salvation Army for good.

'It was more than just a question of who could drink the most,' Old Funny said. 'It was a battle between faith and science. He had his Jesus, and I had my method. But he won, the bastard. I went under the table at four o'clock in the morning. To this day I still don't know how he did it.'

'So you're a believer now?'

'I'm a man of my word,' Old Funny said. 'I believe in the Lord Jesus Christ, and I renounce the devil and all his works. The good Lord looks after me. It's thanks to him I've still got my wanking hand.'

He put down his glass and made the sign of the cross, while his stump waggled as if wanting to join in the fun too.

'But you're still drinking,' Wally protested.

'Only when I take communion, and I'm a frequent churchgoer. Besides, I think I owe it to old Jesus. You see' – he looked around, and they could tell that the story hadn't yet reached its climax – 'when he'd drunk me under the table, and he realised he'd won, he got up, threw his coat on the floor and shouted, "I'm through with the Salvation Army!" No one got what the hell he was talking about until he explained it. "I realised it as soon as I emptied my first glass," he said. "I like drinking. I didn't win because the Lord was on my side. I won because I couldn't get enough!"'

They howled with laughter around the mess table. Old Funny enjoyed this applause for a while as he studied the transparent liquid in his glass. Then he raised the vodka to his lips and drained the glass in one gulp.

'Here's to Jesus,' he belched.

FREIGHT SHIPS FROM ARCHANGEL AND MURMANSK JOINED THEM along the route back to Iceland, making them a pack of eight in total. A destroyer and two refitted trawlers, both equipped with depth charges, escorted them. It wasn't much protection, but apart from the ballast they were sailing empty, and the British Admiralty probably assumed that the Germans would think it a waste of ammunition to attack ships with no war materials on board. They'd soon discover that the Germans took a different view.

It was now October and the ice rim had shifted further south. They sailed as close to it as they dared, but for the German bombers based in northern Norway, it was still no distance at all. The autumn gales provided some unexpected help. The weather was severe most of the time, and in heavy winds the aircraft never left the ground. But a storm in the Barents Sea made no difference to the U-boats.

Wally was on the lookout at the bow, and he managed to sound three false torpedo alarms in the course of a single hour. 'It's the stripes of foam on the waves,' he explained apologetically.

'He's anxious,' said Anton, who'd appeared on the bridge from the engine room to moan about all the times he'd been ordered to reverse or stop for no reason.

Knud Erik thought it over. 'I'd better find someone else,' he said.

'Being up there all on my own with no one to talk to drives me round the bend,' Wally said, with a look of gratitude.

Knud Erik went down to the mess. As usual Herman was sitting by the table holding court. Only Duncan and Helge, who were busy getting dinner ready, were there. Helge had grown used to Herman and called him Old Funny along with the rest of the crew. Sometimes they'd talk about Marstal.

Knud Erik hadn't spoken to Herman since he'd come on board. Now he went up to him and announced without a greeting, 'It's about time you made yourself useful.' He ordered him dressed in an

Icelandic jumper, duffel coat and oilskins, and his head wrapped in a cap and woollen scarves. A mitten was put on his hand. His lower body was covered by blankets and a tarpaulin. Then Knud Erik had him tied to the wheelchair.

Herman was undisturbed. 'I feel like a baby being taken for a stroll' was all he said. Not once had he asked the captain what he was supposed to do.

'May you freeze to death,' said Knud Erik.

Two of the crew carried Herman up onto the stem, where they secured his wheelchair so the heavy rolling of the ship wouldn't send him flying. The *Nimbus* didn't plunge deep enough for the bow to be submerged, but an icy spray washed over it. Knud Erik stood on the bridge and looked down on the bundled-up figure, who seemed to occupy the whole bow. The circle was complete. Once, Herman had sent Ivar out on the bowsprit. Now Herman was similarly exposed.

Knud Erik saw him bend his arm and raise something to his lips. Someone had managed to slip him a bottle of vodka. Oh yes, Old Funny was one of theirs all right.

Two hours later Herman raised his hand: a torpedo was heading towards them.

Knud Erik ordered the ship to reverse, and Anton responded instantly down in the engine room. Knud Erik had time to note the strangeness of their putting unconditional faith in a man who'd once threatened their lives. Then he spotted the stripe of foam just ahead of the bow. Herman's warning had come at the last minute.

The torpedo sped onward, now aiming for another of the convoy ships, the tanker *Hopemount*. Another foam stripe appeared, parallel to the first. The torpedoes hit the *Hopemount* amidships just ten seconds apart. The ship broke in two, and the halves drifted in opposite directions in the raging sea; the front half began sinking immediately. The water around the stricken ship was filled with men, with and without life jackets, fighting to stay afloat in the freezing water.

The *Nimbus* was still reversing at full speed. They were now the last ship in the convoy. A trawler approached; Knud Erik hoped she was there to pick up survivors. If she dropped a depth charge, it would mean certain death for the men in the water.

On the deck of the *Hopemount*'s rear end, still afloat, a half-naked figure appeared. The sailor had managed to fasten his life jacket around his heavy belly, but his legs were naked. He climbed up on the rail and let himself fall into the water. Knud Erik saw him surface and make brisk strokes to escape the suction from the half-upright stern, which was rapidly taking in water and would soon plunge to the bottom of the sea. The distress light on the life jacket glowed red against the grey waves.

He'd seen it so many times before and he already knew what it meant: yet another betrayal, yet another piece of his already wrecked humanity sinking to the ocean floor along with the *Hopemount*.

Then he snapped.

Shoving the helmsman aside, he ordered full speed ahead and simultaneously pulled the wheel hard to port. They quickly approached the sinking stern. Knud Erik kept his eyes fixed on the struggling man in the water.

The swimmer threw back his head towards the overcast sky as if fighting for breath. A heavy wave lifted him up and hid him from sight. When he resurfaced, he seemed to be screaming, though the racket from the engines prevented Knud Erik from hearing anything. Then the water around him turned red.

For a moment Knud Erik thought the trawler had released its depth charge, and he expected to see the drowning sailor shoot out of the sea with his chest exploding, but nothing happened. Had he been attacked by a shark? It was unlikely. Perhaps he'd been injured before he jumped into the water?

By now a couple of minutes had passed, and the sailor was very close. But his time was nearly up. No one survived that long in the icy water.

Knud Erik ordered full stop and ran out of the bridge. He climbed the rail and stood on it for a moment, swaying as though hesitating.

Then he jumped.

Later, when he tried to explain it to himself, he'd say: I did it to restore the balance in my life. But when he jumped, he didn't have a single thought in his head. He jumped the way you rub your eye with your finger when something irritates it. A red distress light was on, and it was bothering the hell out of him.

He'd broken the most basic rule of convoy sailing: a ship must never stop to pick up survivors. The rule wasn't there just to prevent them from becoming an easier target for the U-boats, but also to stop the ships behind from colliding with them. In plenty of cases a single deviation from course had set off a chain of collisions, often with fatal consequences for the ships involved.

But the *Nimbus* was at the rear of the convoy, so no one would run into them from behind. When Knud Erik leaped into the sea from the bridge wing it was only the lives of his own crew he was risking. Like every other act committed during a war, it confirmed one rule only to break another. It was simultaneously right and hideously wrong.

The icy water hit him like a kick to the head. He instantly felt the cold soak through his clothes. He got his head out of the water, gasped, and looked around wildly, already half panicking. He couldn't see the drowning sailor. Then a wave lifted him up and he spotted him. He swam towards him with furious strokes that made his blood pump faster. The drowning man's mouth was still open, and now he heard his scream, full of pain and ecstasy. Then, as the distress light threw its red glow across his face, Knud Erik saw that the sailor wasn't a man at all, but a woman with short black hair and narrow, oriental-looking eyes, of which only the whites were visible. If it hadn't been for her scream he'd have assumed she was dead.

Then he reached her. Her eyes returned to normal, but her gaze was oddly elsewhere, as if she were concentrating on something happening inside her. He thought she must be in shock. He started dragging her back to the ship. He had to hurry now. The cold spreading through his body was beginning to paralyse him. He'd have to give up soon, and he had no life jacket to keep him buoyant.

Most of the men at the rail were cheering him on as if he were a runner approaching the finishing line. They'd hung a ladder over the side. Absalon was waiting on the bottom step, holding on with one hand and stretching the other towards Knud Erik. The raging sea had soaked him through. Someone threw a line; Knud Erik grabbed hold of it and let himself be pulled over to the ladder. Then Absalon grasped his hand and pulled him up. His other hand supported the woman by her arm; she still seemed unaware of what was happening. She'd stopped screaming and an introverted smile had spread across her lips. As he yanked her out of the water, her naked abdomen revealed the guts spilling out of her. Death had made her gaze distant and quelled her screams.

He tried to throw her over his shoulder, but a soft object blocked

648

him. He looked down a second time. There was something coming out of her, but it wasn't her intestines. It was an umbilical cord. And in her arms she was cradling a baby. A small, creased, puce-coloured human bundle, born underwater.

Her childbirth must have started even before the *Hopemount* was torpedoed. In the icy water, with only a few minutes' grace before she froze, the mother had fought not only for her own life but also for the baby's.

Gripping the woman beneath the thighs, Knud Erik lifted her up to Absalon, and from the rail countless hands reached out for them.

Just then he heard the dull undersea roar of depth charges, followed by the sound of heavily falling water. He closed his eyes and knew that the woman in his arms was now the sole survivor of the *Hopemount*.

Dear Knud Erik,
Last night they bombed Hamburg, and the whole sky was lit
up by the glow of the flames. They say that the fire reached
several kilometres into the air and that the asphalt in the streets
melted. It thundered all night as loudly as if the bombs were
falling on Ærø. The cliffs at Voderup started collapsing. The
last time that happened was in 1849, when the Christian VIII
blew up in Eckernförde Fjord, and Hamburg is so much further
away.

An American pilot was found drowned in his parachute out
at the Tail. The Germans ordered him buried at six o'clock in
the morning. I think this was to avoid a scene, but we all turned
up at the cemetery with a rake and a watering can and told
them it was a Marstal custom to tidy family graves early in the
morning. I don't think the Germans fell for it.

Apart from that the Germans here on the island are calm
and sensible.

Everything in Marstal is peaceful. As always, death comes
from the sea.

The fishermen are afraid of catching corpses in their nets,
so no one is eating the eels this summer though they are much
fatter than usual.

Many people are keeping pigs in their back gardens even
though there is a ban. Marstal must have looked like this a
hundred years ago, when there were still pens in the centre of
the town. However, it burns to the south, and we hear the
bombers day and night.

Few sailors attend the Navigation College, but those who do
get a lot of attention from the many women in this town who
have not seen their husbands for more than two years. I don't
judge them. There is a shortage of everything, including love.

Personally I broke the habit of needing love, but not everyone is like me, and the older I get, the more understanding I grow. I missed out on so much. Some of it is my own fault, some of it not. I had a great mission. I wanted to make it possible for women to love. Today I think I failed. I did achieve a few things, but not for me. On the contrary: I pushed you away, and Edith, who now lives in Aarhus, I see only rarely.

I used to think that when a woman met a man, she would lose not only her virtue but also her dreams. When she has a son, she is rewarded for losing her virtue, but she loses her dreams all over again.

There was so much I wanted for you. You wanted something else. I was disappointed and I withdrew my love. I have never learned to love without conditions. I did not think that life had given me anything, so I decided to take what I wanted for myself, but life was not prepared to bargain with me. Perhaps the greatest thing you can achieve is to love without demanding anything in return. I don't know. I don't think I can make the distinction. So much of what is called love seems to me merely bitter constraint and self-sacrifice.

I think about you every day.

Your mother

EVERY COMMUNITY HAS ITS OWN MYTHS, INCLUDING THE COMMUNITY of ships that sailed the convoy routes to Russia. Their myths were improbable, verging on the completely unnatural. They made you listen and gawp at the same time. And yet unlike most popular legends, they were true. Take the one about Moses Huntington.

Moses Huntington was black, from Alabama: as well as a sailor, he was a tap dancer. He had a deep, melodious voice, and he tapped his feet to his own music. But it wasn't these talents which gave him his mythic status and made people ask for his autograph.

It was the *Mary Luckenbach*.

Moses was the mess boy Knud Erik had seen through his binoculars carrying a pot of coffee across the deck of the *Mary Luckenbach* in the last moment of her existence. A second later the torpedo had hit and instead of a ship there was a column of black smoke rising several kilometres into the sky, where it began to spread and rain black soot.

The *Mary Luckenbach* was gone. But Moses Huntington was still there.

He reappeared half a nautical mile down the convoy, where the British destroyer HMS *Onslaught* picked him up. No one could explain his survival, least of all Moses himself. It defied nature. Yet it had happened, and here he was to prove it, alive and tap-dancing. And all the men who heard his story straightened their backs and renewed their faith that there'd be life after the war.

Then there was Captain Stein and his Chinese crew, on board the *Empire Starlight*. The *Starlight* was the most-bombed ship in history. From 4 April 1942 up to and including 16 June 1942, the ship was attacked almost daily by German bombers: Messerschmitts, Focke-Wulffs, Junker 88s, you name it, sometimes up to seven times a day. The *Empire Starlight* took one direct hit after another. She was anchored off the coast by Murmansk and the crew could have gone ashore if they had wanted to. But they didn't. The *Empire Starlight* was their ship and there was no way they'd abandon her. Every time she was attacked, they'd fix whatever could be fixed. They took in survivors from other ships. They shot down four enemy bombers. 'Come and have a go' was their attitude. They were nothing but a bunch of Chinamen with a Yankee skipper, but they never gave in.

During the ship's final days the men camped on land because by then the *Empire Starlight* was so wrecked it was impossible to stay on board. But they kept rowing out to carry on fixing her, so that she grew to be their ship, literally, more and more as each day passed.

They wouldn't give in.

Like the story of Moses Huntington, it sounded impossible. It defied nature. But it had happened. Which meant it *could* happen. And those who heard the story gritted their teeth and held their heads high.

And then there was Harald Bluetooth, the boy born in a sea filled with U-boats, torpedoes, depth charges and drowned sailors – a sea where lives usually ended rather than began.

Everyone believed he was dead when he arrived on deck, and they gathered around him and his mother in respectful silence. But he wasn't dead, and Knud Erik cut the umbilical cord and they wrapped him in woollen blankets, though they all thought that within a few days he'd be heading back into the freezing waters he'd just emerged from. But he didn't.

The Danes on the *Nimbus* christened him Harald Blåtand. The ship already had a Knud, a Valdemar and an Absalon on board, so why not a Harald Blåtand, another early Danish hero? However, the Danes were a minority on board, so, of course his name got anglicised and he ended up as Bluetooth.

It was under this name that he became a myth. Like Moses Huntington and the *Empire Starlight*, he should have died, but he'd gone on living, contrary to all expectations. In his case, the borrowed time was counted from his very first breath.

His mother had no objection to the name and said so once she'd recovered, which she did very quickly. New mothers are hardy creatures. She turned out to be Danish as well, though she didn't look it. Her grandmother and her mother were from Greenland and even the Eskimos there are a kind of Dane. Her grandmother had been a k'ivitok, an oddball who ran around the ice cap on her own and refused to mix with other people. However, she'd done so eventually – and rather thoroughly, too. The man she chose was a middle-aged Danish artist who never even saw the daughter he fathered. The daughter had married a Canadian called Smith.

They were sitting in a semicircle around her as she told her story. She was lying in the berth in the captain's cabin – nothing less would do. But it was Bluetooth who was the guest of honour. He was snuggled at his mother's breast, sound asleep as if nothing more astounding had happened to him recently than a perfectly ordinary birth.

It was when she mentioned her Canadian father that Knud Erik leaned forward and studied Bluetooth's mother.

'Miss Sophie,' he said, hesitantly.

'No one's called me that for a long time. Neither Mrs nor Miss, though I happen to be unmarried. Not that it's relevant. I still go by my maiden name, Sophie Smith. Yes, that's me.'

'Little Bay?' Knud Erik said. He wasn't checking that he was right. He just didn't know what else to say.

'Yes, Knud Erik, I recognise you. You don't need to introduce yourself. You called me a bitch when we said goodbye. You're still the same handsome boy. You've grown taller. But then you hadn't quite grown up. And your eyes – they're not quite the same.'

'When you disappeared, I thought you'd died.'

'Yes, I suppose I owe you an explanation. I was wild in those days. I wanted to see the world, so I ran off with a sailor. He soon got tired of me and I got tired of him. So I became a sailor myself. I was the steward on board the *Hopemount*.' She looked around at them. 'Where are the others?'

'You're the only survivor.'

She looked down at Bluetooth and caressed his face with a finger. A tear rolled down her cheek.

'It was Knud Erik who . . .' Anton said.

She looked at Knud Erik. 'I once said that you'd drown. But I was just trying to make myself interesting. Instead, you saved me from the water.'

'I still have time,' he said. 'To drown, I mean.'

*　　*　　*

Sophie didn't say who Bluetooth's father was, nor did she seem to attach much importance to it. He hadn't been one of the lost men of the *Hopemount*, as they'd originally believed, and they got the impression that Bluetooth was the fruit of one of the many casual encounters that wartime so lavishly offers. She assured them that she hadn't planned to give birth on the open sea in the middle of a convoy on the most dangerous route the war could offer. She'd intended to be back in England before her due date, but the *Hopemount* had been stuck in Murmansk for five months, and given the choice between a Russian hospital and the sea, she'd definitely preferred the latter.

She helped out in the mess with Duncan and Helge. A stoker knocked together a cradle for Bluetooth. Herman sat in the mess, as usual, except when he was sent to the bow to keep a lookout, and when he wasn't washing down his vodka according to his scientific method, he used his wanking hand to gently rock the baby. Together, Old Funny and Bluetooth, the ugly idol of war and the small growing seed of defiant, promising life, formed the core of the ship.

The *Nimbus* sailed to Iceland and from there to Halifax, Nova Scotia. From Halifax they returned to Liverpool. They celebrated Christmas on the Atlantic.

Old Funny told his stories. For the time being all the crew demanded of Bluetooth was his existence. And exist he did. He wet and soiled his nappies, which were improvised from tea towels and dishcloths; he burped and gurgled, sucked and cried; he got nappy-rash and then colic. But most significant were the happy times when his eyes, like telescopes, would examine the mess as though it were the whole universe, whose secrets he was trying to discover. Twenty sailors stared back at him as though they were at the pictures. They all wanted to hold and tickle him, they all wanted him to chew at their fingers and tug on their ears. They volunteered for nappy-changing and babysitting and gave advice on care and diet. Together they possessed a wealth of knowledge about babies that Sophie had to admit exceeded hers. She'd given birth to Bluetooth, but he was her first, so she was no expert, and if anyone offered good advice, she was happy to take it.

'He's a degausser,' Anton said.

The degausser was the electrical cable that circled the waterline.

It reversed the ship's magnetic charge, to stop her attracting magnetic mines. That was Bluetooth's function, too: not only to unite the crew, but also to protect them, mostly from themselves. He helped them in a sense take root in the middle of the heaving sea.

Your roots aren't to be found in your childhood so much as in your child. It's he who provides your link to the world, and home is wherever he is. It suddenly dawned on Knud Erik that it was Bluetooth he felt connected to, not Sophie.

They'd met twice, both times by coincidence, but two coincidences don't make a pattern. The first time had been nothing but an immature infatuation, and on Sophie's side not even that: just a frivolous game with an impressionable boy. She admitted so herself when they happened to talk about it. He'd barely got to know her. The only thing that had tied him to her was the unresolved way they'd parted, and her sudden disappearance.

Knud Erik was no longer attracted to her. But then, he wasn't attracted to any women. That was the problem. He was attracted to a moment's ecstasy in the thunder of an air raid, and nothing else. He preferred to make love in the dark, and he wanted to see a face only in the phosphorescent flash of a bomb detonating close by. He suspected that deep down Sophie was a kindred spirit and that Bluetooth had been conceived during a blitz.

Something united them, but it was no longer budding desire. It was those icy minutes they'd spent together in the water, close to death, when he'd leaped into the sea to save her. Really it was himself he'd been trying to save, he supposed. She'd just been the random pretext.

They spoke a lot, and that was what made the greatest change in his life. She'd moved out of the captain's cabin into Helge's; Helge now bunked with the second mate. Though she'd stopped sleeping there, the captain's cabin was no longer a solitary den. She was a few years older than Knud Erik, and both were experienced and disillusioned. She'd lived the dream of her youth to excess, but in the meantime she'd outgrown it and hadn't found a replacement. She'd seen the world too: he could reel off one port after another, and she could match his list, speaking as one sailor to another. That was the note they struck together.

They never got beyond that stage, and nor did Knud Erik try to.

He never sought out the feminine in her, and perhaps that was why she accepted him. Once she'd hidden behind the stilted, literary language of a bookish and dreamy young girl. Since then she'd acquired the manner of a hardened sailor. It was a world he knew, where he felt safe, and he had no need to explore what lay behind it. He had neither the energy nor the courage. Anton's advice was still valid: it was better to forget.

He didn't want to get to know another human being too well. He was afraid that what he might discover could destroy him.

He put the whisky bottle in the cupboard and didn't take it out again. He overcame his contempt for Herman and started turning up in the mess. Bluetooth was the attraction. Though Knud Erik wasn't his father, the boy wouldn't be in this world if it hadn't been for him. He'd stood on the threshold of death and pulled a newborn into life. No, he didn't know whether he'd saved himself. But he'd saved Bluetooth, and that mattered more. Suddenly he felt his own lack of children as the greatest absence in his life. Bluetooth wasn't his, but his own death-defying leap into two-degree water had won him a parental right.

It was pure coincidence that he'd run into Miss Sophie again. But it was no coincidence that he'd saved Bluetooth. Life had singled him out and found a use for him.

AROUND THE MESS TABLE, ANTON TOLD THEM ABOUT A MAN CALLED
Laurids Madsen, who nearly a hundred years previously had fought
in a battle on Eckernförde Fjord and had been standing on the deck
of a ship when it blew up. Like Moses Huntington, he'd come back
down alive. He also told them about a schoolteacher called Isager
whose students had tried to kill him by setting fire to his house, and
about Albert Madsen, who'd searched for his missing father across
the entire Pacific and returned home bearing the shrunken head of
James Cook.

Knud Erik, who'd heard the same stories – indeed, he was Anton's
source for most of them – interrupted. He had better knowledge of
these things. He told them about the First World War and about
Albert's visions. Then Anton cut in, saying that he wasn't telling it
quite right, and Knud Erik realised that when his friend had got hold
of Albert's famous boots, he'd also purloined his notebooks and read
them.

Anton recounted the story of how he'd found Albert dead, and
together he and Knud Erik told everyone about the gang named after
the old captain. Vilhjelm brought up their discovery of the skull of
the murdered Jepsen. Knud Erik looked over at the man the crew
called Old Funny to note the effect of this story. He'll change the
subject. He'll deny everything, he thought.

Herman looked distant for a moment, then said pensively, 'Vilhjelm
is talking about me,' as if this were the first he'd heard about his
stepfather's murder. 'Yes, I killed my stepfather. He was in my way.
I was young. I was impatient.'

He started telling how, at the age of fifteen, he'd sailed a topgallant yard schooner back to Marstal single-handed, as though his
first murder was merely the beginning of the story and the best part
was yet to come.

The crew stared at him. They were gripped by the tension of his tale. Old Funny was a born storyteller. All right, so he was a dangerous killer as well. All right, so the captain had been right about him after all. But take a look at him now. He'd certainly been punished.

Knud Erik understood that Herman's pathetic state, legless and one-armed, was a ticket to a free pardon, already granted. There was no need for him to ask for his audience's pity: they gave it to him voluntarily. Old Funny had once been a man. A man capable of killing other men. But what was he now?

Anton, Knud Erik and Vilhjelm exchanged a glance. They hadn't been expecting a confession and they wanted to investigate further. But Herman's Marstal adventures were now in full flood and the audience wanted more. 'Then what happened?' they asked, and Anton had to tell them about Kristian Stærk and the killing of Tordenskjold. 'Did you really kill his seagull?' Wally asked Old Funny accusingly.

Knud Erik couldn't suppress the triumph in his voice when he told them how they'd driven Old Funny out of town simply by staring at him, and how most of the gang members didn't even know that he was a murderer but thought the whole thing was about the death of a bird.

Old Funny looked irritated, as if he regretted his departure all those years ago. Then he winked at Knud Erik and laughed. 'You really got me there,' he said. Then he started talking about the Copenhagen Stock Exchange and Henckel and how he'd lost the inheritance he'd waited to get his hands on for so many years. His life had had its ups and downs.

Vilhjelm talked about the loss of the *Ane Marie* and about the *Book of Sermons*, which he still knew by heart. They were welcome to test him if they wanted.

'So you've been in the ice before; you know what it's like,' one of the British gunners said. 'You practically had a dress rehearsal for convoy sailing.'

'Bloody Marstal sailors,' a Canadian said. 'You poke your noses into everything and you've been everywhere.'

Miss Kristina and Ivar entered the story, and Knud Erik recounted their chapter in a tone that grew increasingly condemning.

Old Funny defended himself. 'I confess to nothing,' he said. 'Ivar's death wasn't murder. Some men can take it, others can't. I was just testing him and that's all there is to it.' He looked around the company, and several men nodded.

'And Miss Kristina?' Knud Erik persisted.

Yes, that was stupid. He was happy to admit it. He flung out his wanking hand as if to say, all things considered, it was a trifle.

'You've ruined lives!' Knud Erik was angry now.

Well, he supposed he had, Herman admitted. He didn't add: look at me now. But his body said it, and that was enough. It was all in the past. No more evil would come from him.

Knud Erik got up and left, but the story continued. Nothing could stop it now.

Old Funny told them about the night he broke the curfew in Setubal. Was he boasting or telling the truth? It was hard to tell. He'd certainly been quite a guy once. Anyone could tell that his audience thought so, just from looking at their faces.

The story spread in every direction and contracted again until it formed a protective ring around the *Nimbus*.

Bluetooth lay awake in his cradle and his telescope eyes wandered from face to face. He was exploring the universe as usual, and he looked as if he understood it all.

The crew had found true fellowship around the table in the mess, however reluctantly and unwillingly at first. Old Funny had helped them become the 'us' that every ship needs. Even Knud Erik conceded it.

WHEN THEY ARRIVED AT LIVERPOOL, HERMAN ASKED TO SEE THE CAPTAIN.
Their meeting took place on the deck where Knud Erik had introduced him to the crew and Herman had first revealed that his trouser
legs were empty. He hadn't come to say goodbye and thank you.
Instead, he requested permission to stay on board the *Nimbus*. After
all, they were fellow Danes, from the same town. He believed he could
be useful around the mess and as a lookout. And he'd like to remind
the captain that on one occasion he'd saved the ship from a torpedo.

Knud Erik shook his head. At this, for the first and only time,
Herman seemed to crack.

'Look at me,' he said. 'They'll shove me into some home.'

'They can lock you up and throw away the key for all I care.'

'What's going to become of me?' Herman looked down. He
appeared pathetic now, and his misery only heightened Knud Erik's
rage.

'As far as I know nothing stands in the way of hanging a man
with no legs and only one arm.'

The crew was standing some distance away, whispering. They
could tell from Old Funny's slumped figure just how the negotiations
were going. Absalon approached them.

'Captain,' he said, 'we've drawn up a petition.' He handed Knud
Erik a piece of paper. Knud Erik cast his eyes over the list. Practically
the entire crew was demanding to keep Old Funny on board: the
only ones who hadn't signed were Anton and Vilhjelm. Sophie's
signature was missing, too: he assumed she didn't want to get involved.
Besides, she didn't count as a crew member.

'I'll think about it.'

He asked Anton and Vilhjelm to come to his cabin.

'Will you sign off if I keep him?'

They both shook their heads. 'We'll stay,' Anton said. 'The *Nimbus* is a good ship, and though I hate to admit it, I think Herman has a share in that. We knew you'd say no. We just wanted to show you that we're on your side. I hate the bastard, but sometimes you have to rise above your own feelings.'

Knud Erik pondered this for a while. 'All right, I'll let him stay,' he said. 'For the sake of the ship.'

The crew celebrated his decision by taking Old Funny on a trip into town. The next morning he was back in his usual place in the mess with bloodshot eyes and an even redder complexion than usual. When he spoke, it was with biblical solemnity.

'There shall come a day when all the women in the world will lie in the gutter screaming for cock,' he intoned. 'But not an inch shall they be given!'

'Am I to understand,' Knud Erik asked, 'that nobody wanted to screw you?'

It was Knud Erik who invited Sophie to stay.

'I'm pleased that you're asking,' she said. 'I was going to ask if I could.'

'You can carry on in the mess. I've spoken to Helge about it.'

They were silent for a while. He felt relieved, but he had no idea how to express his joy at her decision. 'The crew will be pleased to hear that,' he said instead. 'They all love Bluetooth.'

'I don't know if it's irresponsible to sail with a baby during a war. But if I stayed ashore I'd be working all day in a munitions factory and I'd never see him. He's only two months old. I wouldn't be able to stand that.'

'There are bombs everywhere,' he said. He realised that they were discussing Bluetooth the way a married couple would discuss their child.

'I don't know what I'd do with myself if I couldn't sail,' she said. 'It's my whole life. I can't live in any other way.'

He knew what she meant. He'd chosen to be a sailor himself, but at some point the sea had chosen him, too. It was something that could no longer be undone. He and Sophie had seemed so very different the first time they met, but since then, they'd lived parallel lives. That said, something seemed to be holding him back and he sensed the same in her, too. He wasn't physically impotent. So the impotence must lie in his soul. Finding oblivion in a moment's ecstasy was all he could manage. He couldn't look into someone's eyes while making love.

'I'm like my grandmother,' she said. 'She was one of those crazy people who can't be with anyone. She couldn't fit in. She needed her independence too much. She had the ice and I have the sea. But it comes down to the same thing.'

'You've got a child now. You have to fit in. You're all Bluetooth's got.'

'He has us,' she said.

He was uncertain if by 'us' she was referring to him or the crew of the ship, of which she was now a part. He wanted to ask but feared the question might spoil something. It was she who broke the increasingly tense silence.

'I do know who Bluetooth's father is,' she said. 'He's not, as most of you probably think, some sailor I happened to meet on shore leave. I know his name, I know his address, I've met his parents and his friends. We were engaged to be married.'

'So what went wrong?'

'What was wrong was that he looked like James Stewart. You know, the American actor. Six foot something with the face of a boy.'

'But James Stewart's handsome!'

'Yes. And he was so damn nice I didn't know whether to cry or throw up. He was sweet and decent and reliable and he loved me. He had a flourishing legal practice in New York. Plenty of money, plenty of everything. We'd have lived in Vermont and our children would've grown up in the country and the war would've been so far away we wouldn't have heard it even if they dropped the biggest bomb in the world.'

'And you couldn't stand that?'

'I wanted it more than anything. But I was promised to another. What was his name again, the ugly little manikin, Rumpelstiltskin? No prince can save me. I briefly believed James Stewart could. But the reality is I prefer life with Rumpelstiltskin. Do you know what I ended up hating about him, my James Stewart boyfriend? It was his damned innocence. I ended up seeing it as dishonesty. He took me out to dinner. We raised our glasses and looked into each other's eyes. We planned our future. The war might just as well never have happened. We just sat there enjoying ourselves in our nice, quiet way, and afterwards we went home and slept in our soft bed, and I knew we'd carry on doing that until the day we died. I couldn't bear it. So one evening, instead of clinking glasses, I threw my drink in his face. It wasn't his fault. He can't help it that he hasn't seen a ship blow up and a hundred men drown in front of his eyes. At bottom, I guess I'm the one with the problem. But his innocence came across as an insult.' She flung out her hand. 'It's not that I love all of this. I can't even explain why I'm here. I don't fit in anywhere. Unless it's here. Or, rather' – she smiled from sudden relief, as if all that talking had finally led her to the right word – 'it's the k'ivitok in me.'

The trust between them grew, but the distance remained, and it didn't decrease. She was right, he thought. It was the war. It was inside them both. Nothing could happen between them until the war was over. But when would the war end? Would they be there when it finally happened? He wanted to have a child with her. It was a blind urge in him, but how long could they wait? She was a couple of years older than he was, thirty-four or thirty-five. When was a woman too old to have a baby?

He gave up. There was Bluetooth. Bluetooth was his child – and the whole crew's.

They celebrated Christmas somewhere north of Ireland. In Halifax, Wally had gone ashore and come back with a fir tree slung over his shoulder: he'd lashed it to the bow, so it didn't start to lose its needles until they put it up in the mess. Helge had managed to obtain a bag of hazelnuts from somewhere, and the crew got four each. He'd wrapped them in pink tissue and handed them out as gifts. Meanwhile other presents were piling up under the Christmas tree. They were all for Bluetooth, though he was still far too young to appreciate them. Sophie unwrapped the packages on his behalf. Inside them was a world he'd not get to know until the war was over: cows and horses, pigs and sheep, an elephant and two giraffes. Most were hand-carved in wood and then carefully decorated with any available paint – though the colours tended to be those of the world of war they were trapped in: black, grey and white.

Bluetooth took the cows, the horses and the elephant, put them in his mouth one by one, and gnawed at them tentatively.

BLUETOOTH WAS ABOUT A YEAR OLD WHEN SOPHIE WENT ASHORE with the crew in Liverpool one night. She left him asleep in the seamen's fo'c's'le with Wally, his special pal, who'd volunteered to babysit. Knud Erik didn't know what she was looking for. Was it something they couldn't give each other, something they could find only with strangers?

He went ashore alone. He'd put the whisky bottle back in the cupboard and never taken it out again. But he couldn't give up his shore nights. They ran into each other in a pub in Court Street. She was wearing a dark red dress and her lips were painted. He was reminded of the first time he met her, in her father's house in Little Bay. They both looked away as if by mutual agreement and pretended they hadn't seen each other.

He went straight back to the ship and turned in immediately. Half an hour later the door to his cabin opened and the unfamiliar scent of perfume filled the narrow room. Had he deliberately forgotten to lock his door?

'We can't go on like this,' she said, and began to undress in the dark.

'I've killed a man,' he said. 'He was kneeling down, pleading for mercy, and I shot him.'

She snuggled up to him in the berth. She cradled his head in her hands. He could barely make out her features in the dim glow from the skylight. 'My Knud Erik,' she said, and her voice was thick with a tenderness he'd never heard before.

He freed himself from her embrace and stepped out on to the floor. 'I need light,' he said. He switched it on and went back to her. 'The red distress lights.'

He didn't know why he'd said that. Those words were taboo: they conjured forbidden memories he must keep at bay if he wanted to survive. But deep down, he understood that if he wanted to be able to love, he must speak them aloud.

665

'There isn't one of us who doesn't think about them,' she said.

'I sailed over them.'

'We,' she said. 'We all sailed over them.'

He let his hand glide down her face and he noticed that her cheek was wet. He pulled her to him and looked into her eyes.

All was completely quiet around them. No air-raid warnings shrilled, no bombs thudded, no waves splashed across the deck, no thunder roared from exploding ammunition ships. There was only the sound of the generator working away deep in the bowels of the *Nimbus*.

He kept holding her tight.

'My Sophie,' he said.

IN AUGUST 1943 THE DANES ROSE UP AND BUILT BARRICADES IN Copenhagen and other towns. The government ceased working with the German occupying forces and resigned. Naval officers scuttled their own ships and sent them to the bottom of Copenhagen's harbour.

The Dannebrog once again became a flag that could fly from a ship in the service of the Allies. By now, however, the crew had grown used to their Red Duster, so they kept it. Besides, there were almost as many nations on board as there were crew members, and the Danes on it were a mixed bunch. Bluetooth had been born in the Atlantic Ocean and was an honorary citizen of the sea. The *Nimbus* was a sailing Babel, at war with the Lord.

'We could fly one of Bluetooth's nappies from the mast,' Anton suggested.

'Clean or dirty?' Wally asked. He was the *Nimbus*'s champion nappy-changer.

They all scrubbed the deck and soaped down the bulkhead. It was cleanliness, sailor-style, just as it had been on board the old *Dannevang*, may she rest in peace. And it was all in honour of Bluetooth.

Now they could go ashore and visit a pub as Danes, with no one calling them 'half-Germans' or 'Adolf's best mates' any more. When other seamen heard they were from the *Nimbus*, the next question would inevitably be 'And how's Bluetooth?'

He's very well, thank you. He lost his hair, but it grew back again, as black as his mother's. His first tooth probably bothered him a bit. He took his first steps a while back, and now he's got his sea legs. He must think the whole world's made of hills – up, down, up, down: in any case, he seems disappointed when the ground's solid. Sometimes he falls over. Then he wants his ma. Or one of his umpteen pas. Seventeen languages is a lot when you're learning to say *Papa*.

Seasick? Bluetooth? Never! No one in the entire Allied merchant navy has a better stomach for the sea.

Oh yes, indeed, the *Nimbus* was a lucky ship. Until one spring day in 1945.

They were bound for Southend, and for the first time in four years they were sailing through the North Sea again. There were still U-boats, but they were fewer and further between, and reports of losses continued to fall. It was approximately ten o'clock at night when the war decided to blow them a parting kiss, just to remind them never to trust it, even when its end seemed imminent. The sea was calm. There was still a faint light to the north-west; summer wasn't far off. That's when the torpedo – the one they'd expected all the years they'd sailed in Allied service – finally tracked them down. It struck them by hatch number three and the *Nimbus* began to take in water at once. The starboard and stern lifeboats were undamaged and ready in their davits. The stokers appeared in nothing but their sweaty vests, and any crewman who had been off duty was also in just his underwear. Knud Erik scolded them. He'd ordered them to sleep fully dressed in case they were torpedoed, but it was an order no one took seriously any more. There'd been a time when they'd even slept in life jackets. Now they could barely remember when they'd last heard the sound of a nose-diving Stuka. As for the U-boats – were there actually any left?

Three minutes later they were in the lifeboats and pushing off. The *Nimbus* had been running at top steam in calm weather when the torpedo hit her: now she continued at the same pace, with her bow sinking ever deeper; she seemed to be gliding on tracks that led directly to the sea bottom. When the water rose over the deck, a bang sounded from inside the engine room and a column of smoke and steam soared into the cloudless spring sky, where the first stars had begun to appear. The *Nimbus* continued on her downward course. The last they saw of her was the stern, stamped with her name and town of registration, Svendborg. Then she was gone, with barely a ripple disturbing the tranquil surface of the sea.

'All gone,' Bluetooth said. He was sitting on his mother's lap wrapped in a blanket, with just his head sticking out. He sniffed, as though the cold night air had given him a cold. Then he started to cry.

668

'You go ahead and have a good cry, my boy. You've plenty of reason.'

It was Old Funny, parked in state in his wheelchair in the centre of the lifeboat. He looked around as though he'd become Bluetooth's mouthpiece. 'That was the lad's childhood home we just lost.'

They sat in silence and let his words sink in. You had to admit he had a point. At two years and seven months, Bluetooth had never known any world but the *Nimbus*, and now it was gone. The ship had become a kind of home for them, too. Only a few of them had ever believed in the *Nimbus*'s inherent luck. Instead, gradually, a different notion took hold: only their own steely determination, the care they took in maintaining the ship and – above all – their love for Bluetooth, kept the torpedoes and the bombs away.

Suddenly they felt that determination slacken. The war had ended for them now – not because it had been won, but because without their ship they could no longer fight. There was no joy in the realisation. They barely knew whether they were winners or losers. They were survivors, and now they wanted out. They were balanced on a knife-edge between disappointment and relief, and when the captain spoke, he spoke for all of them.

'I think we should go home,' Knud Erik said.

Go home: that was easier said than done. The crew had more homes than there were corners of the world. 'As far as I can see,' he went on, 'we're roughly halfway between England and Germany. Anyone who feels at home in England rows that way.' He pointed westward. 'And the rest – '

Old Funny interrupted him: 'What are you saying? There were no Germans on board the last time I looked.'

'We're not going to Germany. We're going home.'

'To Denmark?' Sophie asked.

'To Marstal.'

The crew split up again, this time according to destination. Old Funny remained in Knud Erik's lifeboat: it seemed he'd given up on vanishing from Marstal and was now ready to go home. Anton, Vilhjelm and Helge wanted to head back too. Knud Erik looked at Sophie for a moment. Then she nodded. Wally and Absalon, too, were curious to see the tiny town that had been presented to them as the centre of the universe. So why not?

They divided the provisions between the two lifeboats. There were three wool pullovers and three sets of oilskins in each. These were given to the freezing stokers. The boats rocked alongside each other as the crew shook hands across the rails. Bluetooth was passed around and got a hug from every man. He'd just said goodbye to his childhood home. Now he had to say goodbye to half its occupants. He didn't understand and cried for his mother as if she were the only fixed point that remained in the world.

They started rowing, and Old Funny insisted on being lifted out of his wheelchair and settled on the thwart so he could do his bit. He pulled hard at the oar with his one arm but struggled to maintain his balance, so Absalon moved closer and supported him with his shoulder.

The other boat soon vanished from sight in the growing darkness.

Dear Knud Erik,
When I believed you had been drowned, I did something I have never liked to think about since.

I became so visible to myself, and that is never comfortable.

It happened one afternoon. I was wandering about aimlessly in the cemetery and suddenly found myself at a grave in the north-western corner. It was Albert's. I had never tended his grave, though he was my benefactor.

Old Thiesen, the gravedigger, was busy painting the cast-iron fence around it. He had already weeded it and it was clear that he would soon turn the neglected grave into a fitting memorial to one of the town's great shipowners.

Suddenly everything inside me – my fears, my grief and uncertainty, my eternally hidden and lonely life, my self-reproach and the heavy burden of the almost impossible task I had set myself – all of it came out in a huge eruption of rage. It was not caused by any particular offence, but sprang rather from that feeling of helplessness that has dogged me all my life. I grabbed the paint bucket and flung it at the cracked grey and white marble column where the dates of Albert's birth and death were engraved. And I screamed the same three words over and over. I suppose I wanted them to sound like a doomsday curse. But I cannot imagine they would have stirred any feeling but profound pity in anyone who might have heard my shouting, because my madness was so obvious.

'Everything must go! Everything must go!'

I had given away my plan – but fortunately Thiesen was the only one who heard me. He understood the words, but not their meaning.

The gravedigger knew my story well. He knew that I had spent many days in the most agonising uncertainty about your fate. He seized my hands, as if he were trying to protect me, rather than prevent me from causing further damage.

'Calm down, Mrs Friis. Everything will be all right. I don't think you're quite yourself,' he said.

He meant it reassuringly, but the terrible truth was that, in that moment, I had been precisely that: myself. I was being myself more than I ever had been before or would be again. The words came straight from my heart: everything must go. I had revealed the entire purpose of my life. Everything must go. Finally I had said it.

I collapsed, exhausted, on the grass at Thiesen's feet. 'I apologise,' I said, as he helped me back up. 'I'm not myself.'

So I encouraged him in his error. I agreed with him. I had to, if I were to go on living among people. 'No, I don't think I'm quite myself,' I repeated.

Everything must go. Everything has gone, and now I know that this was never what I truly wanted. I walk the streets of this town, which seems to have been hit by a curse, empty of the men who made up half of its inhabitants. And I see more and more women with an expression in their eyes that tells me that it has been so long since they last received a letter that they have finally given up hoping.

We are not in the habit of keeping accounts of the dead in this town. But I do know that far more have not returned from this war than Marstal lost in the last war or on the Newfoundland route. And it goes the way it always goes for those who drown. No earth for them to rest in.

I visit the cemetery every day and place flowers and wreaths on the few graves that we do have. Now I am the one who tends Albert's.

I ask you again to forgive me for having once exiled you to the dead.

Your mother

IT TOOK THEM THREE DAYS TO REACH THE GERMAN COAST, AN ENDLESS
sandy beach with white dunes behind it. They arrived in the early
dawn. The sky was overcast and a pink rim across the landscape
announced the sunrise. The weather had been calm all the way. They
manoeuvred through the surf, and Absalon and Wally jumped into
the water to push the lifeboat ashore. Then they eased Old Funny
out of the boat and into his wheelchair. He was heavy to push in
the sand. Bluetooth ran alongside. He needed to move his legs after
sitting for so long. He was clutching his stuffed toy dog, Skipper
Woof, who'd also been born at sea, according to the boy. A new life
awaited both of them. The up-down, up-down of the waves was a
thing of the past. Now they were on boring land, and here they'd
stay, for the time being at least.

'Where are the houses?' the child asked. He'd never seen a beach
before. The only world he knew consisted of the sea and bombed
harbours. But some things hadn't changed. He looked around. There
was Papa Absalon, there was Papa Wally (his special pal), there was
Papa Knud Erik, Papa Anton and Papa Vilhjelm. There was Old
Funny in his wheelchair, and there was his mother.

They found a road that led away from the beach. There was no
traffic on it. Knud Erik walked along with a battered leather suitcase in his hand.

'What's inside it?' Wally asked.

'Money.'

'You have German marks?' Wally gave him a look of surprise.

'Something better. Cigarettes.'

'You're a man with foresight,' Sophie said.

'Only sometimes,' he said.

They hardly knew where the front line was: whether they were ahead
of it or behind it, or whether the Germans were still holding out or

had already been overrun. The Russians were far away, but the Americans were pushing forward. The group had landed somewhere in the German Bight and would still have to cross northern Germany to get to the Baltic. Only the last leg of their journey to Marstal would they be able to complete by sea.

During the first few hours ashore, they saw no signs of war. The road ran through flat marshland sparsely dotted with farms. The main road ahead of them was still empty. Bluetooth grew tired of running about and climbed onto the lap of Old Funny, who'd miraculously conjured a bottle of rum from beneath his blanket. Wally always maintained that Herman's wheelchair had a false bottom that concealed a stash of booze.

Later that morning they reached a village. Seeing smoke emerging from the chimney of a house, Knud Erik walked up the garden path and knocked on the door. No one came to open it, but he saw a face staring at him from behind a curtain. They continued: the first bomb craters appeared in the road, filled with water and reflecting the blue spring sky. Soon they found themselves skirting craters and burned-out transport trucks. They were nearing a town, and people began to appear on the road, while unshaven soldiers in filthy uniforms trudged along indifferently. It was hard to decide whether these men were on the run or had merely been sent on a mission they no longer believed in. Horse-drawn carts rumbled past, piled with towers of tightly packed furniture and mattresses, followed by dead-faced people moving with the mechanical steps of prisoners in a chain gang. Others struggled along with wheelbarrows and push-carts. No one spoke: they kept their eyes on the ground and seemed lost in mute introspection.

'Look, a horsie!' Bluetooth cried out in his baby English, pointing a finger.

They hushed him – not for fear of standing out in the growing crowd, but from concern that in the midst of this silent, funereal traffic, any exclamation of joy was out of place. Soon, though, they realised that they were no different from anyone else. A man in a wheelchair with a child on his lap, a woman and a group of men trudging along: just another motley crew of refugees. The main roads of Europe were teeming with people like them, who'd lost a home and were on the lookout for another that hadn't been wrecked by war. But they had two things that most of the others didn't: they had hope, and a fixed goal. They must keep a low profile. If they showed any curiosity or raised their voices, they'd attract attention. Knud Erik had feared that Absalon's black skin might give them away as foreigners, but in the end no one paid them any heed. The Germans were too busy with their own wrecked lives and dreams, oblivious to anything but the blind onward trudge from one blasted city to the next.

They arrived at a town. Most of it had been destroyed by bombs, but they'd seen ruins before, in Liverpool, London, Bristol and Hull. In some places the house fronts were still standing, four to five storeys high, their sooty walls punctured by empty windows. In others, even the facades had crumbled, exposing the gaps between the floors. They looked into rooms, guessing at which had been bedrooms and which kitchens. They kept expecting the people they saw in the streets to return to the half-houses with boards nailed across the doors and start a new shadow life that matched their dead faces and downcast eyes.

Bluetooth was used to ruins. He thought houses were meant to be burned out. So for him, it wasn't the sombre, ravaged landscape that stood out, but the big white bird sitting high up on the spire of a shelled church.

'Look,' he said. 'That's Frede.'

He said it in Danish. He switched freely between that and English. They'd told him about the stork on Goldstein's roof, but they never mentioned Anton's attempt to kill it. Now he thought he was seeing Frede.

'No, it's not Frede. It is a stork just like him.'

Knud Erik couldn't help but laugh. A passer-by stared at him as if his laughter were a kind of high treason, as if he'd cursed Hitler in a loud voice.

The stork took off and flapped heavily above the street. They followed it. When it reached the railway station it landed on its damaged roof as if showing them the way.

The puddles on the stone floor inside the station suggested that it had rained recently, and there were people all over the place, lying and sitting on piles of rubble as though the heaps were benches and chairs supplied by provident authorities. The majority had to be homeless. They didn't look as if they were going anywhere. Where would they travel to anyway? To the next bombed-out railway station?

In a corner someone was handing out coffee and bread; a notice announced that later that day soup would be served. Though they were hungry, the former crew of the *Nimbus* avoided the bread line, afraid of giving themselves away. Knud Erik went off alone with a packet of cigarettes and returned shortly afterwards with a loaf of bread, a sausage and a bottle of water. Bluetooth bolted his share eagerly, but the others chewed theirs for a long time. They didn't know when their next meal would be.

They spent the night in the railway station and took a train to Bremen the next morning. In Bremen they'd change for Hamburg. They had no tickets, but Knud Erik's cigarettes solved that problem. The platform was overcrowded, so they used Old Funny as a battering ram. People moved out of his way, doubtless presuming him to be a tragic war invalid. All that was missing was an Iron Cross pinned to his chest.

A woman in an oversized winter coat was standing in the middle of the platform: she didn't seem to be headed anywhere, but just stood there. Her pale, emaciated face, half covered by the scarf tied under her chin, wore the most intense expression of loss Knud Erik had ever seen. She wasn't withdrawn, so much as totally absent: her eyes were completely blank. She was pushed and shoved from all sides by the blind throng, and the suitcase that she carried suddenly sprang open and an infant fell out. Knud Erik saw it clearly. It was the burnt body of a little child, withered and practically unrecognisable, a mummy shrunk by the heat of the same fire that had clearly devoured its mother's mind, too. A man, focused on reaching the train, pushed her away, and without even noticing where he put his feet, trod right on the tiny corpse that lay in front of him. Knud Erik turned away.

'Look,' Bluetooth said, 'the lady dropped her Negro doll.'

As they approached Hamburg, for almost thirty minutes they travelled through nothing but ruins. They thought they knew what bombs could do to a town, but they'd never seen anything to compare with this. No ghostly scorched facades rose from the piles of rubble: there was no guessing where the streets had once lain. The devastation was so complete that you could barely believe it was caused by man.

But it didn't look like a natural disaster either – that would have left something standing, however randomly. This destruction was so systematic that it looked like the work of a force that knew neither earth, water nor air, but only fire.

For the first time in almost six years of war, they felt they'd existed only at its periphery. Like the other passengers in the overcrowded train they averted their gaze: they couldn't bear the sight. The scale of the city's destruction was so unfathomable that they gave up trying to understand what neither their minds nor their eyes could take in. They knew that if they stayed here any longer, they'd end up like the people around them, and lose the hope that drove them on.

Even Bluetooth looked away and started fiddling with a button on his coat. He didn't ask any questions, and Knud Erik wondered if it was because he was wise enough to fear the answers.

AT FOUR THIRTY IN THE MORNING ON 3 MAY 1945, THEY STOLE A tugboat from Neustadt's harbour. They'd planned to go to Kiel but had to accept the transport options that presented themselves. Knud Erik's last carton of cigarettes had secured them places in the covered bed of a truck that was going to Neustadt. The harbour was deserted, and they walked the length of the quay looking for a boat that would fit their purpose. Bluetooth was sleeping, curled like a puppy on Old Funny's lap. Anton decided on a tugboat named *Odysseus*. When they'd quietly lowered Herman's chair down from the quay, Bluetooth woke and demanded to be put down on the deck, where he stretched and yawned, and his telescope eyes began their eternal search for news in the universe.

'Look,' he said, pointing at the sky.

They glanced up. High above them a large bird was flying north-west with huge, slow wingbeats.

'It's the stork,' Bluetooth said cheerfully. 'It's Frede.'

'Do you know, I'm beginning to believe it is,' Anton muttered. 'Looks like he's heading for Marstal.'

On their way out of the Bay of Lübeck they passed three passenger ships lying at anchor, the *Deutschland*, the *Cap Arcona* and the *Thielka*. Though there was no sign of a crew on the bridges or decks, they were nervous that their theft would be discovered and someone would chase them, so once they were some distance away, they sailed at full speed. They'd planned to head north around the island of Fehmarn. Of course this would mean going far into the Baltic, almost as far as Gedser, before they could turn west and then south around Langeland. It was quite a detour, but they didn't dare sail any closer to the German coast.

It was early afternoon when a hollow roar rolled across the sea. Several more followed, and for a moment they felt the firmament vibrate above them. Tracks of smoke etched themselves across the bay and they guessed that Neustadt was under attack or the three anchored ships had been hit. As the day progressed they realised they might as well have followed the coast. No one would have pursued them. The Germans seemed to have lost control of the Baltic altogether; it was now patrolled by British Hawker Typhoon bombers. Again and again they heard the faint echoes of bombs exploding far across the sea.

There was heavy traffic on the water, but most of it came from the eastern part of the Bay of Lübeck, where the Russians were advancing. There were all kinds of vessels: fishing boats, freighters, smaller motor ships, yachts, smacks and rowing boats with makeshift masts and sails. Columns of smoke drifted up all along the horizon. They constantly came across pieces of wreckage and once nearly sailed into a huddle of charred bodies bobbing face down in the water. From a distance they'd looked like a raft of seaweed; the crew saw their mistake just in time to change course. The drowned – women and children as well as men – were everywhere. None of them wore life jackets. Clearly they, too, had been refugees.

Will it never end? thought Knud Erik.

The euphoria of having escaped was gone. They understood that if they were to get across the Baltic alive, they'd need their luck to hold. They were sailing a German ship, and there was nothing to stop the next Typhoon Hawker dropping its lethal load on them as it passed overhead. They hadn't flown a Danish flag in five years: now they wished they had one. But maybe not even that was enough. It was as if the sea had turned itself inside out, and was disgorging all the thousands of people it had swallowed across the centuries. Crossing it, they felt a fellowship with them.

Knud Erik was at the helm. He ordered everyone to put on a life jacket, but there weren't enough to go round. He glanced briefly at Herman in his wheelchair. Then he shrugged. Captain Boye had drowned because he'd given his life jacket to a stoker who had left his own behind in the engine room. He handed his life jacket to Wally and ordered him to help Herman put it on. If they sank, he'd have given up his life for a man he despised, but he had no choice. The war had taught him one thing: the Allies might be fighting for justice, but life itself was unjust. He was the captain and he was responsible for his crew. Duty was the only thing he had left. He must cleave to it or else surrender to pure meaninglessness.

'Aren't you going to put on your life jacket?' Sophie asked. She hadn't noticed him glancing at Herman. He brushed her question aside with a smile. 'The captain's always the last to leave the ship. And the last to put on his life jacket.'

'A right Odysseus you are,' she said, returning his smile. 'And a lucky one too, having Penelope on board.'

'We aren't like Odysseus,' he said. 'We're more like his men.'

'What do you mean?'

'Have you read the story?'

She shrugged. 'Not properly.'

'It's depressing reading, actually. Odysseus is the captain, right? He has fantastic adventures. But he doesn't bring back a single one of his crew alive. That's the part we sailors play in this war. We're Odysseus' crew.'

'Well, you'd better get moving, Captain Odysseus,' she said, looking at him. 'Because this particular crew member happens to be pregnant.'

THEY SAILED AT HALF SPEED AND SWITCHED OFF THE BOAT'S LIGHTS
at night. The closer they came to their destination, the more they
feared they'd never reach it. Up until now they'd existed only in the
present, as all who put their trust in the vagaries of luck are obliged
to. Now that they dared to believe in the future, they were terrified
of losing their lives. The old daily dread from the time of the convoys
returned. Again, the sky above and the sea beneath seemed packed
with hidden menaces.

The sea was like dark blue silk, and the bright spring night was
cloudless. A warmth in the air heralded summer, and had it not been
for the tugboat's pervasive smell of coal and tarred hemp rope, they'd
have caught the scent of apple blossom coming from the shore. But
the water was cold. Winter clung to its depths, and all they could think
about was that chill: it felt as if they were still sailing the Arctic, still
on the lookout for the foam stripes that signalled torpedoes and the
red distress lights that had once bankrupted their souls and could do
so again. Again, they listened out for the sound of oars or cries of help.
Again, they enacted an eternal dress rehearsal of death by exposure.
Spring welcomed them, but the memory of the five-year winter they'd
endured still held them in its grip.

In the bay they'd left behind that morning, eight thousand Allied
prisoners of war were incinerated when their transport ships were
bombed. Earlier, another ten thousand refugees had drowned in
the same sea the *Odysseus* was now crossing. But her crew knew
nothing of this either. They'd seen ships go down before, but they'd
never seen a refugee ship sinking with ten thousand passengers
trapped on board, or heard the collective scream as the water
gushed in from all sides and sent the ship down to the bottom, or
the wail that followed the final plea for help, when those still living
realised that *rescue* is just a word. No, they'd never heard that vast
cry, and yet it entered them that night.

They spent the night on deck; they dared not go below. They wrapped themselves in blankets they'd found on board and sat awake, watching the sea with restless eyes, and listening.

Bluetooth didn't sleep, either. He lay silently, watching the fading stars. As dawn broke, he was the first to hear the deep whoosh of wings. 'The stork' was all he said.

They looked up. There it was, flying low above them, still heading north-west. Far away they could see Kjeldsnor Lighthouse in the early-morning light. They were approaching the southern point of Langeland.

Ærø appeared in the late afternoon after they'd sailed along the Langeland coast for most of the day. Trying to save coal, Anton kept the tug at half speed: they were running out. They saw Ristinge Hill rise to the north. Open water followed. Further out to the west lay Drejet and the hills at Vejsnæs. In the midst of it all rose the red roofs of Marstal, with the copper church spire, now green with verdigris, towering high above. A few masts still stood in the harbour, like the remains of a stockade that had been overrun by some unknown force. From here they couldn't see the Tail and the breakwater that embraced the town like a useless arm.

Some distance outside the harbour, they saw black masses of smoke pouring into the calm air. Coming closer, they saw flames. Two steamers in Klørdybet were ablaze. The war had beaten them to it. Knud Erik had been so sure that the destruction would all end the moment he set eyes on the Marstal skyline. Fatigue overwhelmed him, and he felt close to giving up. If he were an exhausted swimmer trying to reach the shore, this was the moment he'd simply let the water take him.

They were just level with the steamers when they heard the howl of a dive-bomber. They looked up: a Hawker Typhoon was coming straight for them. One of its wings gave a flash, and a rocket sped towards them, trailing white smoke.

There was a bang, and the whole boat shook.

IT WASN'T A GOOD TIME TO BE A CHILD. CORPSES FLOATED ONTO the beach and the little islands around the town on a daily basis, and it was the children who found them. They'd always fetch an adult, but by then the damage had been done. They'd seen the decomposing faces of the drowned, and afterwards they were full of questions that we found it hard to answer.

Early in the morning of 4 May, a ferry docked at the harbour. It came from Germany and it was packed with refugees. Only a few on board were men: soldiers with blood-soaked bandages around their arms and legs. The rest were women and children. The children said nothing, but simply stared pale-faced into the distance with their scrawny necks sticking out from winter coats that seemed far too big for them, as though nature had gone into reverse and they'd grown too small for their clothes. They couldn't have had a proper meal in a long time. But it was their eyes that made the deepest impression on us. They seemed to see nothing at all. We reckoned it was because they'd seen too much. Children's heads are quickly overloaded by ugly things. The eyes simply go on strike.

We offered them bread and tea. They looked like they could do with something warm. We behaved decently towards them, though we couldn't exactly claim they were welcome.

At eleven o'clock that morning two German steamers ran aground attempting to navigate the south channel. British bombers had flown over the island several times during the past few days, and we'd often see them flying over the sea. Two of them appeared now. They fired their rockets and both steamers caught fire. They had machine cannons mounted both fore and aft and they returned fire. The British planes kept coming back, and one of the steamers took several direct hits and was soon engulfed in flames.

We didn't dare approach the ships to rescue the survivors until the shooting was over. The water was filled with people, many of them burned or wounded by shrapnel. They screamed and wailed when we hauled them on board, but we couldn't just let them lie there in the cold water. It was a dreadful sight. Their hair had been singed off. They were black from soot, and you could see bloodied flesh where the skin had been burned away. Many were naked. We'd brought blankets, but wrapping them around the poor shivering creatures would be of no help: the wool would just stick to the exposed flesh. Helping them ashore on the quay, we handled them as gently as possible. There were many dead too. We left them in the water. Survivors had priority.

The wounded were taken to the hospital in Ærøskøbing, and the others billeted in the house we called the Lodge, in Vestergade. Then we started recovering the bodies. There were quite a few – twenty in all. We brought them to the quay by Dampskibsbroen, right by the entrance to the harbour, where we laid them out in a row and covered them with blankets. One of the bodies was missing its head, but somehow that one was the least horrific: no face, and no mouth gaping in a rigid scream that it would take to the grave.

Several hundred people had gathered in the harbour to watch the steamers burn. One of them was almost extinguished, but she was still giving off plenty of smoke, while the other one burned amidships. Some drunken German soldiers were on board manhandling a group of half-naked women on the foredeck. Fear of death combined with booze had made them lose all inhibition.

Late in the afternoon the British resumed bombing the two steamers. The crowd was swelling. We'd all come to watch the sad scene unfolding on our waters. Many of us had lost husbands, brothers and sons in this war, and it would have been easy for us to think that these Germans had got what was coming to them. We didn't, though. How many times had we, our fathers, or our grandfathers been on a ship that was sinking or on fire? We knew what it was like. A sinking ship was a sinking ship. It didn't matter whose.

Suddenly a tugboat appeared in the south channel. We'd been so preoccupied by the burning steamers that we didn't even notice it at first. Marstal harbour's south channel is tricky to navigate if you're not familiar with the waters, but the captain seemed to be managing well until one of the British bombers flew low over the boat and fired its rockets. The explosion that followed could be heard all the way to the shore. The boat took a direct hit and went up in flames.

Gunnar Jakobsen, who'd been out there with his dinghy, would always say afterwards that he'd never seen a more jumbled-up crew. One bloke was a Negro, another was a Chinaman and another one was in a wheelchair: the others shoved him overboard before they jumped themselves. He had no legs and only one arm, but his life jacket kept him afloat. A woman with a child popped up in the water, too. Half the world seemed to be floating around down there. Gunnar's surprise doubled when he pulled them all on board; not only did both the Negro and the Chinaman speak Danish, but the rest spoke it like Marstallers. 'Aren't you Gunnar Jakobsen?' one of them said.

Gunnar Jakobsen narrowed his eyes – not because he couldn't see the man properly, but because he needed time to think.

'Bloody hell,' he exclaimed eventually. 'You're Knud Erik Friis!' Then he recognised Helge and Vilhjelm. The man with no legs and one arm said nothing, nor did any of the others introduce him. 'Anton,' Knud Erik Friis said suddenly, looking round desperately. 'Where's Anton?'

'You mean Anton Hay? The Terror of Marstal?' Gunnar Jakobsen asked.

They looked around. 'He's not here,' Vilhjelm said.

He wasn't visible in the water, either. The *Odysseus* was about to keel and the flames soared high. No one could be on that ship and still be alive. They circled about for a while, calling out for Anton.

The bombers kept attacking the steamers as if they'd been ordered to use up their entire supply of bombs and rockets before the war ended. Just when the men in Gunnar Jakobsen's dinghy were about to give up and head for the harbour, the *Odysseus* took another direct hit. This time she must have been struck below the waterline, because she keeled instantly and began to sink. Gunnar Jakobsen switched off his motor, as if he felt he owed the tugboat a minute's silence as it died. A moment later the ship was gone. In the place where she'd been, they could see something floating on the water. Gunnar Jakobsen started the engine and headed for the spot. At first they couldn't make out what it was, but then they recognised the horribly charred remains of what had once been a human being. They saw its back and its head. Anton was naked and his hair had been burned off. His life jacket was gone, or if it was still on him, there was no telling it from the flesh of his back, which was as black and porous as charcoal.

Sophie covered Bluetooth's eyes with her hand. Knud Erik reached into the water to get the charred body into the dinghy. He didn't think about what he was doing; he simply couldn't leave it there. But when he hauled up the corpse the whole arm came off. Startled, he let go, and when the body hit the water again, what had once been Anton's flesh fell off his bones, which began sinking at once.

The engine was throbbing violently.

Gunnar Jakobsen wanted to get back ashore as quickly as possible. None of the survivors from the *Odysseus* objected. They sat in total silence, their expressions as blank as those of the German children; Gunnar hoped he'd never see anything like them on the faces of his own kids. He didn't know much more about the war than what he'd read in the newspapers. He'd heard the pounding in the south when the British dropped their bombs, and he'd seen flames on the horizon when Hamburg and Kiel were razed. Now he was learning more in a single day than he had over the past five years, and he'd have the same experience in the months that followed every time he met someone who had spent the war outside Denmark's borders. Something was wrong with them, and he just couldn't explain what it was. It wasn't anything they said, because they said nothing; they seemed to be brooding over a huge secret that they kept to themselves only because it wouldn't help to tell it. They were part of a dreadful community that no one else could penetrate and which they couldn't escape.

The boy was crying. He'd seen nothing, but he sensed that something had happened.

'Will we never see Anton again?' he asked.

'No,' said the woman, whom Gunnar Jakobsen thought must be the child's mother. 'Anton's dead. He's not coming back.'

It was a brutal thing to say, Gunnar Jakobsen thought, and he'd probably wouldn't have been so frank with his own children.

Yet something inside him acknowledged the honesty of the woman's reply. To the children of war, you told the truth.

High above them a stork flew past. It came close to one of the burning steamers and seemed to vanish briefly in the clouds of smoke before emerging on the other side, unharmed. It continued across the town, and when it reached the other end of Markgade, it folded its wings and prepared to land in the nest on the roof of Goldstein's house.

Gunnar Jakobsen put in at Dampskibsbroen. This was where most of us were standing, and though he'd been shaken by the sight of Anton's body, he nevertheless felt that he was returning with a great story that deserved a big audience. He was bringing home the first people to return to Marstal from the war after an absence of more than five years.

Gunnar Jakobsen hadn't noticed that the dead were still lying on the quay when the big legless man was helped out and settled among their covered bodies. We stared at him with curiosity and suddenly Kristian Stærk said loudly, 'That's Herman.'

A wave of unease went through us as the news spread, and those who didn't know who Herman was had it explained to them in terms that were far from flattering. Herman hadn't shown his face in Marstal for twenty years, but the mere mention of his name still disgusted those of us who'd heard the story of the *Kristina*. He sat strangely lost among the dead. His arm and leg stumps made him look like a stranded walrus waving its flippers, but his vulnerability didn't lessen our contempt.

'Help me up,' he said.

We did nothing; we just kept staring at him. None of us wanted to go near him, so he just sat there in the puddle of his wet clothes and his big body started shaking from cold.

A man in Kongensgade was running towards us waving his arms and shouting, but we couldn't make out what he was saying: he was too far off.

At the same moment the church bells started to peal in a wild and breathless rhythm we'd never heard before, as if someone were improvising a melody fit for an occasion unique to the history of the town – neither funeral nor wedding service, sunrise nor sunset.

In a way that we couldn't explain, we knew that something

momentous had happened, something much bigger than the burning steamers out on the water or Herman's sudden reappearance.

Finally the running man came within earshot.

'The Germans have surrendered! The Germans have surrendered!'

We looked at Herman and Knud Erik and Helge and Vilhjelm and the other men whose names we didn't yet know, and we looked at the woman and the child, and we understood that they were just the first. The sea was about to return our dead.

We lifted them up and bore them high through the streets. We even hauled Herman out of his pool of water and found a cart to pull him around on. Cheering, we marched through Kongensgade, along Kirkestræde, down Møllegade, along Havnegade, up Buegade, through Tværgade and down Prinsensgade, where Klara Friis, as always, sat in her bay window, her pale face staring out to sea.

We went back along Havnegade and as we marched, more people joined us. An accordion appeared, and then a trumpet, a double bass, a tuba, a mouth organ, a drum and a violin. We mixed 'King Christian' with 'Whisky, Johnny' and 'What Shall We Do with a Drunken Sailor?'. There was whisky and beer, there was rum and more beer, there was Riga Balsam and Dutch gin; it had all been saved up for this moment, the moment we'd always known would come. Lights were lit in the windows, and blackout curtains were burned in the street, crackling as they blazed.

We ended up on Dampskibsbroen, where the dead lay waiting for us in their rows. And we drank and danced and stumbled about among the corpses, and that was as it should be. The dead had been piling up throughout our entire lives: the drowned and the missing, all those who'd remained unburied across the centuries, lost even to the cemetery, those who'd ruined our lives with longing. Now they rose up and took our hands. We danced and danced in a huge churning circle, and in the midst of it all sat Herman, no longer shivering from the cold but flushed with intoxication, brandishing an already half-empty whisky bottle. He sang in a voice that was hoarse with toil and drunkenness and evil, with impatience and greed and battered lust for life:

'Shave him and bash him,
Duck him and splash him,
Torture him and smash him
And don't let him go!'

There was a black man, a Chinese man, an Eskimo woman and a child we didn't know; there was Kristian Stærk and Henry Levinsen with the crooked nose; there was Doctor Kroman, there was Helmer and there was Marie, who'd finally learned how to clench her fist but didn't yet know that she'd been widowed this very day – Vilhjelm would tell her later. There were Vilhjelm's parents, deaf but smiling; there were the Boye widows, Johanne, Ellen and Emma, and tonight they didn't hesitate to join hands with us and dance; there was their distant relative, Captain Daniel Boye; and there was Klara Friis, running down Havnegade, breaking through the circle until she found Knud Erik and he nodded at her, and the little boy whose name we didn't know went up to her and said a word we guess Knud Erik must have taught him: 'Granny'. And the child took her hand and pulled her into the dance, and our dance was like a tree that grew and grew, adding rings for every year.

There was Teodor Bager, still clutching his chest; there was Henning Friis, once the most handsome man on the *Hydra*, with the blond forelock Knud Erik had inherited; there was the indefatigable Anna Egidia Rasmussen, and there were her seven dead children, and they, too, joined the dance alongside the one living daughter; there was the cassocked Pastor Abildgaard, who before he died had finally found himself a rural parish that suited him better than Marstal, looking at us through his steel-rimmed glasses and taking a hesitant step forward. Albert followed, with hoar frost in his beard and the head of James Cook under his arm, and then came Lorentz – he was panting and struggling, but nothing was going to stop him from joining the dance; there was Hans Jørgen, who went down with the *Incomparable*, and Niels Peter. Even Isager took his place with us, and so did his fat wife, with the resurrected Karo in her arms, and their sons, Johan and Josef with the Negro hand; behind them came Farmer Sofus and Little Clausen and Ejnar and Kresten, the poor creature with the constantly weeping hole in his cheek. Laurids Madsen towered above us in his heavy sea boots; others appeared behind him; and finally there was Anton, whose charred face broke open in a smile that revealed his tobacco-stained teeth. Then came whole crews: the men of the *Astræa* and the *Hydra*, the *Peace*, the *H. B. Linnemann*, the *Uranus*, the *Swallow*, the *Smart*, the *Star*, the *Crown*, the *Laura*, the *Forward*, the *Saturn*, the *Ami*, the *Denmark*, the *Eliezer*, the *Felix*, the *Gertrud*, the *Industry*, the *Harriet*, the *Memory* – all the drowned. And there, in the outer circle, with their faces half hidden by fog, danced everyone who'd been away at sea for these five years of war.

So many of them had died. We didn't know how many.

We'd count them tomorrow. And in the years to come we'd mourn them as we'd always done.

But tonight we danced with the drowned. And they were us.

Acknowledgements

We, the Drowned is fiction. The novel is inspired by and largely adheres to the history of the town of Marstal in the years 1848 to 1945. I have made use of the town's traditional family names, but I have shuffled the deck so that any resemblances to people living or dead are purely coincidental.

The historical parts of the novel are based on my research in the archives of the Maritime Museum in Marstal and on its many publications. I also found valuable material in the newspapers *Ærø Folkeblad* and *Ærø Tidende* as well as the quarterly publication *Ærøboen*.

I have found inspiration and gained essential knowledge from – among others – the following writers and publications: Henning Henningsen (*Crossing the Equator, Sømanden og kvinden, Sømandens våde grav, Sømandens tøj*), Ole Lange (*Den hvide elefant, Jorden er ikke større*), H. C. Røder (*Dansk skibsfarts renæssance*, vols 1, 2 and 4), Joseph Conrad (*The Shadow-Line*), H. Tusch Jensen (*Skandinaver i Congo*), Adam Hochschild (*Kong Leopolds arv*), *Søndagstanker – kristelige Betragtninger på Søn – og Helligdage af ærøske Præster, Sømandspostillen*, Knud Ivar Schmidt (*Fra mastetop til havneknejpe*), Harriet Sergeant (*Shanghai*), E. Kromann (*Marstals søfart indtil 1925, Dagligliv i Marstal og på Ærø omkring år 1900*), Hans Christian Svindings ('Dagbog vedrørende Eckernførdetogtet og Fangenskabet i Rendsborg og Glückstadt', *Danske Magazin*, series 8, vol 3), *Marstalsøfolkenes visebog*, J.R. Hübertz (*Beskrivelse af Ærø 1834*), C. T. Høy (*Træk af Marstals Historie*), Victor Hansen (*Vore Søhelte. Historiske Fortællinger*), *Salmebog til Kirke – og Husandagt* 1888, Anne Salmond (*The Trial of the Cannibal Dog: Captain Cook in the South Seas*), Homer (*The Odyssey*), Nordahl Grieg (*Skibet går videre*), W. Somerset Maugham (*The Trembling of a Leaf*), Herman Melville (*White Jacket*), Robert Louis Stevenson (*Tales of the South Sea, A Footnote to History*), Mark Twain

(*Roughing It in the Sandwich Islands*), Victor Hugo (*Les Travailleurs de la Mer*), F. Holm Petersen (*Langfarere fra Marstal*), Knud Gudnitz (*En Newfoundlandfarers erindringer*), Rauer Bergstrøm (*Kølvand*), Per Hansson (*Hver tiende man måtte dø*), Martin Bantz (*Mellem bomber og torpedoer*), Andrew Williams (*Slaget om Atlanten*), Richard Woodman (*Arctic Convoys*), Claes-Göran Wetterholm (*Dødens Hav: Østersøen 1945*), Edward E. Leslie (*Desperate Journeys, Abandoned Souls*), Anders Monrad Møller, Henrik Detlefsen, Hans Chr. Johansen (*Dansk søfarts historie, vol 5, Sejl og Damp*), Mikkel Kühl (*Marstallerne solgte væk*), 'Marstals handelsflåde 1914–1918', in *Maritim Kontakt 26*), Karsten Hermansen (*Søens købmænd*), Karsten Hermansen, Erik Kroman a.o. (*Marstals søfart 1925–2000*), H. Meesenburg and Erik Kroman ('Marstal – et globalt lokalsamfund', in *Bygd*, vol 17, no. 4), Tove Kjærboe (*Krampebånd og Klevesnak*), Finn Askgaard, ed. (*Fregatten Jylland*), Samling af søforklaringer over forliste danske Skibe i Årene 1914–1918, Christian Tortsen (*Søfolk og skibe 1939–1945*), Ole Mortensøn (*Sejlskibssøfolk fra Det Sydfynske Øhav*) and Poul Erik Harritz (*Rundt om Selma fra Birkholm*).

Appreciation

I WISH TO THANK THE PEOPLE OF MARSTAL WHO TURNED UP AT MY evening readings at the Navigation College and at the public library in Skolegade, as well as the following individuals, each of whom in their own way provided invaluable assistance: Lis Andersen, Iben Ørum, Henning Therkildsen, Jens and Hanne Lindholm, Henry Lovdall Kromann, Knud Erik Madsen, Connie and Martin Bro Mikkelsen, Lars Klitgaard-Lund, Nathalia Mortensen, Annelise and Poul Erik Hansen, Astrid Raahauge, Pulle Teglbjerg, Leif Stærke Kristensen and Berit Kristensen, Regitze and Ole Pihl, Hjørdis and Kaj Hald, Erik and Lillian Albertsen, Hans Krull, Karla Krull, Erna Larsen, Adam and Anne Grydehøj, Søren Buhl and Marjun Heinesen, Gunnar Rasmussen, Pastor Emeritus Finn Poulsen, Lars Kroman, Lone Søndergaard, Frans Albertsen, Kristian Bager. A special thank-you goes to Erik Kroman, Director of the Maritime Museum in Marstal, for making the museum archives available to me. And to Karsten Hermansen, who shared his home-baked currant buns as well as his inexhaustible knowledge.

I owe Christopher Morgenstierne my thanks for helping me with maritime terminology and expressions. Any errors in sailing techniques and wind force lie entirely with the author.

Huge thanks to my dearest Laura. It has taken me half your life to write this book, and you have voiced your strong views about it with unswerving enthusiasm the whole way through.

And to my beloved Liz I owe a debt of gratitude it would take more than a lifetime to repay. You have supported me with your unique blend of professionalism and love, and it is thanks to you that I finally made it safely to port.